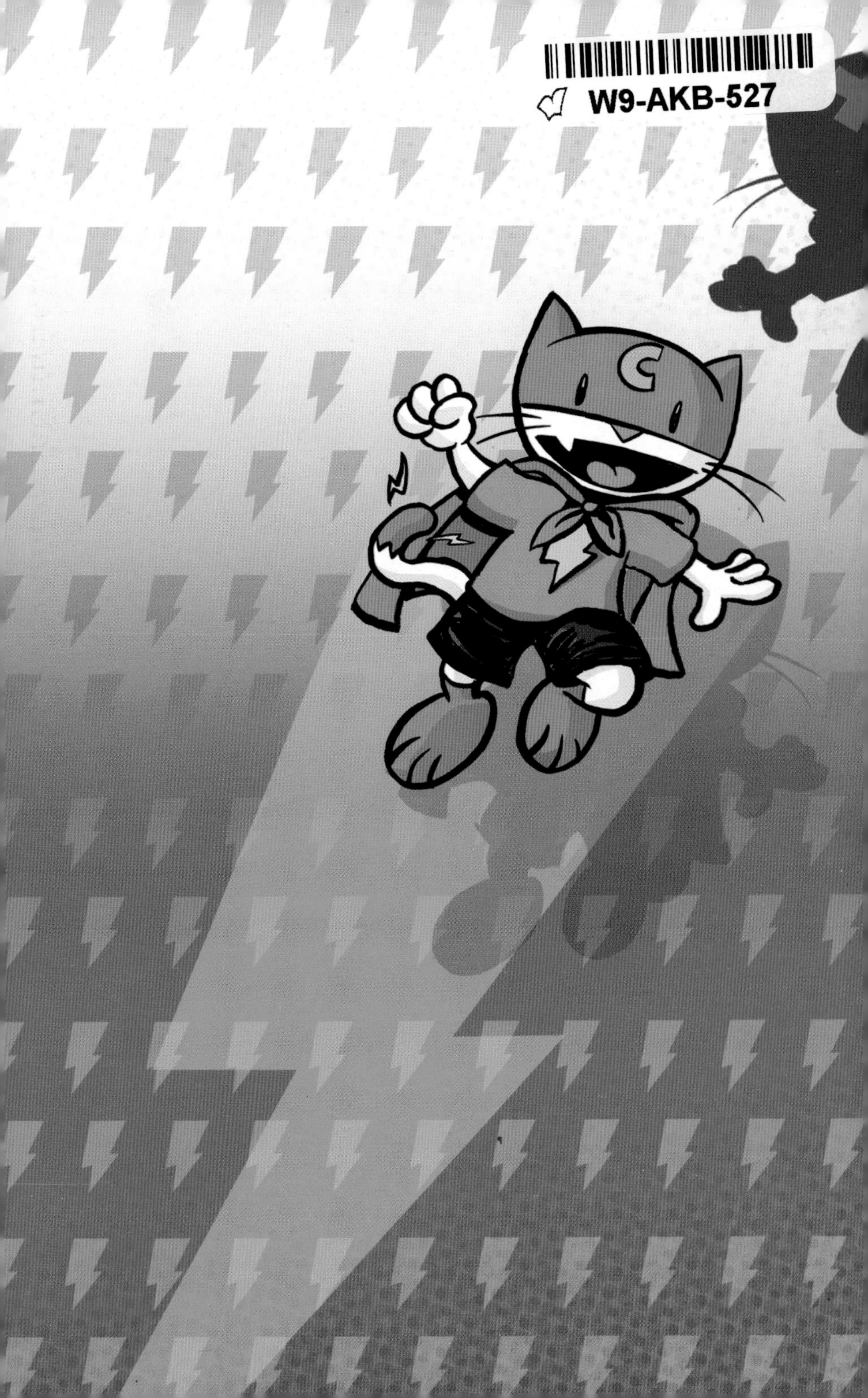

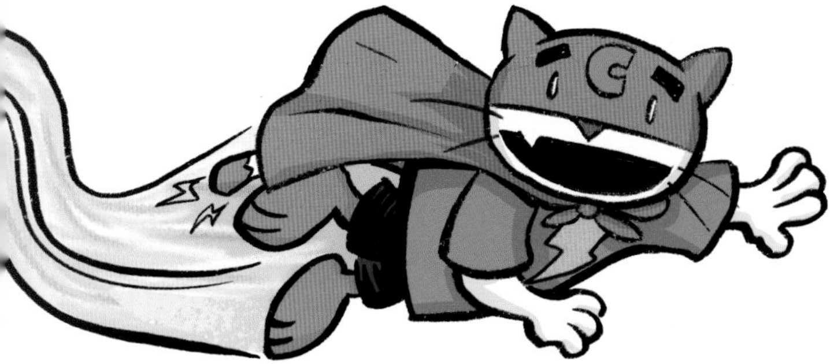

READ ALL OF MAX MEOW'S ADVENTURES!

#1 Max Meow, Cat Crusader

#2 Max Meow, Donuts and Danger

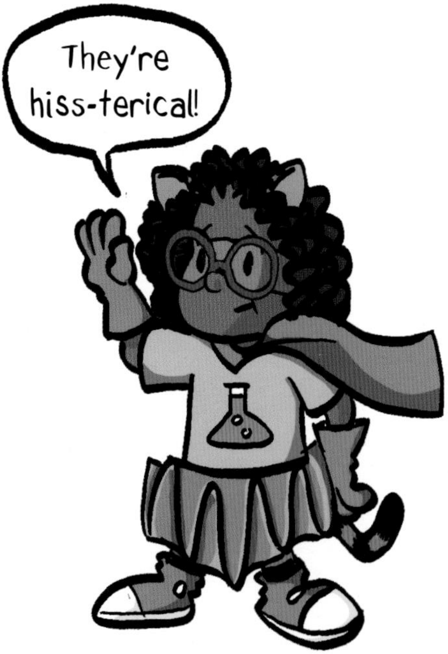
They're hiss-terical!

MAX MEOW!
DONUTS AND DANGER

JOHN GALLAGHER

RANDOM HOUSE 🏠 NEW YORK

All rights reserved. Published in the United States by Random House
Children's Books, a division of Penguin Random House LLC, New York.

Random House and the colophon are registered trademarks
of Penguin Random House LLC.

Visit us on the Web! rhcbooks.com

Educators and librarians, for a variety of teaching tools,
visit us at RHTeachersLibrarians.com

Library of Congress Cataloging-in-Publication Data
Names: Gallagher, John, author, illustrator.
Title: Max Meow : donuts and danger / John Gallagher.
Description: First edition. | New York: Random House Children's Books, [2021] |
Series: Max Meow; [book 2] Summary: "When Max and Mindy's evil look-alikes try to
take over the world's donut supply, the real Max and Mindy work together
to save the day and the donuts" —Provided by publisher.
Identifiers: LCCN 2020025248 | ISBN 978-0-593-12108-5 (hardcover) |
ISBN 978-0-593-12109-2 (library binding) | ISBN 978-0-593-12110-8 (ebk)
Subjects: LCSH: Graphic novels. | CYAC: Graphic novels. | Doughnuts—Fiction. |
Identity—Fiction. | Cats—Fiction. | Superheroes—Fiction.
Classification: LCC PZ7.7.G325 Don 2021 | DDC 741.5/973—dc23

Book design by John Gallagher and April Ward

MANUFACTURED IN CHINA

10 9 8 7 6 5 4 3 2 1

First Edition

To Millie and Mom.
Millie, because she's my cat.
And Mom, because
she's my mom.

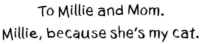

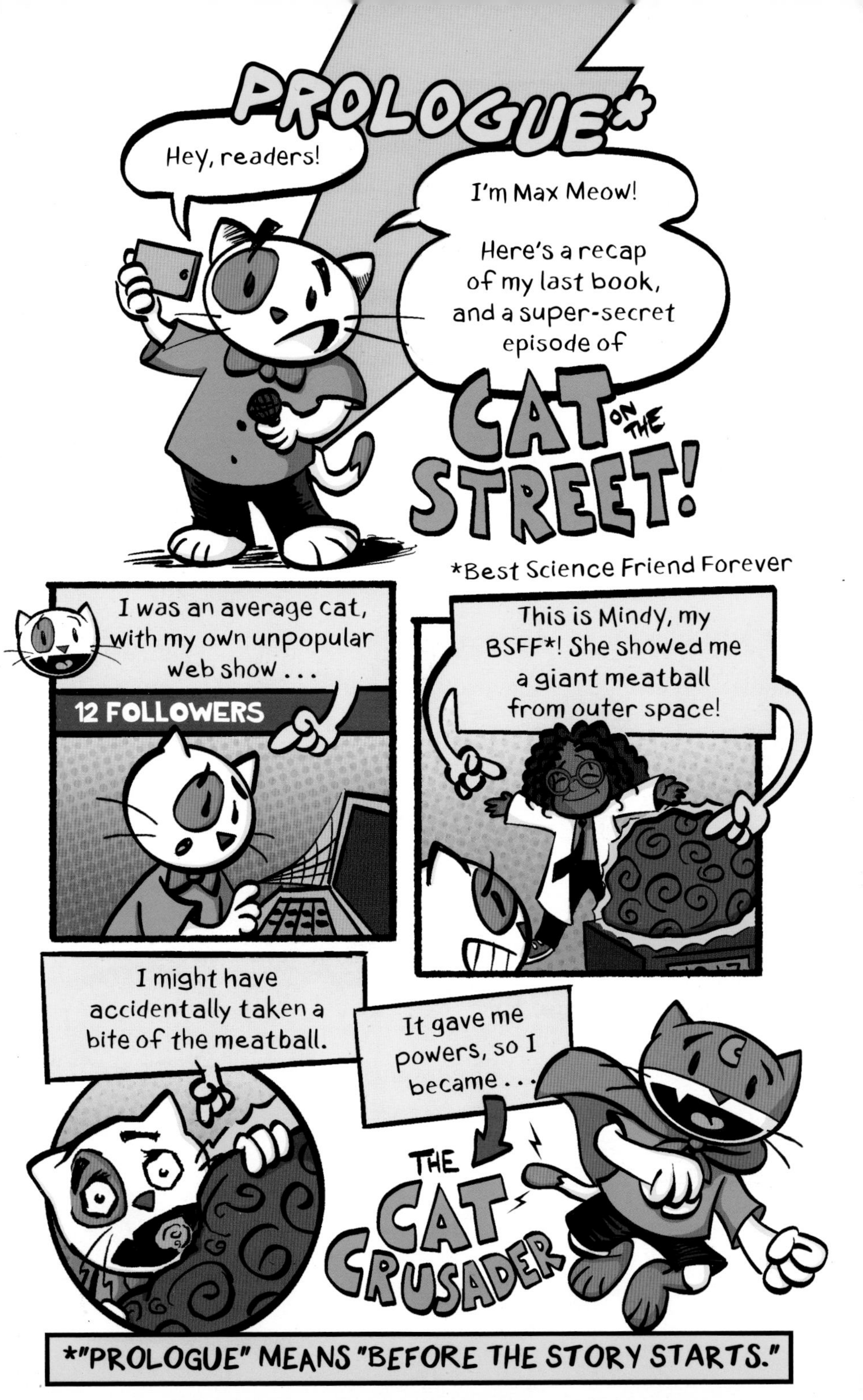

PROLOGUE*
Hey, readers!
I'm Max Meow!
Here's a recap of my last book, and a super-secret episode of
CAT ON THE STREET!
I was an average cat, with my own unpopular web show . . .
12 FOLLOWERS
This is Mindy, my BSFF*! She showed me a giant meatball from outer space!
*Best Science Friend Forever
I might have accidentally taken a bite of the meatball.
It gave me powers, so I became . . .
THE CAT CRUSADER
*"PROLOGUE" MEANS "BEFORE THE STORY STARTS."

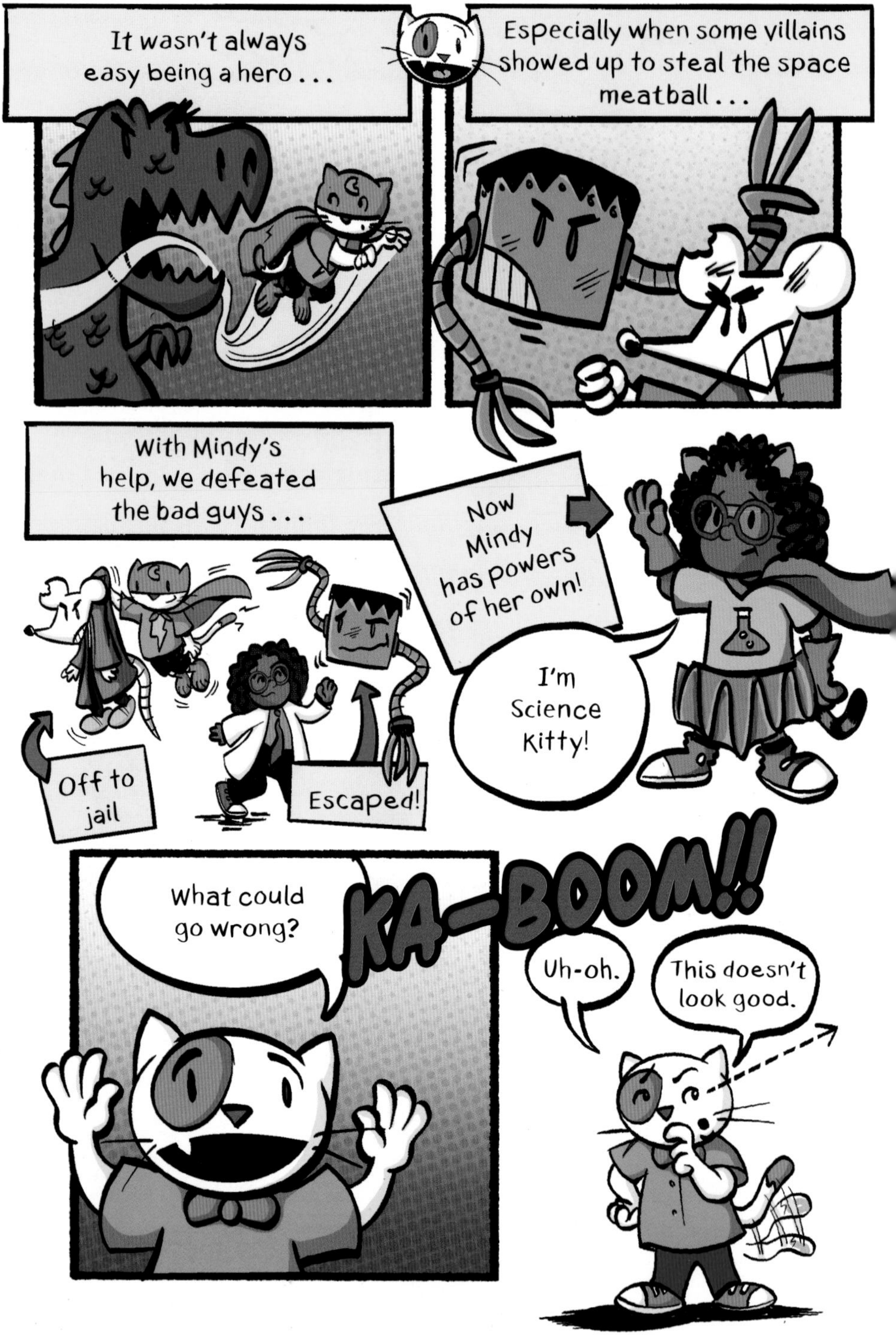
It wasn't always easy being a hero . . .
Especially when some villains showed up to steal the space meatball . . .
With Mindy's help, we defeated the bad guys . . .
Off to jail
Escaped!
Now Mindy has powers of her own!
I'm Science Kitty!
What could go wrong?
KA-BOOM!!
Uh-oh.
This doesn't look good.

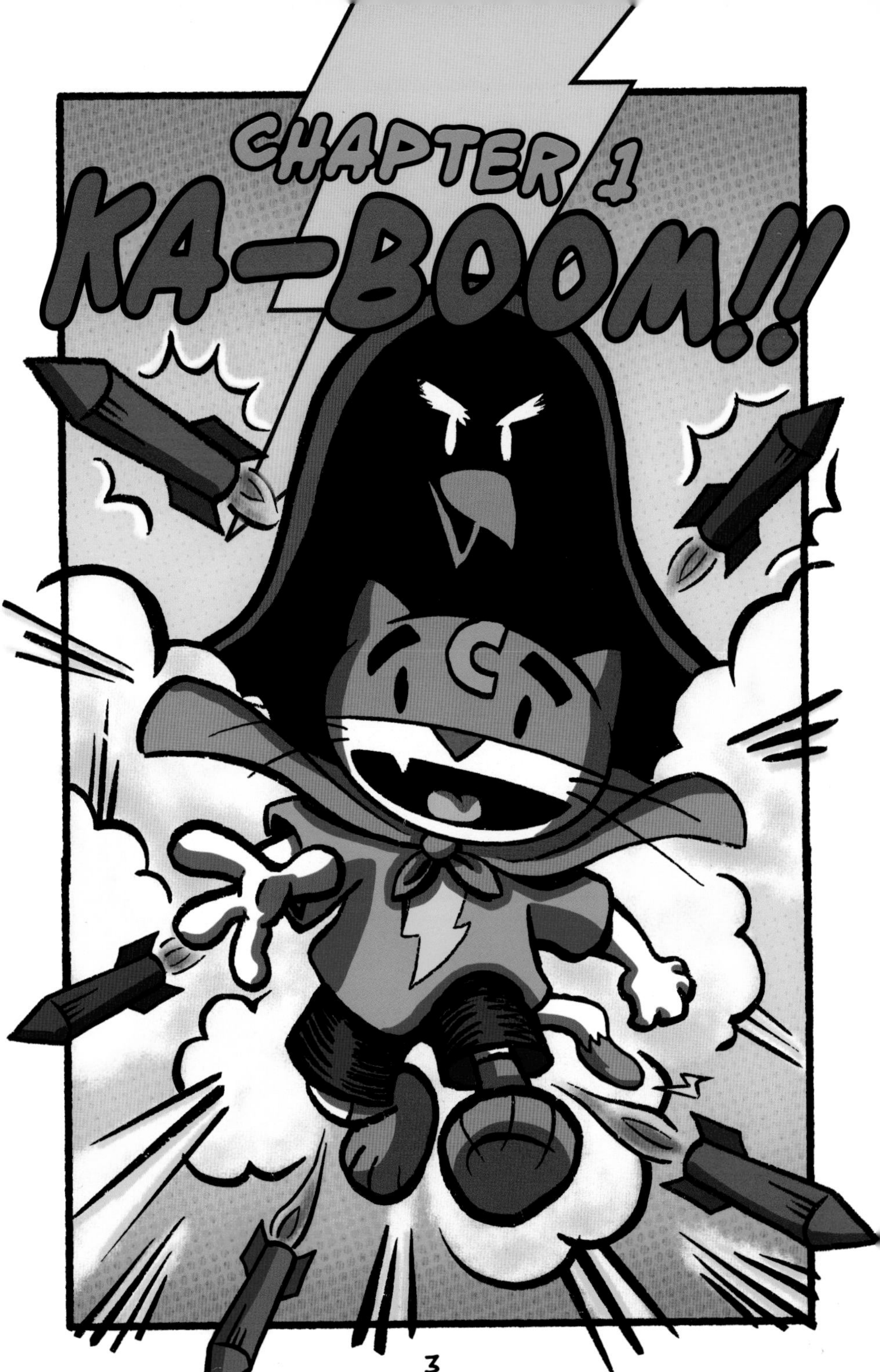
CHAPTER 1
KA-BOOM!!

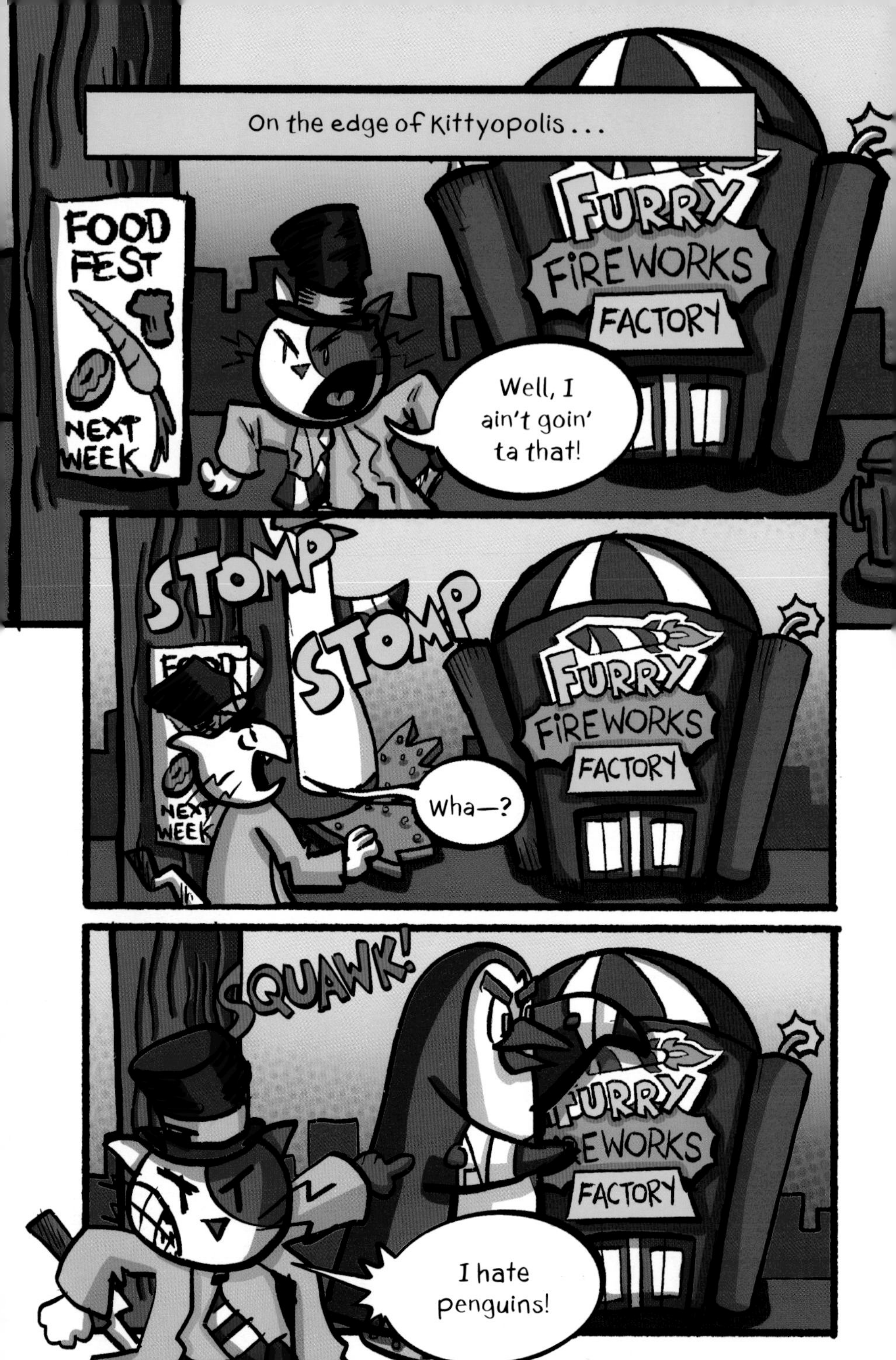
On the edge of Kittyopolis . . .
FOOD FEST NEXT WEEK
FURRY FIREWORKS FACTORY
Well, I ain't goin' ta that!
STOMP
STOMP
Wha—?
SQUAWK!
I hate penguins!

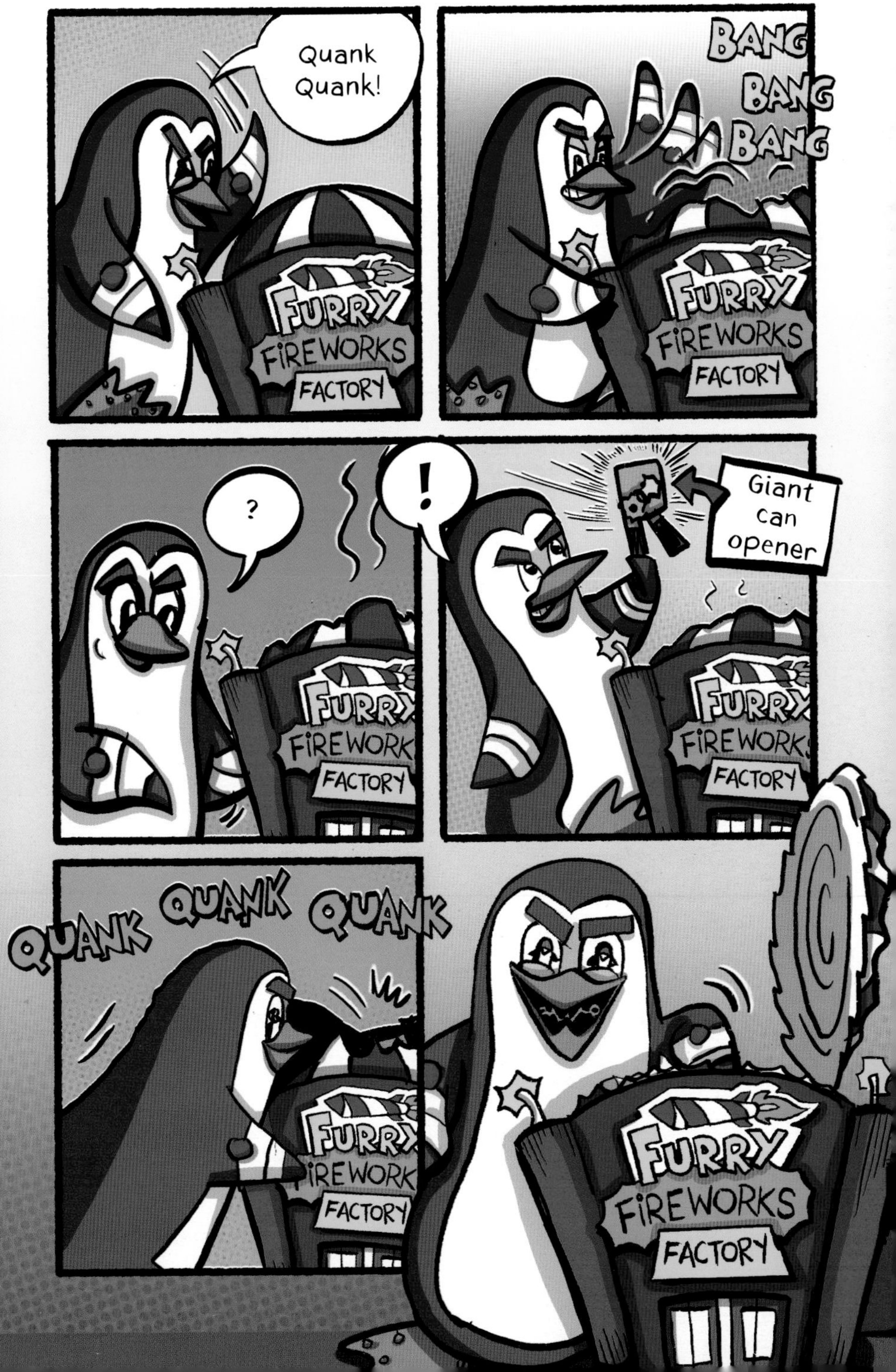
Quank Quank!
BANG
BANG
BANG
FURRY FIREWORKS FACTORY
?
!
Giant can opener
QUANK QUANK QUANK

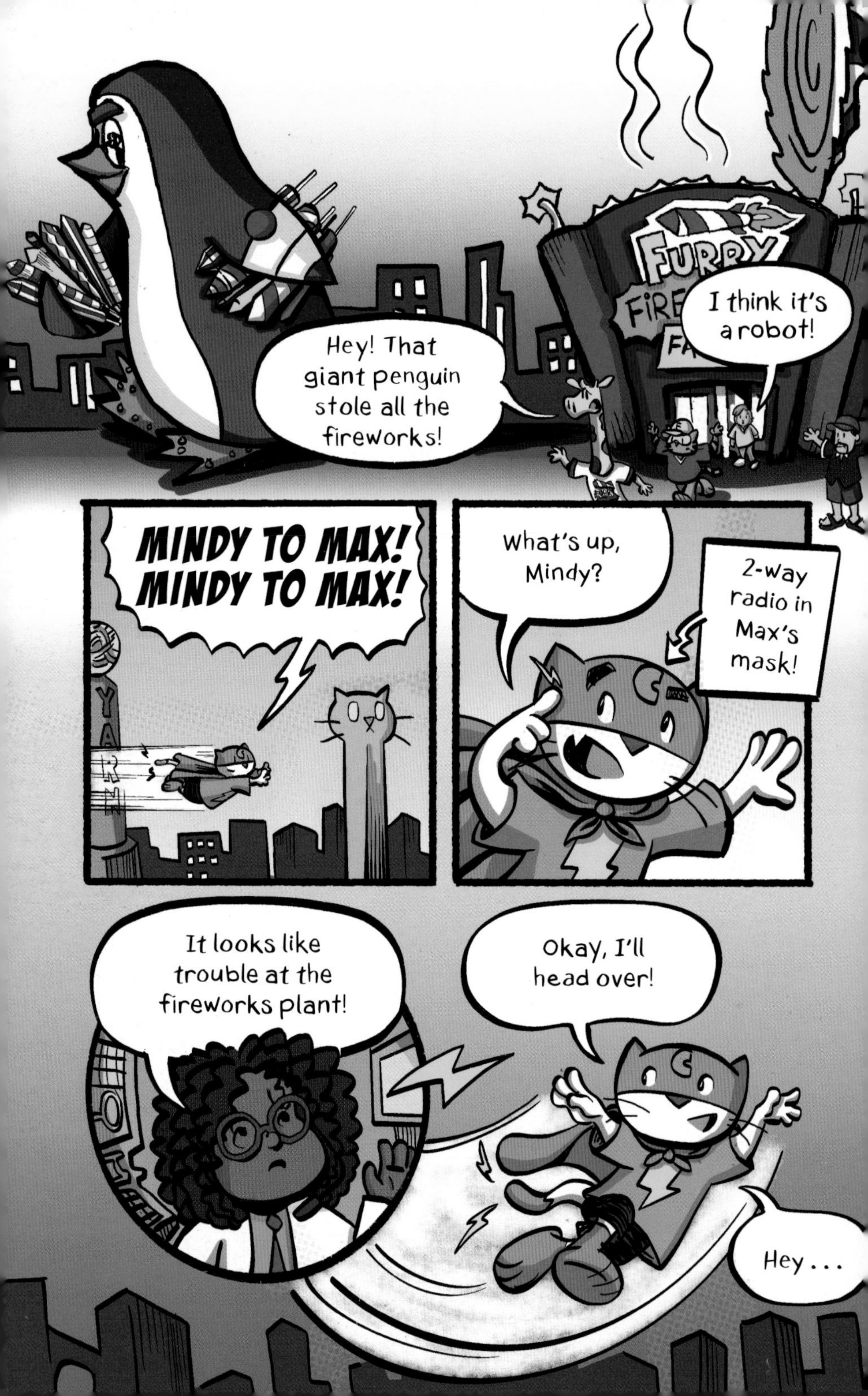
Hey! That giant penguin stole all the fireworks!
I think it's a robot!
FURRY FIRE FA
MINDY TO MAX! MINDY TO MAX!
What's up, Mindy?
2-way radio in Max's mask!
It looks like trouble at the fireworks plant!
Okay, I'll head over!
Hey . . .

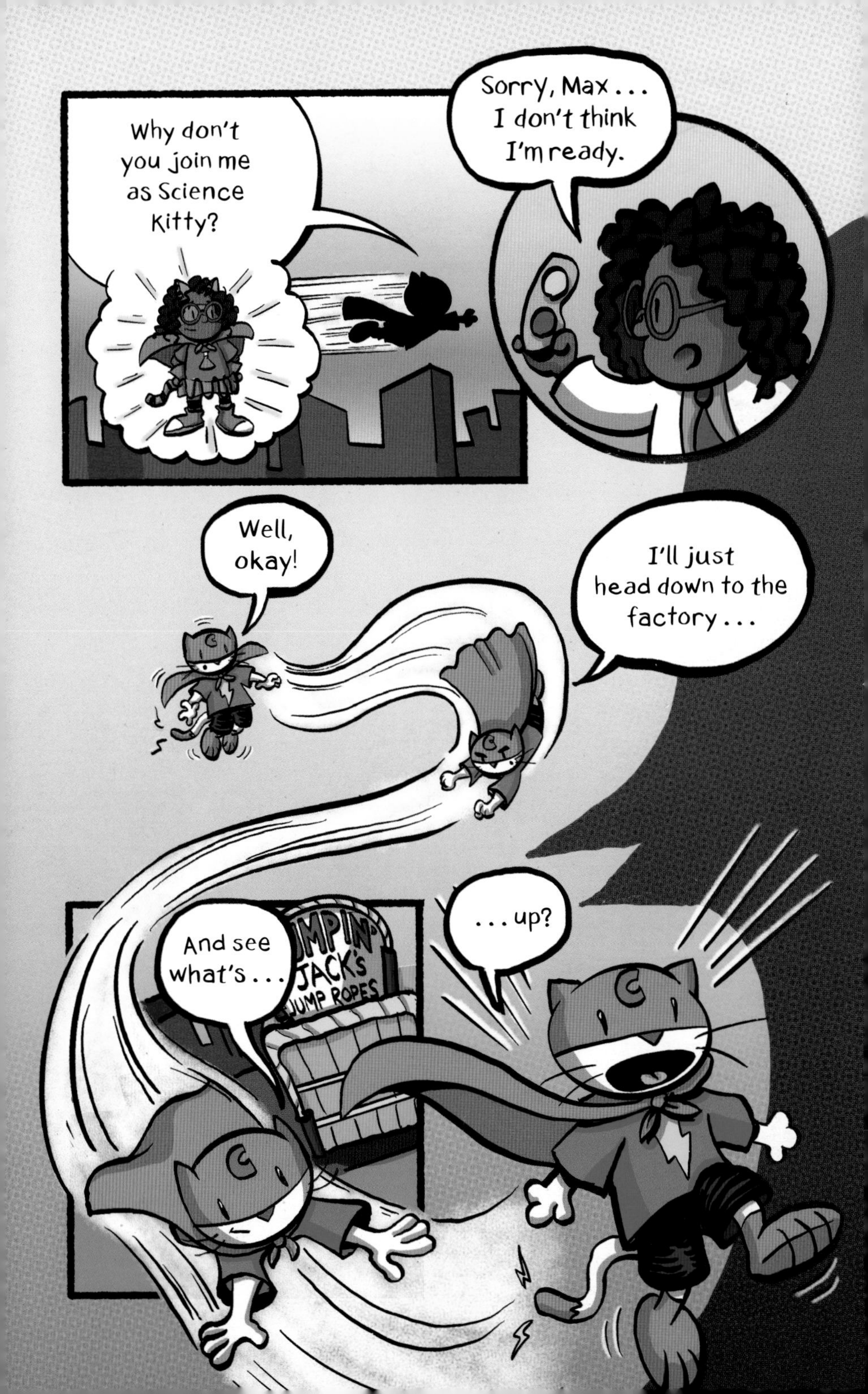
Why don't you join me as Science Kitty?
Sorry, Max . . . I don't think I'm ready.
Well, okay!
I'll just head down to the factory . . .
And see what's . . .
JACK'S
JUMP ROPES
. . . up?

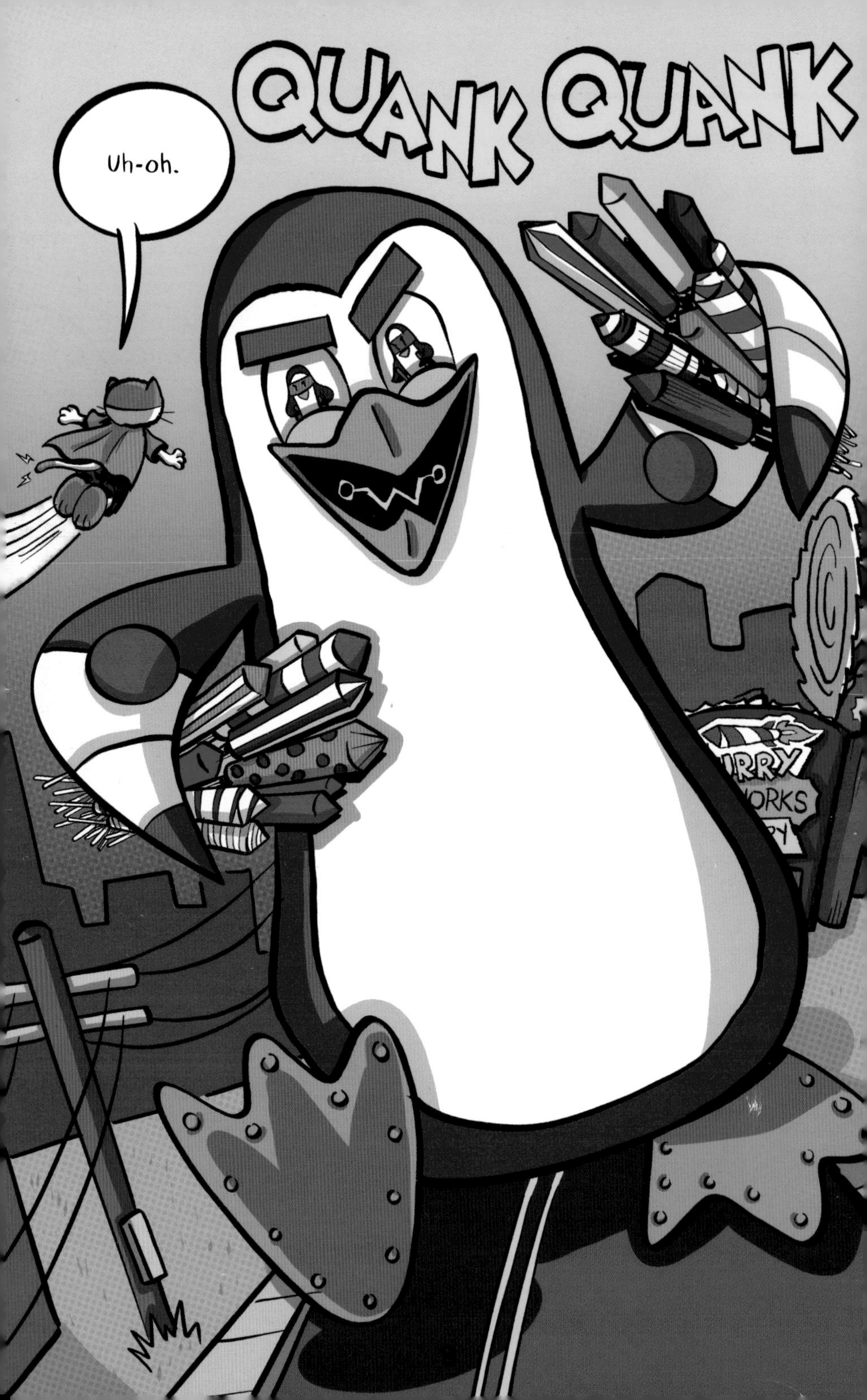

QUANK QUANK
Uh-oh.

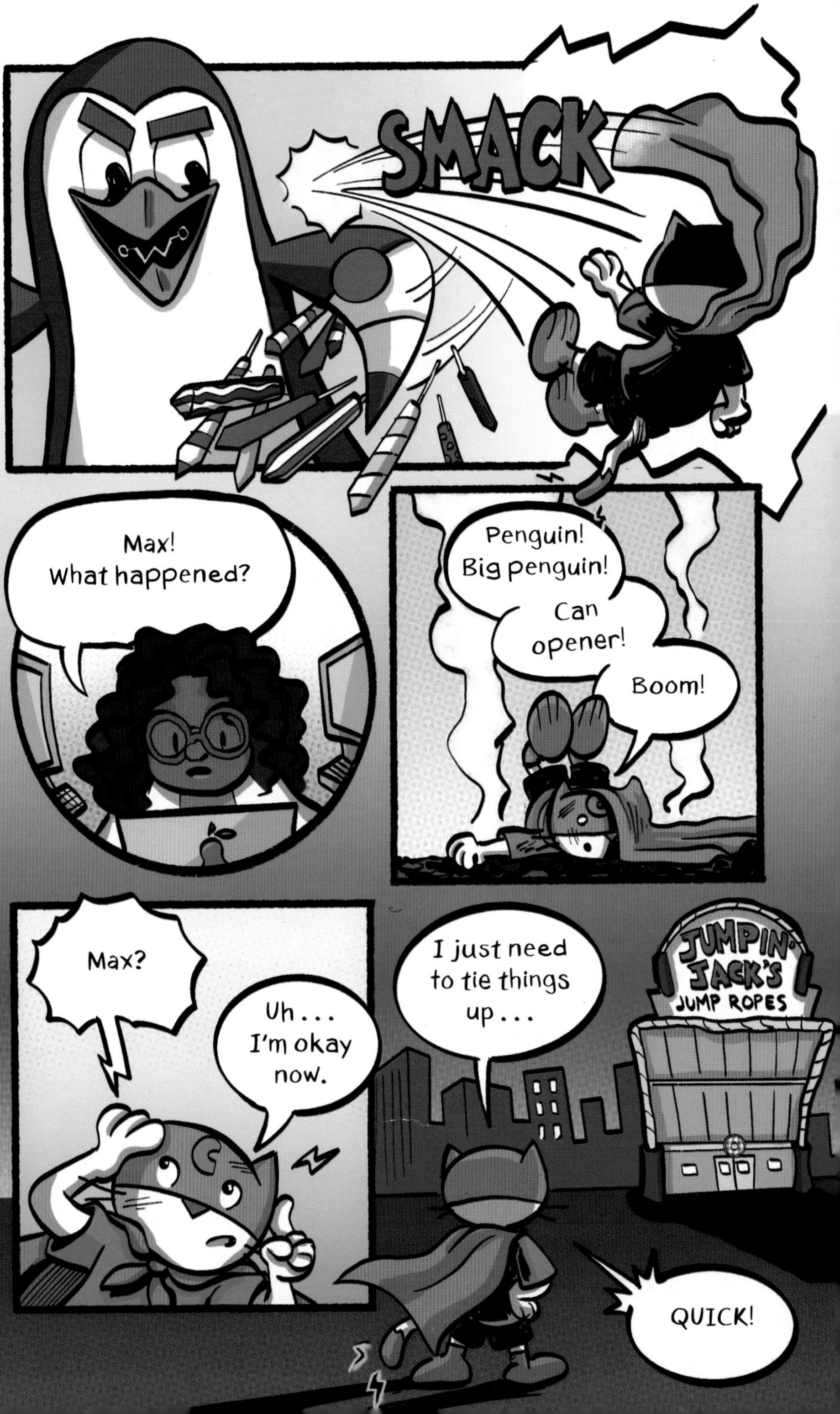
SMACK
Max!
What happened?
Penguin!
Big penguin!
Can
opener!
Boom!
Max?
Uh . . .
I'm okay
now.
I just need
to tie things
up . . .
JUMPIN'
JACK'S
JUMP ROPES
QUICK!

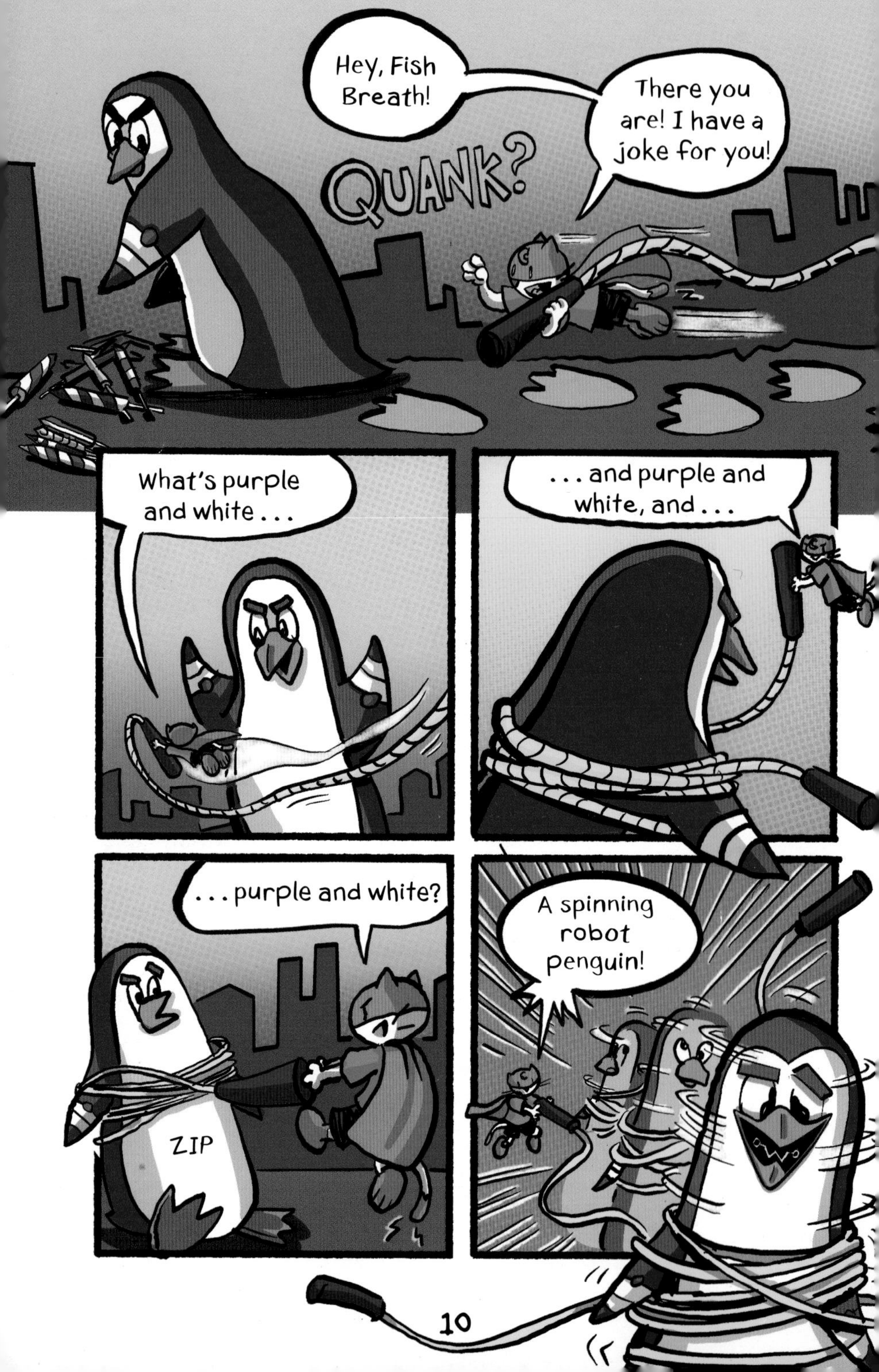
Hey, Fish Breath!
There you are! I have a joke for you!
QUANK?
What's purple and white . . .
. . . and purple and white, and . . .
. . . purple and white?
ZIP
A spinning robot penguin!

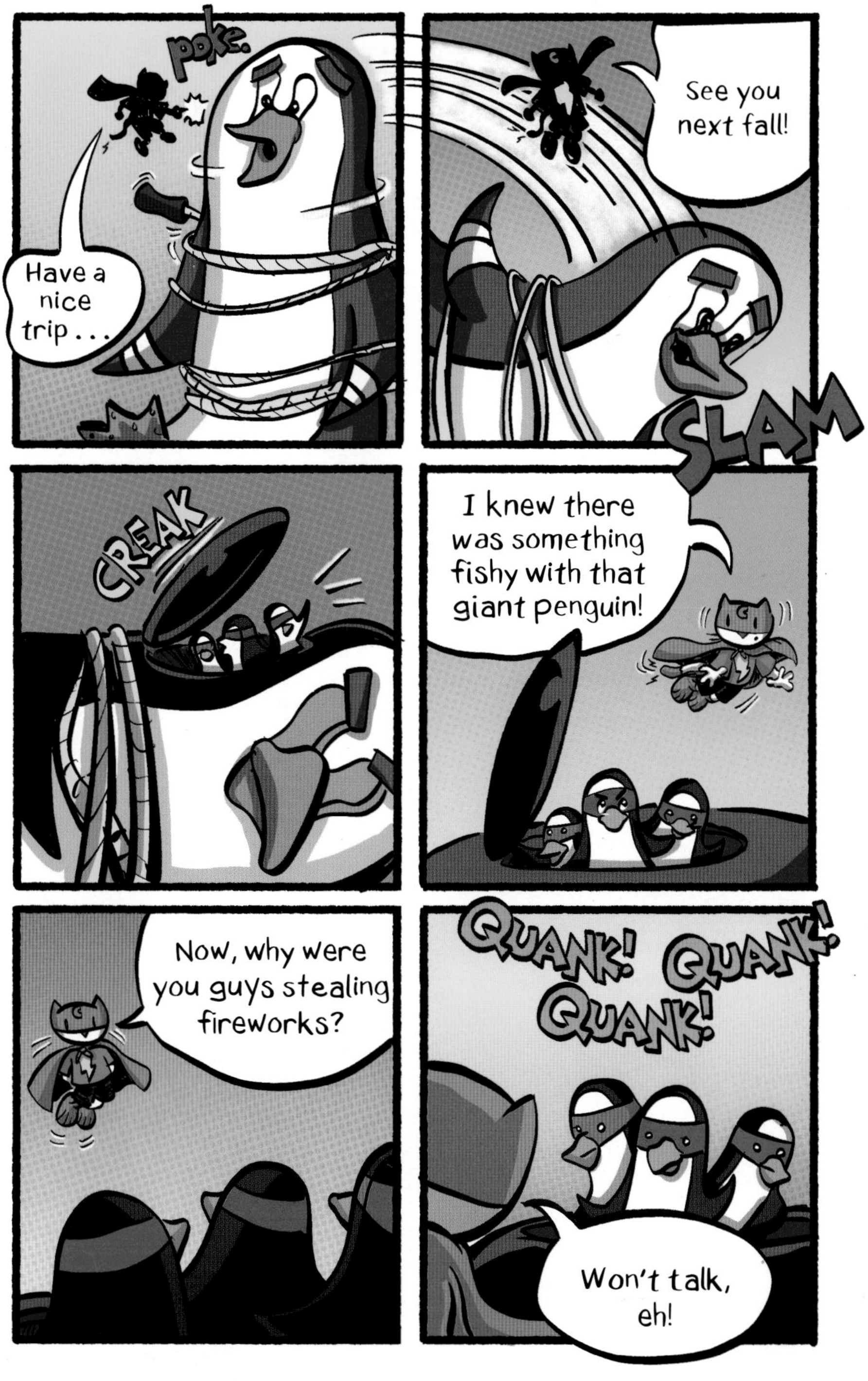
POKE.
Have a nice trip . . .
See you next fall!
SLAM
CREAK
I knew there was something fishy with that giant penguin!
Now, why were you guys stealing fireworks?
QUANK! QUANK! QUANK!
Won't talk, eh!

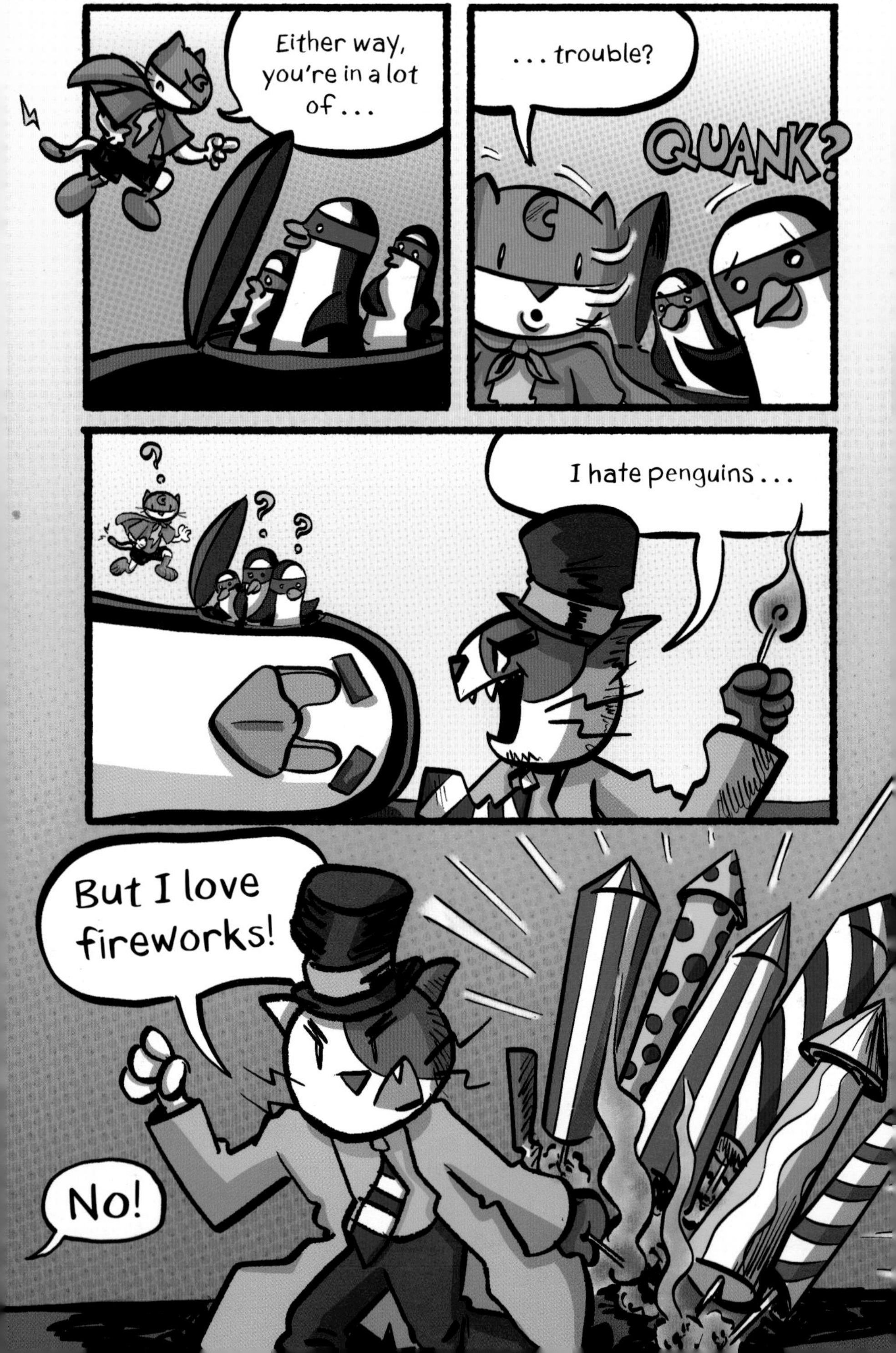
Either way, you're in a lot of . . .
. . . trouble?
QUANK?
I hate penguins . . .
But I love fireworks!
No!

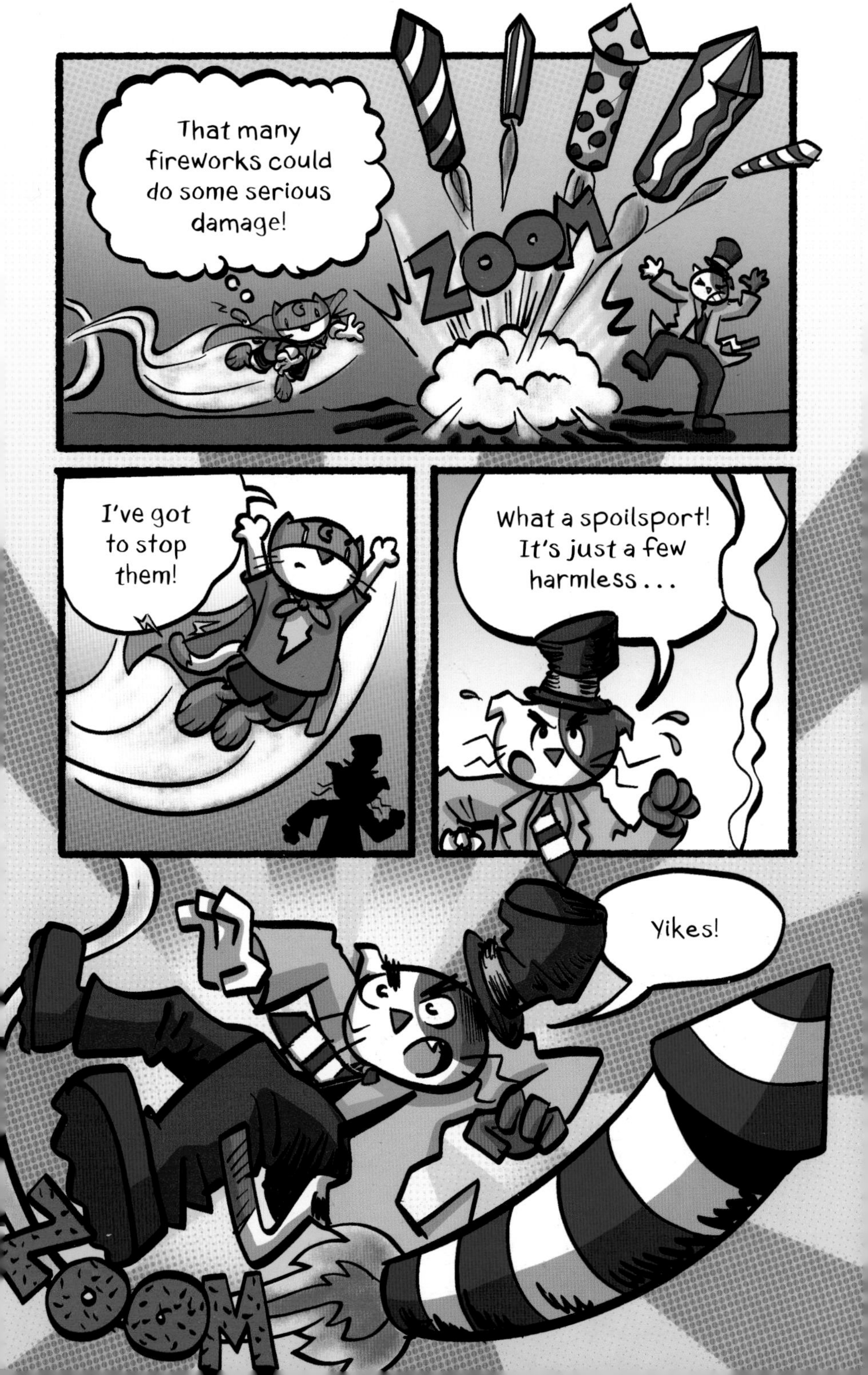
That many fireworks could do some serious damage!
ZOOM
I've got to stop them!
What a spoilsport! It's just a few harmless . . .
Yikes!
YOOOM

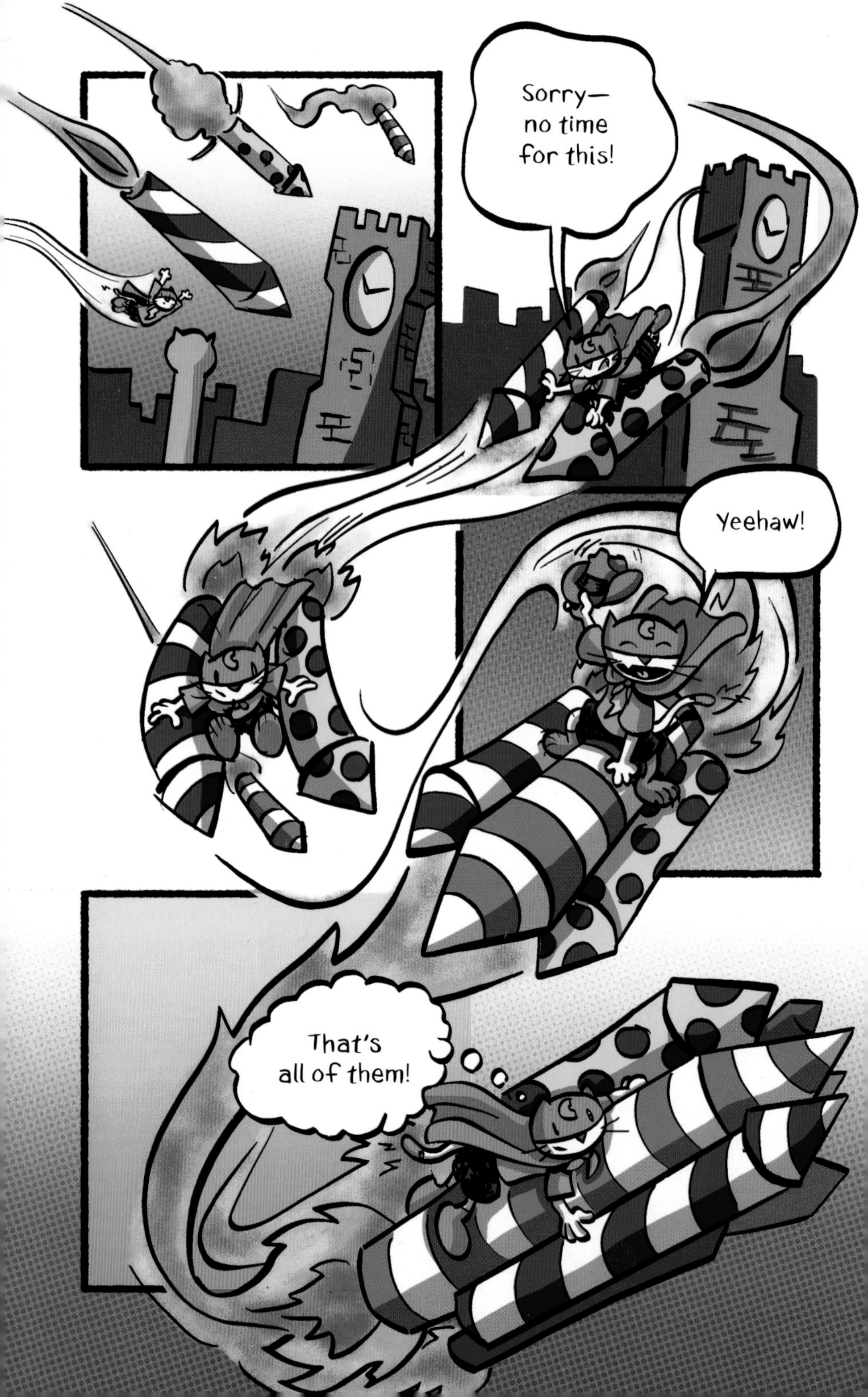
Sorry—
no time
for this!
Yeehaw!
That's
all of them!

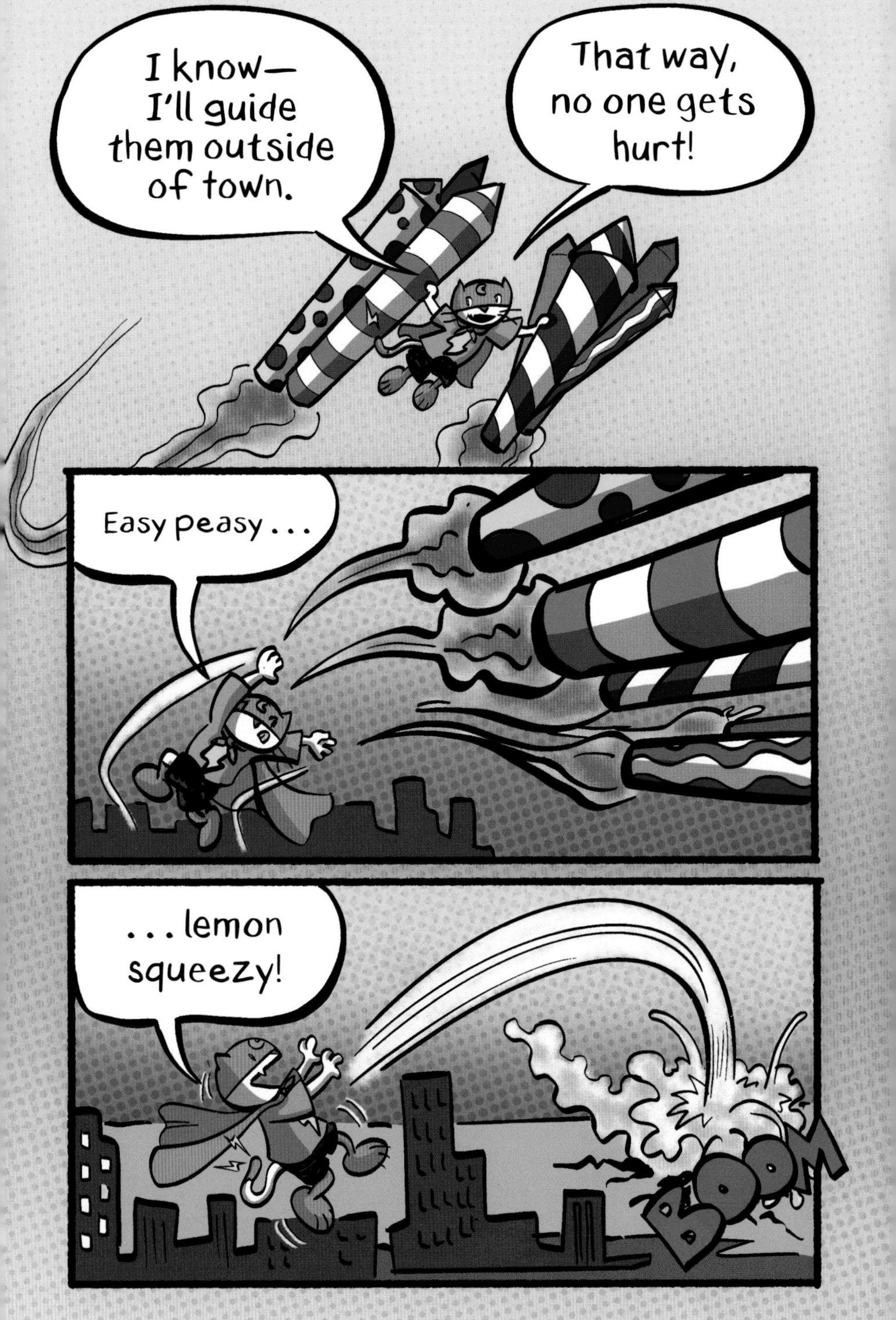

I know—
I'll guide
them outside
of town.
That way,
no one gets
hurt!
Easy peasy . . .
. . . lemon
squeezy!
BOOM

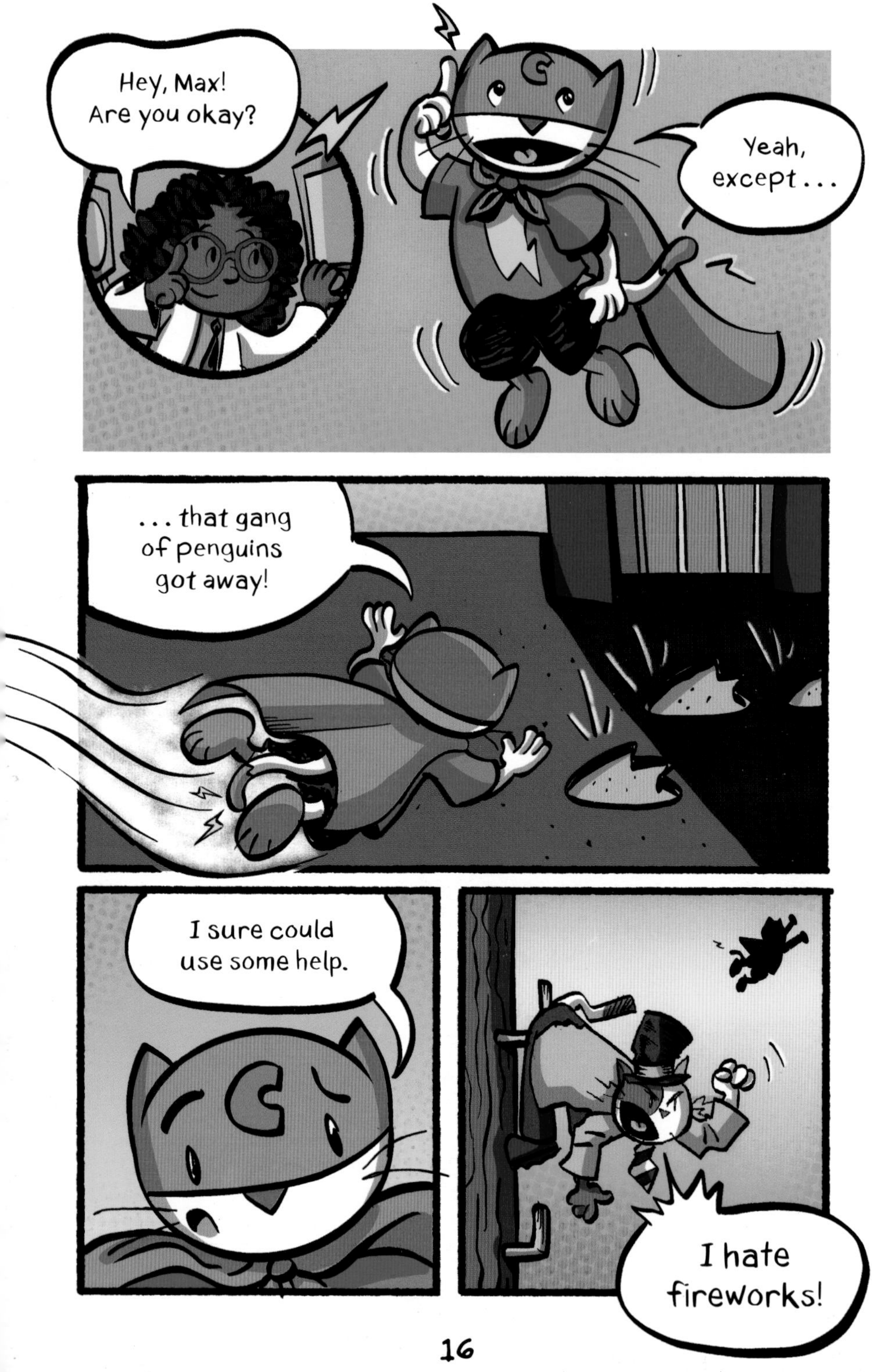
Hey, Max!
Are you okay?
Yeah,
except . . .
. . . that gang
of penguins
got away!
I sure could
use some help.
I hate
fireworks!

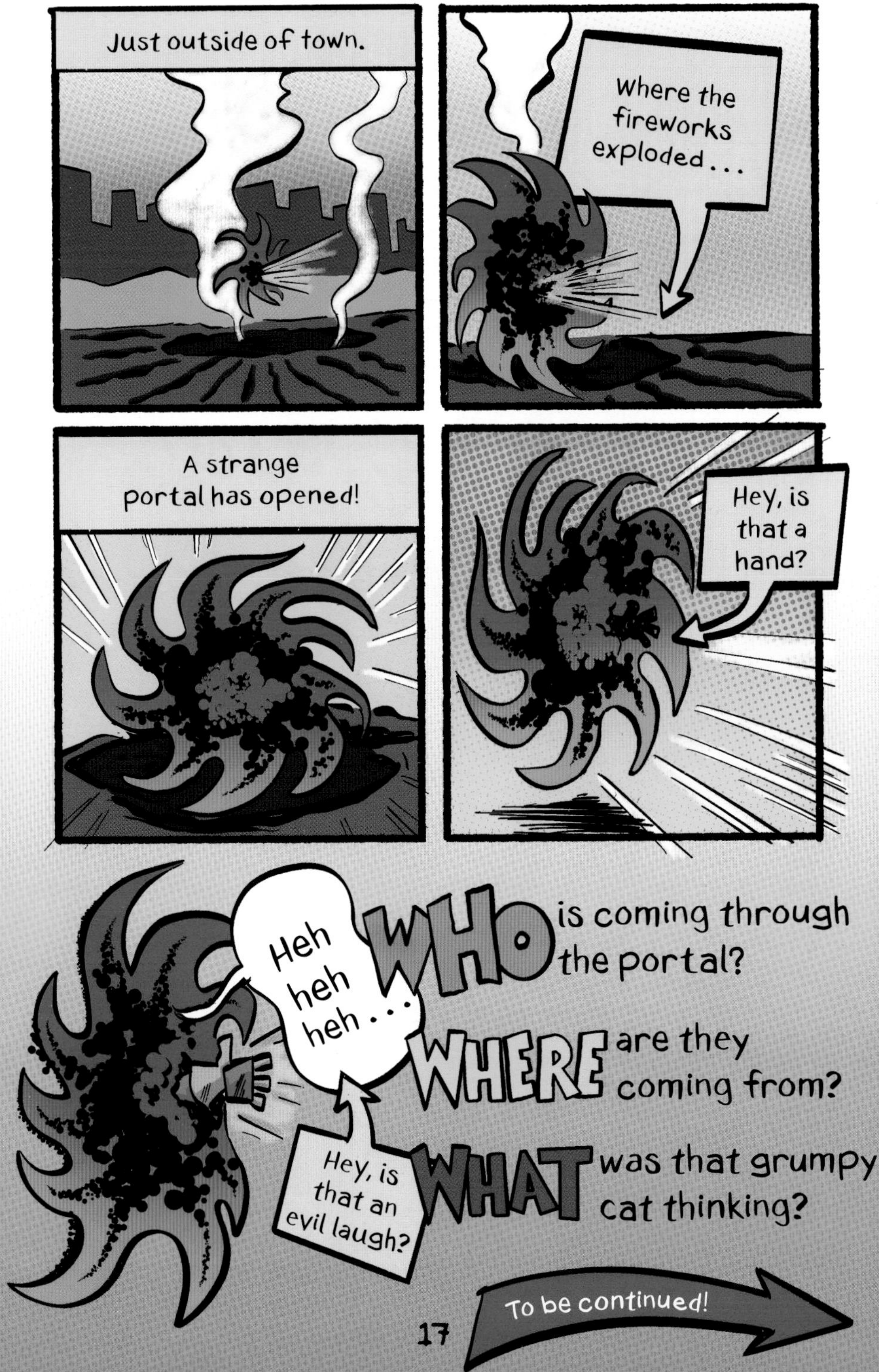
Just outside of town.
Where the fireworks exploded . . .
A strange portal has opened!
Hey, is that a hand?
Heh heh heh . . .
Hey, is that an evil laugh?
WHO is coming through the portal?
WHERE are they coming from?
WHAT was that grumpy cat thinking?
To be continued!

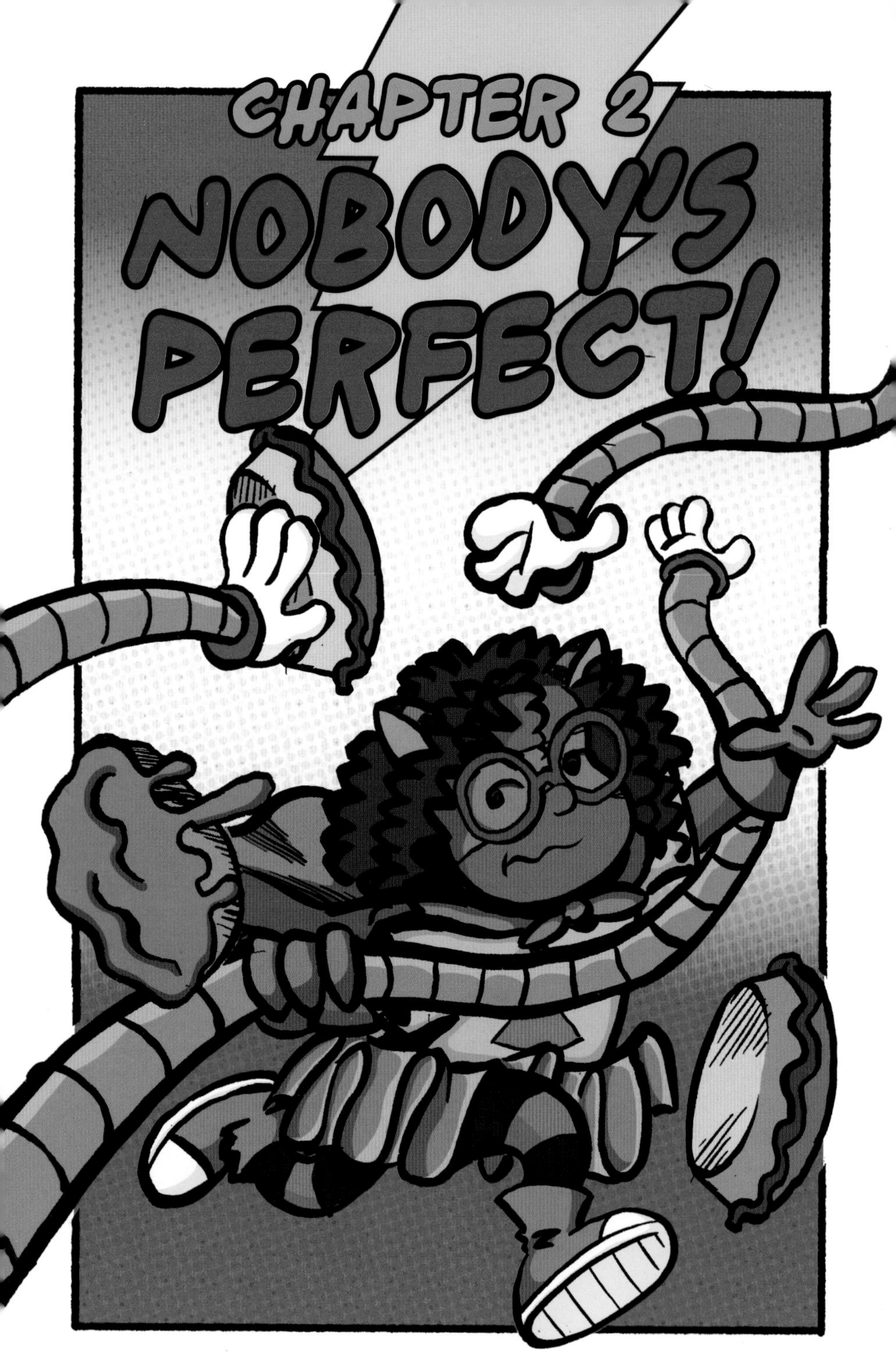
CHAPTER 2
NOBODY'S PERFECT!

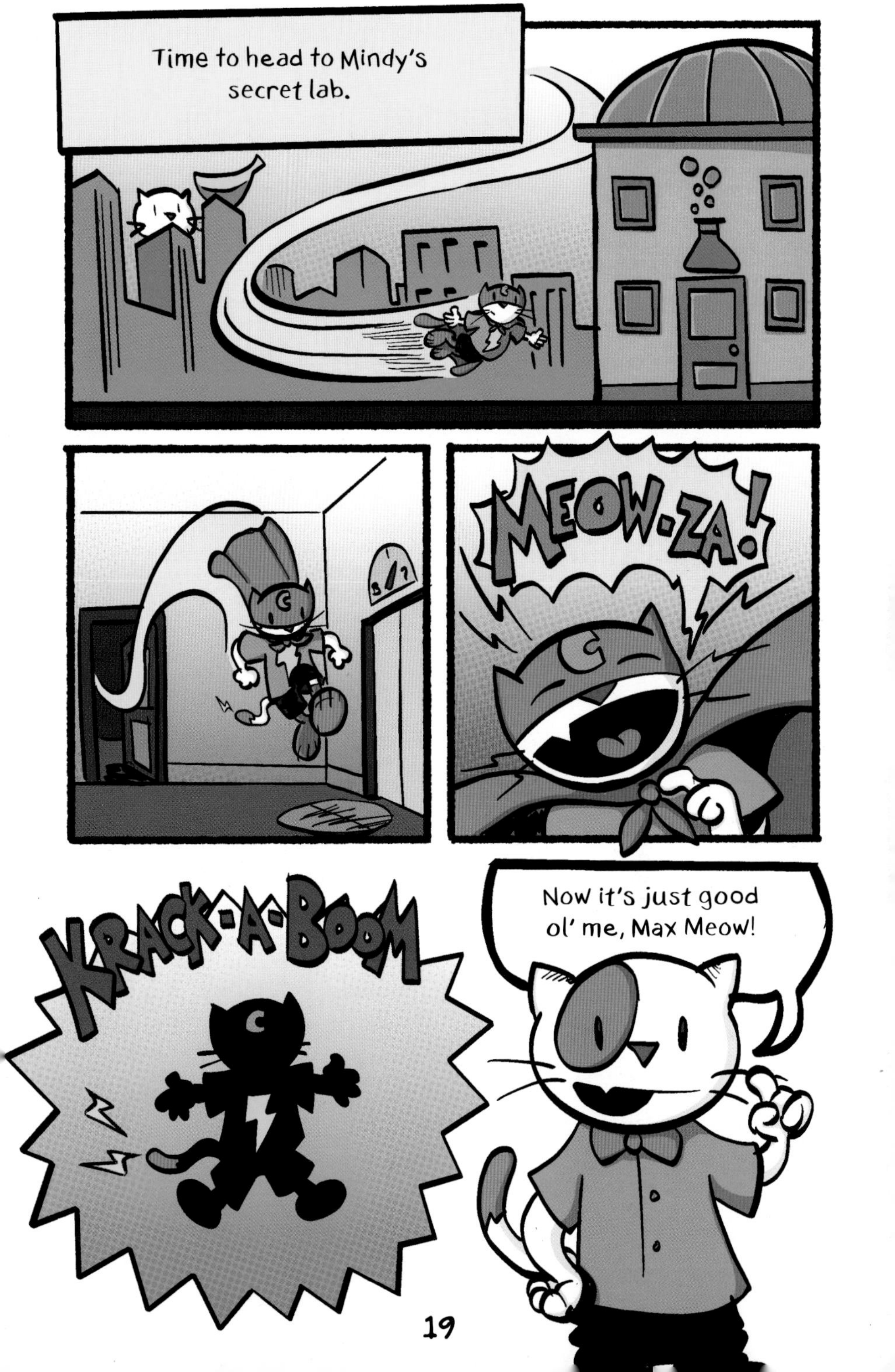

Time to head to Mindy's secret lab.
MEOW-ZA!
KRACK-A-BOOM
Now it's just good ol' me, Max Meow!

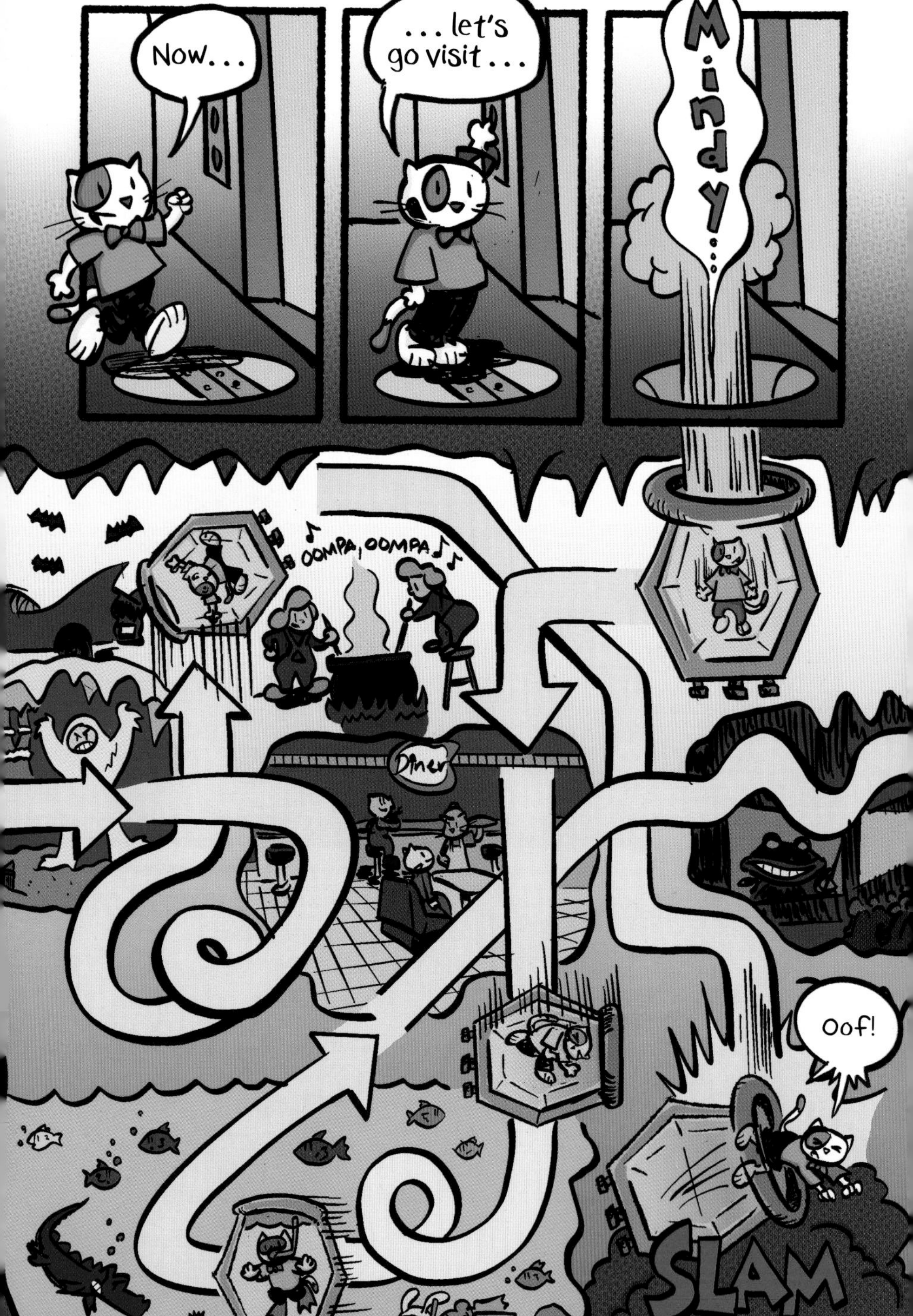
Now...
...let's go visit...
Mindy...
OOMPA, OOMPA
Diner
Oof!
SLAM

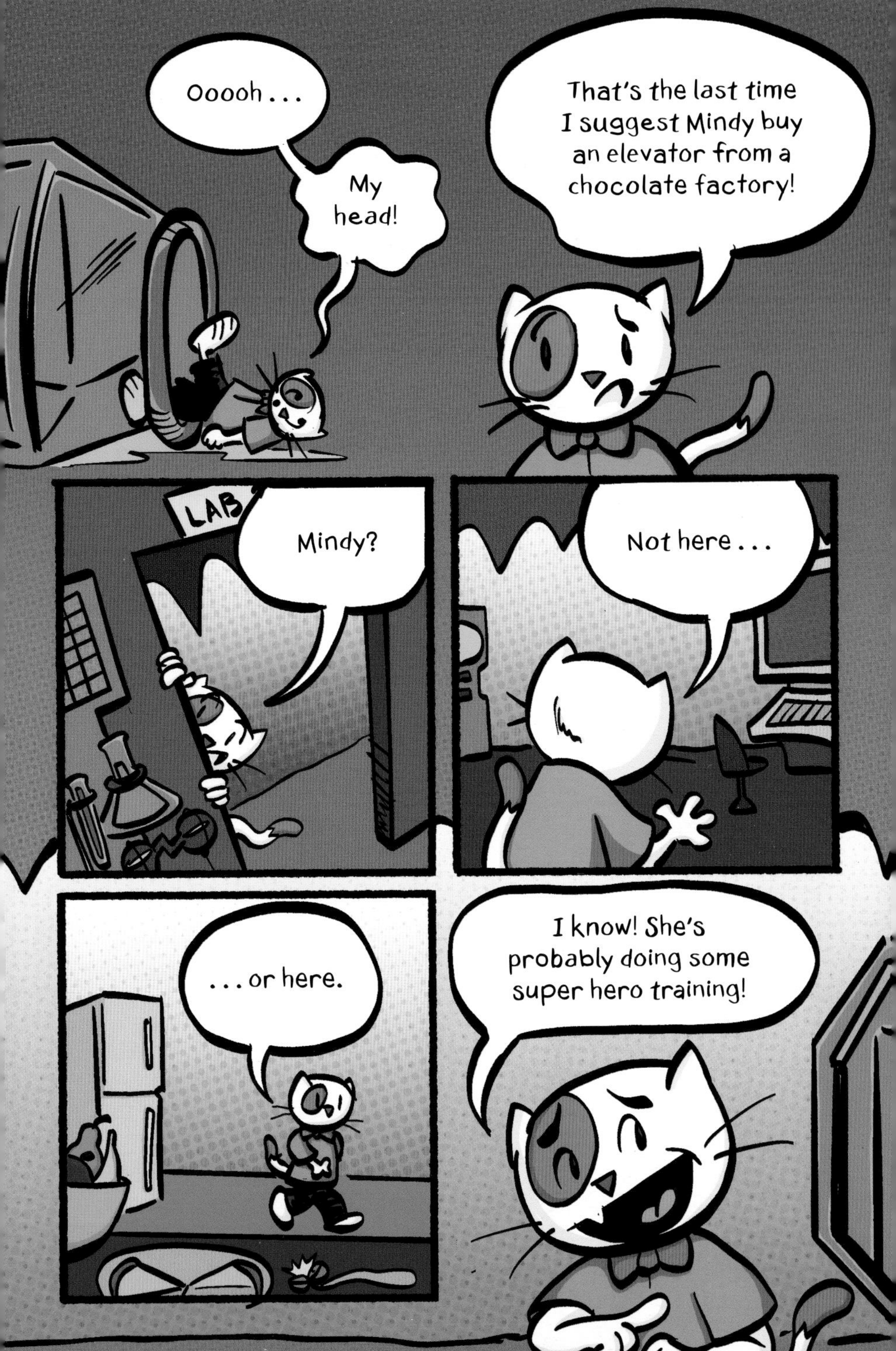
Ooooh . . .
My head!
That's the last time I suggest Mindy buy an elevator from a chocolate factory!
LAB
Mindy?
Not here . . .
. . . or here.
I know! She's probably doing some super hero training!

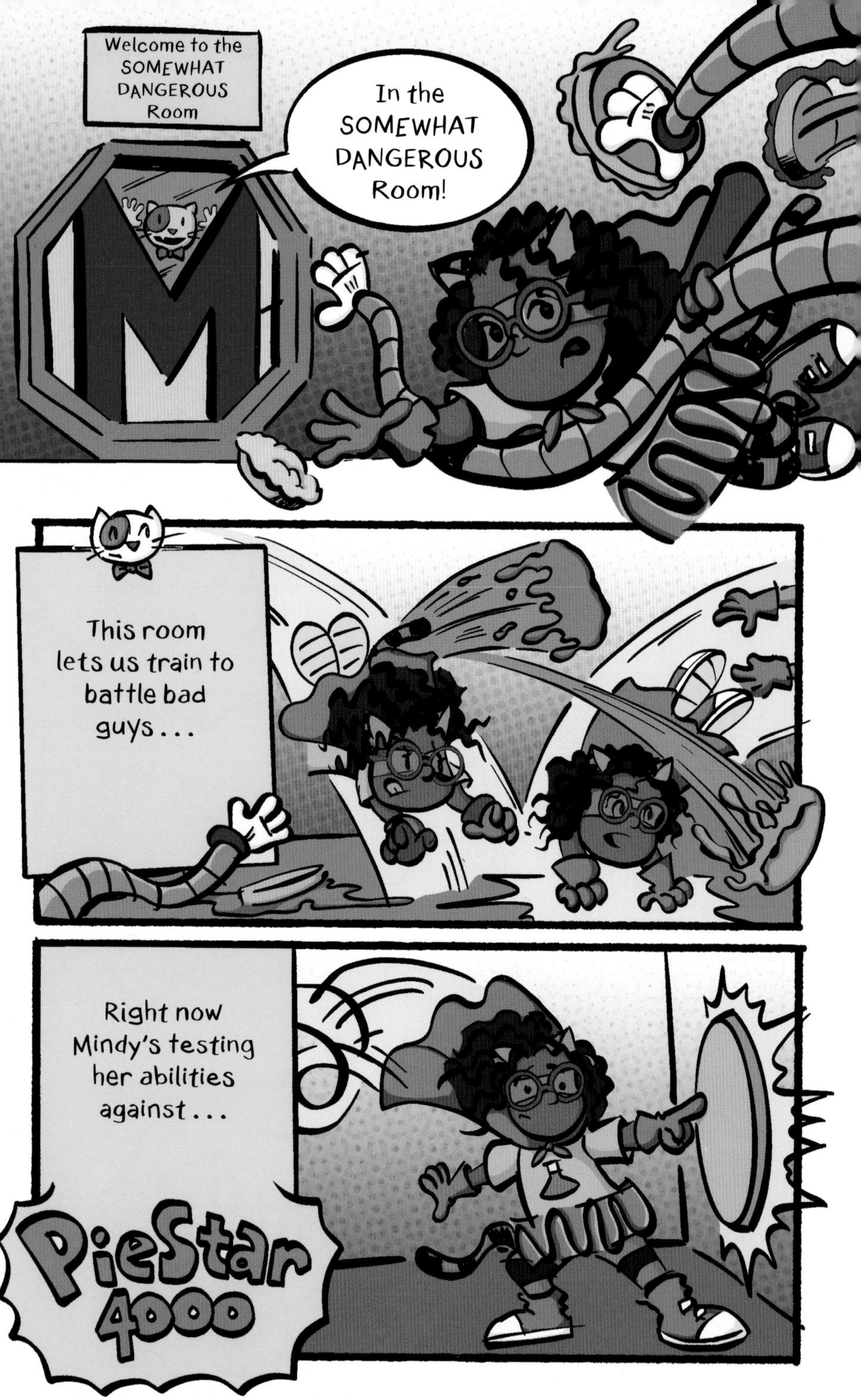
Welcome to the SOMEWHAT DANGEROUS Room
In the SOMEWHAT DANGEROUS Room!
This room lets us train to battle bad guys . . .
Right now Mindy's testing her abilities against . . .
PieStar 4000

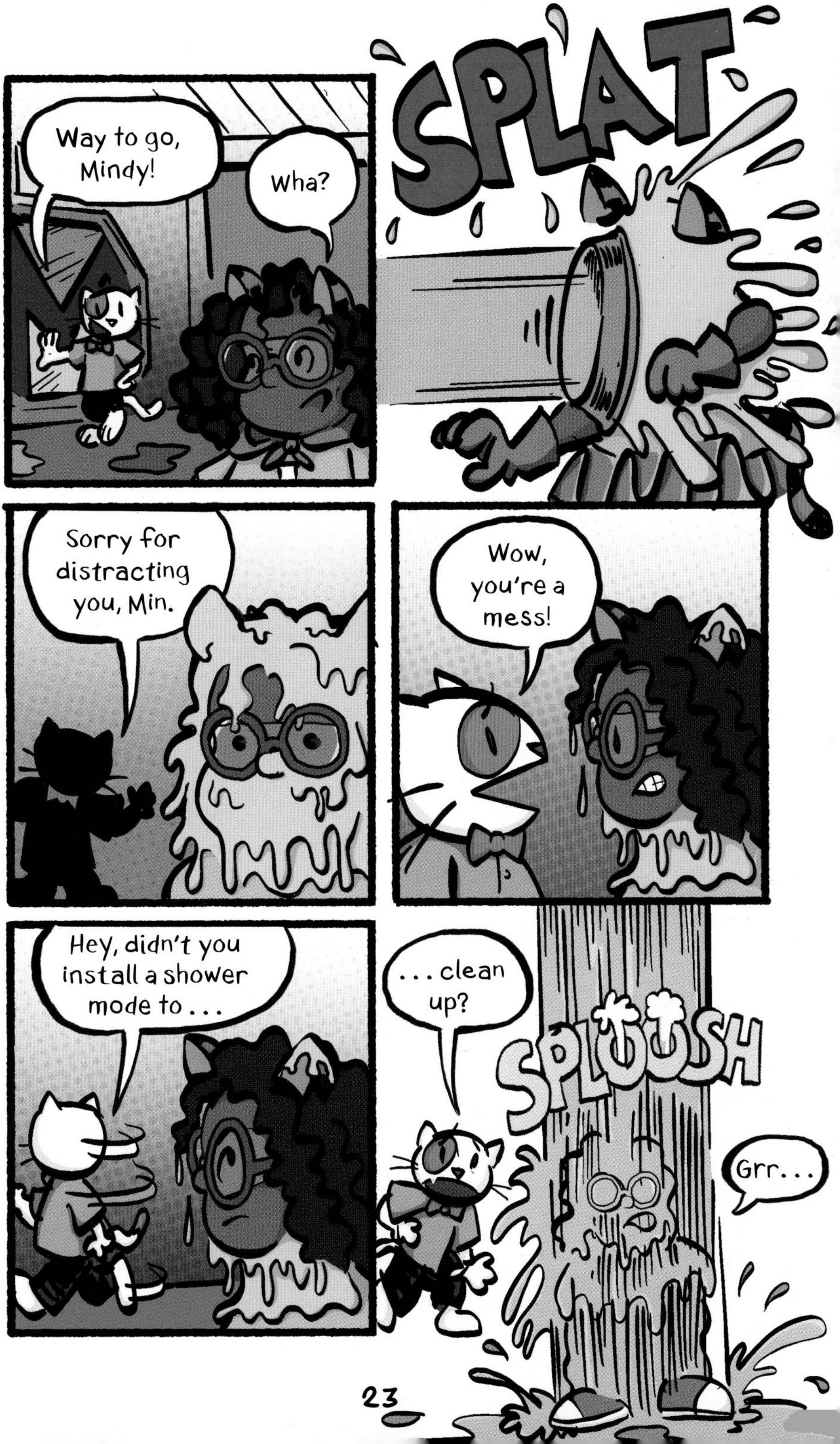
Way to go, Mindy!
Wha?
SPLAT
Sorry for distracting you, Min.
Wow, you're a mess!
Hey, didn't you install a shower mode to . . .
. . . clean up?
SPLOOSH
Grr. . .

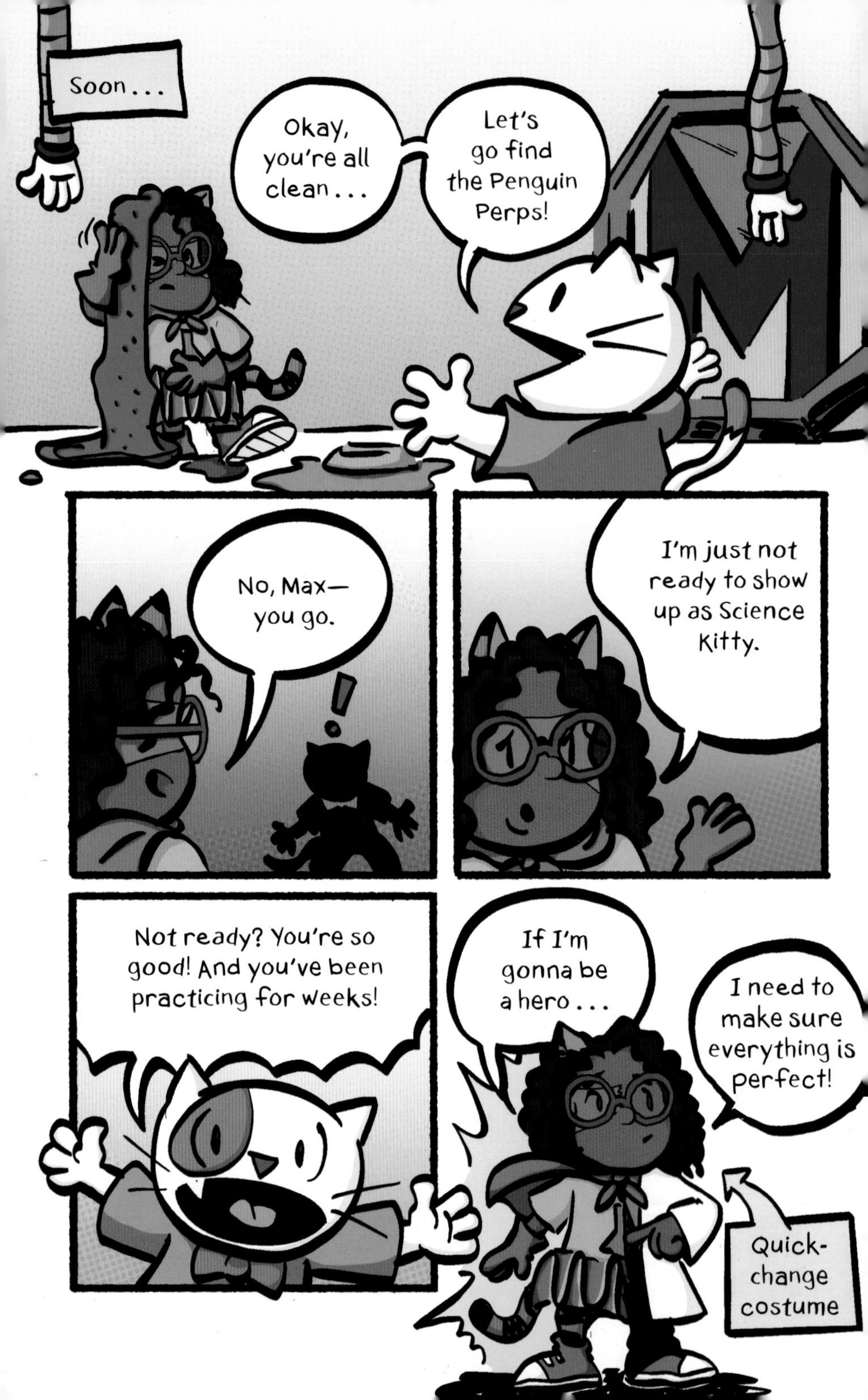
Soon . . .
Okay, you're all clean . . .
Let's go find the Penguin Perps!
No, Max— you go.
!
I'm just not ready to show up as Science Kitty.
Not ready? You're so good! And you've been practicing for weeks!
If I'm gonna be a hero . . .
I need to make sure everything is perfect!
Quick-change costume

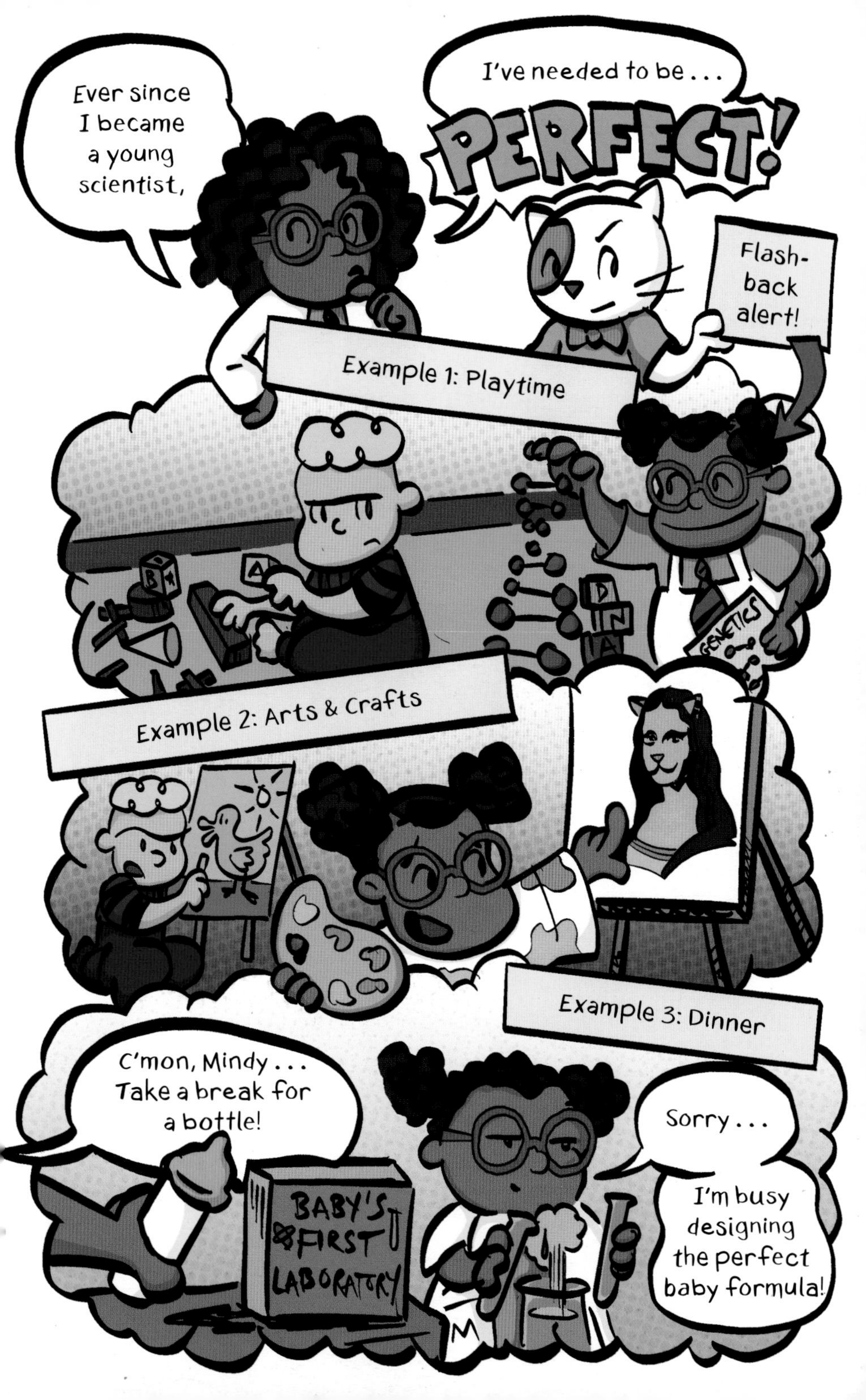
Ever since I became a young scientist,
I've needed to be . . .
PERFECT!
Flash-back alert!
Example 1: Playtime
GENETICS
Example 2: Arts & Crafts
Example 3: Dinner
C'mon, Mindy . . . Take a break for a bottle!
Sorry . . .
I'm busy designing the perfect baby formula!
BABY'S FIRST LABORATORY

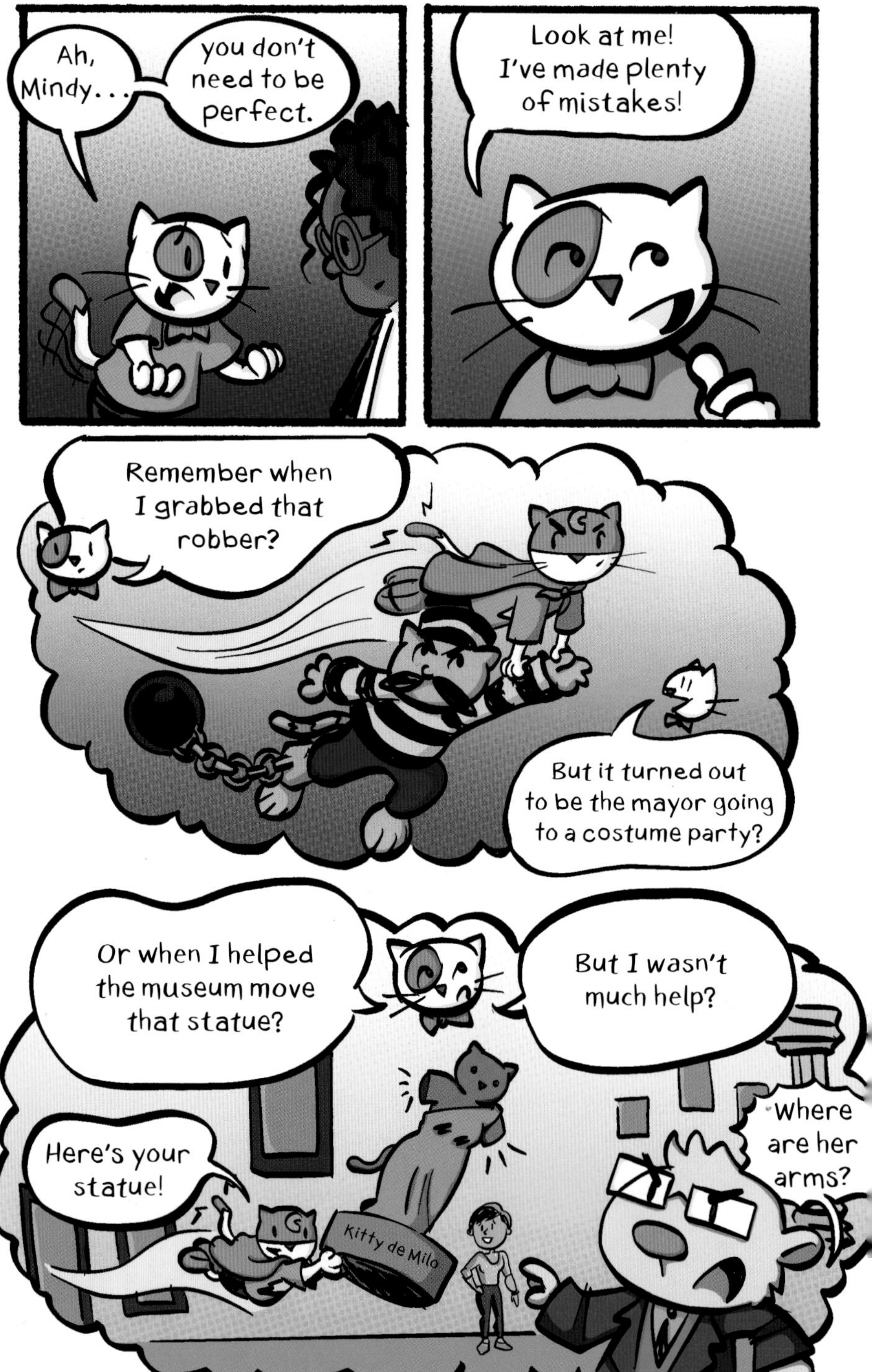
Ah, Mindy. . .
you don't need to be perfect.
Look at me! I've made plenty of mistakes!
Remember when I grabbed that robber?
But it turned out to be the mayor going to a costume party?
Or when I helped the museum move that statue?
But I wasn't much help?
Here's your statue!
Kitty de Milo
Where are her arms?

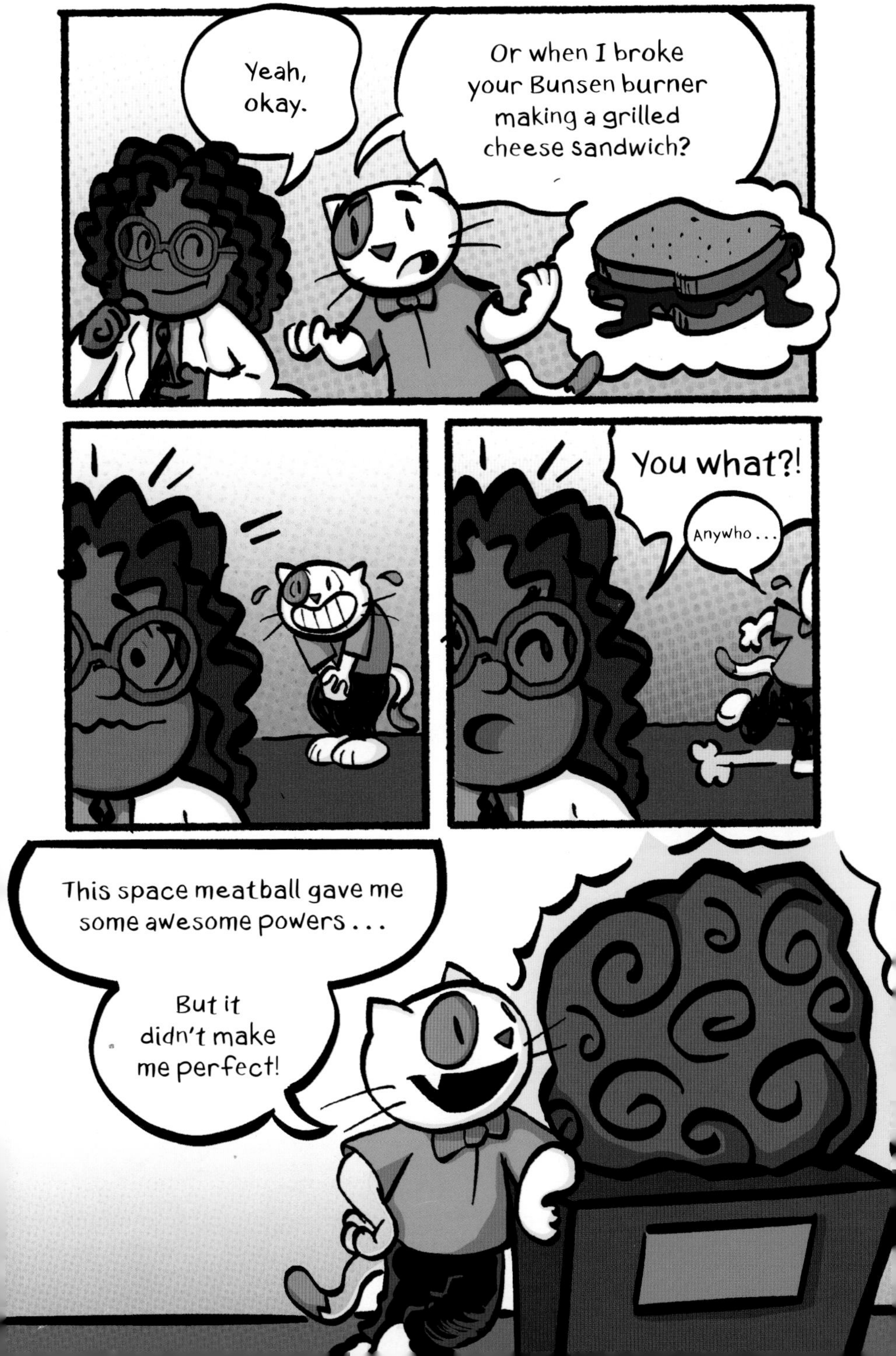
Yeah, okay.
Or when I broke your Bunsen burner making a grilled cheese sandwich?
You what?!
Anywho . . .
This space meatball gave me some awesome powers . . .
But it didn't make me perfect!

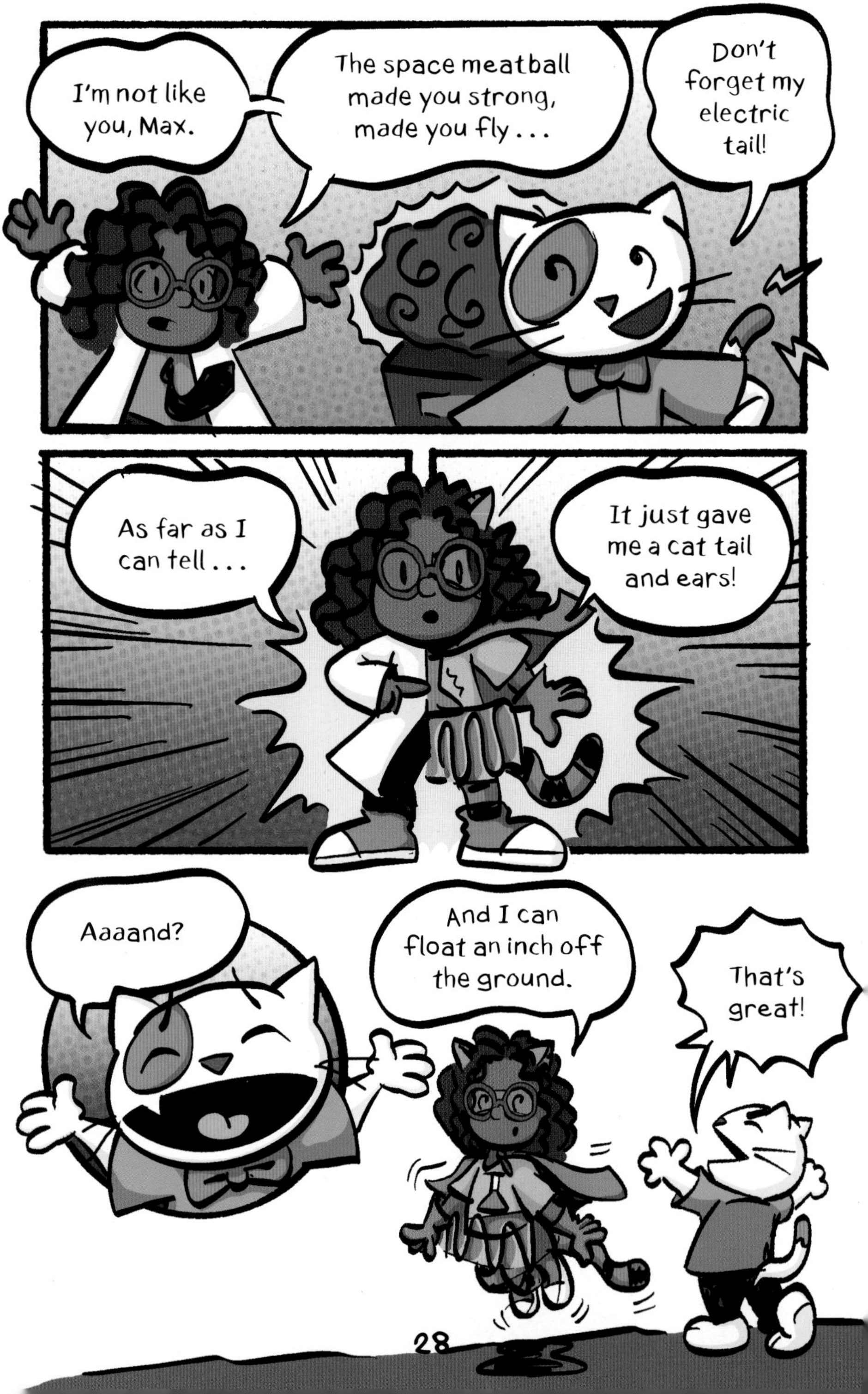
I'm not like you, Max.
The space meatball made you strong, made you fly . . .
Don't forget my electric tail!
As far as I can tell . . .
It just gave me a cat tail and ears!
Aaaand?
And I can float an inch off the ground.
That's great!

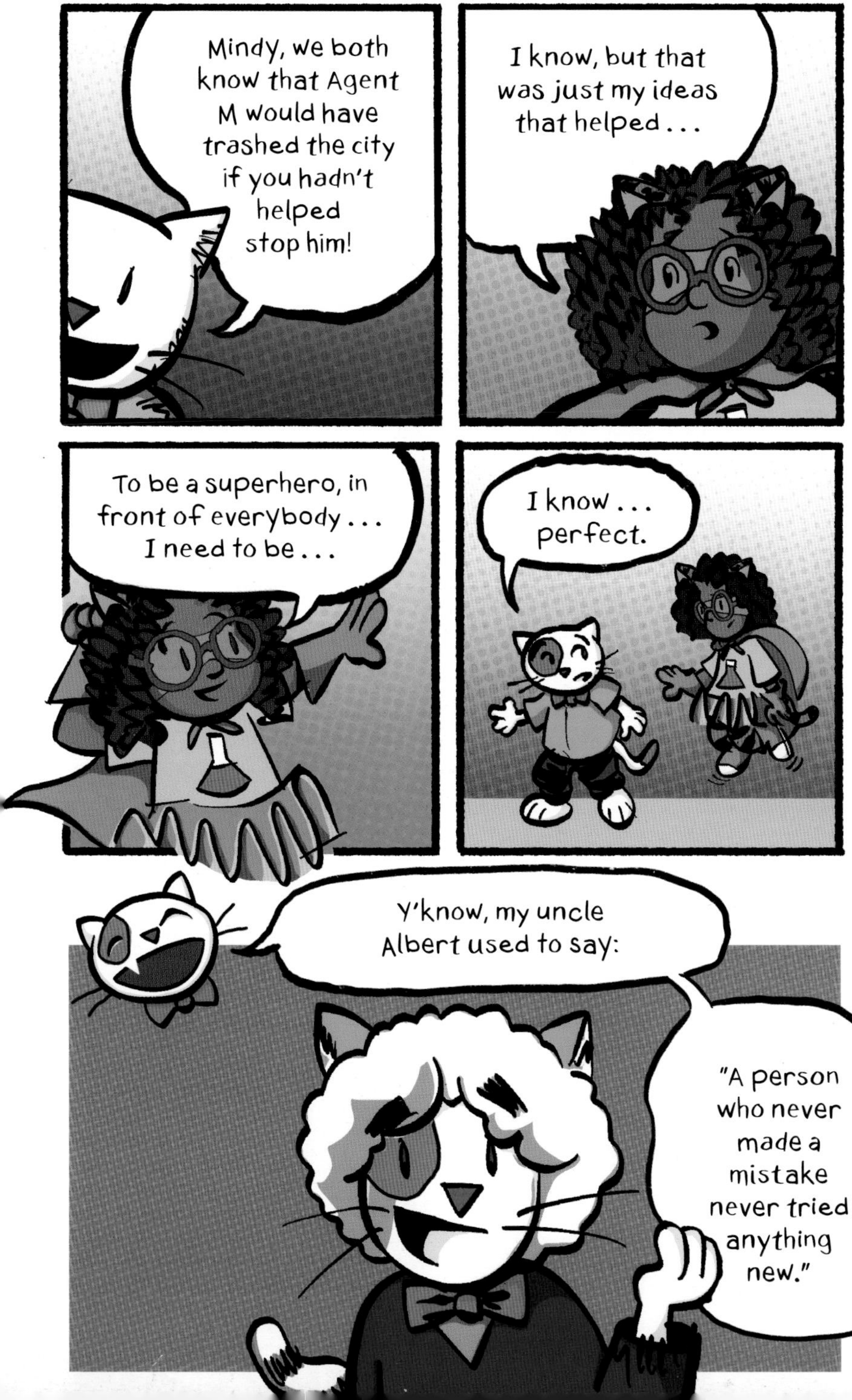
Mindy, we both know that Agent M would have trashed the city if you hadn't helped stop him!
I know, but that was just my ideas that helped . . .
To be a superhero, in front of everybody . . . I need to be . . .
I know . . . perfect.
Y'know, my uncle Albert used to say:
"A person who never made a mistake never tried anything new."

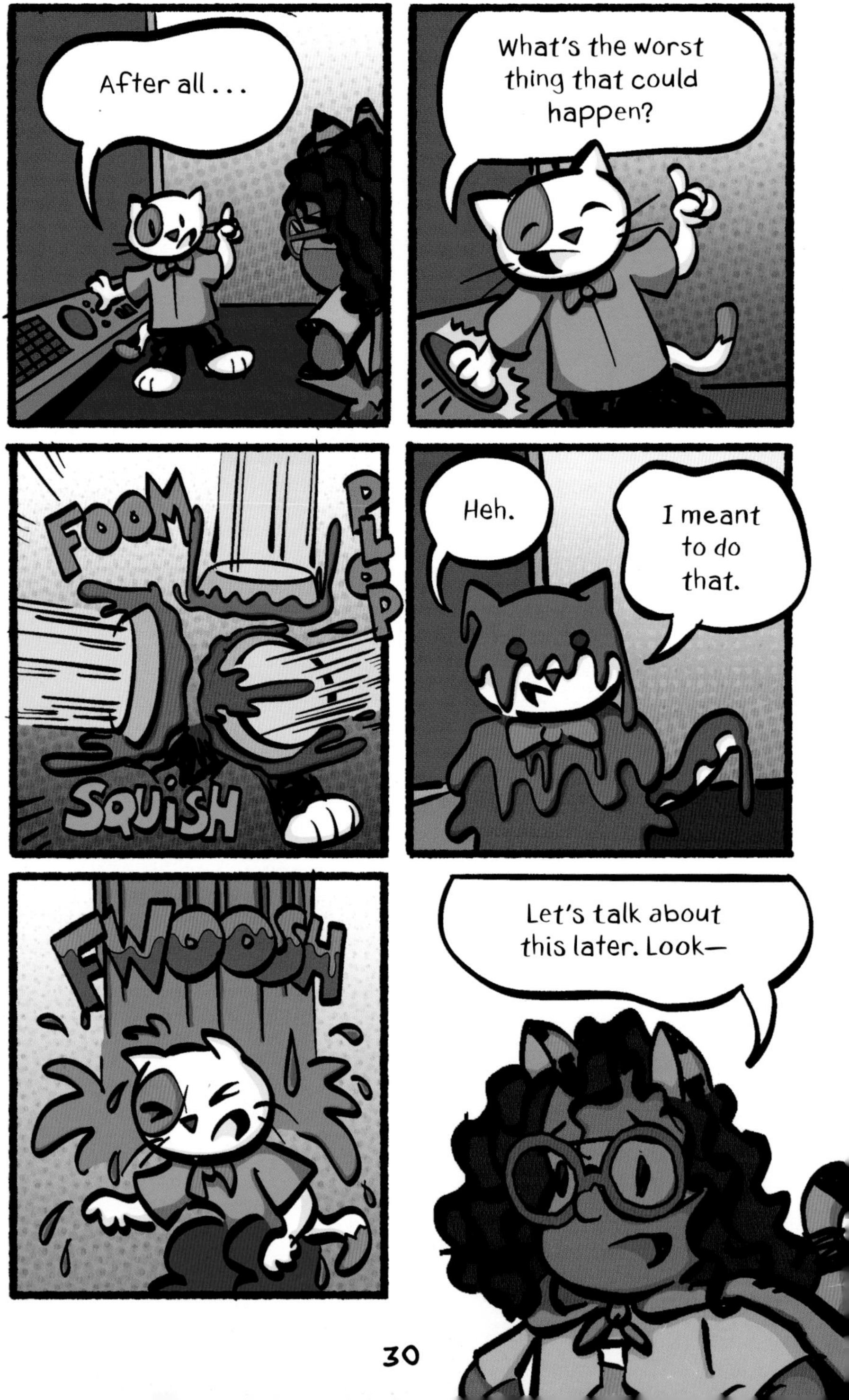
After all . . .
What's the worst thing that could happen?
FOOM
PLOP
SQUISH
Heh.
I meant to do that.
FWOOSH
Let's talk about this later. Look—

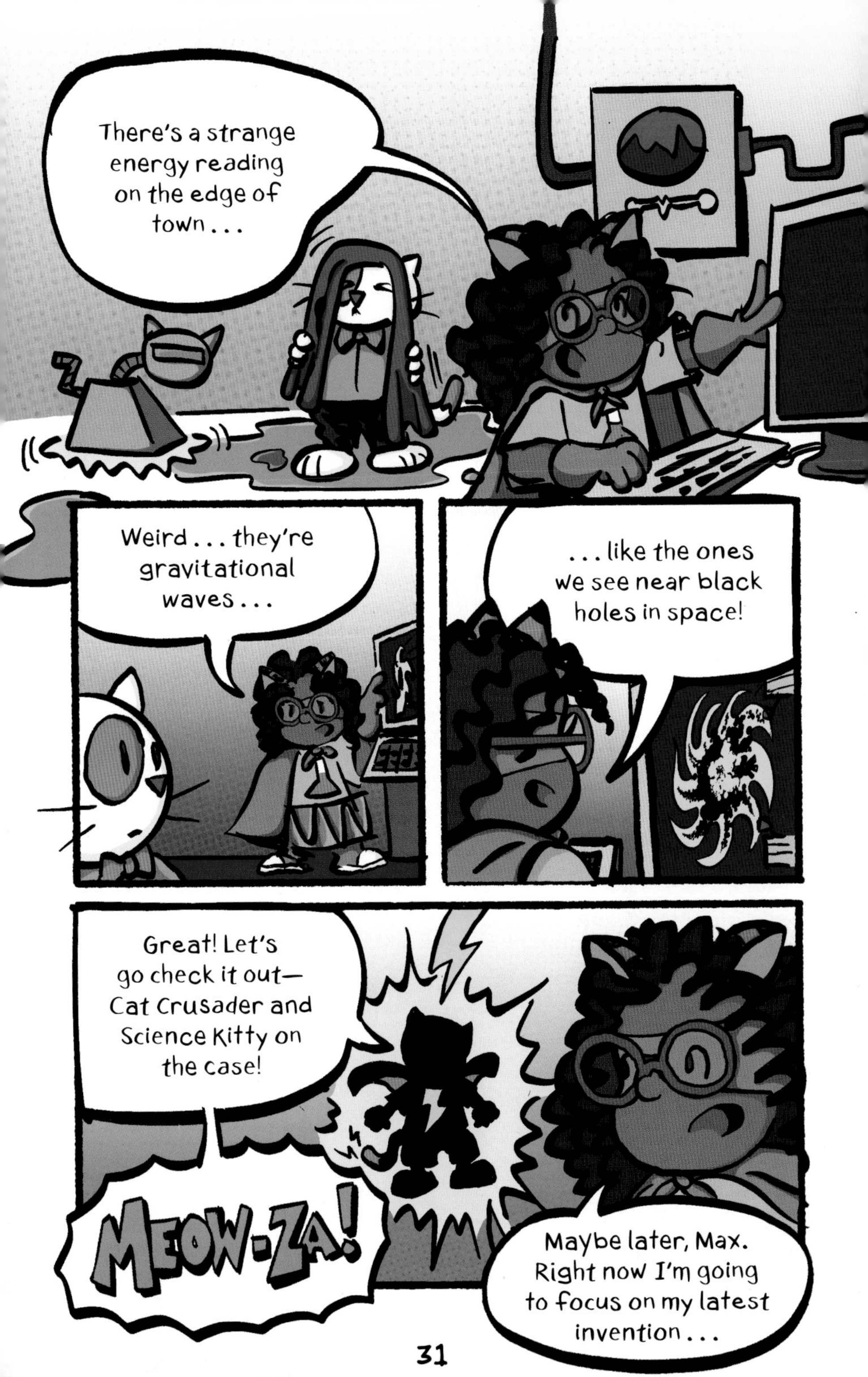
There's a strange energy reading on the edge of town . . .
Weird . . . they're gravitational waves . . .
. . . like the ones we see near black holes in space!
Great! Let's go check it out— Cat Crusader and Science Kitty on the case!
MEOW-ZA!
Maybe later, Max. Right now I'm going to focus on my latest invention . . .

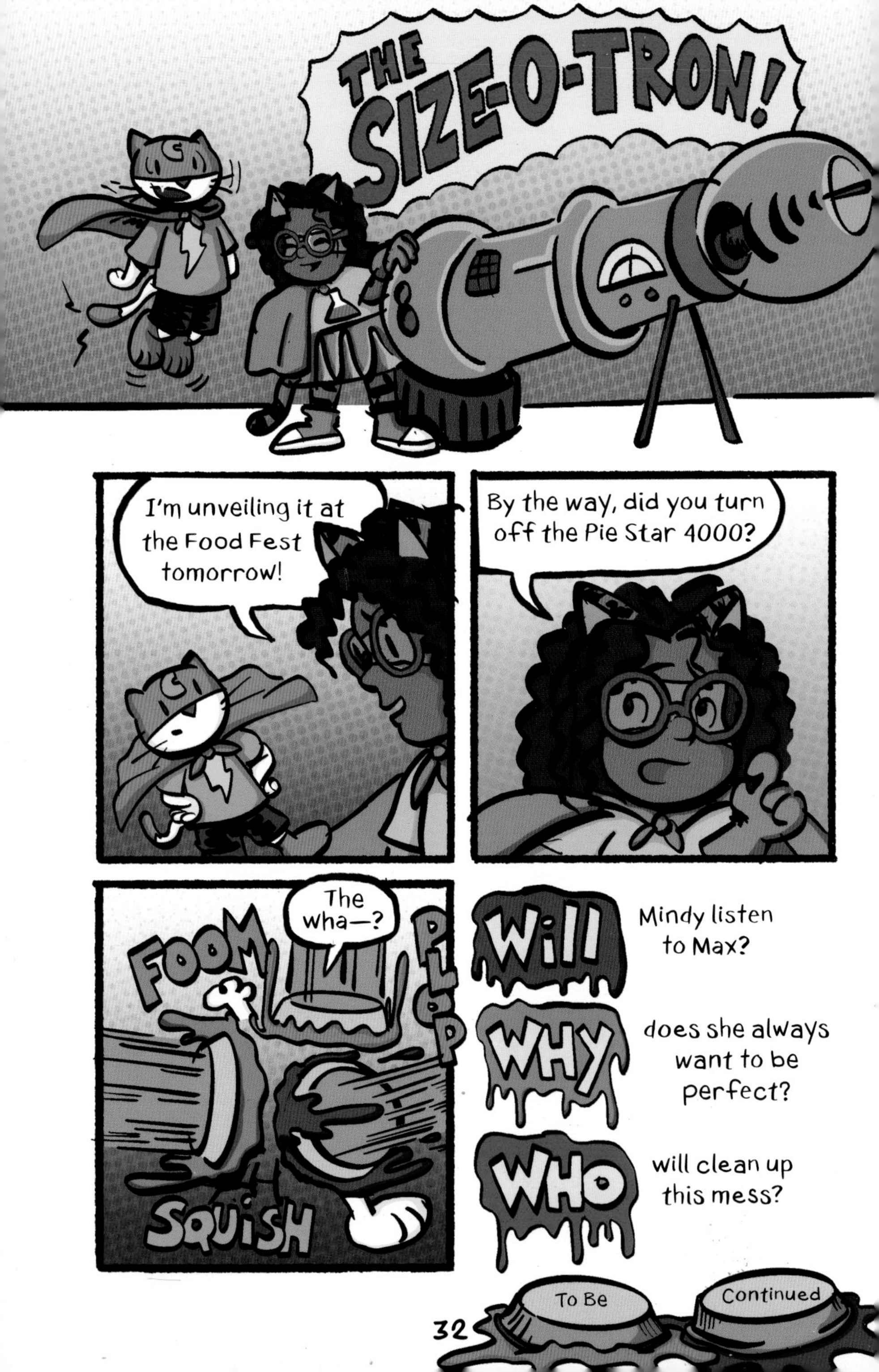
THE SIZE-O-TRON!
I'm unveiling it at the Food Fest tomorrow!
By the way, did you turn off the Pie Star 4000?
FOOM
The wha—?
PLOP
SQUISH
Will Mindy listen to Max?
WHY does she always want to be perfect?
WHO will clean up this mess?
To Be Continued

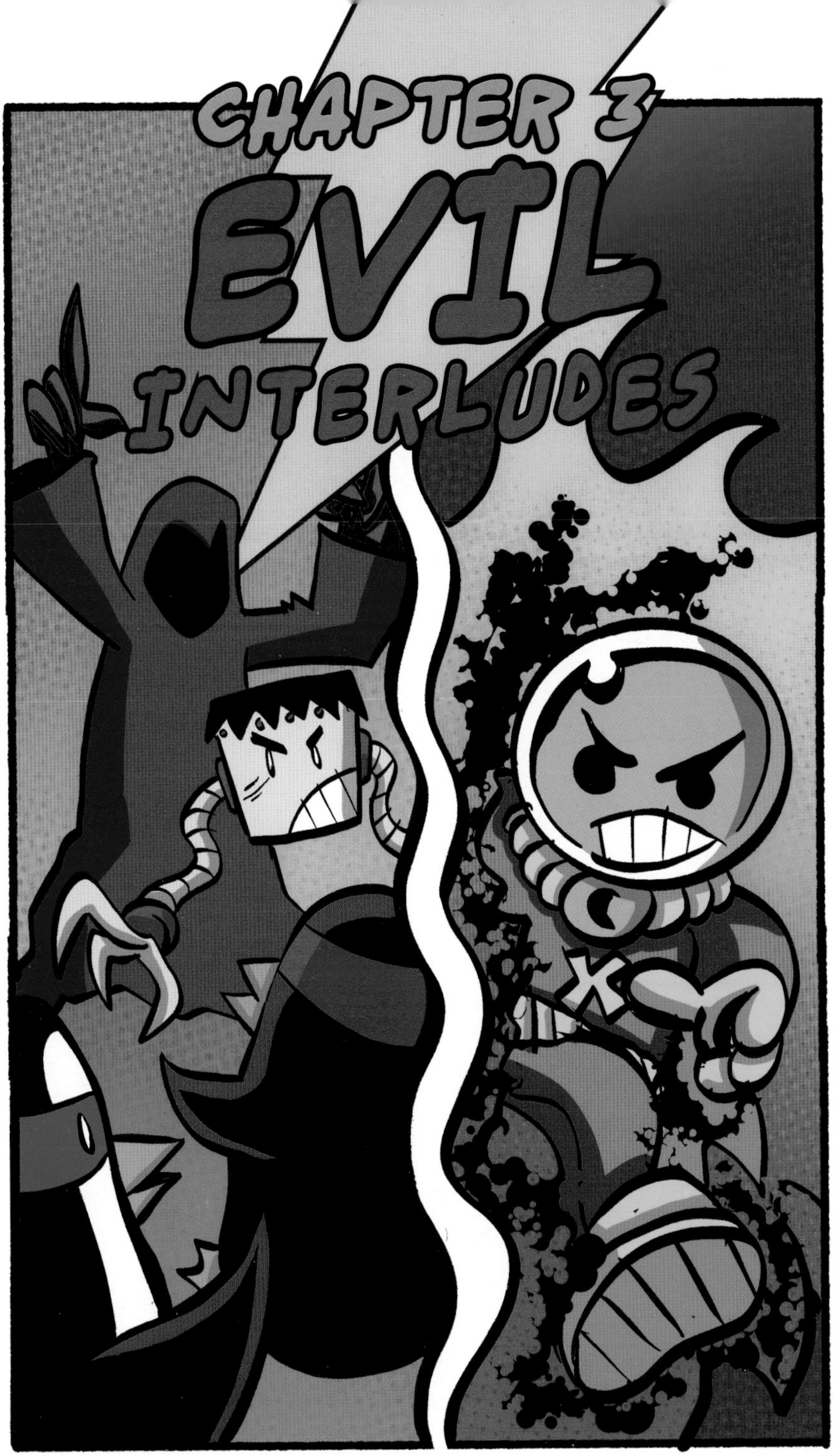
CHAPTER 3
EVIL
INTERLUDES

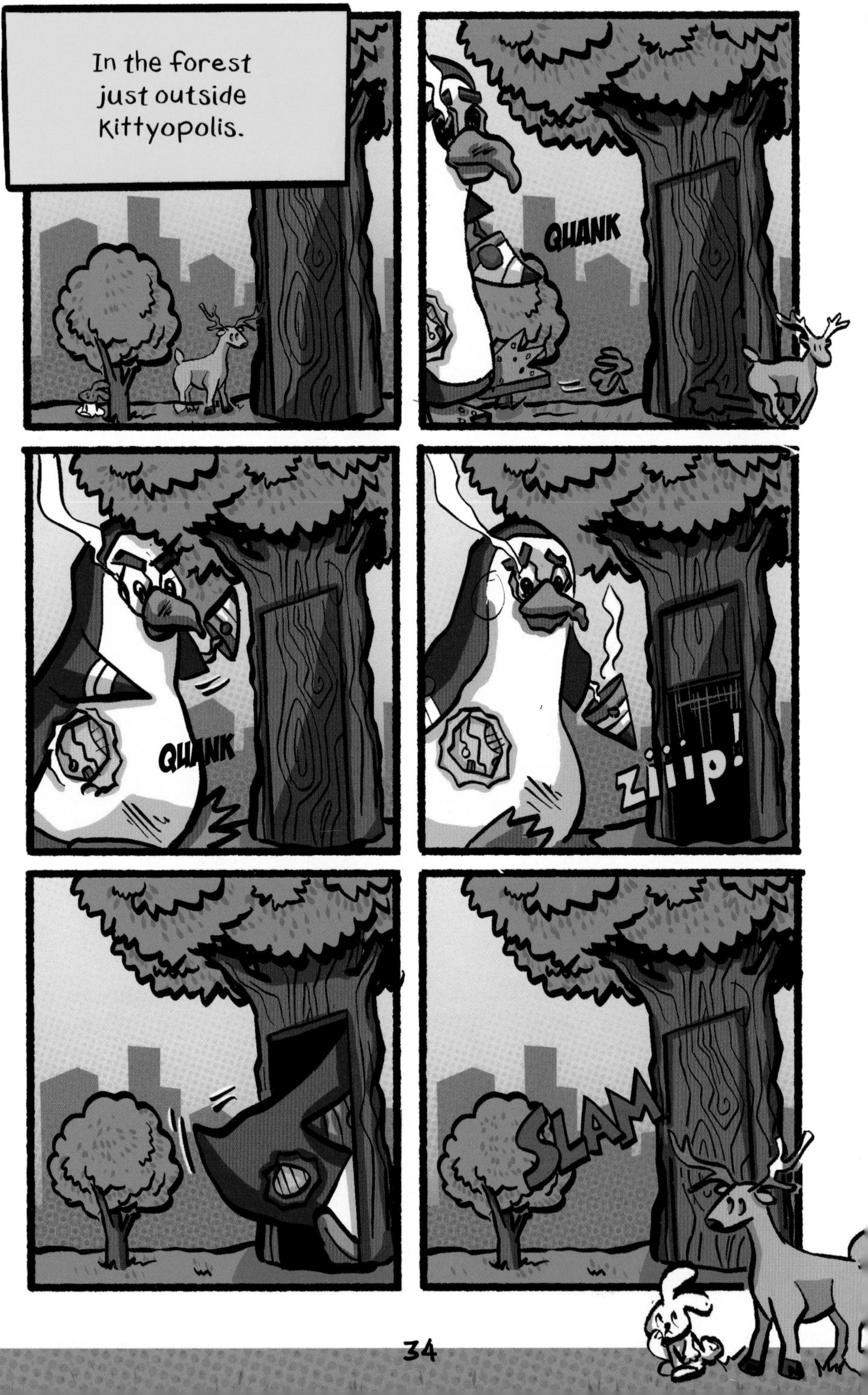
In the forest
just outside
Kittyopolis.
QUANK
QUANK
ziiip!
SLAM

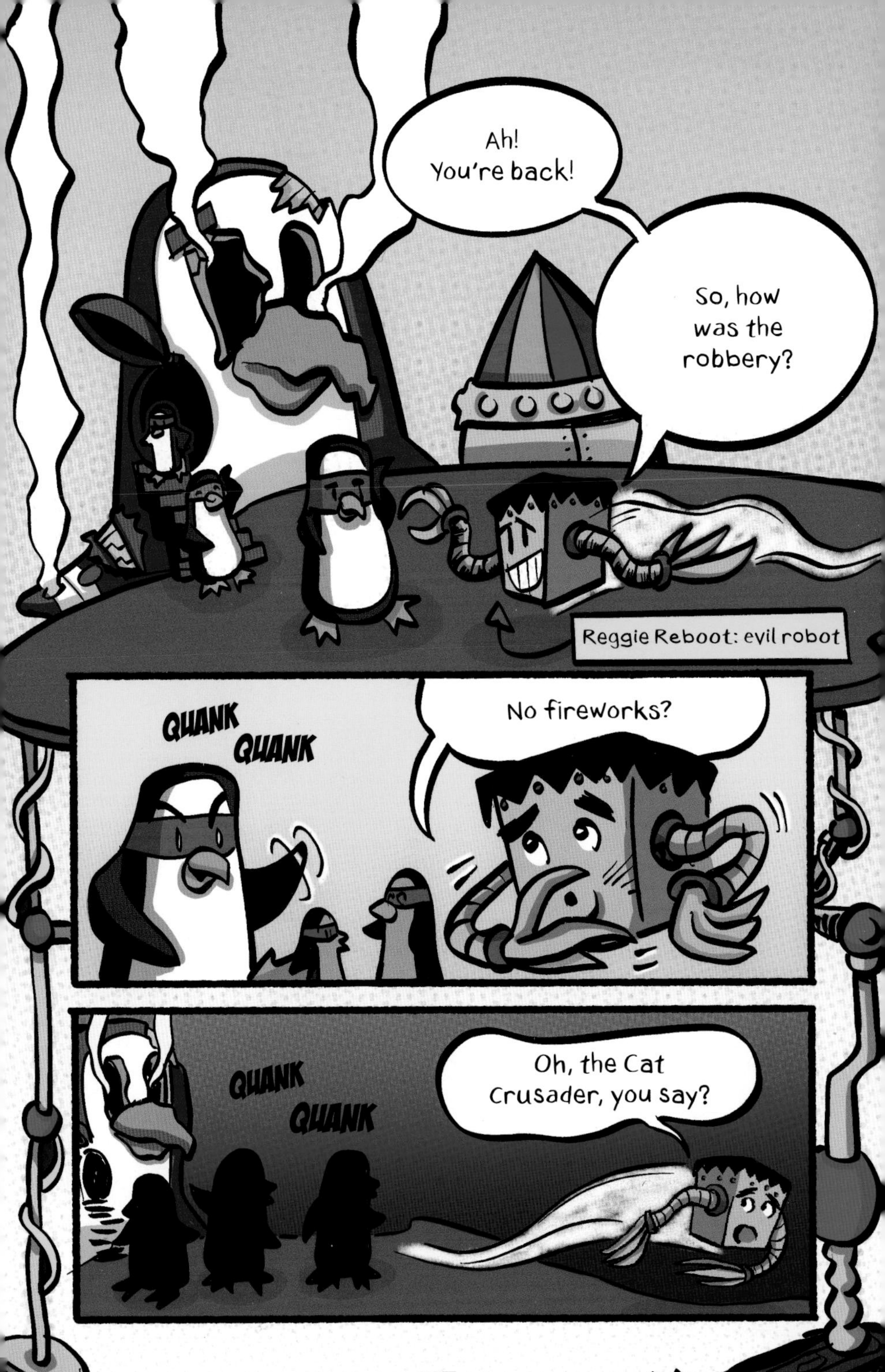
Ah! You're back!
So, how was the robbery?
Reggie Reboot: evil robot
QUANK QUANK
No fireworks?
QUANK QUANK
Oh, the Cat Crusader, you say?

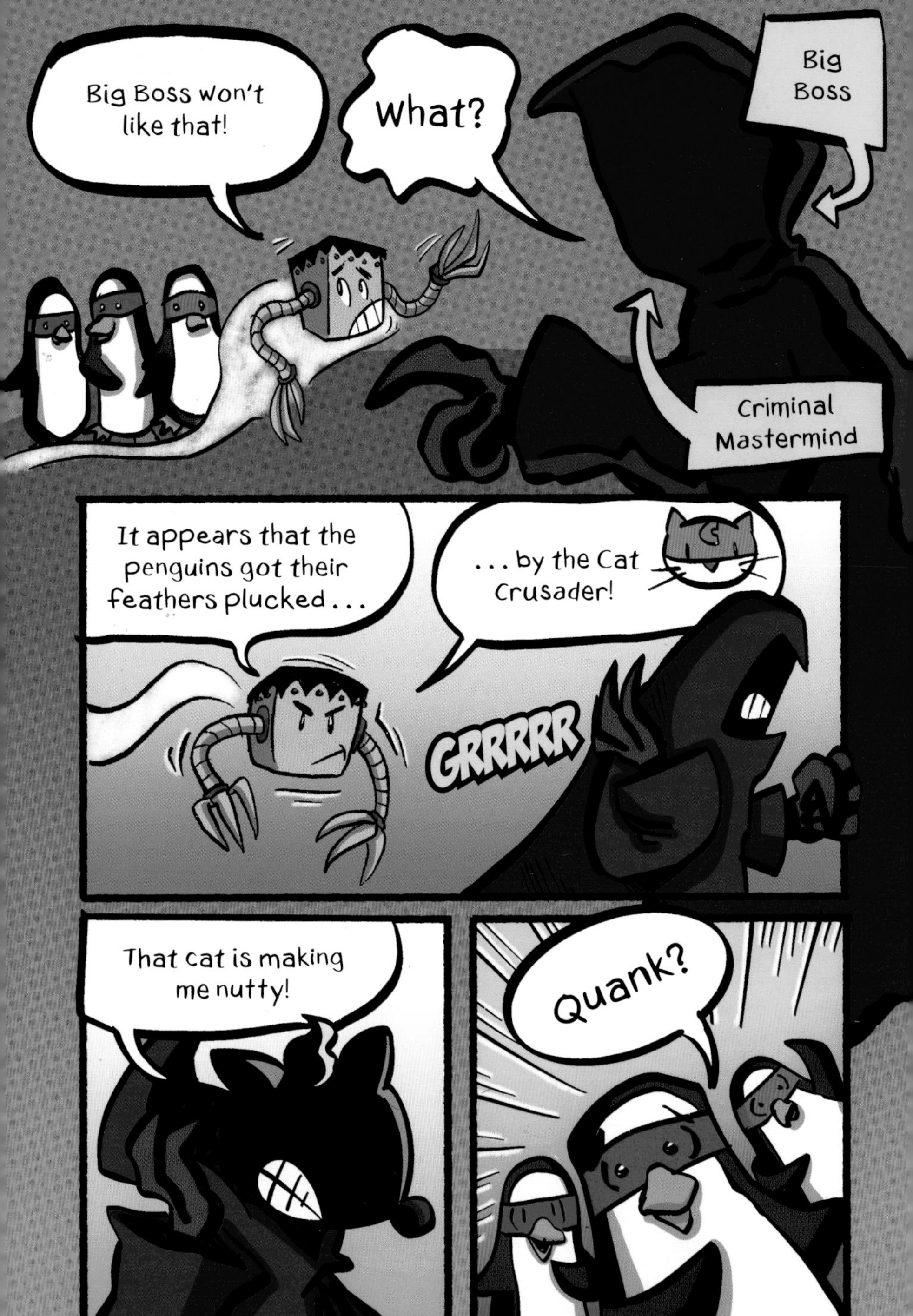
Big Boss won't like that!
What?
Big Boss
Criminal Mastermind
It appears that the penguins got their feathers plucked . . .
. . . by the Cat Crusader!
GRRRRR
That cat is making me nutty!
Quank?

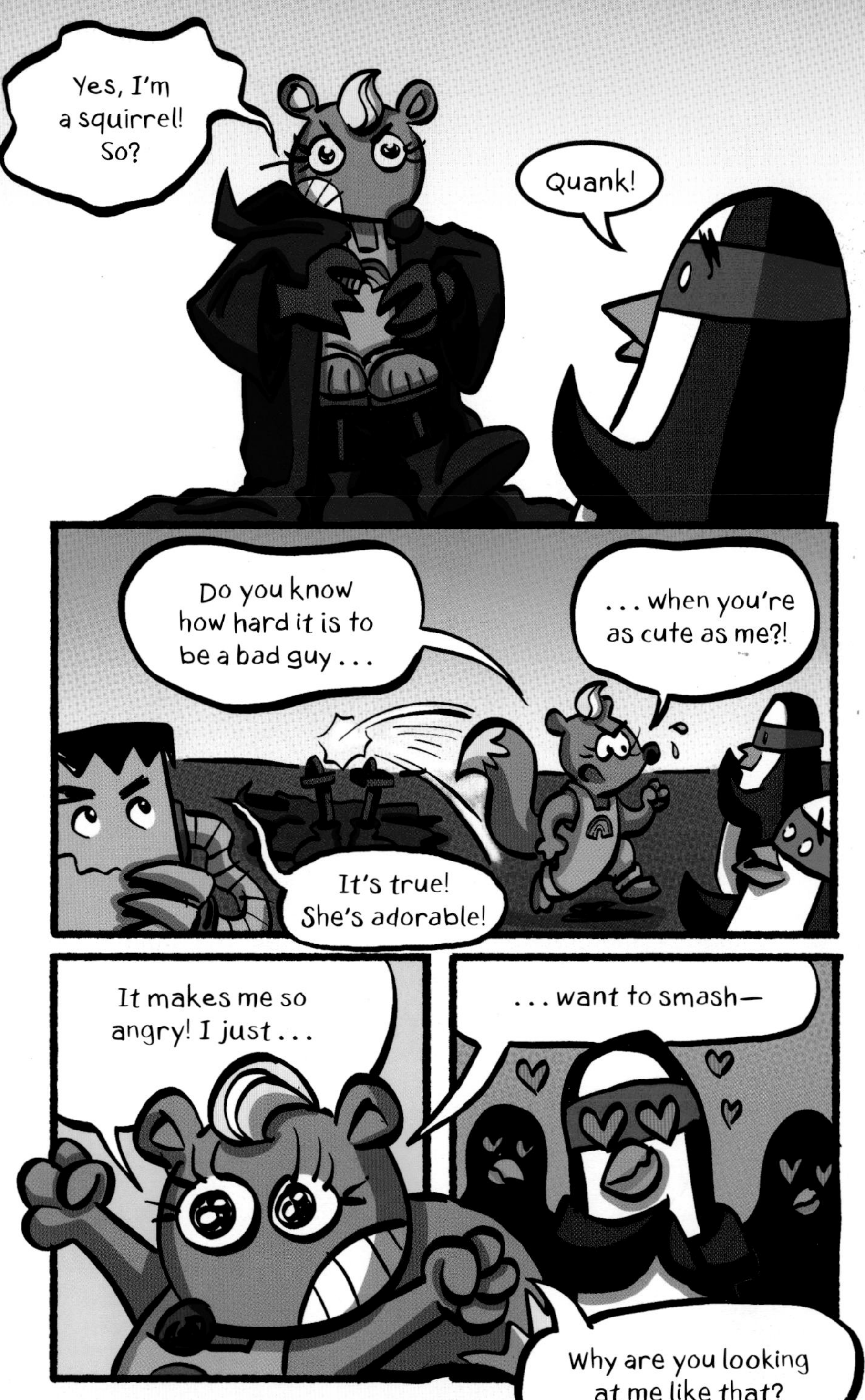
Yes, I'm a squirrel! So?
Quank!
Do you know how hard it is to be a bad guy . . .
. . . when you're as cute as me?!
It's true! She's adorable!
It makes me so angry! I just . . .
. . . want to smash—
Why are you looking at me like that?

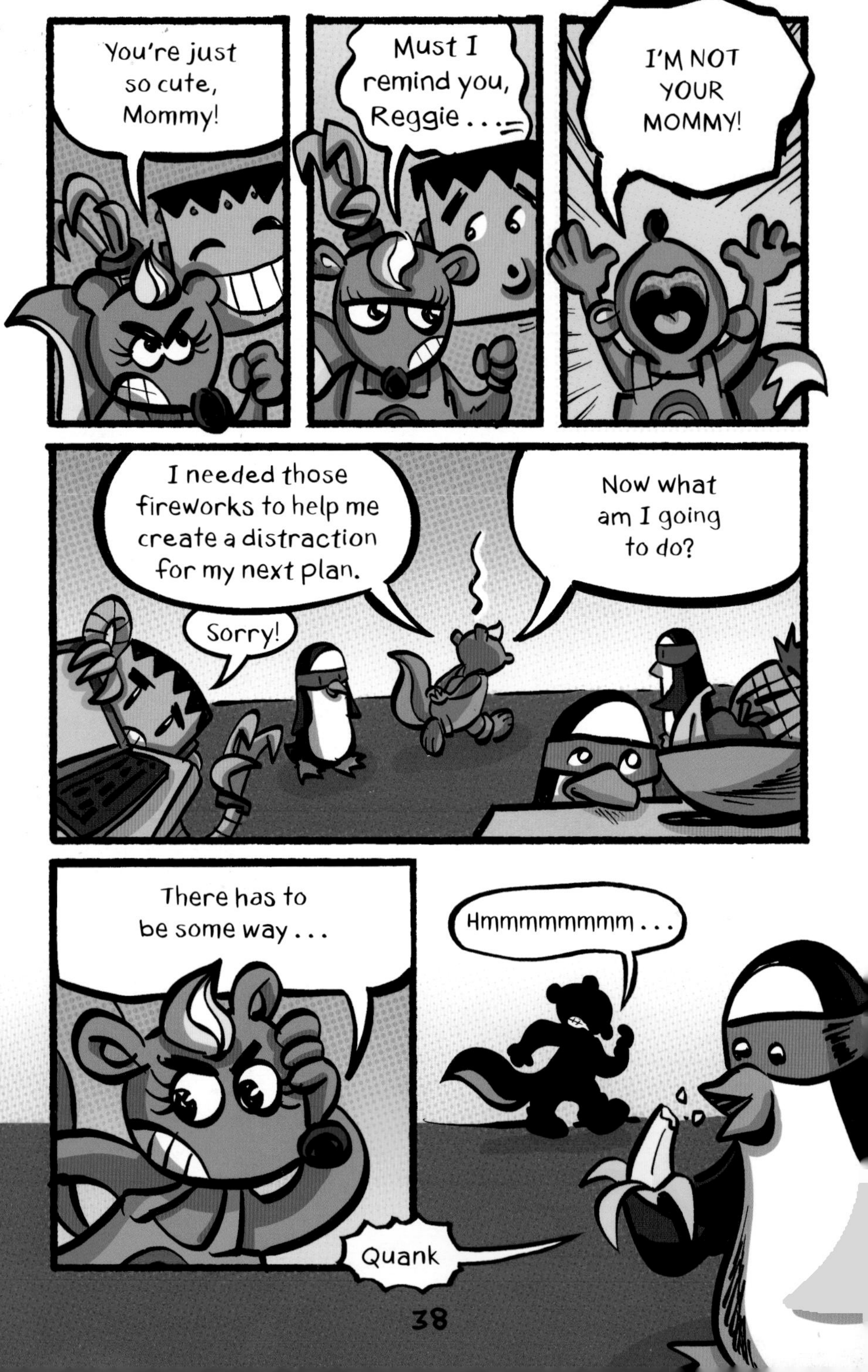
You're just so cute, Mommy!
Must I remind you, Reggie . . .
I'M NOT YOUR MOMMY!
I needed those fireworks to help me create a distraction for my next plan.
Now what am I going to do?
Sorry!
There has to be some way . . .
Hmmmmmmmm . . .
Quank

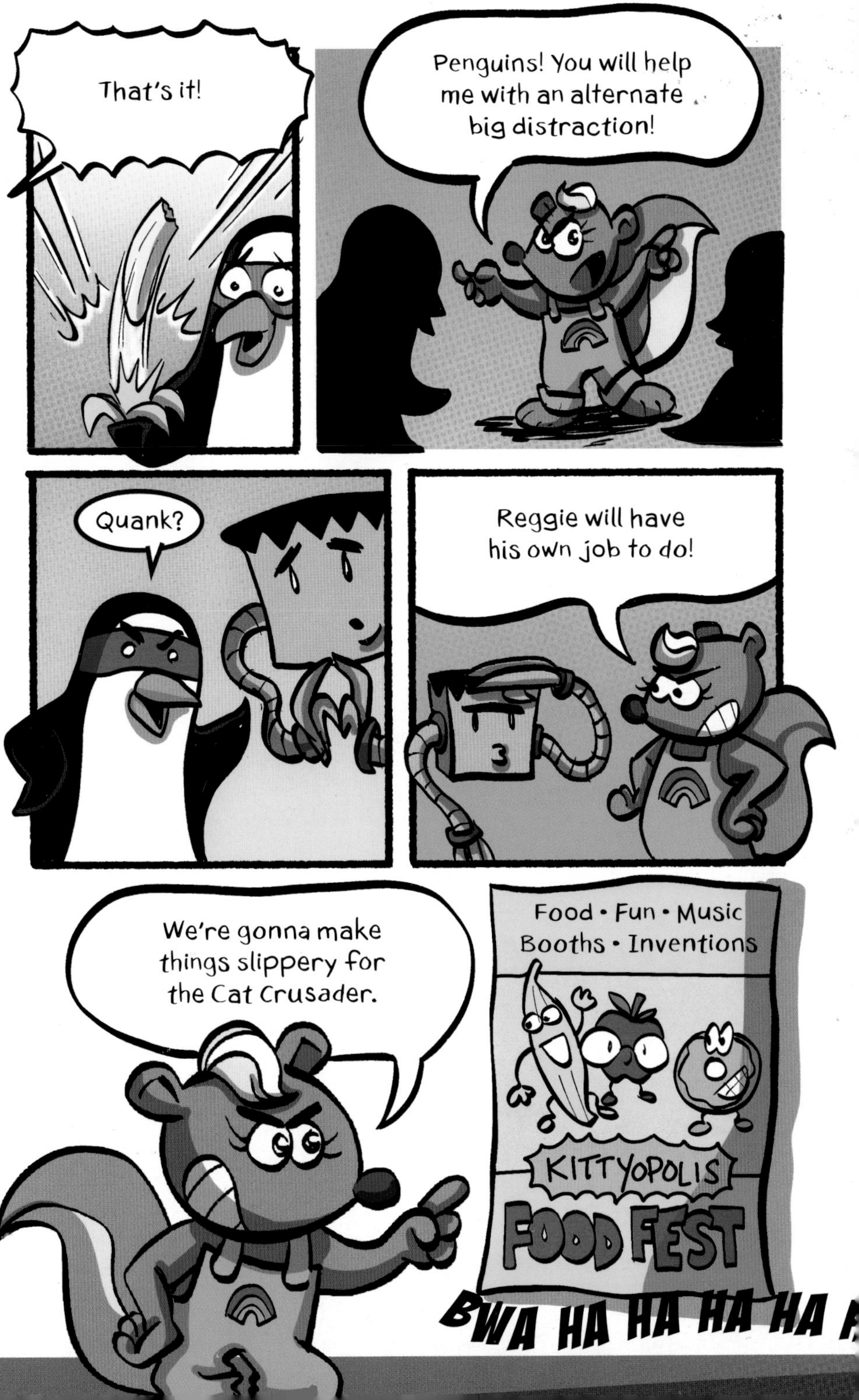
That's it!
Penguins! You will help me with an alternate big distraction!
Quank?
Reggie will have his own job to do!
3
We're gonna make things slippery for the Cat Crusader.
Food • Fun • Music
Booths • Inventions
KITTYOPOLIS
FOOD FEST
BWA HA HA HA HA

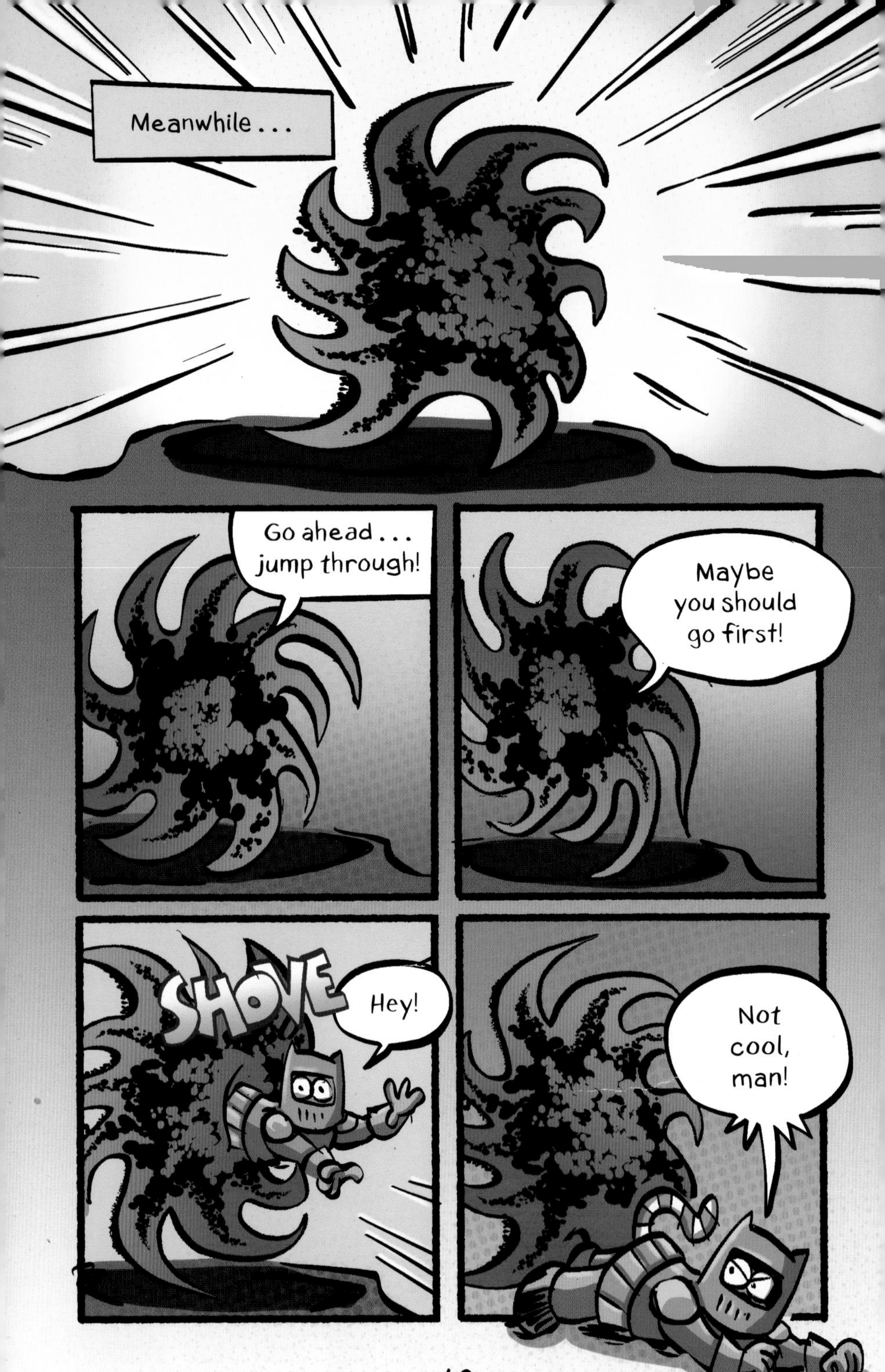
Meanwhile . . .
Go ahead . . . jump through!
Maybe you should go first!
SHOVE
Hey!
Not cool, man!

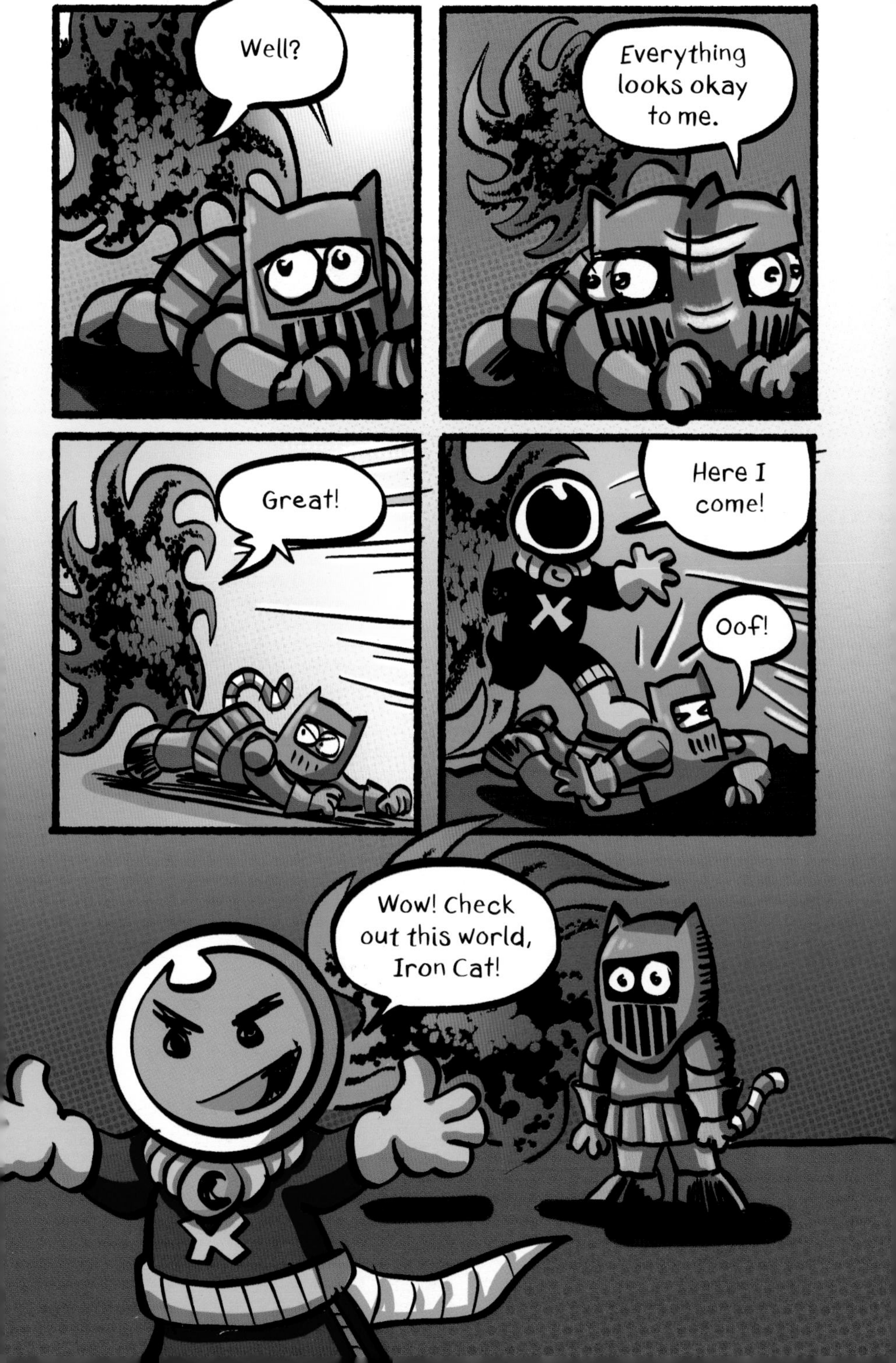
Well?
Everything looks okay to me.
Great!
Here I come!
Oof!
Wow! Check out this world, Iron Cat!

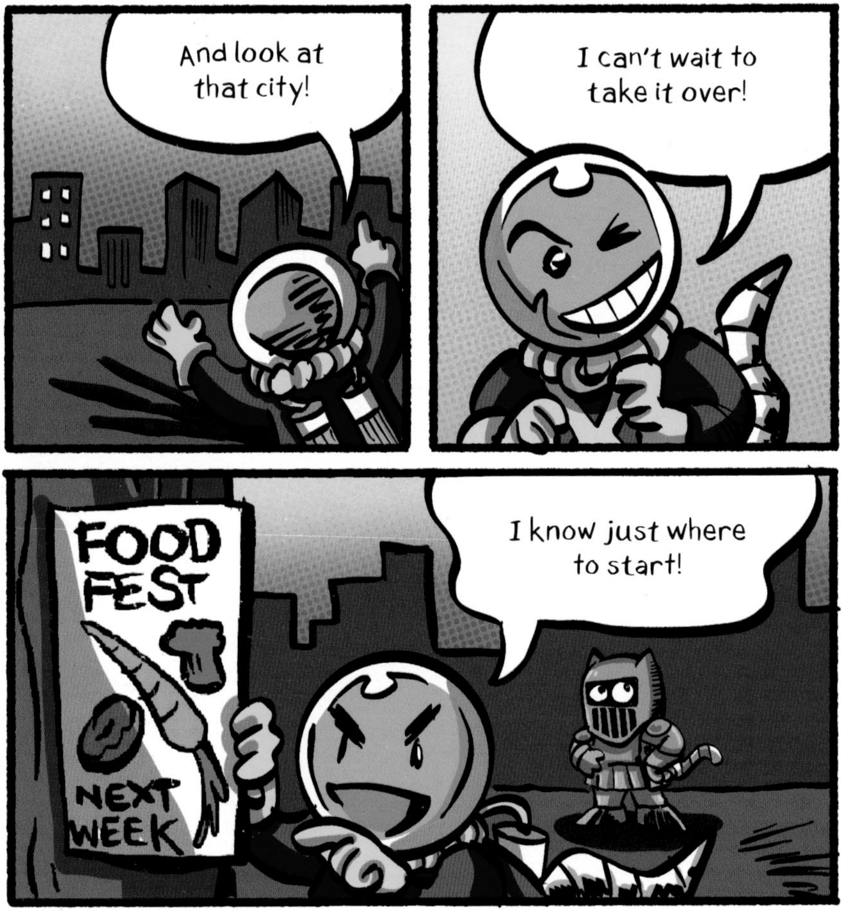
And look at that city!
I can't wait to take it over!
FOOD FEST
NEXT WEEK
I know just where to start!

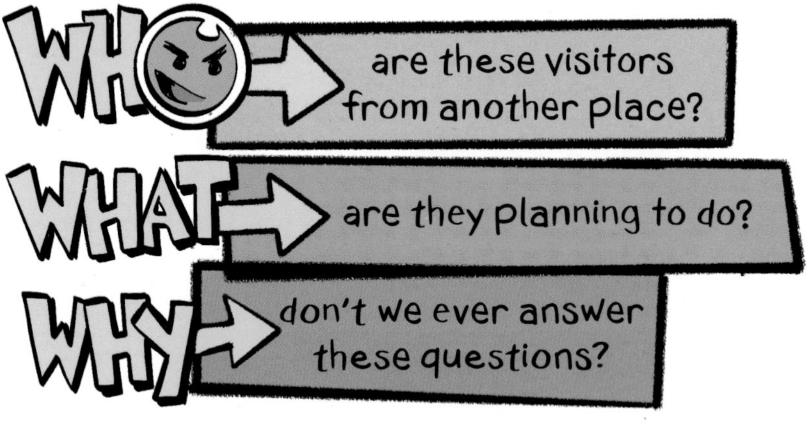
WHO
are these visitors from another place?
WHAT
are they planning to do?
WHY
don't we ever answer these questions?

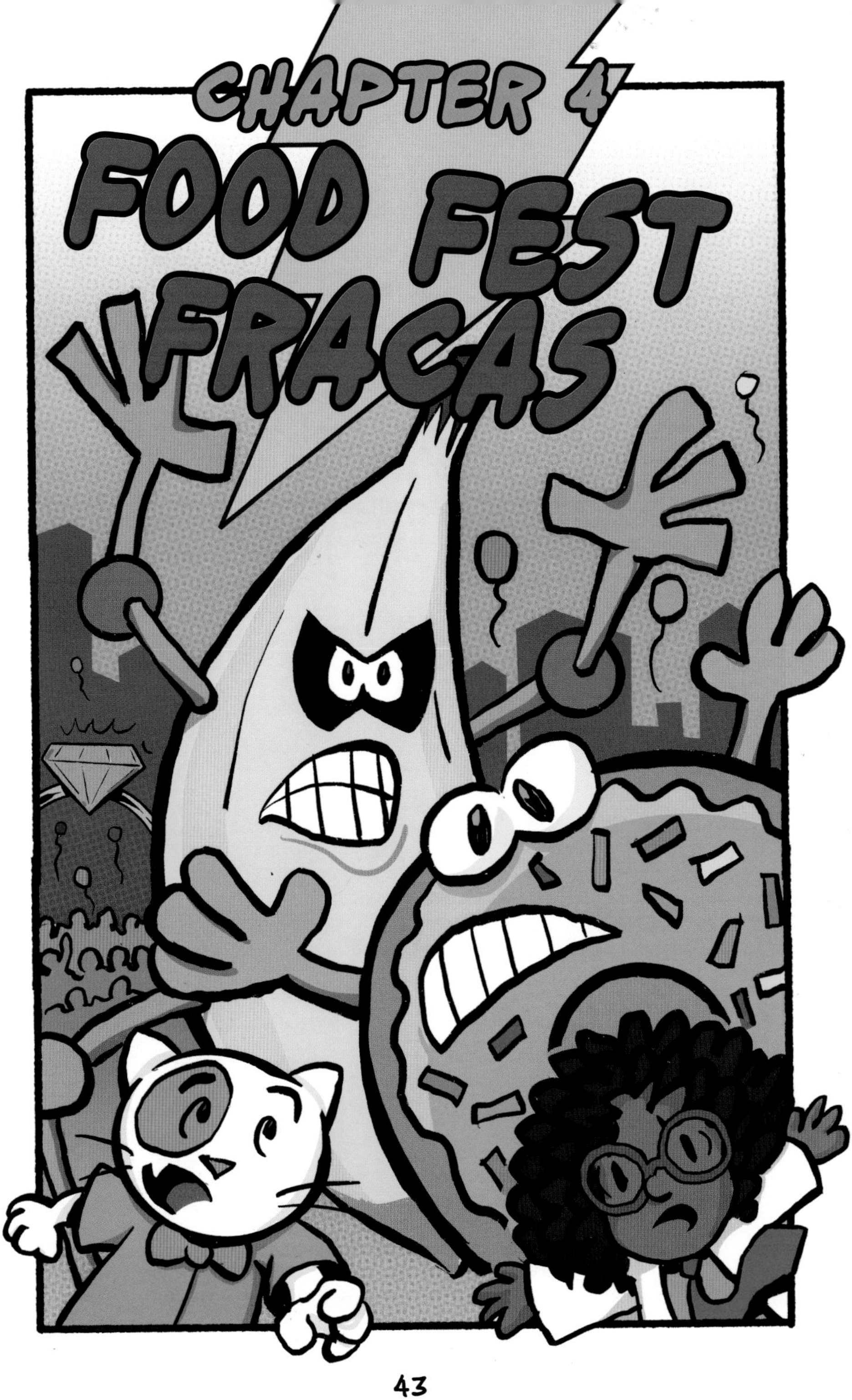
CHAPTER 4
FOOD FEST FRACAS

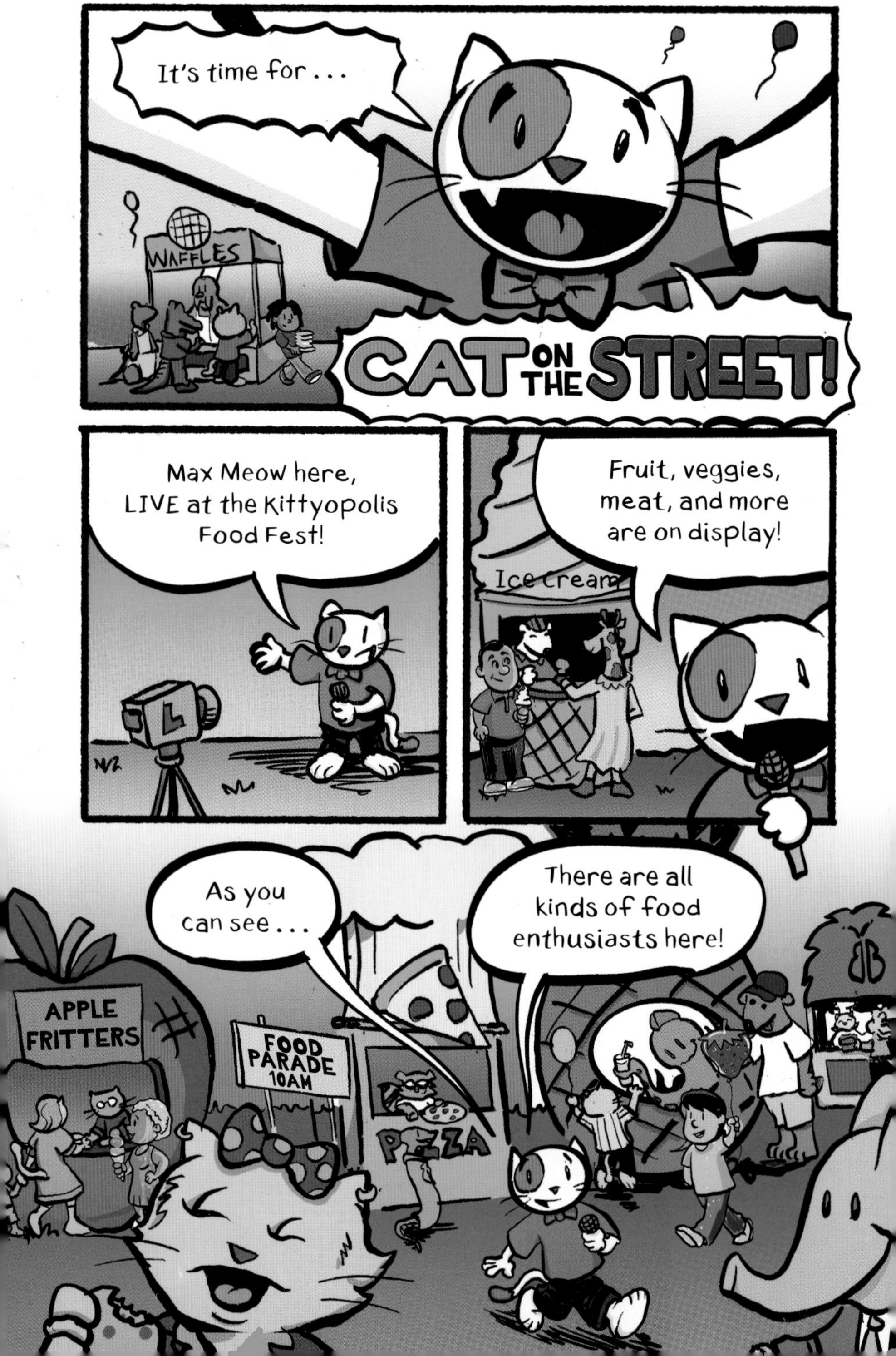
It's time for . . .
WAFFLES
CAT ON THE STREET!
Max Meow here, LIVE at the Kittyopolis Food Fest!
Fruit, veggies, meat, and more are on display!
Ice Cream
As you can see . . .
There are all kinds of food enthusiasts here!
APPLE FRITTERS
FOOD PARADE 10AM
PIZZA

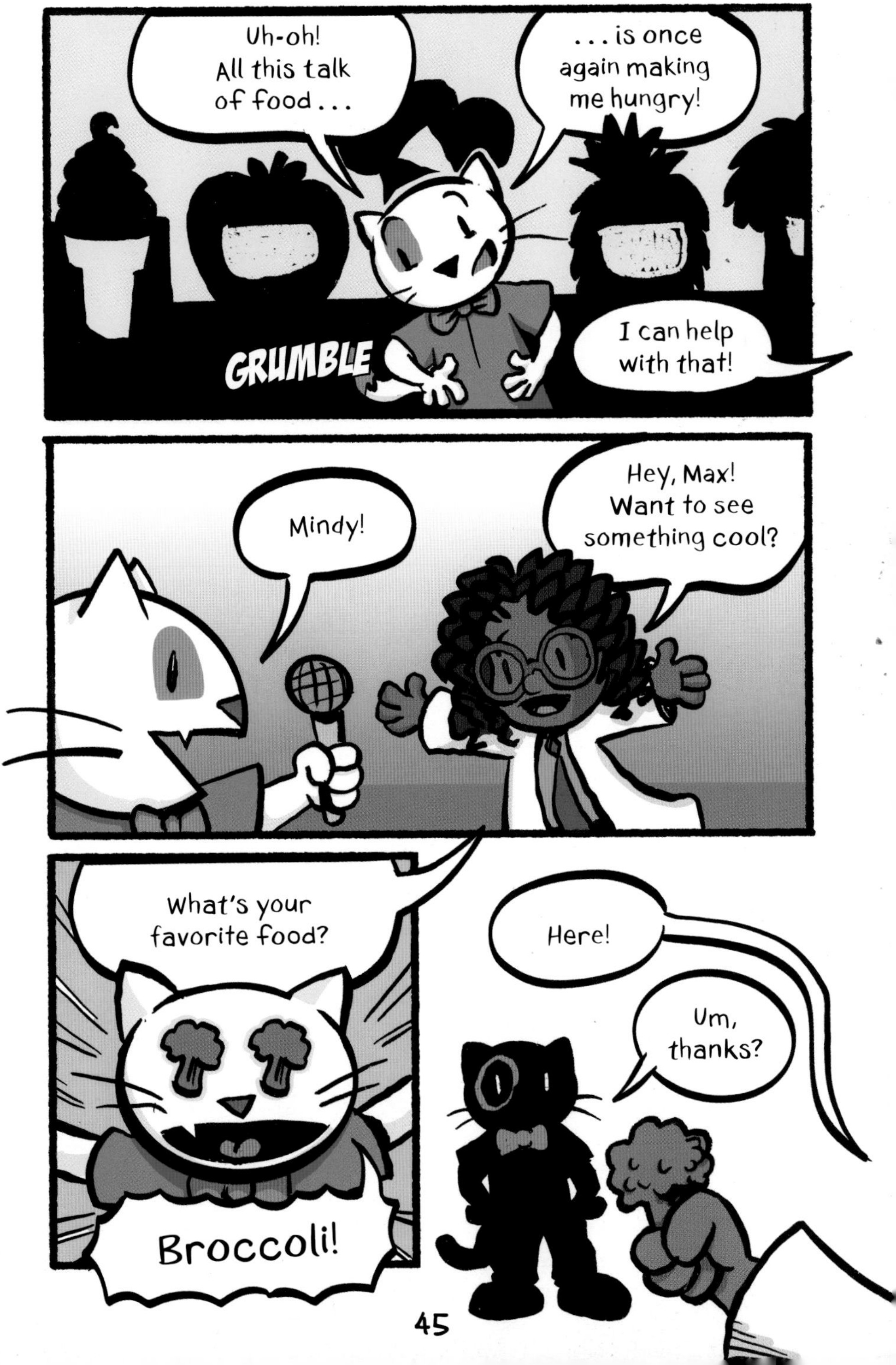
Uh-oh! All this talk of food . . .
. . . is once again making me hungry!
GRUMBLE
I can help with that!
Mindy!
Hey, Max! Want to see something cool?
What's your favorite food?
Broccoli!
Here!
Um, thanks?

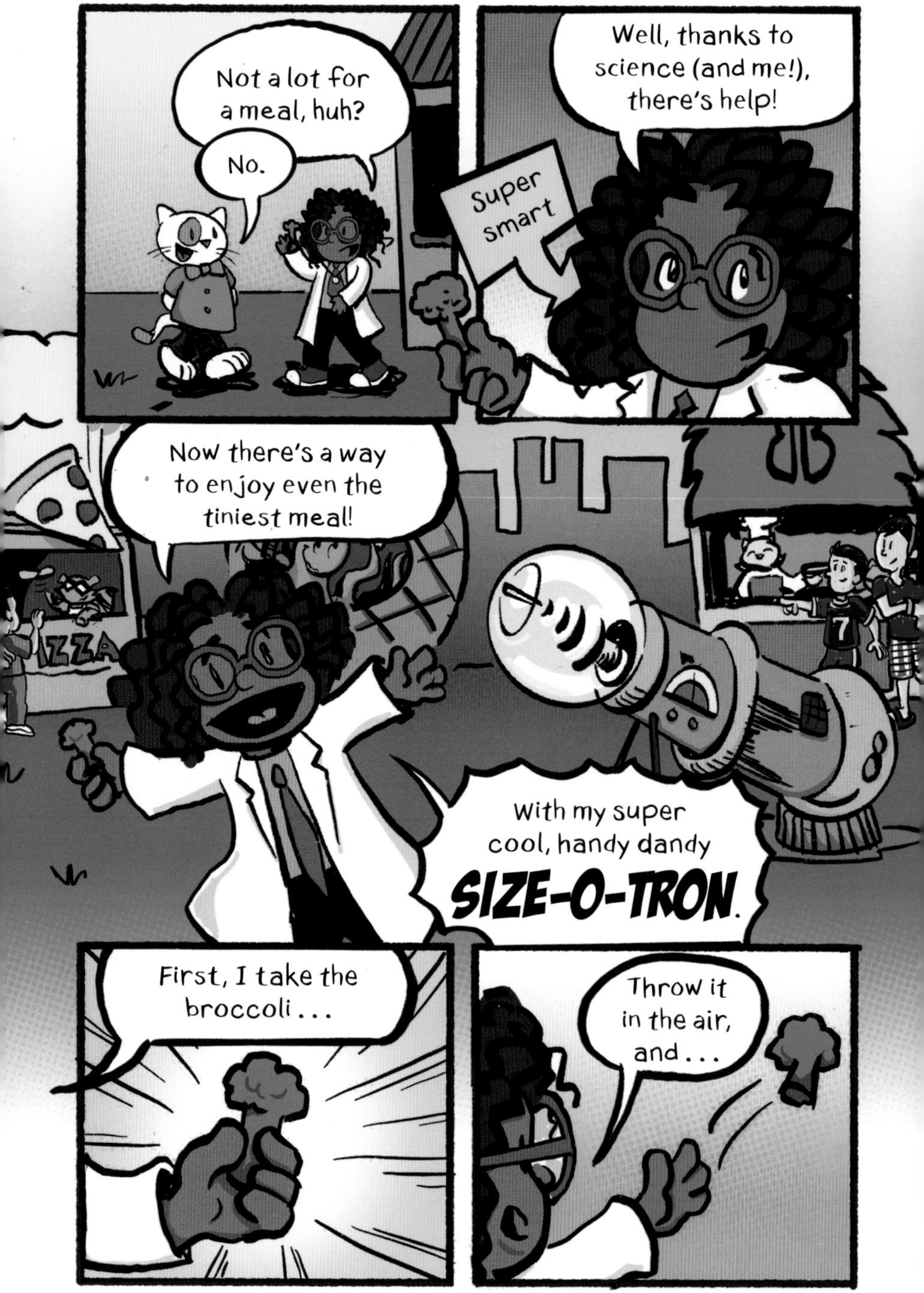
Not a lot for a meal, huh?
No.
Well, thanks to science (and me!), there's help!
Super smart
Now there's a way to enjoy even the tiniest meal!
IZZA
With my super cool, handy dandy SIZE-O-TRON.
First, I take the broccoli . . .
Throw it in the air, and . . .

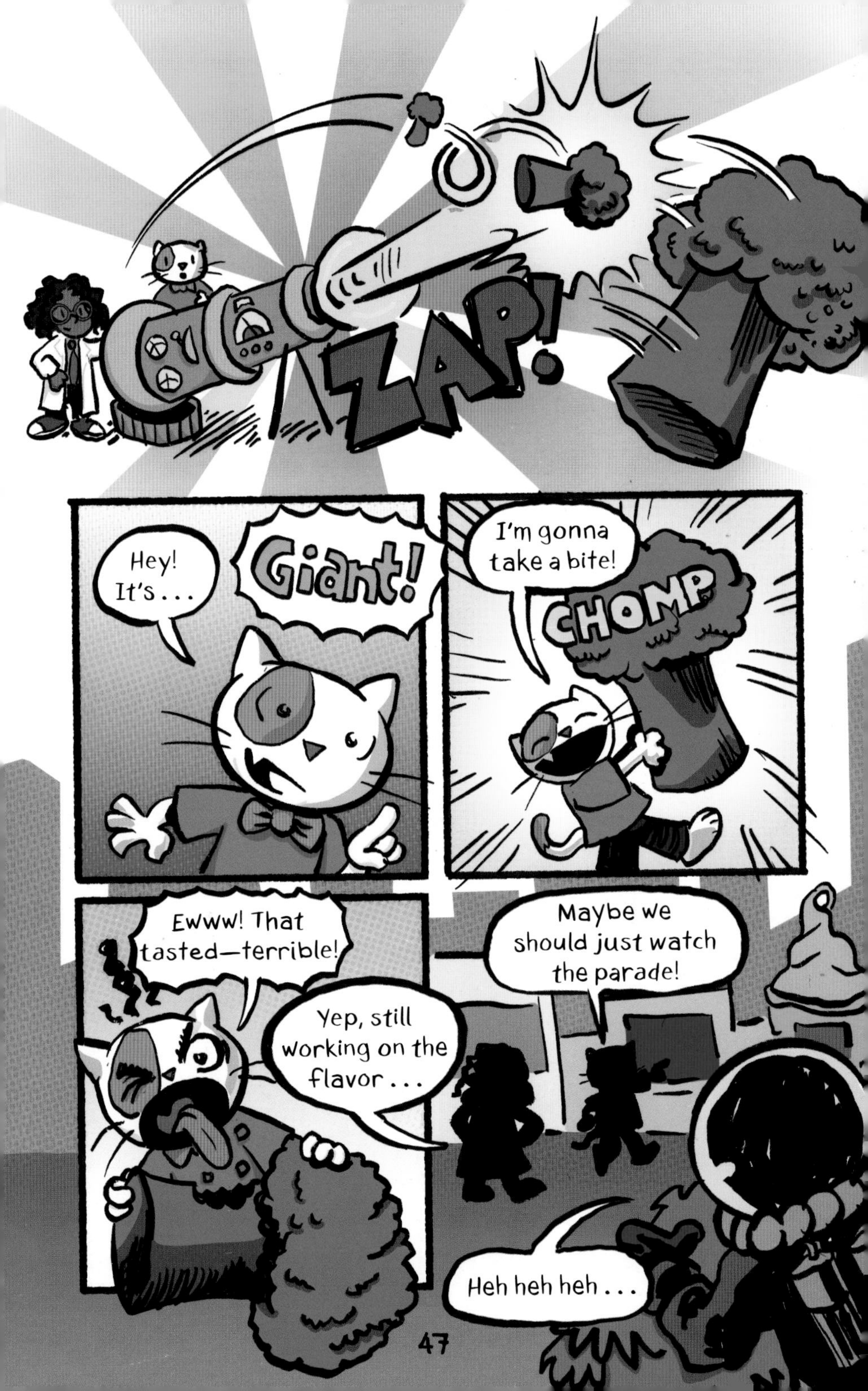
ZAP!
Hey! It's . . .
Giant!
I'm gonna take a bite!
CHOMP
Ewww! That tasted—terrible!
Yep, still working on the flavor . . .
Maybe we should just watch the parade!
Heh heh heh . . .

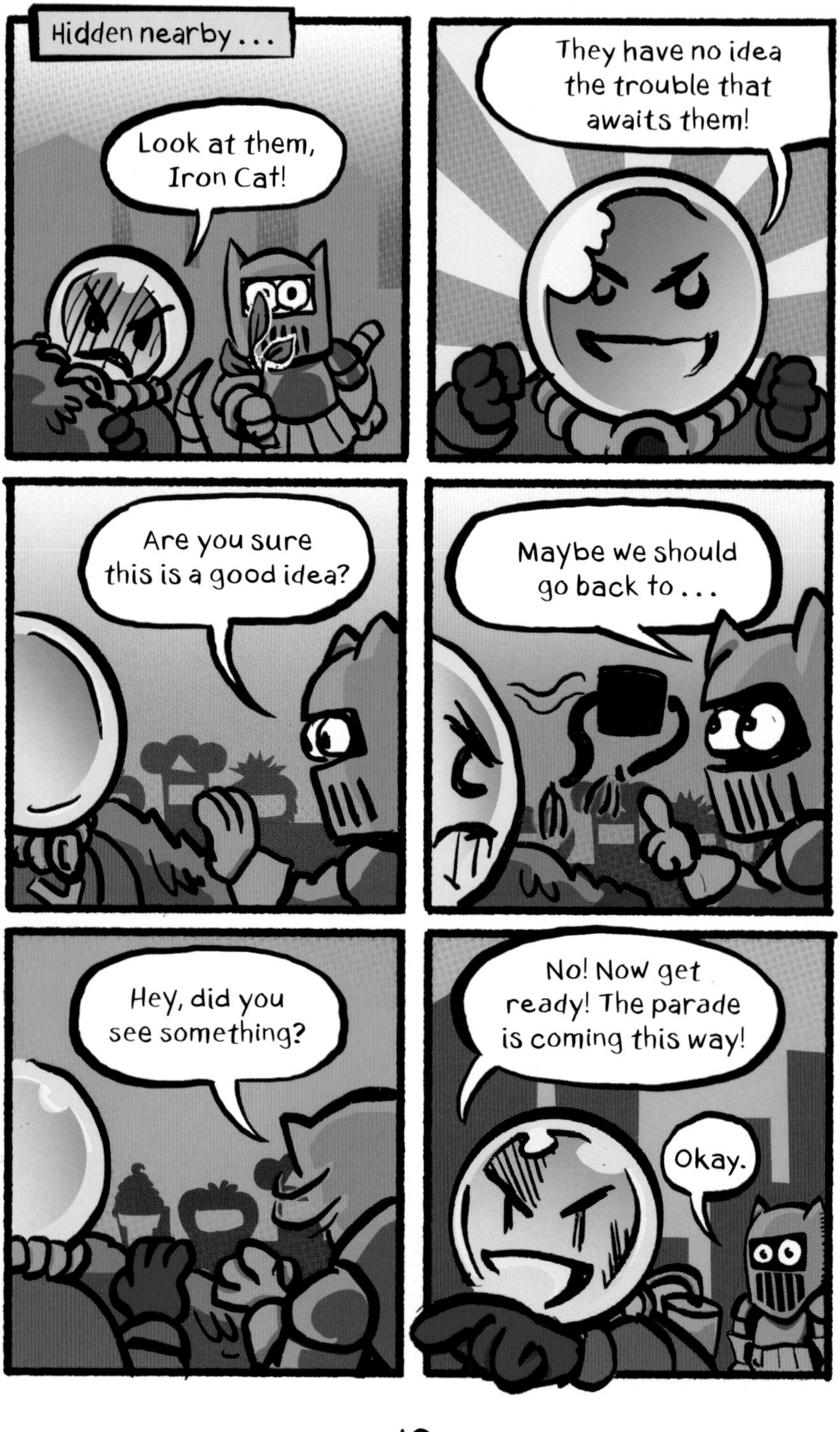
Hidden nearby . . .
Look at them, Iron Cat!
They have no idea the trouble that awaits them!
Are you sure this is a good idea?
Maybe we should go back to . . .
Hey, did you see something?
No! Now get ready! The parade is coming this way!
Okay.

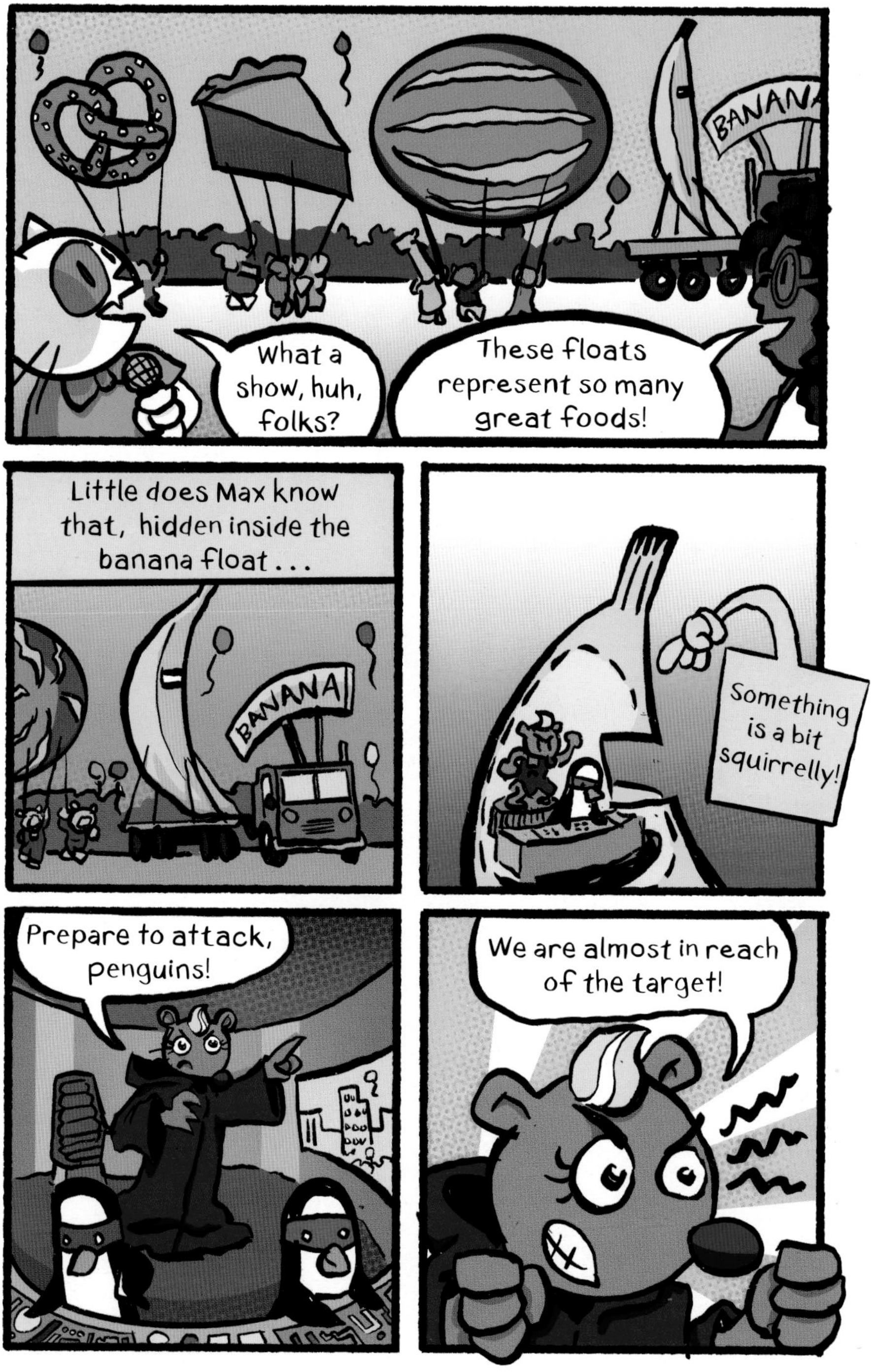
What a show, huh, folks?
These floats represent so many great foods!
BANANA
Little does Max know that, hidden inside the banana float . . .
BANANA
Something is a bit squirrelly!
Prepare to attack, penguins!
We are almost in reach of the target!

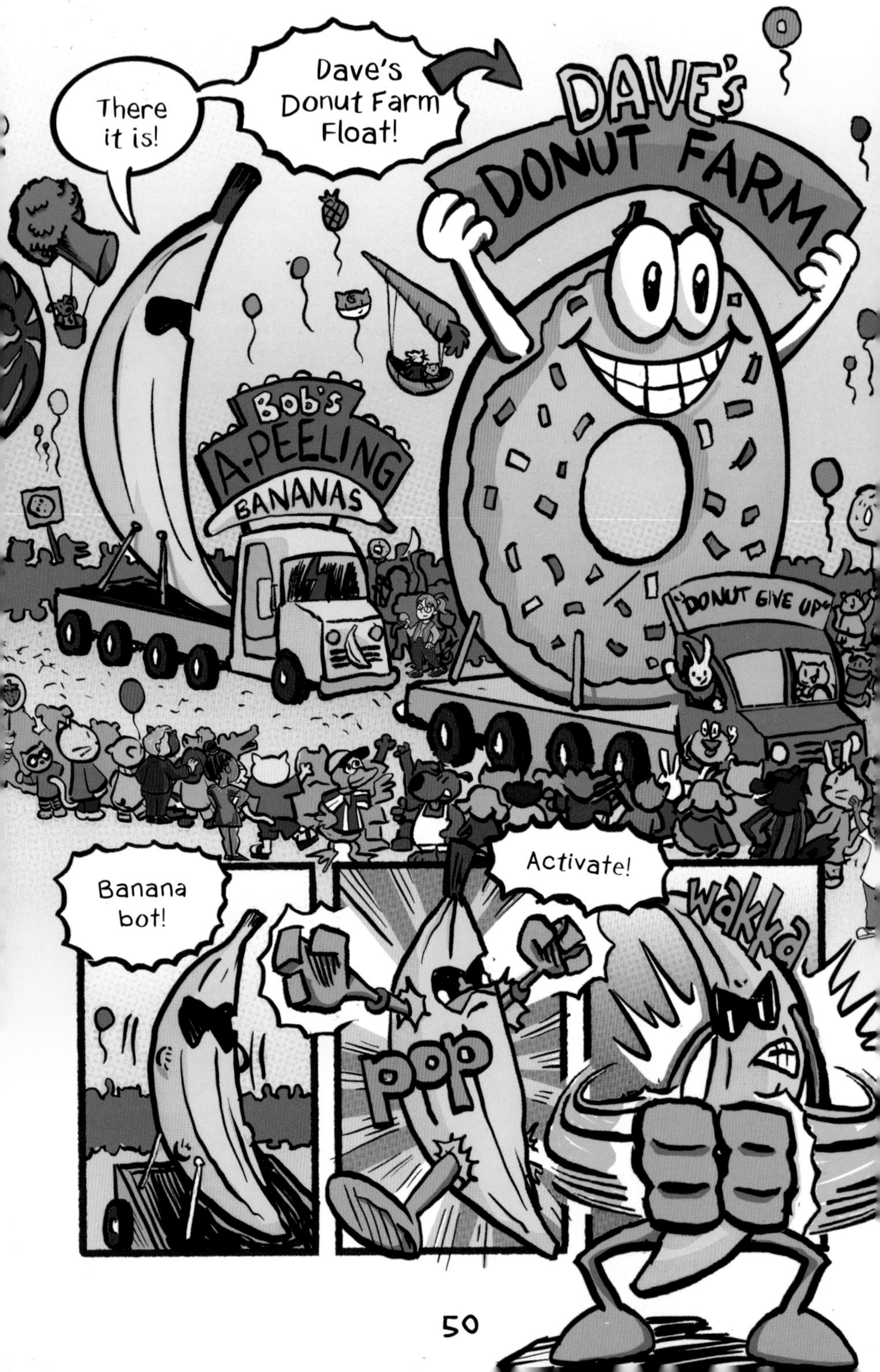
There it is!
Dave's Donut Farm Float!
DAVE's DONUT FARM
Bob's A-PEELING BANANAS
"DONUT GIVE UP"
Banana bot!
Activate!
POP
wakka

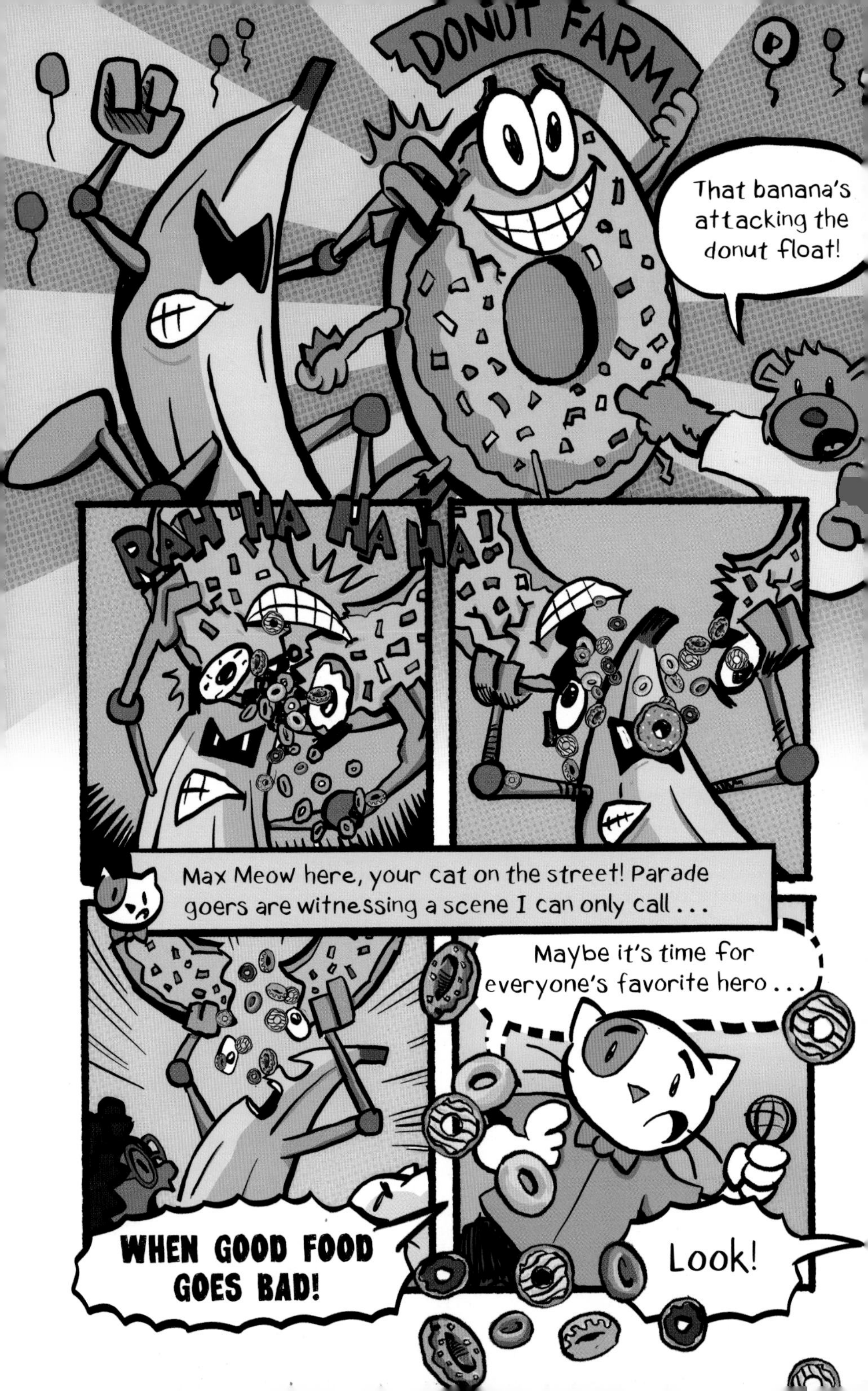
DONUT FARM
That banana's attacking the donut float!
RAH HA HA HA!
Max Meow here, your cat on the street! Parade goers are witnessing a scene I can only call . . .
WHEN GOOD FOOD GOES BAD!
Maybe it's time for everyone's favorite hero . . .
Look!

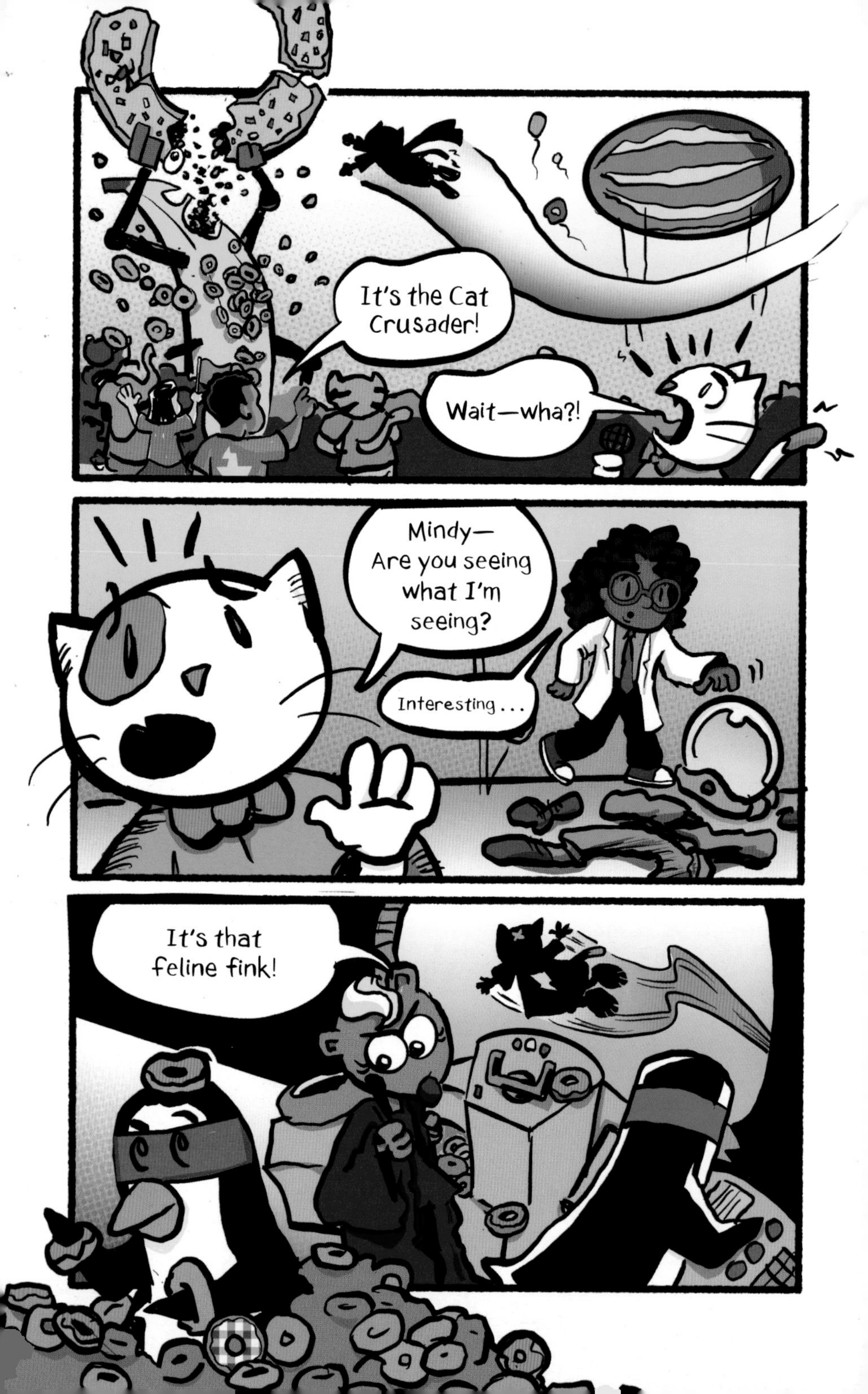
It's the Cat Crusader!
Wait—wha?!
Mindy— Are you seeing what I'm seeing?
Interesting . . .
It's that feline fink!

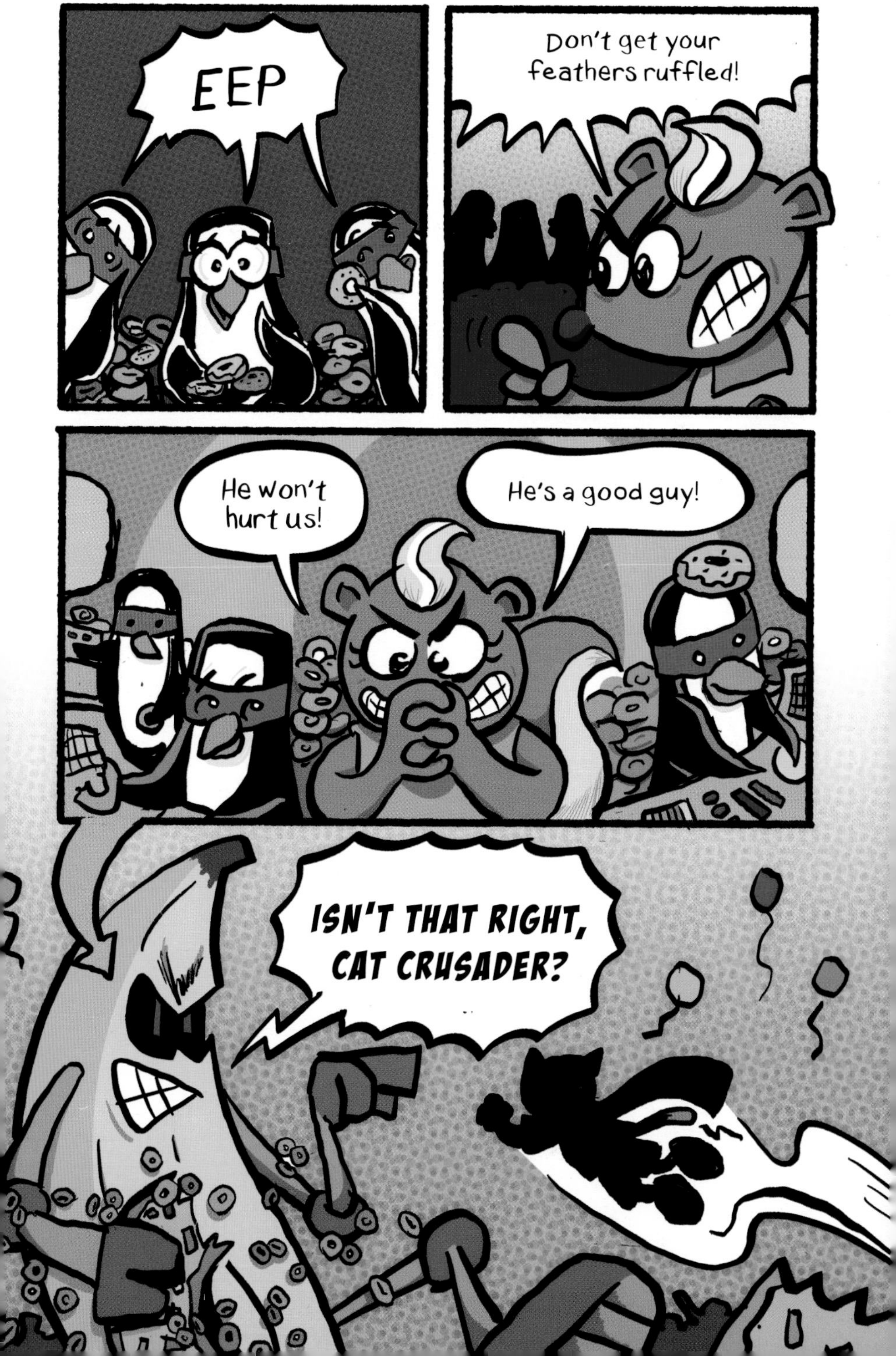
EEP
Don't get your feathers ruffled!
He won't hurt us!
He's a good guy!
ISN'T THAT RIGHT, CAT CRUSADER?

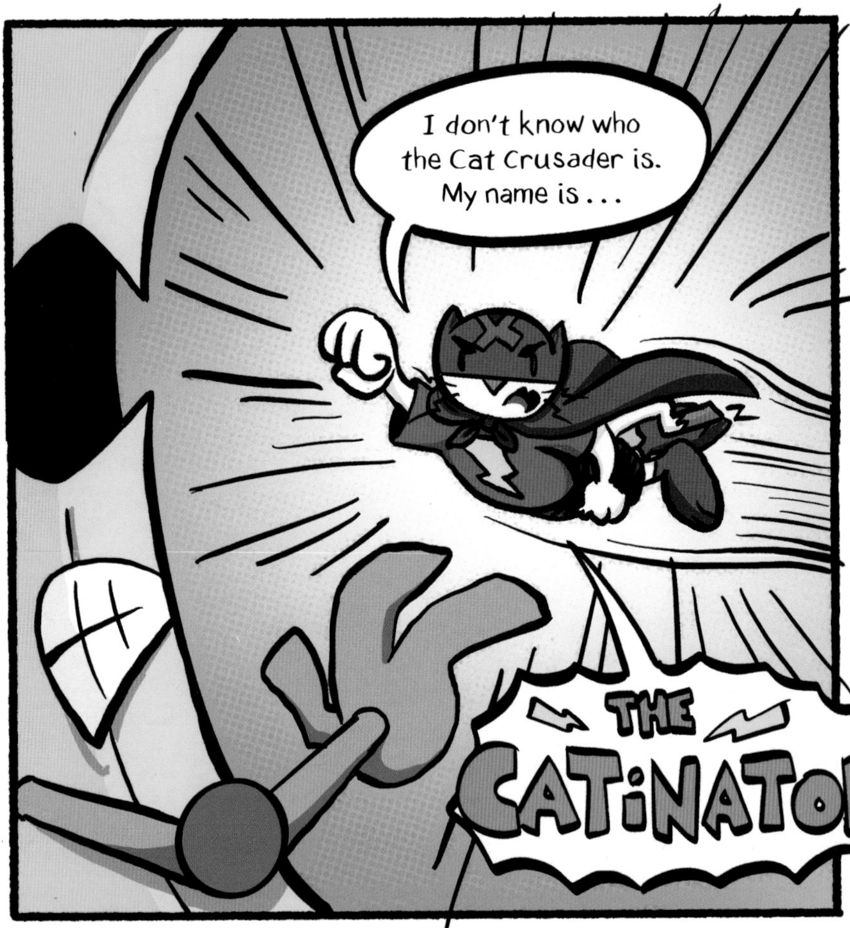
I don't know who the Cat Crusader is. My name is . . .
THE CATiNATOR!

WHO is this Catinator character?

WHY does he look like the Cat Crusader?

WHAT can make this story any weirder?

Find out in the next chapter!

Okay—probably the chapter after that!

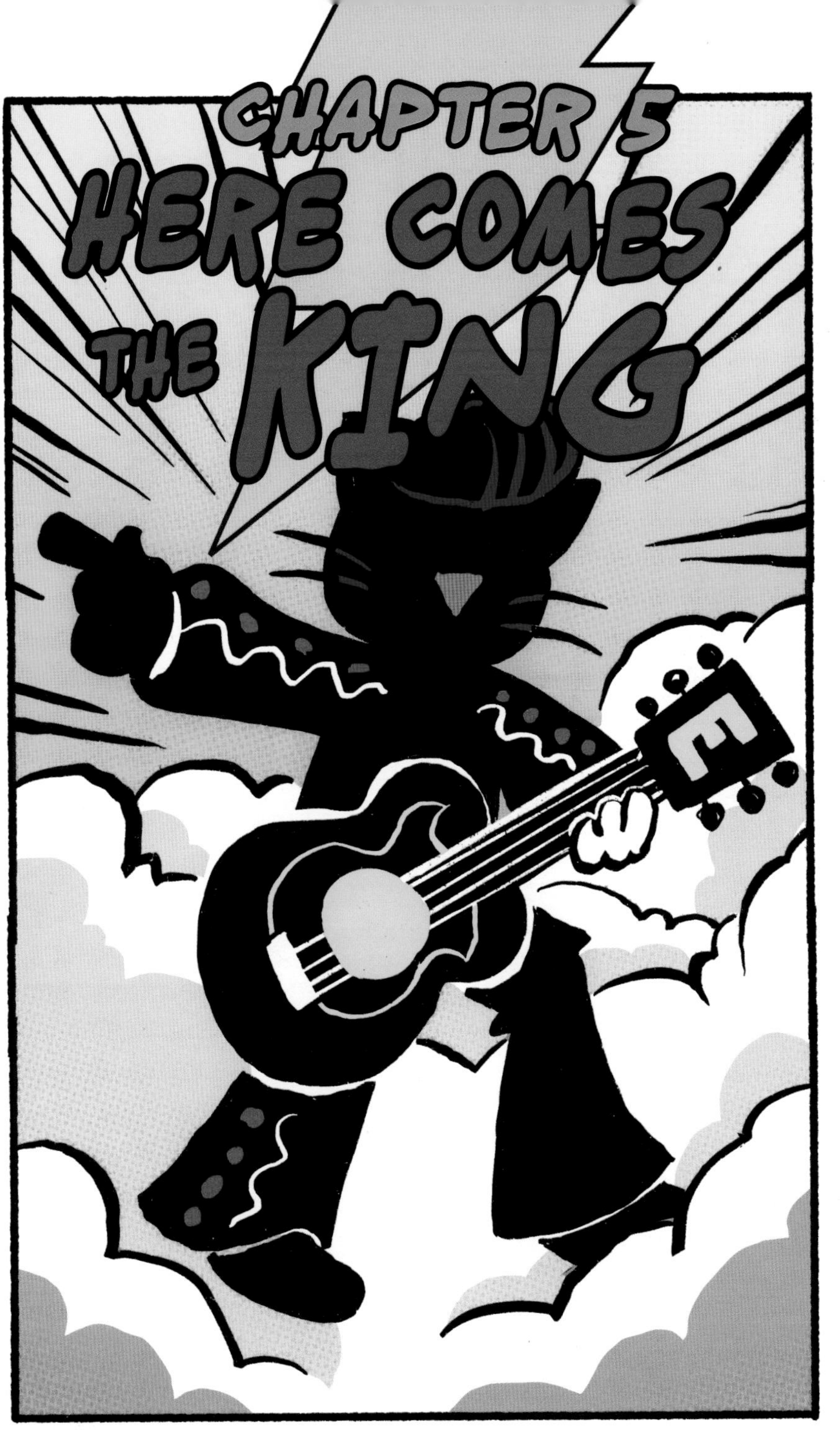
CHAPTER 5
HERE COMES THE KING

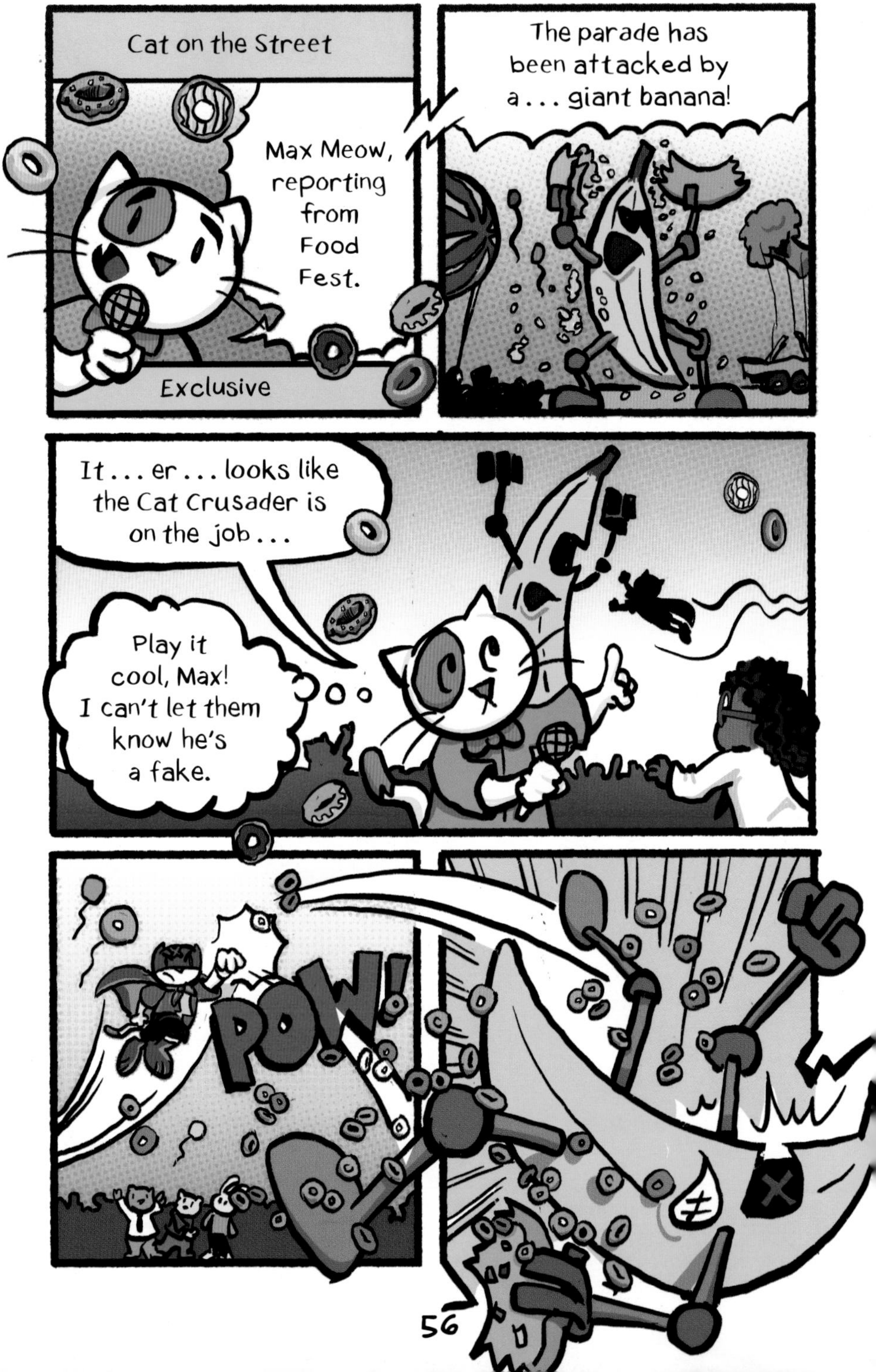
Cat on the Street
Max Meow, reporting from Food Fest.
Exclusive
The parade has been attacked by a . . . giant banana!
It . . . er . . . looks like the Cat Crusader is on the job . . .
Play it cool, Max! I can't let them know he's a fake.
POW!

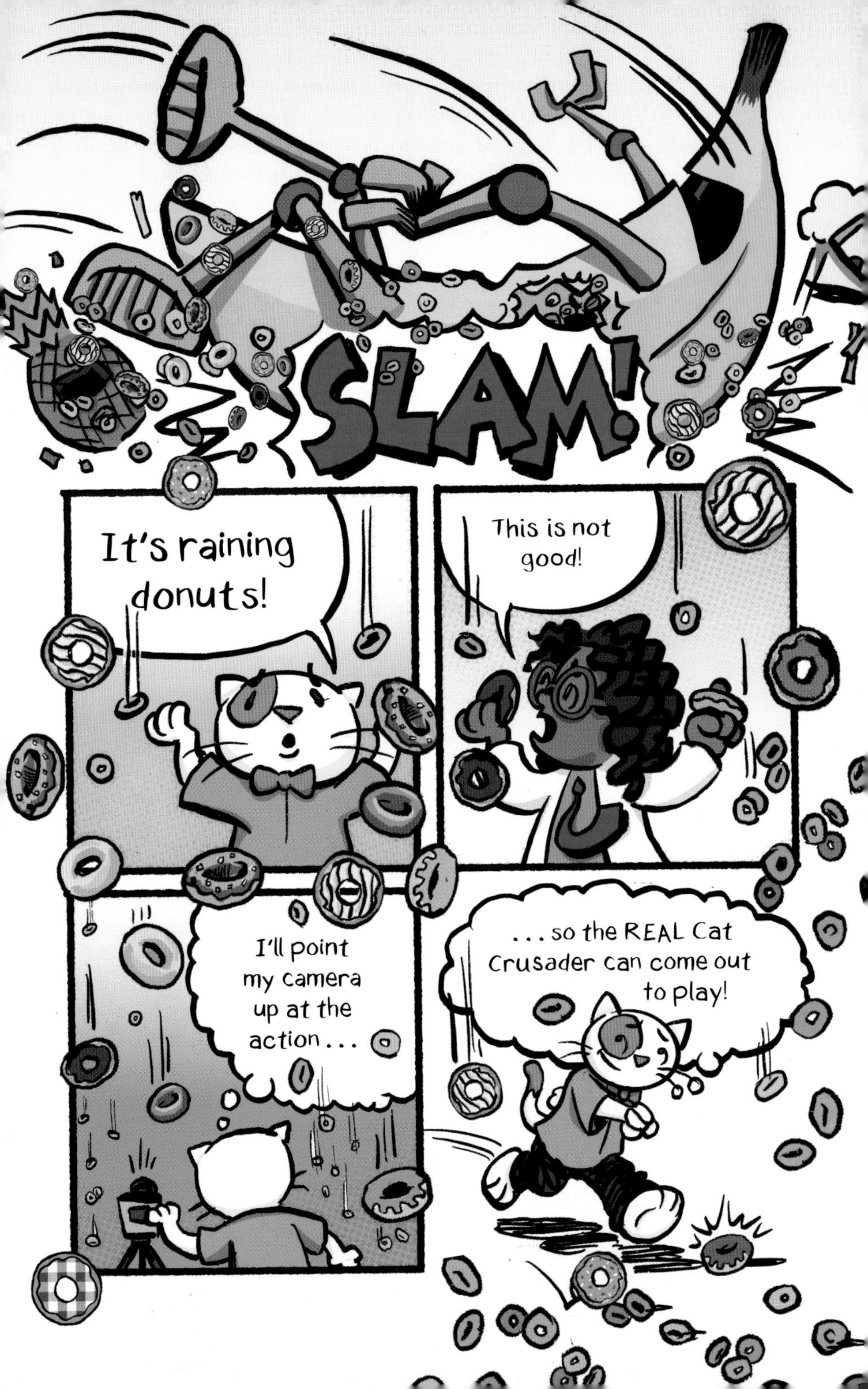
SLAM!
It's raining donuts!
This is not good!
I'll point my camera up at the action . . .
. . . so the REAL Cat Crusader can come out to play!

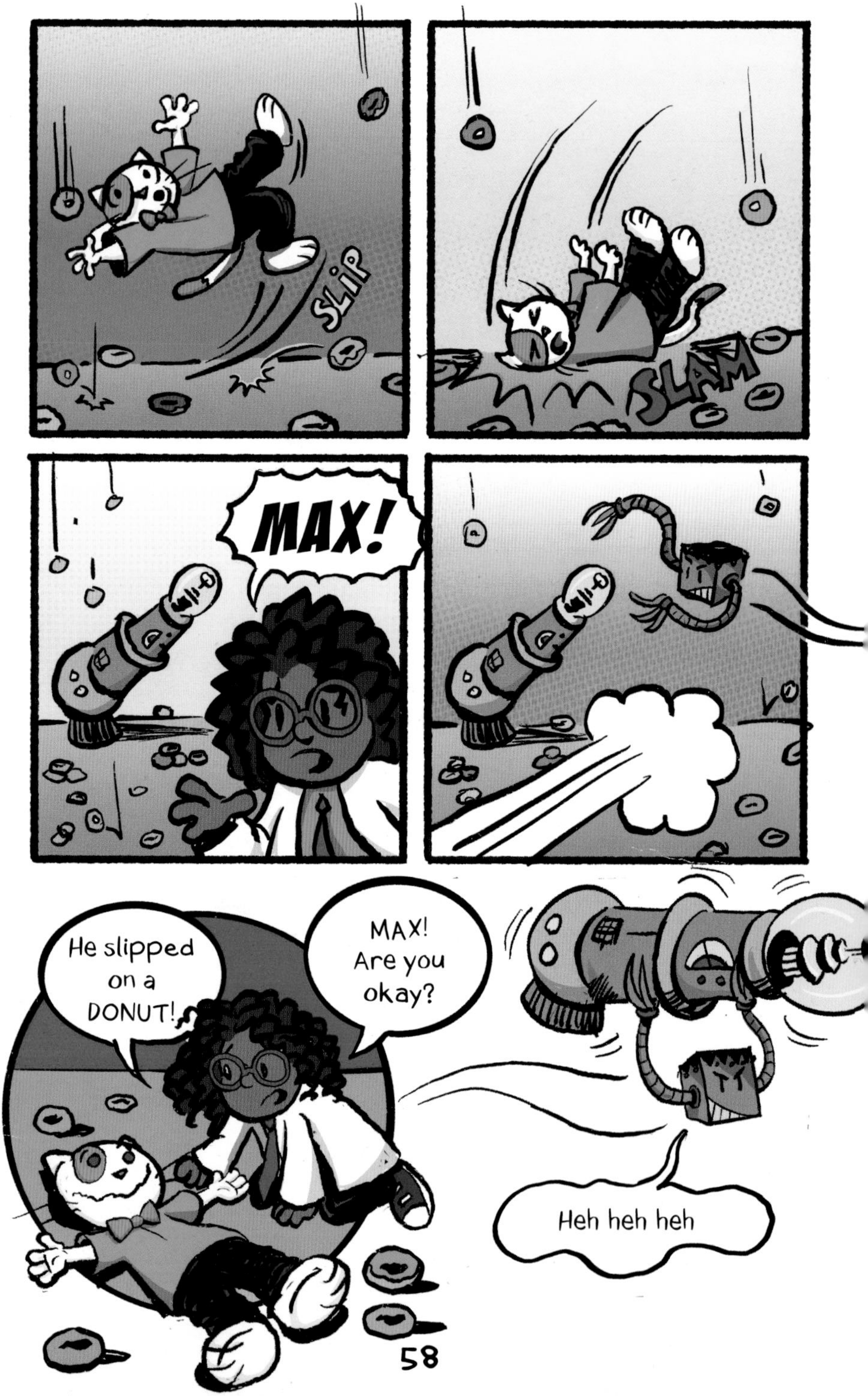
SLIP
SLAM
MAX!
He slipped on a DONUT!
MAX! Are you okay?
Heh heh heh

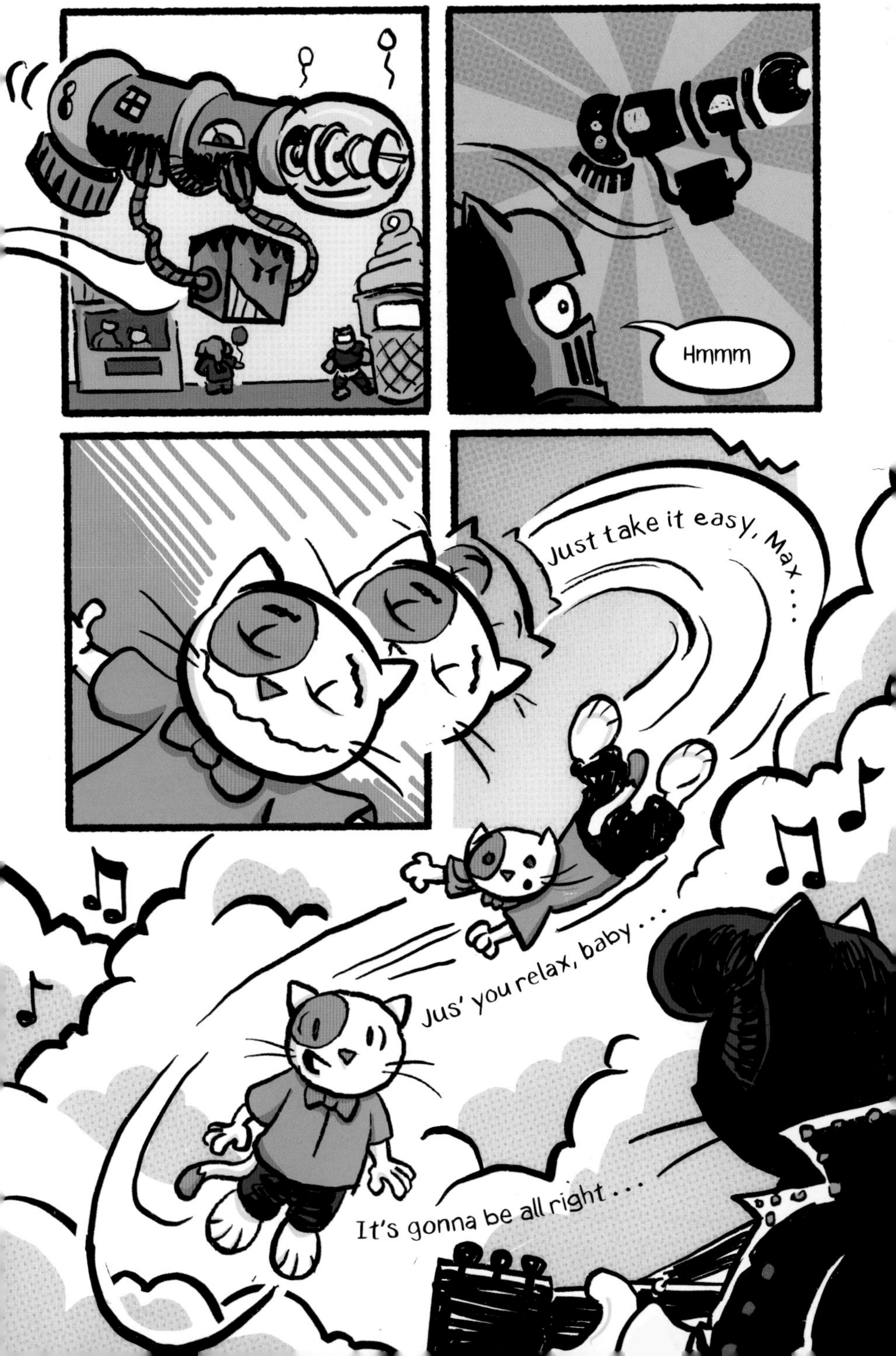
Hmmm
Just take it easy, Max . . .
Jus' you relax, baby . . .
It's gonna be all right . . .

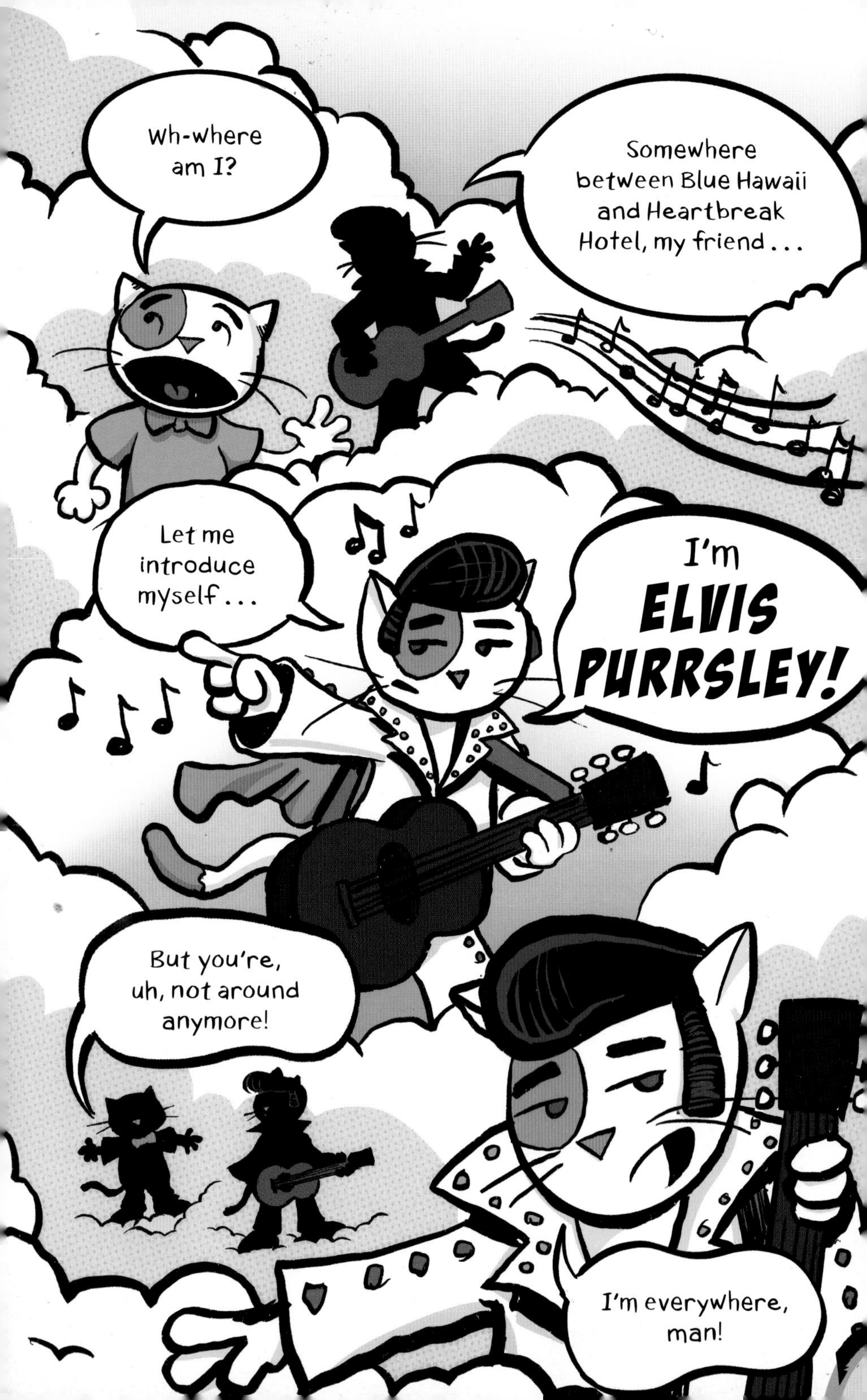
Wh-where am I?
Somewhere between Blue Hawaii and Heartbreak Hotel, my friend . . .
Let me introduce myself . . .
I'm ELVIS PURRSLEY!
But you're, uh, not around anymore!
I'm everywhere, man!

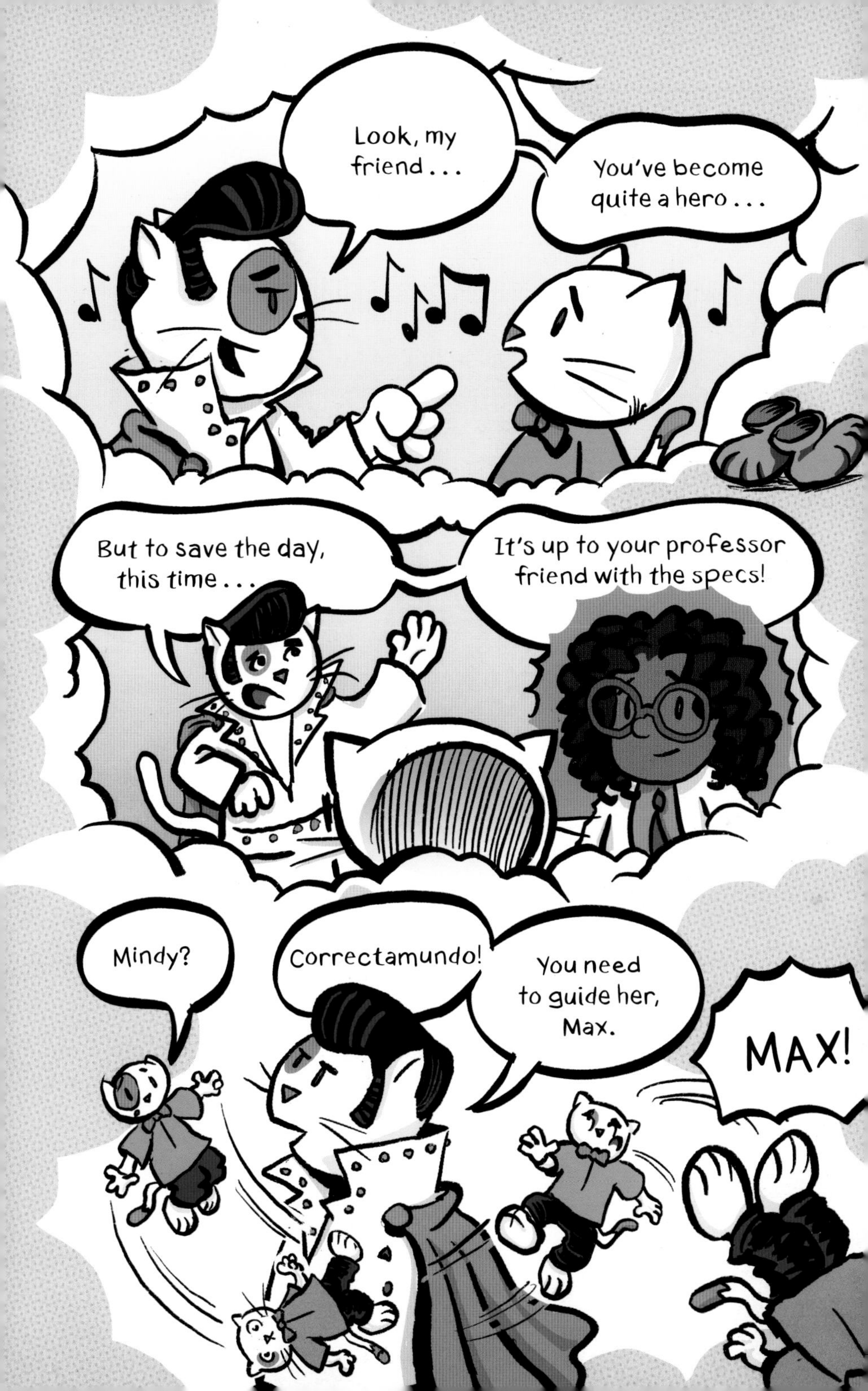
Look, my friend . . .
You've become quite a hero . . .
But to save the day, this time . . .
It's up to your professor friend with the specs!
Mindy?
Correctamundo!
You need to guide her, Max.
MAX!

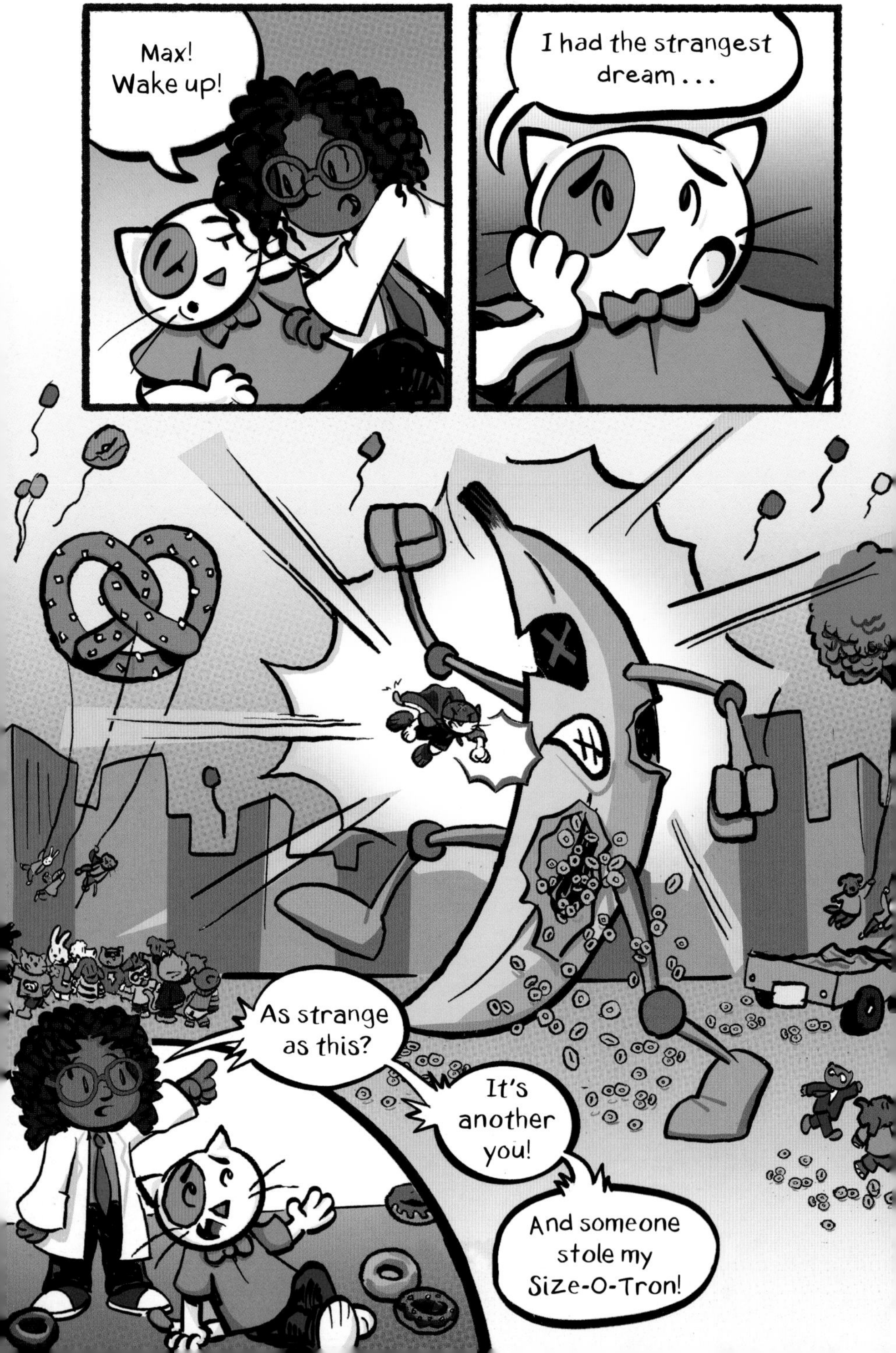
Max! Wake up!
I had the strangest dream . . .
As strange as this?
It's another you!
And someone stole my Size-O-Tron!

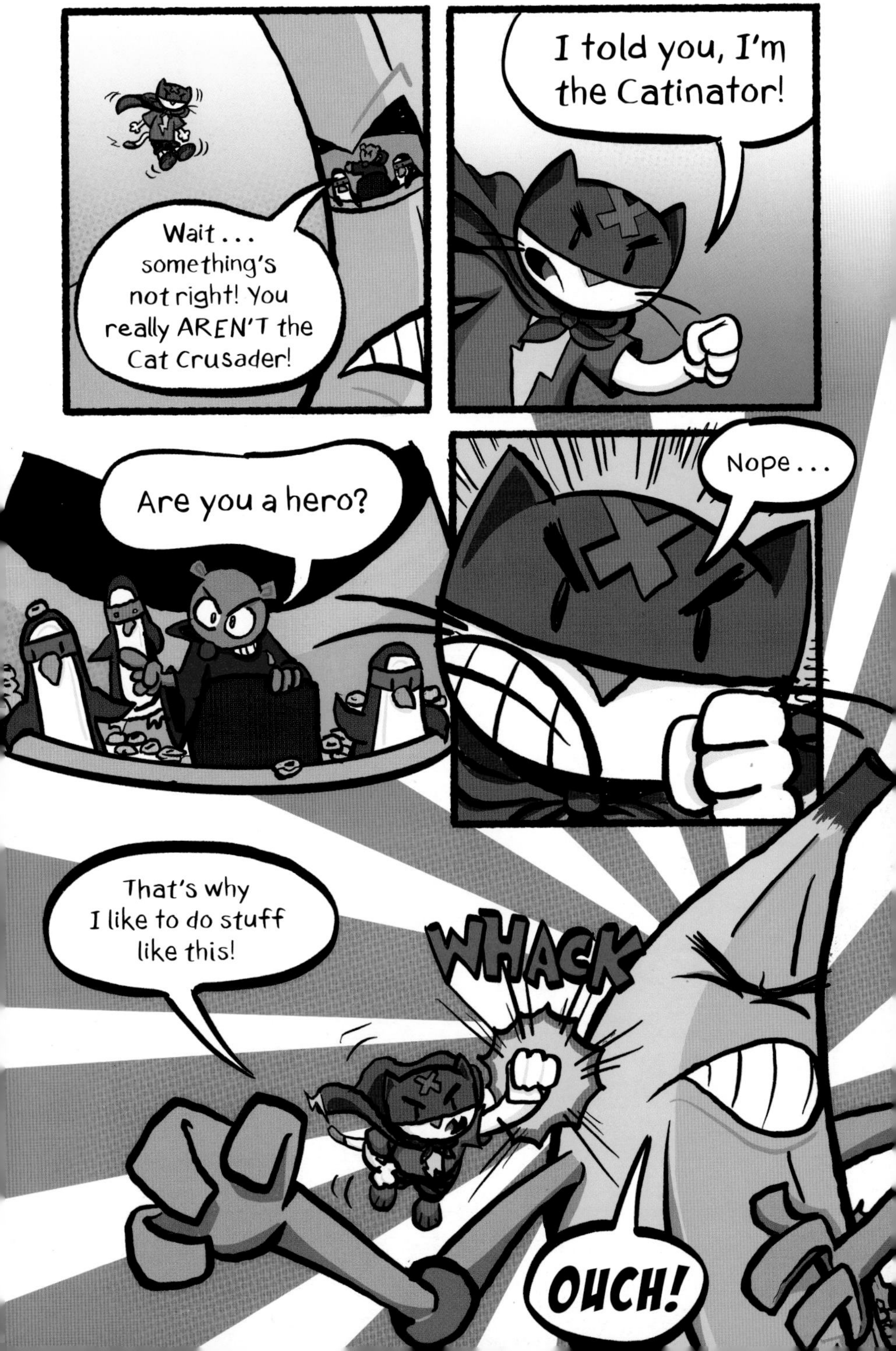
Wait . . . something's not right! You really AREN'T the Cat Crusader!
I told you, I'm the Catinator!
Are you a hero?
Nope . . .
That's why I like to do stuff like this!
WHACK
OUCH!

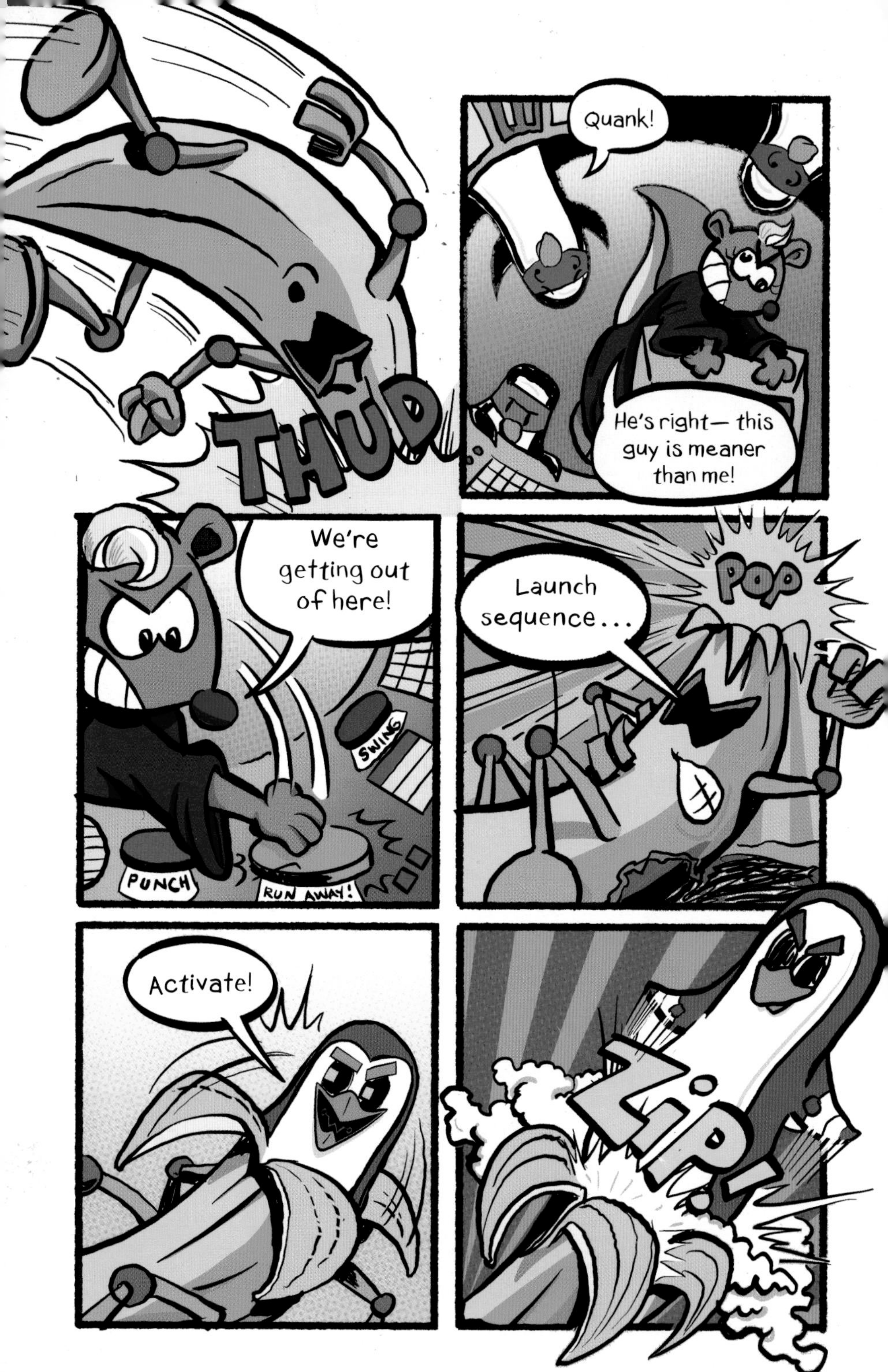
THUD
Quank!
He's right— this guy is meaner than me!
We're getting out of here!
SWING
PUNCH
RUN AWAY!
Launch sequence...
POP
Activate!
ZIP!

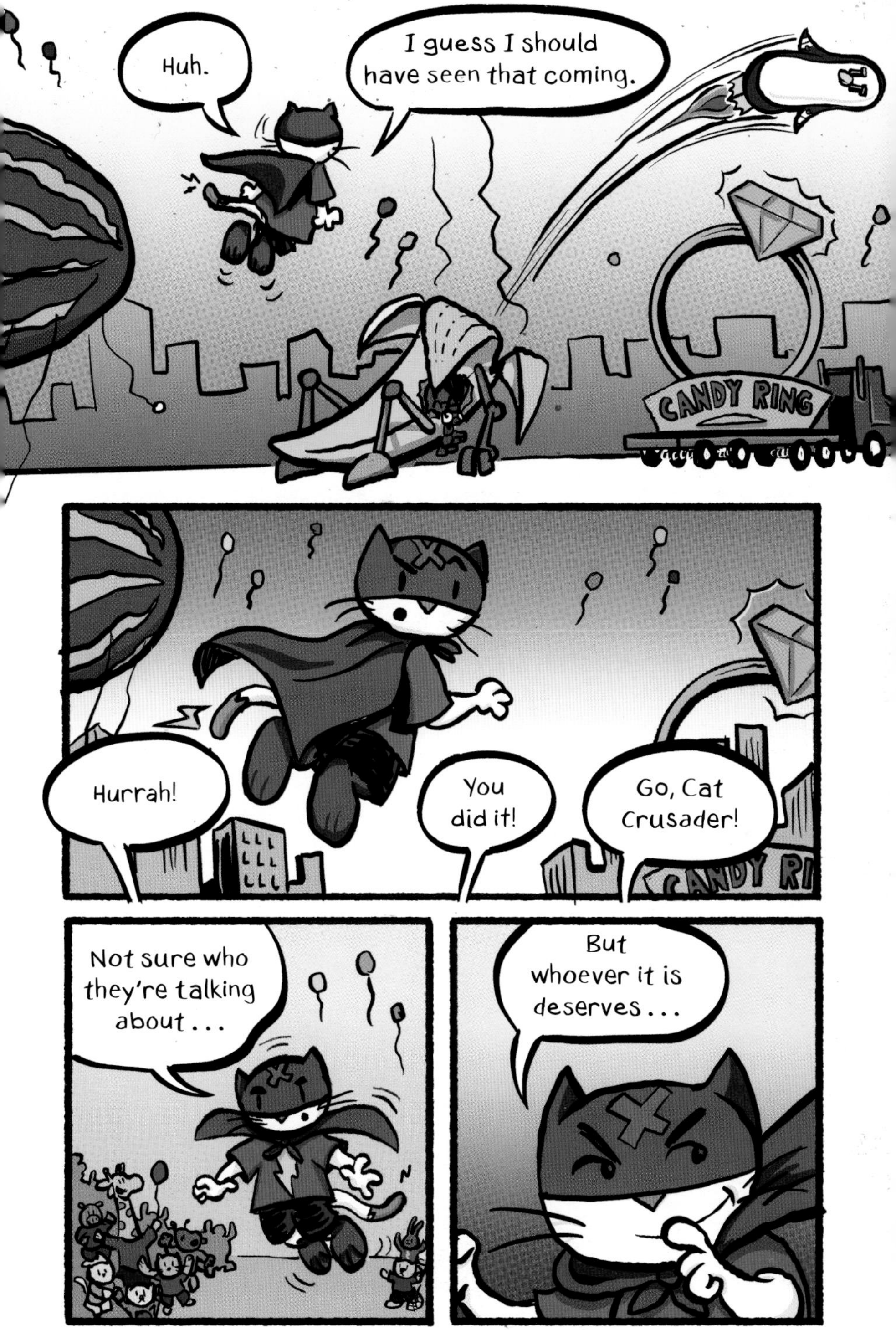
Huh.
I guess I should have seen that coming.
CANDY RING
Hurrah!
You did it!
Go, Cat Crusader!
Not sure who they're talking about . . .
But whoever it is deserves . . .

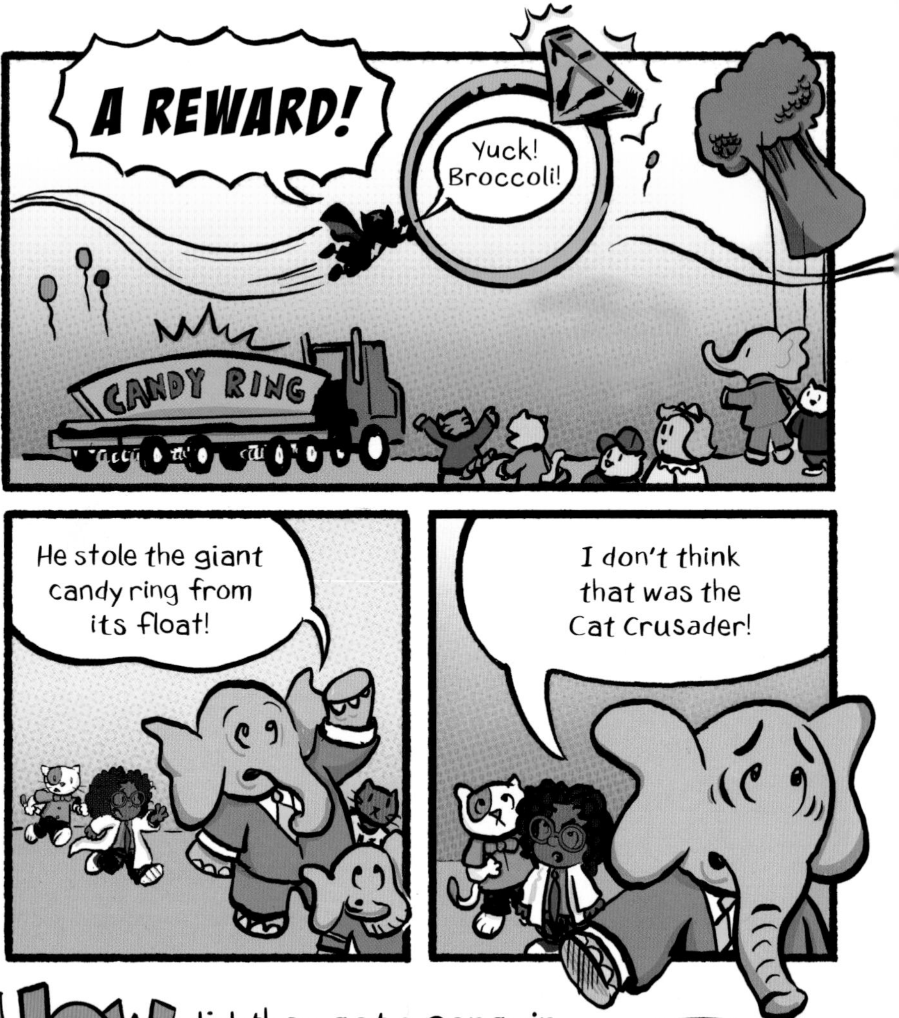
A REWARD!
Yuck! Broccoli!
CANDY RING
He stole the giant candy ring from its float!
I don't think that was the Cat Crusader!

HOW did they get a penguin robot into a banana suit?

WHY did Max see a famous rock 'n' roll feline?

WHEN will we ever answer any of these questions?

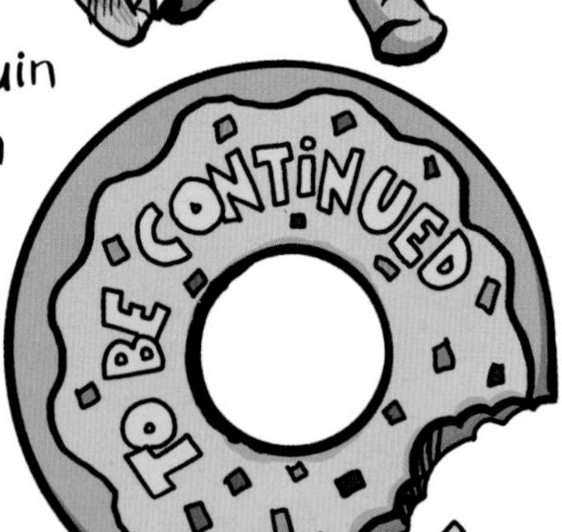
TO BE CONTINUED

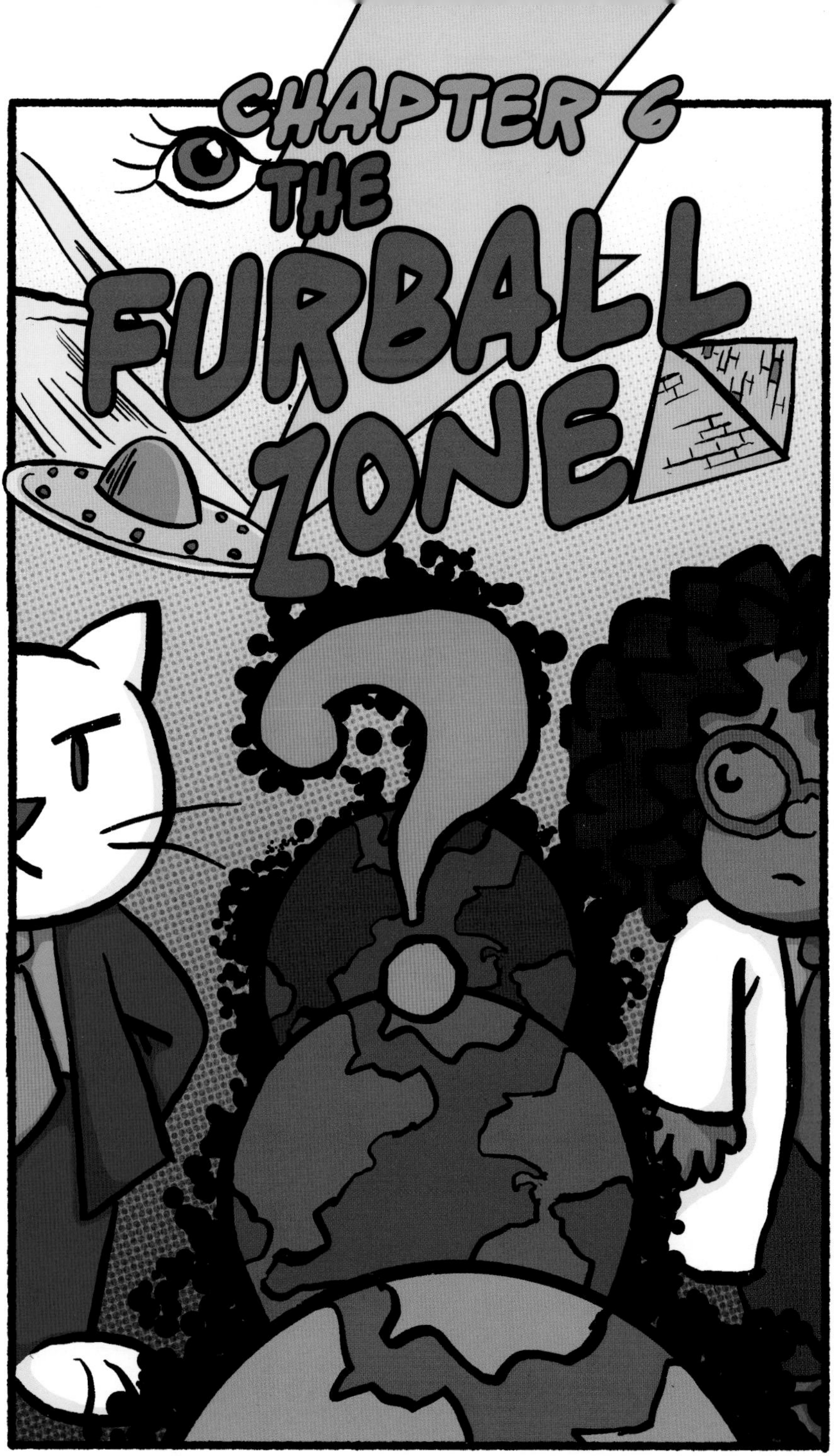
CHAPTER 6
THE
FURBALL
ZONE

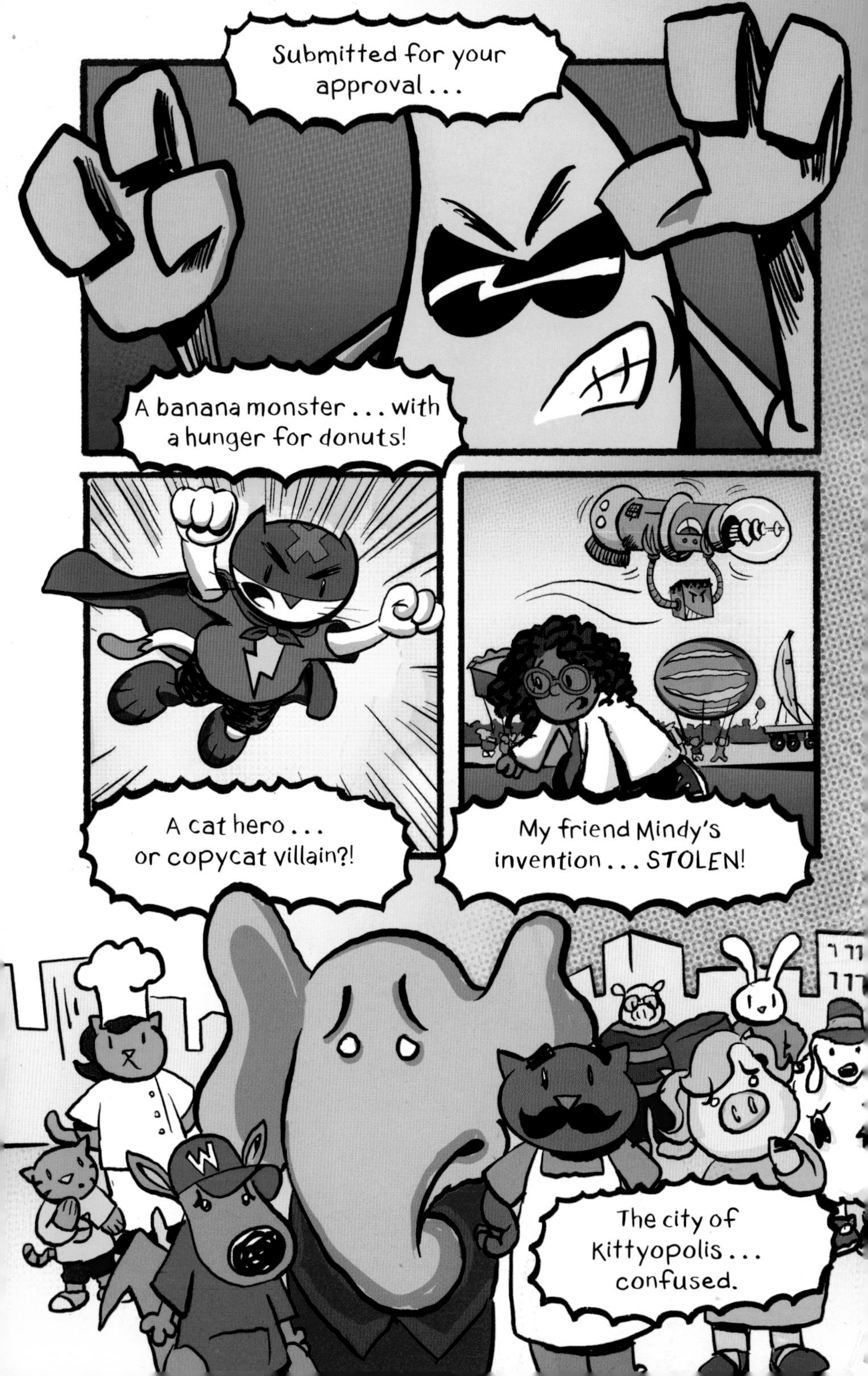
Submitted for your approval . . .
A banana monster . . . with a hunger for donuts!
A cat hero . . . or copycat villain?!
My friend Mindy's invention . . . STOLEN!
The city of Kittyopolis . . . confused.

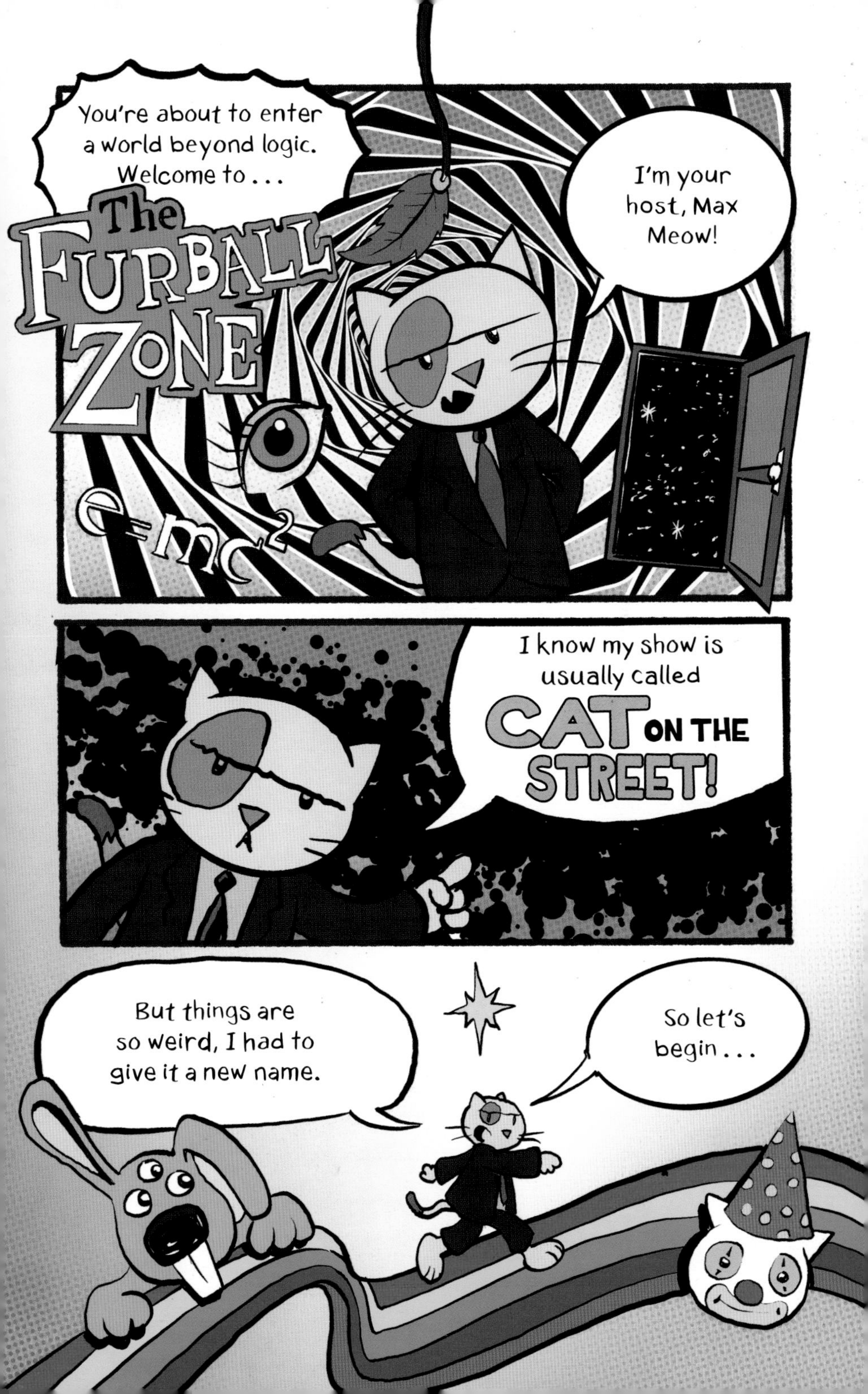
You're about to enter a world beyond logic. Welcome to . . .
The FURBALL ZONE
I'm your host, Max Meow!
e=mc2
I know my show is usually called CAT ON THE STREET!
But things are so weird, I had to give it a new name.
So let's begin . . .

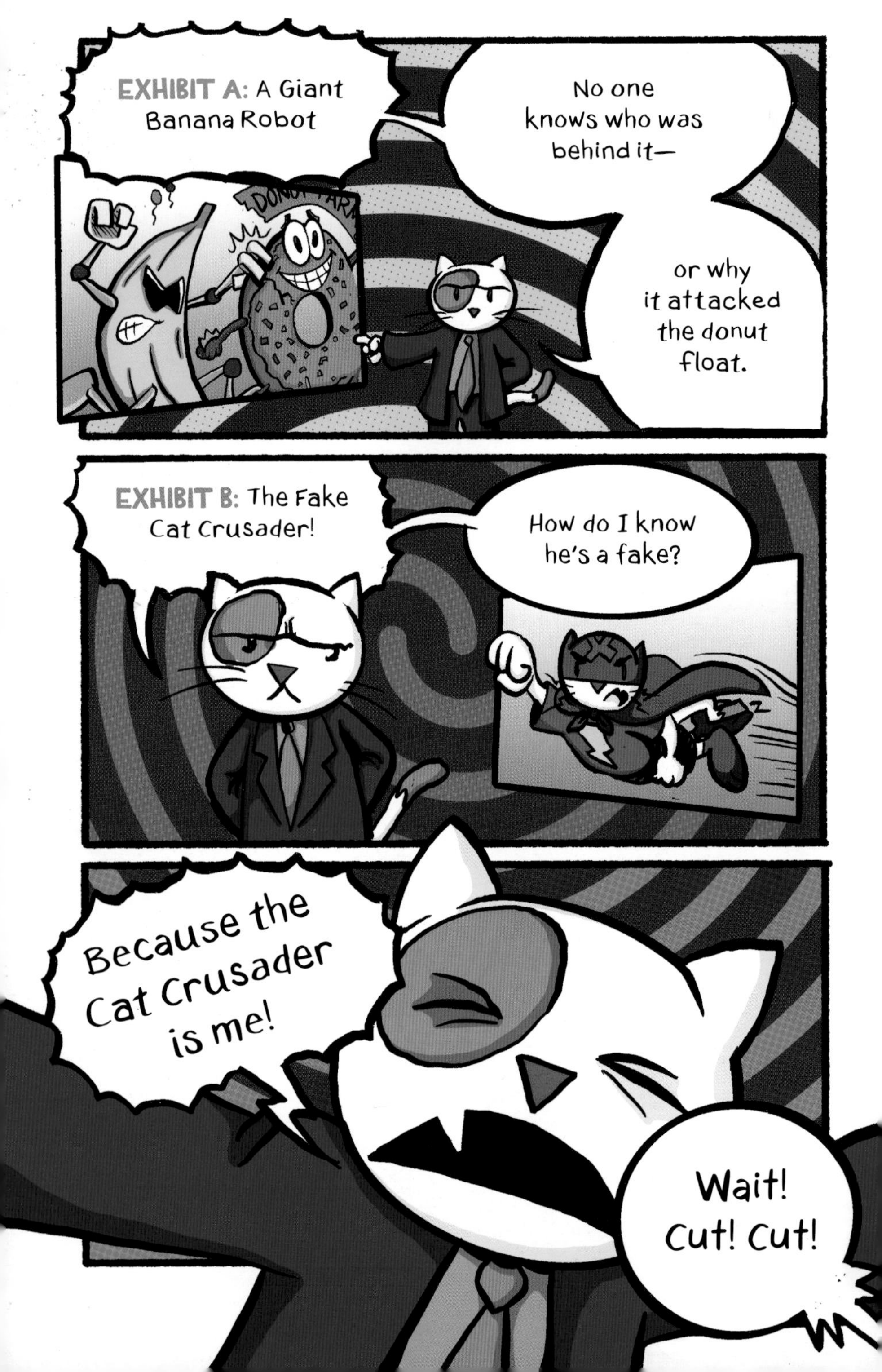

EXHIBIT A: A Giant Banana Robot
No one knows who was behind it—
or why it attacked the donut float.
EXHIBIT B: The Fake Cat Crusader!
How do I know he's a fake?
Because the Cat Crusader is me!
Wait! Cut! Cut!

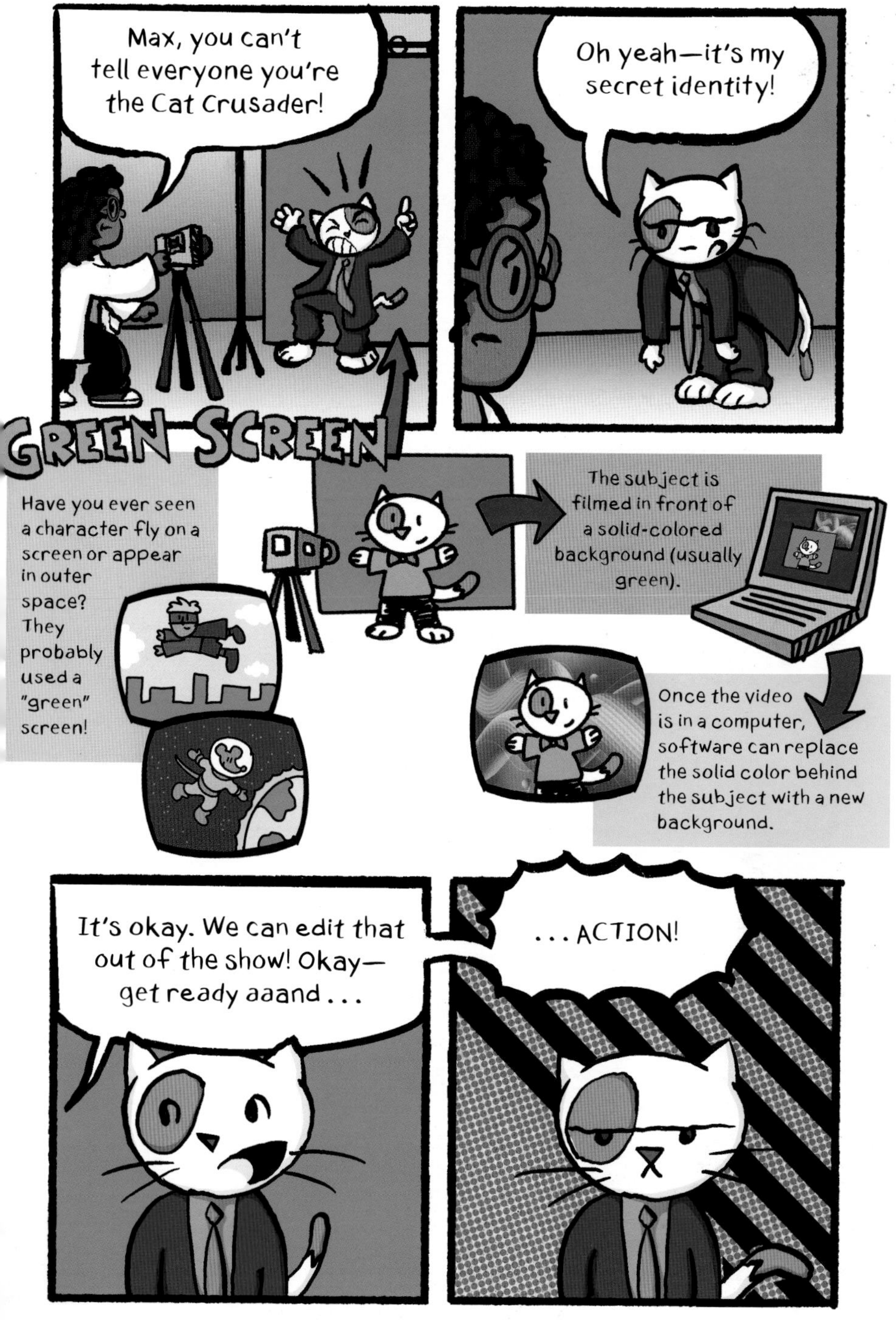
Max, you can't tell everyone you're the Cat Crusader!
Oh yeah—it's my secret identity!
GREEN SCREEN
Have you ever seen a character fly on a screen or appear in outer space? They probably used a "green" screen!
The subject is filmed in front of a solid-colored background (usually green).
Once the video is in a computer, software can replace the solid color behind the subject with a new background.
It's okay. We can edit that out of the show! Okay—get ready aaand . . .
. . . ACTION!

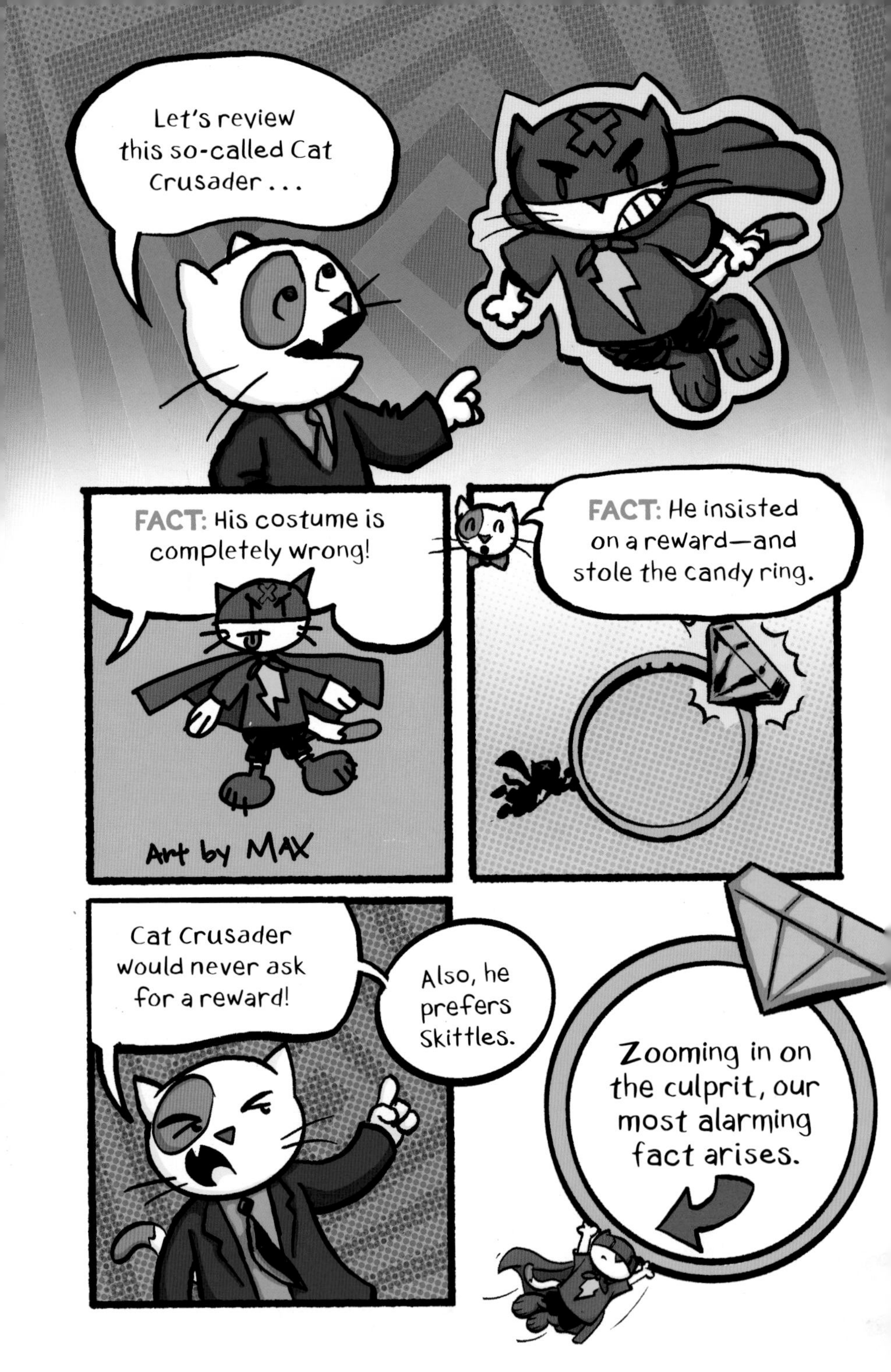
Let's review this so-called Cat Crusader . . .
FACT: His costume is completely wrong!
Art by MAX
FACT: He insisted on a reward—and stole the candy ring.
Cat Crusader would never ask for a reward!
Also, he prefers Skittles.
Zooming in on the culprit, our most alarming fact arises.

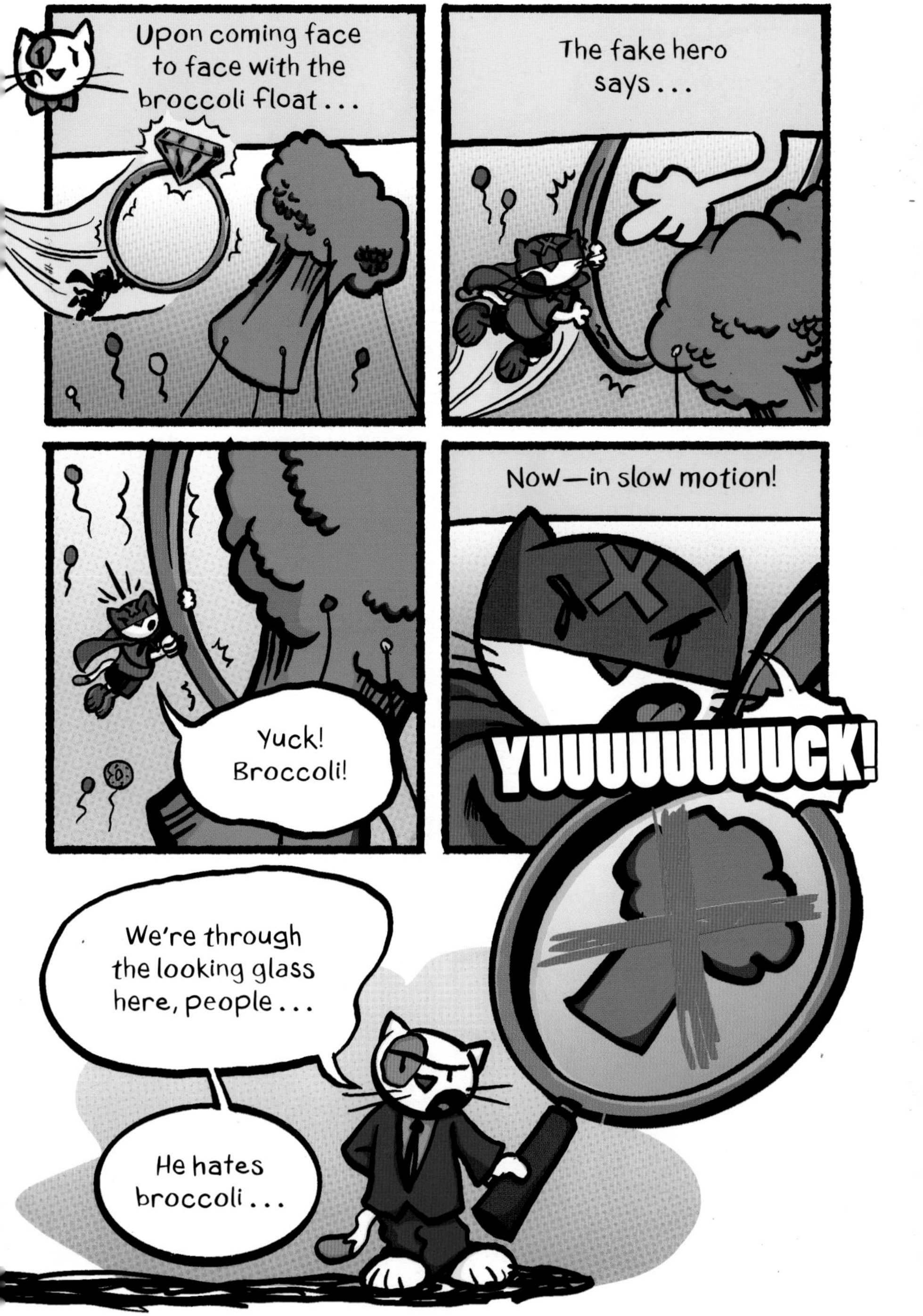
Upon coming face to face with the broccoli float . . .
The fake hero says . . .
Yuck! Broccoli!
Now—in slow motion!
YUUUUUUUUUCK!
We're through the looking glass here, people . . .
He hates broccoli . . .

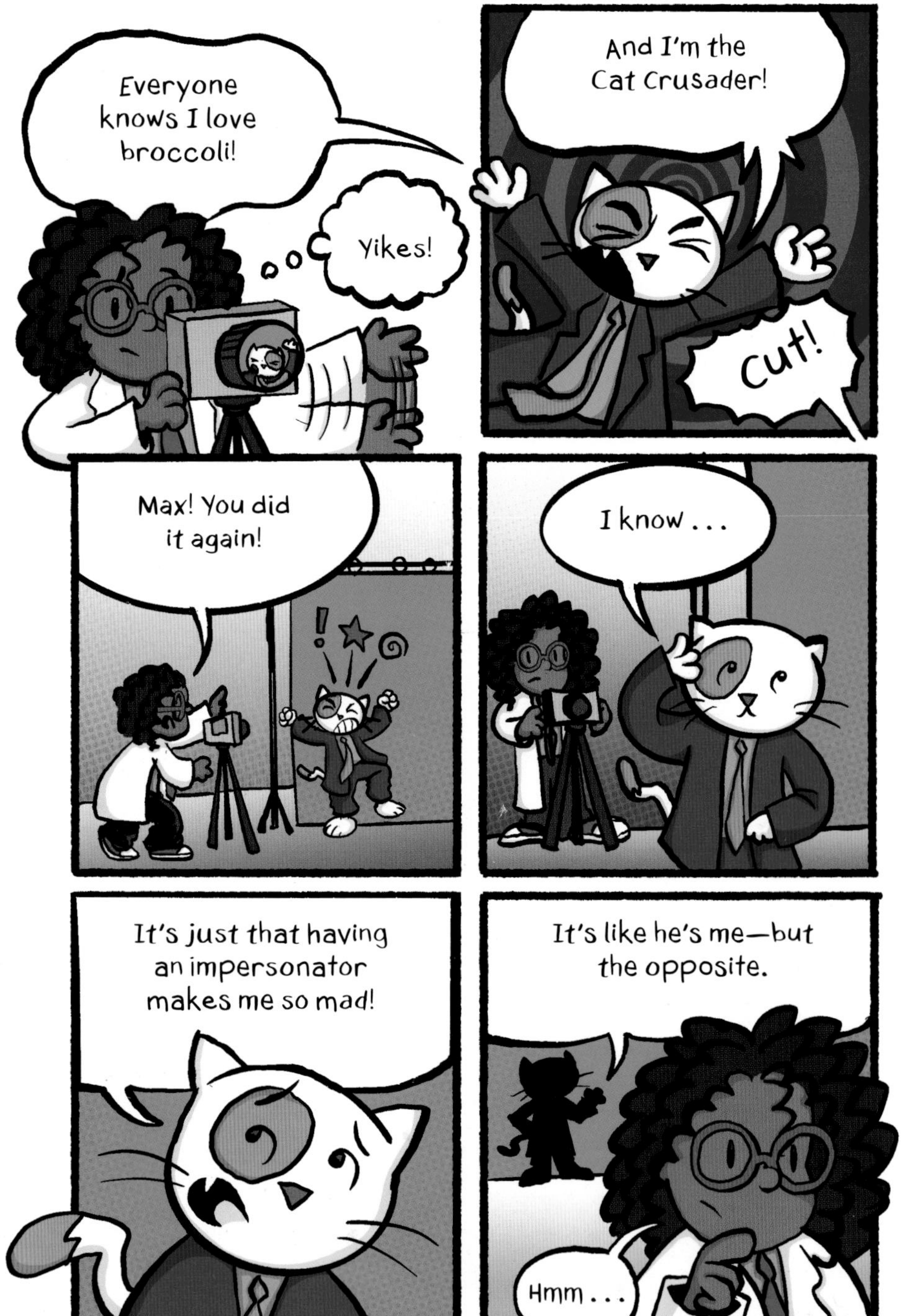
Everyone knows I love broccoli!
Yikes!
And I'm the Cat Crusader!
Cut!
Max! You did it again!
I know . . .
It's just that having an impersonator makes me so mad!
It's like he's me—but the opposite.
Hmm . . .

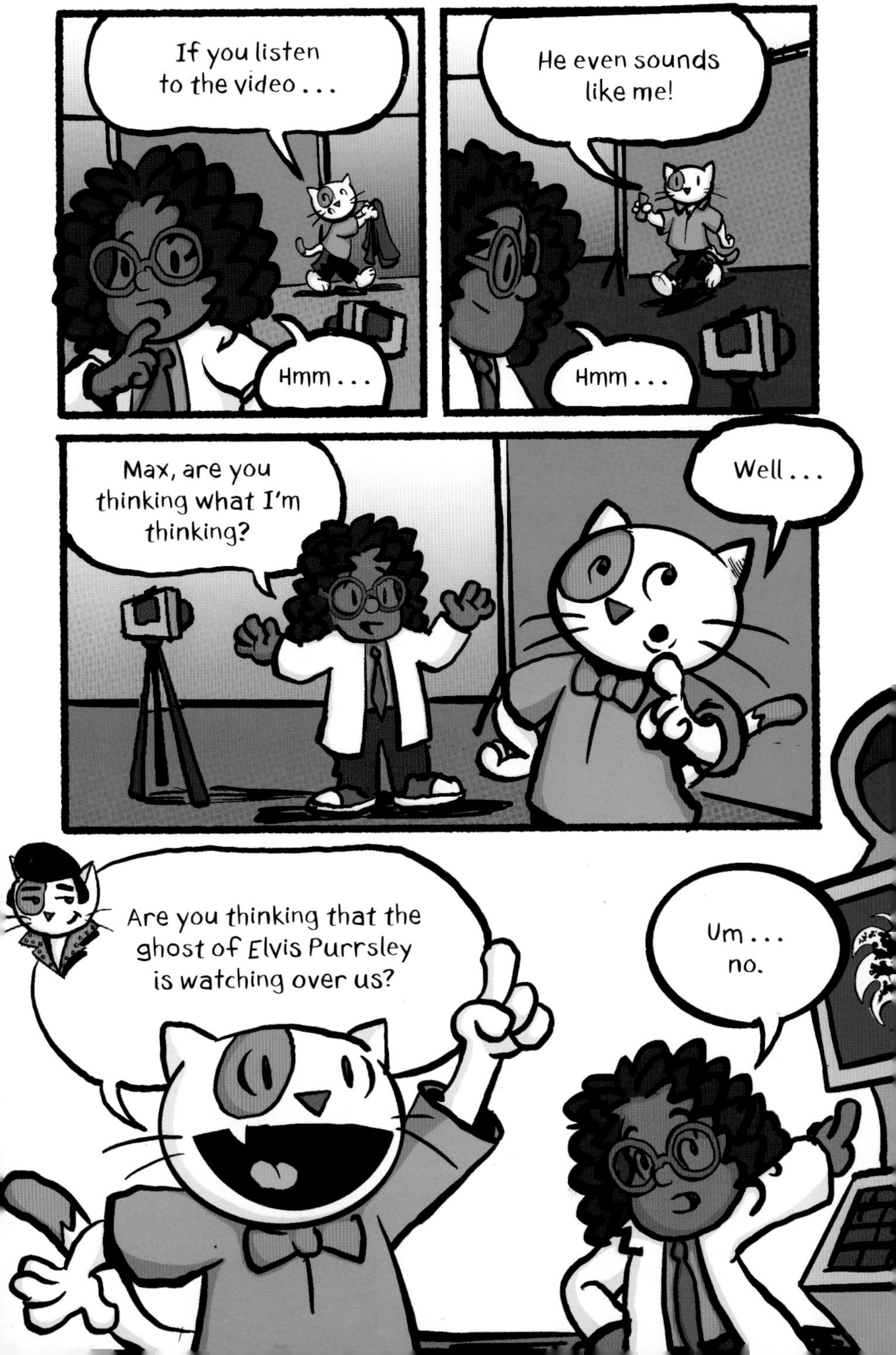
If you listen to the video . . .
Hmm . . .
He even sounds like me!
Hmm . . .
Max, are you thinking what I'm thinking?
Well . . .
Are you thinking that the ghost of Elvis Purrsley is watching over us?
Um . . . no.

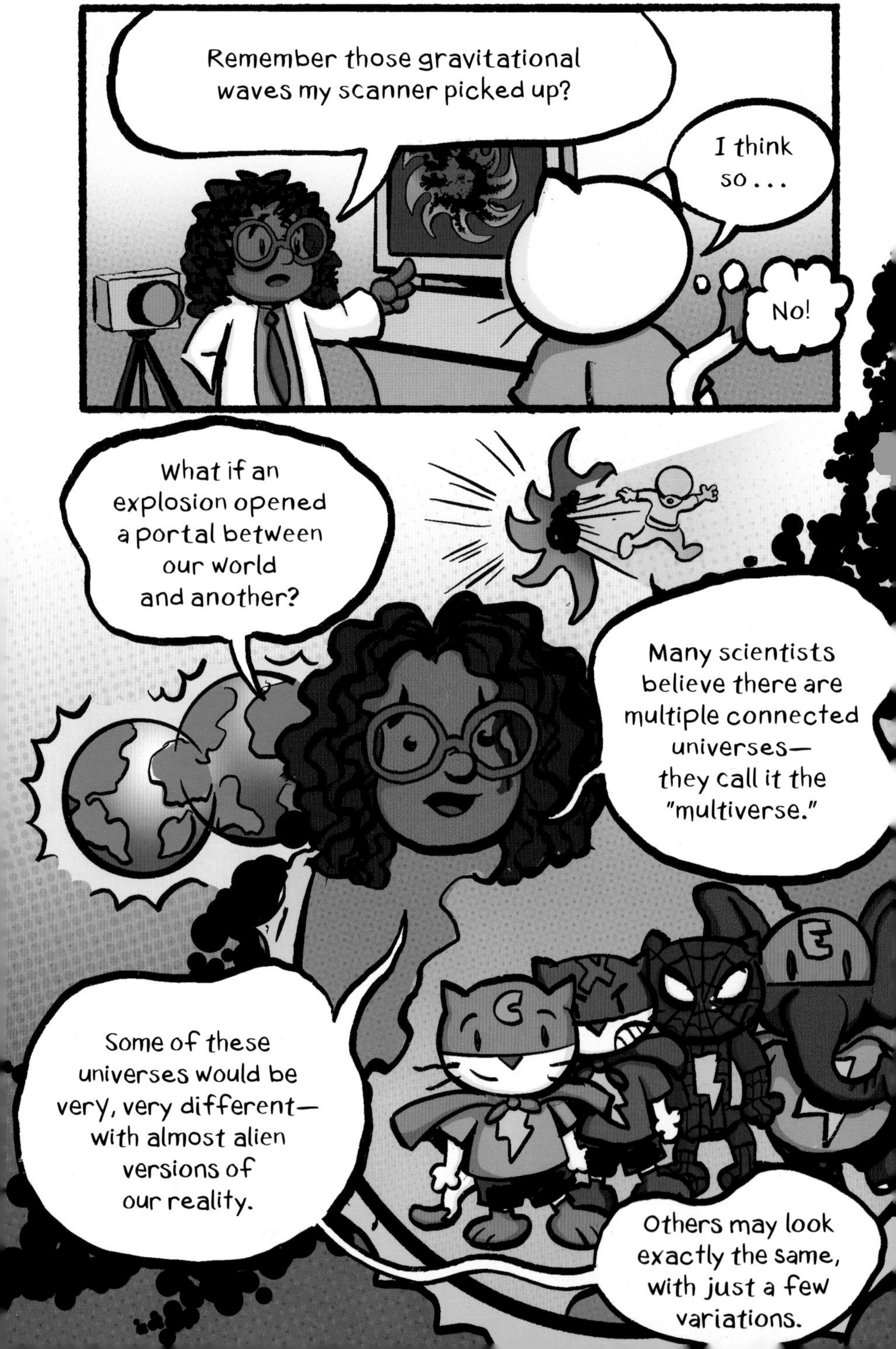
Remember those gravitational waves my scanner picked up?
I think so . . .
No!
What if an explosion opened a portal between our world and another?
Many scientists believe there are multiple connected universes—they call it the "multiverse."
Some of these universes would be very, very different—with almost alien versions of our reality.
Others may look exactly the same, with just a few variations.

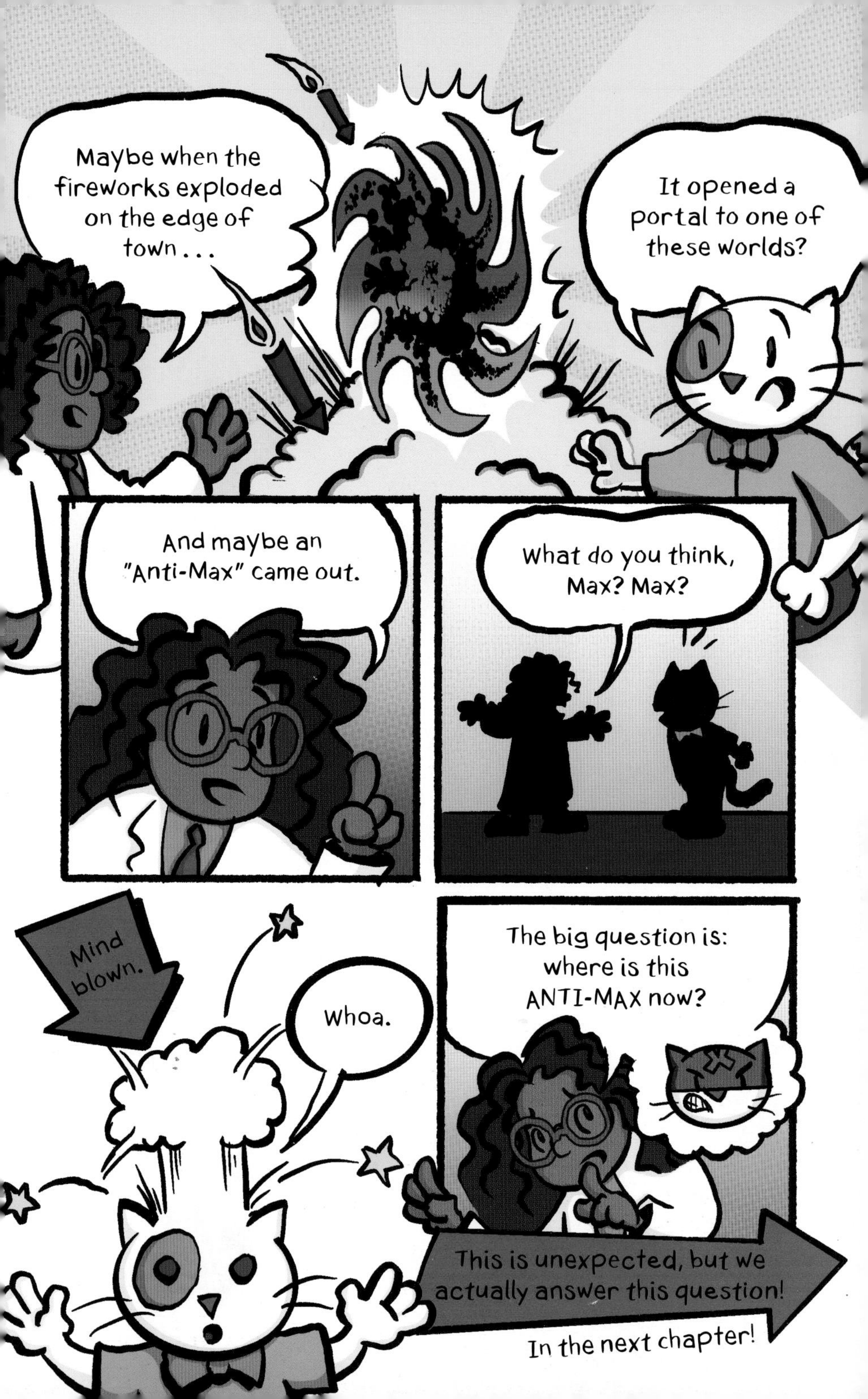
Maybe when the fireworks exploded on the edge of town . . .
It opened a portal to one of these worlds?
And maybe an "Anti-Max" came out.
What do you think, Max? Max?
Mind blown.
Whoa.
The big question is: where is this ANTI-MAX now?
This is unexpected, but we actually answer this question!
In the next chapter!

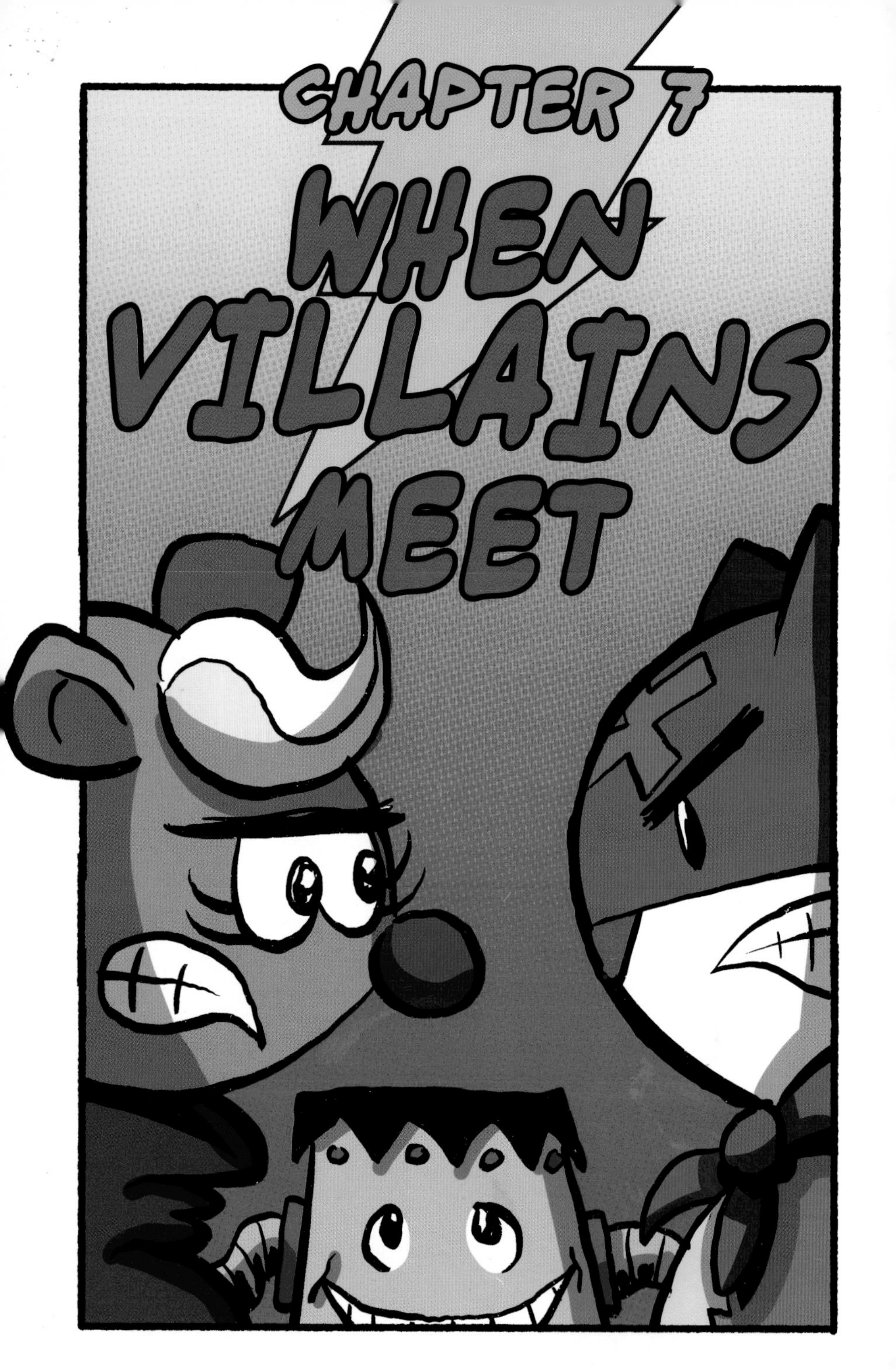
CHAPTER 7
WHEN VILLAINS MEET

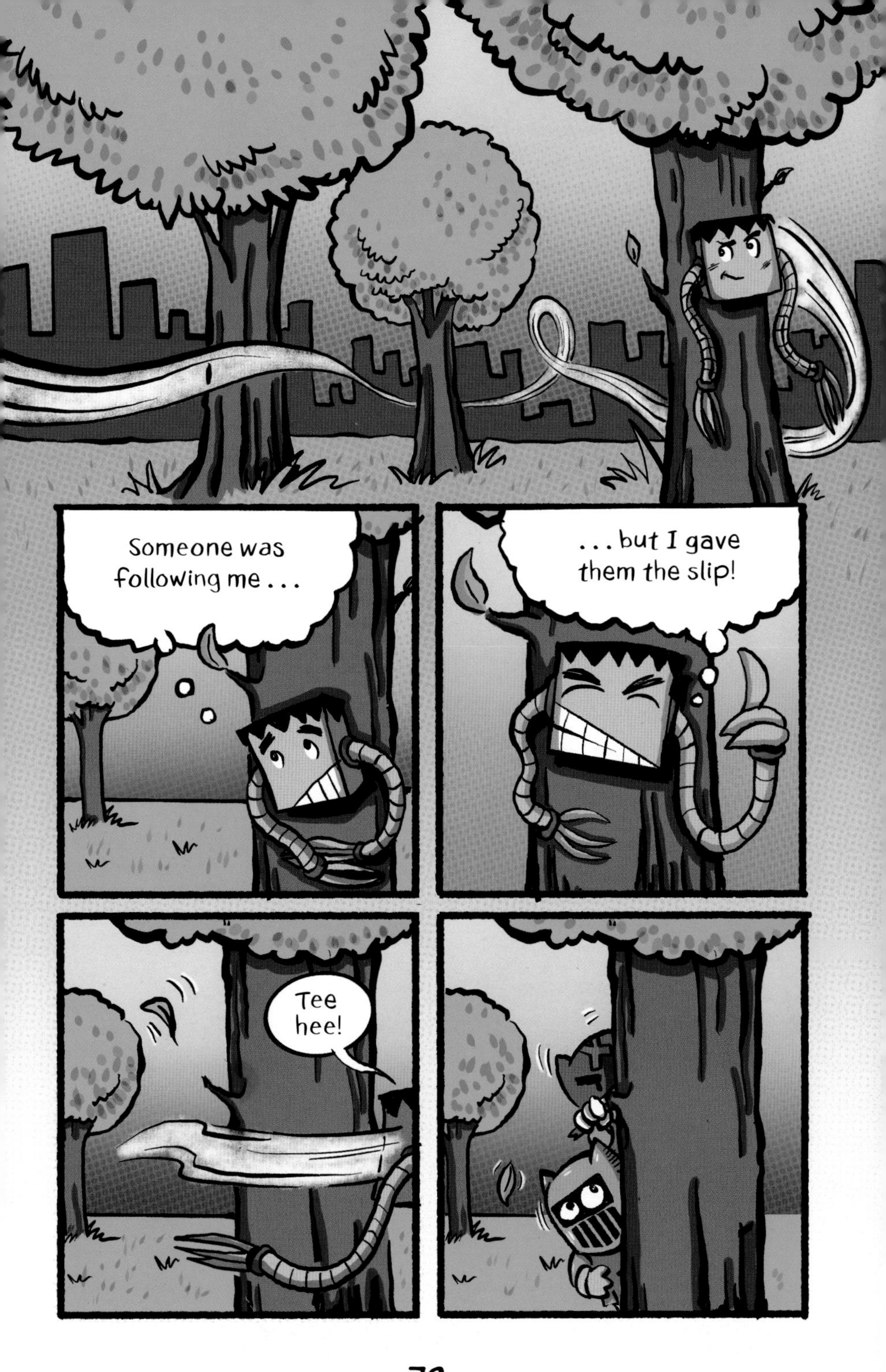
Someone was following me . . .
. . . but I gave them the slip!
Tee hee!

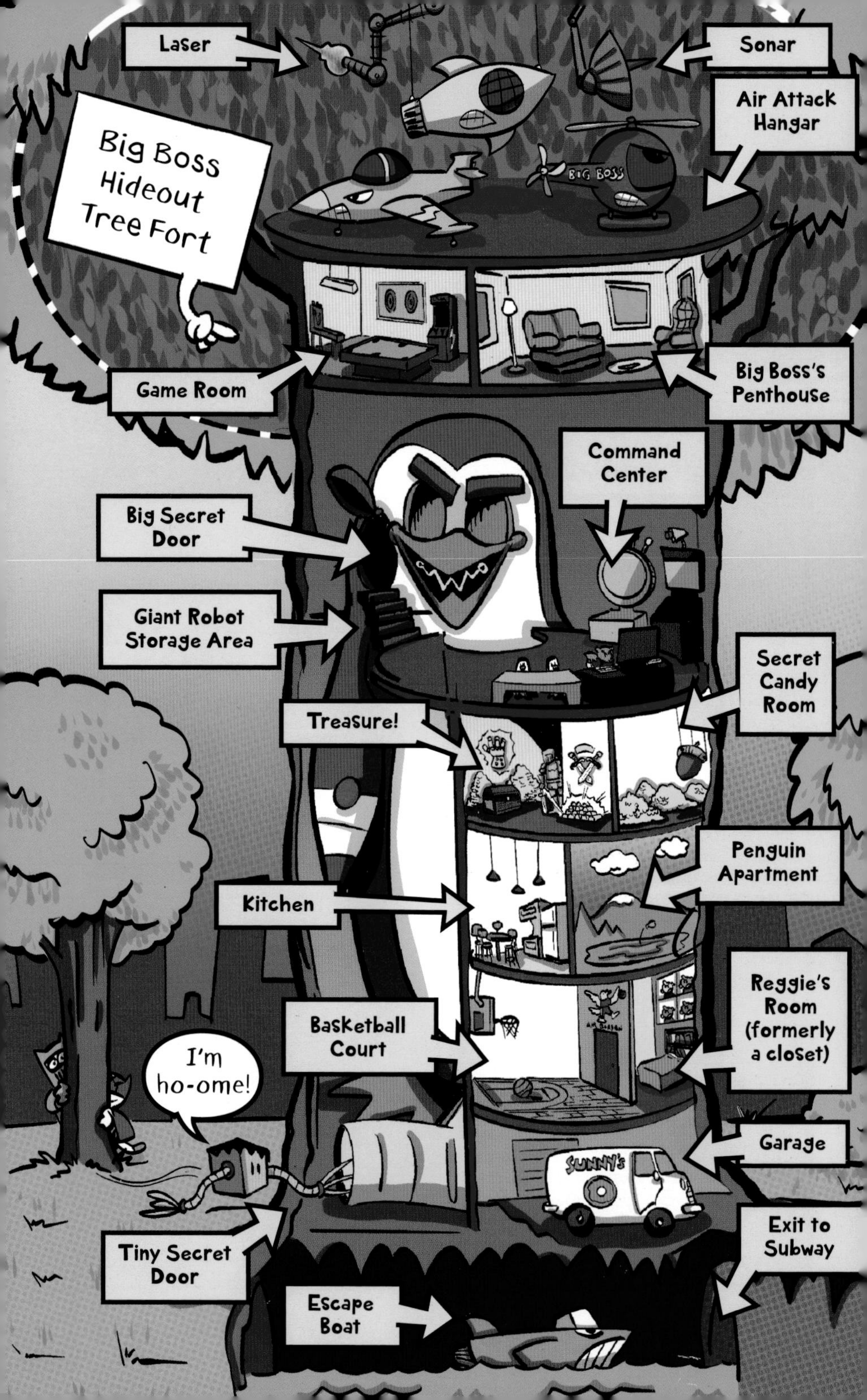
Big Boss Hideout Tree Fort
Laser
Sonar
Air Attack Hangar
BIG BOSS
Game Room
Big Boss's Penthouse
Command Center
Big Secret Door
Giant Robot Storage Area
Secret Candy Room
Treasure!
Penguin Apartment
Kitchen
Reggie's Room (formerly a closet)
Basketball Court
I'm ho-ome!
Garage
SUNNY'S
Exit to Subway
Tiny Secret Door
Escape Boat

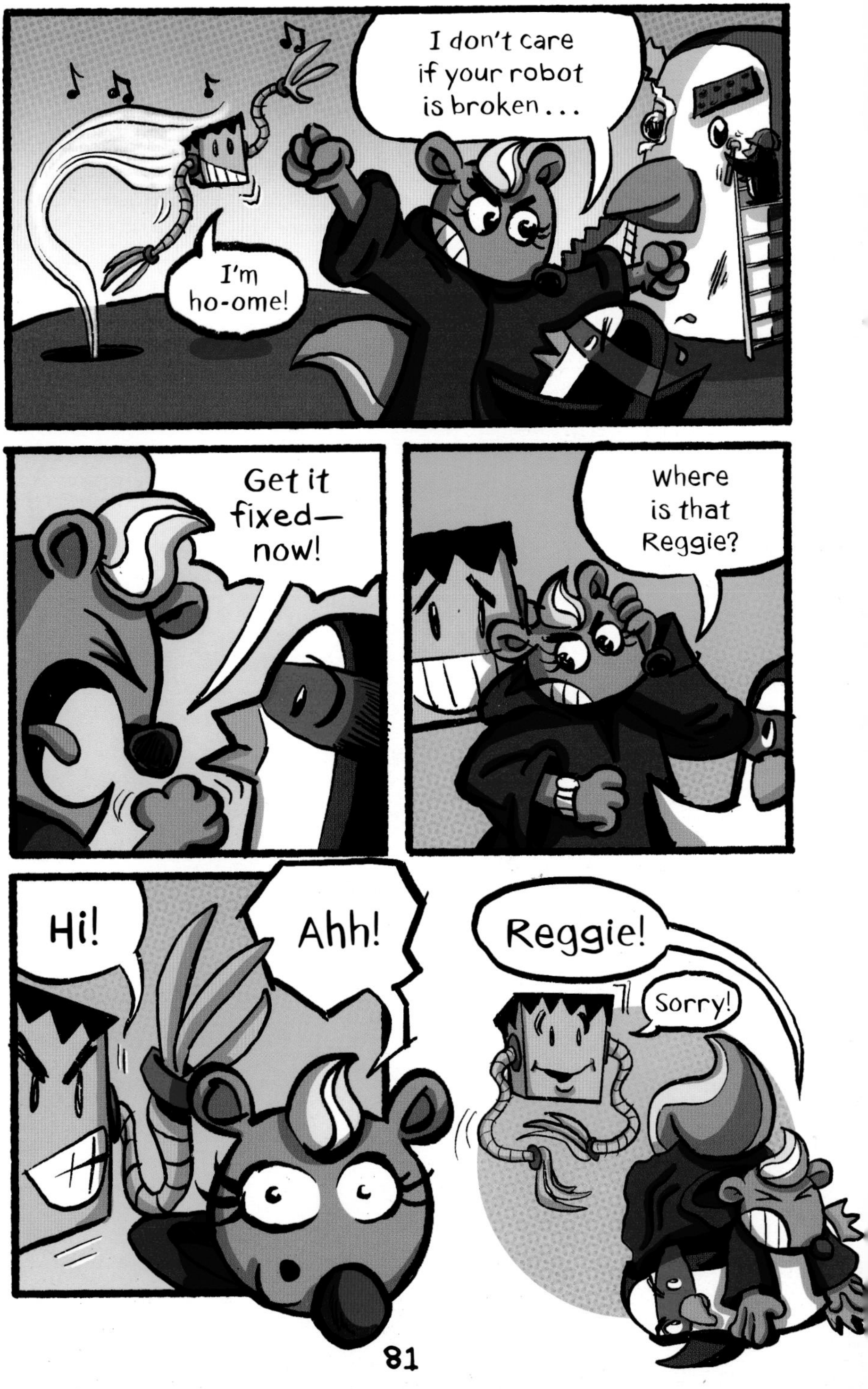
I don't care if your robot is broken . . .
I'm ho-ome!
Get it fixed—now!
Where is that Reggie?
Hi!
Ahh!
Reggie!
Sorry!

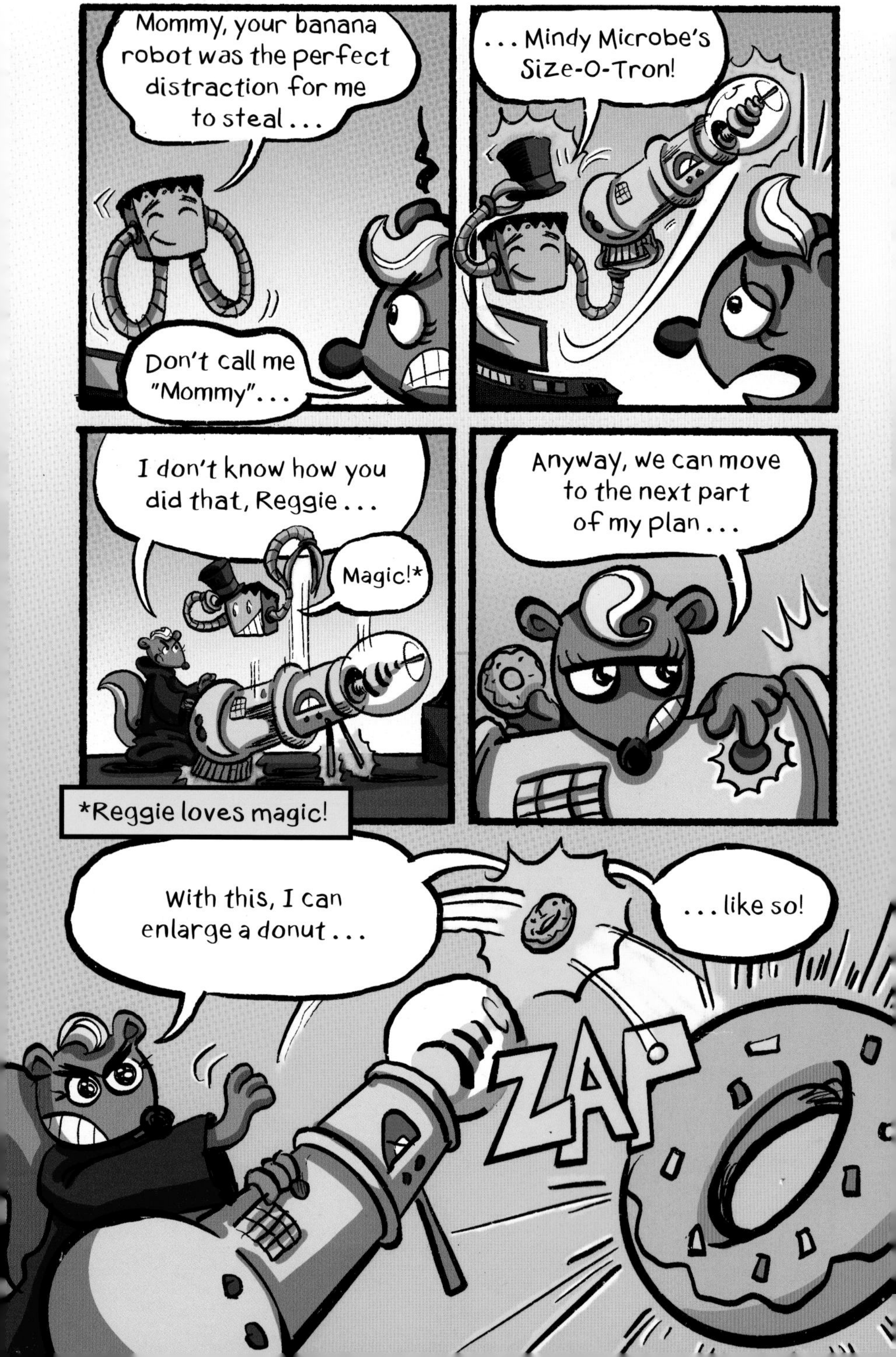
Mommy, your banana robot was the perfect distraction for me to steal . . .
Don't call me "Mommy". . .
. . . Mindy Microbe's Size-O-Tron!
I don't know how you did that, Reggie . . .
Magic!*
*Reggie loves magic!
Anyway, we can move to the next part of my plan . . .
With this, I can enlarge a donut . . .
. . . like so!
ZAP

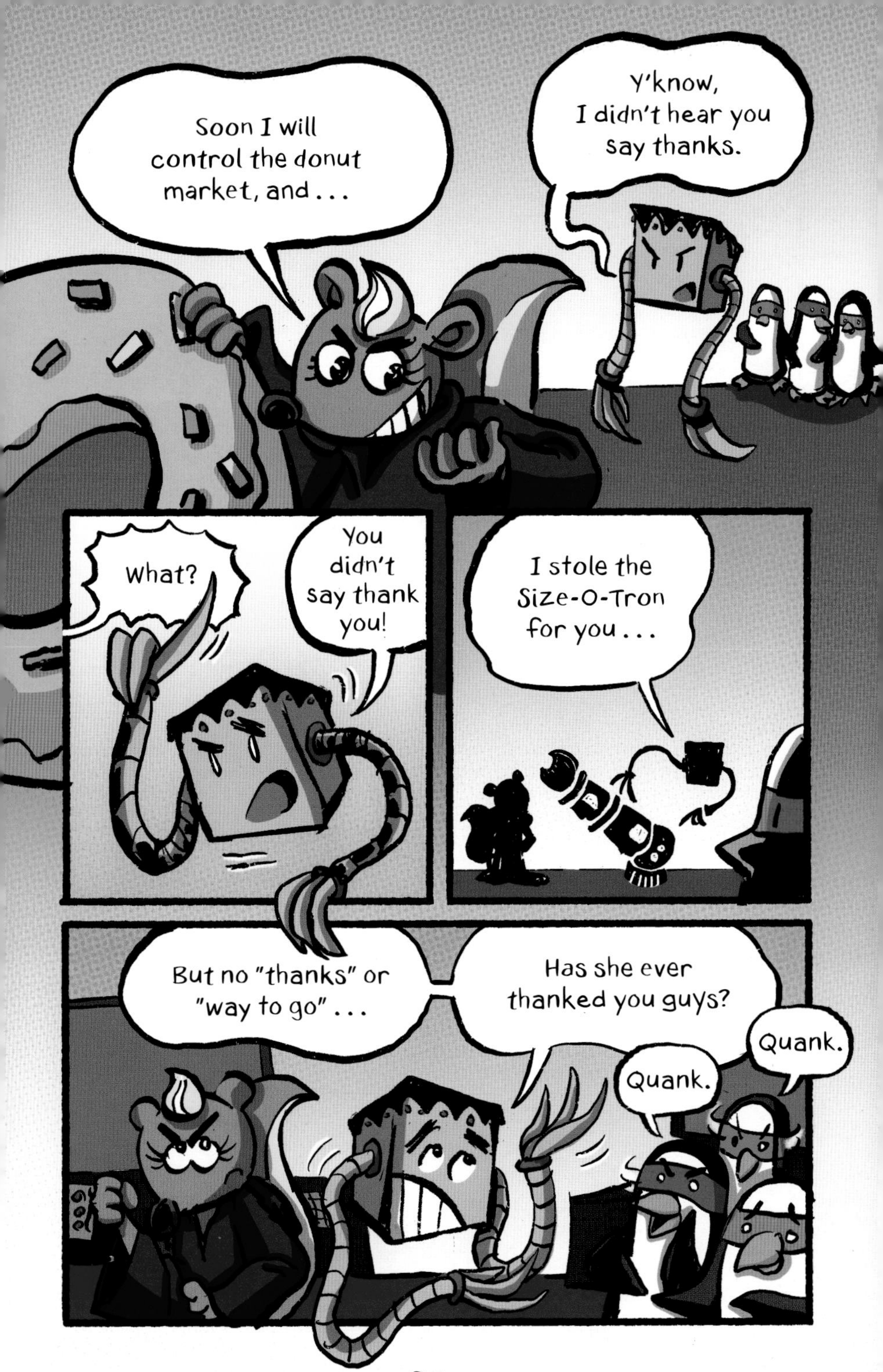
Soon I will control the donut market, and . . .
Y'know, I didn't hear you say thanks.
What?
You didn't say thank you!
I stole the Size-O-Tron for you . . .
But no "thanks" or "way to go" . . .
Has she ever thanked you guys?
Quank.
Quank.

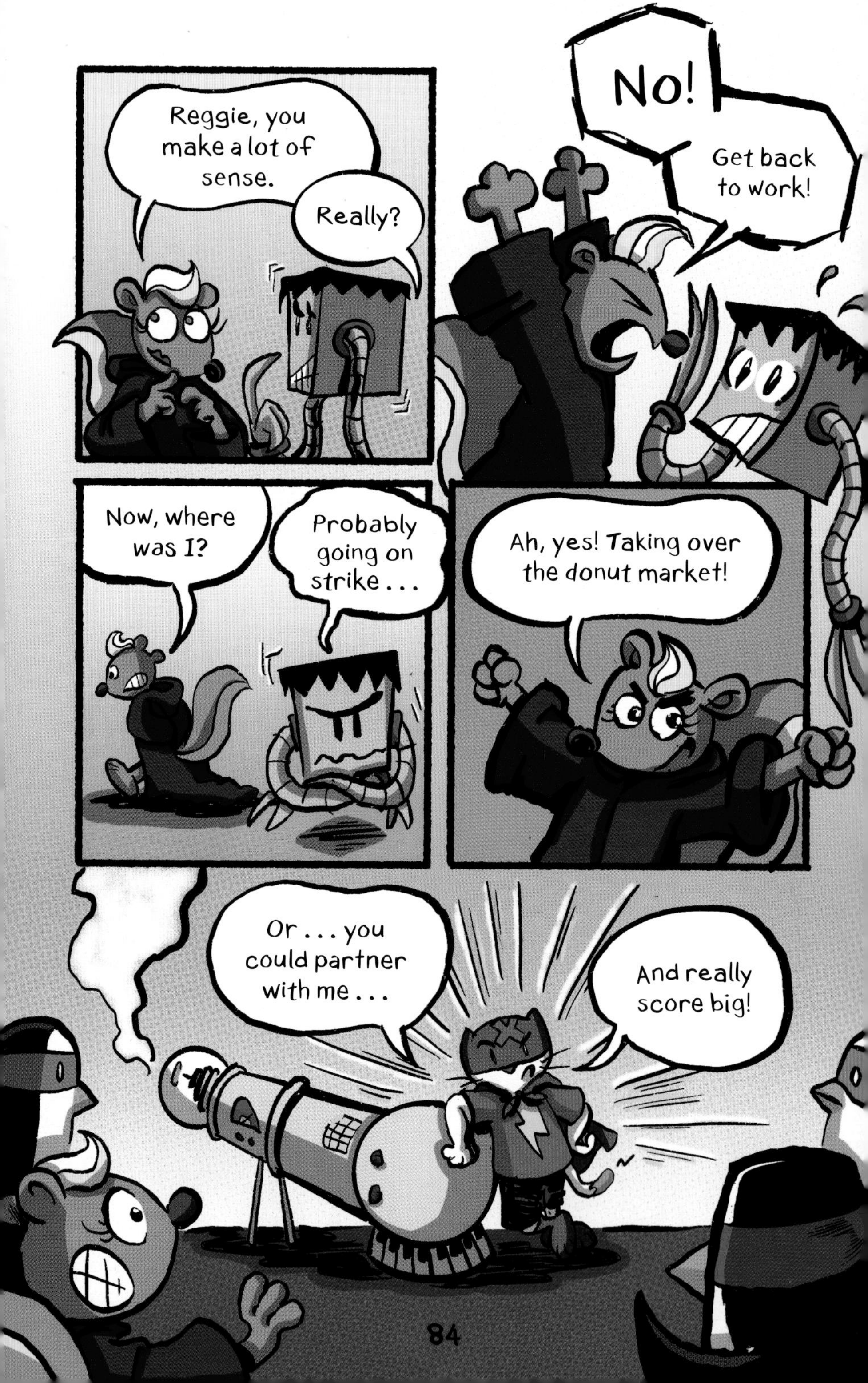
Reggie, you make a lot of sense.
Really?
No!
Get back to work!
Now, where was I?
Probably going on strike . . .
Ah, yes! Taking over the donut market!
Or . . . you could partner with me . . .
And really score big!

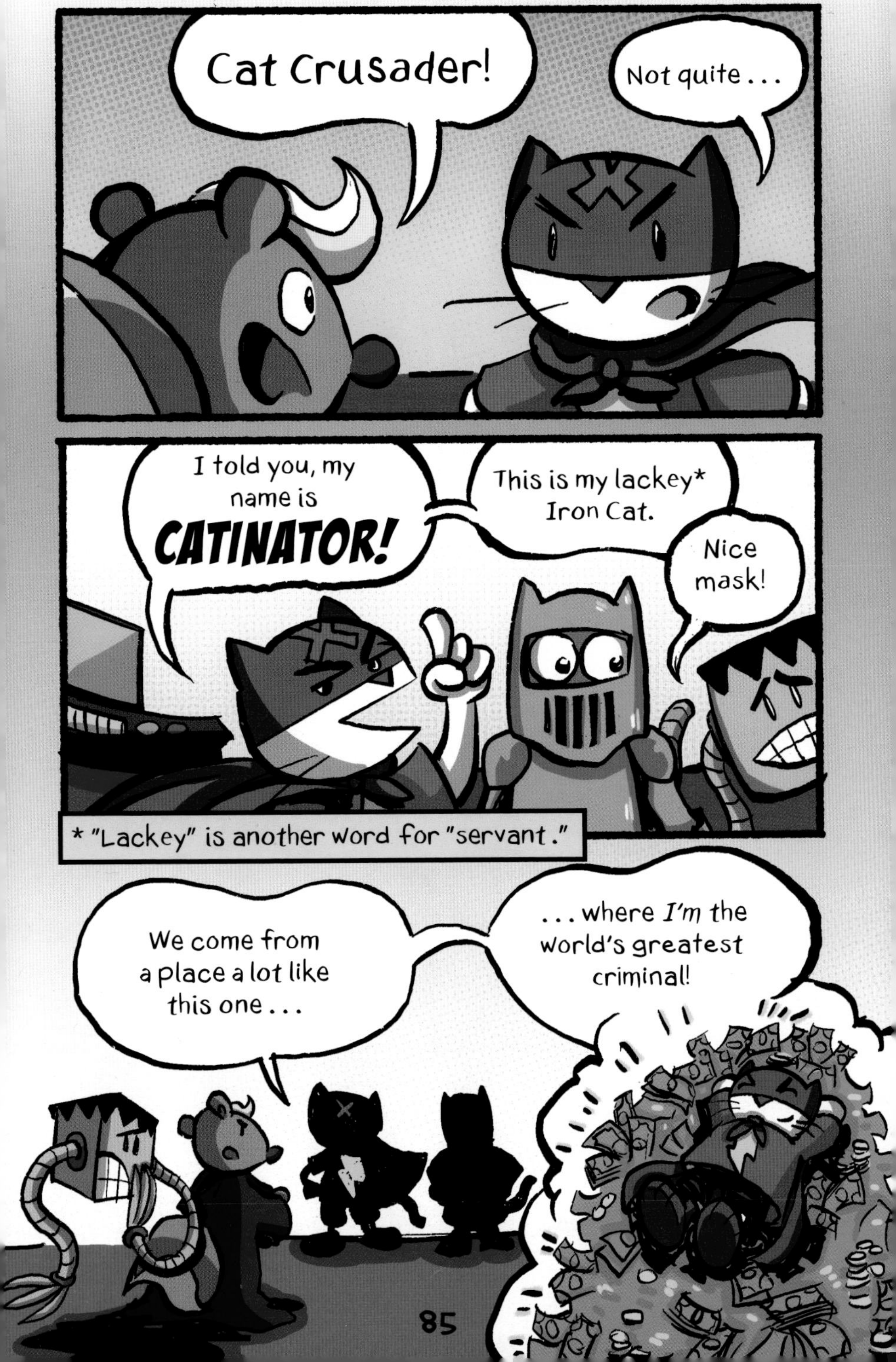
Cat Crusader!
Not quite . . .
I told you, my name is CATINATOR!
This is my lackey* Iron Cat.
Nice mask!
We come from a place a lot like this one . . .
. . . where *I'm* the world's greatest criminal!

* "Lackey" is another word for "servant."

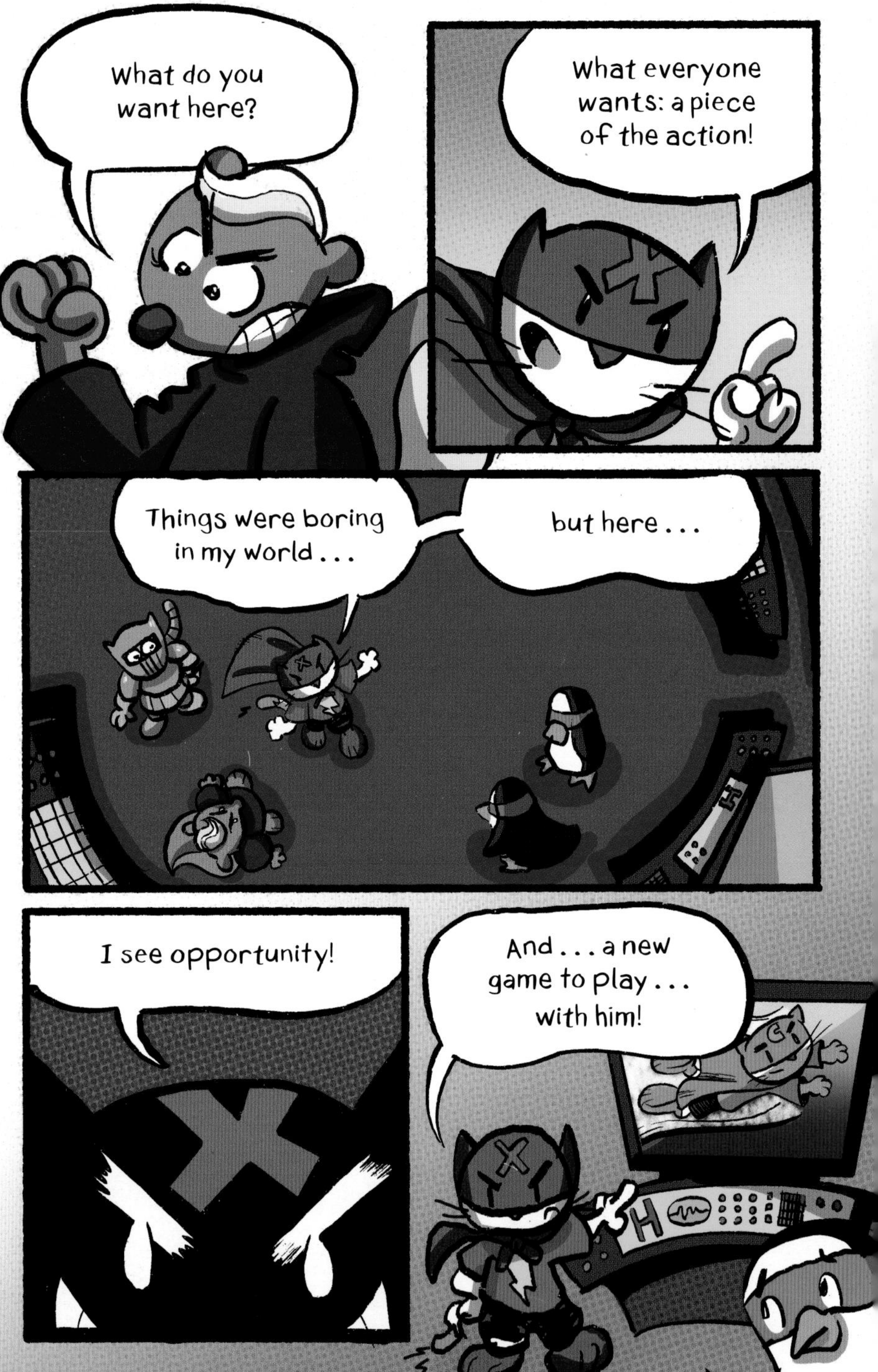
What do you want here?
What everyone wants: a piece of the action!
Things were boring in my world . . .
but here . . .
I see opportunity!
And . . . a new game to play . . . with him!

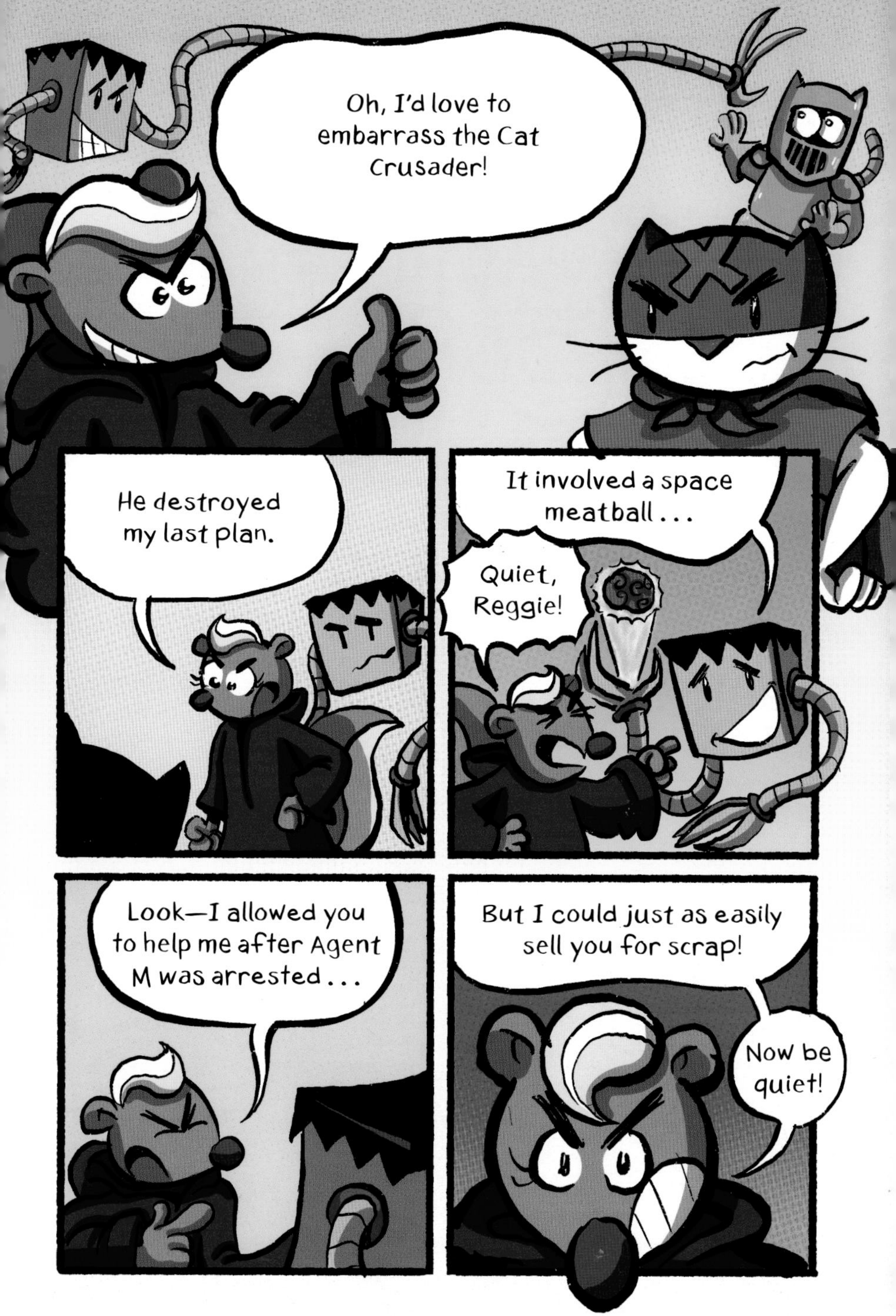
Oh, I'd love to embarrass the Cat Crusader!
He destroyed my last plan.
It involved a space meatball . . .
Quiet, Reggie!
Look—I allowed you to help me after Agent M was arrested . . .
But I could just as easily sell you for scrap!
Now be quiet!

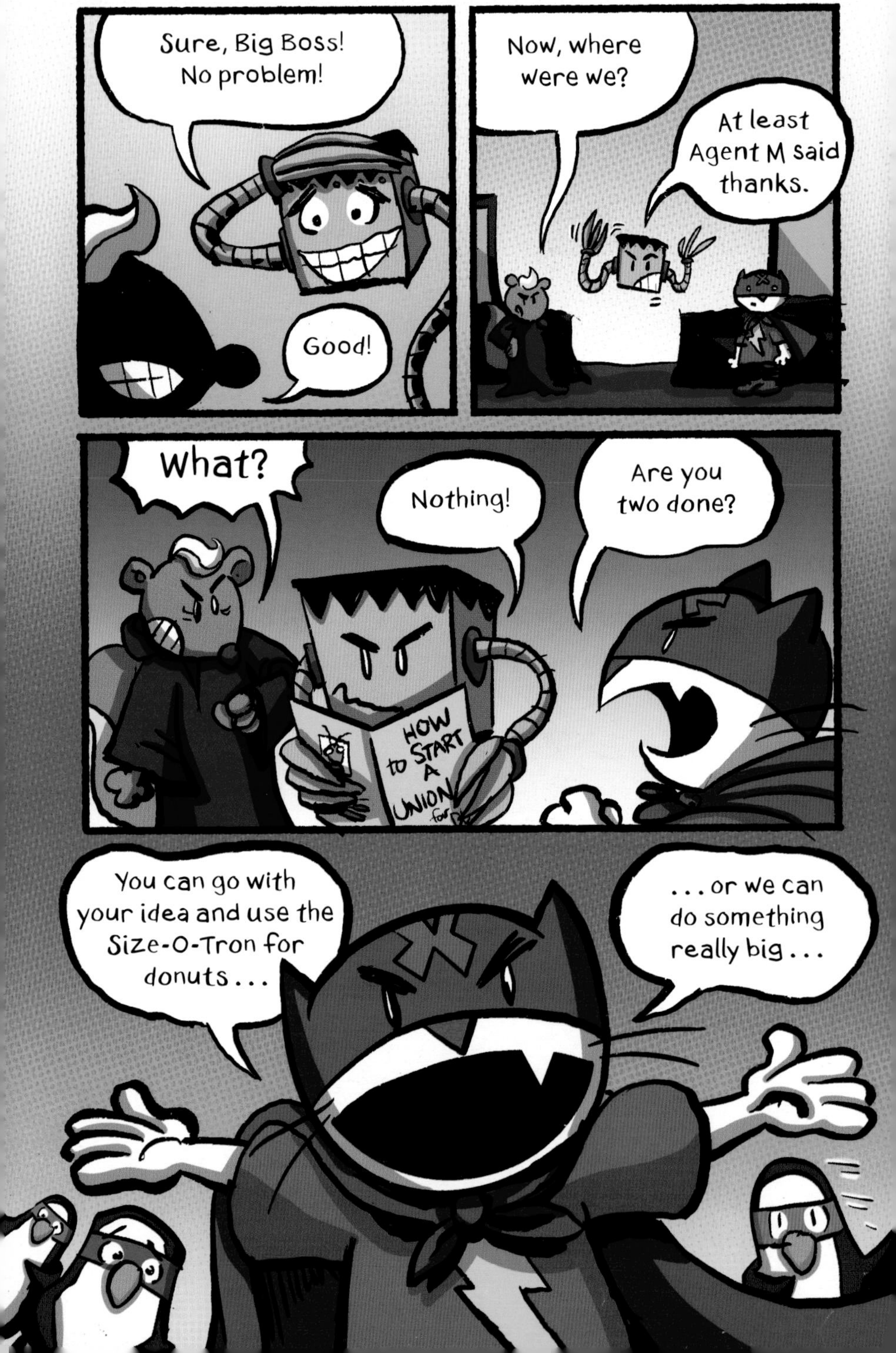
Sure, Big Boss! No problem!
Good!
Now, where were we?
At least Agent M said thanks.
What?
Nothing!
HOW to START A UNION for
Are you two done?
You can go with your idea and use the Size-O-Tron for donuts . . .
. . . or we can do something really big . . .

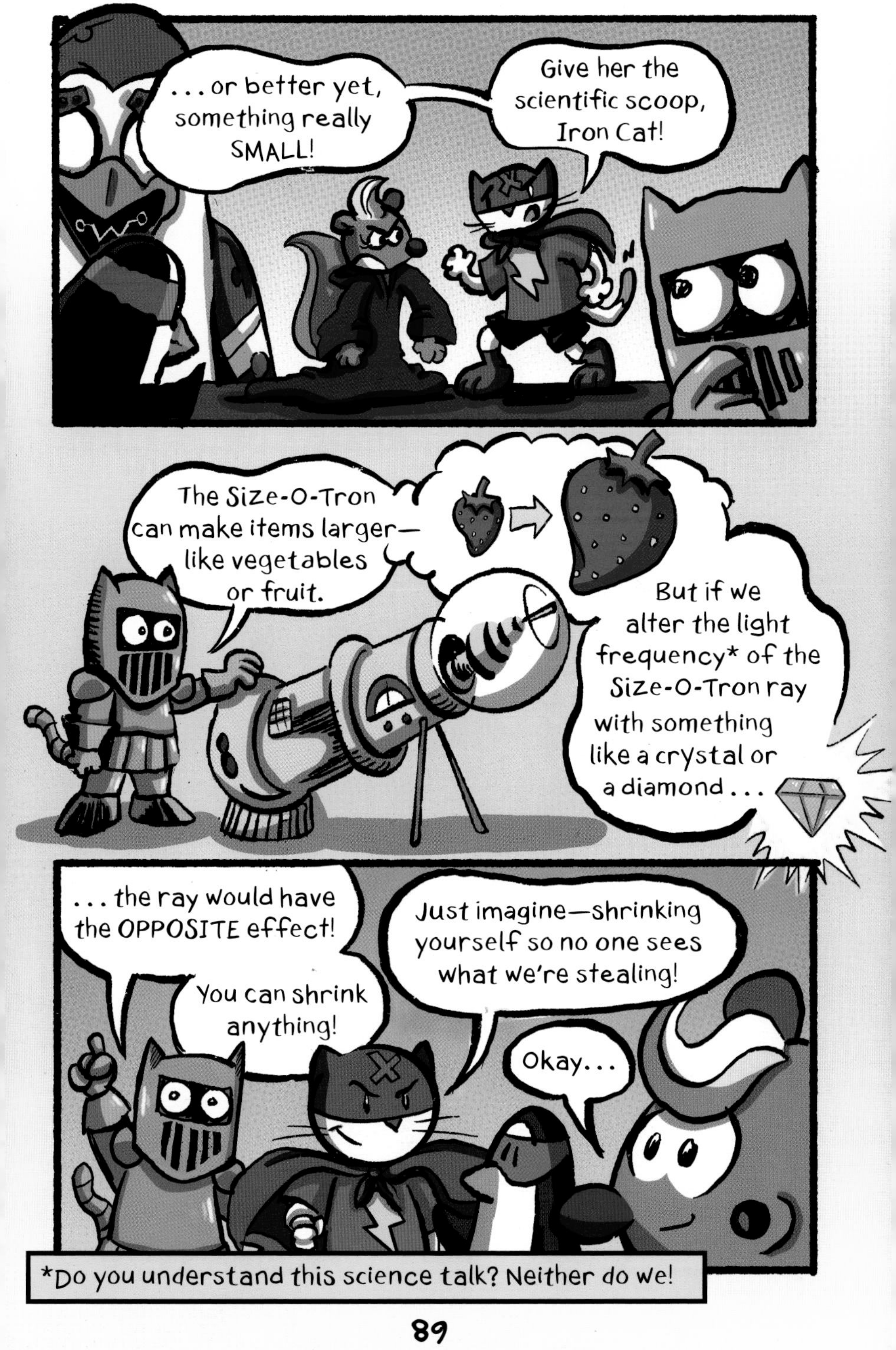
. . . or better yet, something really SMALL!
Give her the scientific scoop, Iron Cat!
The Size-O-Tron can make items larger—like vegetables or fruit.
But if we alter the light frequency* of the Size-O-Tron ray with something like a crystal or a diamond . . .
. . . the ray would have the OPPOSITE effect!
You can shrink anything!
Just imagine—shrinking yourself so no one sees what we're stealing!
Okay . . .

*Do you understand this science talk? Neither do we!

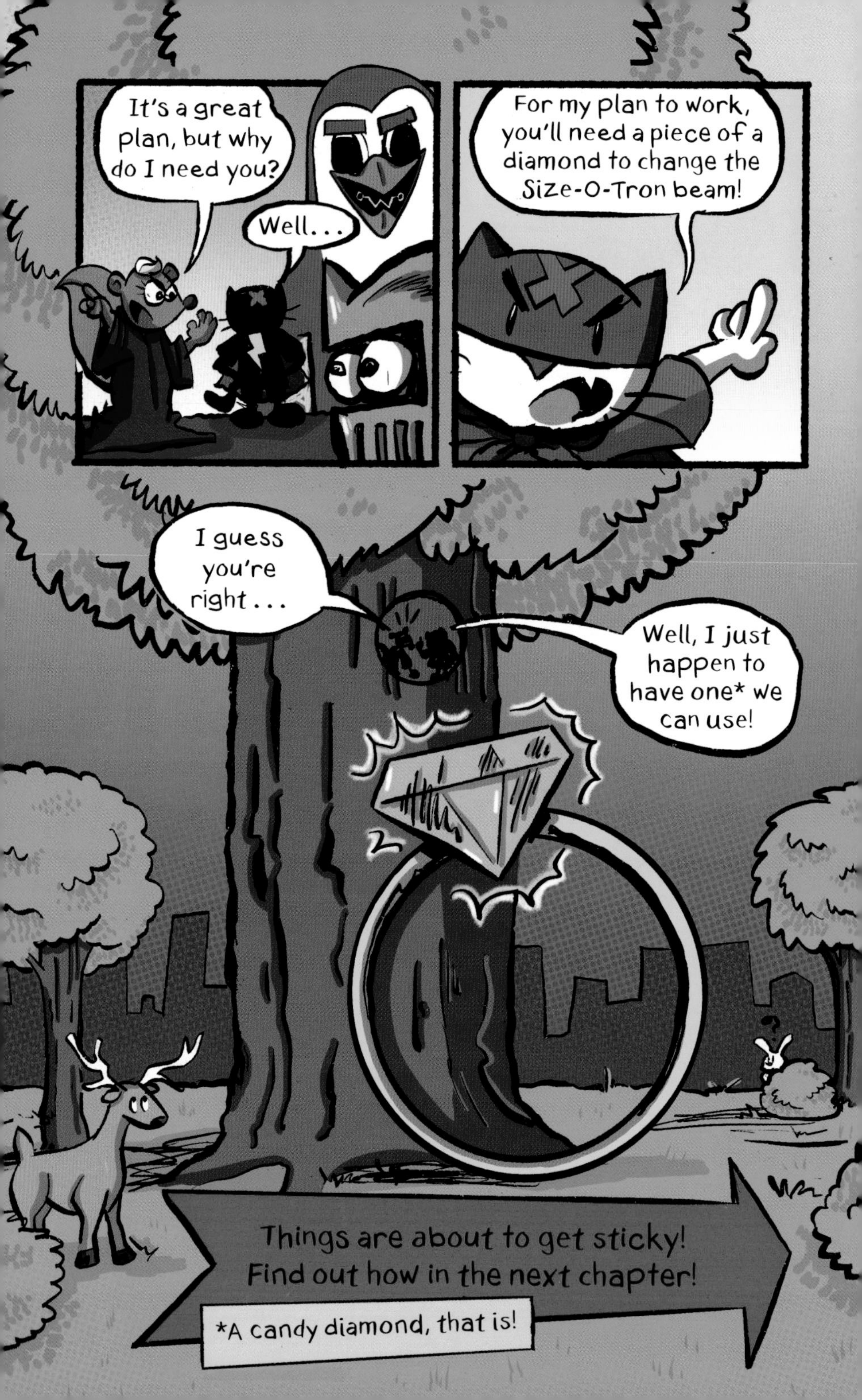

It's a great plan, but why do I need you?
Well...
For my plan to work, you'll need a piece of a diamond to change the Size-O-Tron beam!
I guess you're right...
Well, I just happen to have one* we can use!
Things are about to get sticky! Find out how in the next chapter!
*A candy diamond, that is!

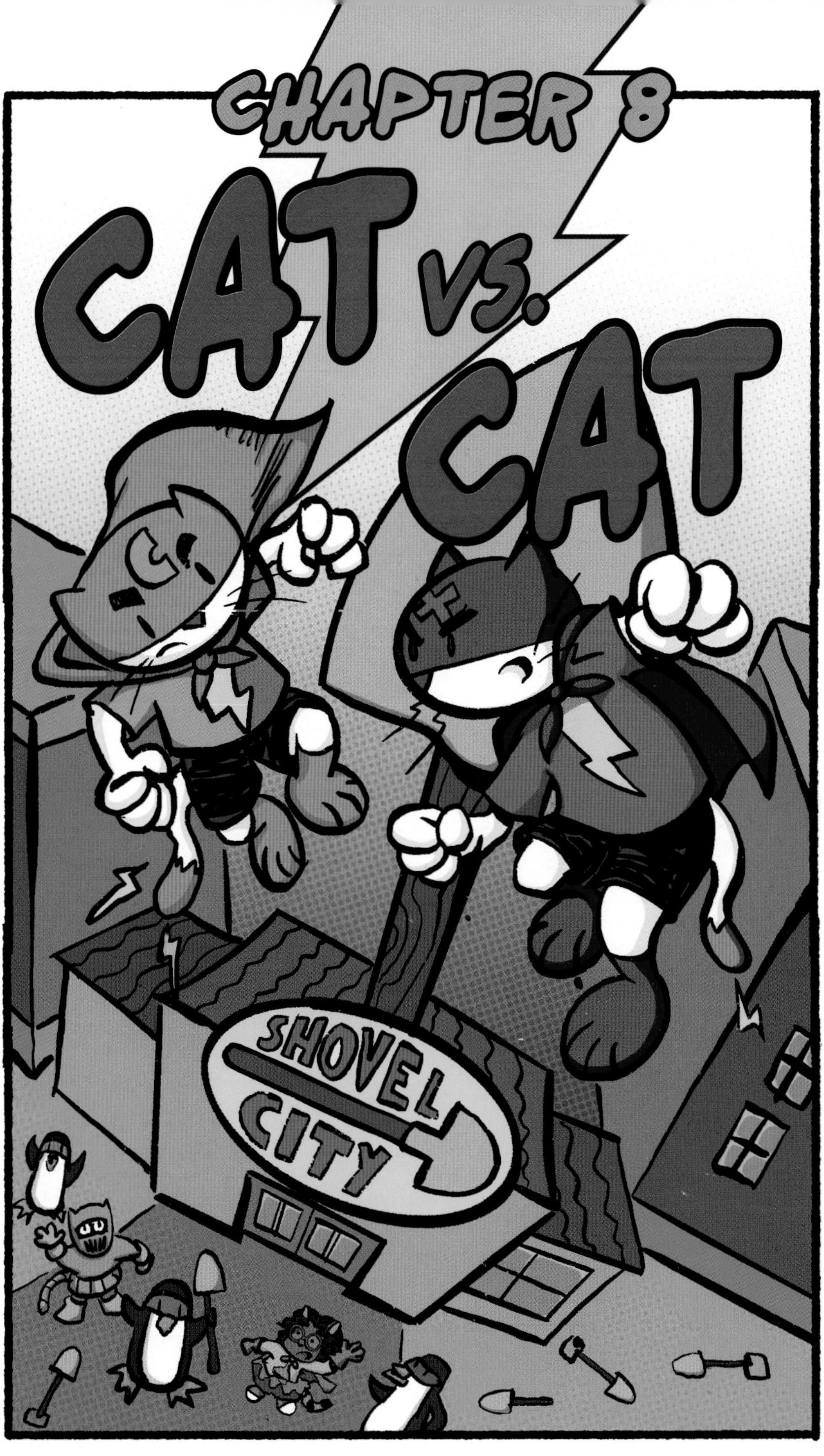
CHAPTER 8
CAT VS. CAT
SHOVEL CITY

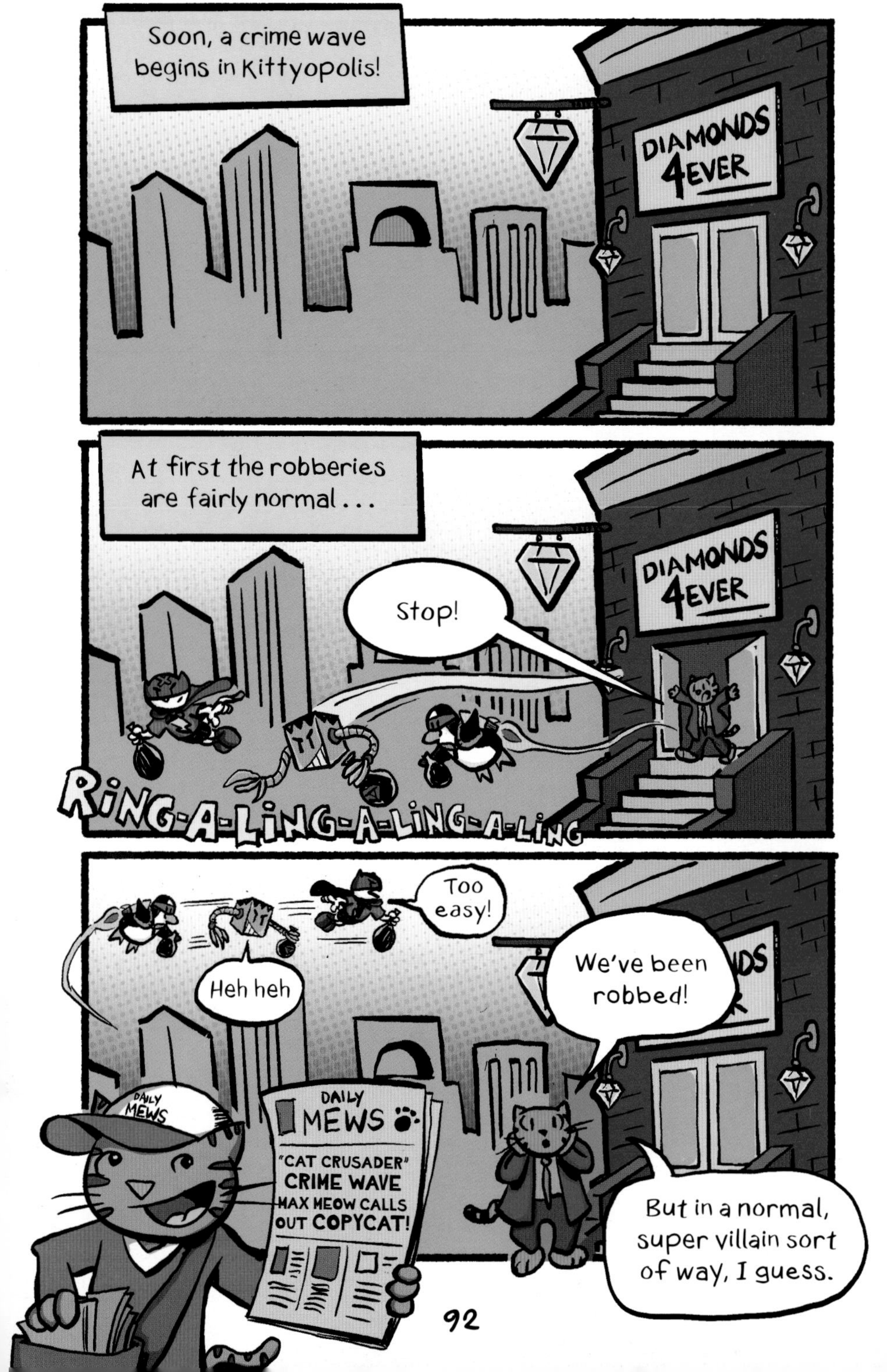

Soon, a crime wave begins in Kittyopolis!
DIAMONDS 4EVER
At first the robberies are fairly normal . . .
DIAMONDS 4EVER
Stop!
RING-A-LING-A-LING-A-LING
Too easy!
Heh heh
We've been robbed!
DAILY MEWS
DAILY MEWS
"CAT CRUSADER" CRIME WAVE
MAX MEOW CALLS OUT COPYCAT!
But in a normal, super villain sort of way, I guess.

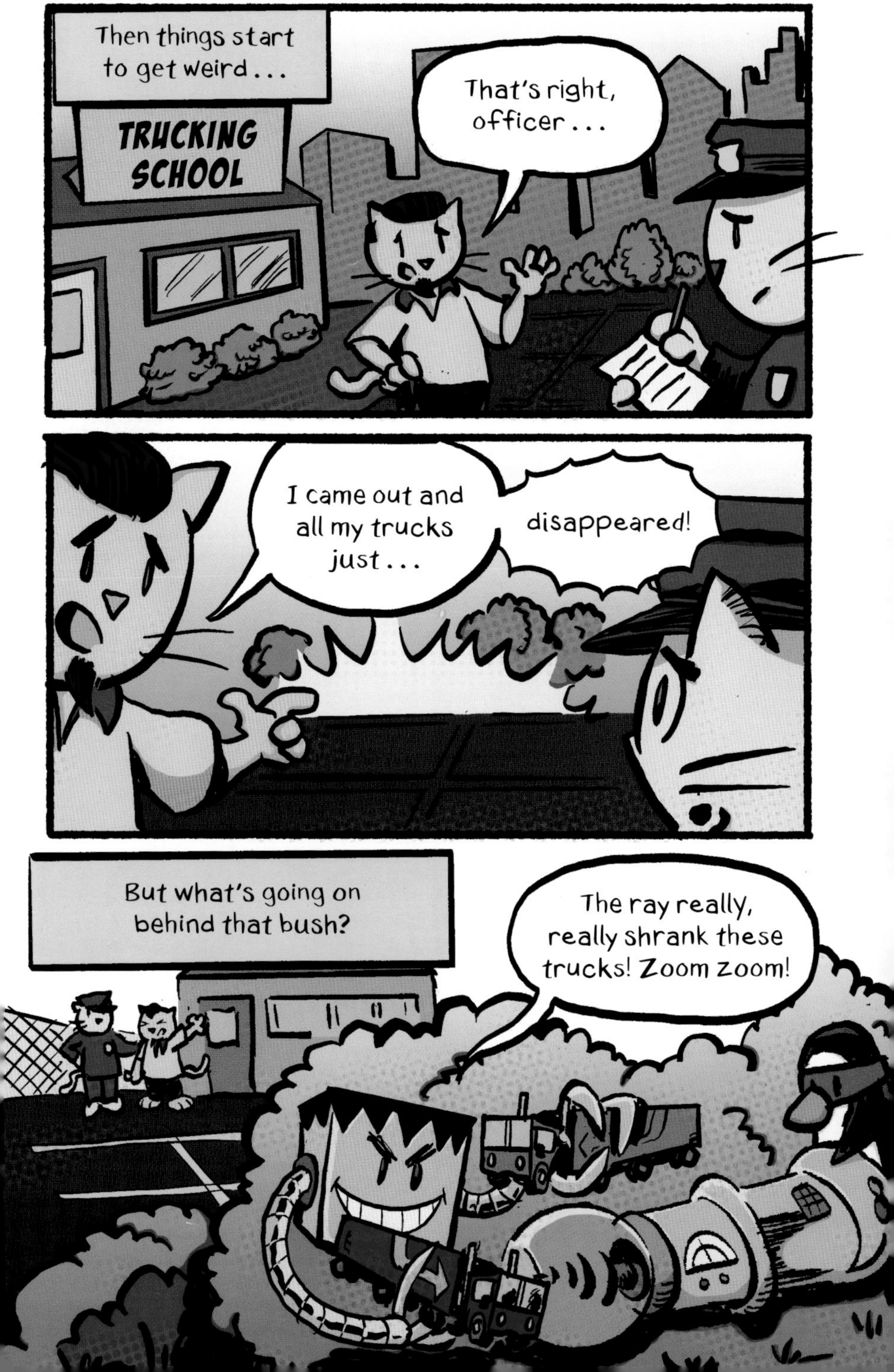
Then things start to get weird . . .
TRUCKING SCHOOL
That's right, officer . . .
I came out and all my trucks just . . .
disappeared!
But what's going on behind that bush?
The ray really, really shrank these trucks! Zoom zoom!

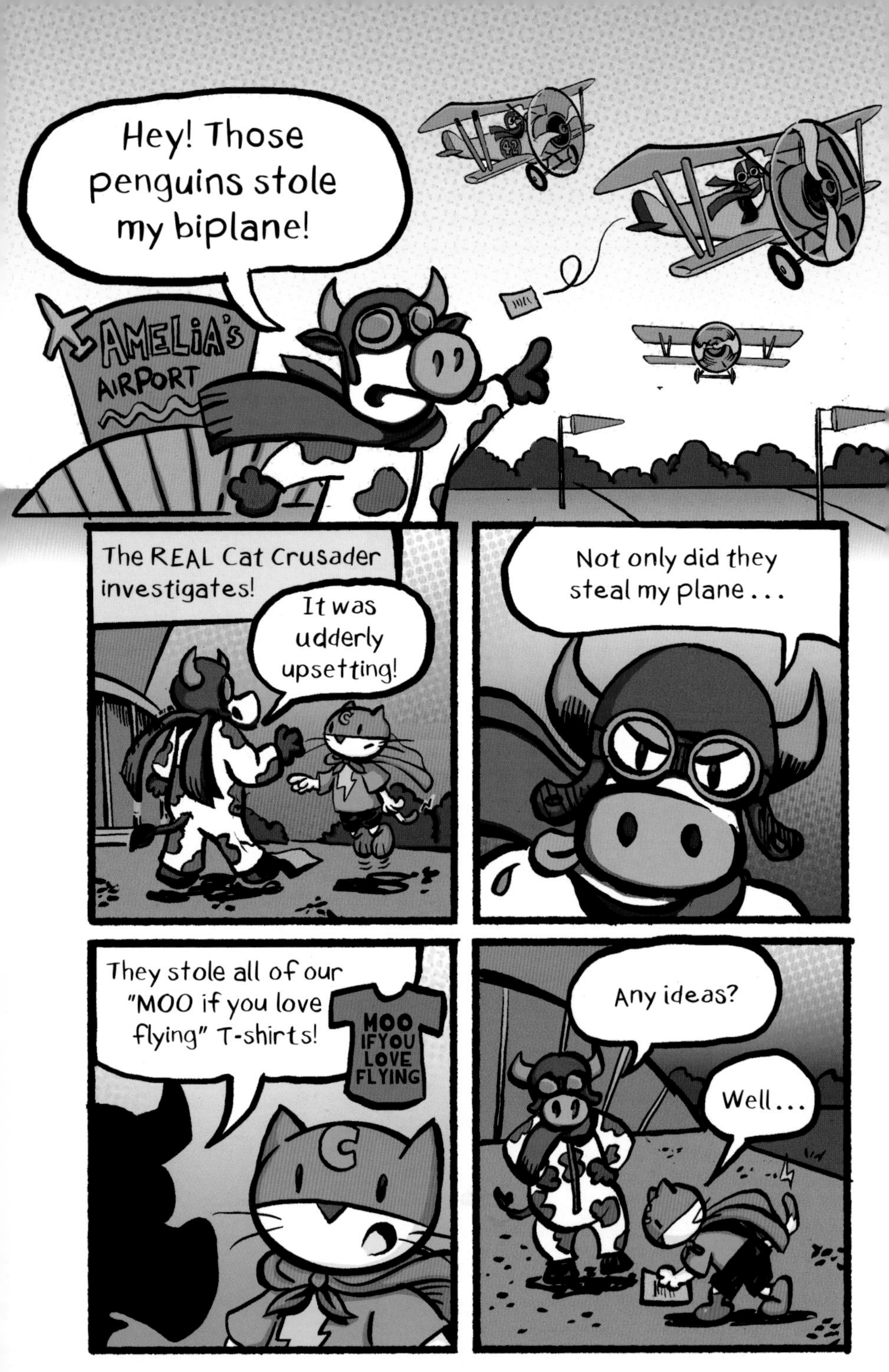
Hey! Those penguins stole my biplane!
AMELIA'S AIRPORT
The REAL Cat Crusader investigates!
It was udderly upsetting!
Not only did they steal my plane . . .
They stole all of our "MOO if you love flying" T-shirts!
MOO IF YOU LOVE FLYING
Any ideas?
Well . . .

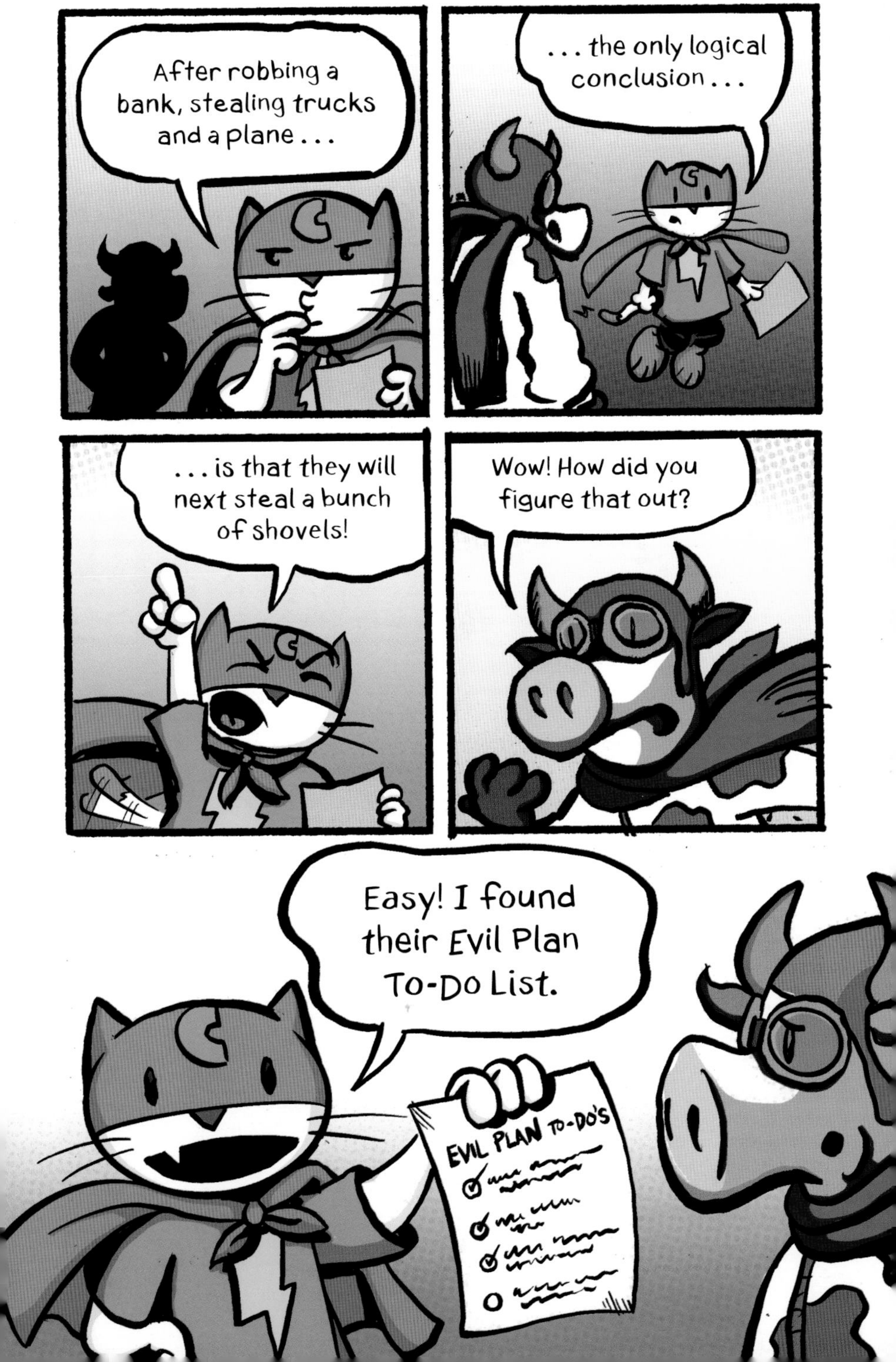
After robbing a bank, stealing trucks and a plane . . .
. . . the only logical conclusion . . .
. . . is that they will next steal a bunch of shovels!
Wow! How did you figure that out?
Easy! I found their Evil Plan To-Do List.
EVIL PLAN TO-DO'S

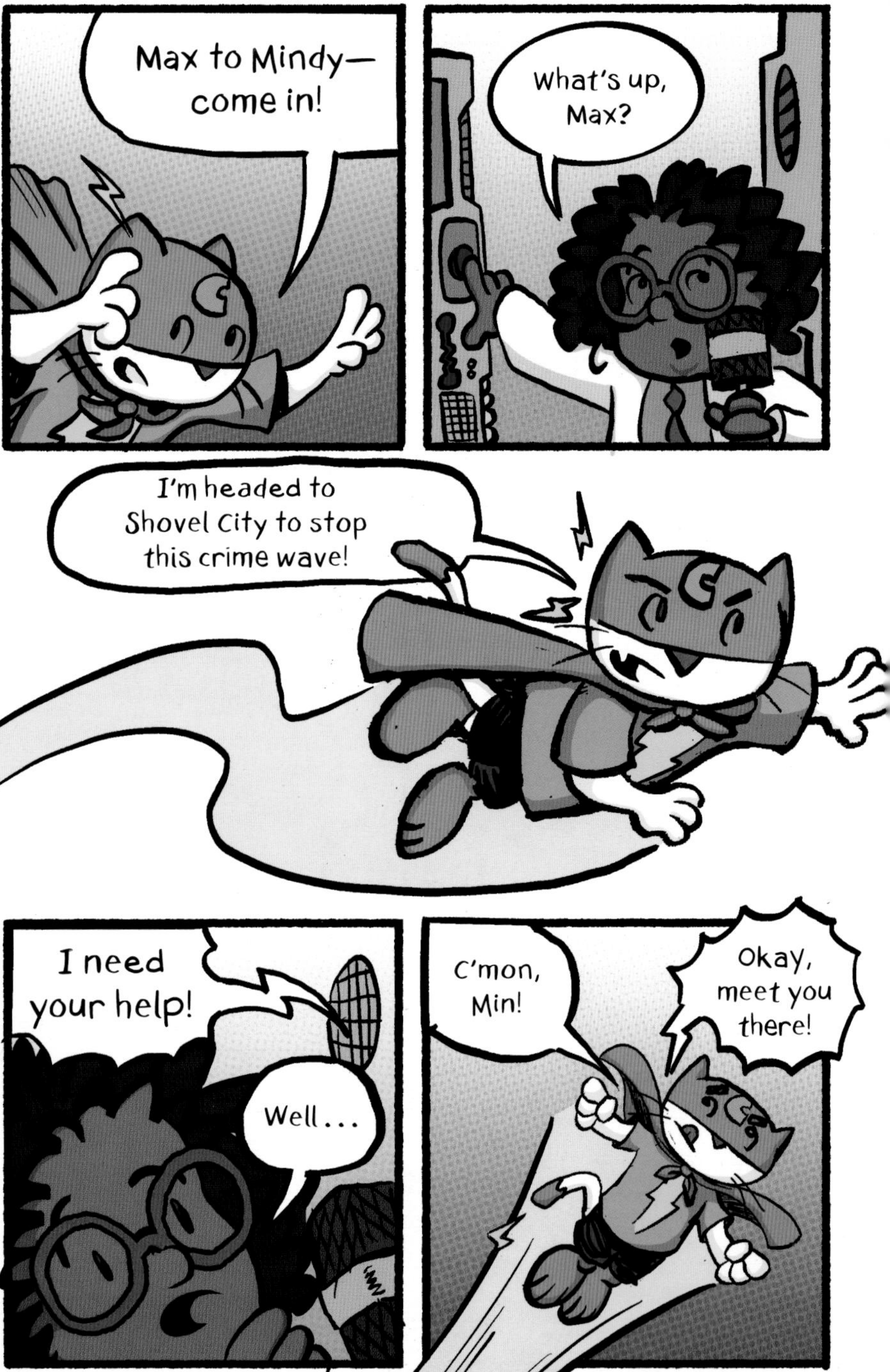
Max to Mindy—
come in!
What's up,
Max?
I'm headed to
Shovel City to stop
this crime wave!
I need
your help!
Well...
C'mon,
Min!
Okay,
meet you
there!

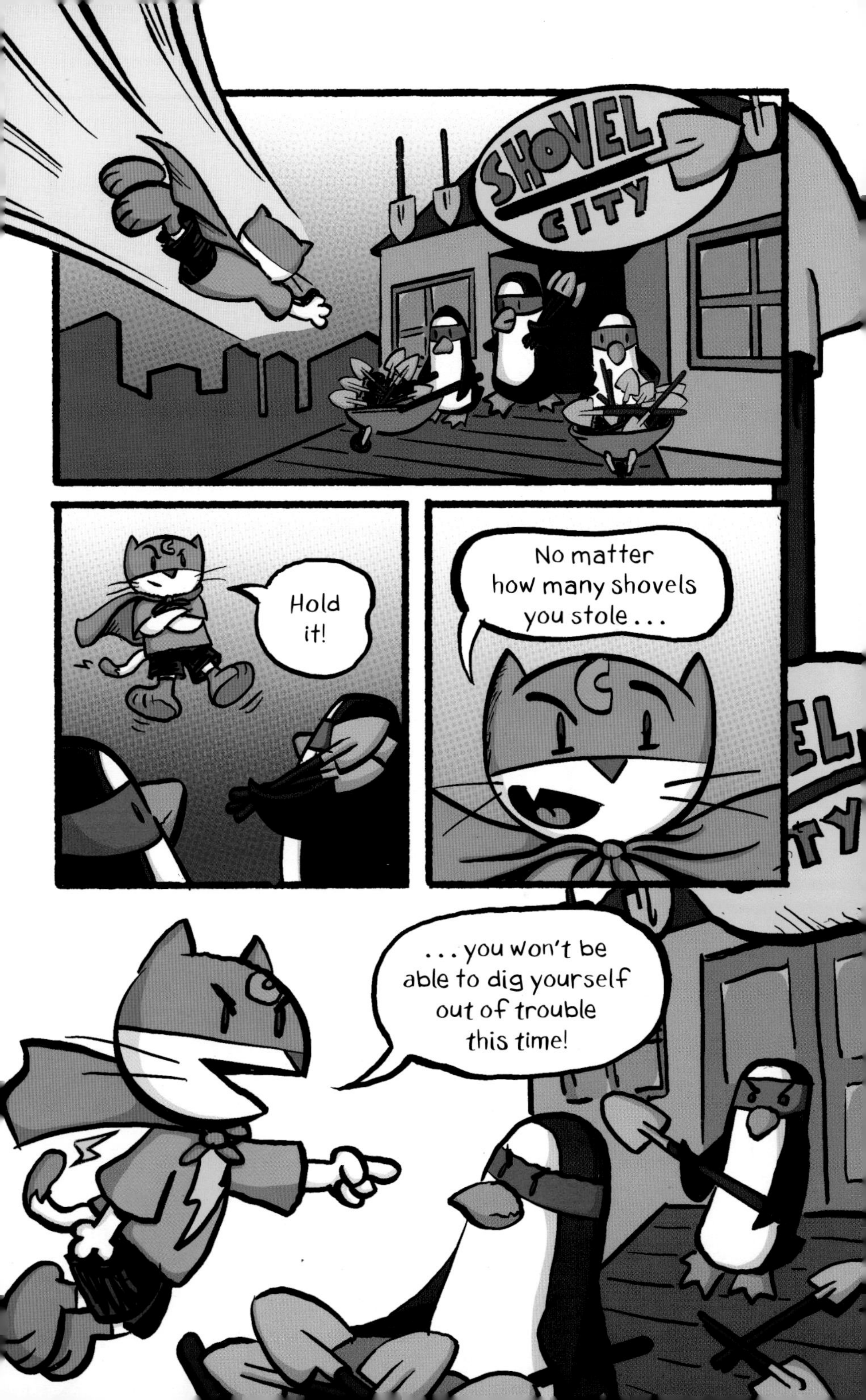
SHOVEL CITY
Hold it!
No matter how many shovels you stole . . .
. . . you won't be able to dig yourself out of trouble this time!

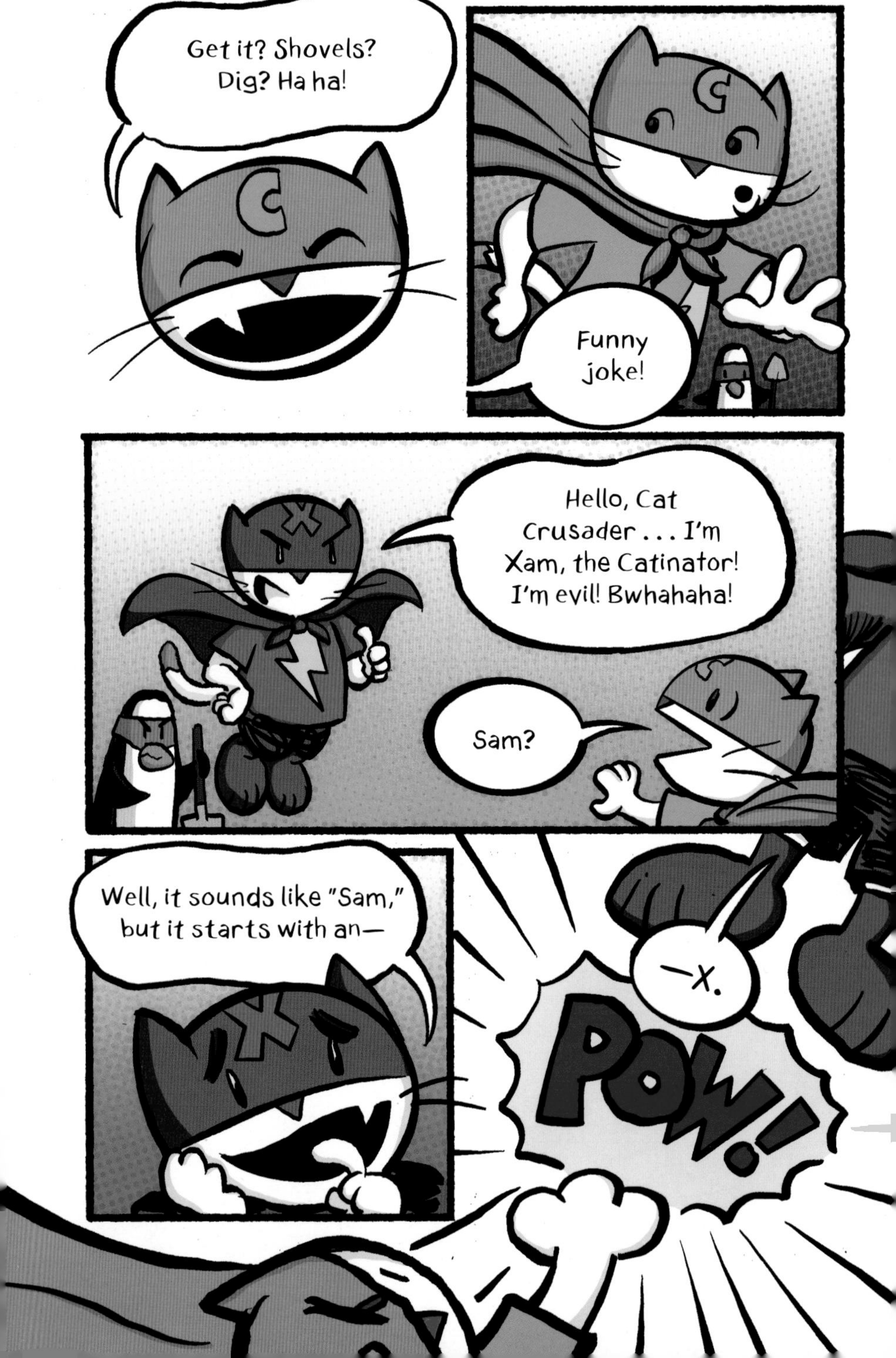
Get it? Shovels? Dig? Ha ha!
Funny joke!
Hello, Cat Crusader . . . I'm Xam, the Catinator! I'm evil! Bwhahaha!
Sam?
Well, it sounds like "Sam," but it starts with an—
—X.
POW!

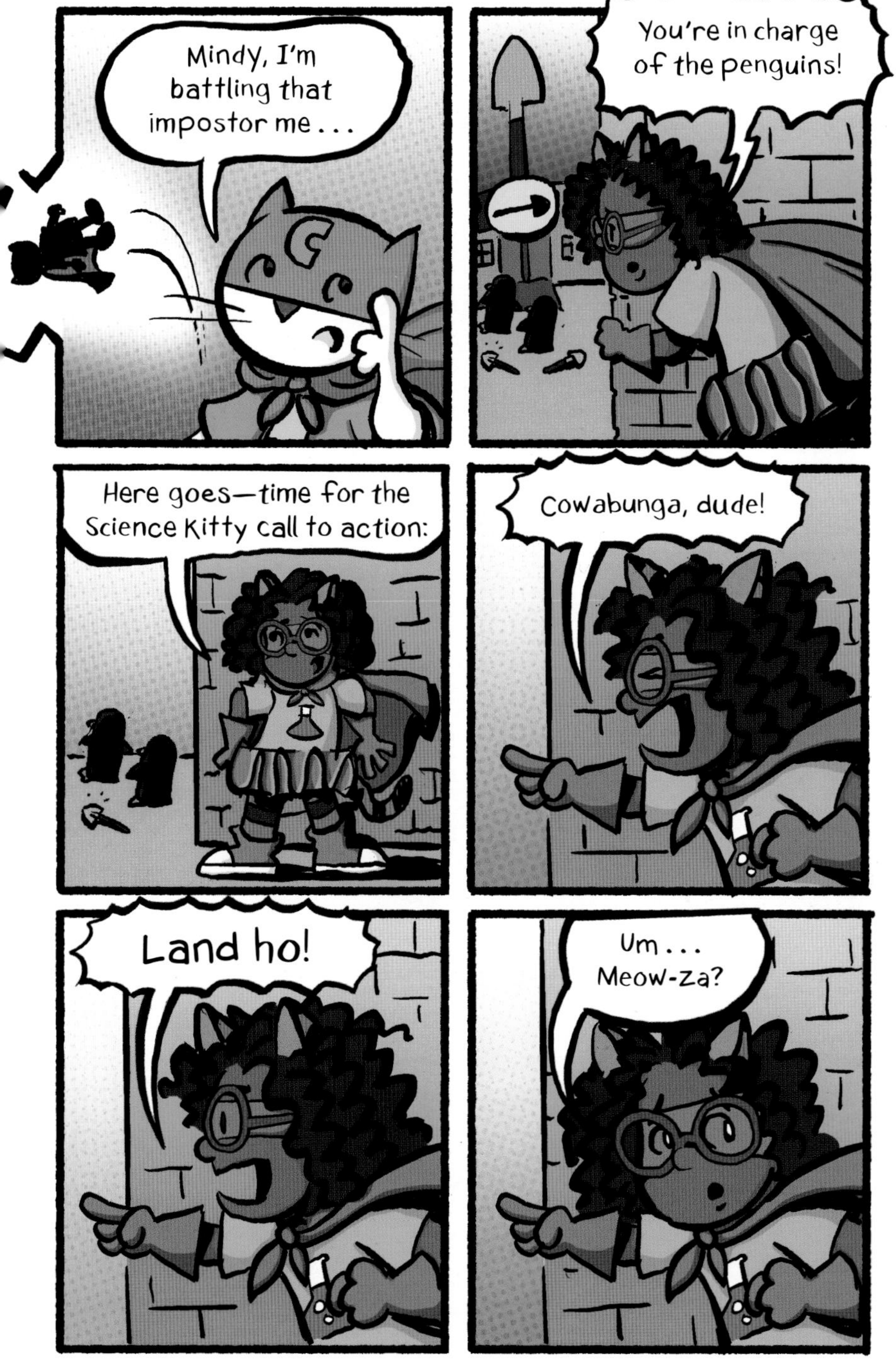
Mindy, I'm battling that impostor me . . .
You're in charge of the penguins!
Here goes—time for the Science Kitty call to action:
Cowabunga, dude!
Land ho!
Um . . . Meow-za?

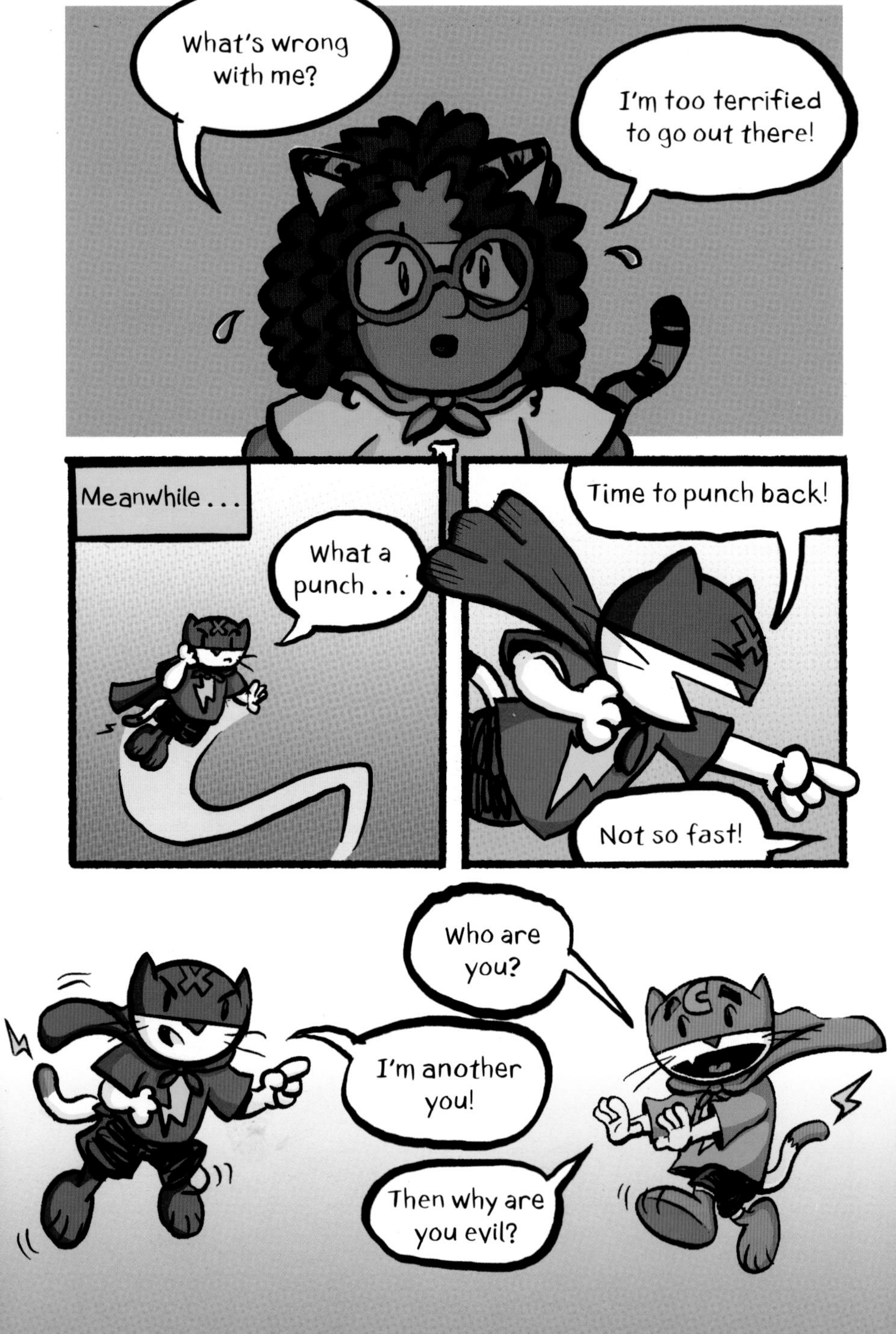
What's wrong with me?
I'm too terrified to go out there!
Meanwhile . . .
What a punch . . .
Time to punch back!
Not so fast!
Who are you?
I'm another you!
Then why are you evil?

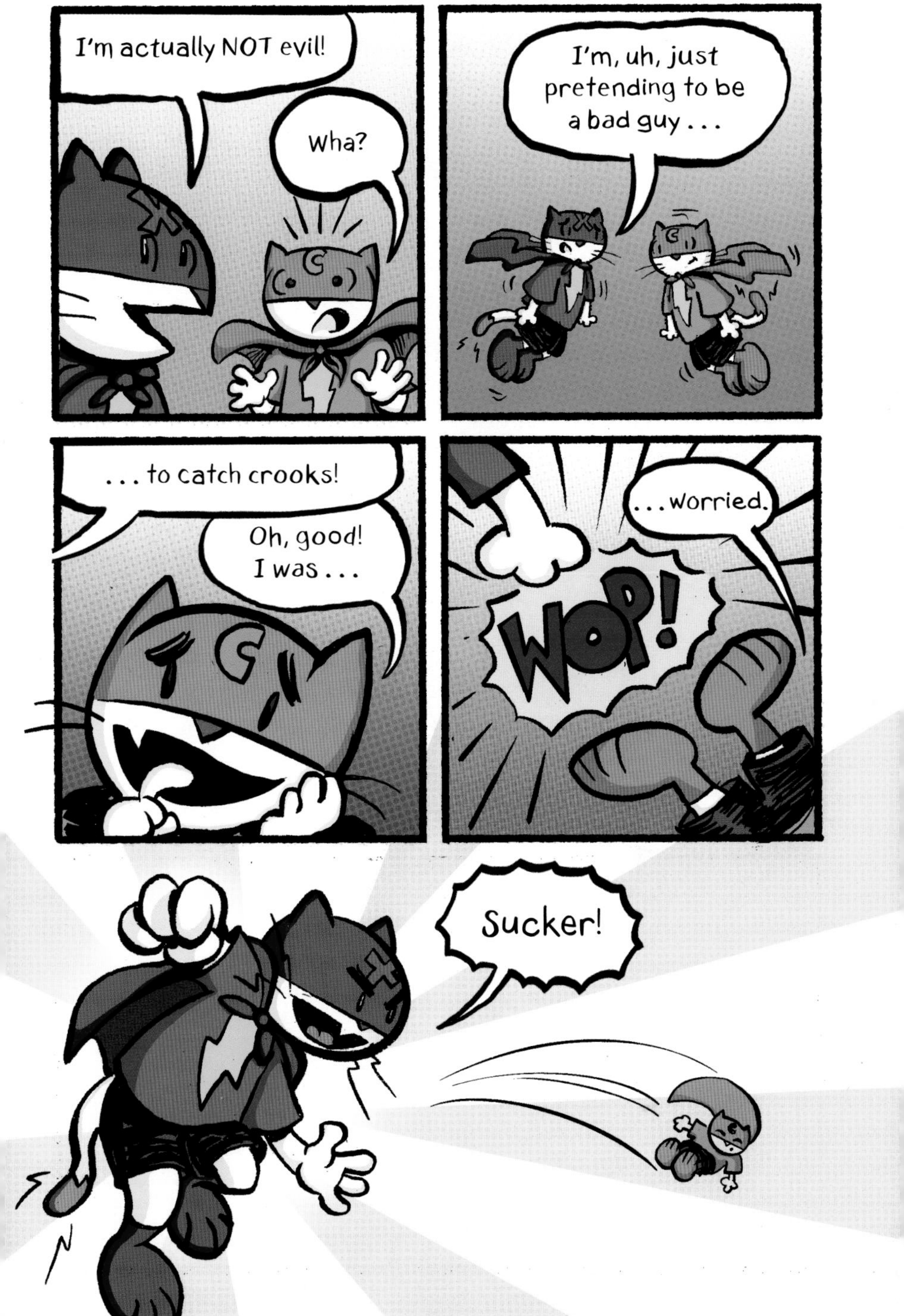
I'm actually NOT evil!
Wha?
I'm, uh, just pretending to be a bad guy . . .
. . . to catch crooks!
Oh, good! I was . . .
. . . worried.
WOP!
Sucker!

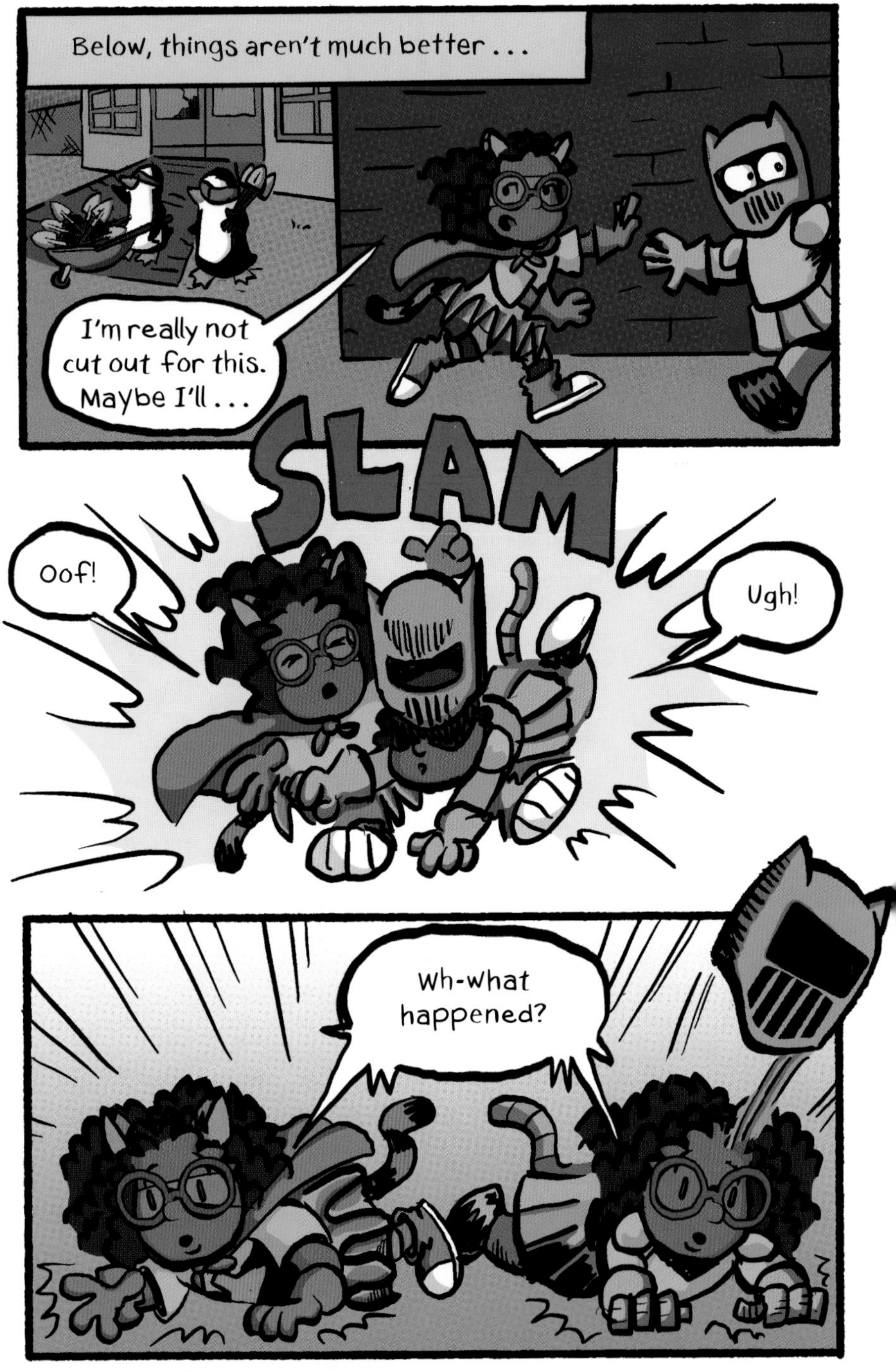
Below, things aren't much better . . .
I'm really not cut out for this. Maybe I'll . . .
SLAM
Oof!
Ugh!
Wh-what happened?

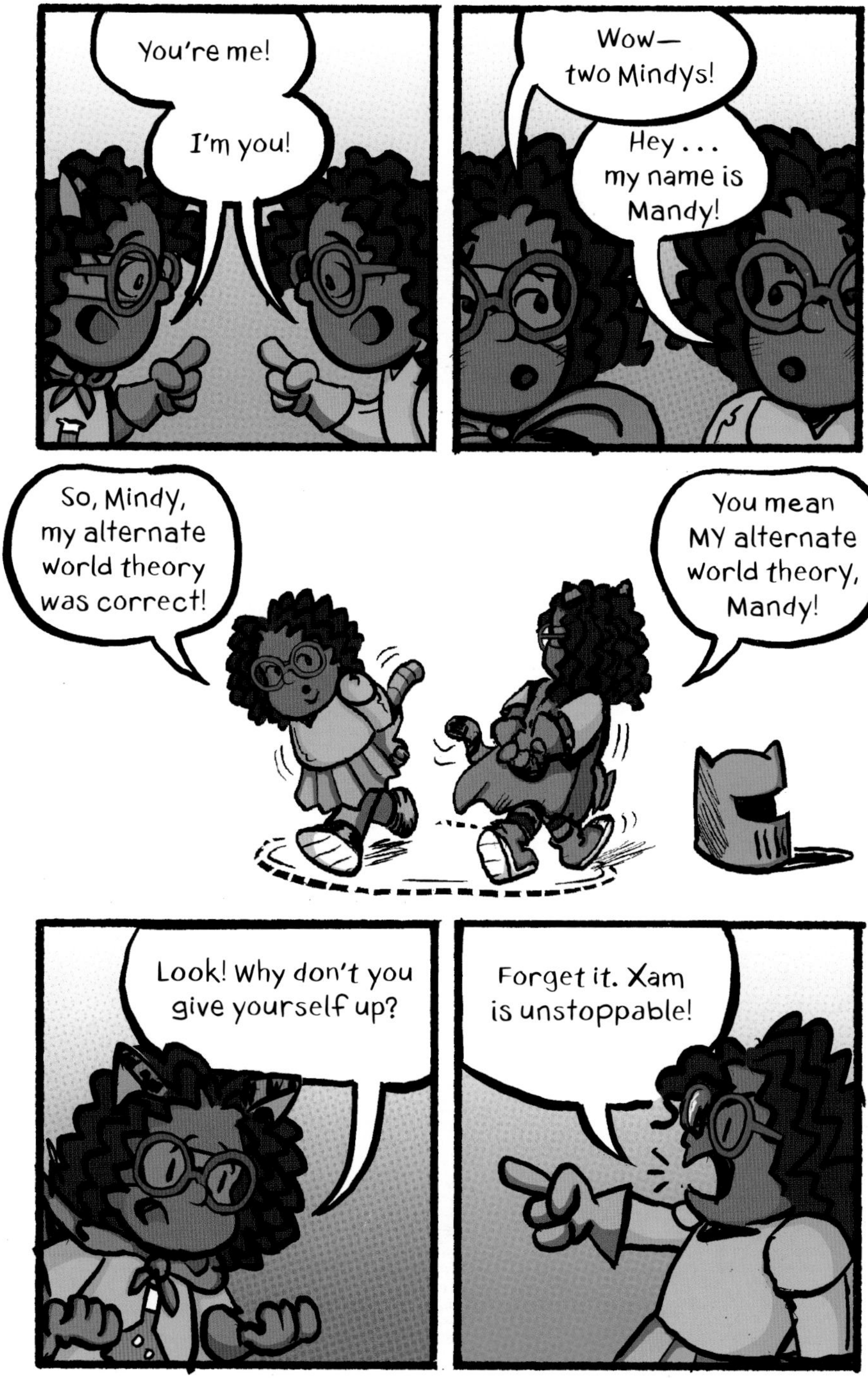
You're me!
I'm you!
Wow—two Mindys!
Hey . . . my name is Mandy!
So, Mindy, my alternate world theory was correct!
You mean MY alternate world theory, Mandy!
Look! Why don't you give yourself up?
Forget it. Xam is unstoppable!

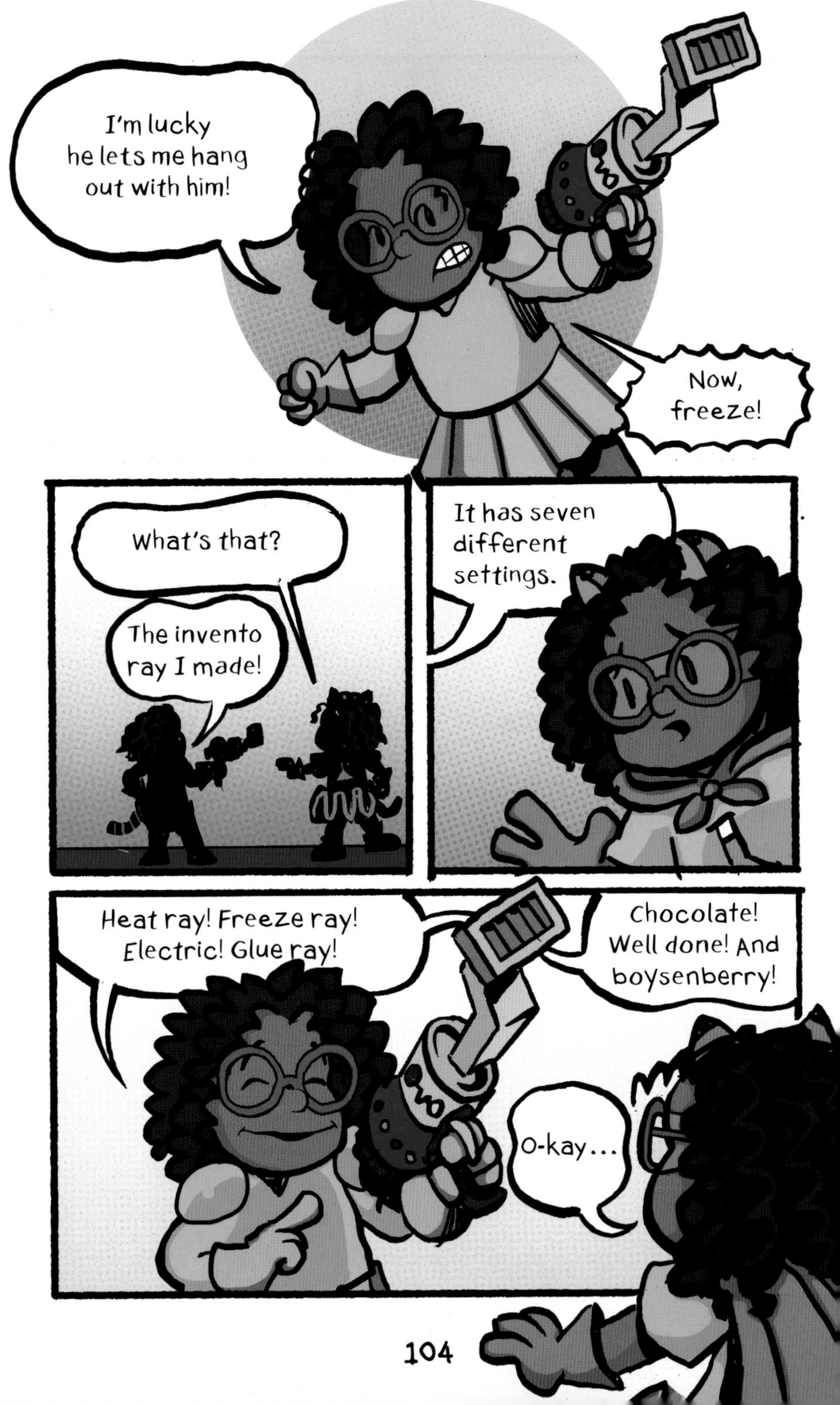

I'm lucky he lets me hang out with him!
Now, freeze!
What's that?
The invento ray I made!
It has seven different settings.
Heat ray! Freeze ray! Electric! Glue ray!
Chocolate! Well done! And boysenberry!
O-kay...

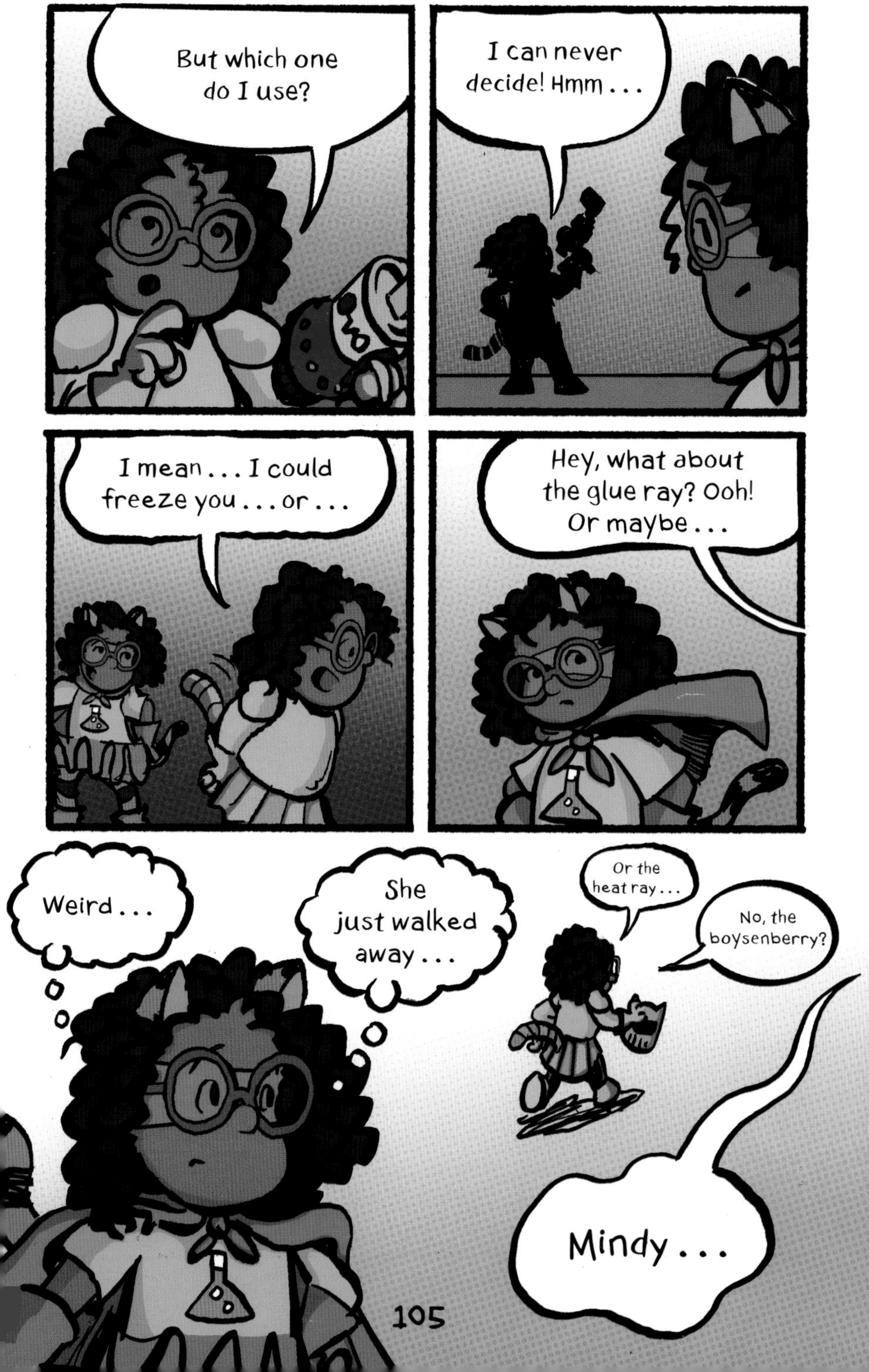
But which one do I use?
I can never decide! Hmm . . .
I mean . . . I could freeze you . . . or . . .
Hey, what about the glue ray? Ooh! Or maybe . . .
Weird . . .
She just walked away . . .
Or the heat ray . . .
No, the boysenberry?
Mindy . . .

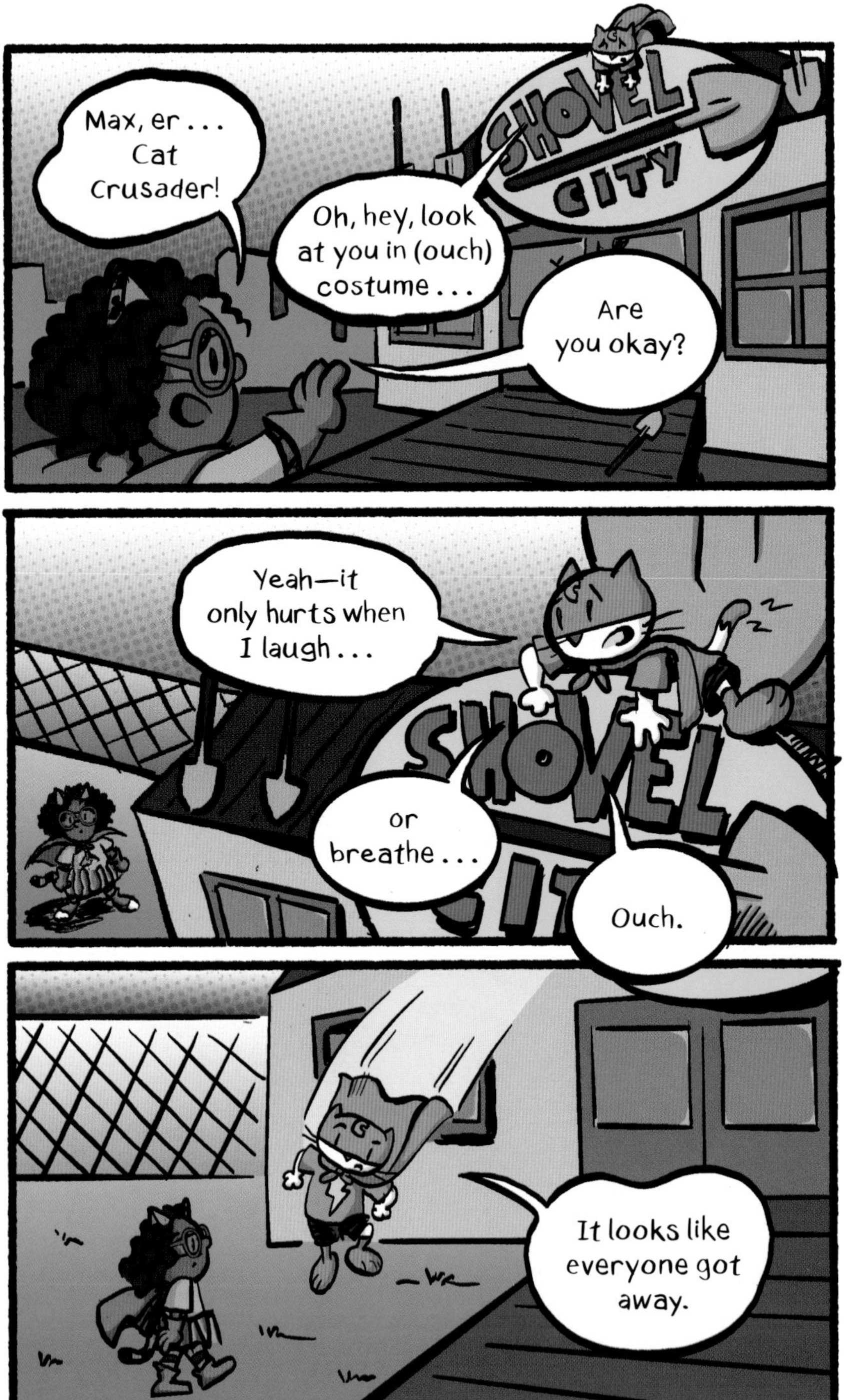

Max, er . . . Cat Crusader!
SHOVEL CITY
Oh, hey, look at you in (ouch) costume . . .
Are you okay?
Yeah—it only hurts when I laugh . . .
or breathe . . .
Ouch.
It looks like everyone got away.

Max, this is all my fault!

I knew I wasn't ready!

Mindy, remember what my uncle Albert said . . .

It's too late, Max . . .

I QUIT!

MINDY **QUITS?**

CAN Max catch the crooks without her?

IS this the end of the Cat Crusader?

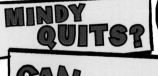

Find out in the next chapter!

Wait, wait! Whoa, that's dark!

Yeah, I'm just frustrated!

We'll work it out!

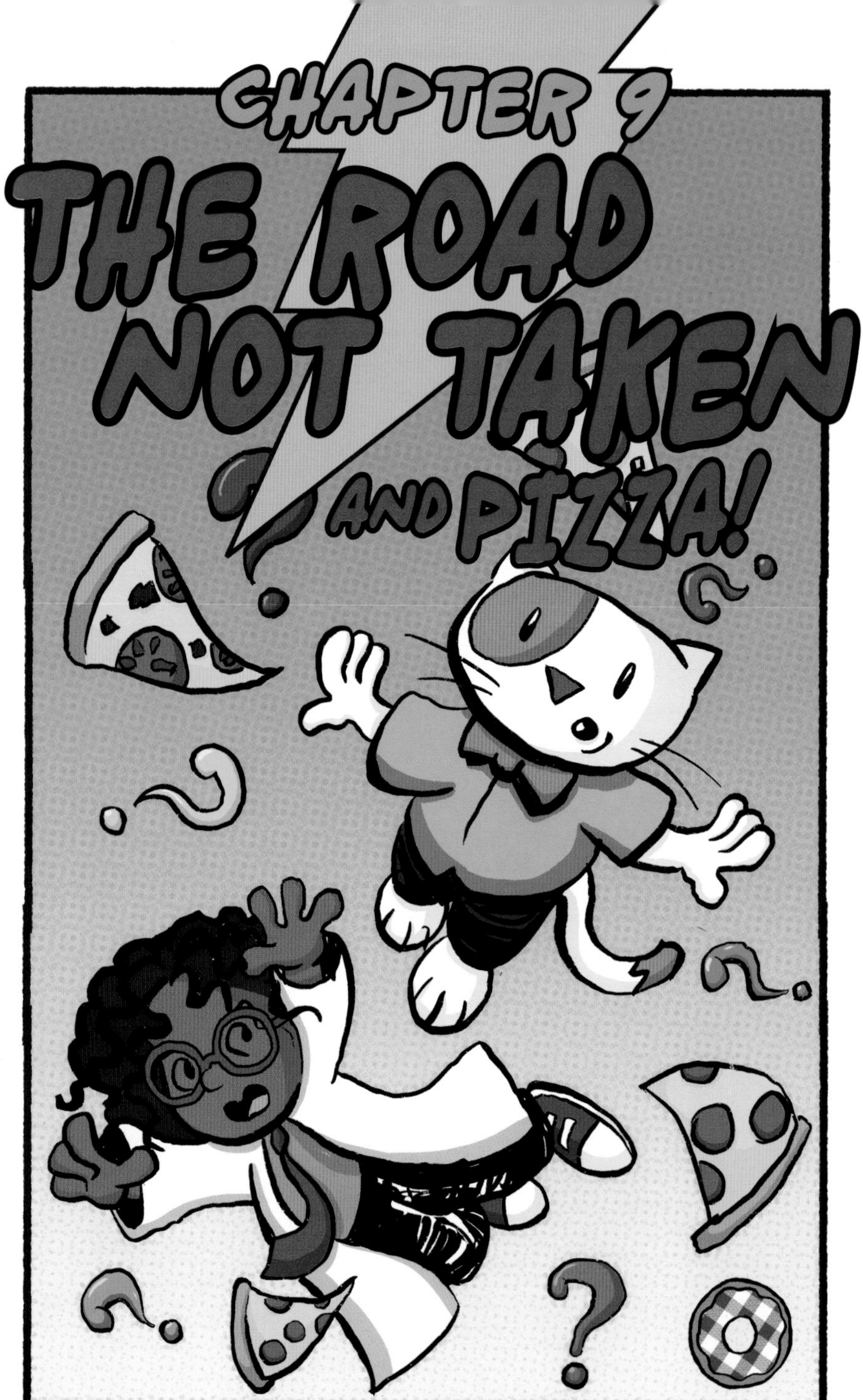
CHAPTER 9
THE ROAD NOT TAKEN
AND PIZZA!

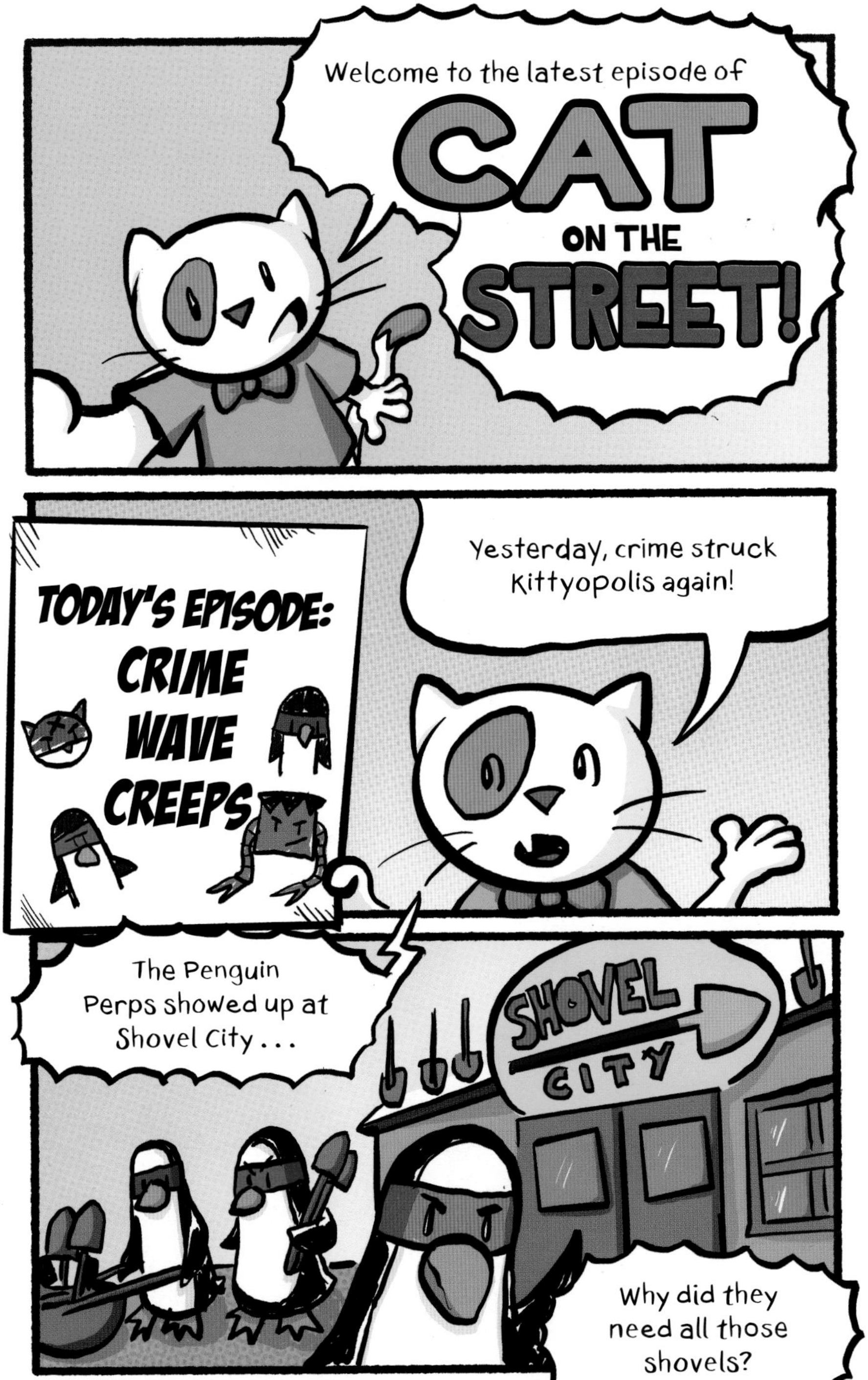
Welcome to the latest episode of
CAT ON THE STREET!
TODAY'S EPISODE: CRIME WAVE CREEPS
Yesterday, crime struck Kittyopolis again!
The Penguin Perps showed up at Shovel City . . .
SHOVEL CITY
Why did they need all those shovels?

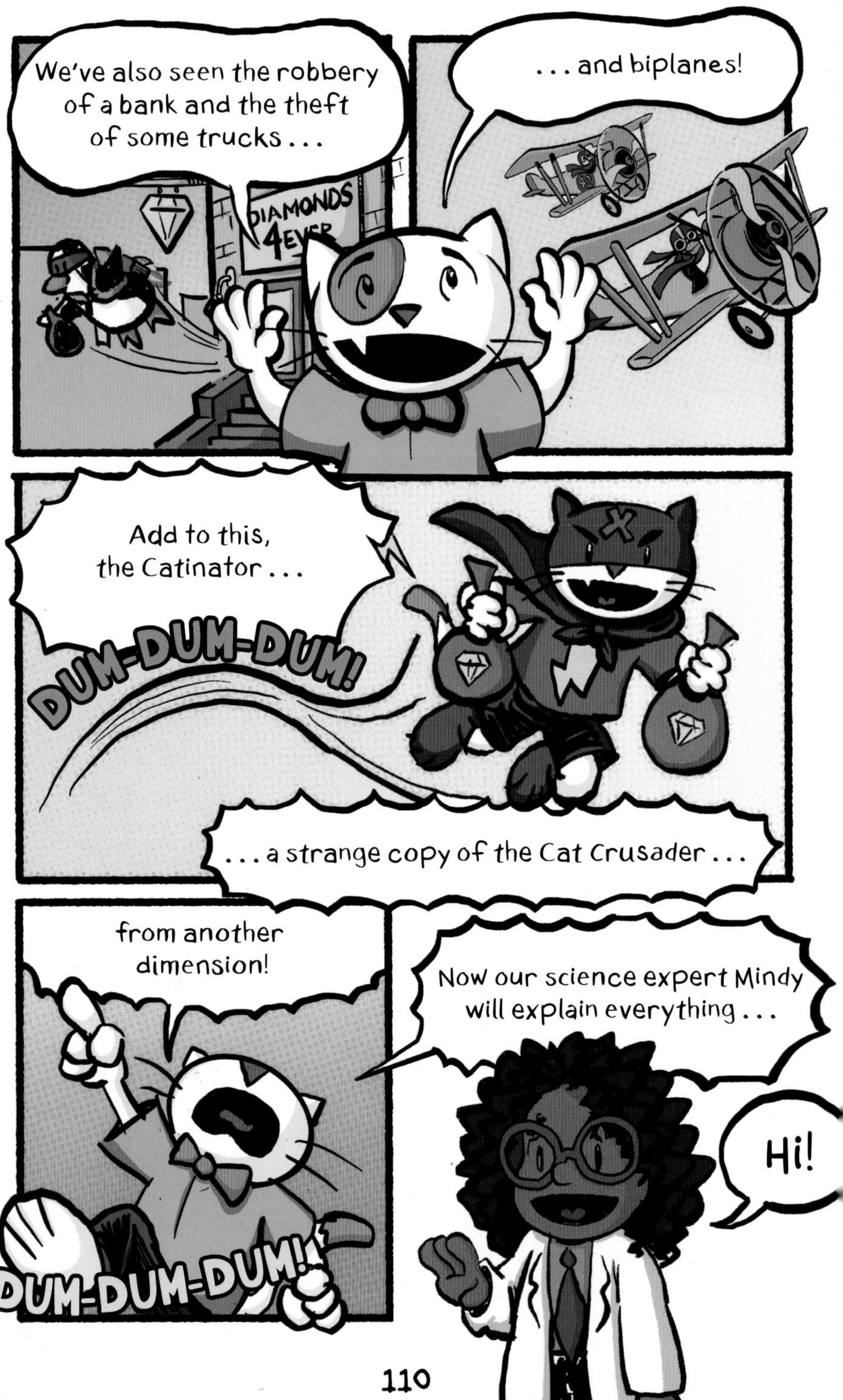
We've also seen the robbery of a bank and the theft of some trucks . . .
DIAMONDS 4EVER
. . . and biplanes!
Add to this, the Catinator . . .
DUM-DUM-DUM!
. . . a strange copy of the Cat Crusader . . .
from another dimension!
DUM-DUM-DUM!
Now our science expert Mindy will explain everything . . .
Hi!

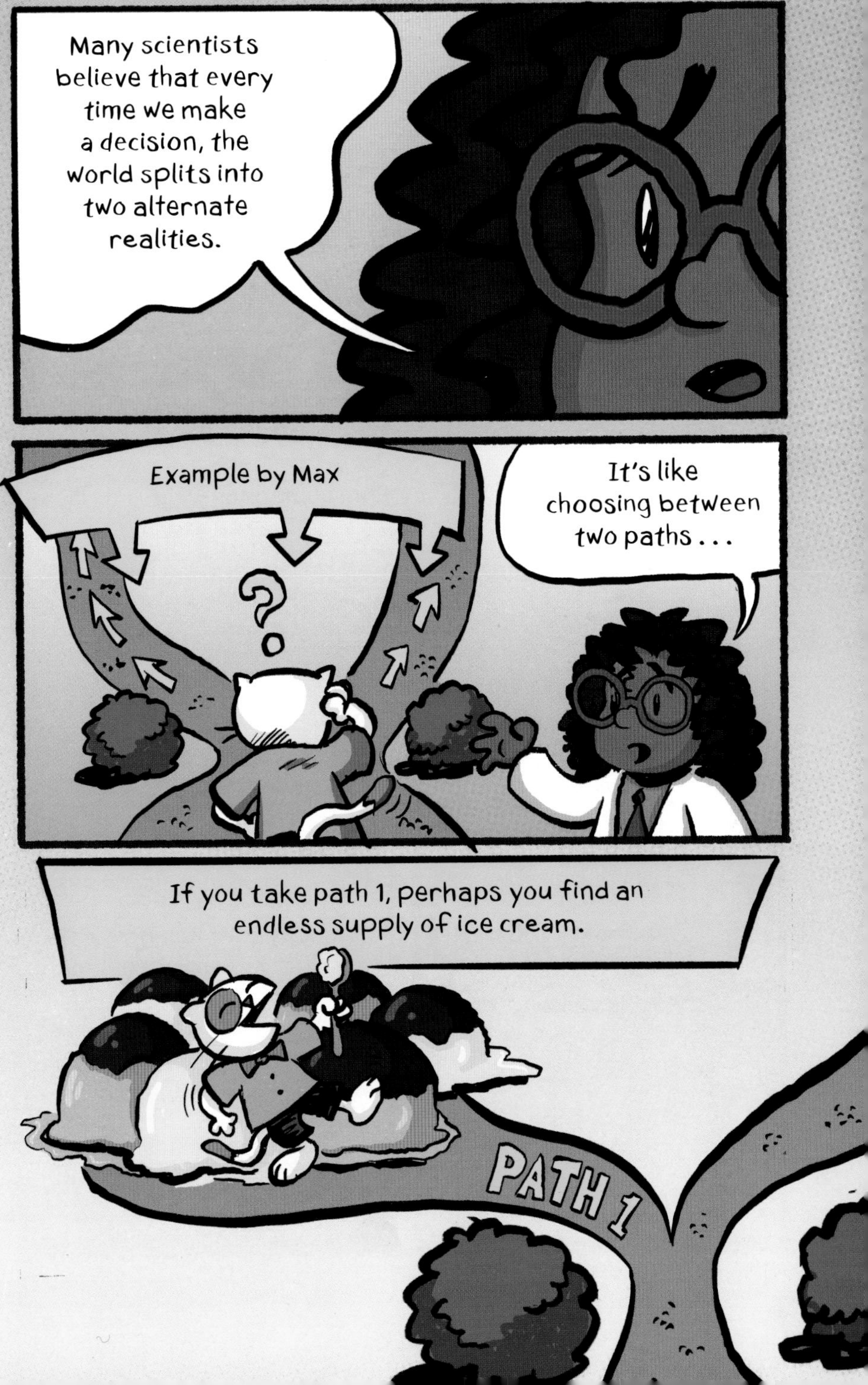
Many scientists believe that every time we make a decision, the world splits into two alternate realities.
Example by Max
It's like choosing between two paths . . .
If you take path 1, perhaps you find an endless supply of ice cream.
PATH 1

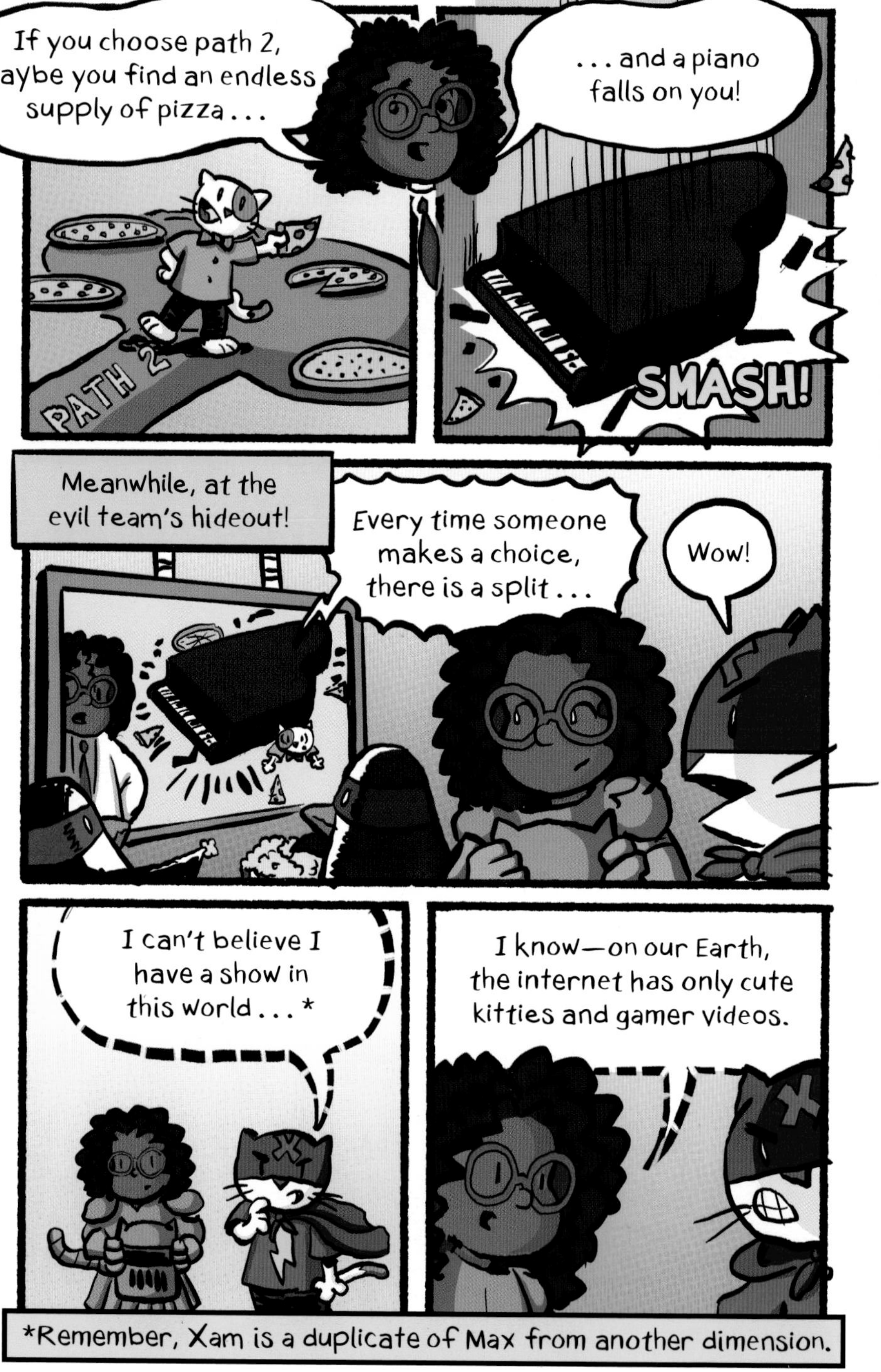
If you choose path 2, maybe you find an endless supply of pizza . . .
PATH 2
. . . and a piano falls on you!
SMASH!
Meanwhile, at the evil team's hideout!
Every time someone makes a choice, there is a split . . .
Wow!
I can't believe I have a show in this world . . . *
I know—on our Earth, the internet has only cute kitties and gamer videos.
*Remember, Xam is a duplicate of Max from another dimension.

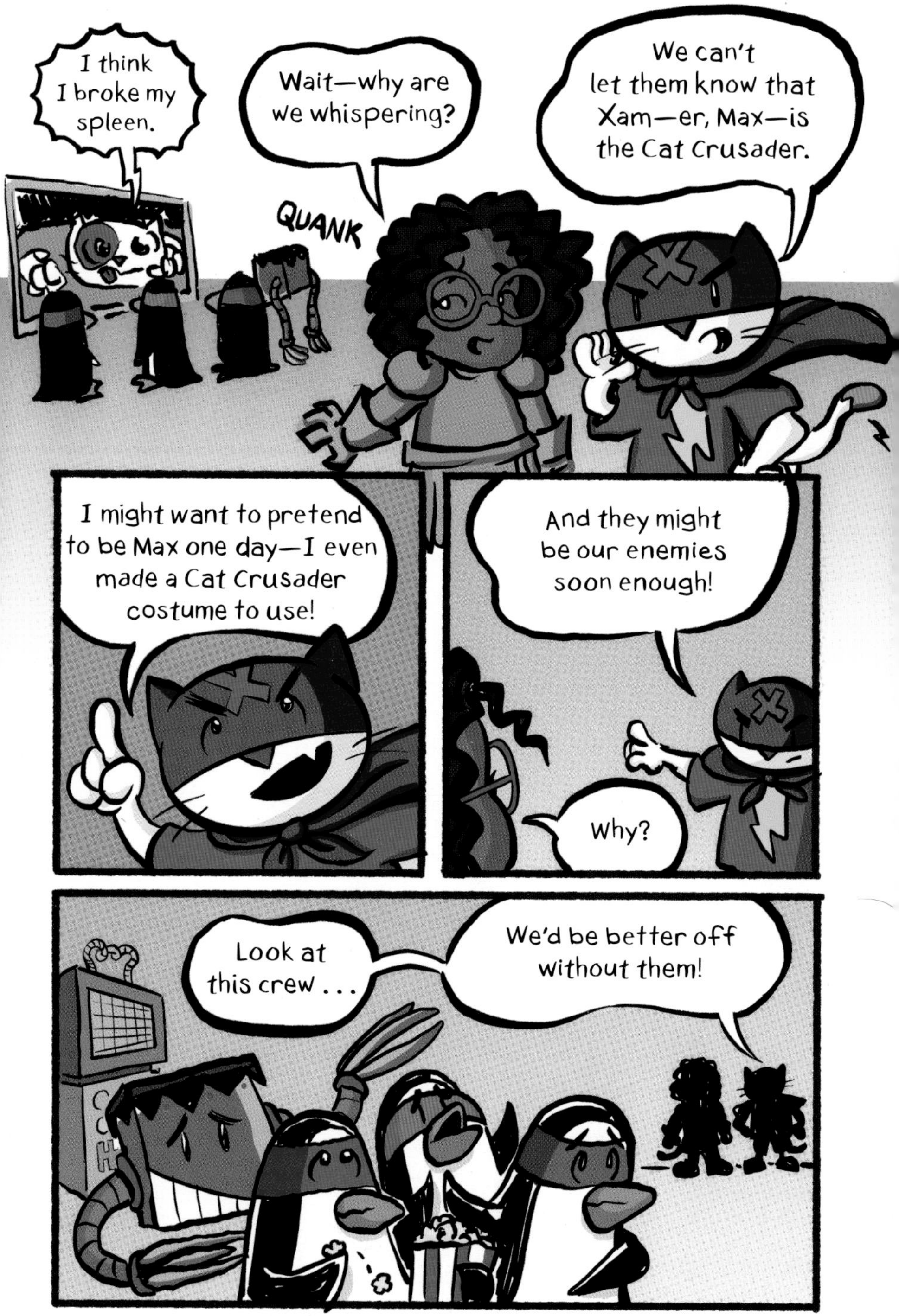
I think I broke my spleen.
Wait—why are we whispering?
We can't let them know that Xam—er, Max—is the Cat Crusader.
QUANK
I might want to pretend to be Max one day—I even made a Cat Crusader costume to use!
And they might be our enemies soon enough!
Why?
Look at this crew . . .
We'd be better off without them!

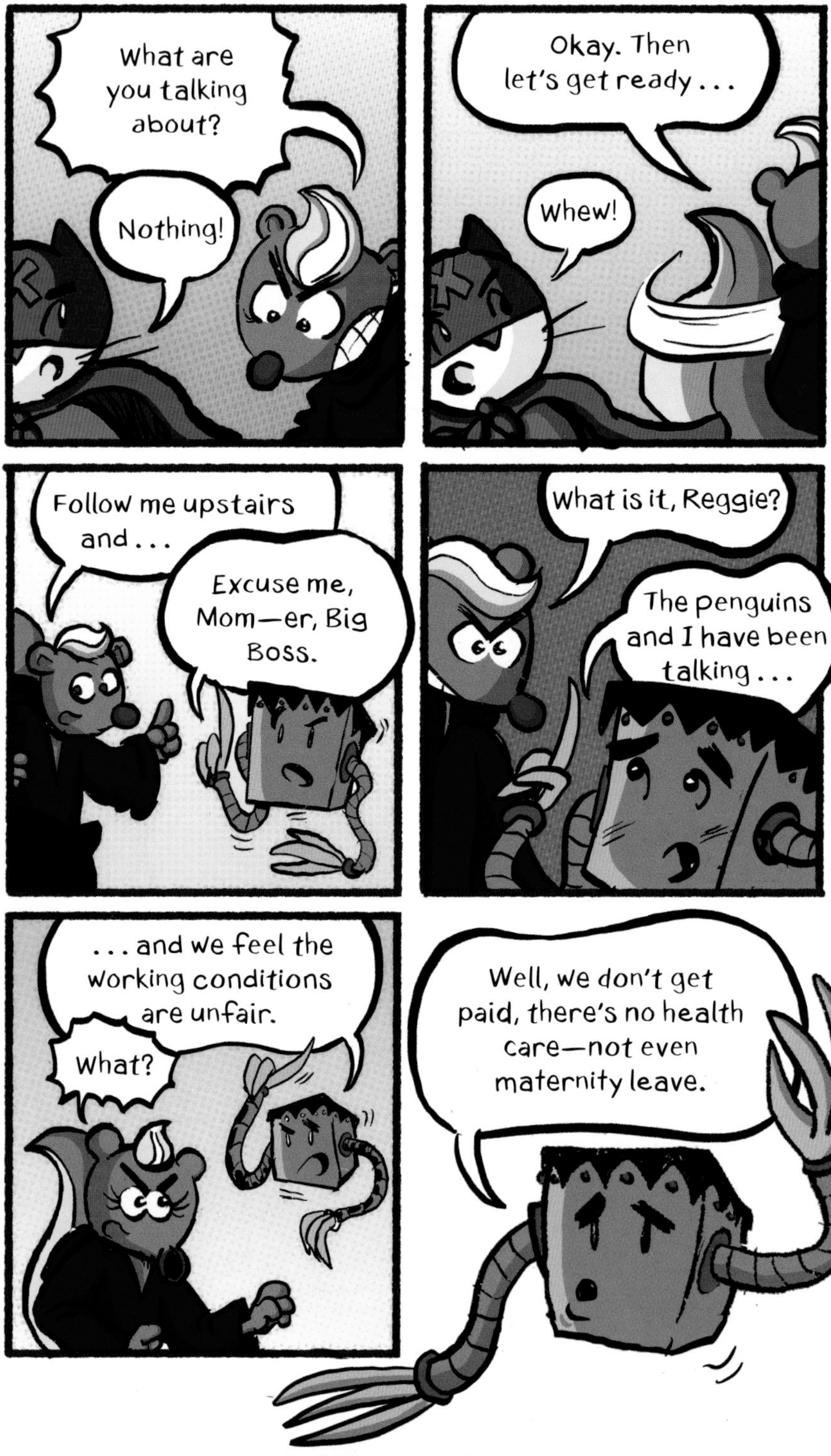
What are you talking about?
Nothing!
Okay. Then let's get ready . . .
Whew!
Follow me upstairs and . . .
Excuse me, Mom—er, Big Boss.
What is it, Reggie?
The penguins and I have been talking . . .
. . . and we feel the working conditions are unfair.
What?
Well, we don't get paid, there's no health care—not even maternity leave.

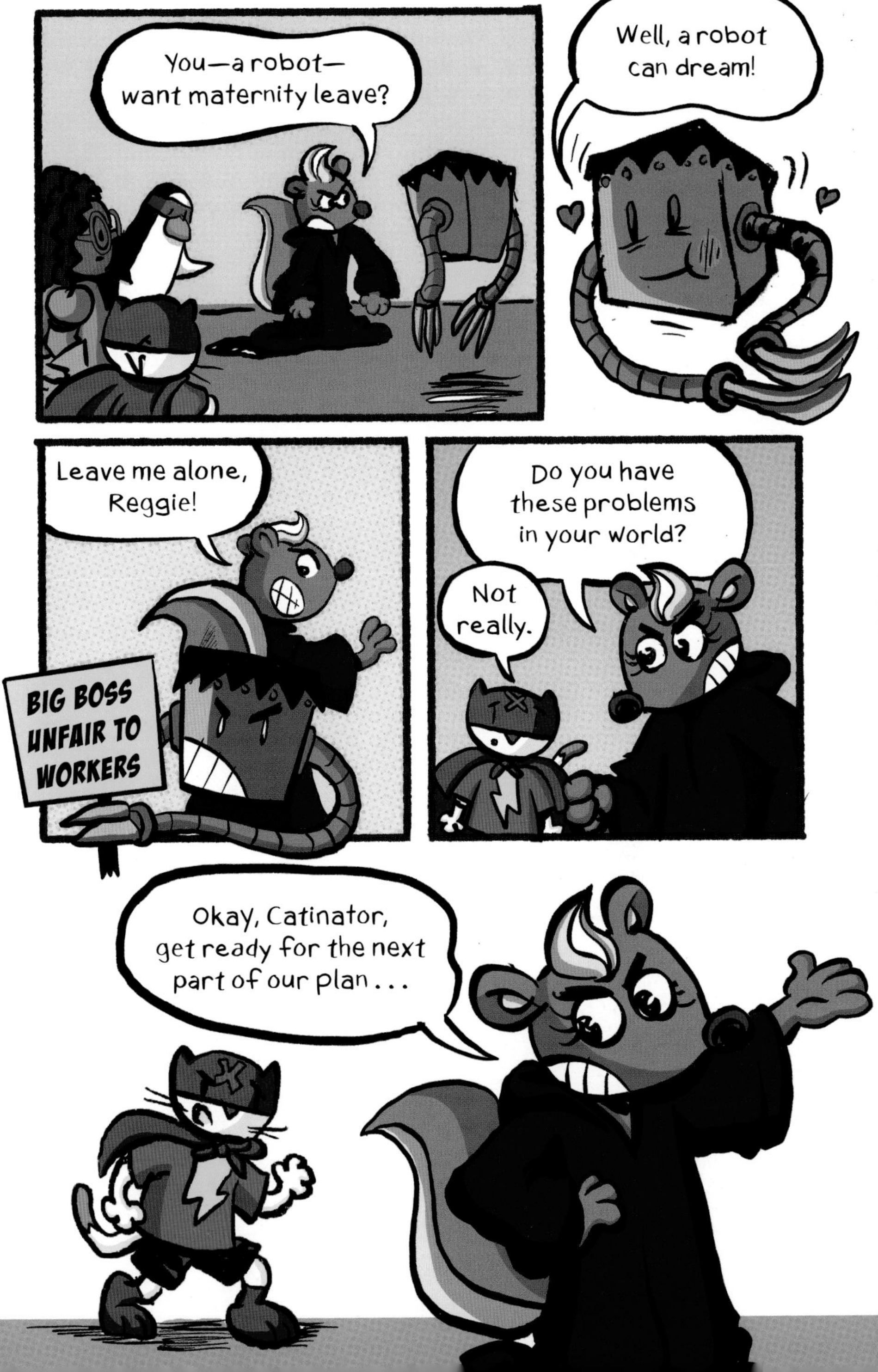

You—a robot—want maternity leave?
Well, a robot can dream!
Leave me alone, Reggie!
BIG BOSS UNFAIR TO WORKERS
Do you have these problems in your world?
Not really.
Okay, Catinator, get ready for the next part of our plan . . .

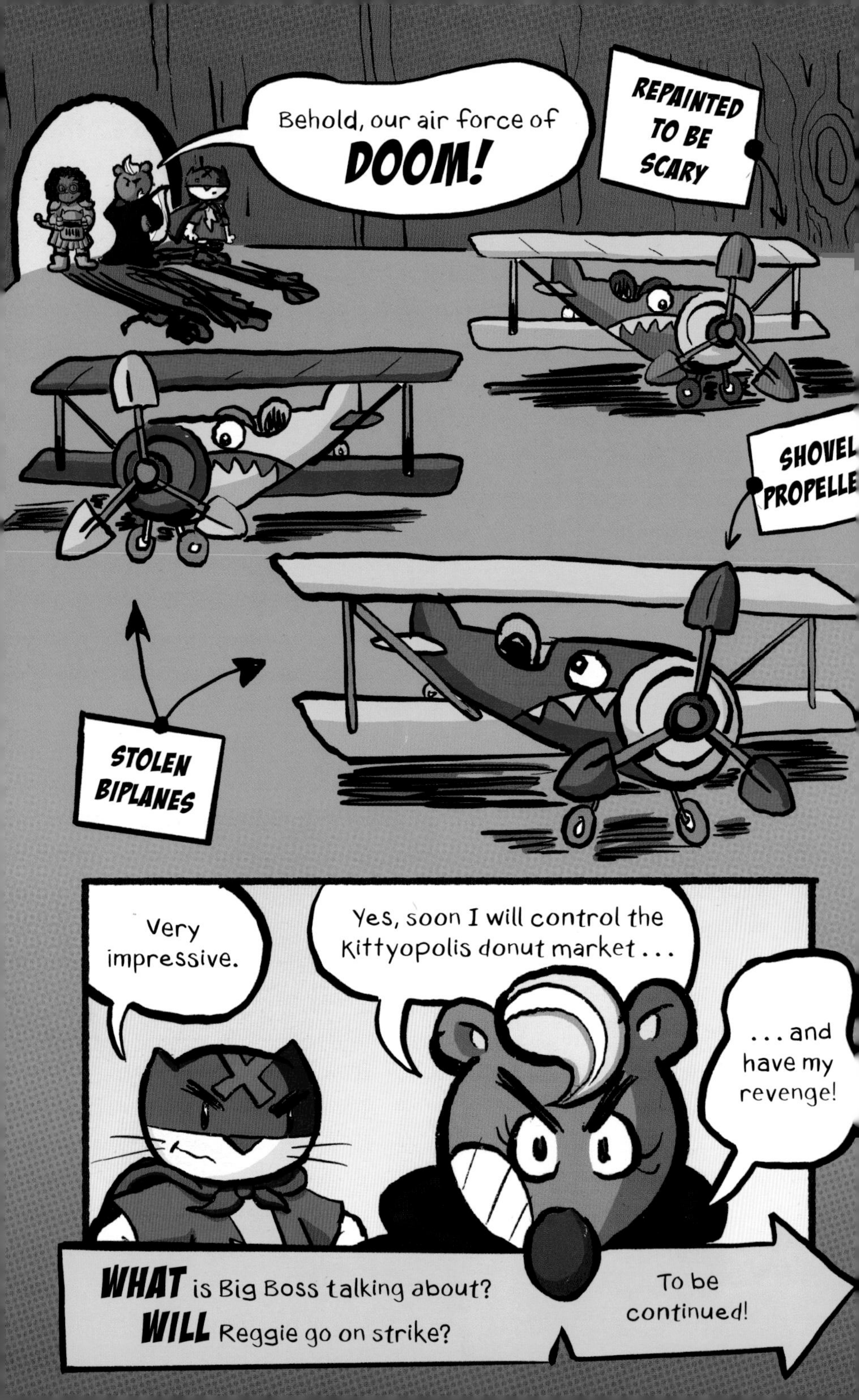

Behold, our air force of DOOM!
REPAINTED TO BE SCARY
SHOVEL PROPELLE
STOLEN BIPLANES
Very impressive.
Yes, soon I will control the Kittyopolis donut market . . .
. . . and have my revenge!
WHAT is Big Boss talking about?
WILL Reggie go on strike?
To be continued!

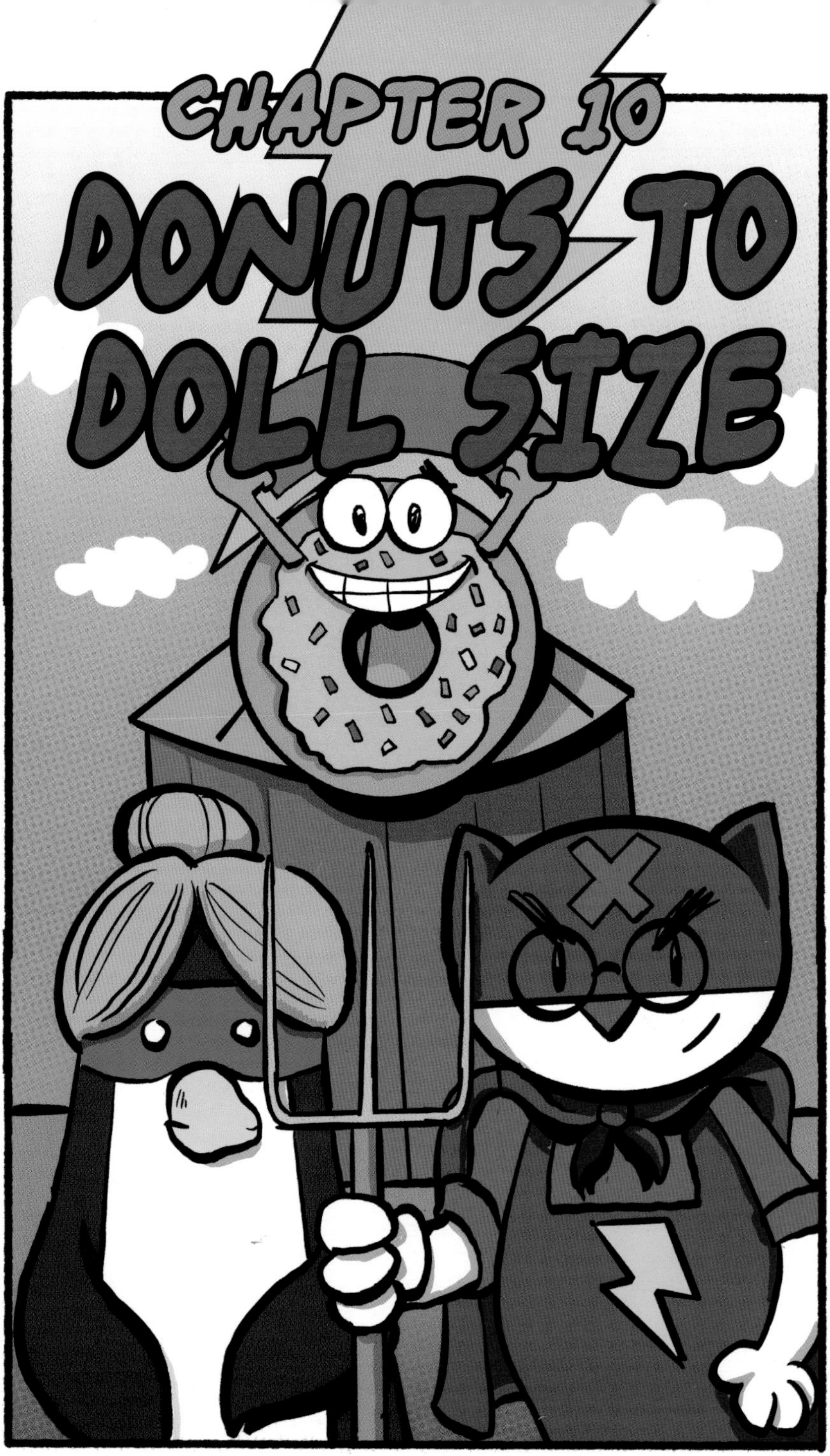
CHAPTER 10
DONUTS TO DOLL SIZE

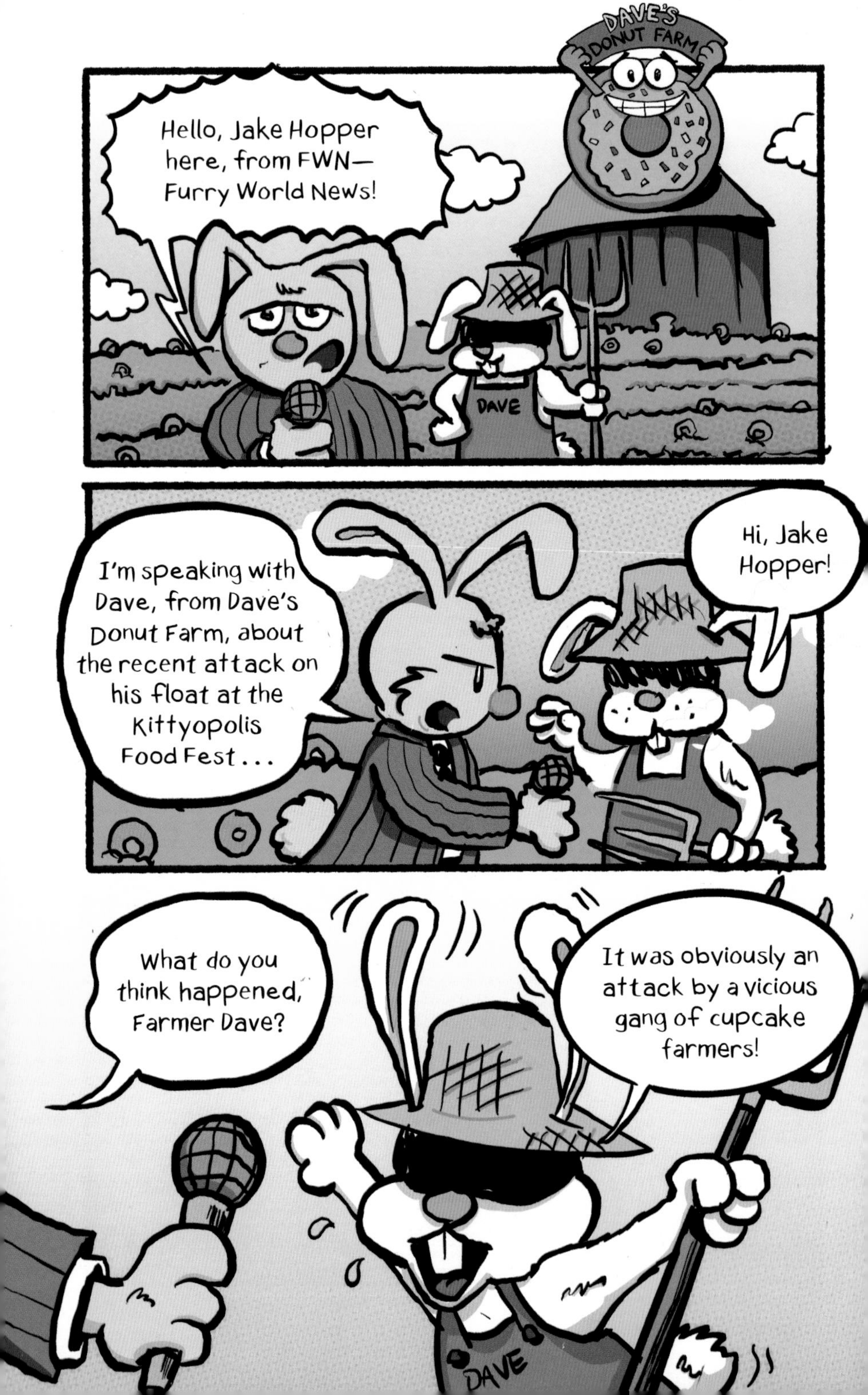
DAVE'S DONUT FARM
Hello, Jake Hopper here, from FWN— Furry World News!
DAVE
I'm speaking with Dave, from Dave's Donut Farm, about the recent attack on his float at the Kittyopolis Food Fest . . .
Hi, Jake Hopper!
What do you think happened, Farmer Dave?
It was obviously an attack by a vicious gang of cupcake farmers!
DAVE

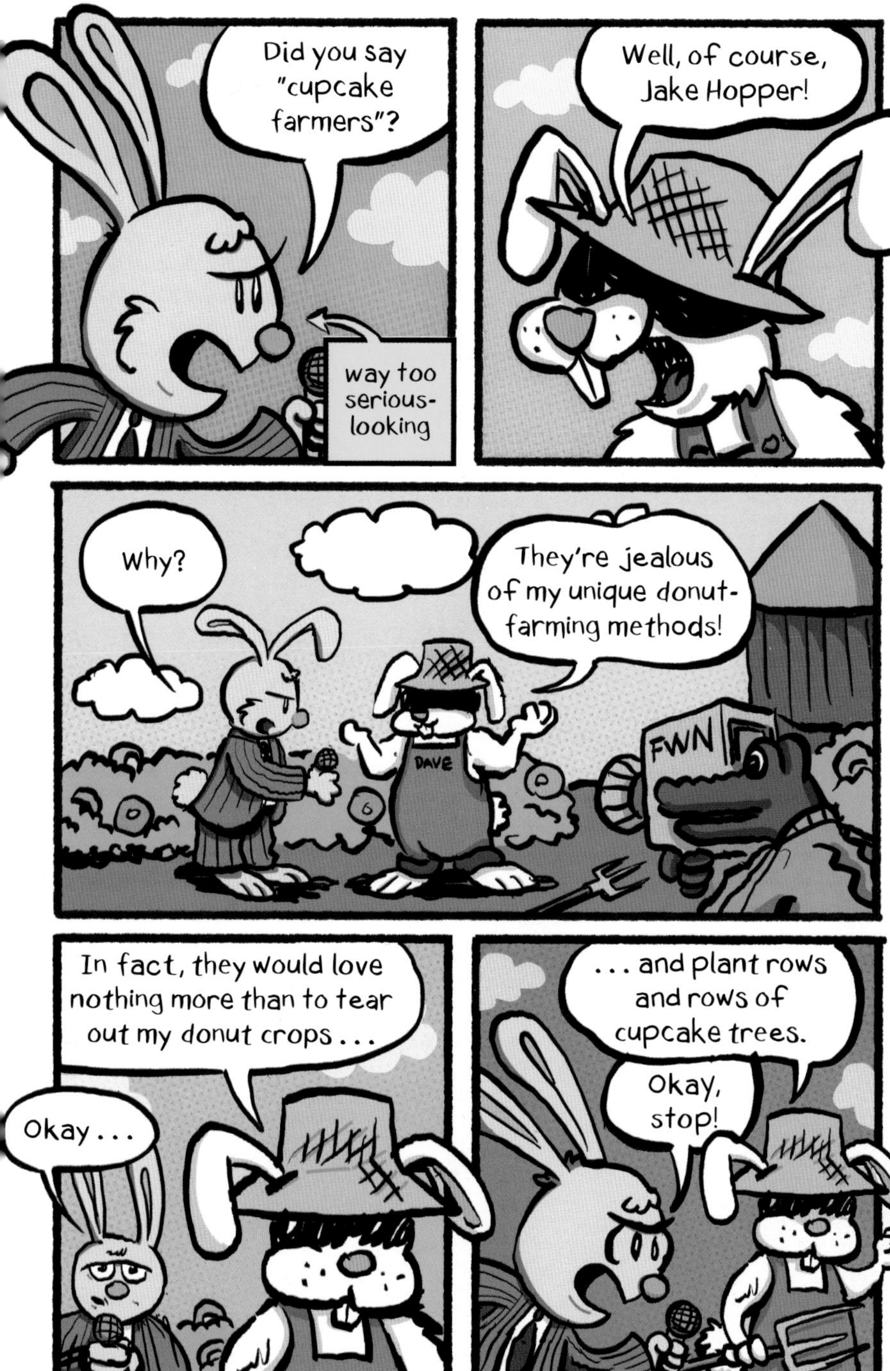
Did you say "cupcake farmers"?
way too serious-looking
Well, of course, Jake Hopper!
Why?
They're jealous of my unique donut-farming methods!
DAVE
FWN
In fact, they would love nothing more than to tear out my donut crops . . .
Okay . . .
. . . and plant rows and rows of cupcake trees.
Okay, stop!

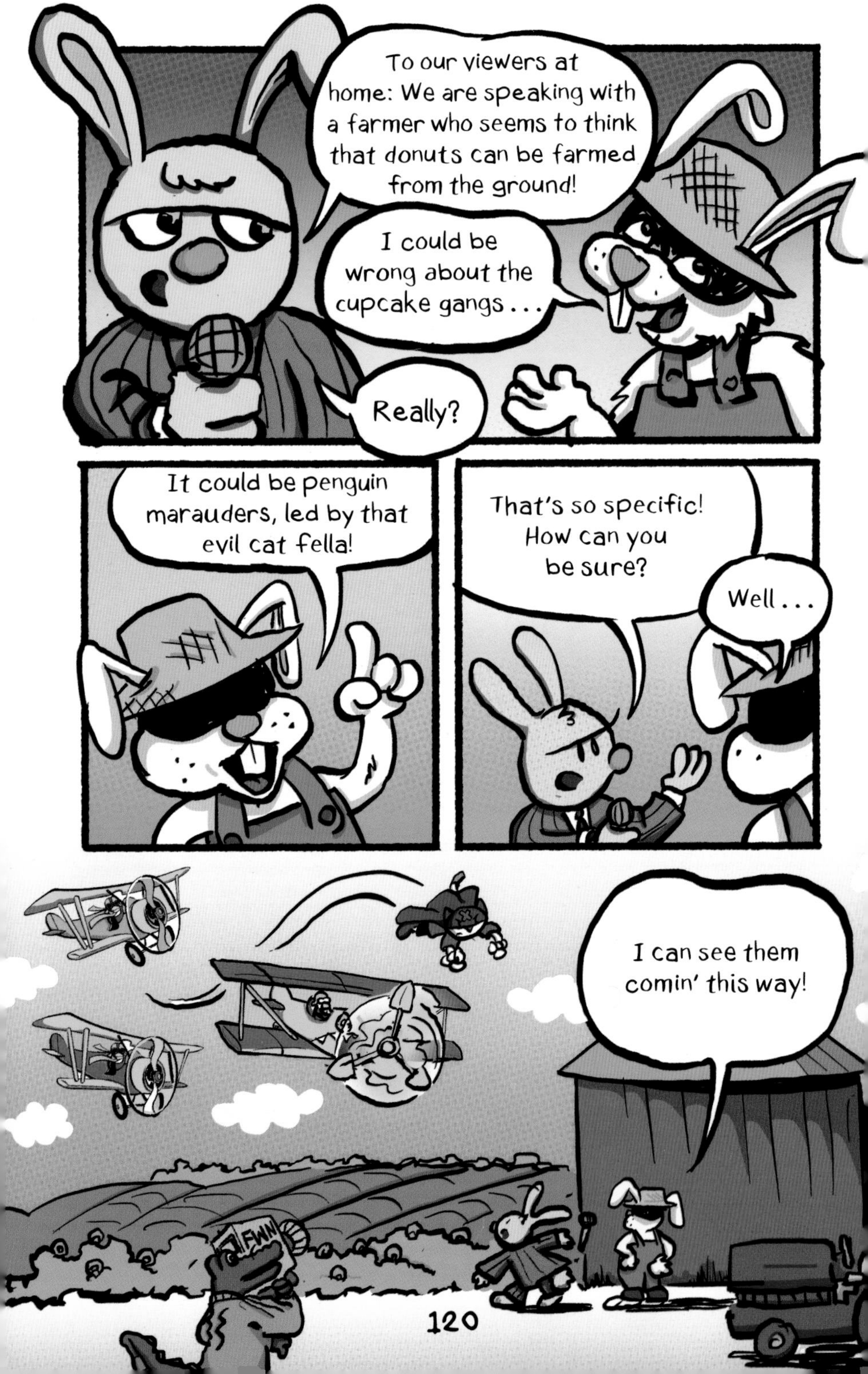
To our viewers at home: We are speaking with a farmer who seems to think that donuts can be farmed from the ground!
I could be wrong about the cupcake gangs . . .
Really?
It could be penguin marauders, led by that evil cat fella!
That's so specific! How can you be sure?
Well . . .
I can see them comin' this way!
FWN

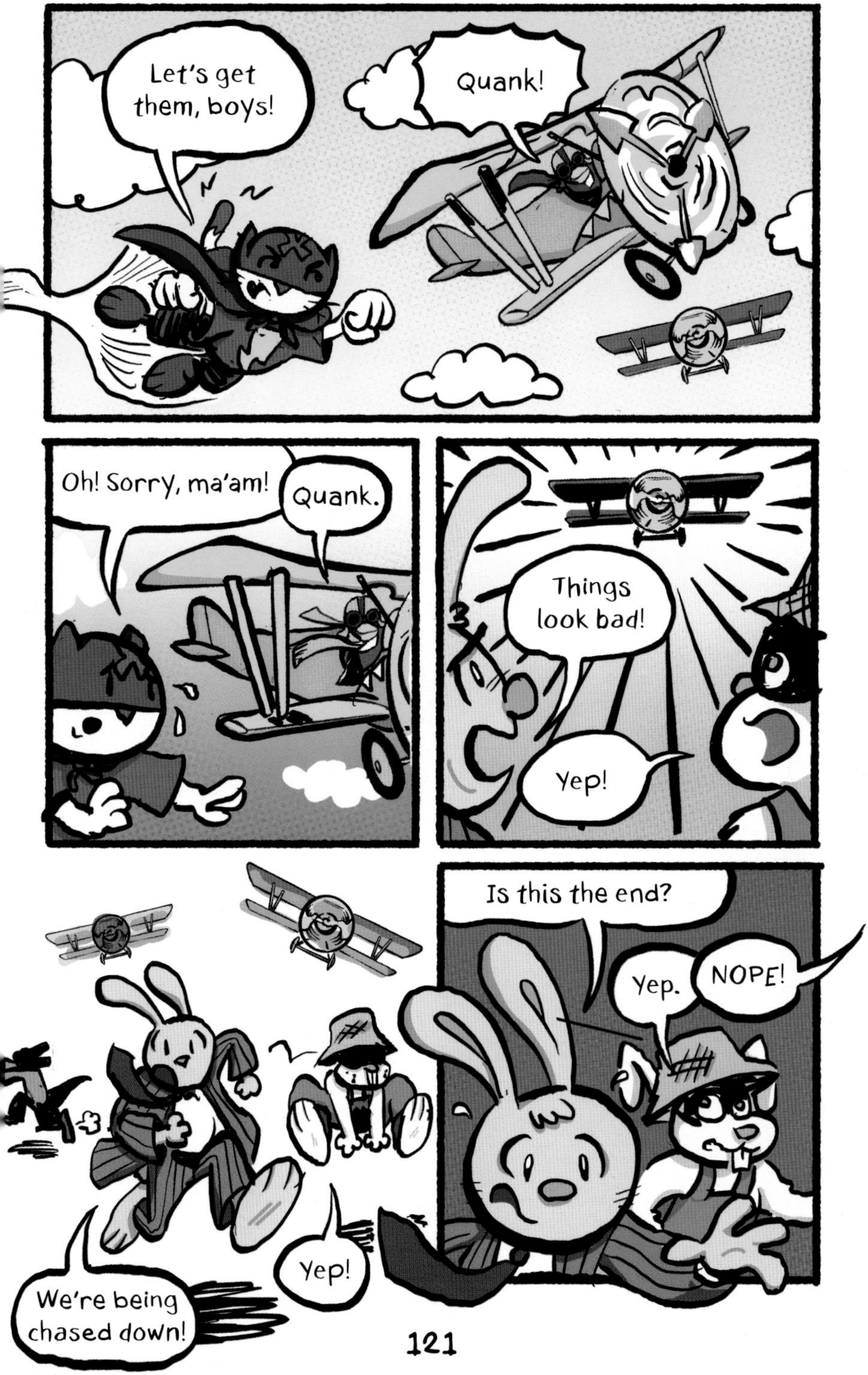
Let's get them, boys!
Quank!
Oh! Sorry, ma'am!
Quank.
Things look bad!
Yep!
We're being chased down!
Yep!
Is this the end?
Yep.
NOPE!

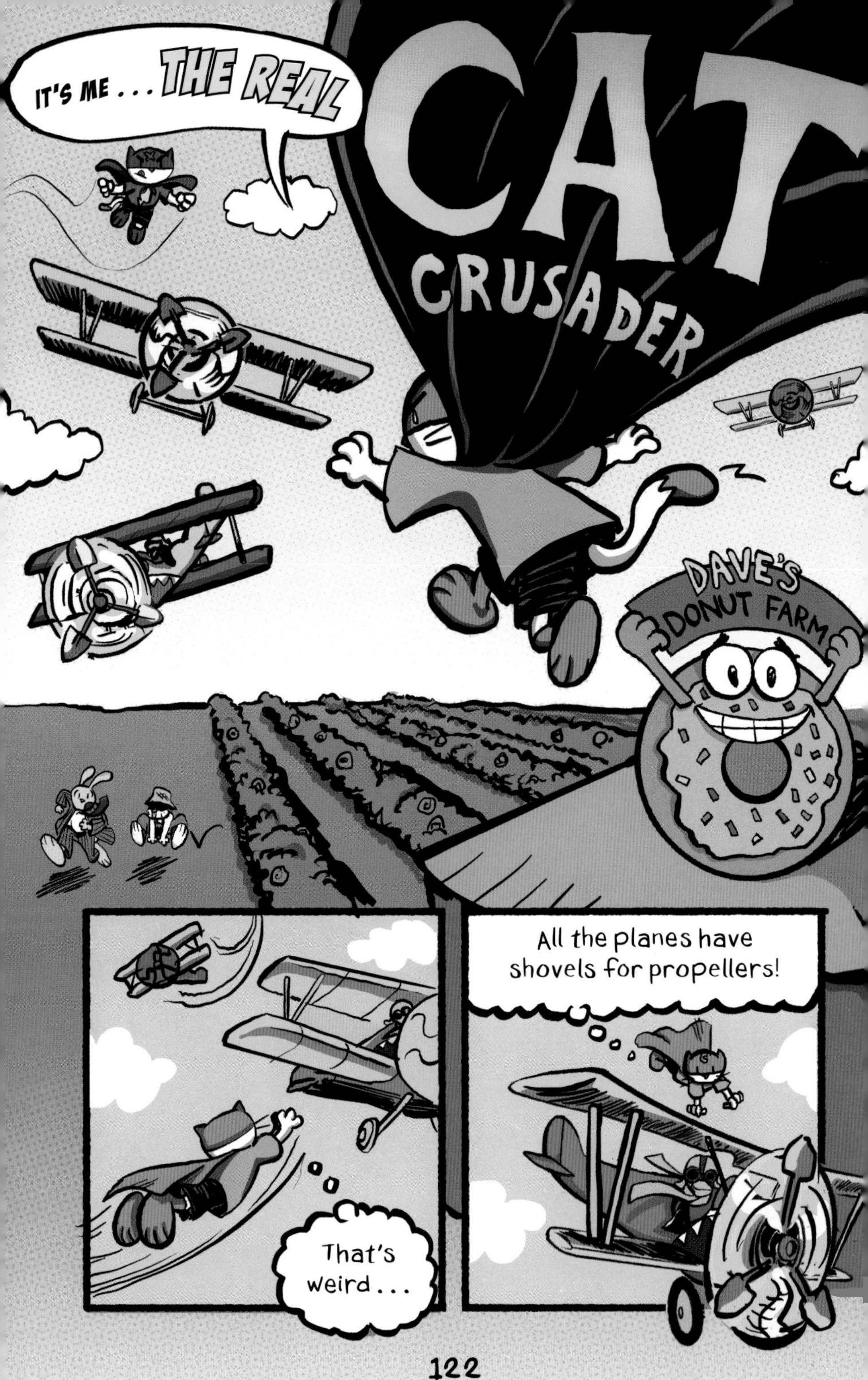
IT'S ME . . . THE REAL
CAT CRUSADER
DAVE'S DONUT FARM
That's weird . . .
All the planes have shovels for propellers!

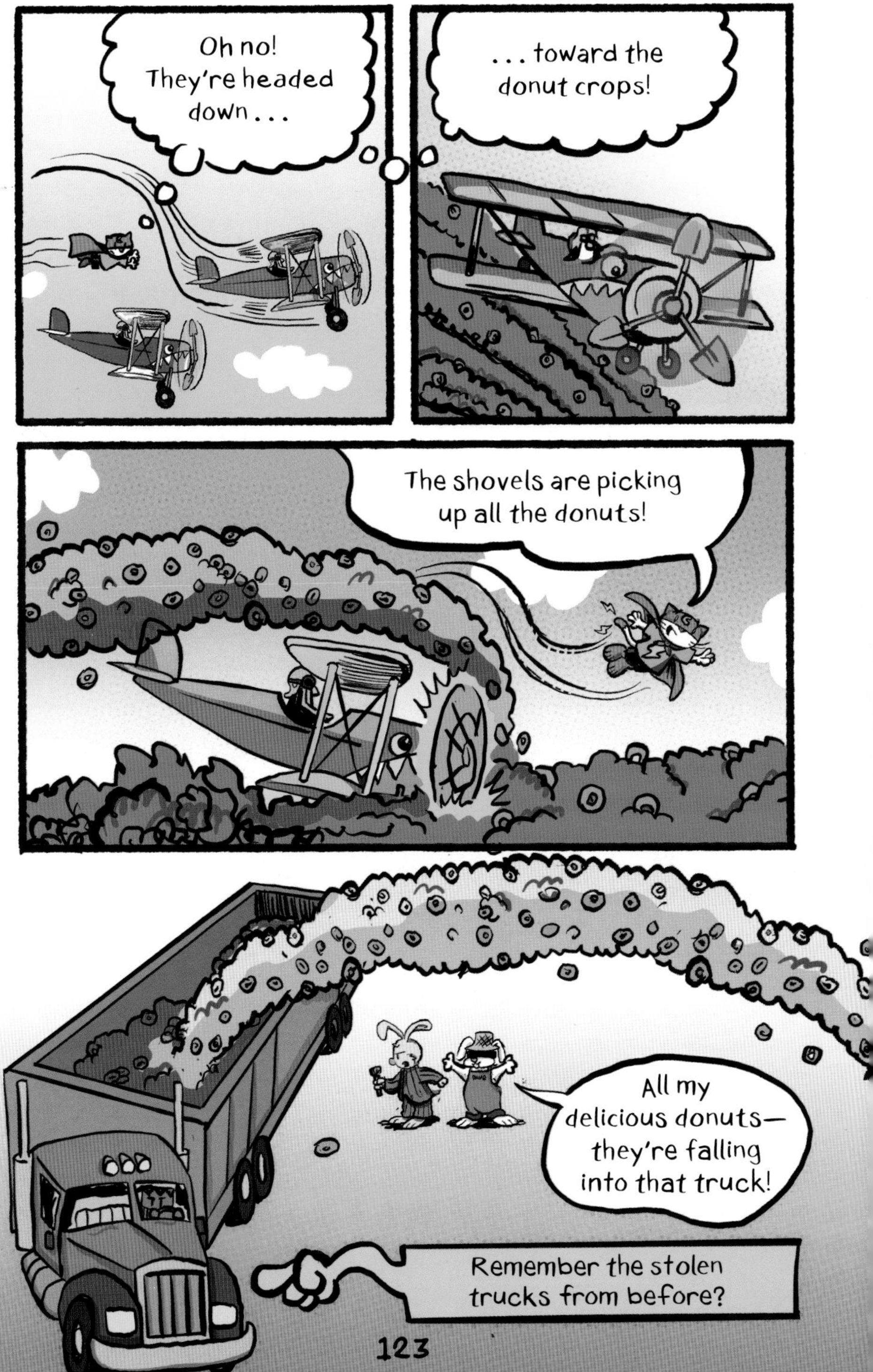
Oh no! They're headed down . . .
. . . toward the donut crops!
The shovels are picking up all the donuts!
All my delicious donuts— they're falling into that truck!
Remember the stolen trucks from before?

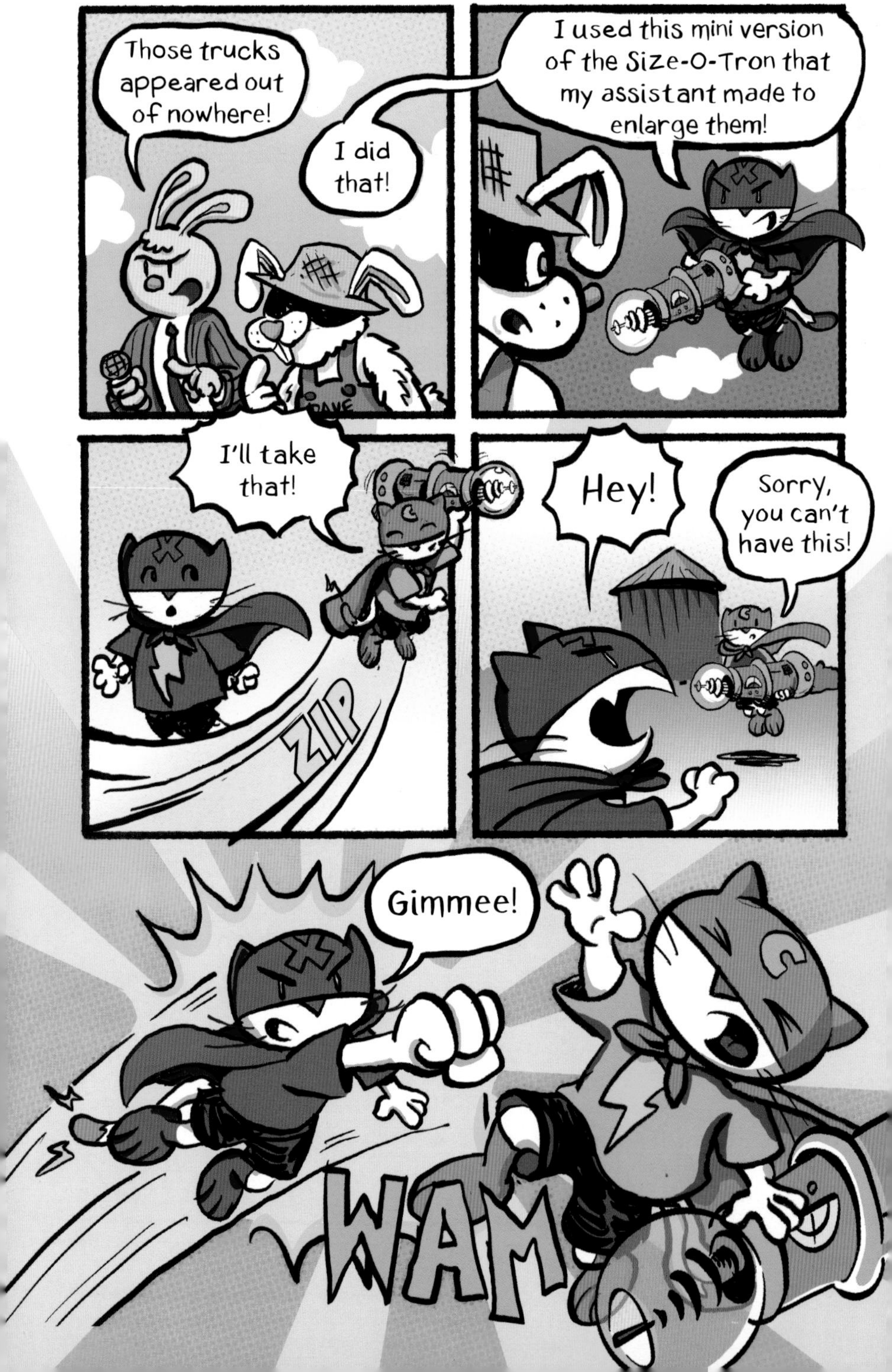
Those trucks appeared out of nowhere!
I did that!
I used this mini version of the Size-O-Tron that my assistant made to enlarge them!
I'll take that!
ZIP
Hey!
Sorry, you can't have this!
Gimmee!
WAM

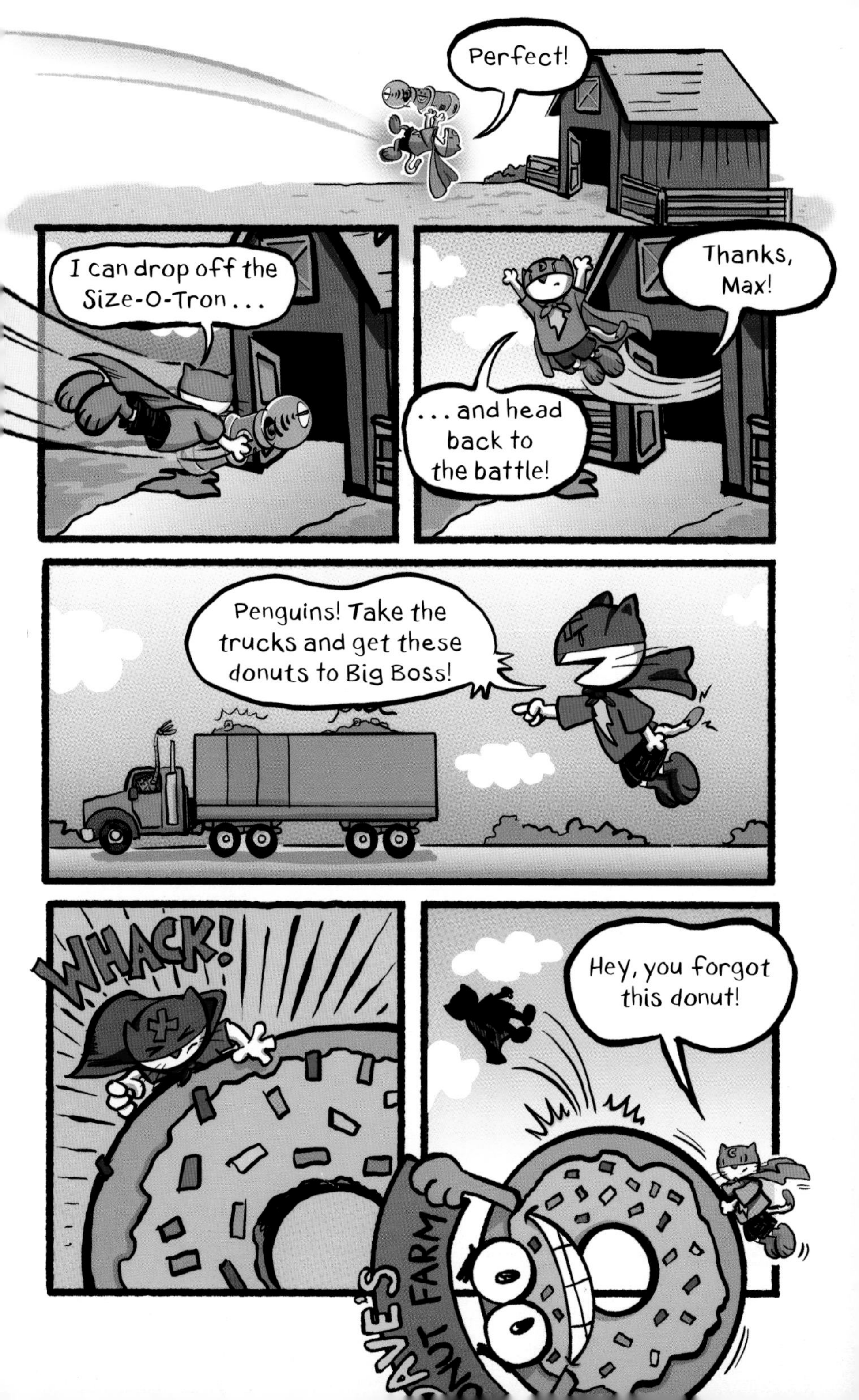
Perfect!
I can drop off the Size-O-Tron . . .
. . . and head back to the battle!
Thanks, Max!
Penguins! Take the trucks and get these donuts to Big Boss!
WHACK!
Hey, you forgot this donut!
DAVE'S DONUT FARM

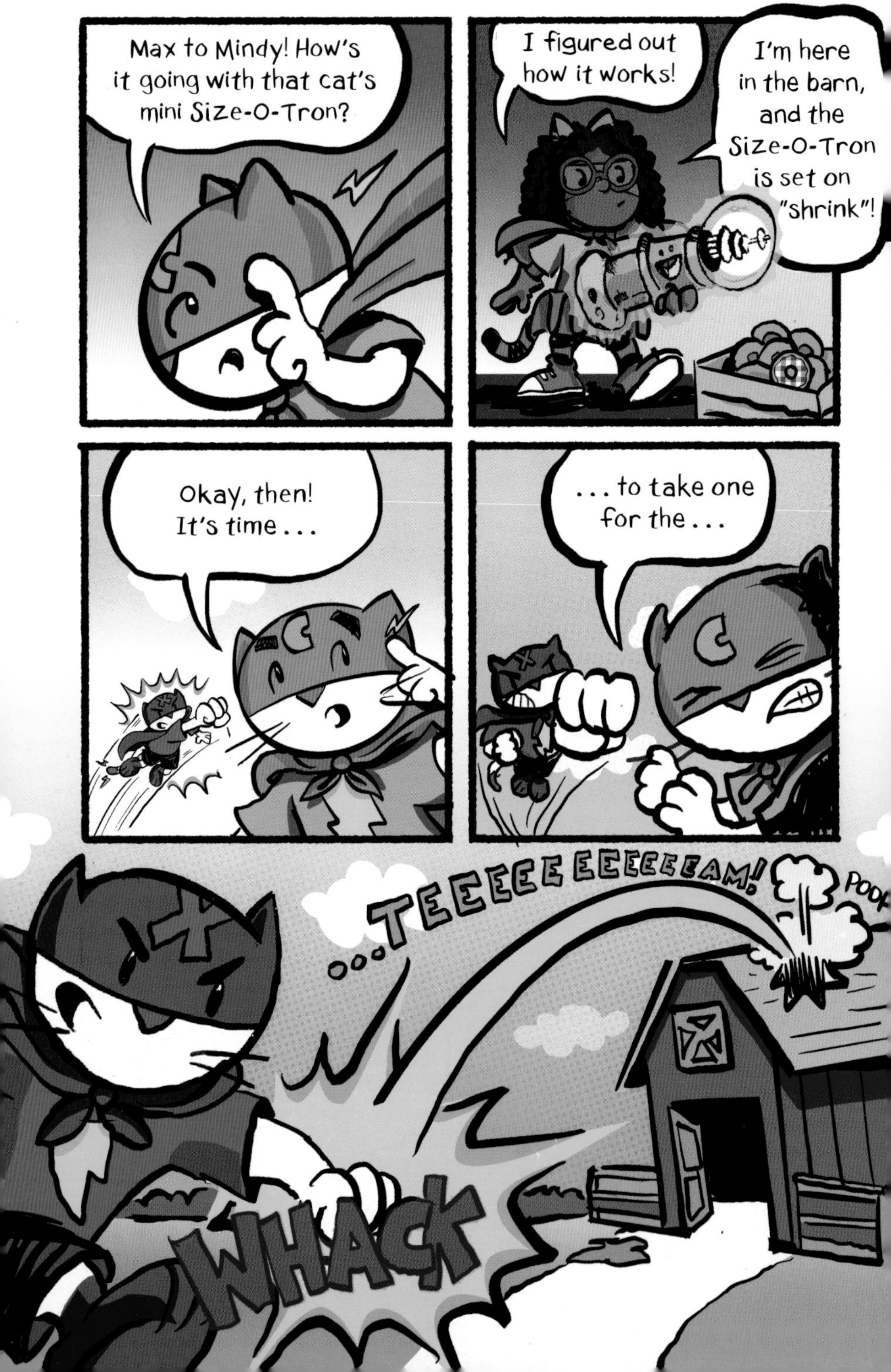

Max to Mindy! How's it going with that cat's mini Size-O-Tron?
I figured out how it works!
I'm here in the barn, and the Size-O-Tron is set on "shrink"!
Okay, then! It's time . . .
. . . to take one for the . . .
WHACK
. . . TEEEEEEEEEEEAM!
POOF

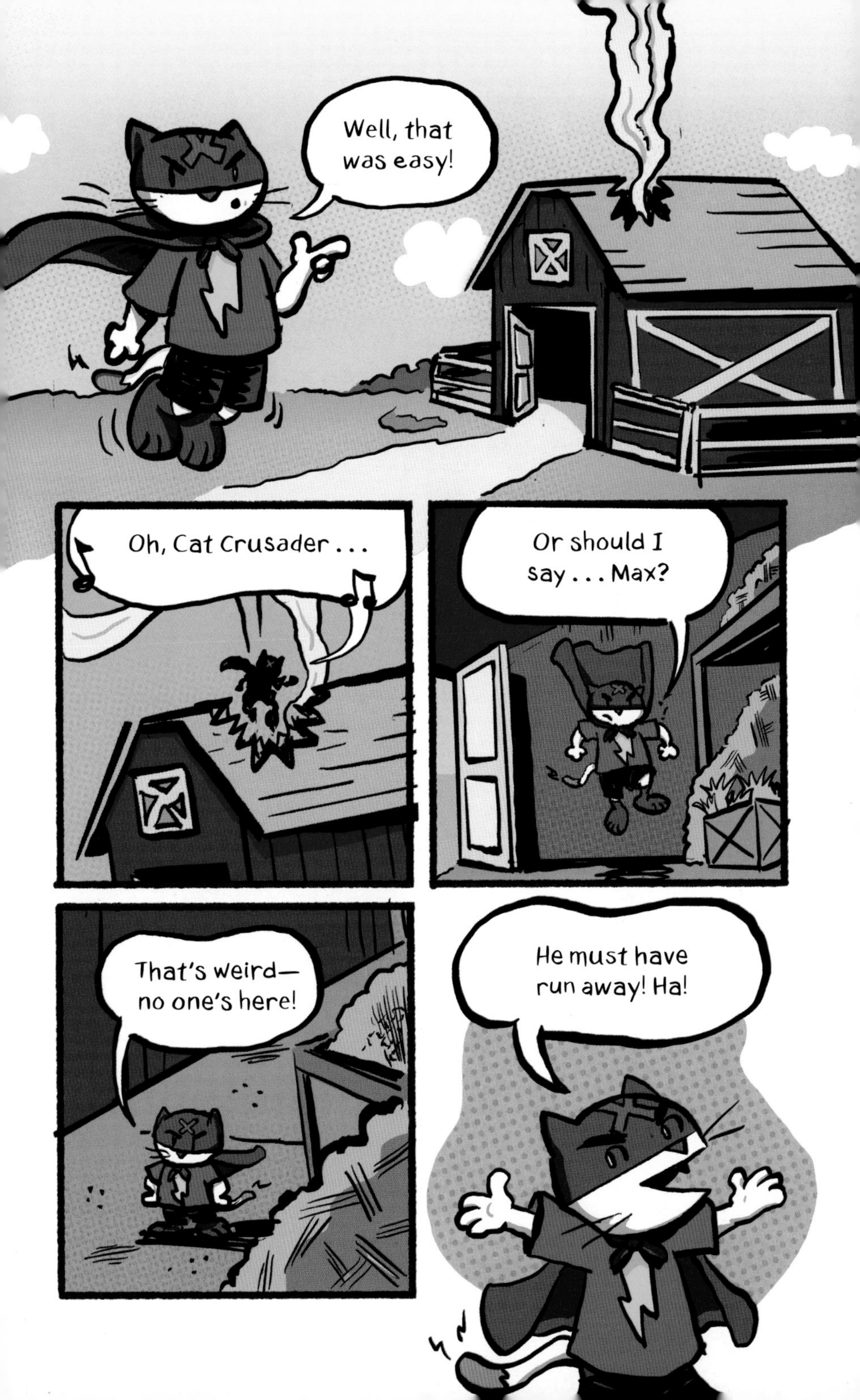
Well, that was easy!
Oh, Cat Crusader . . .
Or should I say . . . Max?
That's weird— no one's here!
He must have run away! Ha!

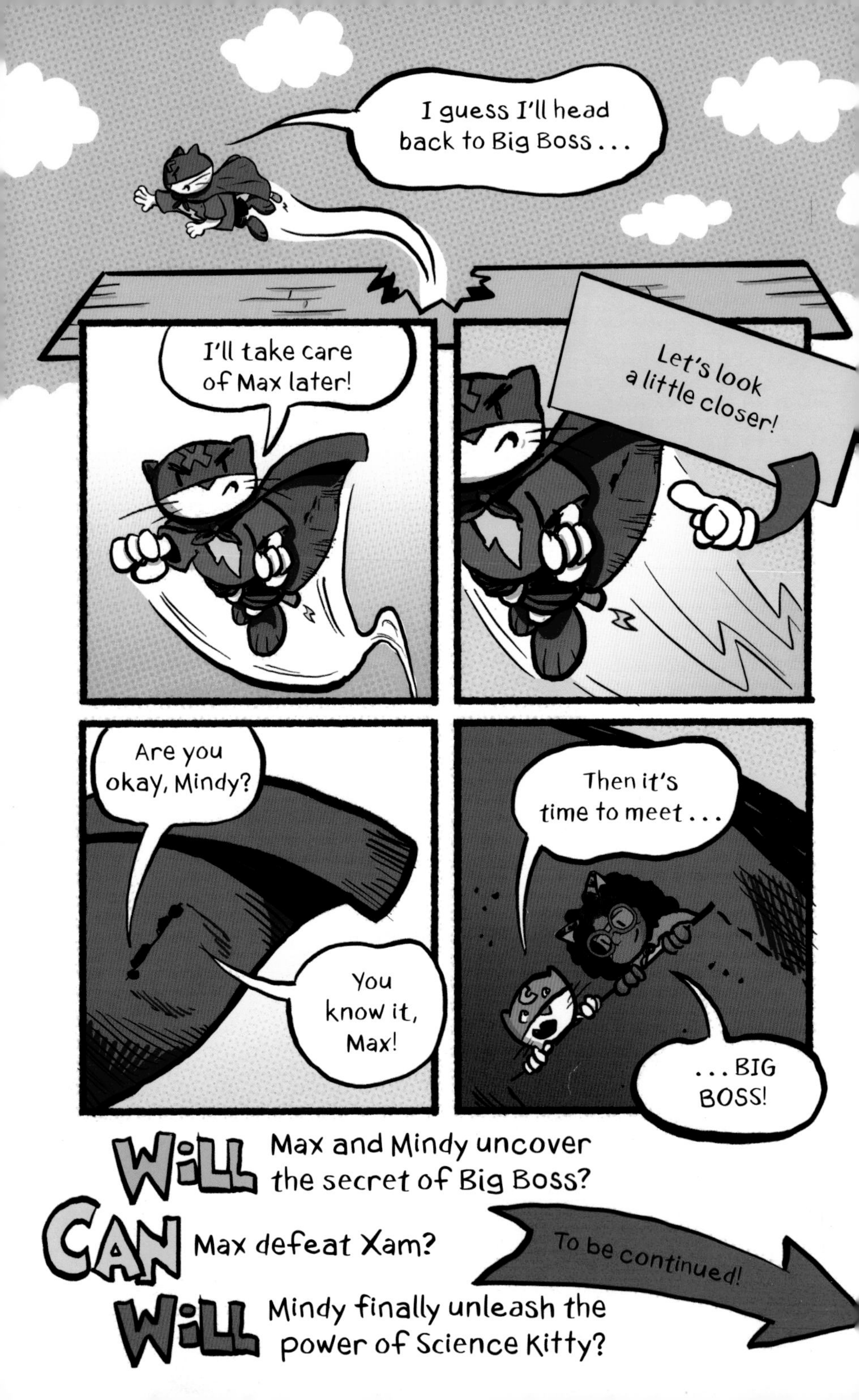
I guess I'll head back to Big Boss . . .
I'll take care of Max later!
Let's look a little closer!
Are you okay, Mindy?
You know it, Max!
Then it's time to meet . . .
. . . BIG BOSS!
WILL Max and Mindy uncover the secret of Big Boss?
CAN Max defeat Xam?
WILL Mindy finally unleash the power of Science Kitty?
To be continued!

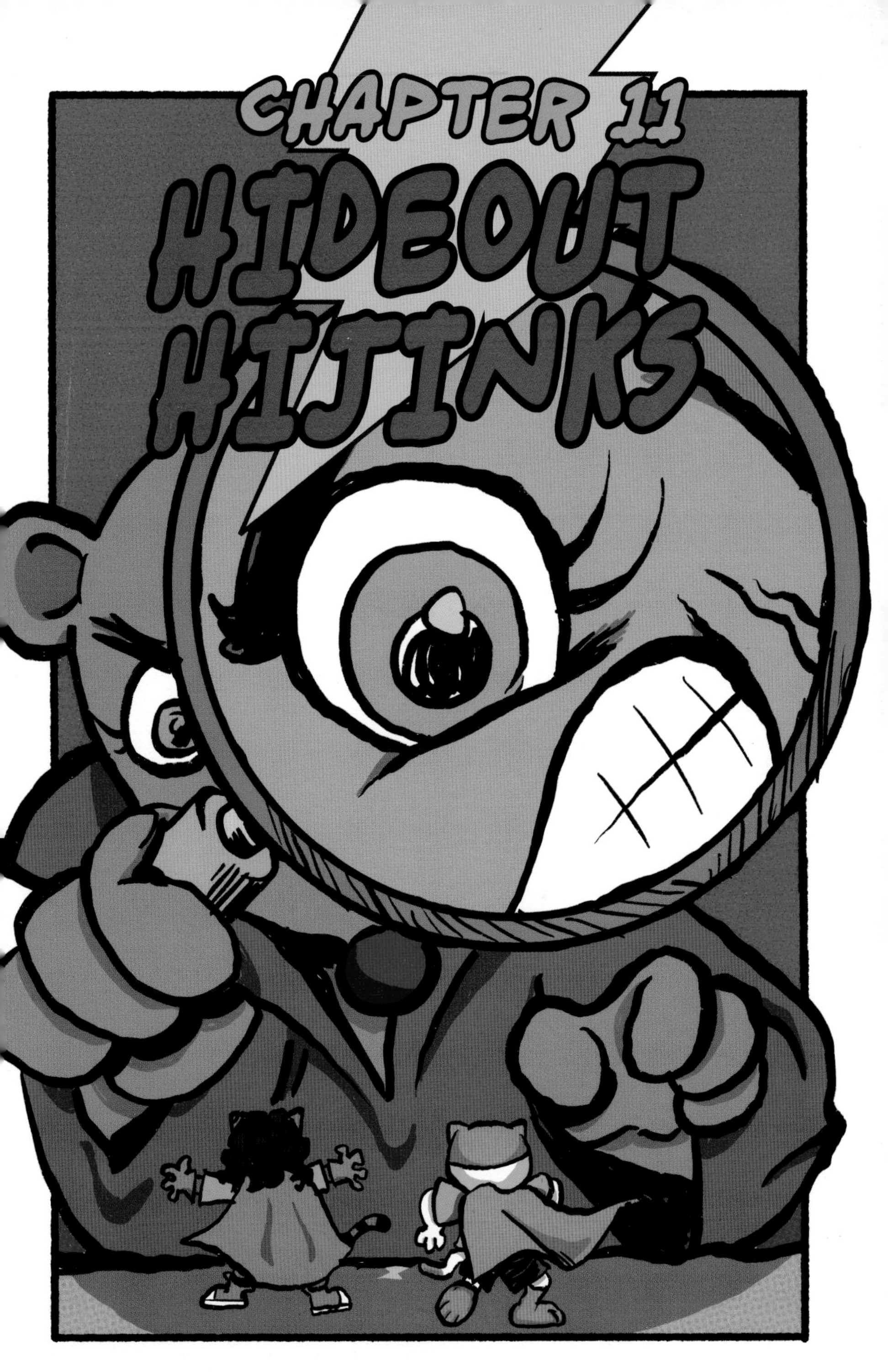
CHAPTER 11
HIDEOUT HIJINKS

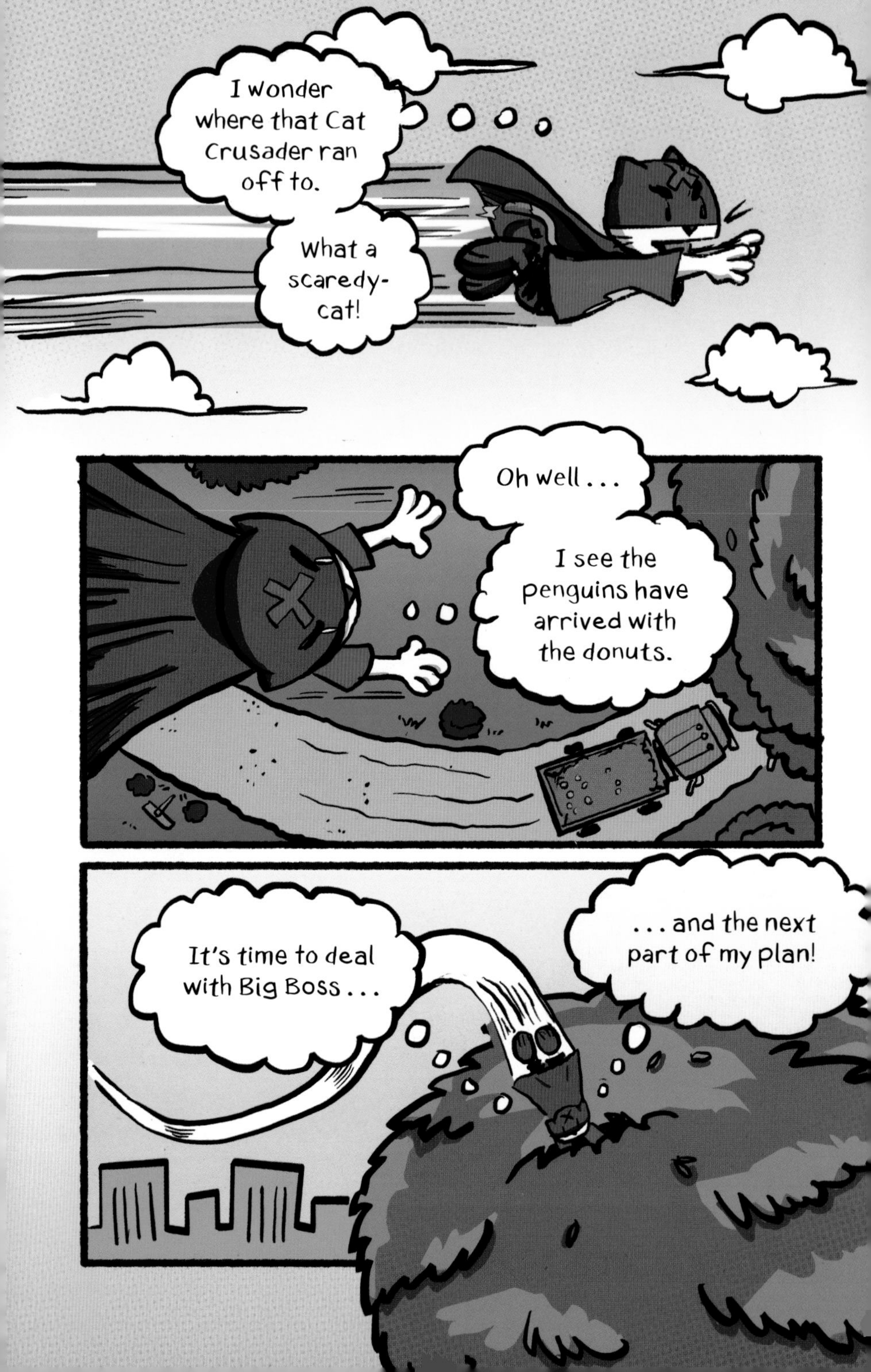
I wonder where that Cat Crusader ran off to.
What a scaredy-cat!
Oh well . . .
I see the penguins have arrived with the donuts.
It's time to deal with Big Boss . . .
. . . and the next part of my plan!

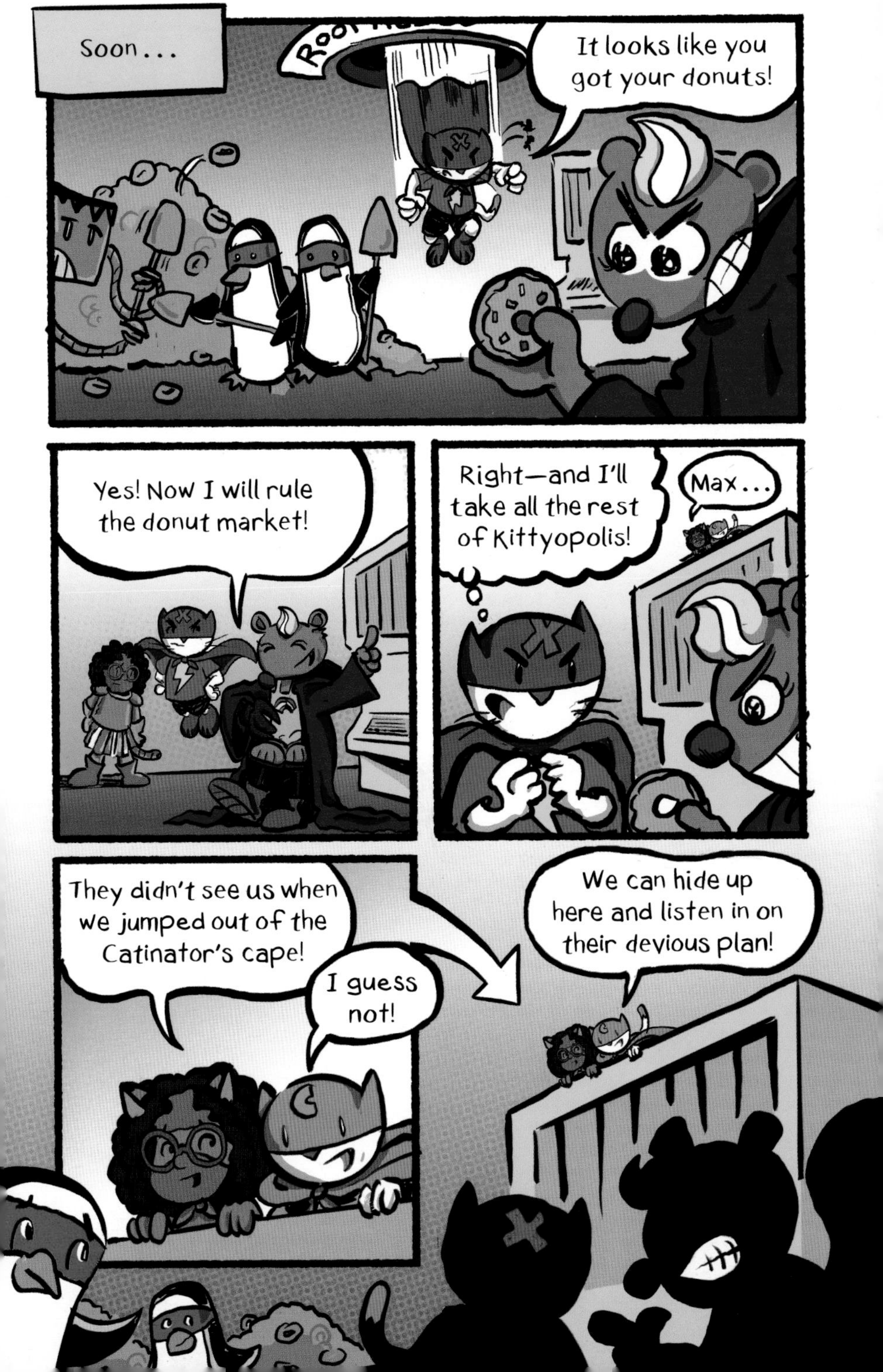
Soon . . .
It looks like you got your donuts!
Yes! Now I will rule the donut market!
Right—and I'll take all the rest of Kittyopolis!
Max . . .
They didn't see us when we jumped out of the Catinator's cape!
I guess not!
We can hide up here and listen in on their devious plan!

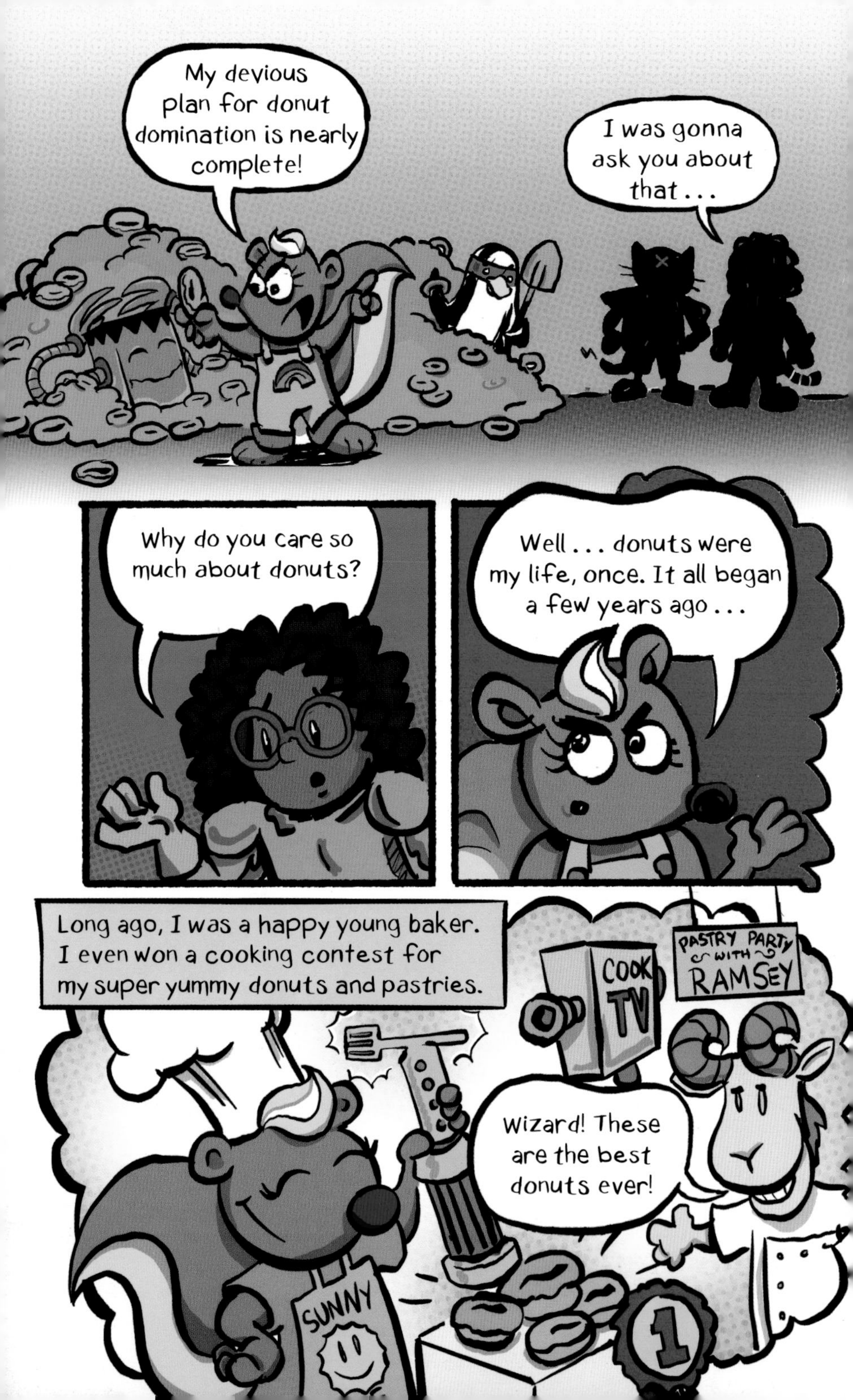
My devious plan for donut domination is nearly complete!
I was gonna ask you about that . . .
Why do you care so much about donuts?
Well . . . donuts were my life, once. It all began a few years ago . . .
Long ago, I was a happy young baker. I even won a cooking contest for my super yummy donuts and pastries.
COOK TV
PASTRY PARTY WITH RAMSEY
Wizard! These are the best donuts ever!
SUNNY
1

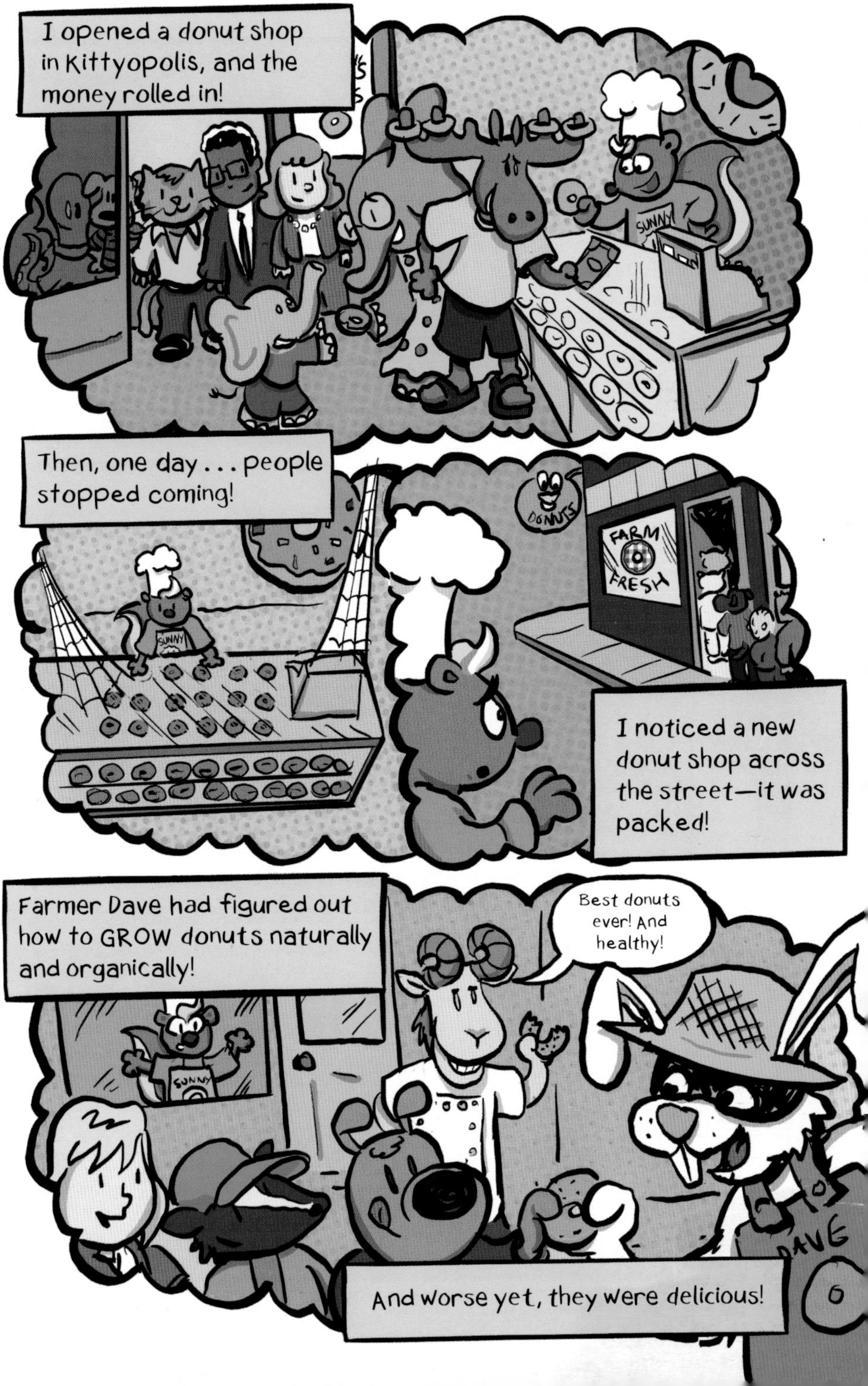
I opened a donut shop in Kittyopolis, and the money rolled in!
SUNNY
Then, one day . . . people stopped coming!
SUNNY
DONUTS
FARM FRESH
I noticed a new donut shop across the street—it was packed!
Farmer Dave had figured out how to GROW donuts naturally and organically!
Best donuts ever! And healthy!
SUNNY
DAVE
And worse yet, they were delicious!
6

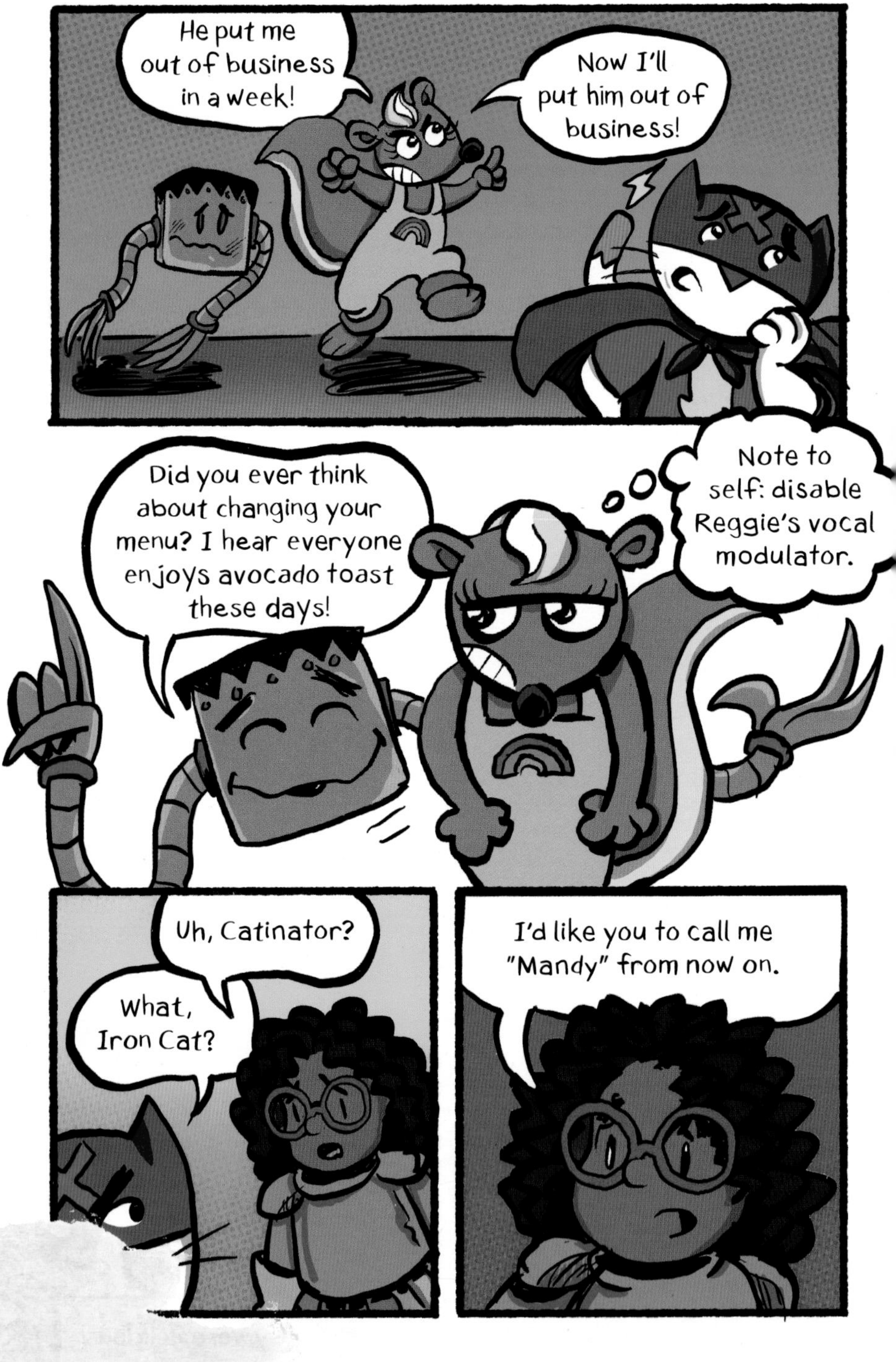
He put me out of business in a week!
Now I'll put him out of business!
Did you ever think about changing your menu? I hear everyone enjoys avocado toast these days!
Note to self: disable Reggie's vocal modulator.
Uh, Catinator?
What, Iron Cat?
I'd like you to call me "Mandy" from now on.

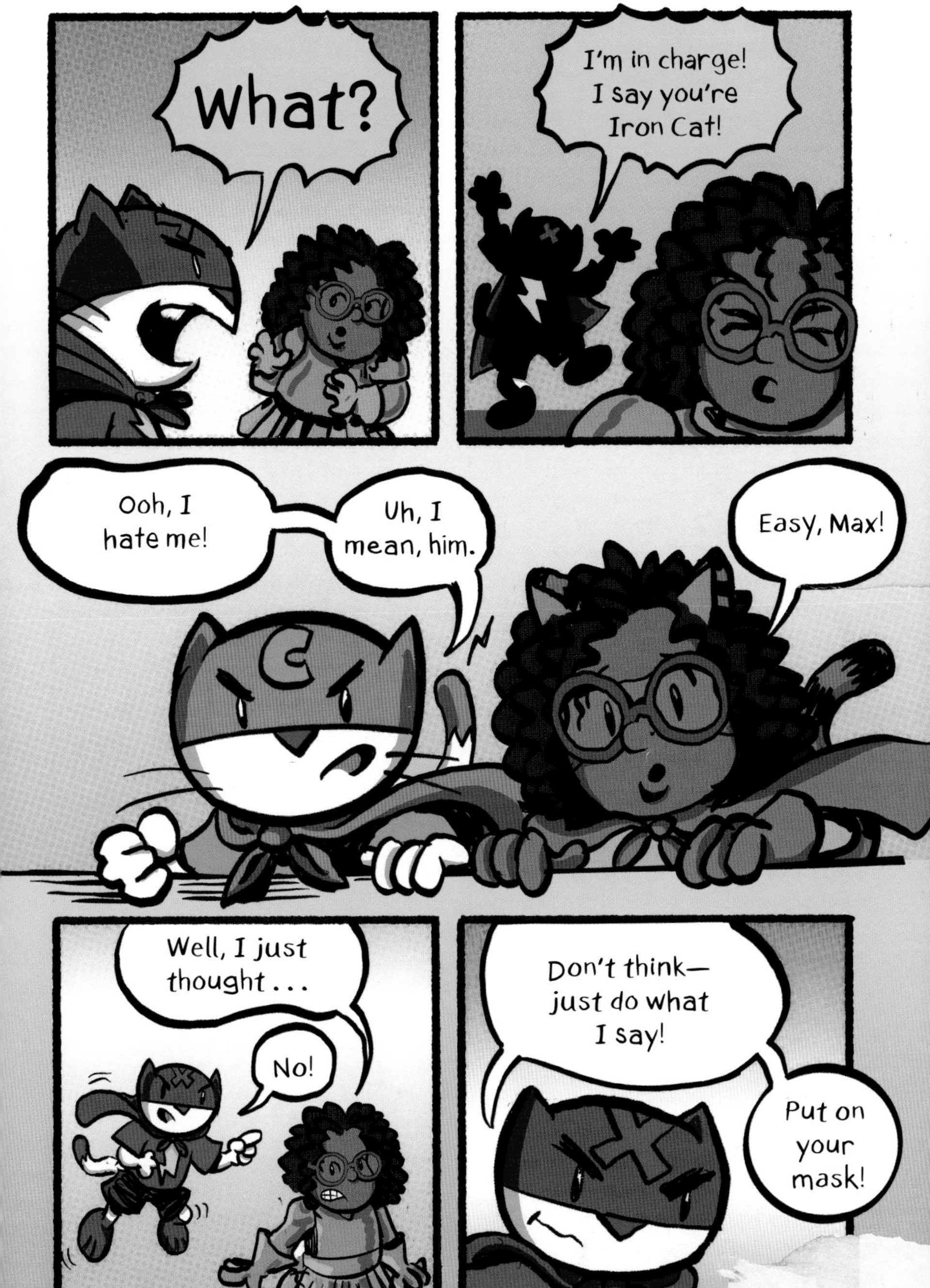
What?
I'm in charge! I say you're Iron Cat!
Ooh, I hate me!
Uh, I mean, him.
Easy, Max!
Well, I just thought . . .
No!
Don't think—just do what I say!
Put on your mask!

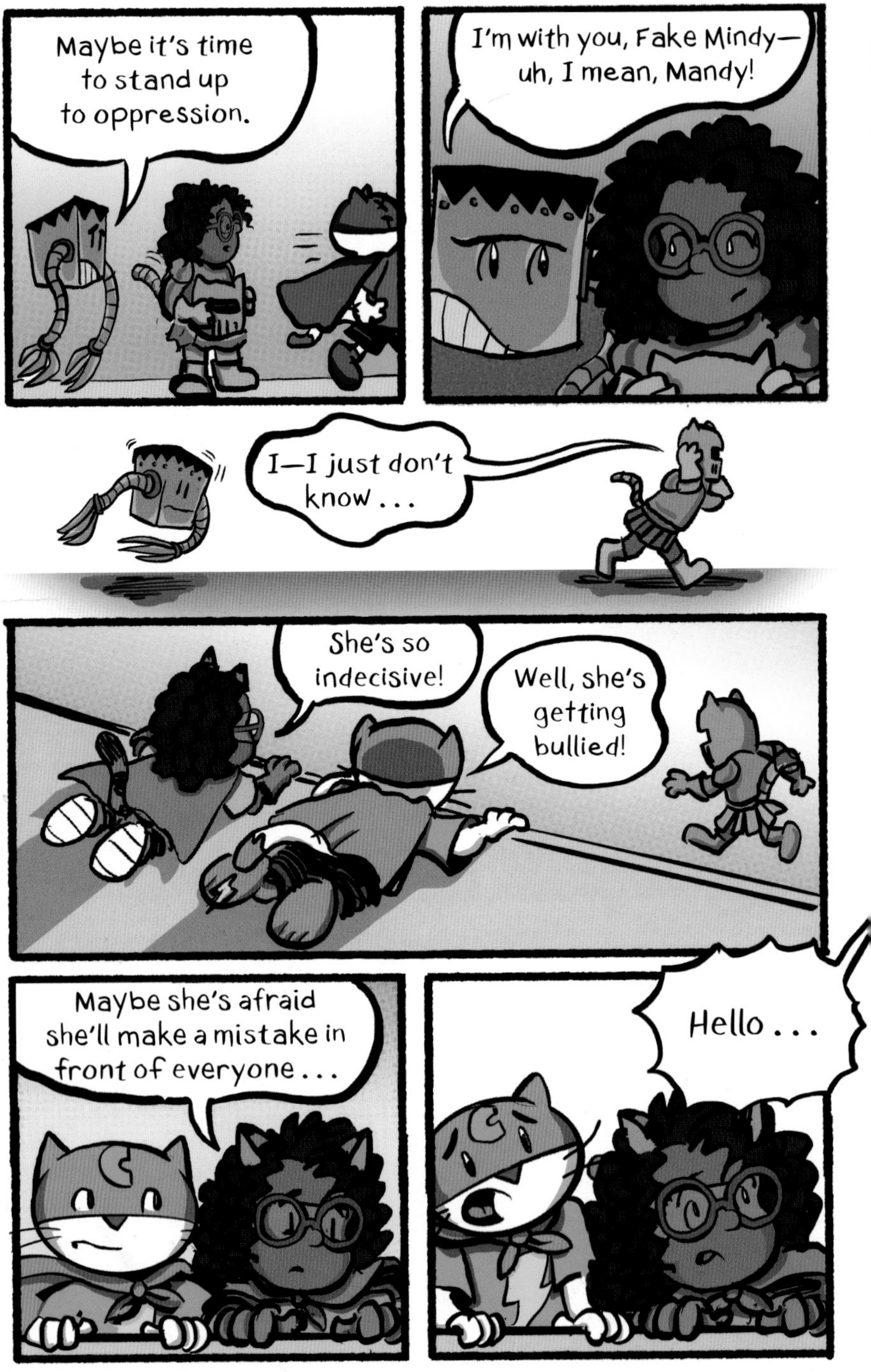
Maybe it's time to stand up to oppression.
I'm with you, Fake Mindy— uh, I mean, Mandy!
I—I just don't know . . .
She's so indecisive!
Well, she's getting bullied!
Maybe she's afraid she'll make a mistake in front of everyone . . .
Hello . . .

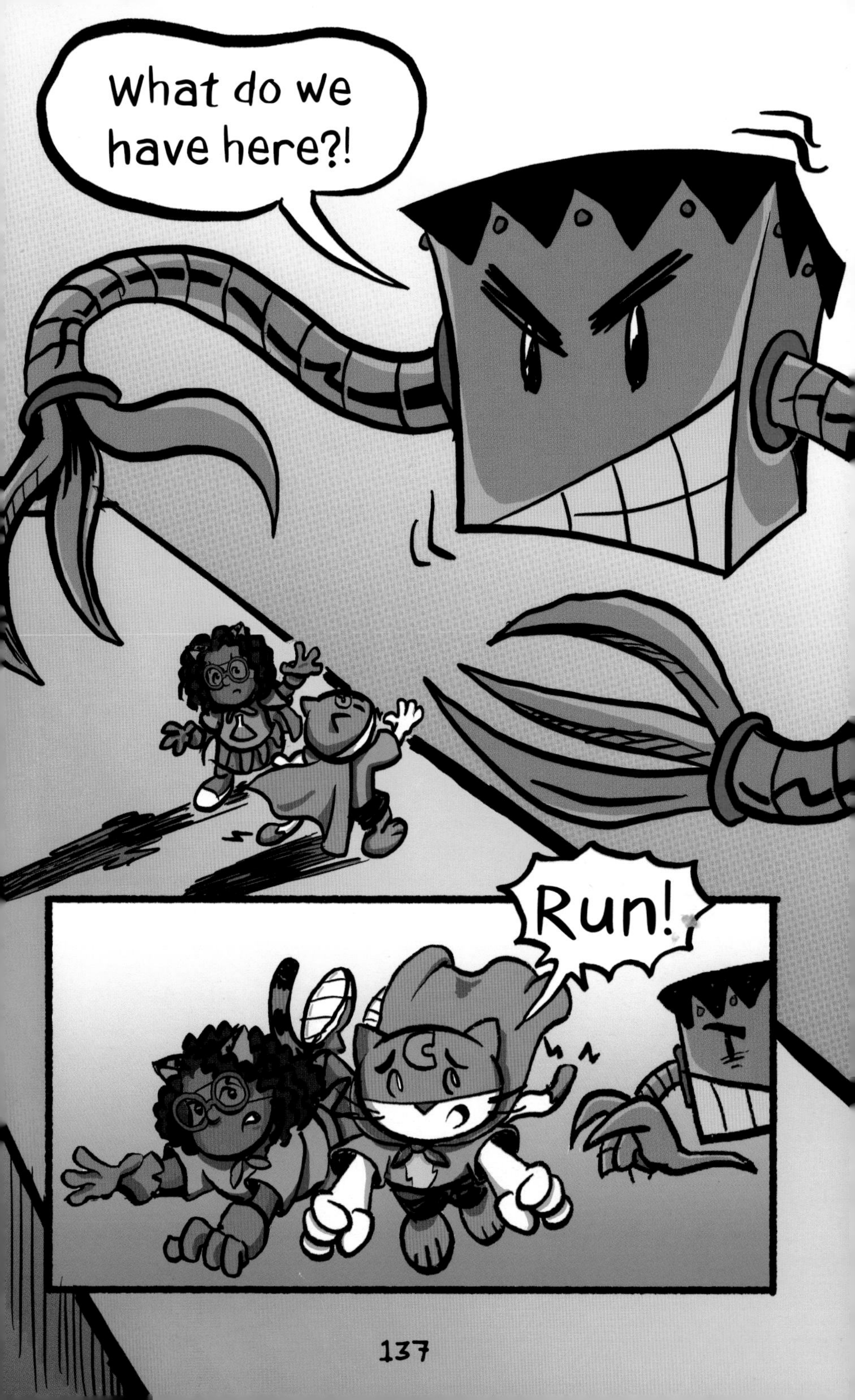
What do we have here?!
Run!

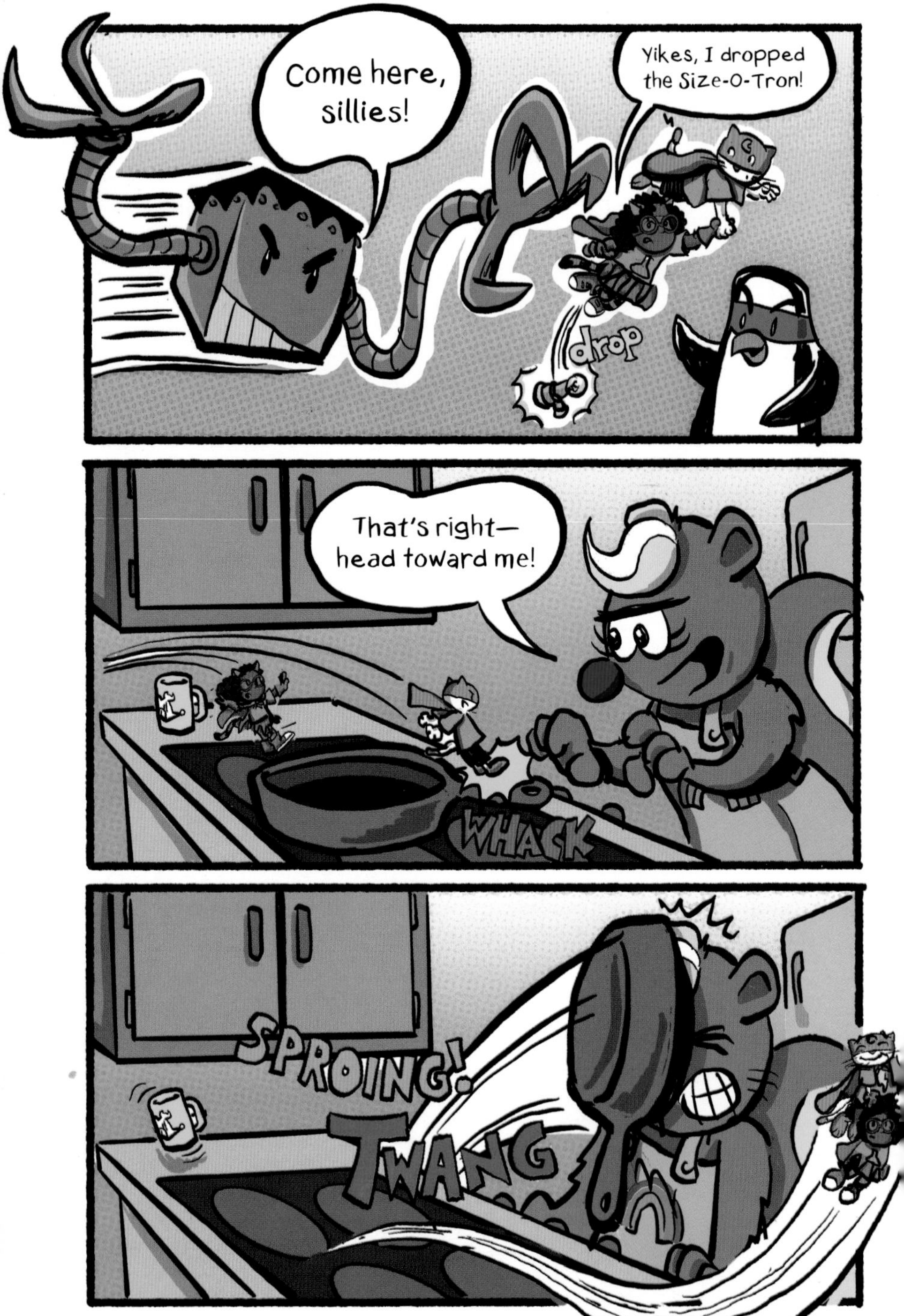
Come here, sillies!
Yikes, I dropped the Size-O-Tron!
drop
That's right—head toward me!
WHACK
SPROING!
TWANG

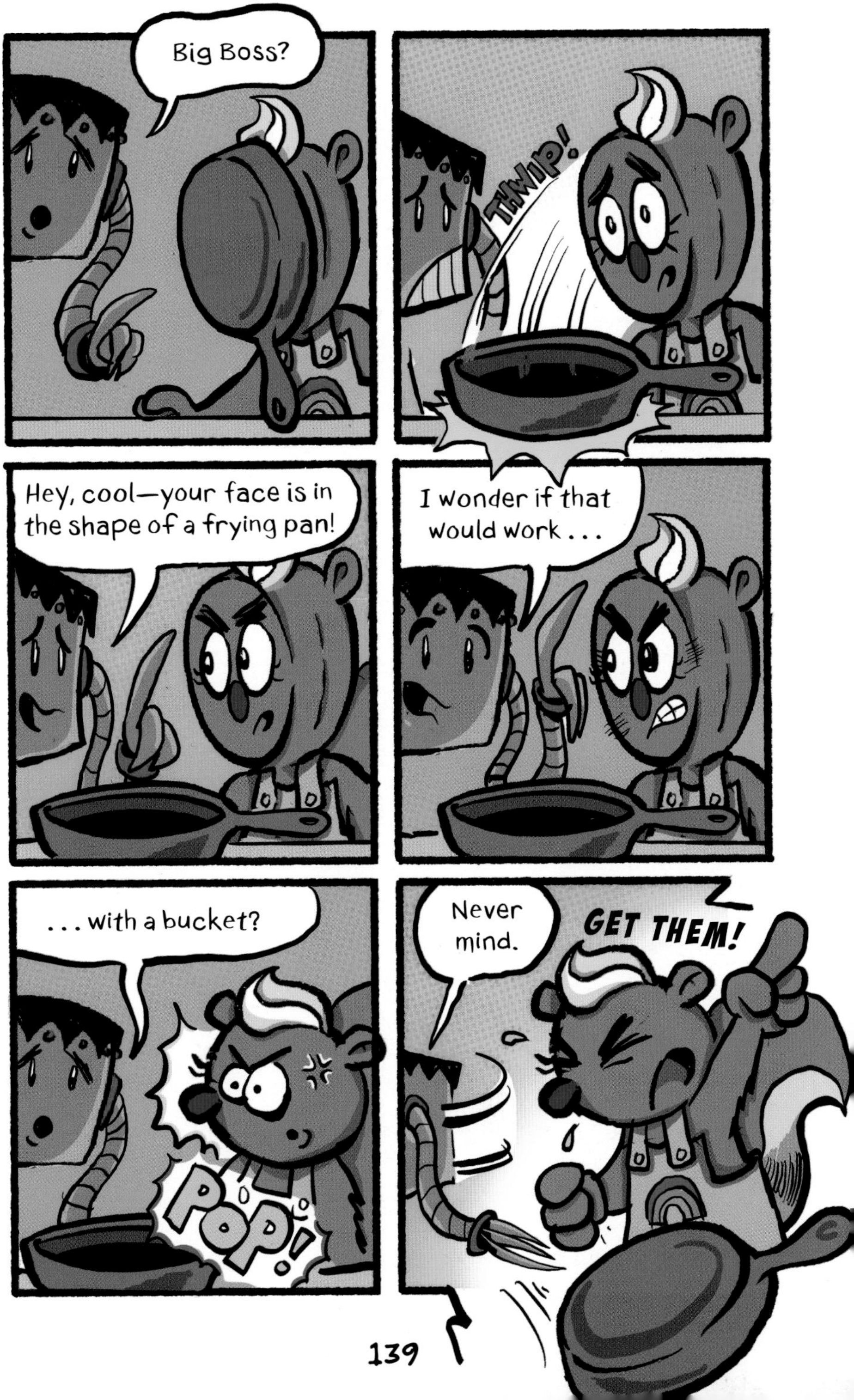
Big Boss?
THWIP!
Hey, cool—your face is in the shape of a frying pan!
I wonder if that would work . . .
. . . with a bucket?
POP!
Never mind.
GET THEM!

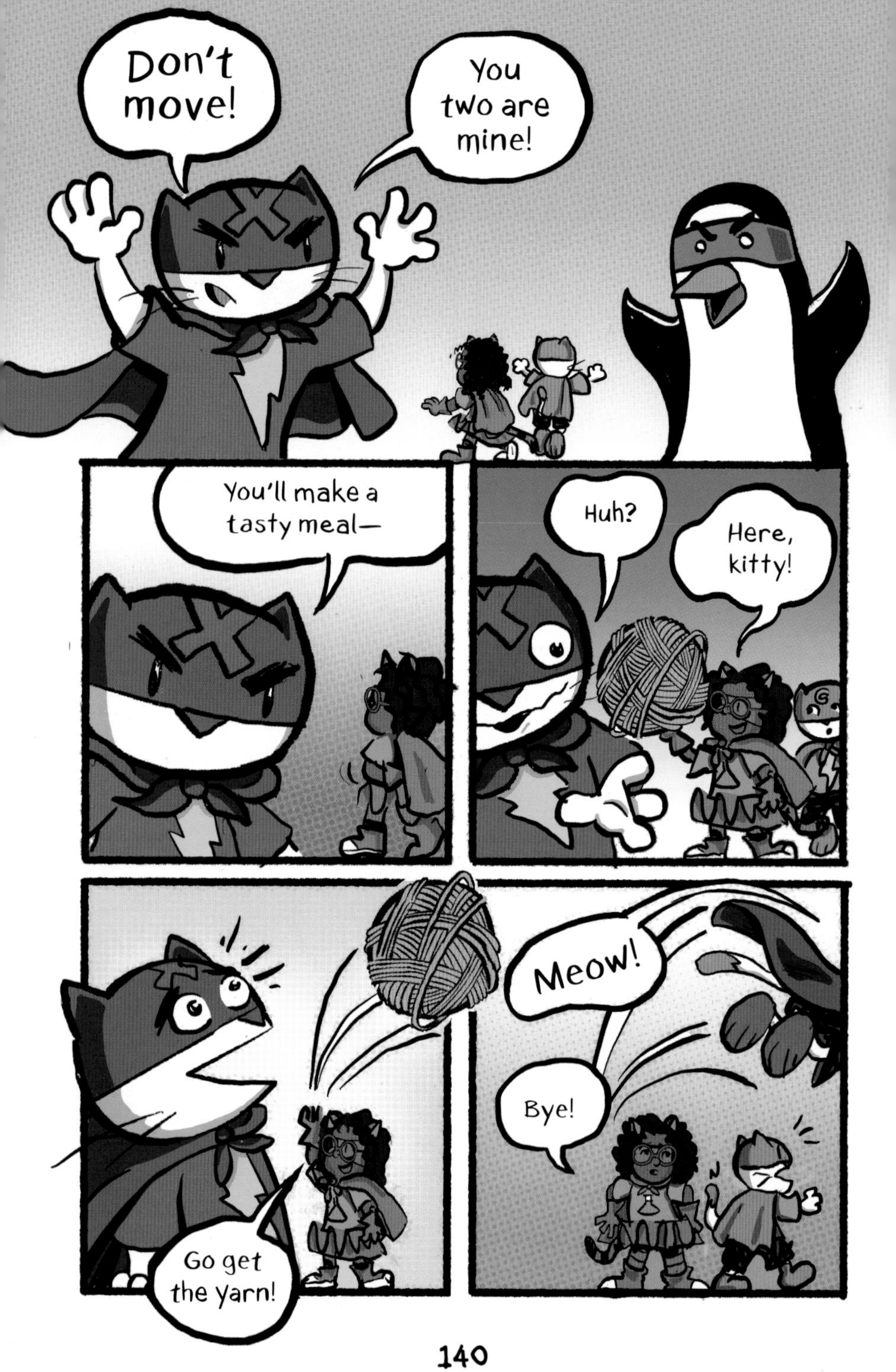

Don't move!
You two are mine!
You'll make a tasty meal—
Huh?
Here, kitty!
Go get the yarn!
Meow!
Bye!

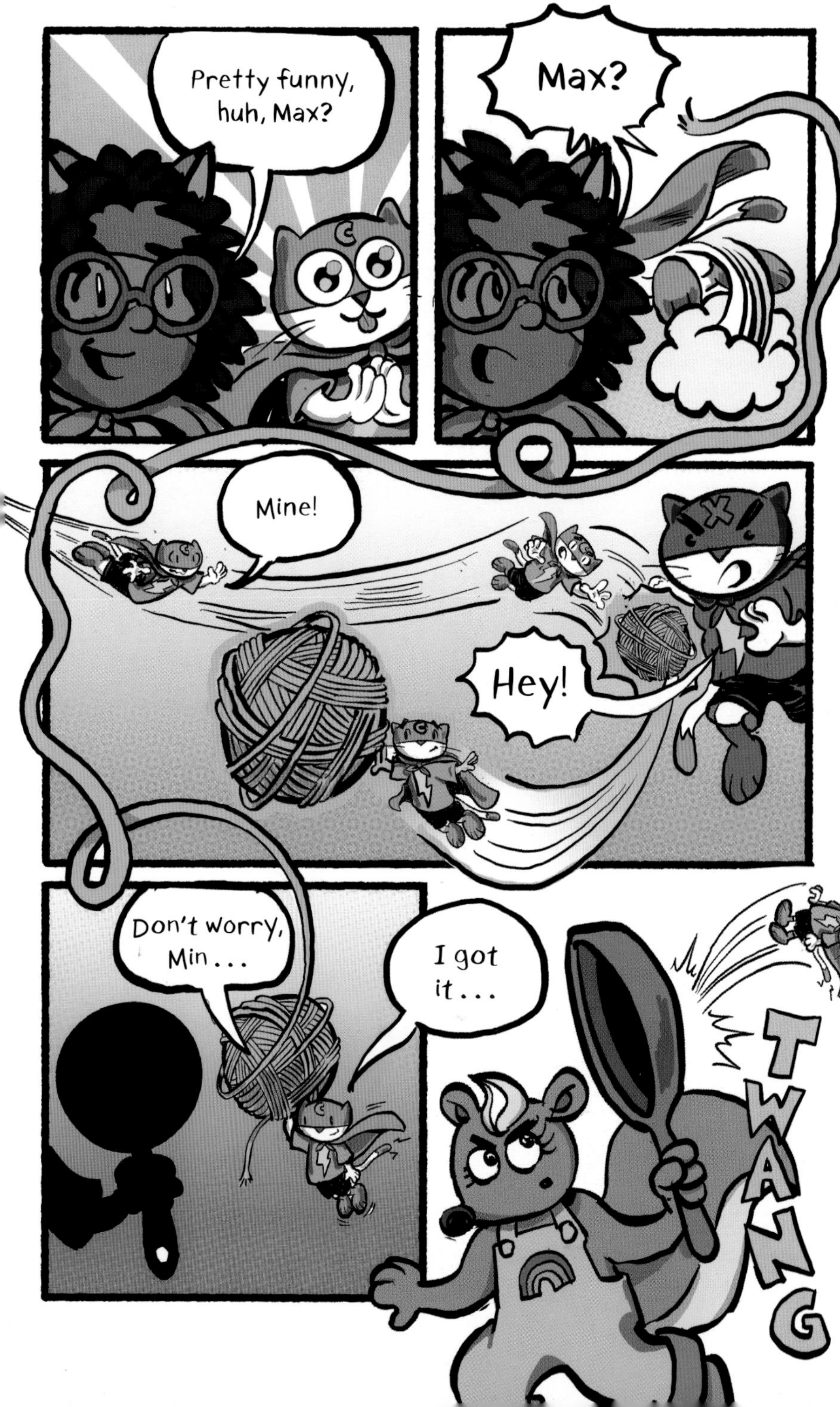
Pretty funny, huh, Max?
Max?
Mine!
Hey!
Don't worry, Min . . .
I got it . . .
TWANG

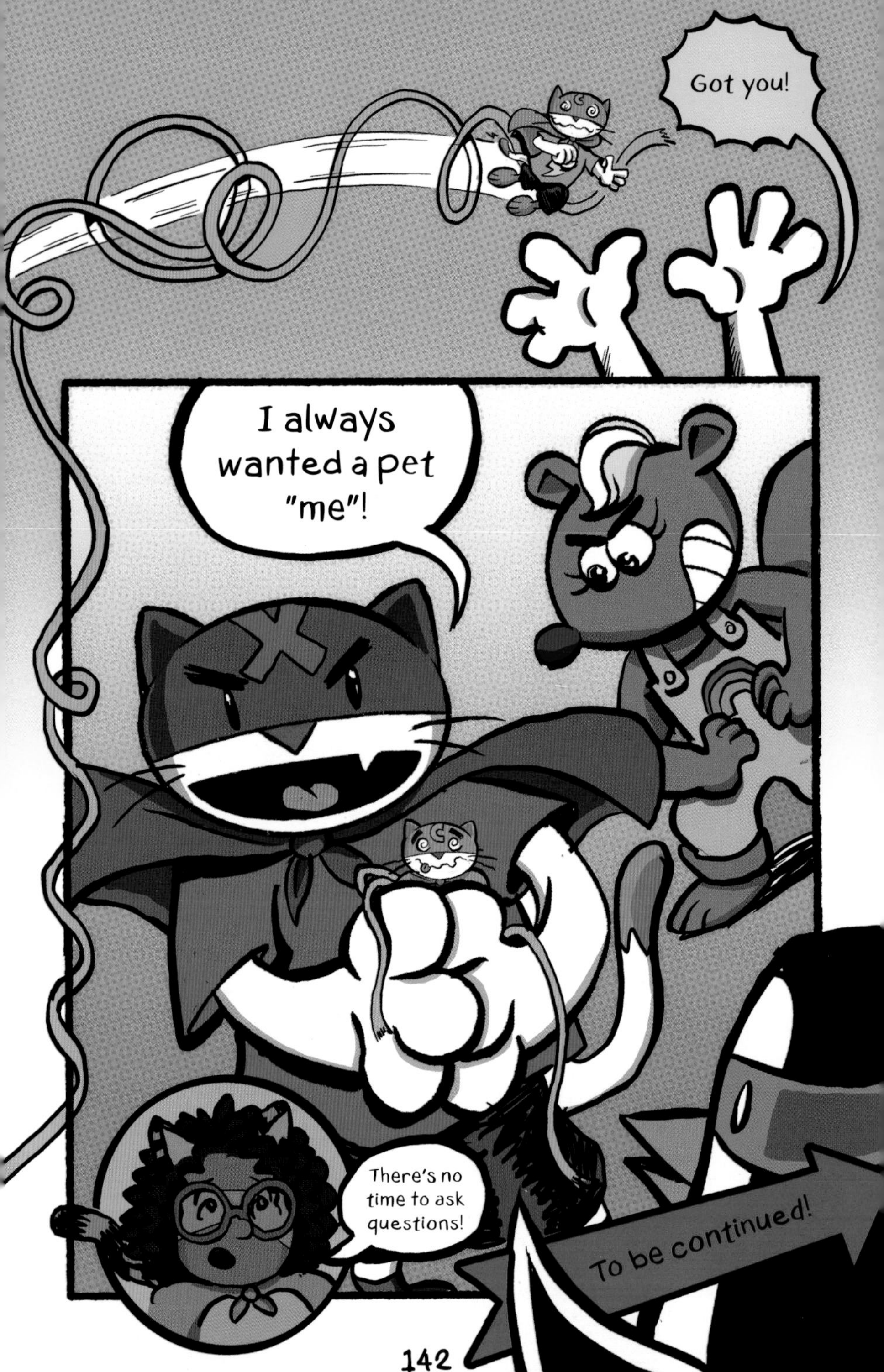
Got you!
I always wanted a pet "me"!
There's no time to ask questions!
To be continued!

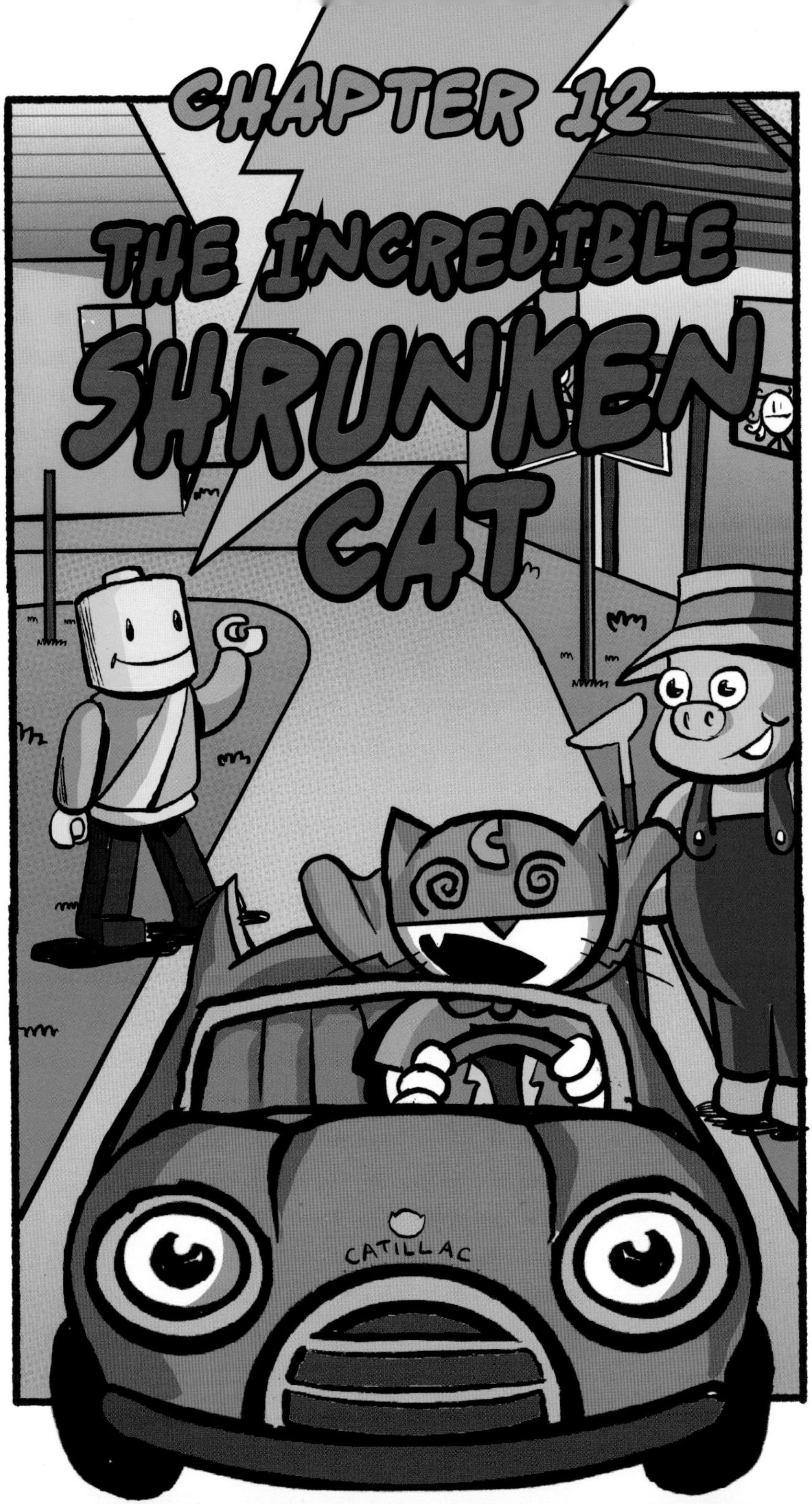
CHAPTER 12
THE INCREDIBLE SHRUNKEN CAT
CATILLAC

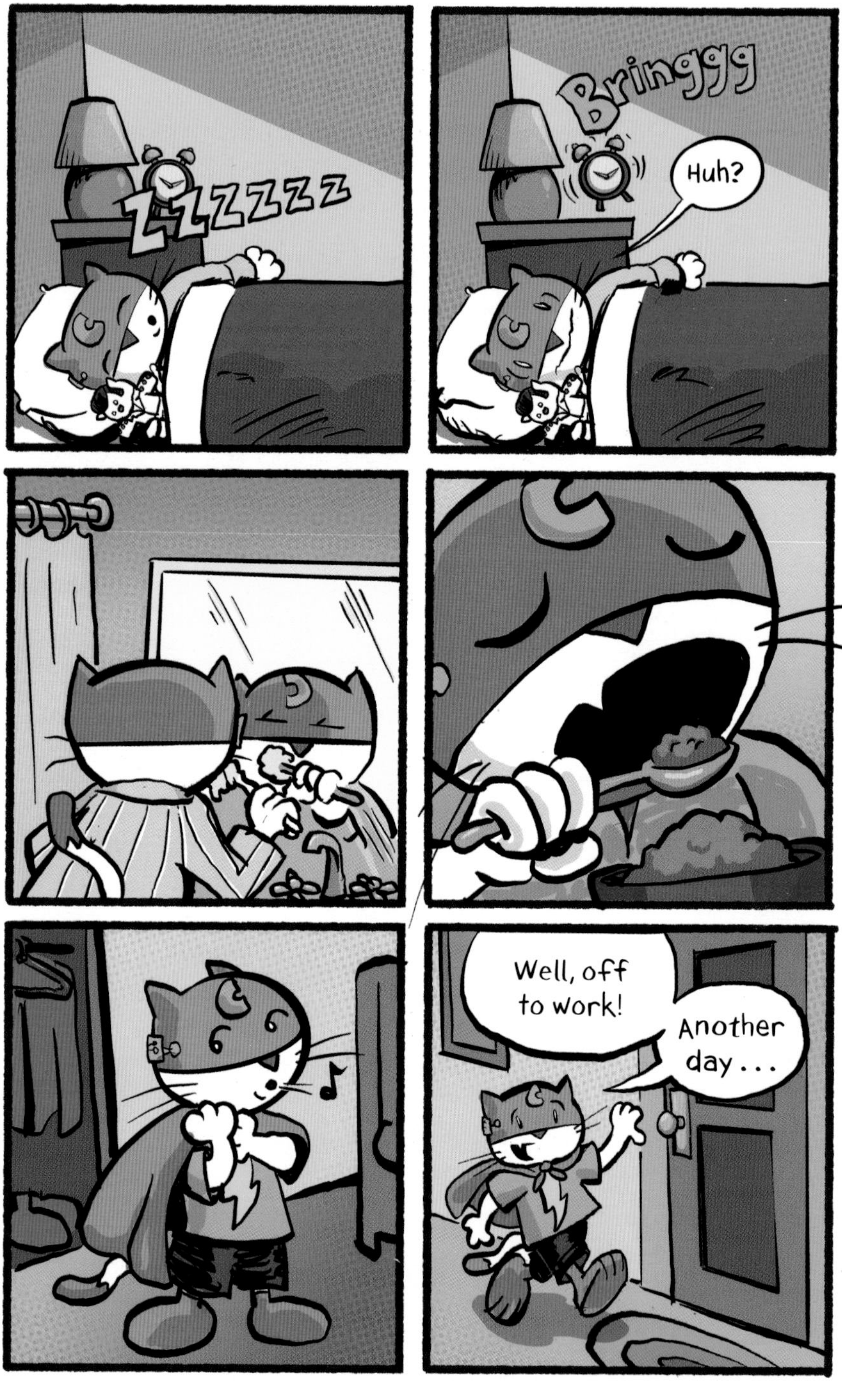
ZZZZZZZ
Bringgg
Huh?
Well, off to work!
Another day . . .

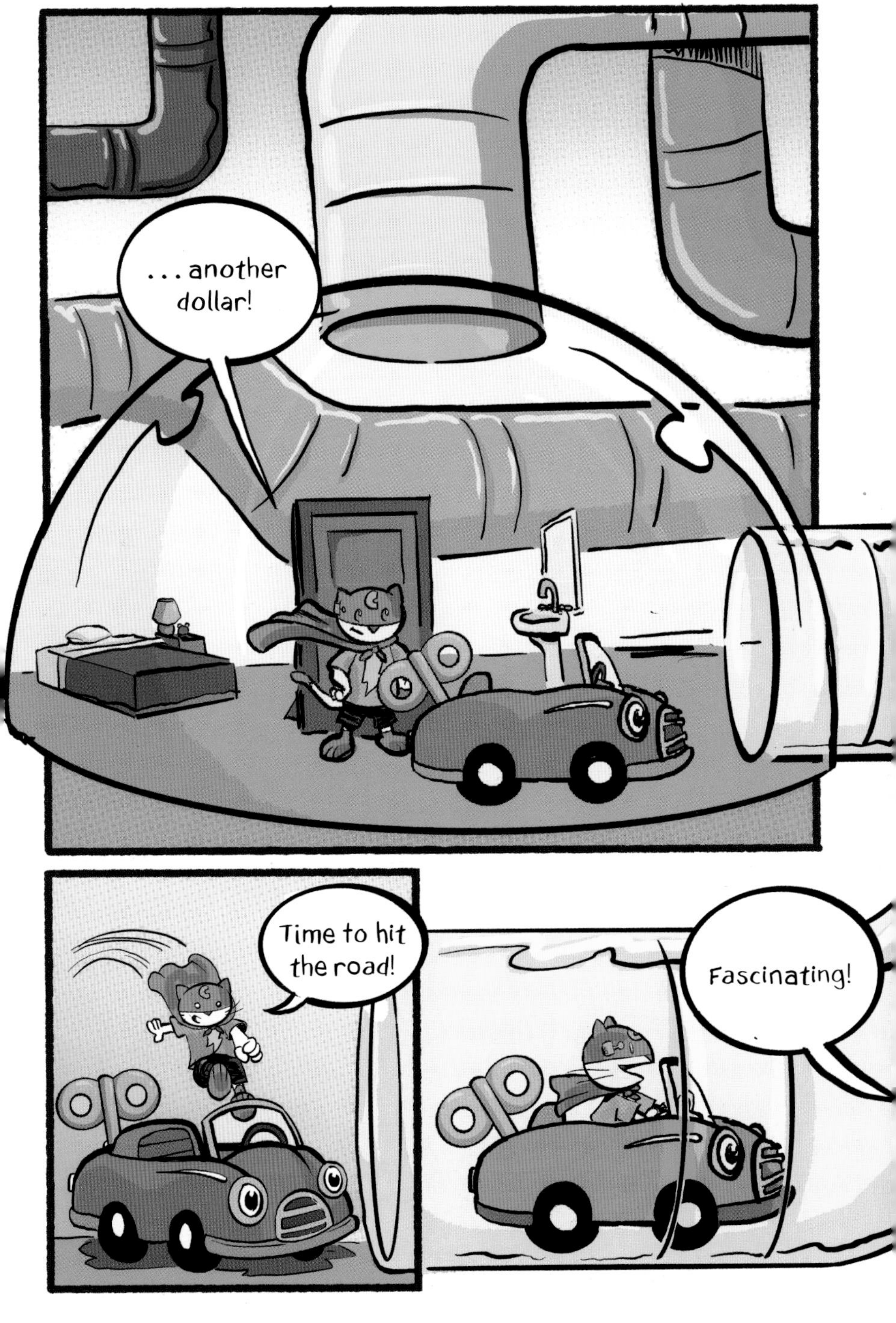
...another dollar!
Time to hit the road!
Fascinating!

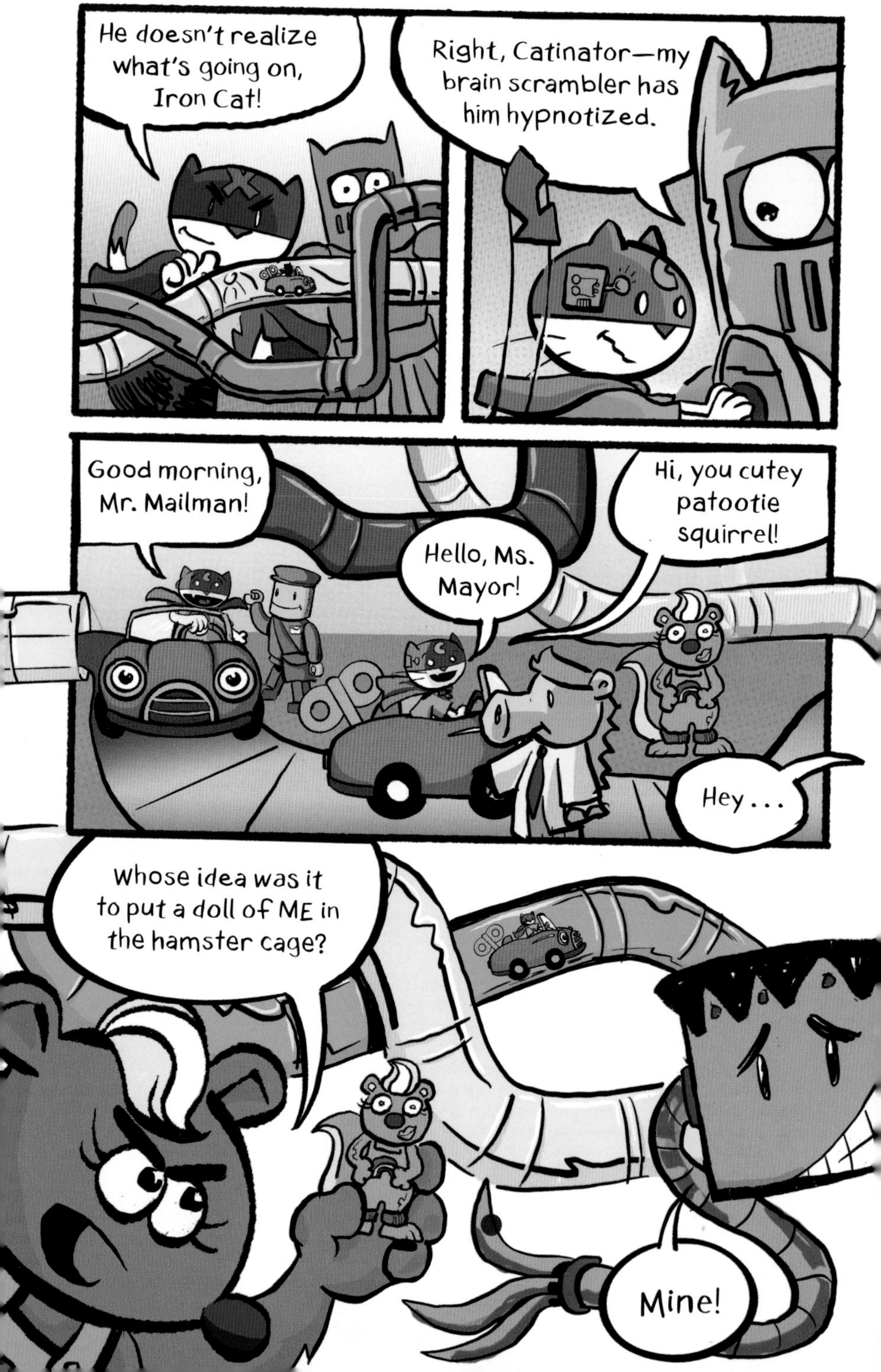
He doesn't realize what's going on, Iron Cat!
Right, Catinator—my brain scrambler has him hypnotized.
Good morning, Mr. Mailman!
Hello, Ms. Mayor!
Hi, you cutey patootie squirrel!
Hey . . .
Whose idea was it to put a doll of ME in the hamster cage?
Mine!

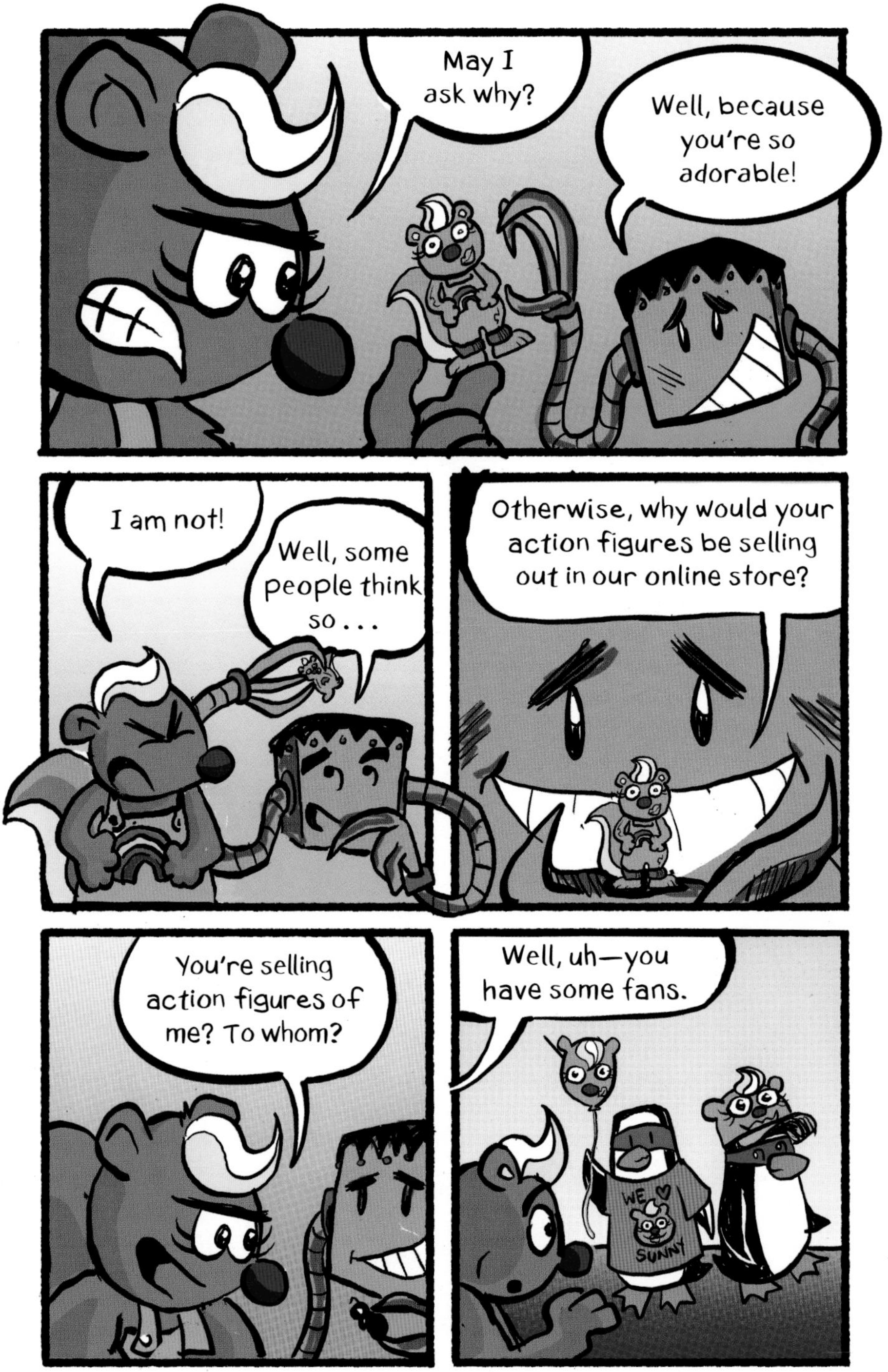
May I ask why?
Well, because you're so adorable!
I am not!
Well, some people think so . . .
Otherwise, why would your action figures be selling out in our online store?
You're selling action figures of me? To whom?
Well, uh—you have some fans.
WE ♥ SUNNY

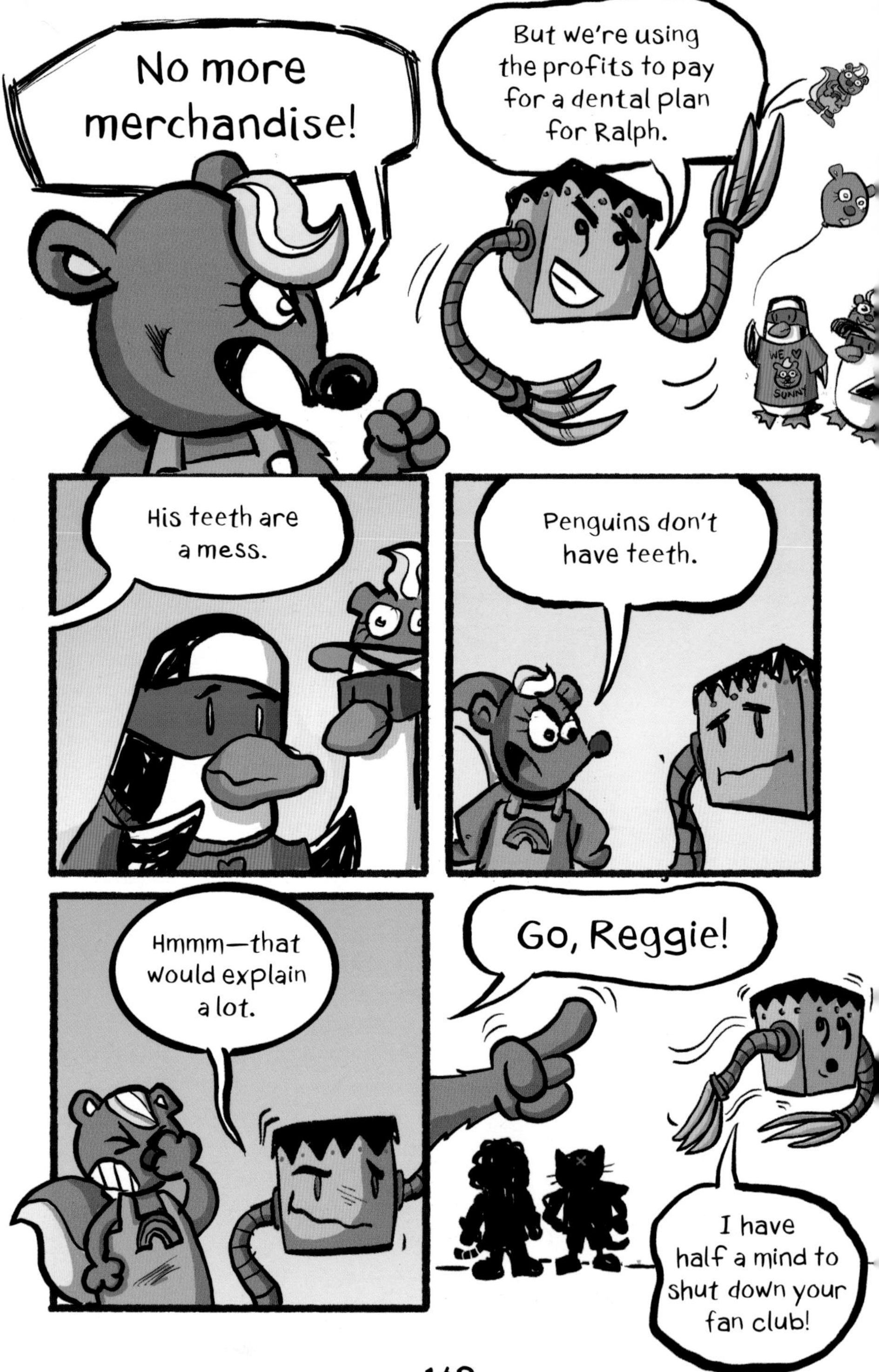
No more merchandise!
But we're using the profits to pay for a dental plan for Ralph.
WE ♥ SUNNY
His teeth are a mess.
Penguins don't have teeth.
Hmmm—that would explain a lot.
Go, Reggie!
I have half a mind to shut down your fan club!

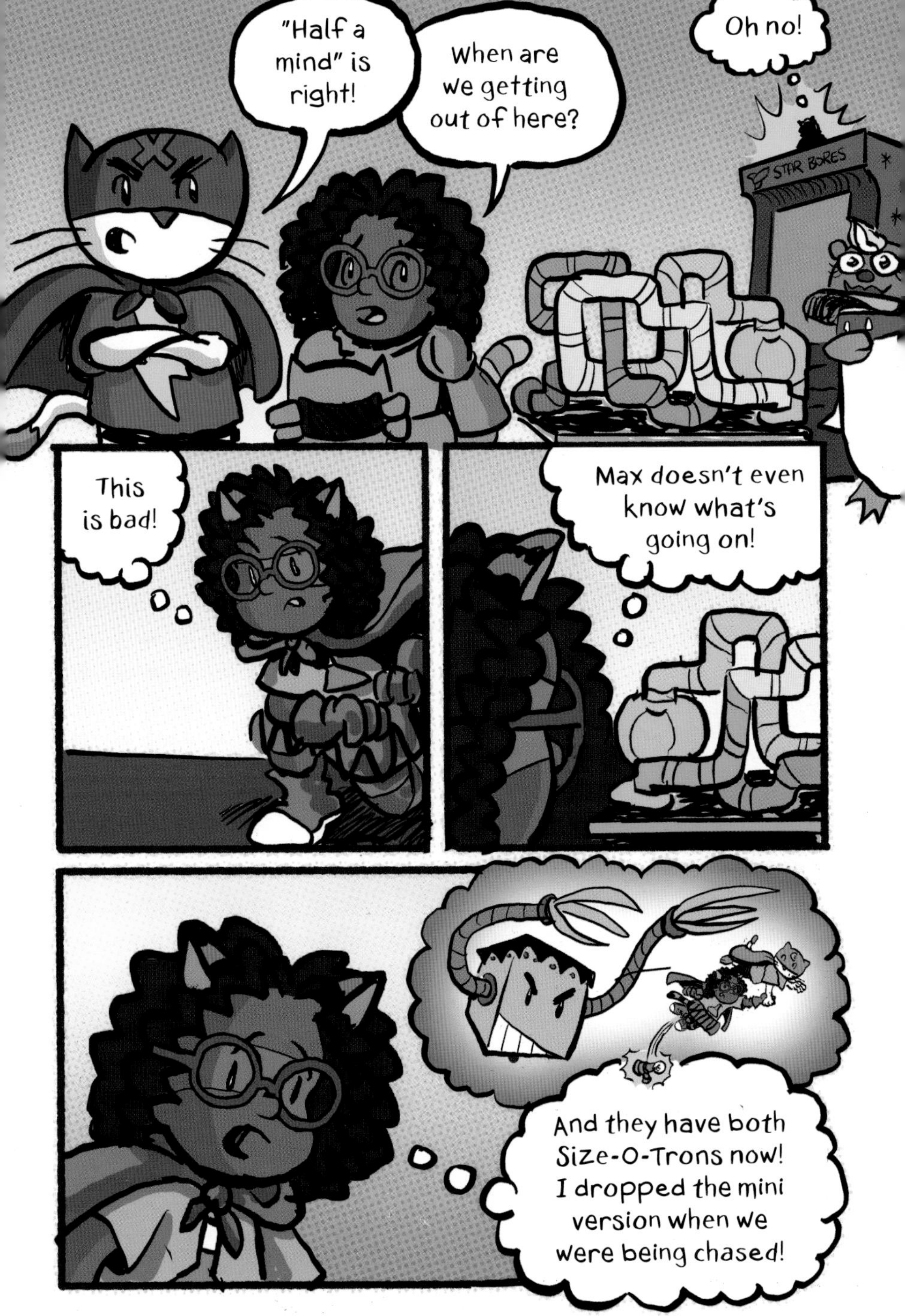
"Half a mind" is right!
When are we getting out of here?
Oh no!
STAR BORES
This is bad!
Max doesn't even know what's going on!
And they have both Size-O-Trons now! I dropped the mini version when we were being chased!

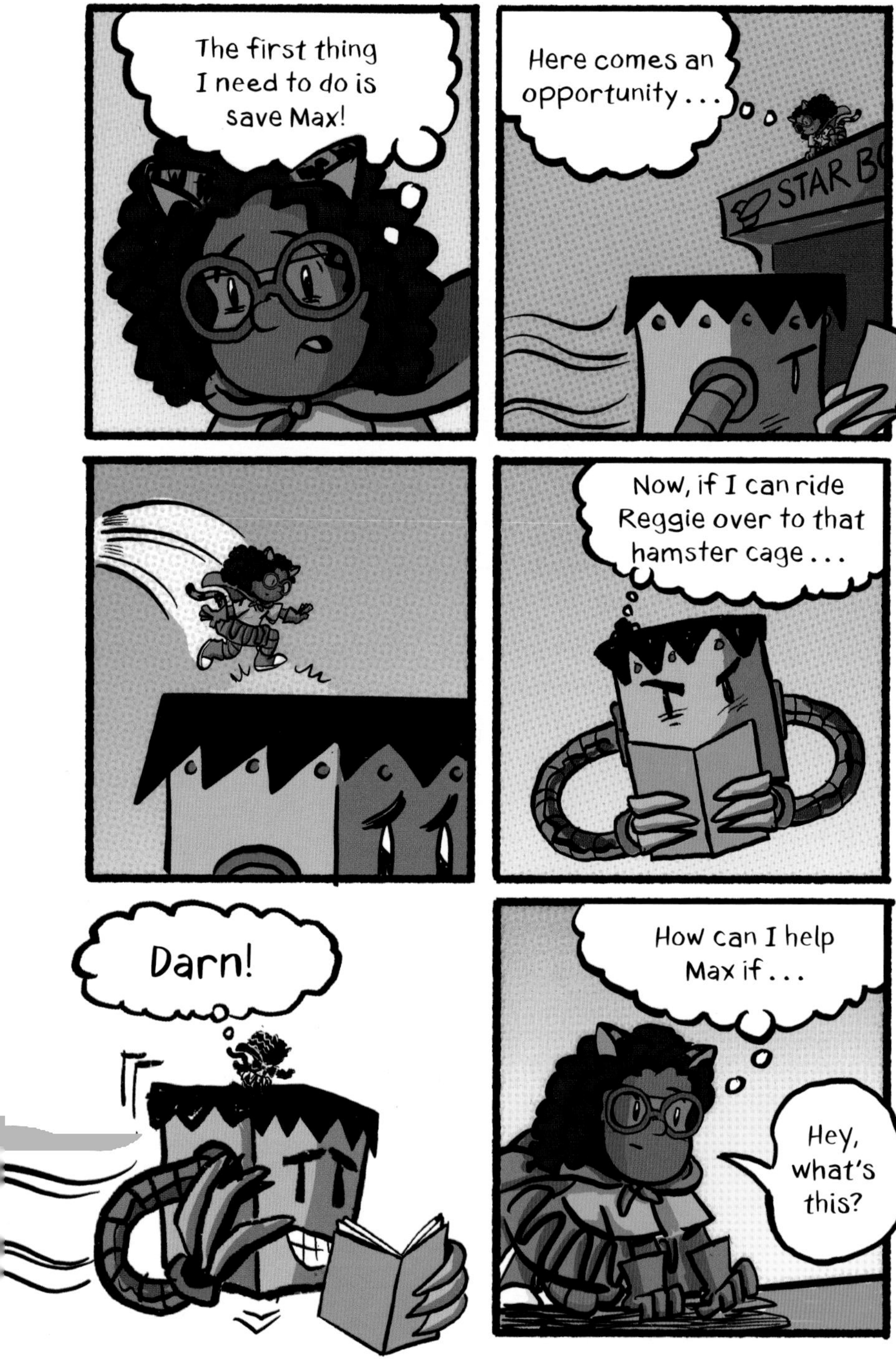
The first thing I need to do is save Max!
Here comes an opportunity . . .
STAR BO
Now, if I can ride Reggie over to that hamster cage . . .
Darn!
How can I help Max if . . .
Hey, what's this?

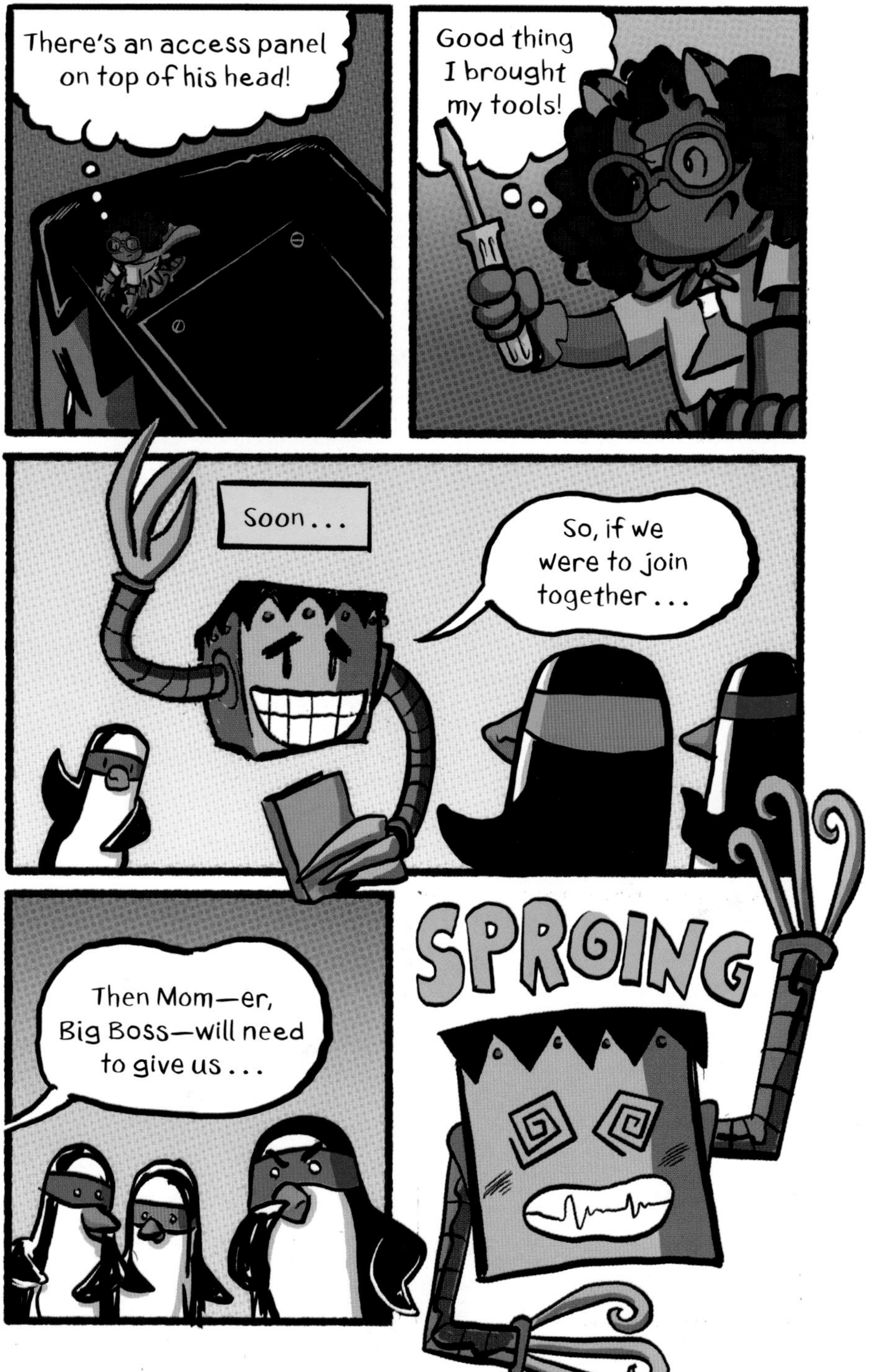
There's an access panel on top of his head!
Good thing I brought my tools!
Soon . . .
So, if we were to join together . . .
Then Mom—er, Big Boss—will need to give us . . .
SPROING

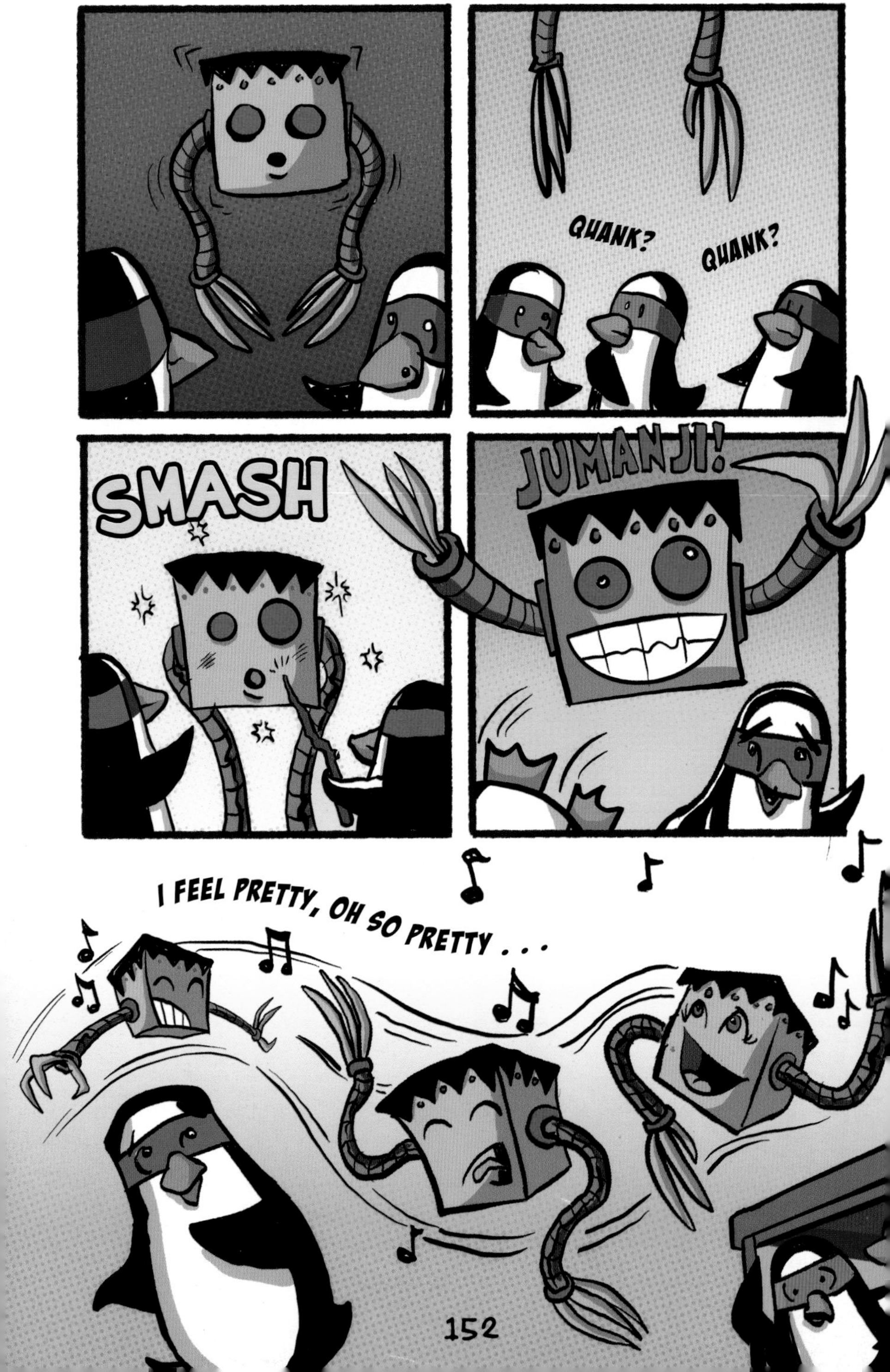
QUANK?
QUANK?
SMASH
JUMANJI!
I FEEL PRETTY, OH SO PRETTY . . .

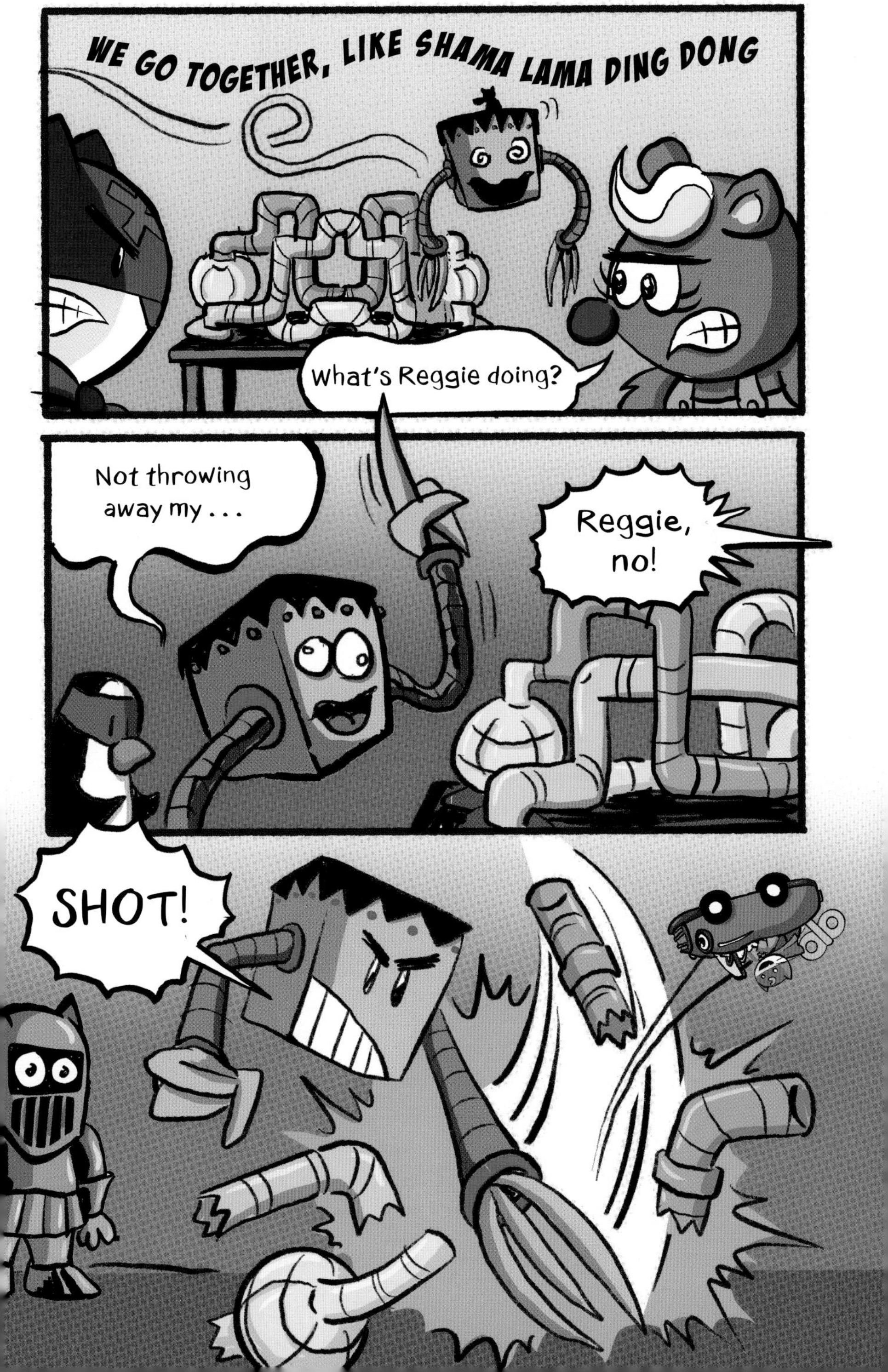
WE GO TOGETHER, LIKE SHAMA LAMA DING DONG
What's Reggie doing?
Not throwing away my . . .
Reggie, no!
SHOT!

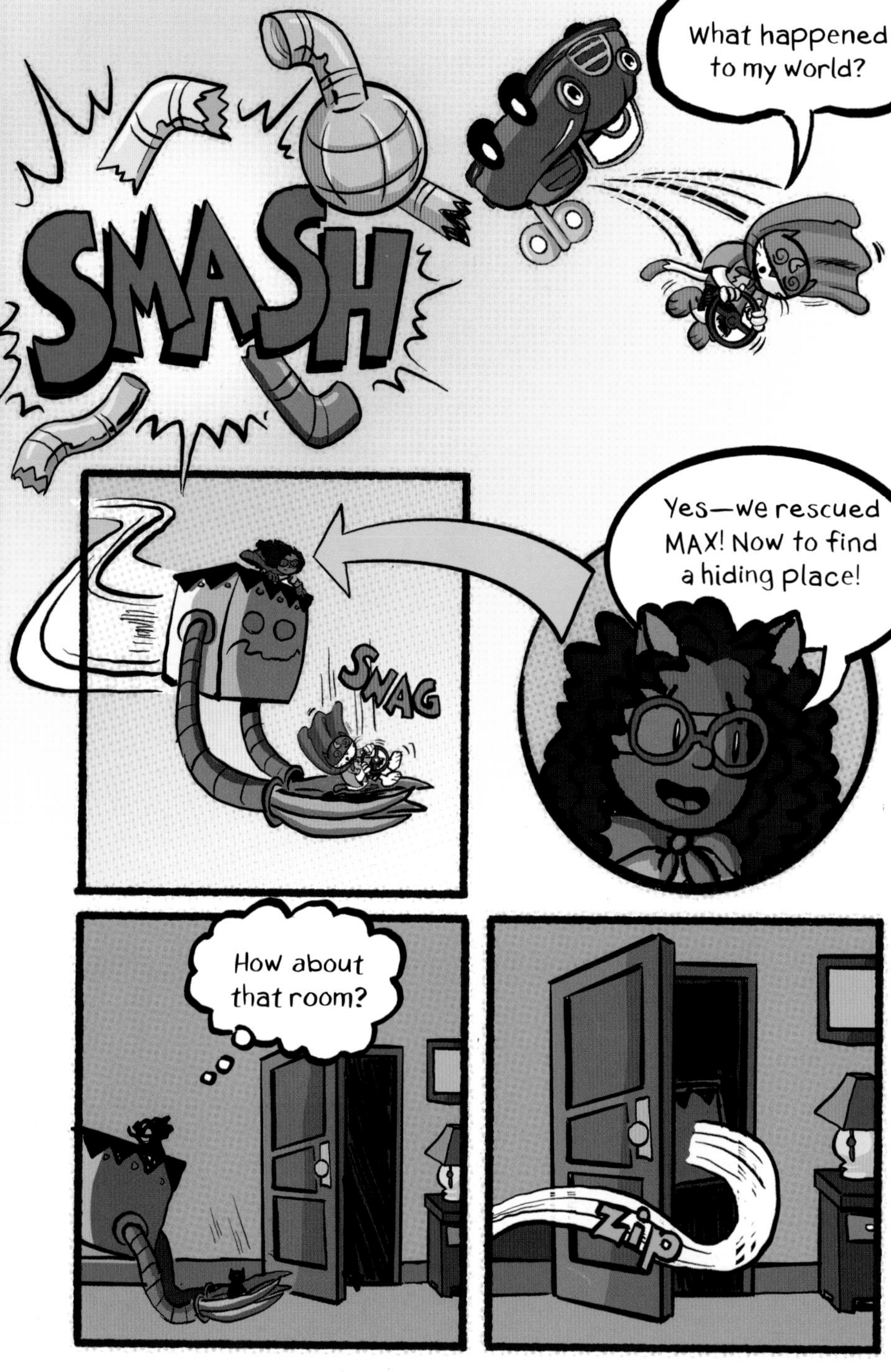
SMASH
What happened to my world?
Yes—we rescued MAX! Now to find a hiding place!
SNAG
How about that room?
Zip

The robot went in there!

They hid in my office?

Uh, hi! What happened?

Someone was controlling you!

I remember show tunes!

Hidden away, in the Catinator's office...

Max, wake up! Are you okay?

Okally dokally...

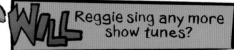

WILL Max be okay?

WILL Mindy and Max stay small forever?

WILL Reggie sing any more show tunes?

WHEN will any of these questions be answered?

155 Find out in the next chapter!

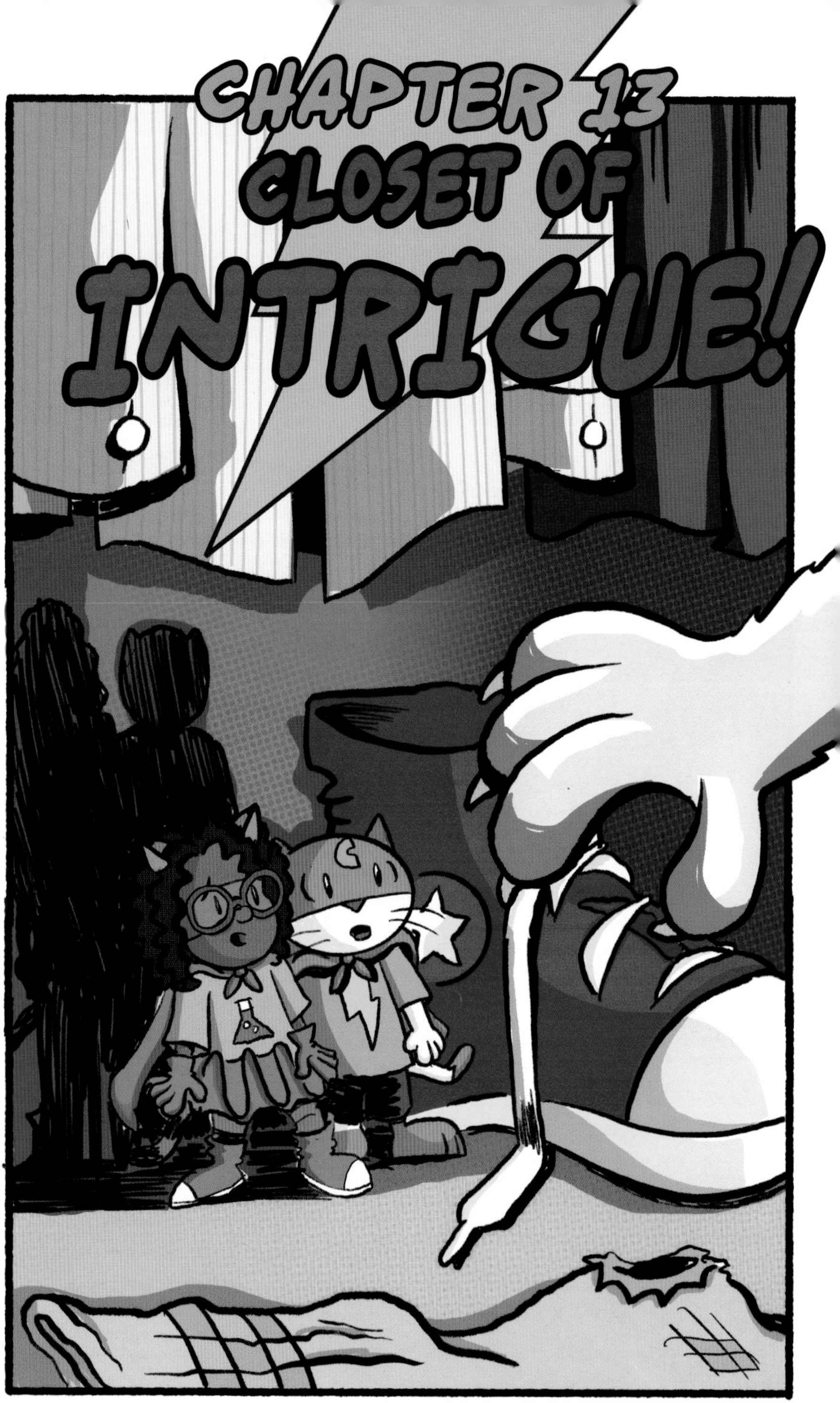
CHAPTER 13
CLOSET OF
INTRIGUE!

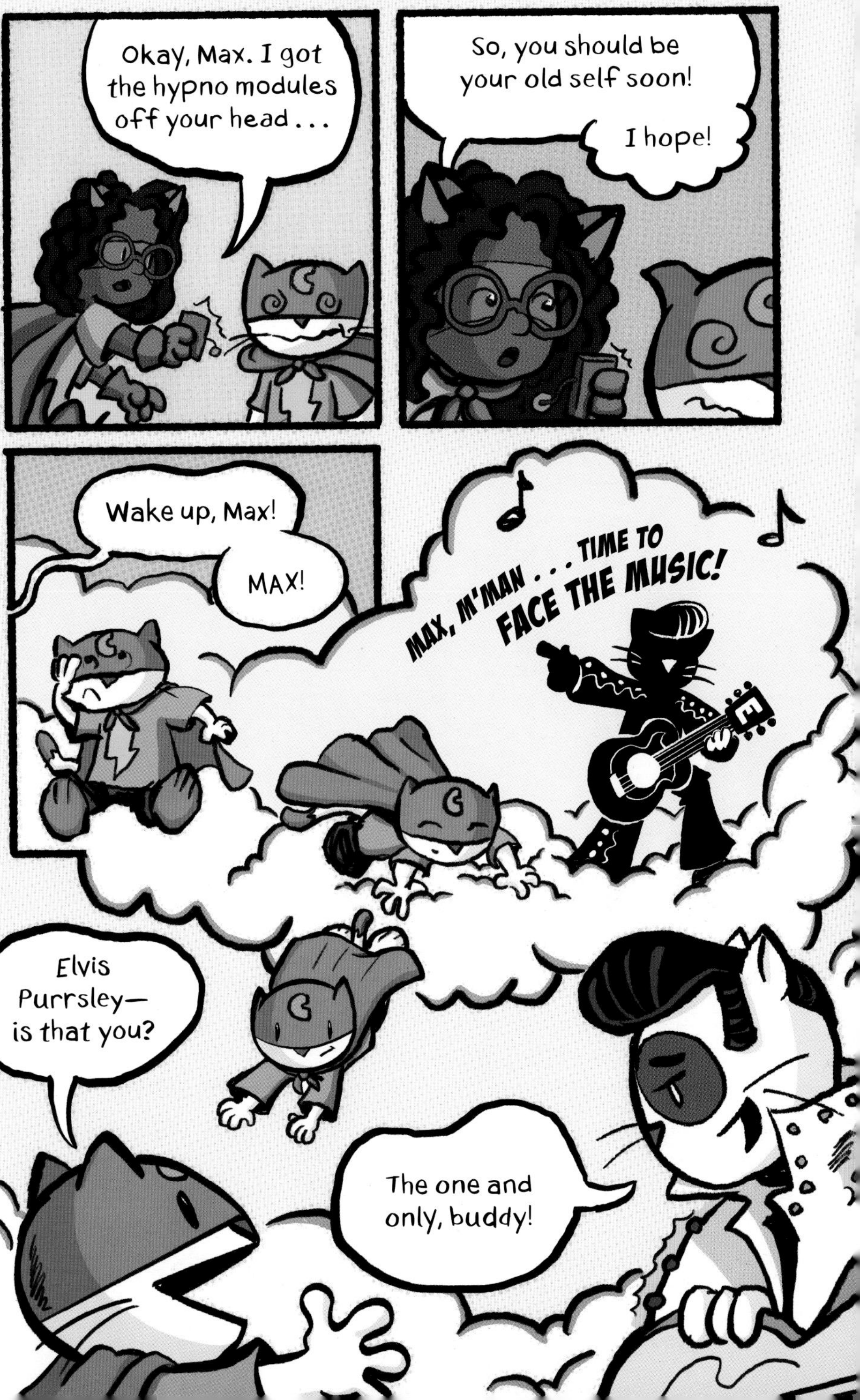
Okay, Max. I got the hypno modules off your head . . .
So, you should be your old self soon!
I hope!
Wake up, Max!
MAX!
MAX, M'MAN . . . TIME TO FACE THE MUSIC!
Elvis Purrsley— is that you?
The one and only, buddy!

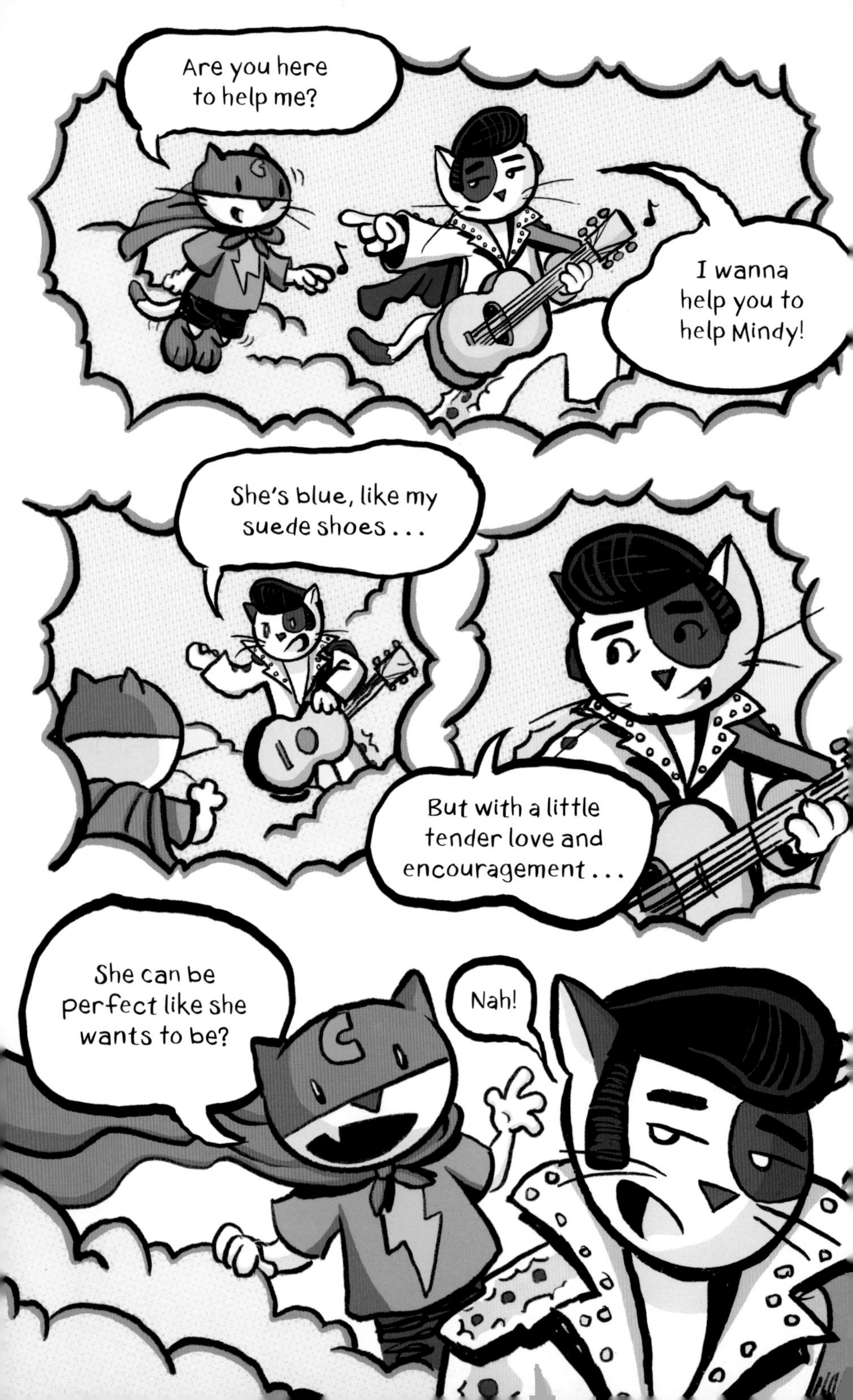
Are you here to help me?
I wanna help you to help Mindy!
She's blue, like my suede shoes . . .
But with a little tender love and encouragement . . .
She can be perfect like she wants to be?
Nah!

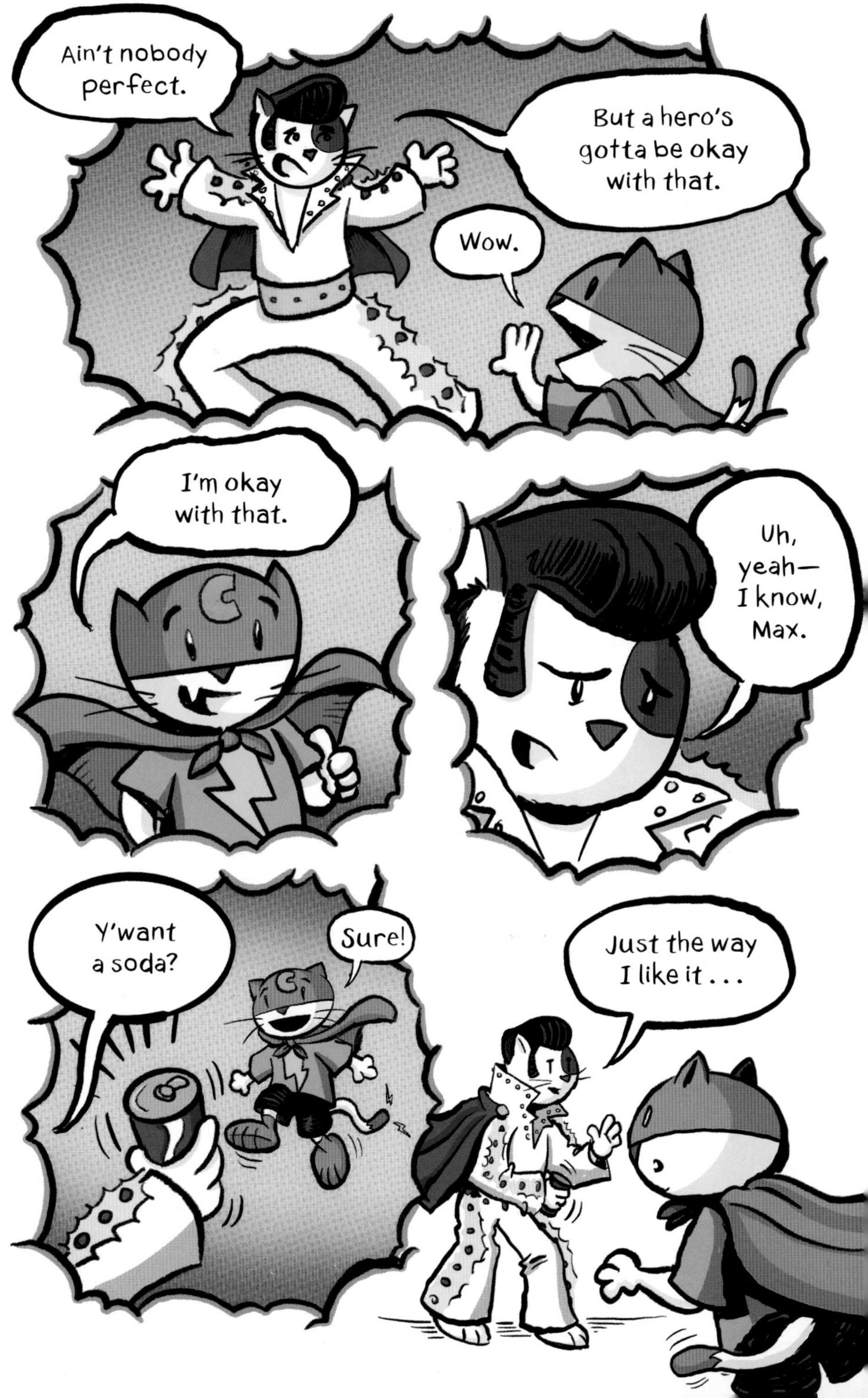
Ain't nobody perfect.
But a hero's gotta be okay with that.
Wow.
I'm okay with that.
Uh, yeah— I know, Max.
Y'want a soda?
Sure!
Just the way I like it . . .

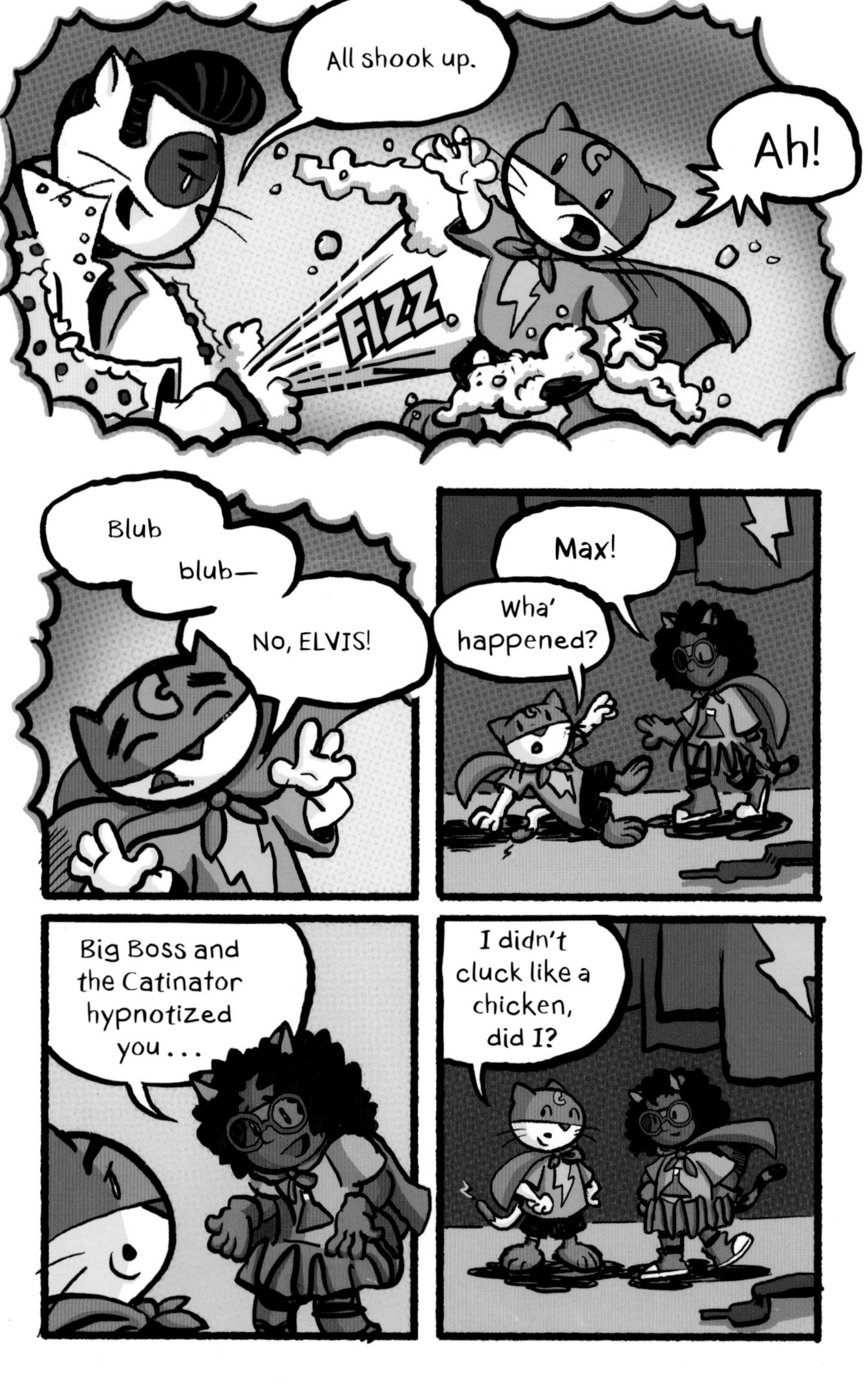
All shook up.
Ah!
FIZZ
Blub blub—
No, ELVIS!
Max!
Wha' happened?
Big Boss and the Catinator hypnotized you . . .
I didn't cluck like a chicken, did I?

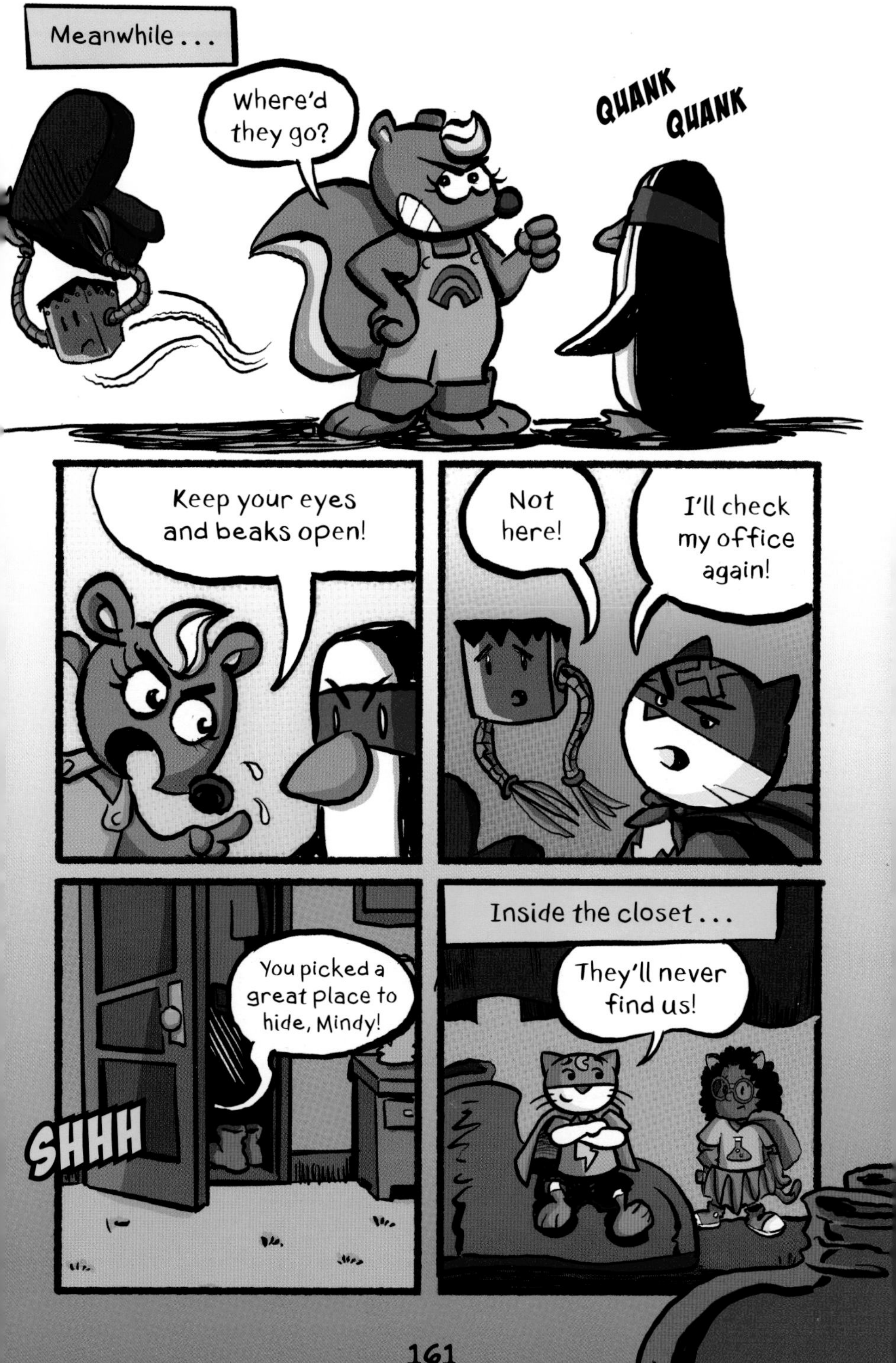
Meanwhile . . .
Where'd they go?
QUANK QUANK
Keep your eyes and beaks open!
Not here!
I'll check my office again!
You picked a great place to hide, Mindy!
SHHH
Inside the closet . . .
They'll never find us!

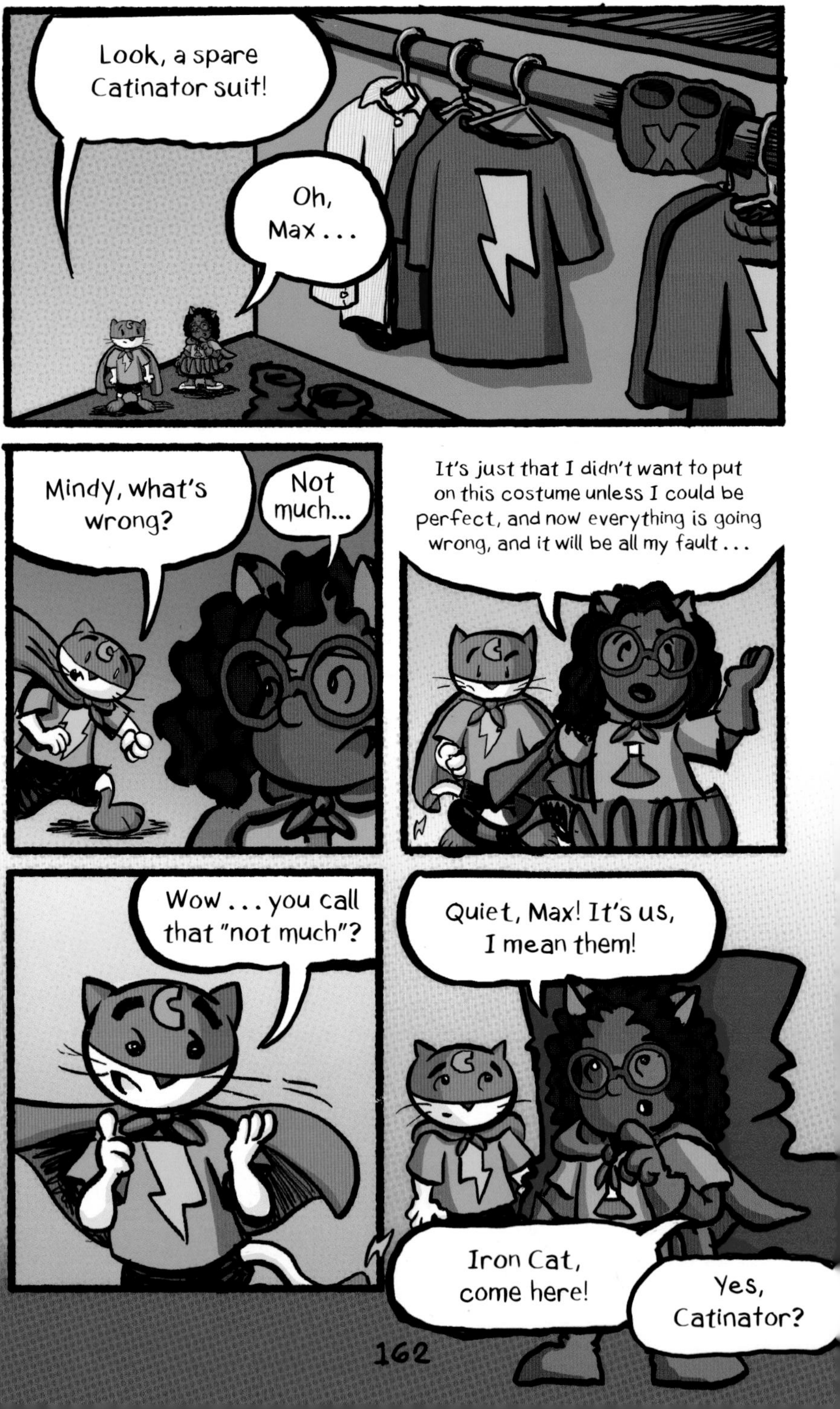

Look, a spare Catinator suit!
Oh, Max . . .
Mindy, what's wrong?
Not much...
It's just that I didn't want to put on this costume unless I could be perfect, and now everything is going wrong, and it will be all my fault . . .
Wow . . . you call that "not much"?
Quiet, Max! It's us, I mean them!
Iron Cat, come here!
Yes, Catinator?

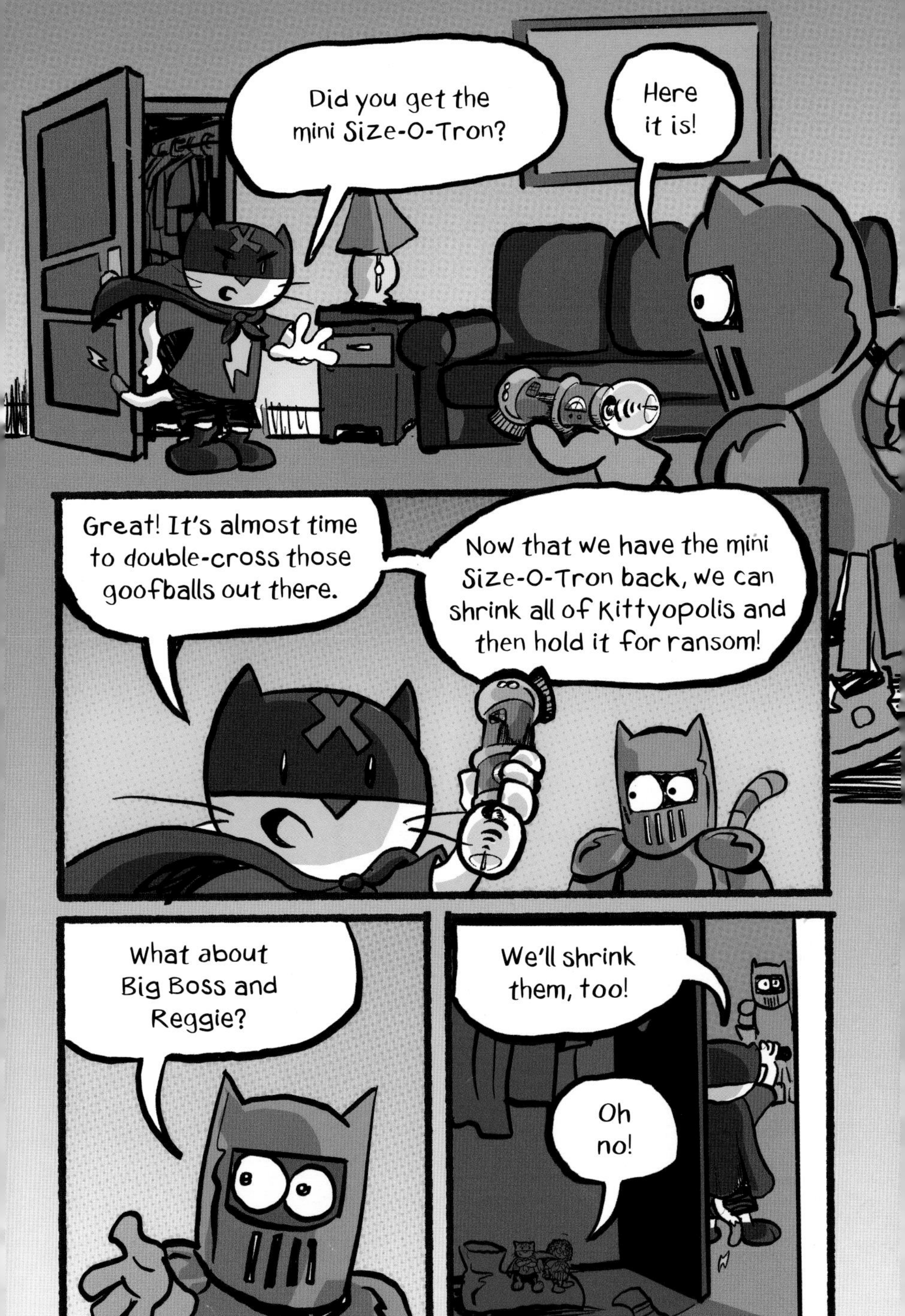
Did you get the mini Size-O-Tron?
Here it is!
Great! It's almost time to double-cross those goofballs out there.
Now that we have the mini Size-O-Tron back, we can shrink all of Kittyopolis and then hold it for ransom!
What about Big Boss and Reggie?
We'll shrink them, too!
Oh no!

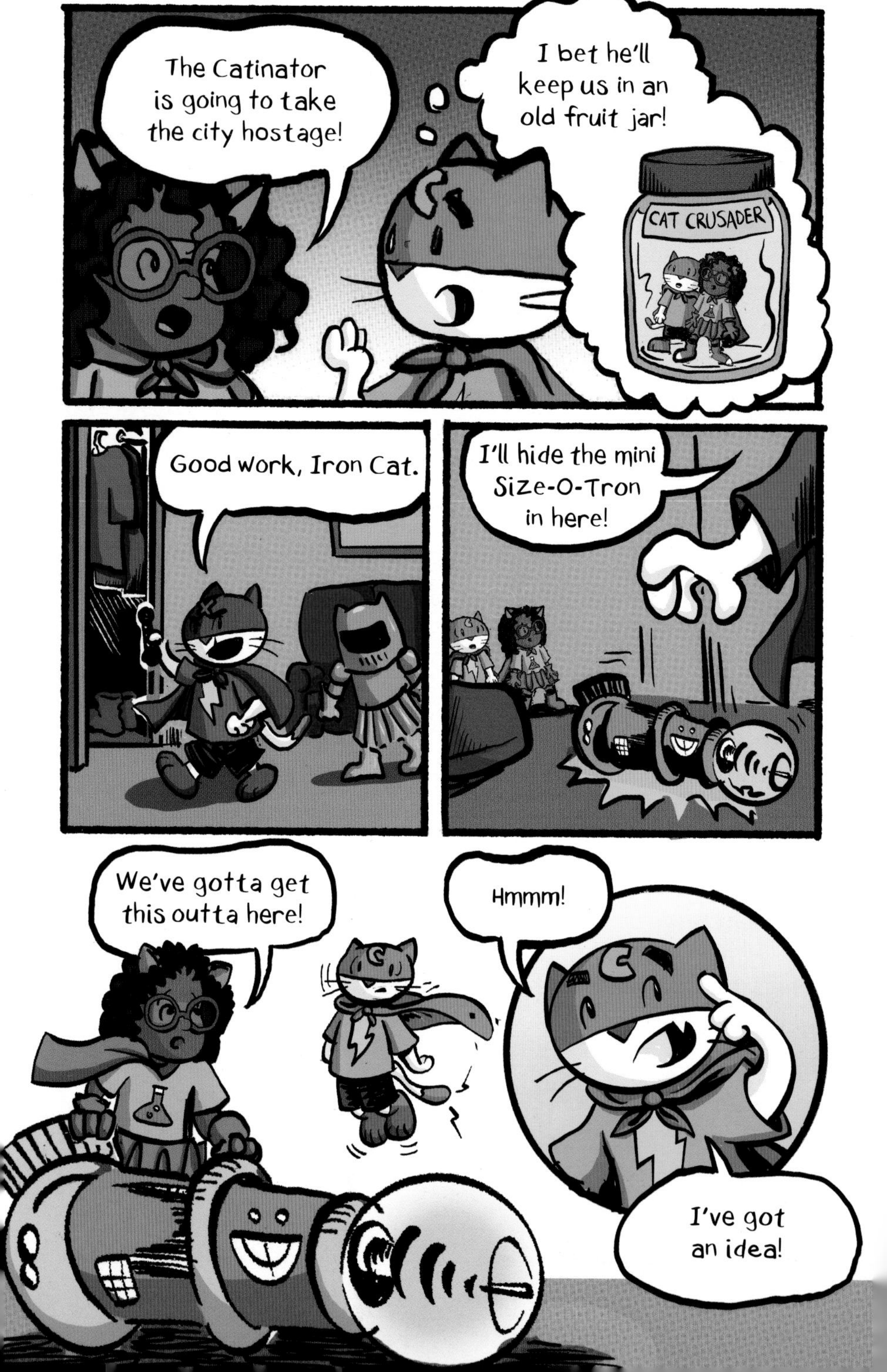
The Catinator is going to take the city hostage!
I bet he'll keep us in an old fruit jar!
CAT CRUSADER
Good work, Iron Cat.
I'll hide the mini Size-O-Tron in here!
We've gotta get this outta here!
Hmmm!
I've got an idea!

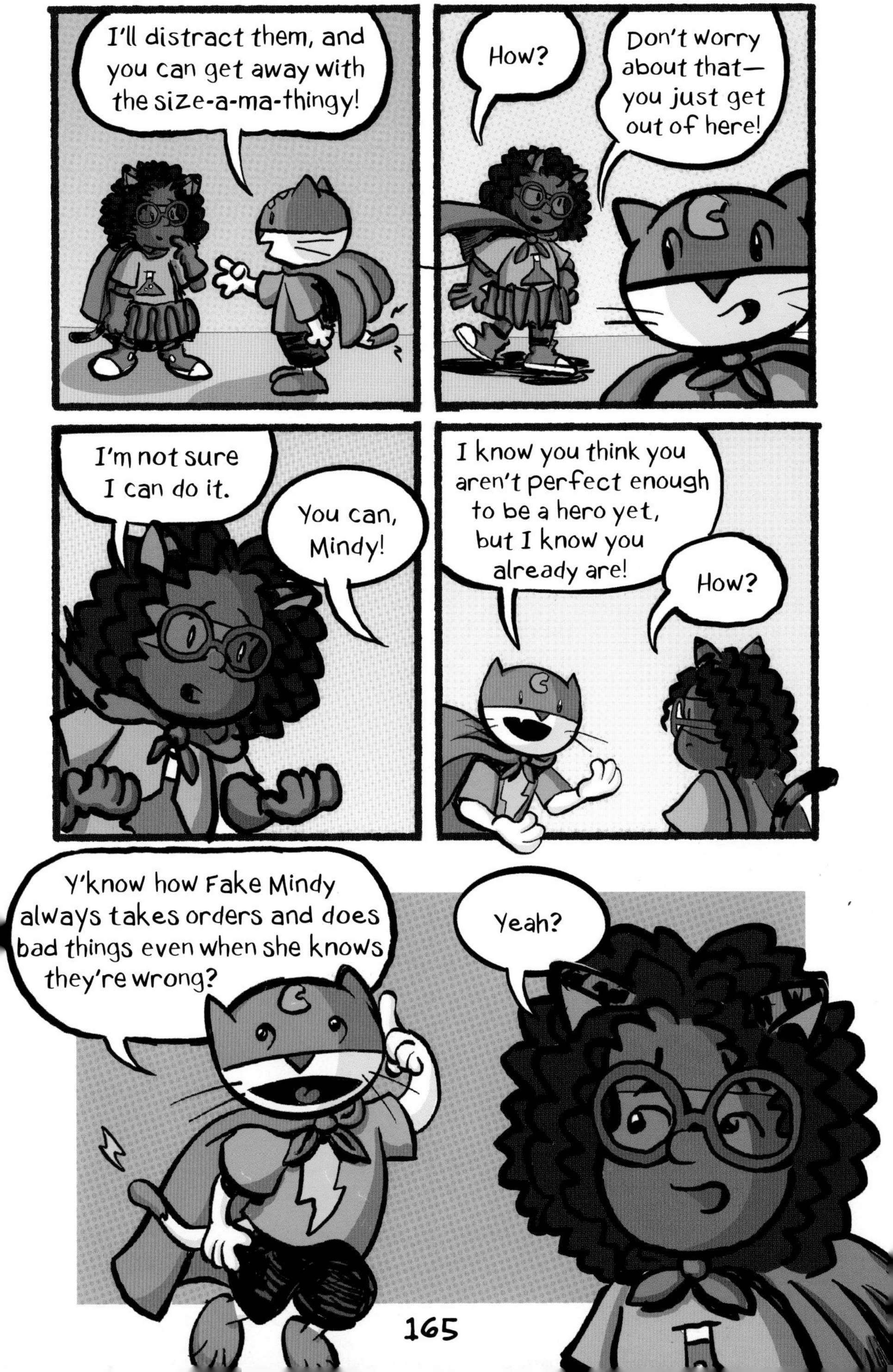
I'll distract them, and you can get away with the size-a-ma-thingy!
How?
Don't worry about that— you just get out of here!
I'm not sure I can do it.
You can, Mindy!
I know you think you aren't perfect enough to be a hero yet, but I know you already are!
How?
Y'know how Fake Mindy always takes orders and does bad things even when she knows they're wrong?
Yeah?

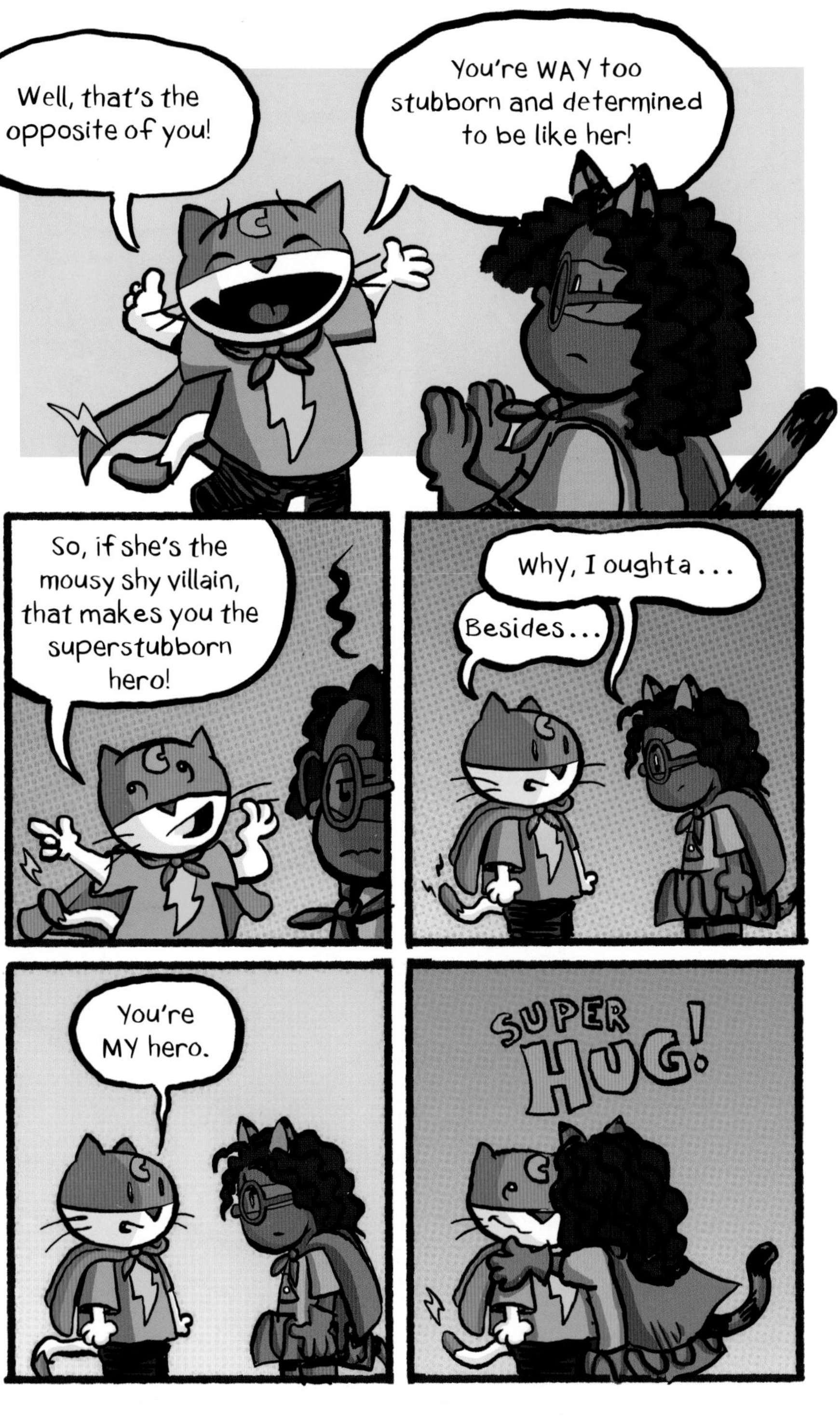

Well, that's the opposite of you!
You're WAY too stubborn and determined to be like her!
So, if she's the mousy shy villain, that makes you the superstubborn hero!
Why, I oughta . . .
Besides . . .
You're MY hero.
SUPER HUG!

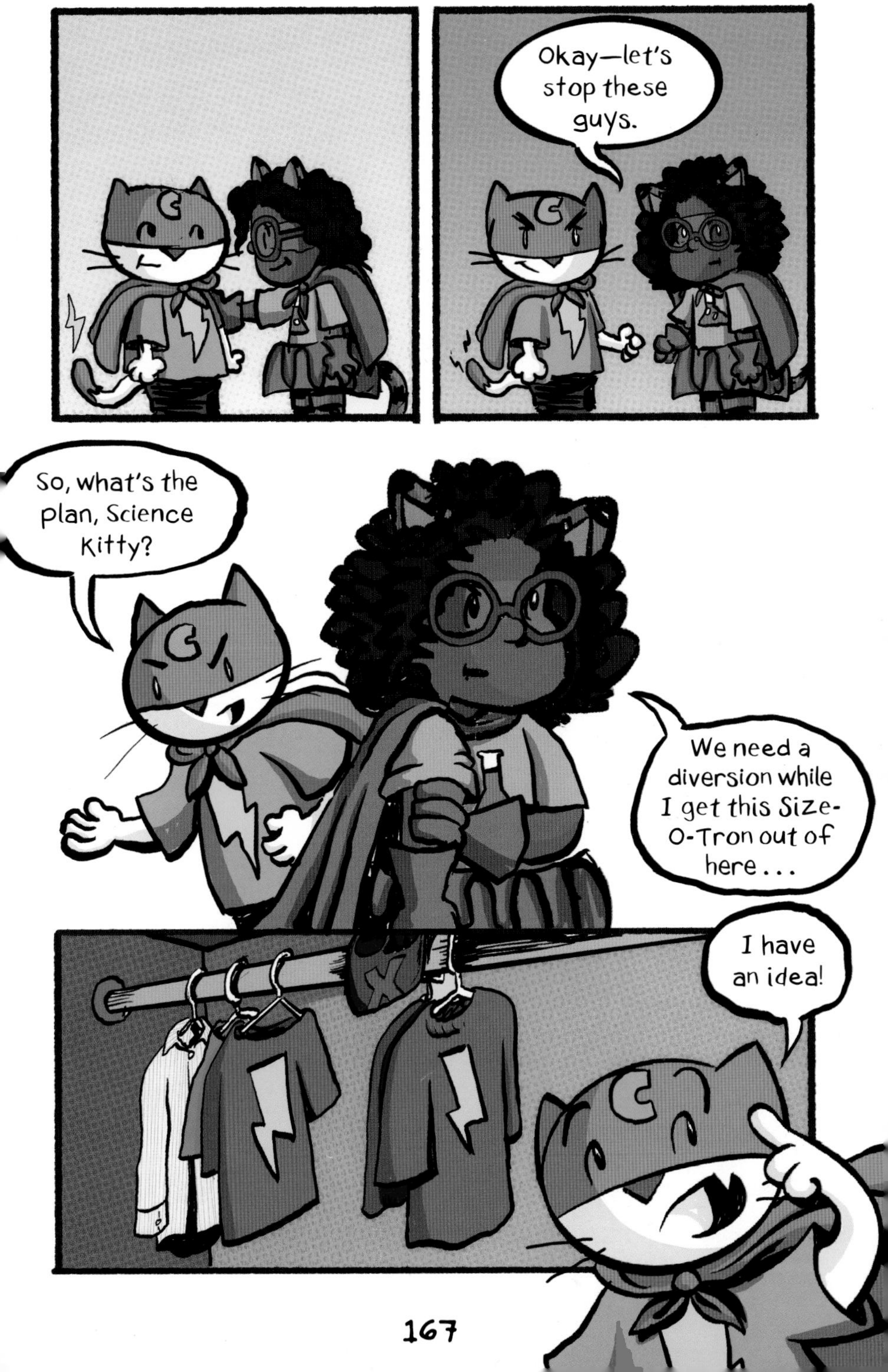
Okay—let's stop these guys.
So, what's the plan, Science Kitty?
We need a diversion while I get this Size-O-Tron out of here . . .
I have an idea!

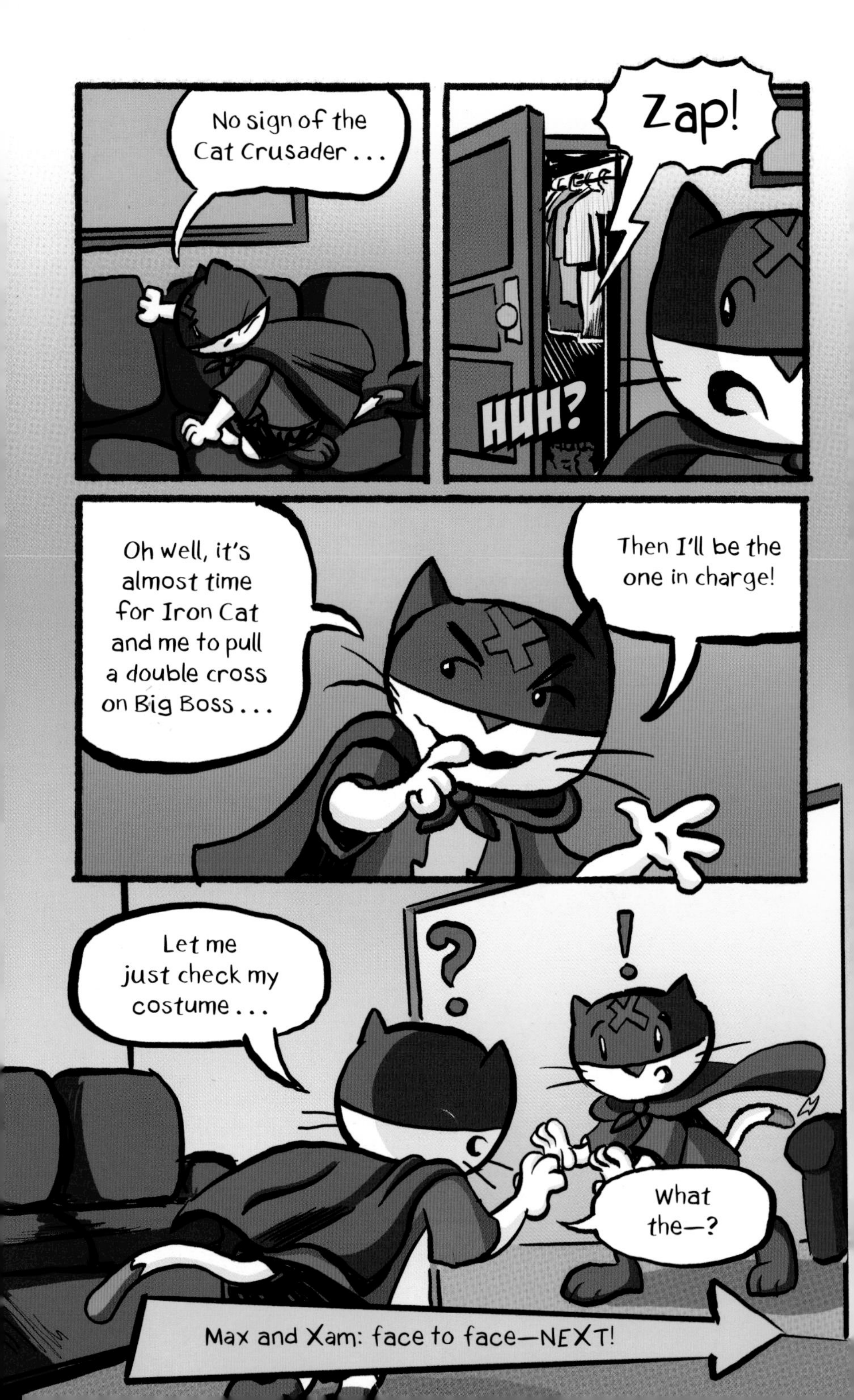
No sign of the Cat Crusader . . .
Zap!
HUH?
Oh well, it's almost time for Iron Cat and me to pull a double cross on Big Boss . . .
Then I'll be the one in charge!
Let me just check my costume . . .
?
!
What the—?
Max and Xam: face to face—NEXT!

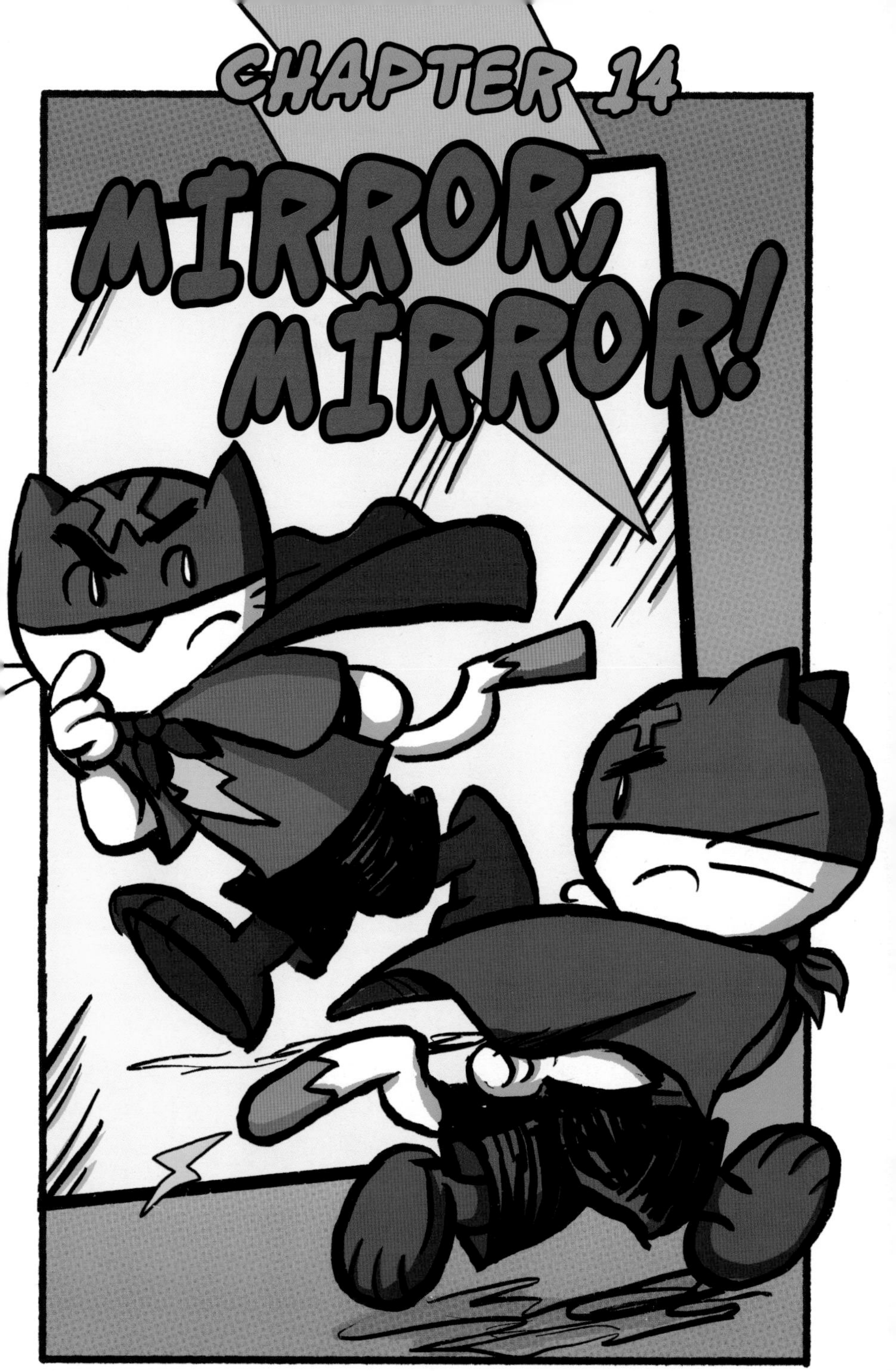
CHAPTER 14
MIRROR, MIRROR!

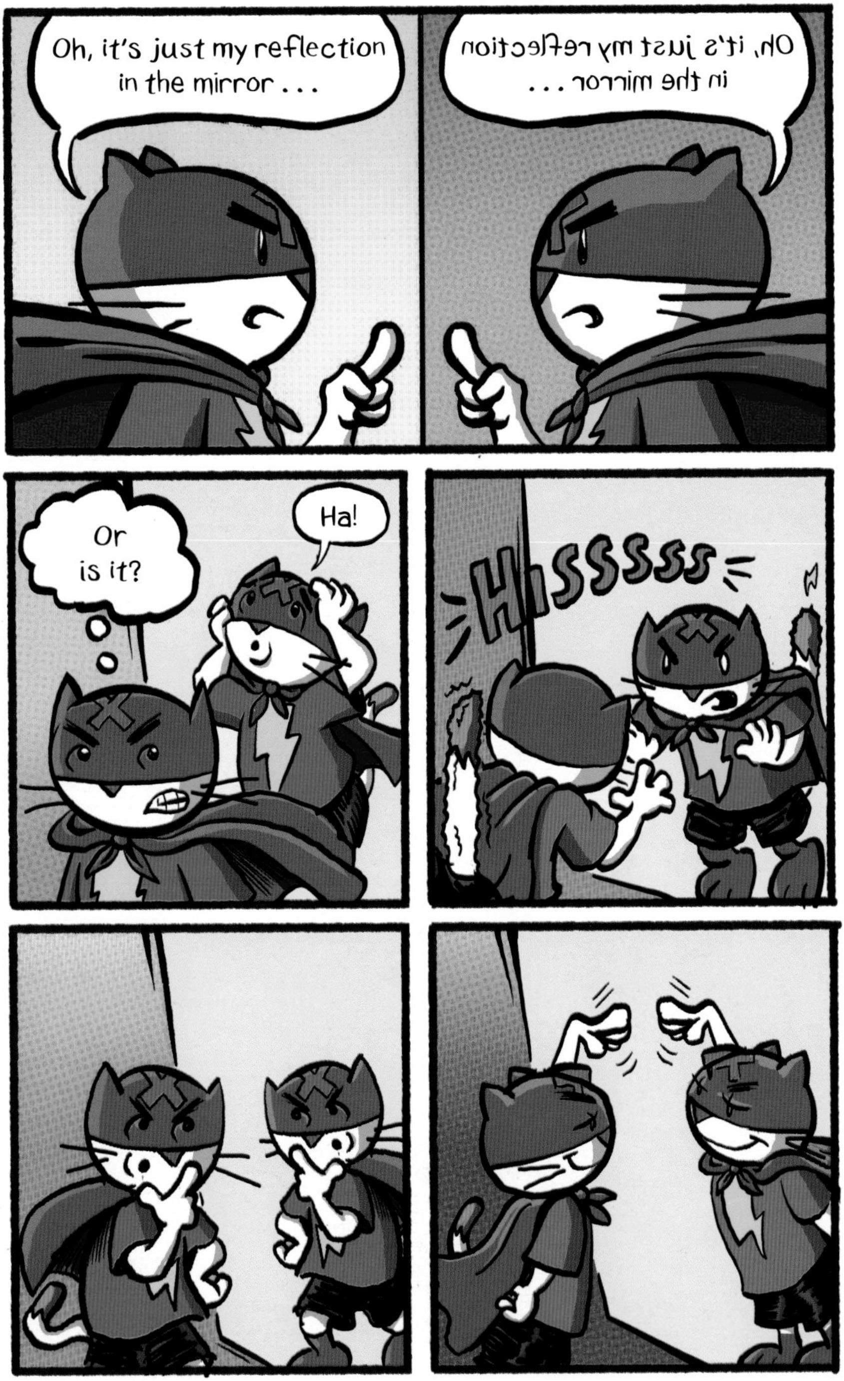
Oh, it's just my reflection in the mirror . . .
Oh, it's just my reflection in the mirror . . .
Or is it?
Ha!
HISSSSS

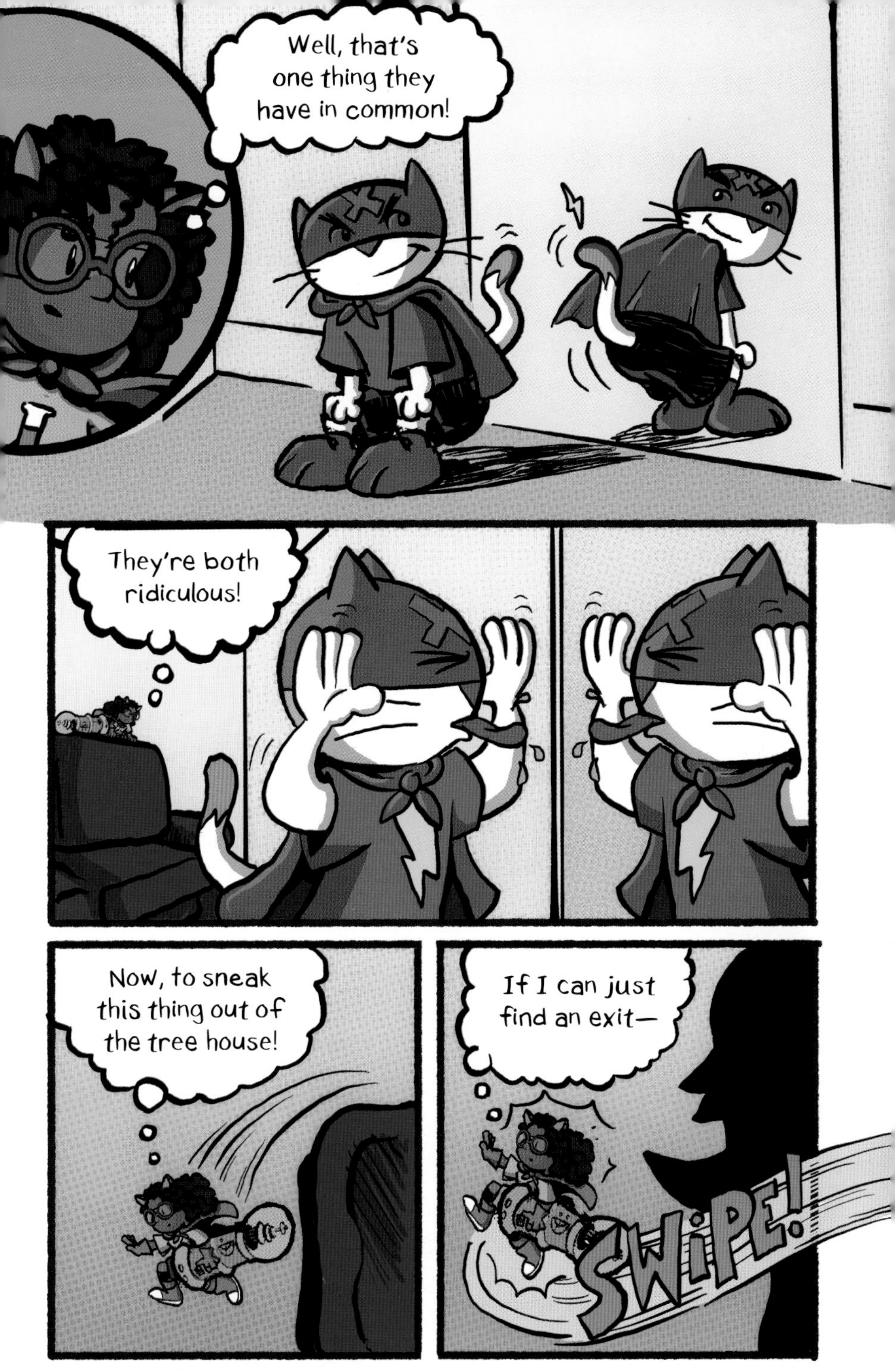
Well, that's one thing they have in common!
They're both ridiculous!
Now, to sneak this thing out of the tree house!
If I can just find an exit—
SWIPE!

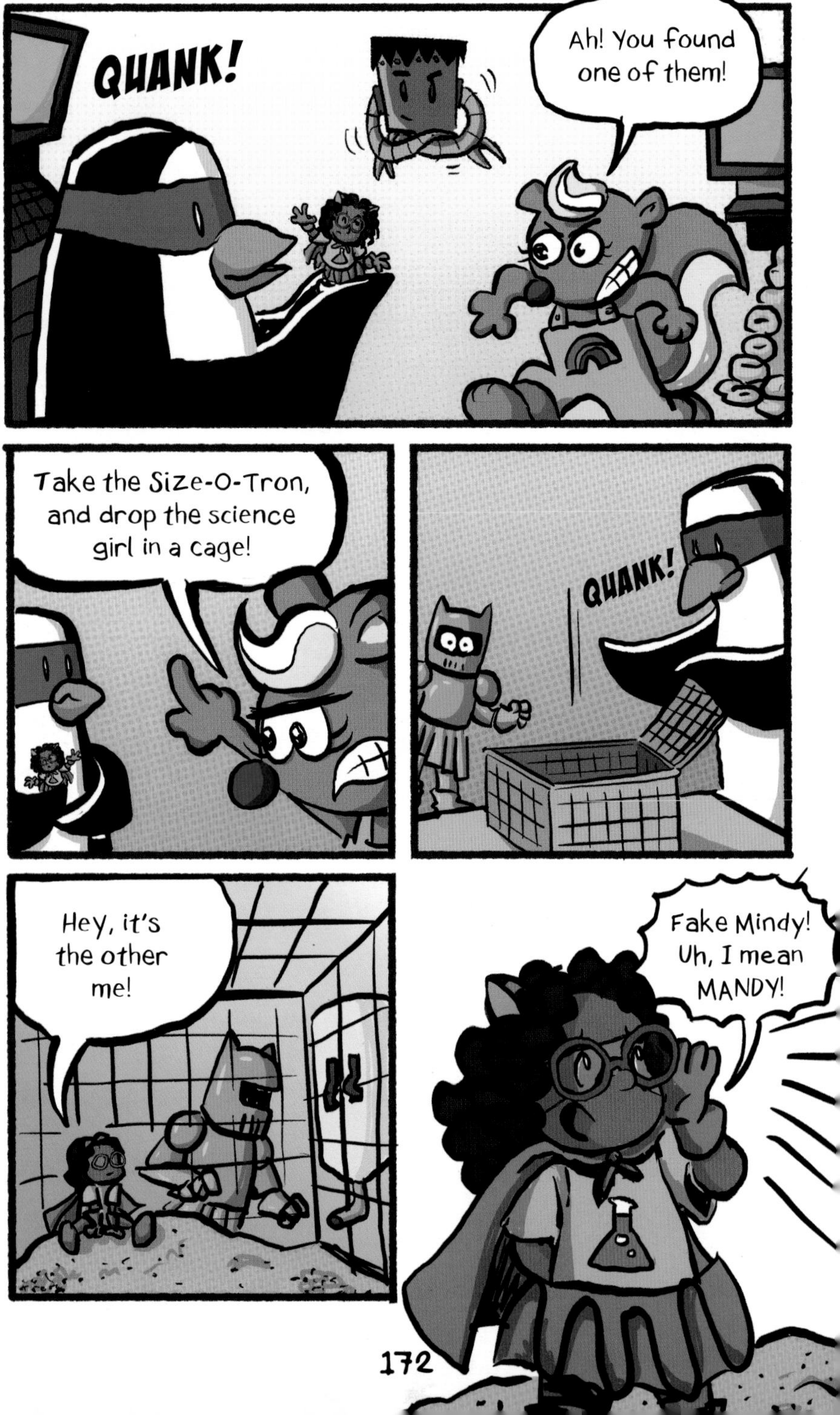
QUANK!
Ah! You found one of them!
Take the Size-O-Tron, and drop the science girl in a cage!
QUANK!
Hey, it's the other me!
Fake Mindy! Uh, I mean MANDY!

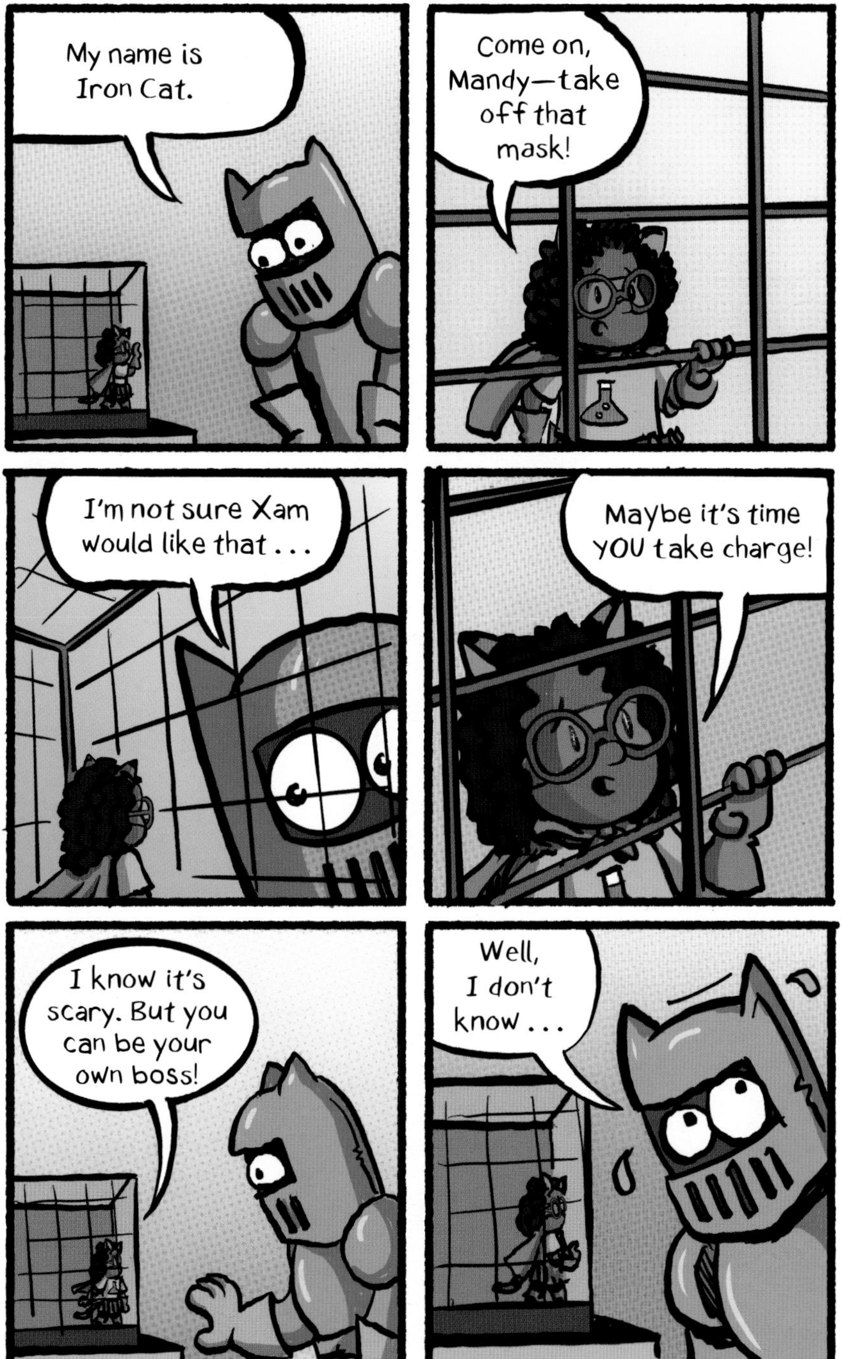
My name is Iron Cat.
Come on, Mandy—take off that mask!
I'm not sure Xam would like that . . .
Maybe it's time YOU take charge!
I know it's scary. But you can be your own boss!
Well, I don't know . . .

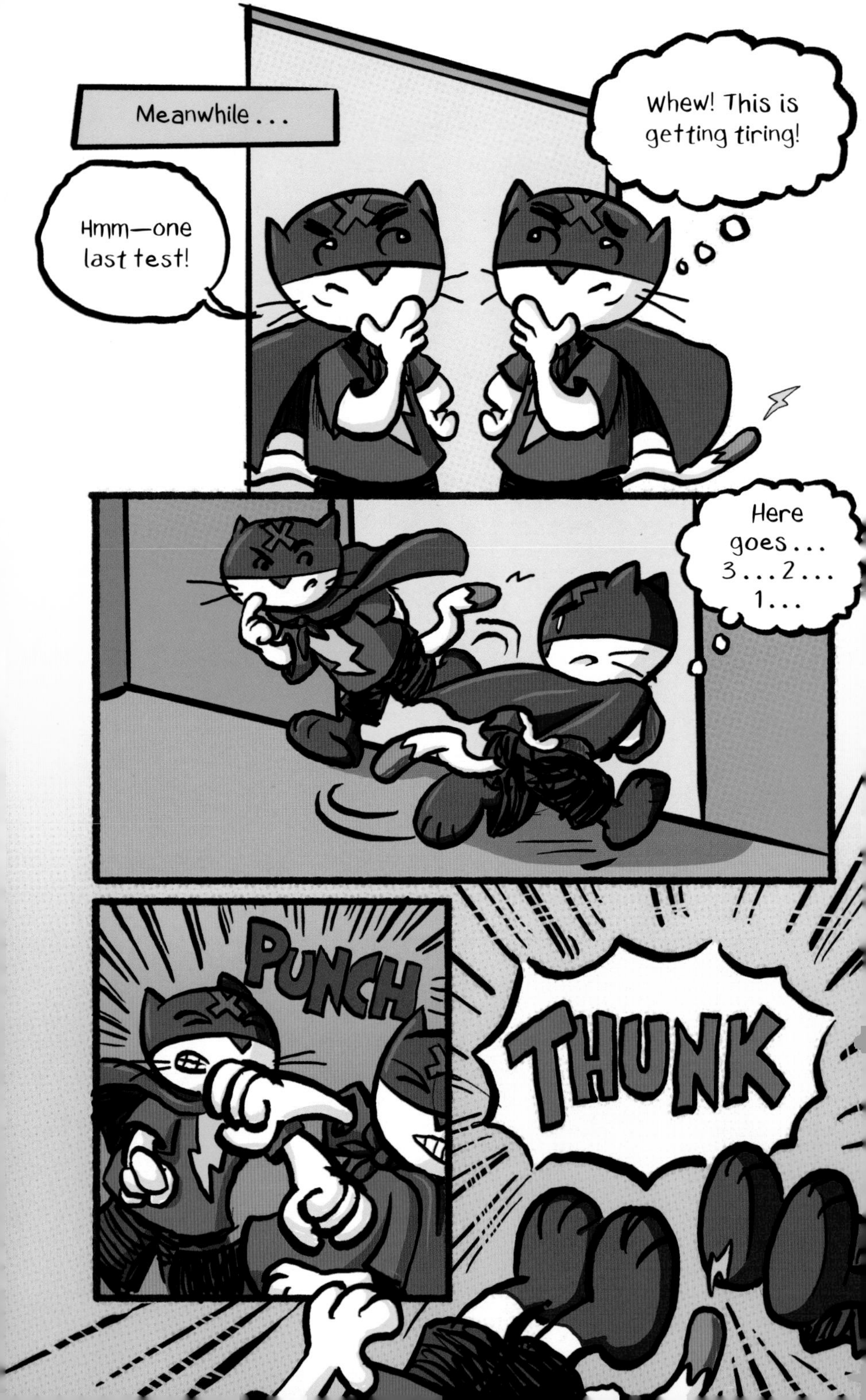
Meanwhile . . .
Hmm—one last test!
Whew! This is getting tiring!
Here goes . . . 3 . . . 2 . . . 1 . . .
PUNCH
THUNK

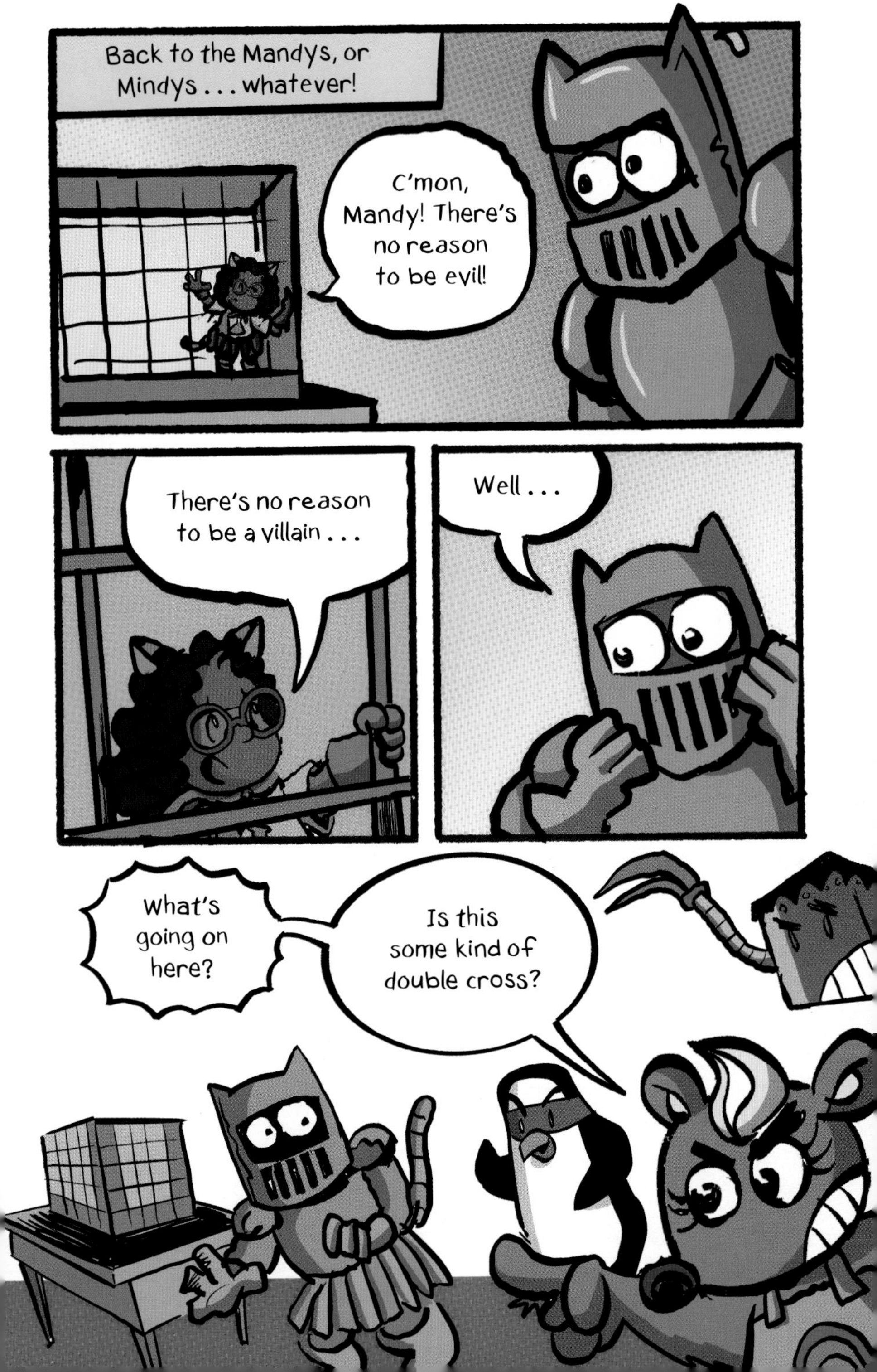
Back to the Mandys, or Mindys . . . whatever!
C'mon, Mandy! There's no reason to be evil!
There's no reason to be a villain . . .
Well . . .
What's going on here?
Is this some kind of double cross?

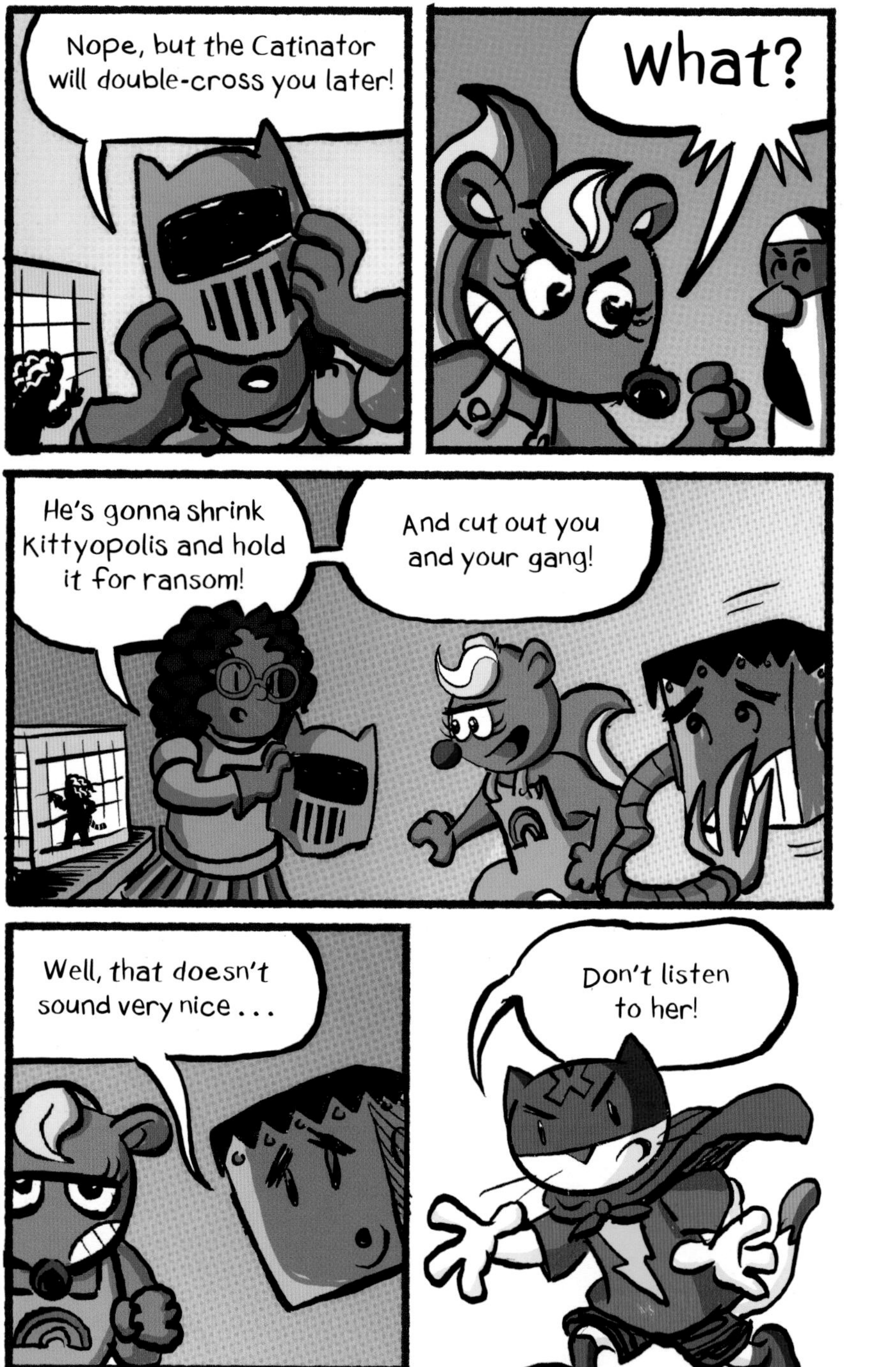
Nope, but the Catinator will double-cross you later!
What?
He's gonna shrink Kittyopolis and hold it for ransom!
And cut out you and your gang!
Well, that doesn't sound very nice . . .
Don't listen to her!

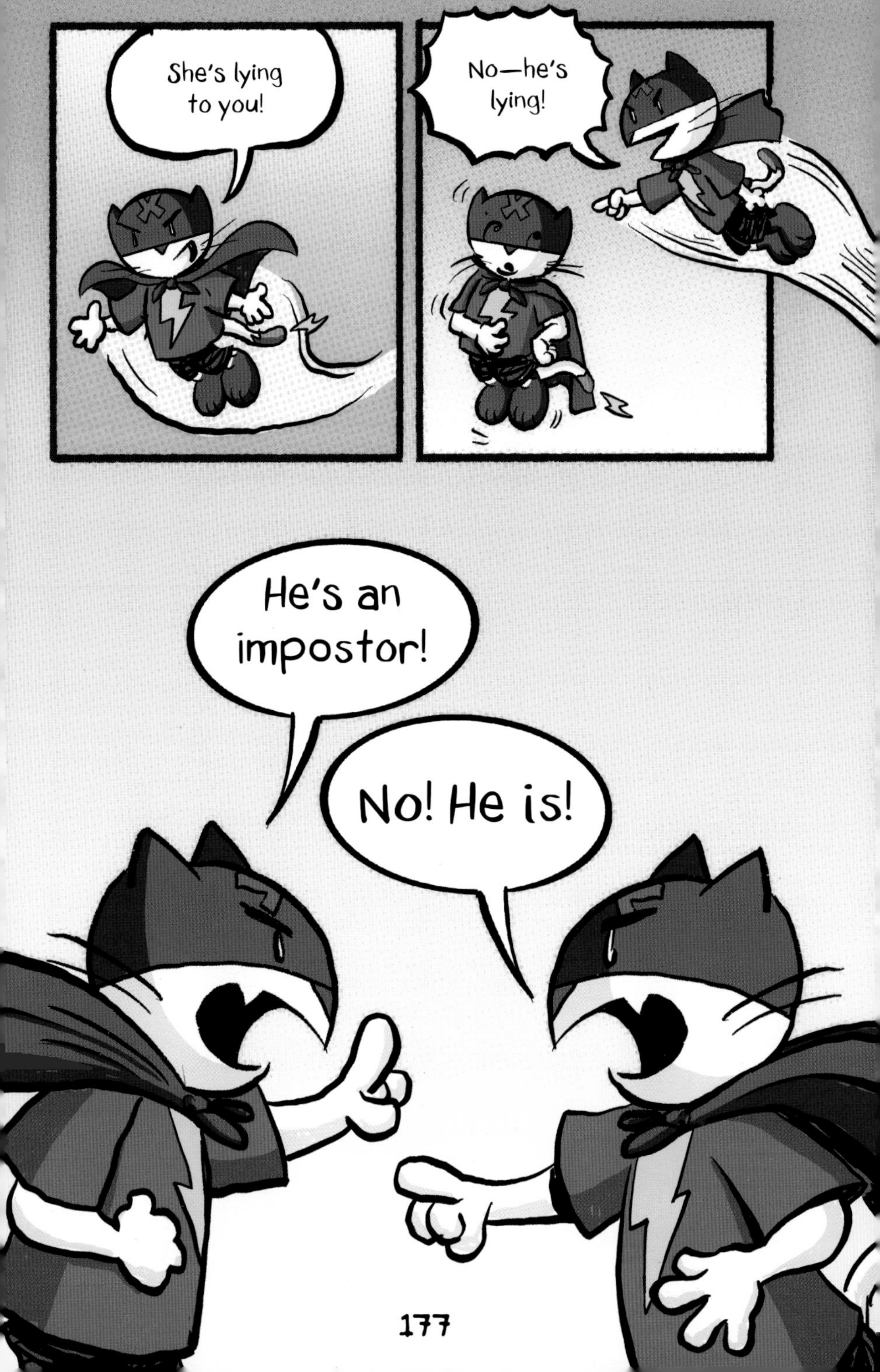
She's lying to you!
No—he's lying!
He's an impostor!
No! He is!

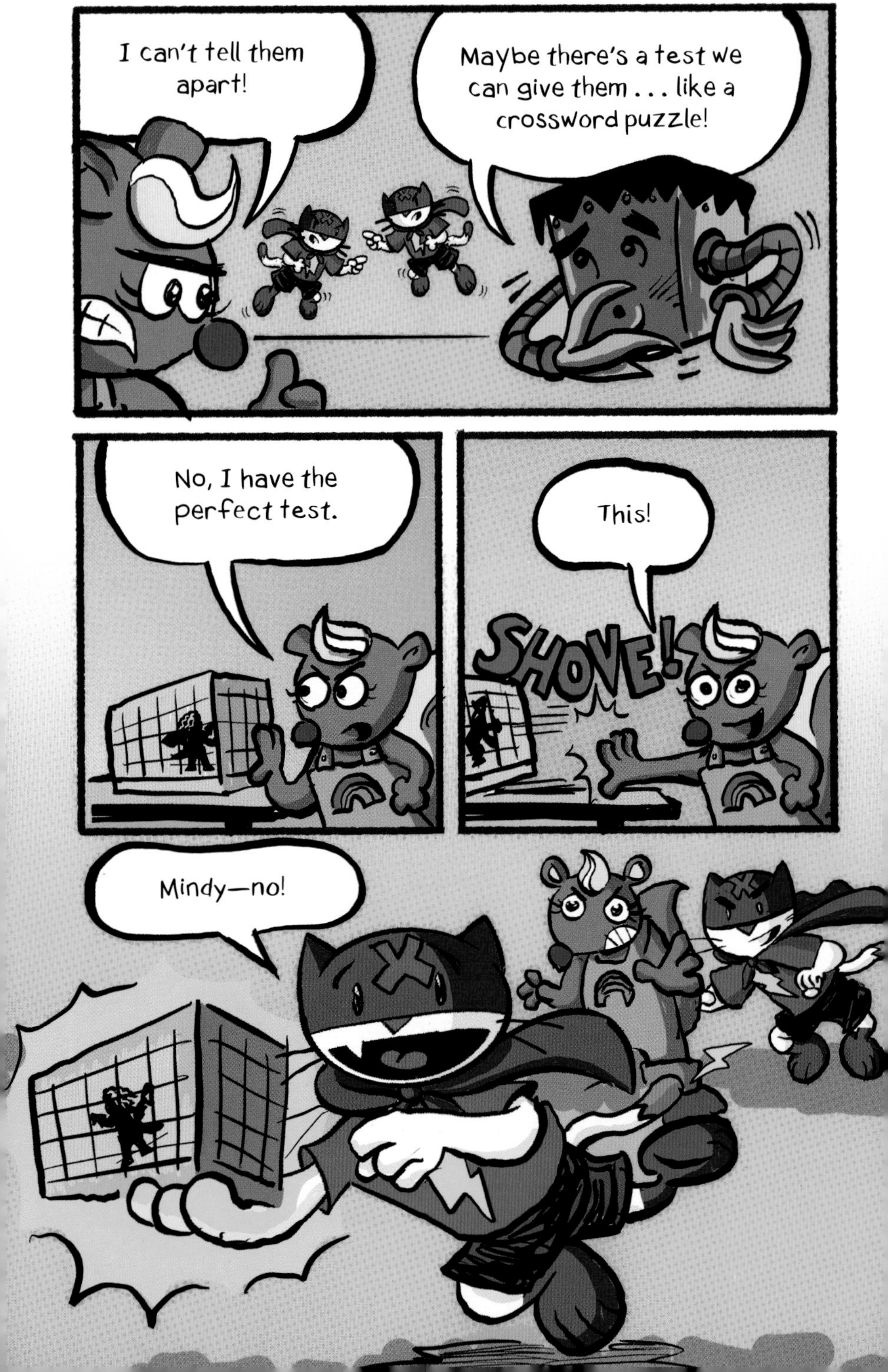
I can't tell them apart!
Maybe there's a test we can give them . . . like a crossword puzzle!
No, I have the perfect test.
This!
SHOVE!
Mindy—no!

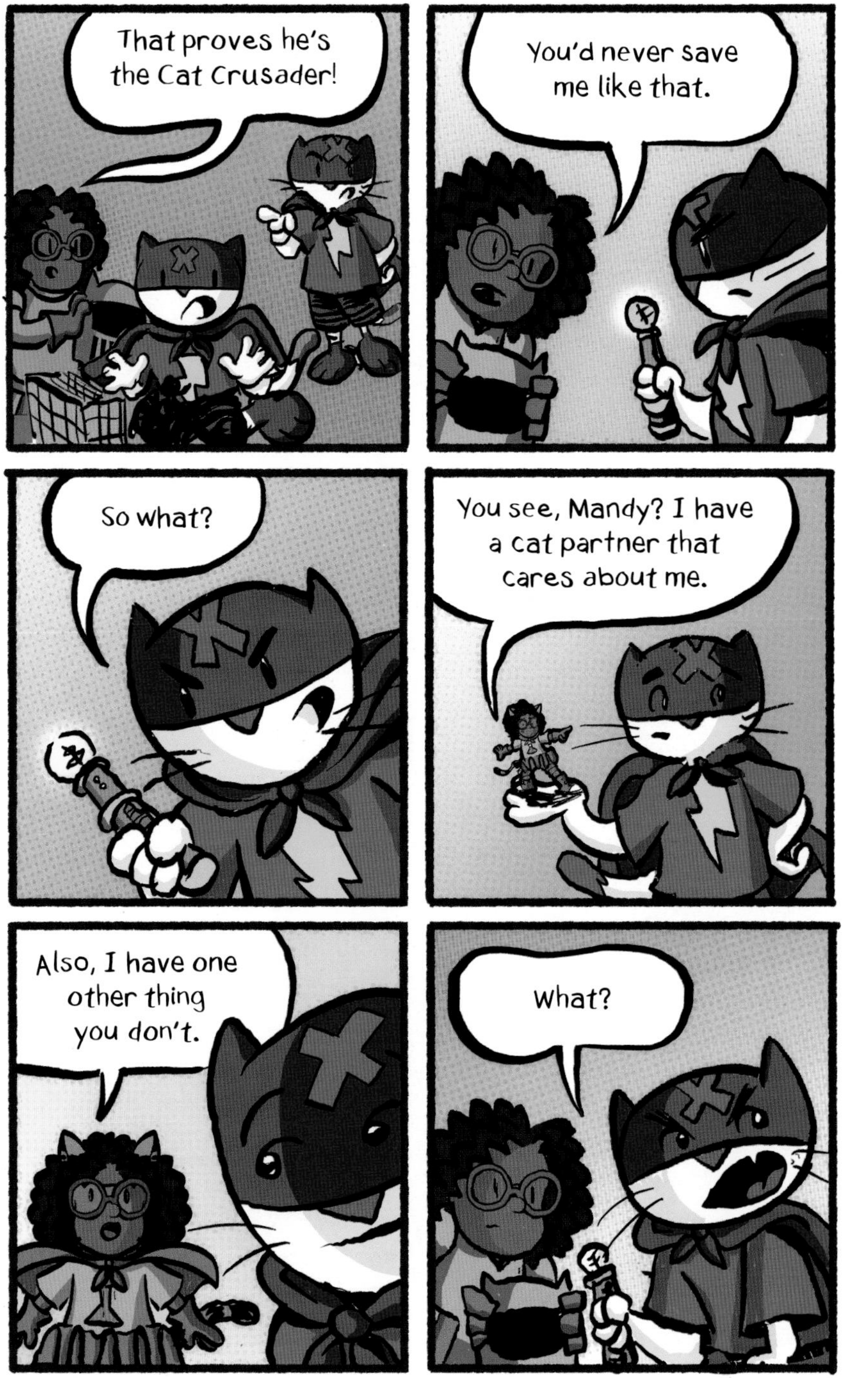
That proves he's the Cat Crusader!
You'd never save me like that.
So what?
You see, Mandy? I have a cat partner that cares about me.
Also, I have one other thing you don't.
What?

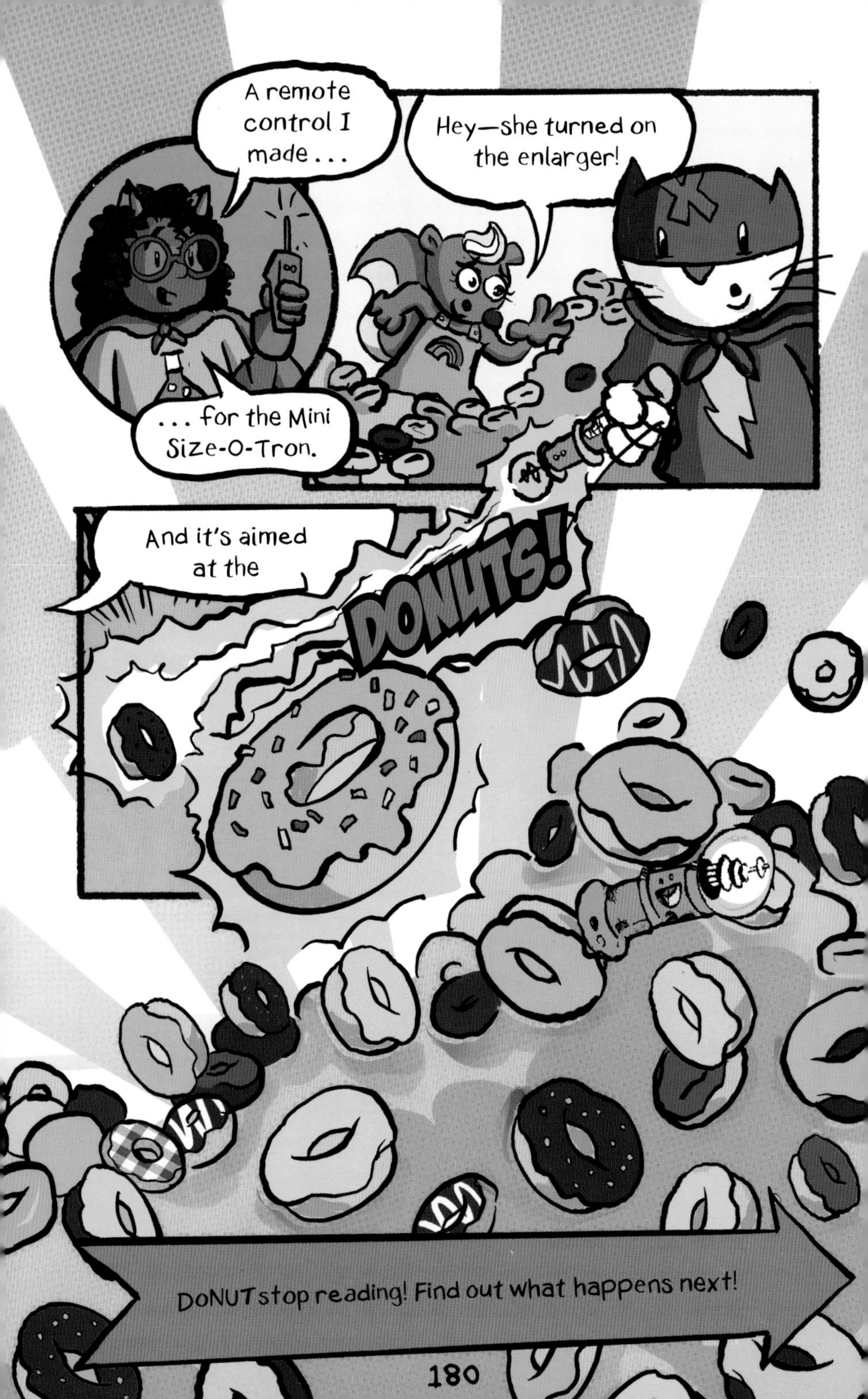
A remote control I made . . .
Hey—she turned on the enlarger!
. . . for the Mini Size-O-Tron.
And it's aimed at the
DONUTS!
DONUT stop reading! Find out what happens next!

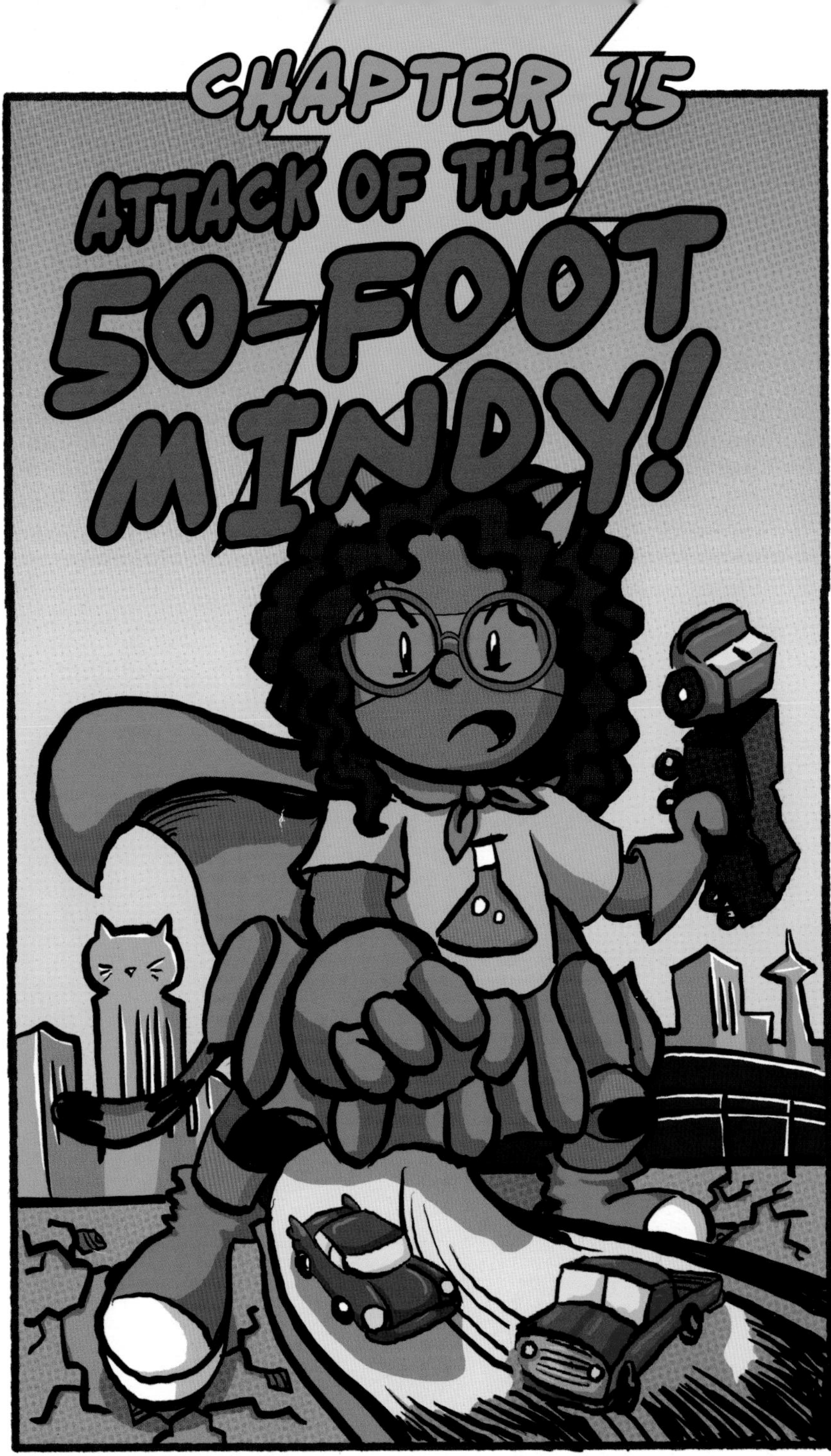
CHAPTER 15
ATTACK OF THE
50-FOOT
MINDY!

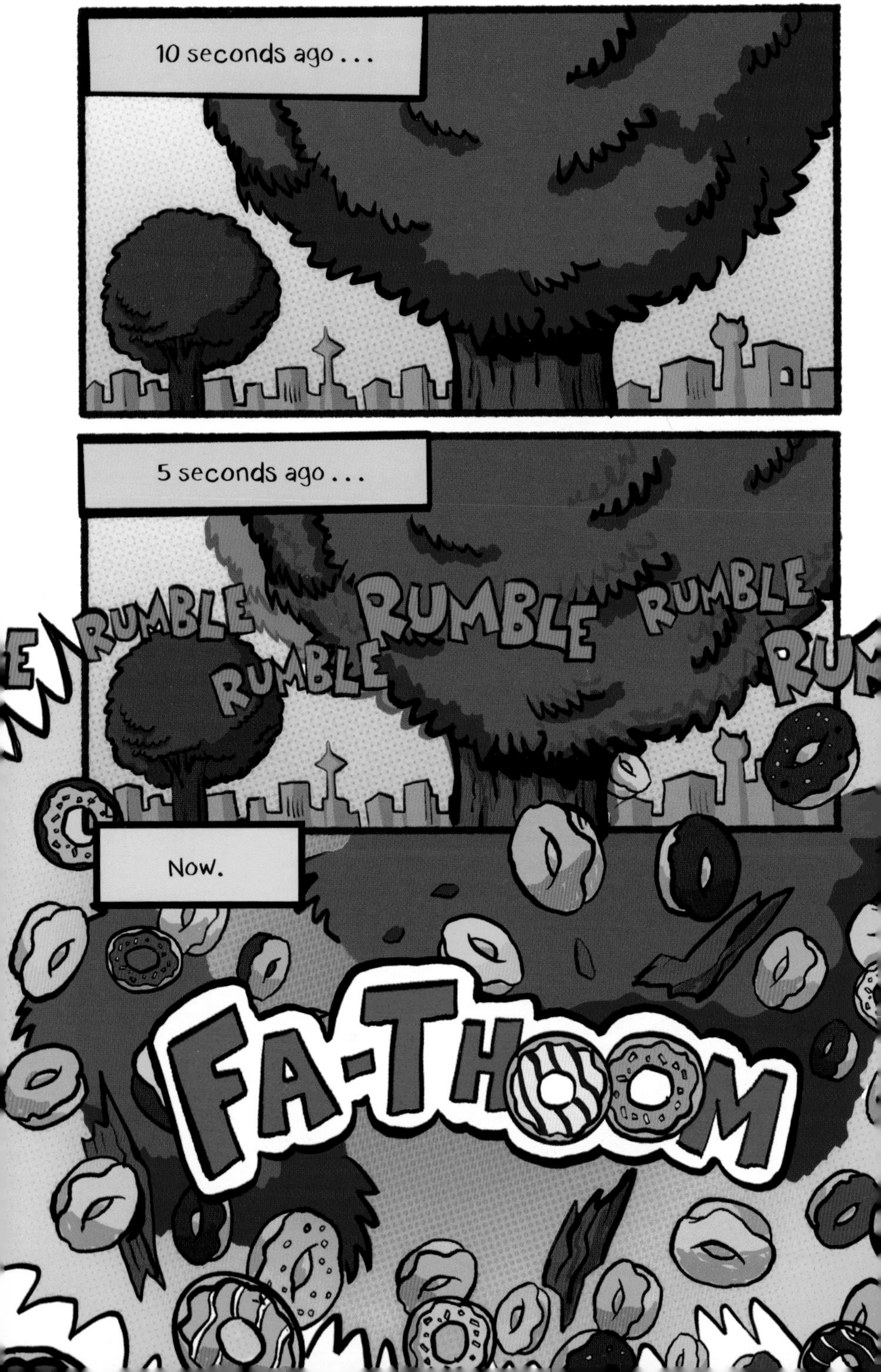
10 seconds ago . . .
5 seconds ago . . .
RUMBLE
RUMBLE
RUMBLE
RUMBLE
Now.
FA-THOOOM

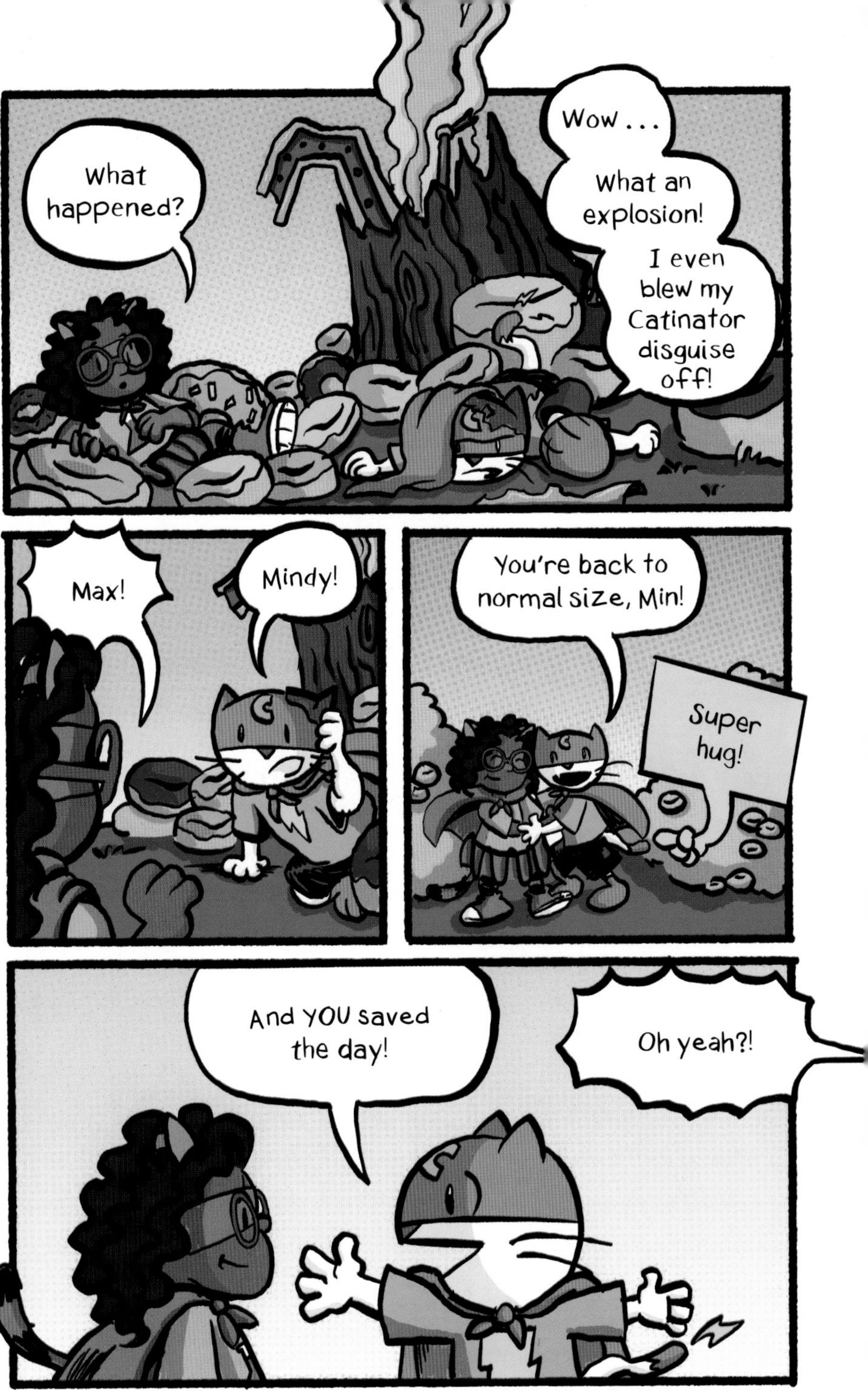
What happened?
Wow . . .
What an explosion!
I even blew my Catinator disguise off!
Max!
Mindy!
You're back to normal size, Min!
Super hug!
And YOU saved the day!
Oh yeah?!

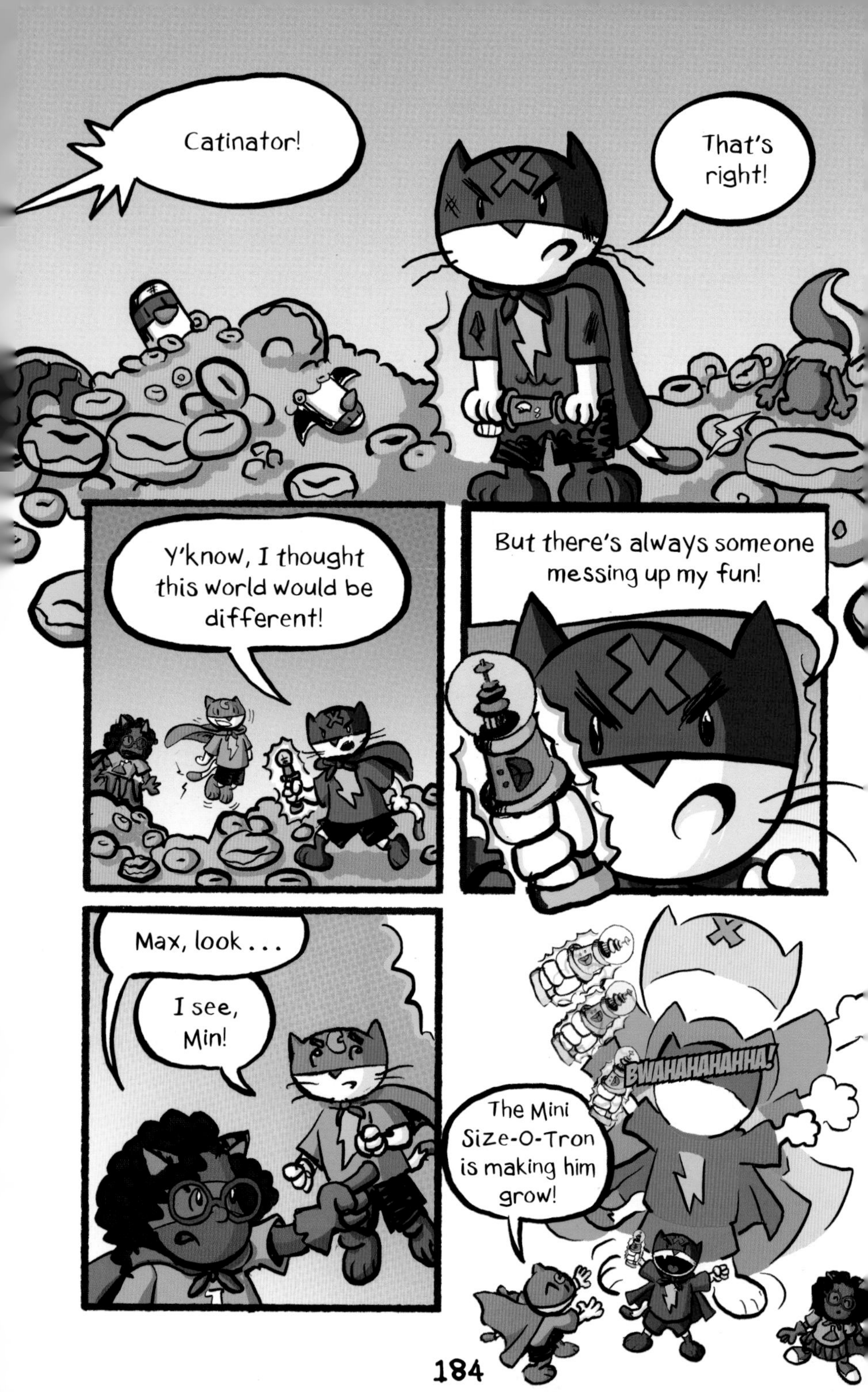

Catinator!
That's right!
Y'know, I thought this world would be different!
But there's always someone messing up my fun!
Max, look . . .
I see, Min!
BWAHAHAHAHHA!
The Mini Size-O-Tron is making him grow!

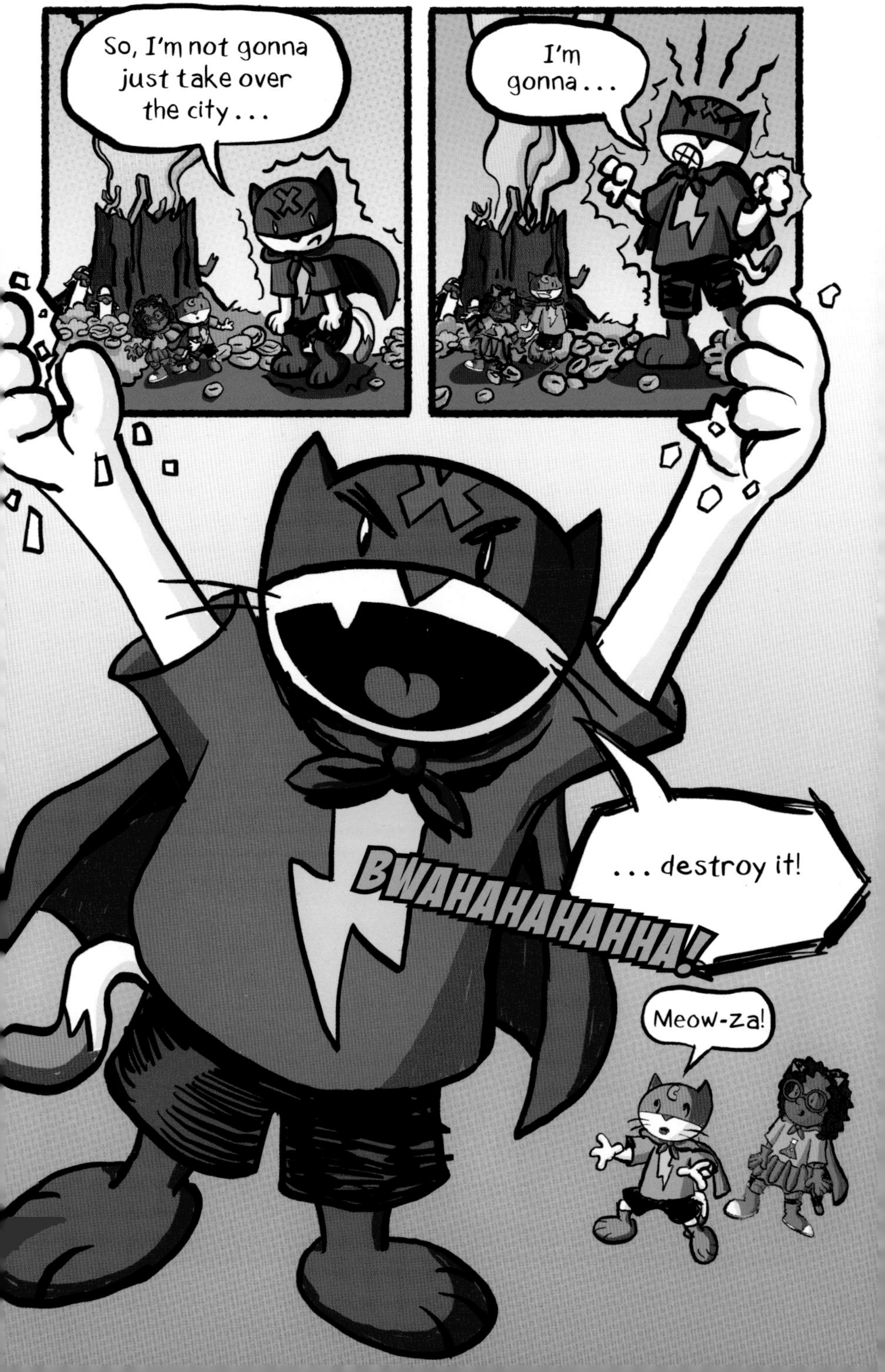
So, I'm not gonna just take over the city . . .
I'm gonna . . .
. . . destroy it!
BWAHAHAHAHAHHA!
Meow-za!

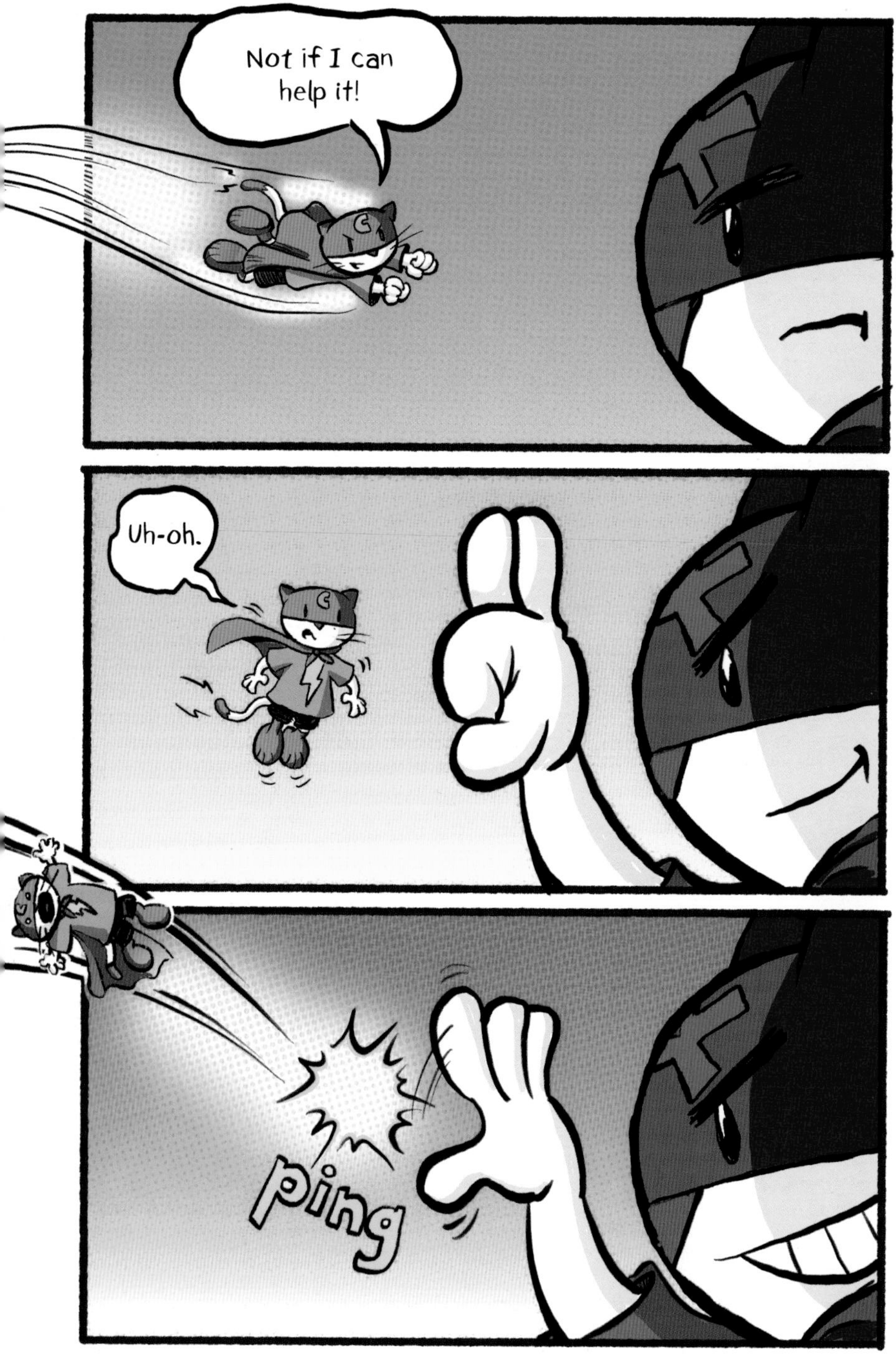
Not if I can help it!
Uh-oh.
ping

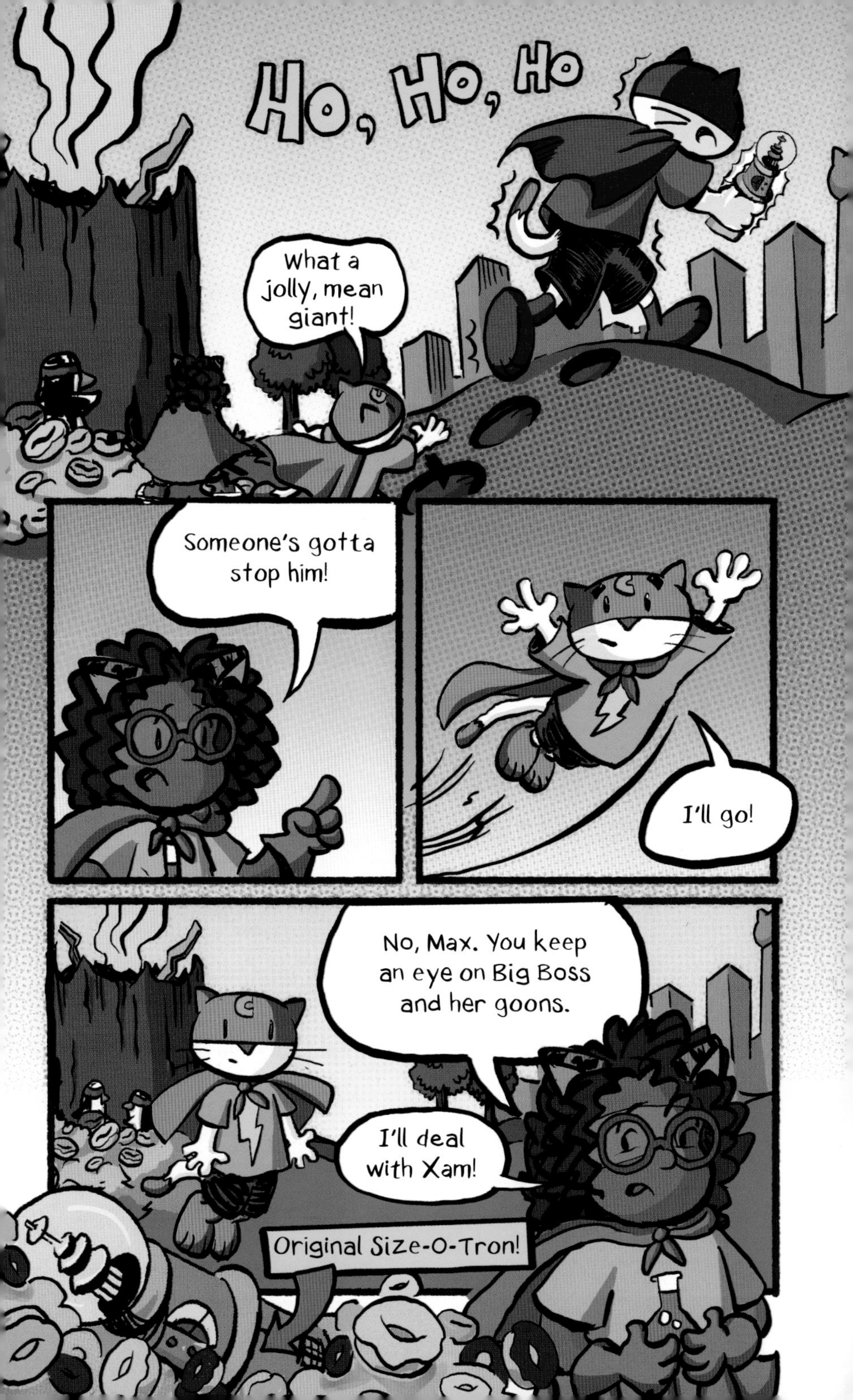
Ho, Ho, Ho
What a jolly, mean giant!
Someone's gotta stop him!
I'll go!
No, Max. You keep an eye on Big Boss and her goons.
I'll deal with Xam!
Original Size-O-Tron!

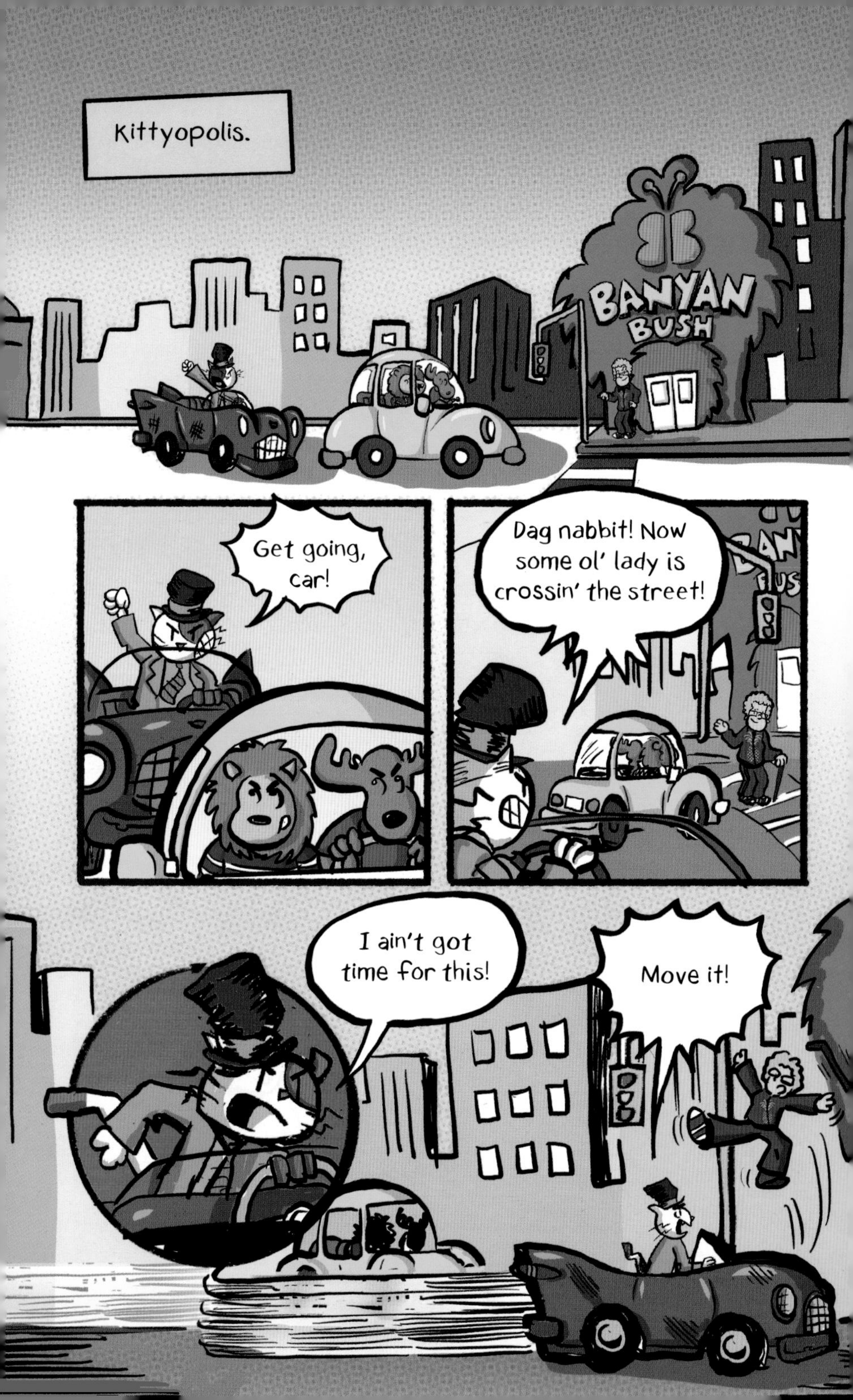
Kittyopolis.
BANYAN BUSH
Get going, car!
Dag nabbit! Now some ol' lady is crossin' the street!
I ain't got time for this!
Move it!

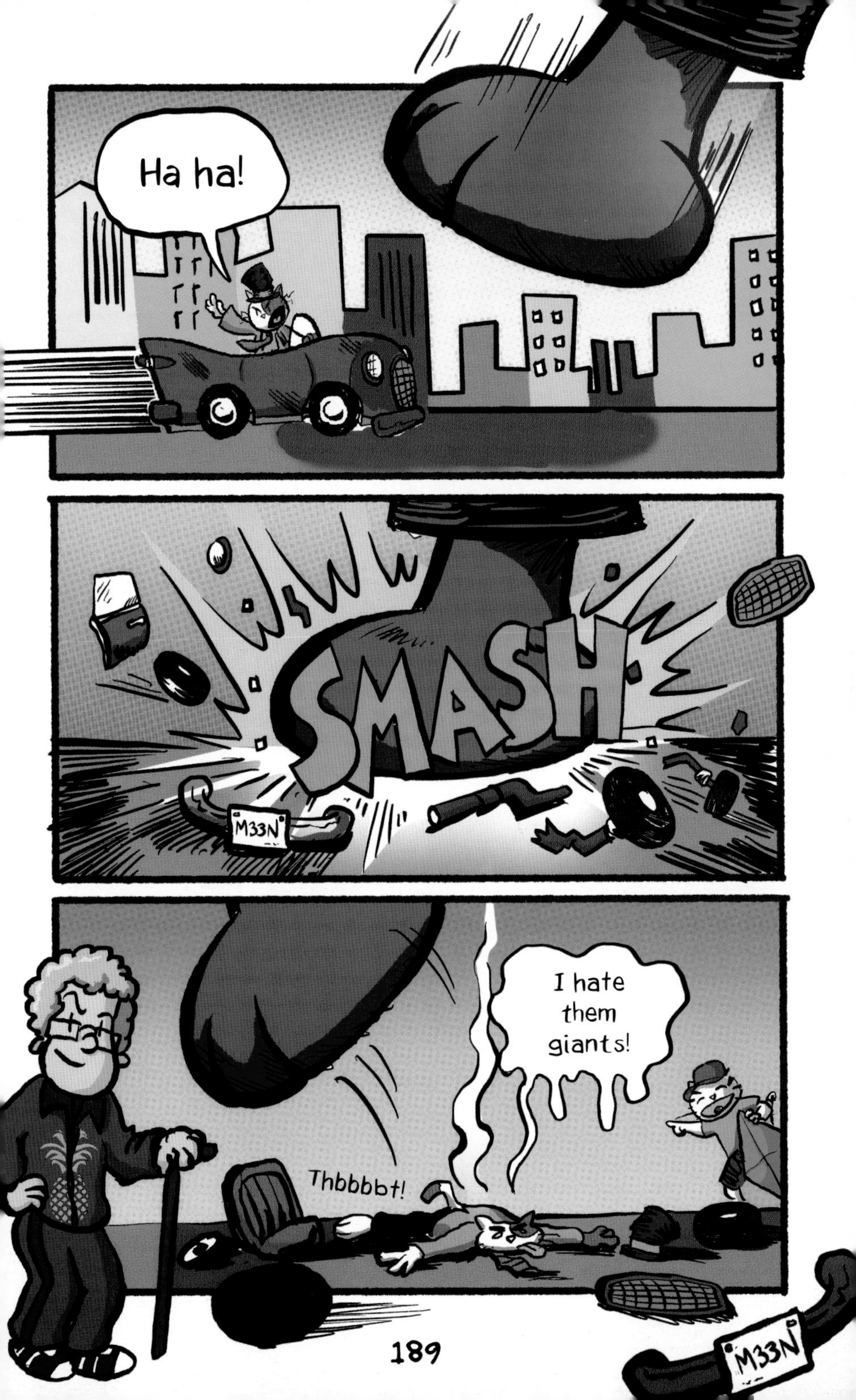
Ha ha!
SMASH
M33N
I hate them giants!
Thbbbbt!
M33N

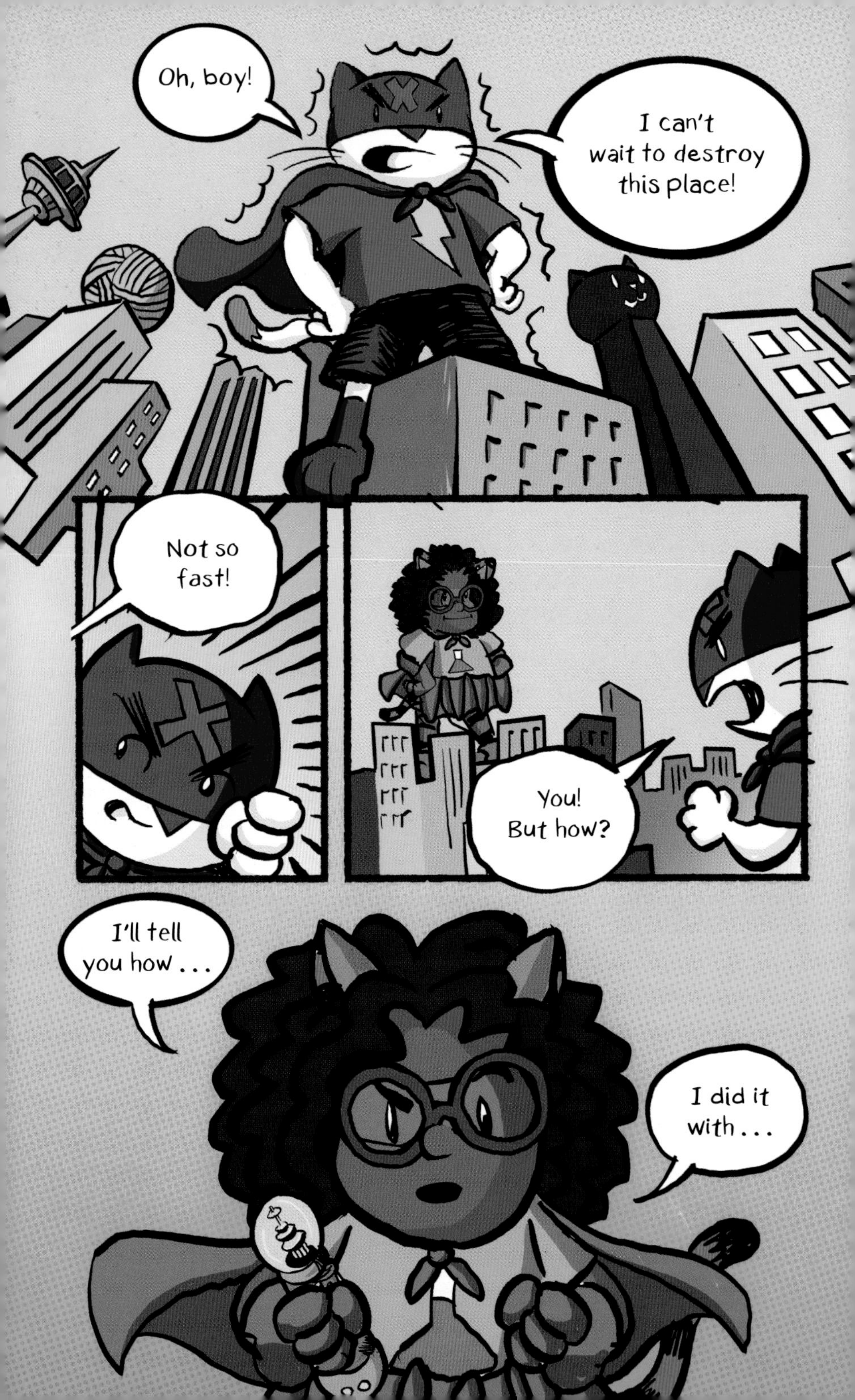
Oh, boy!
I can't wait to destroy this place!
Not so fast!
You! But how?
I'll tell you how . . .
I did it with . . .

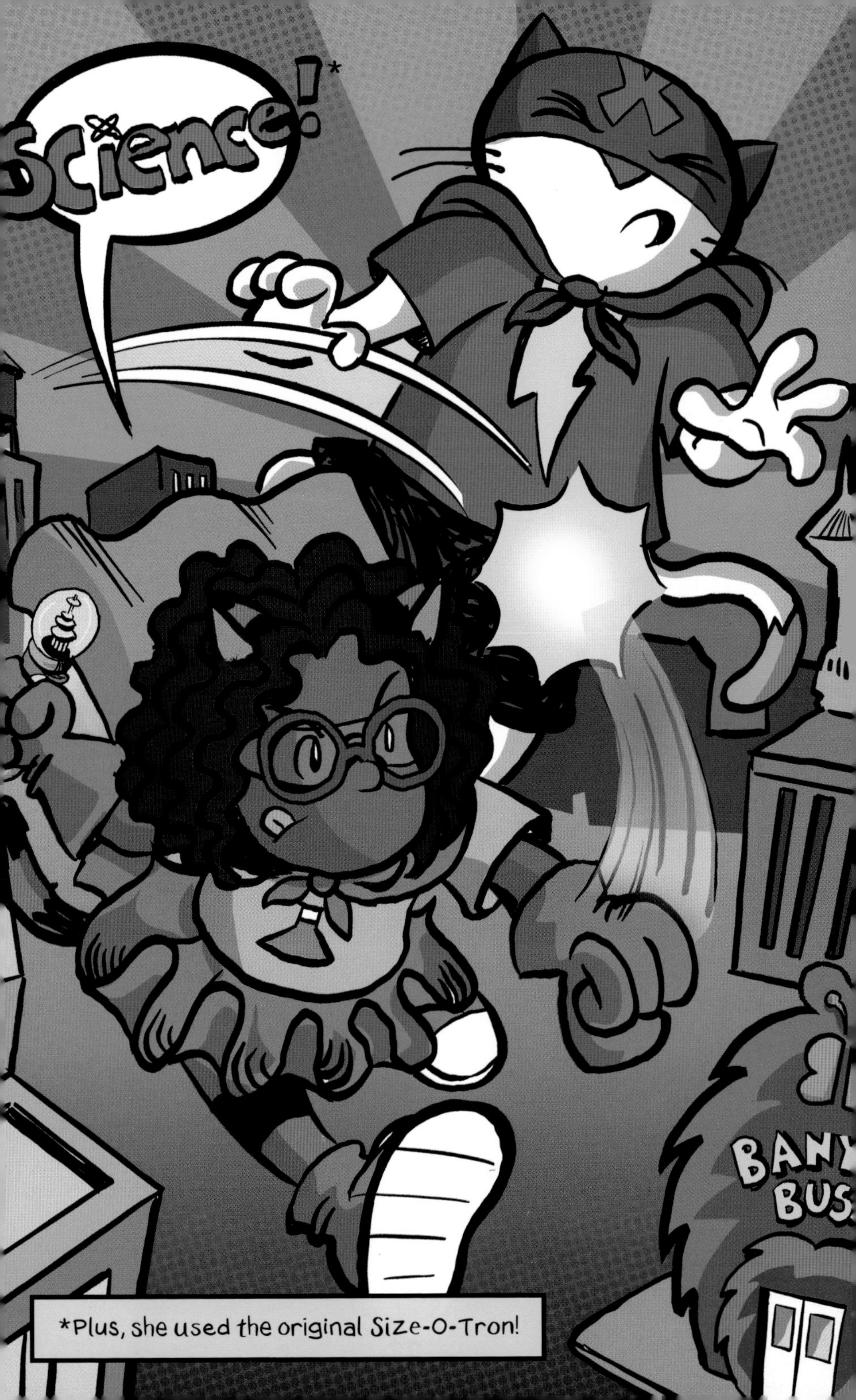
SCIENCE!*
*Plus, she used the original Size-O-Tron!

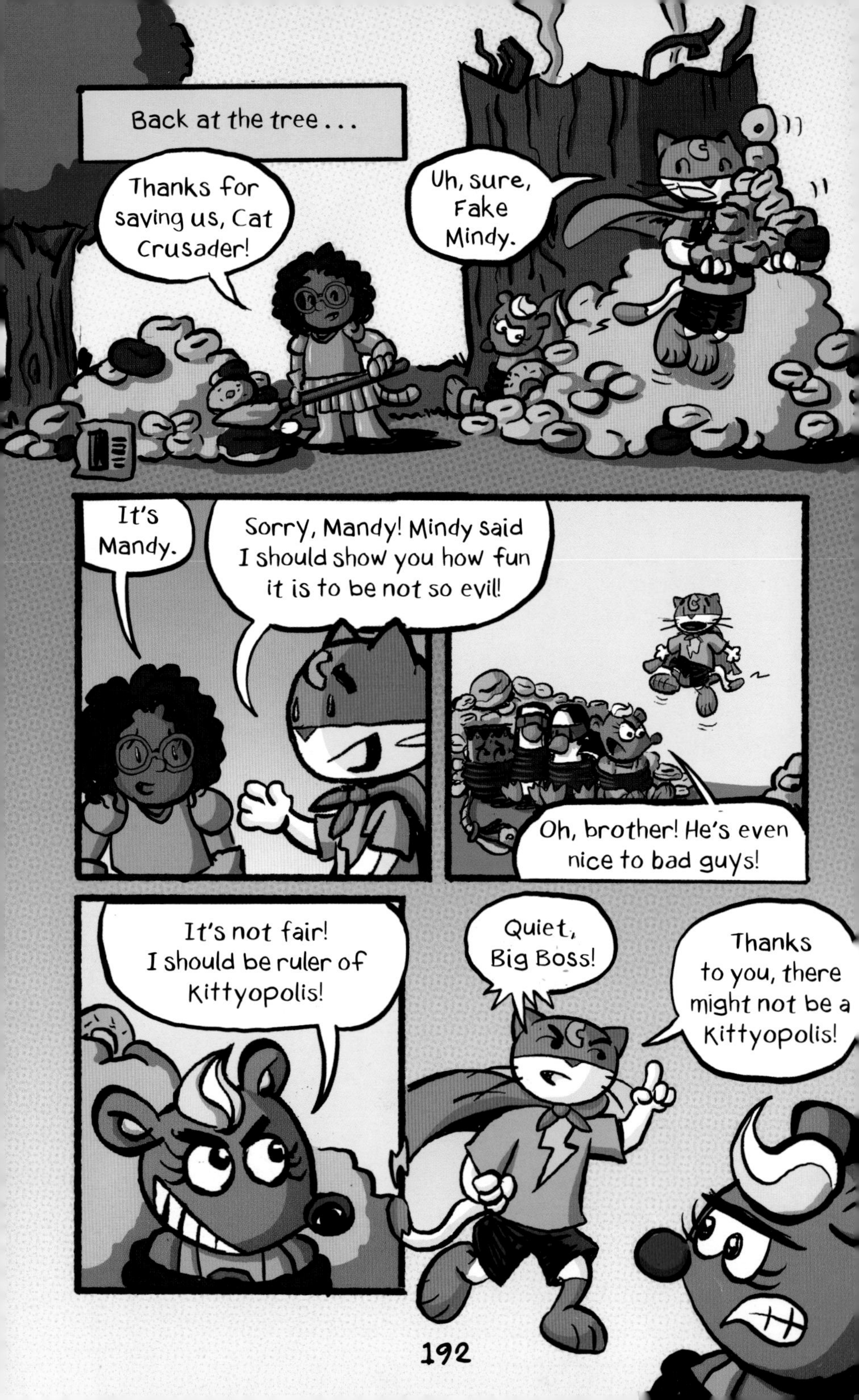

Back at the tree . . .
Thanks for saving us, Cat Crusader!
Uh, sure, Fake Mindy.
It's Mandy.
Sorry, Mandy! Mindy said I should show you how fun it is to be not so evil!
Oh, brother! He's even nice to bad guys!
It's not fair! I should be ruler of Kittyopolis!
Quiet, Big Boss!
Thanks to you, there might not be a Kittyopolis!

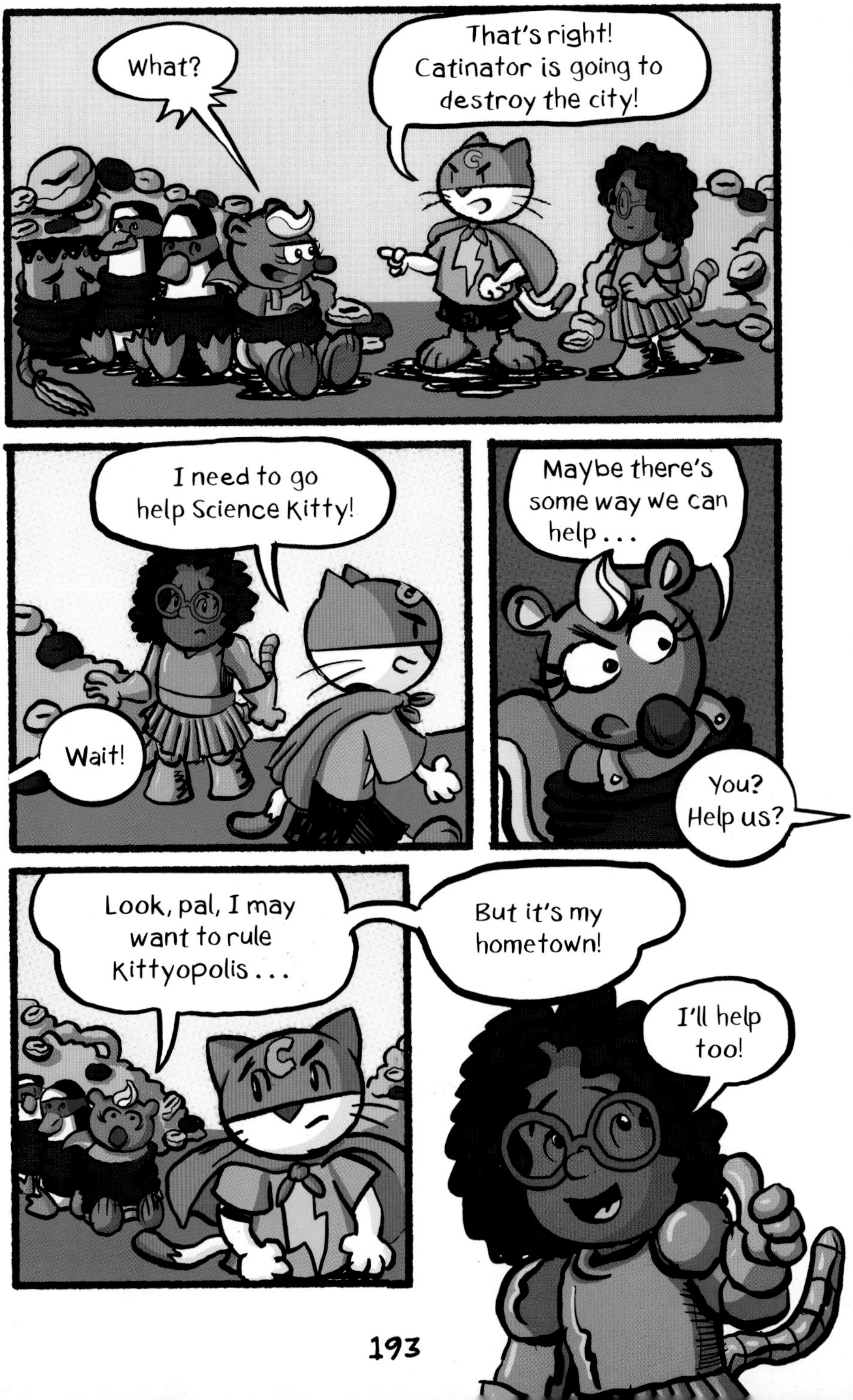
What?
That's right! Catinator is going to destroy the city!
I need to go help Science Kitty!
Wait!
Maybe there's some way we can help . . .
You? Help us?
Look, pal, I may want to rule Kittyopolis . . .
But it's my hometown!
I'll help too!

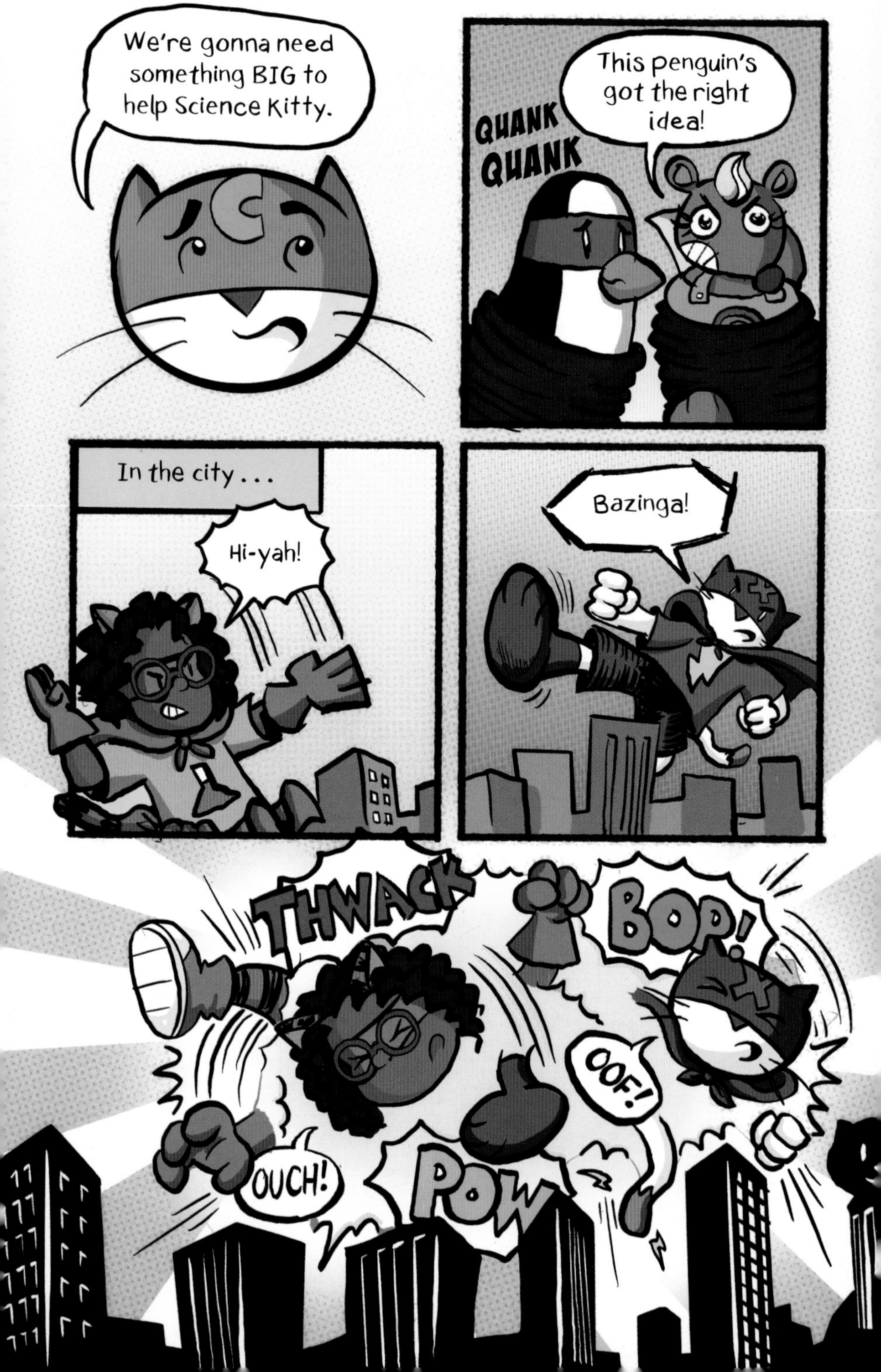
We're gonna need something BIG to help Science Kitty.
QUANK QUANK
This penguin's got the right idea!
In the city . . .
Hi-yah!
Bazinga!
THWACK
BOP!
OOF!
OUCH!
POW

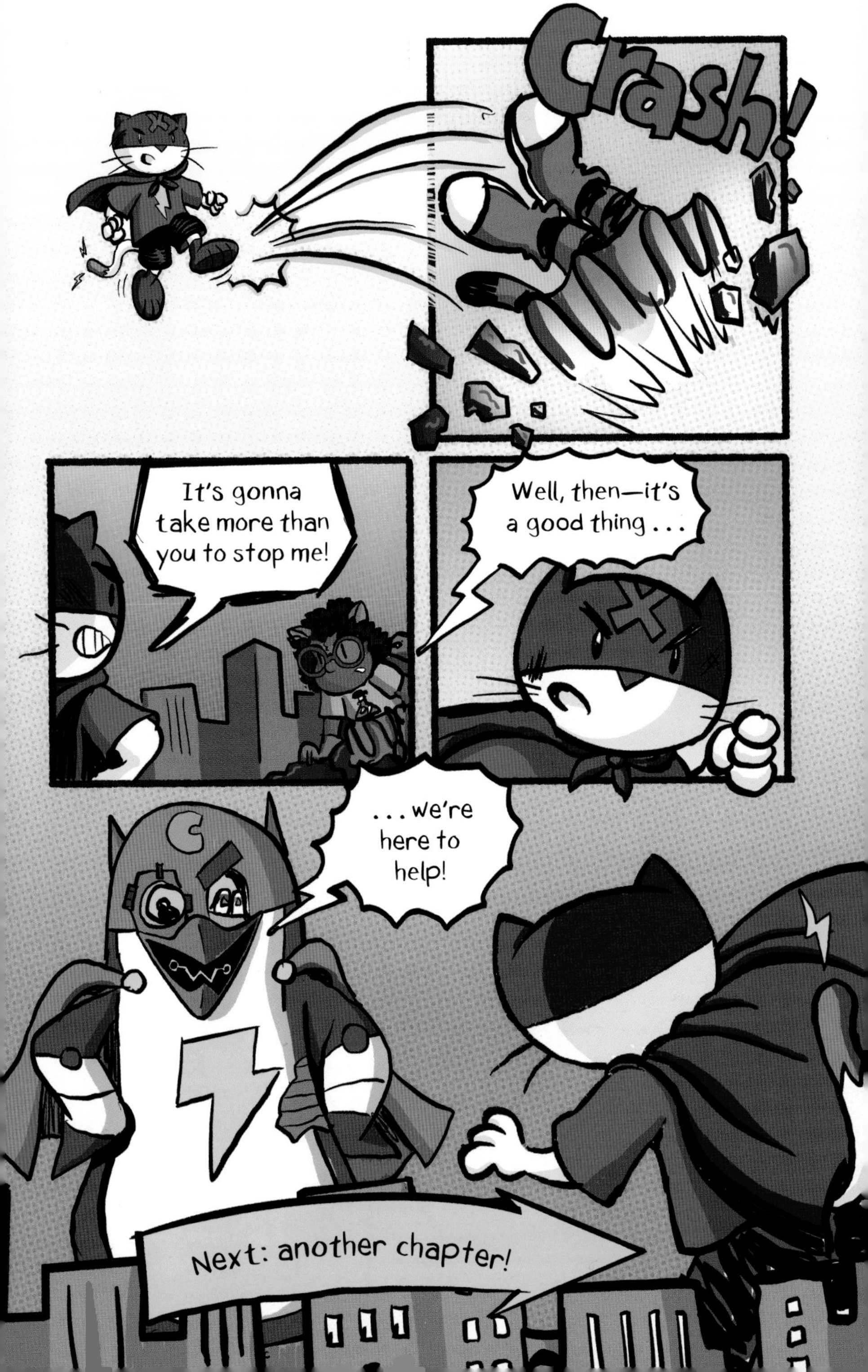
Crash!
It's gonna take more than you to stop me!
Well, then—it's a good thing . . .
. . . we're here to help!
Next: another chapter!

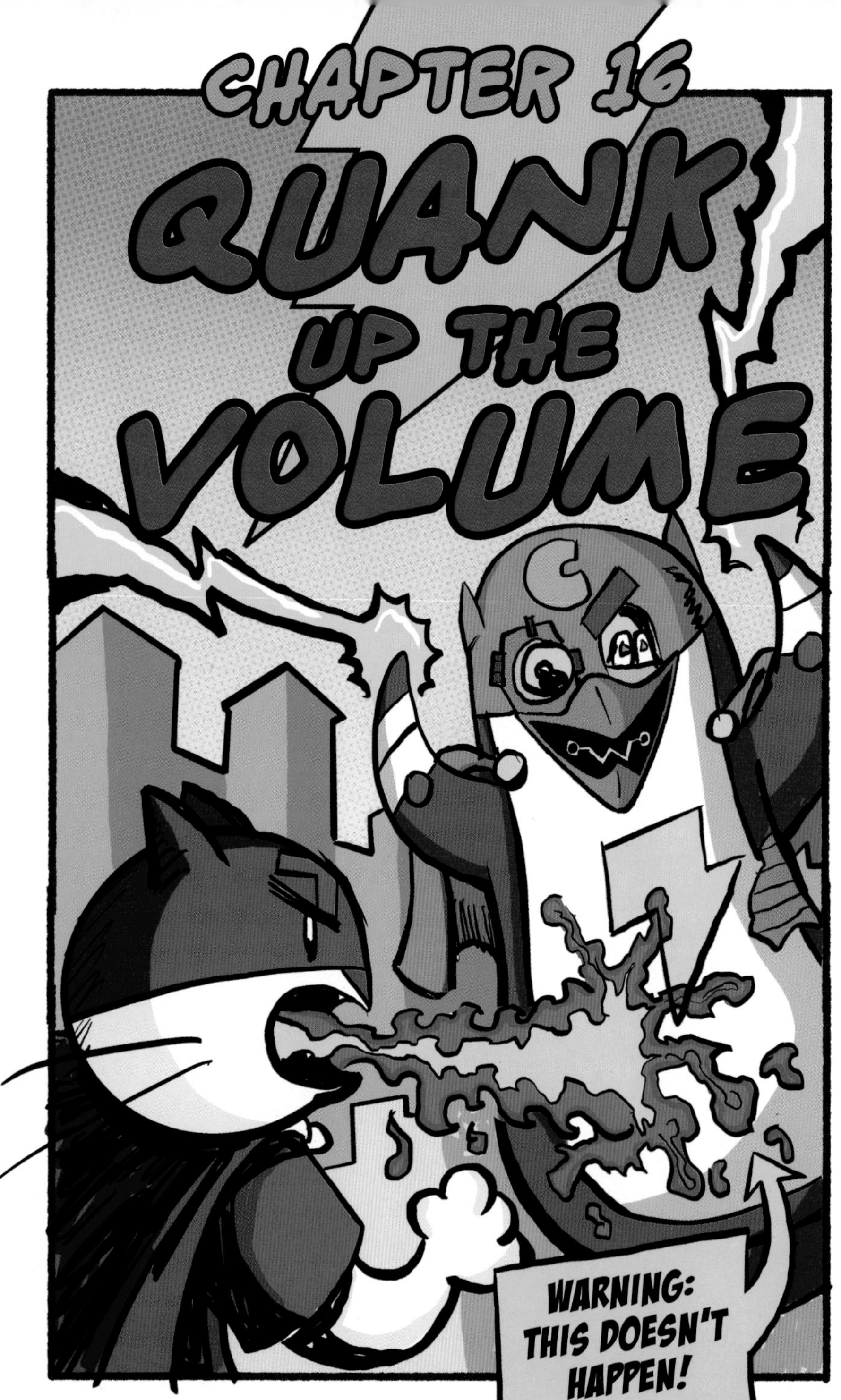
CHAPTER 16
QUANK UP THE VOLUME
WARNING: THIS DOESN'T HAPPEN!

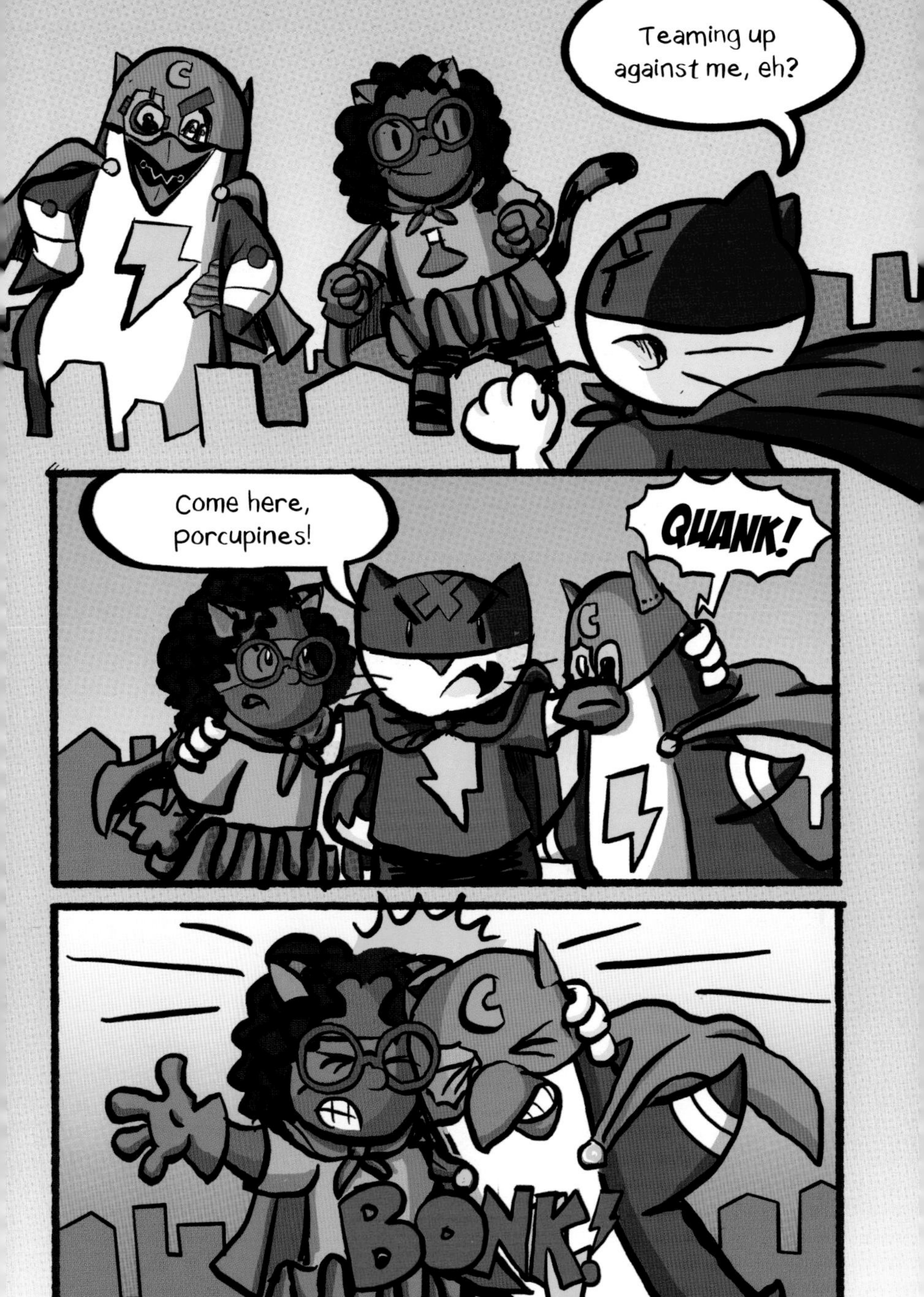
Teaming up against me, eh?
Come here, porcupines!
QUANK!
BONK!

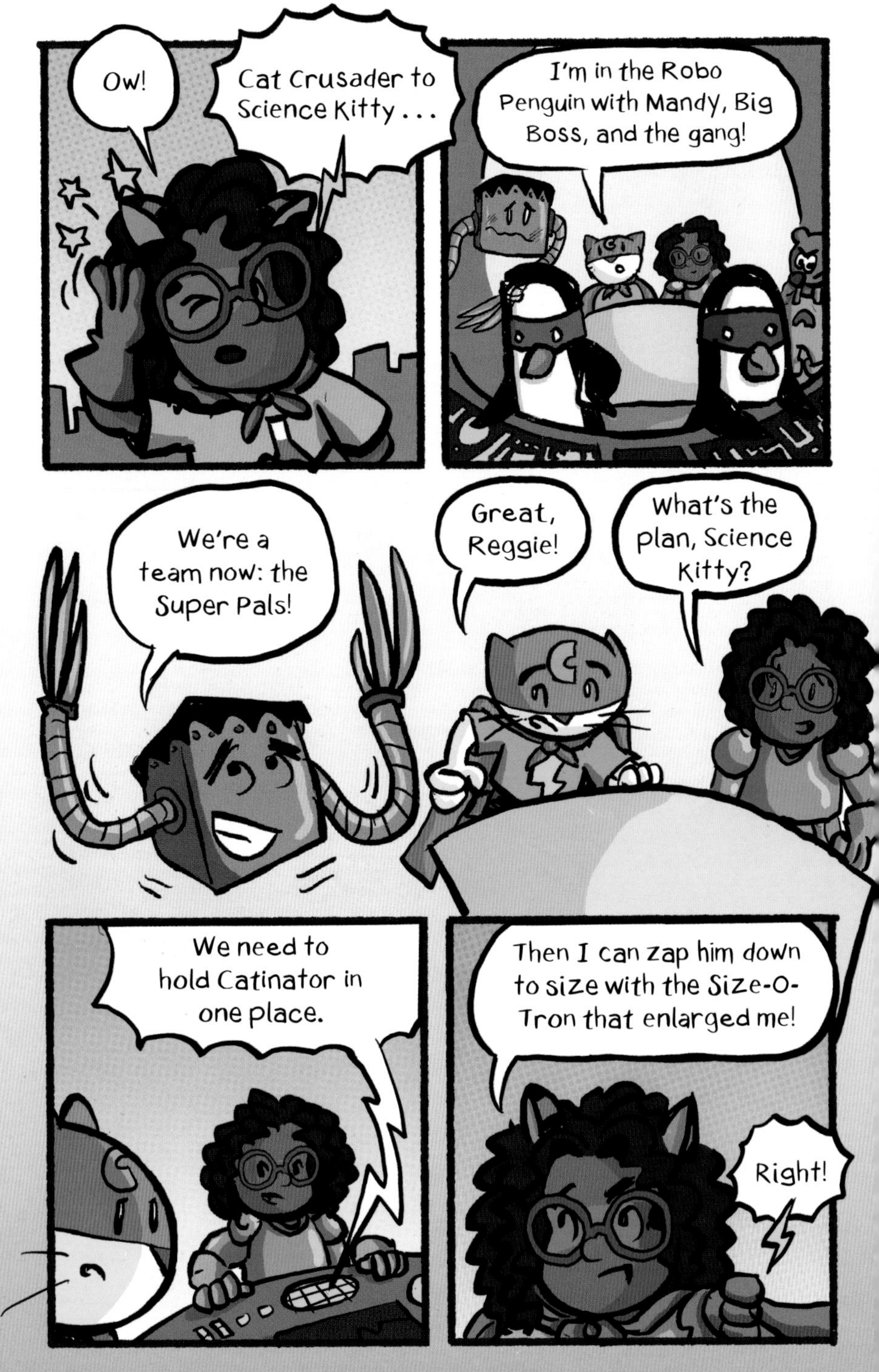
Ow!
Cat Crusader to Science Kitty . . .
I'm in the Robo Penguin with Mandy, Big Boss, and the gang!
We're a team now: the Super Pals!
Great, Reggie!
What's the plan, Science Kitty?
We need to hold Catinator in one place.
Then I can zap him down to size with the Size-O-Tron that enlarged me!
Right!

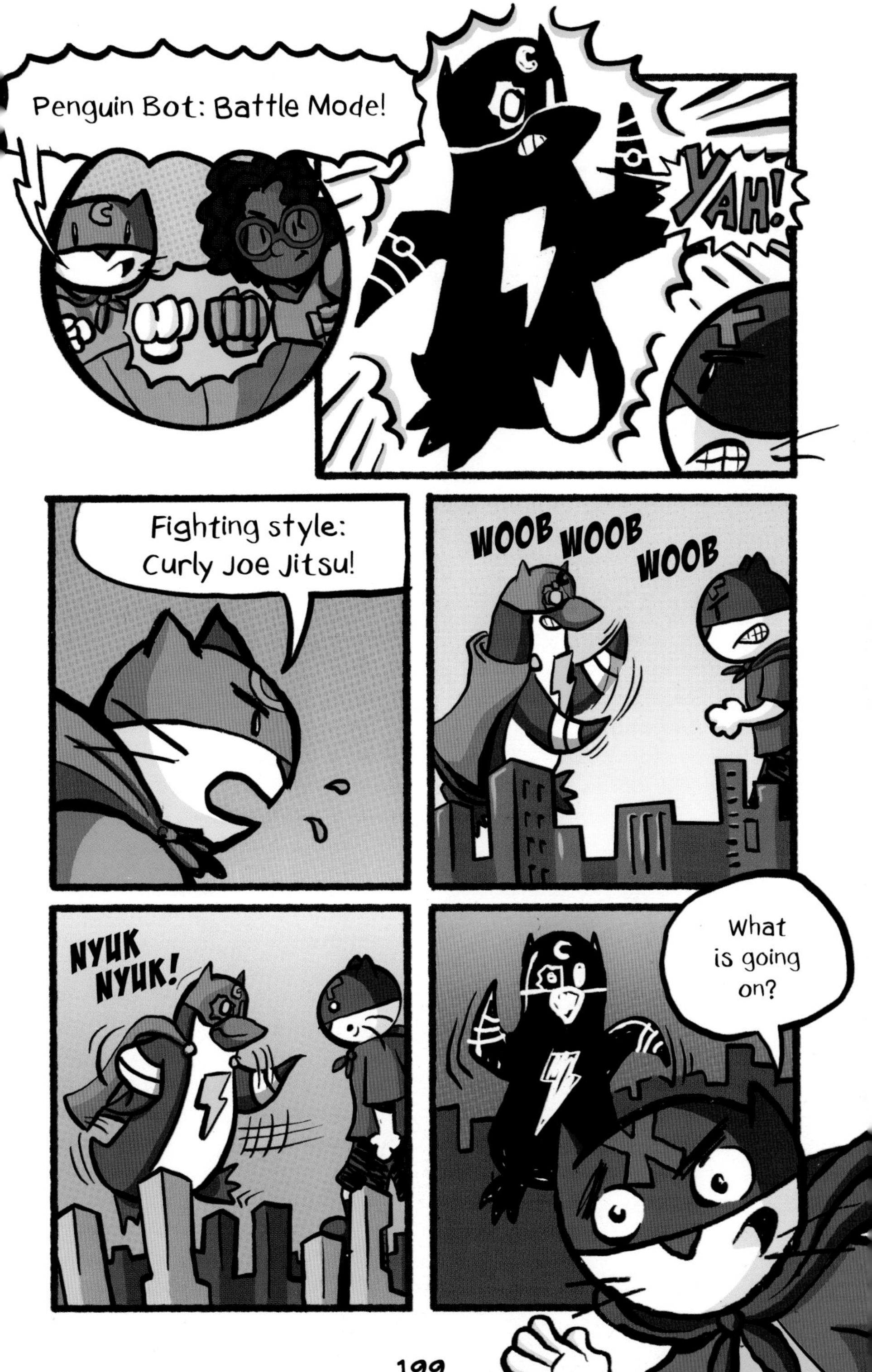
Penguin Bot: Battle Mode!
YAH!
Fighting style: Curly Joe Jitsu!
WOOB WOOB WOOB
NYUK NYUK!
What is going on?

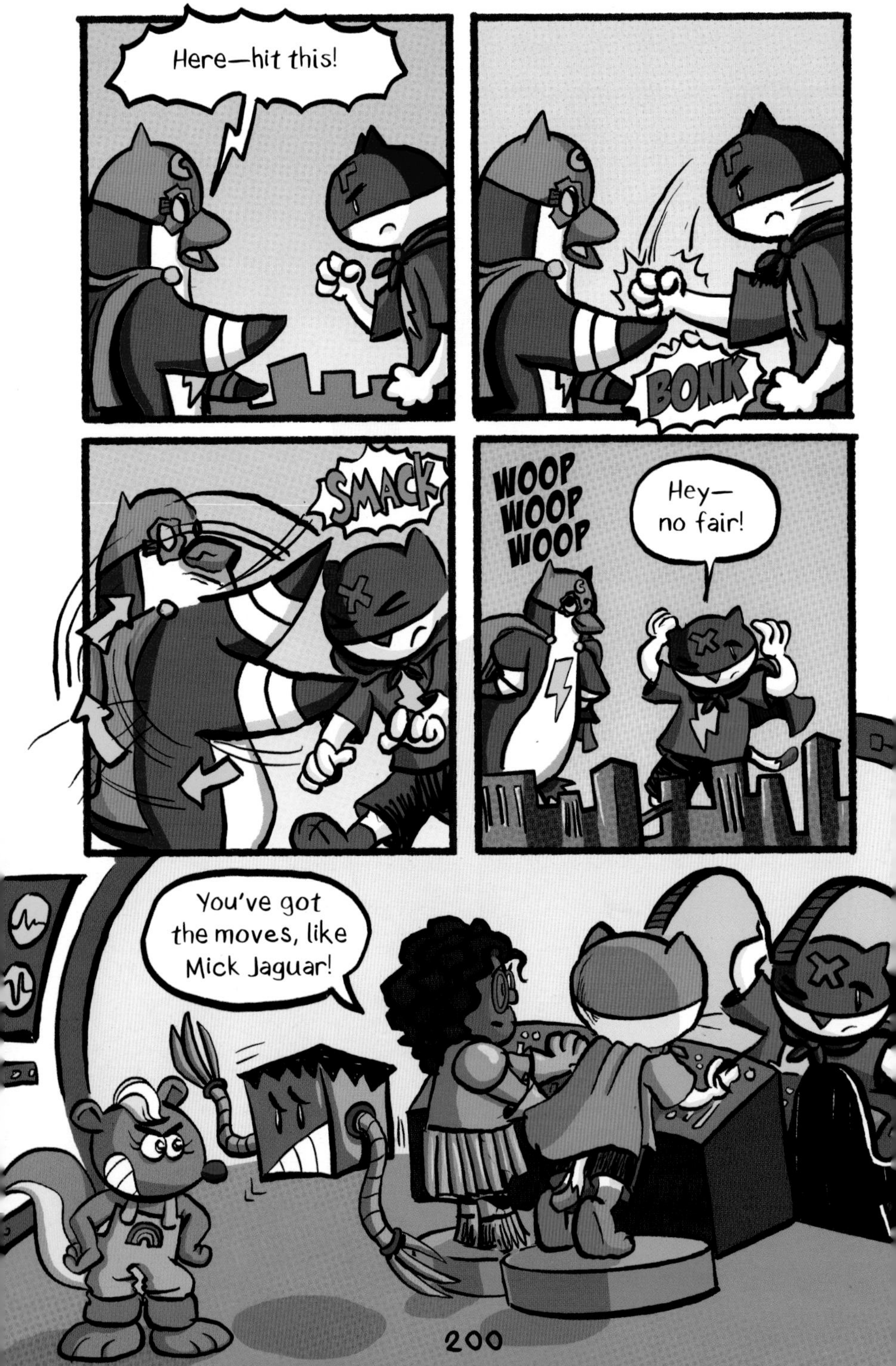
Here—hit this!
BONK
SMACK
WOOP
WOOP
WOOP
Hey—
no fair!
You've got
the moves, like
Mick Jaguar!

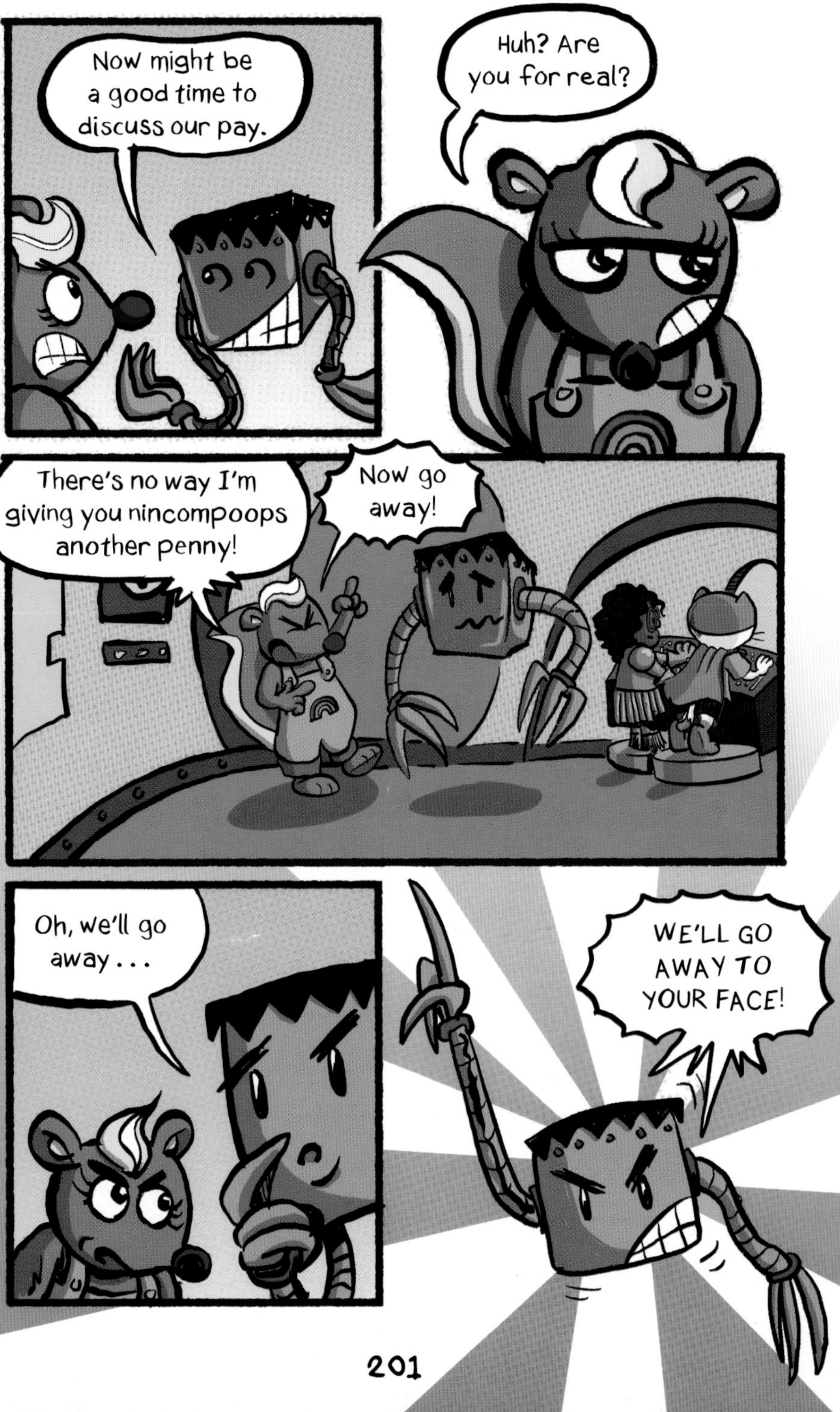
Now might be a good time to discuss our pay.
Huh? Are you for real?
There's no way I'm giving you nincompoops another penny!
Now go away!
Oh, we'll go away . . .
WE'LL GO AWAY TO YOUR FACE!

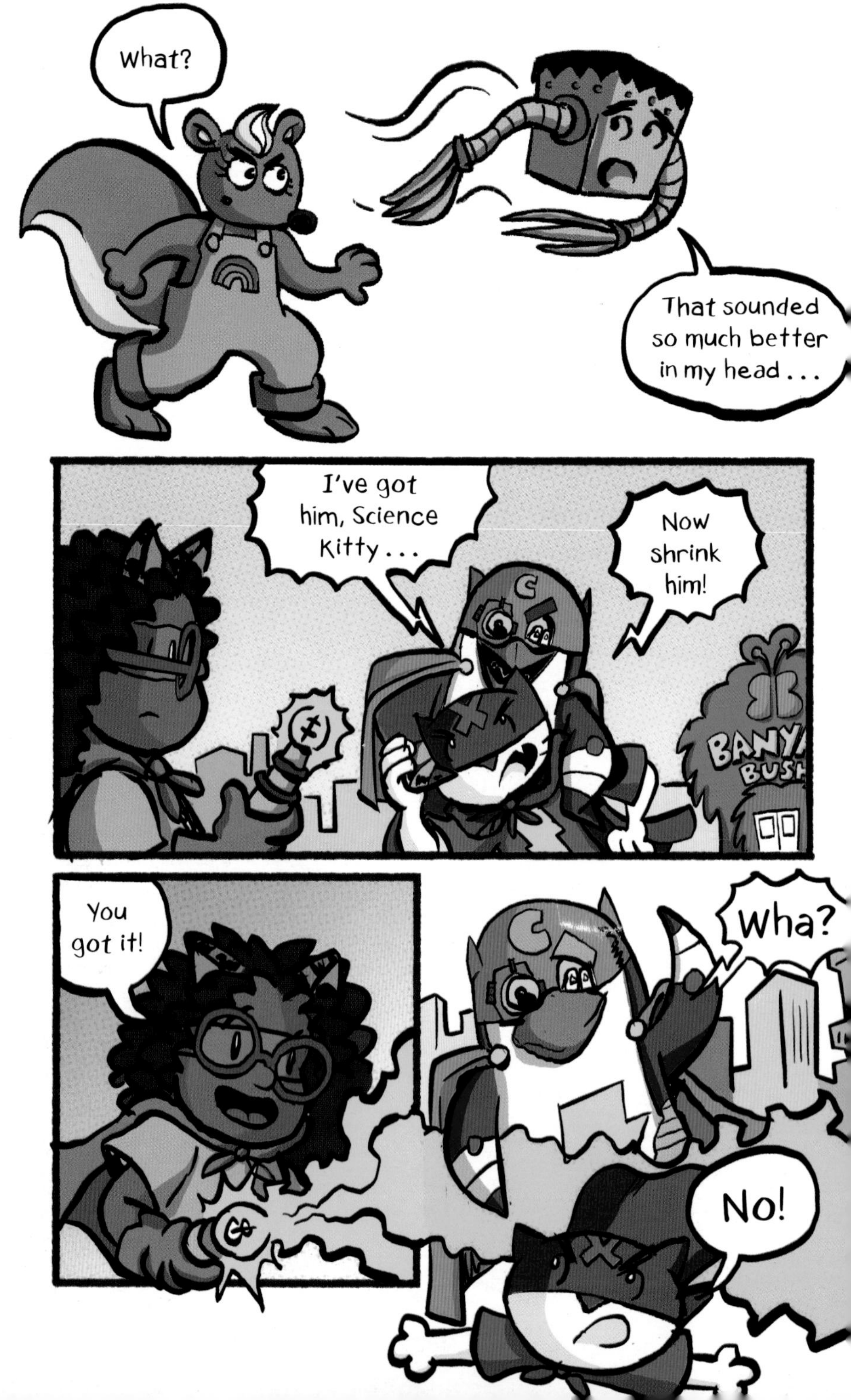
What?
That sounded so much better in my head . . .
I've got him, Science Kitty . . .
Now shrink him!
You got it!
Wha?
No!

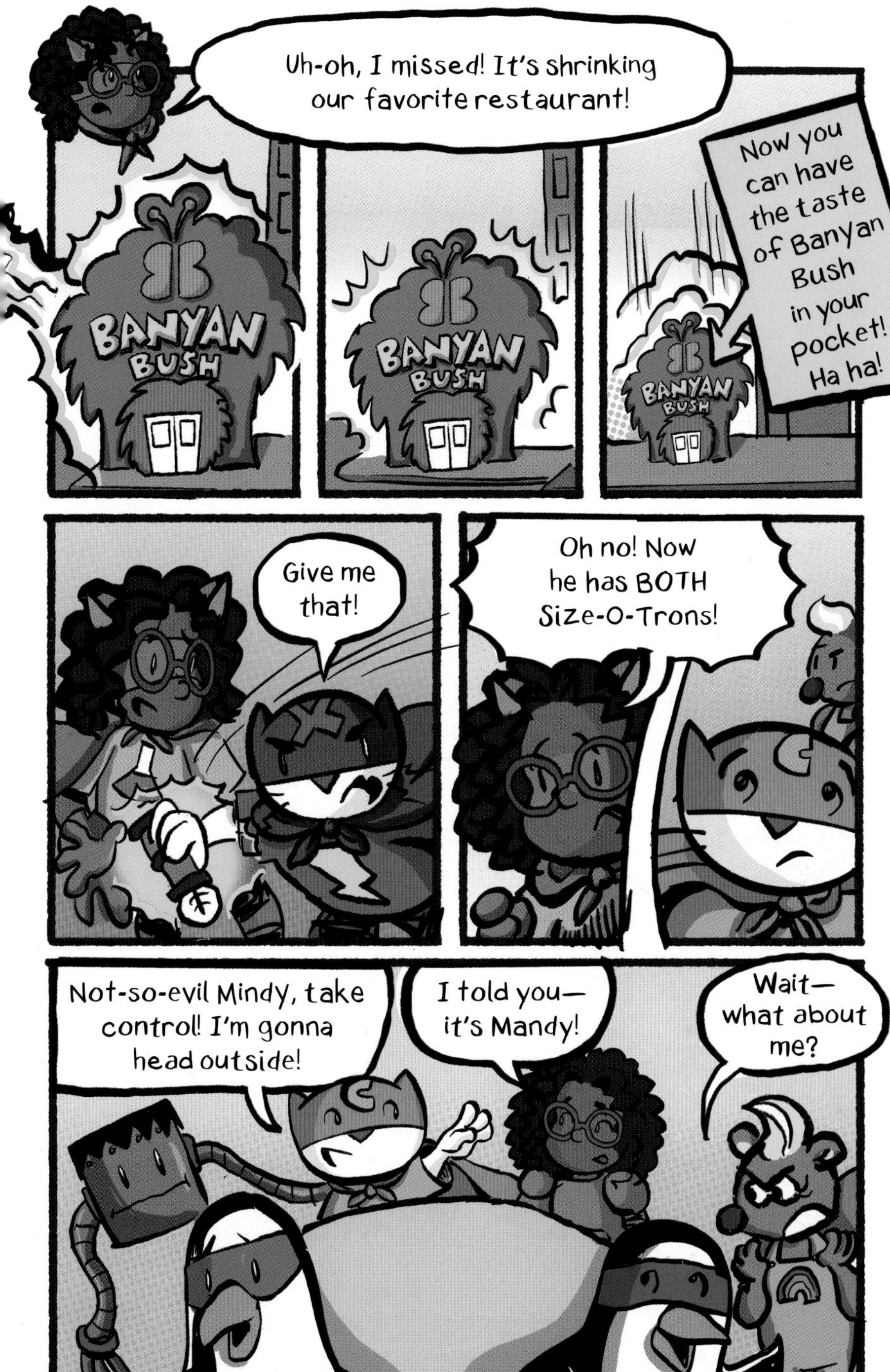
Uh-oh, I missed! It's shrinking our favorite restaurant!
BANYAN BUSH
BANYAN BUSH
BANYAN BUSH
Now you can have the taste of Banyan Bush in your pocket! Ha ha!
Give me that!
Oh no! Now he has BOTH Size-O-Trons!
Not-so-evil Mindy, take control! I'm gonna head outside!
I told you— it's Mandy!
Wait— what about me?

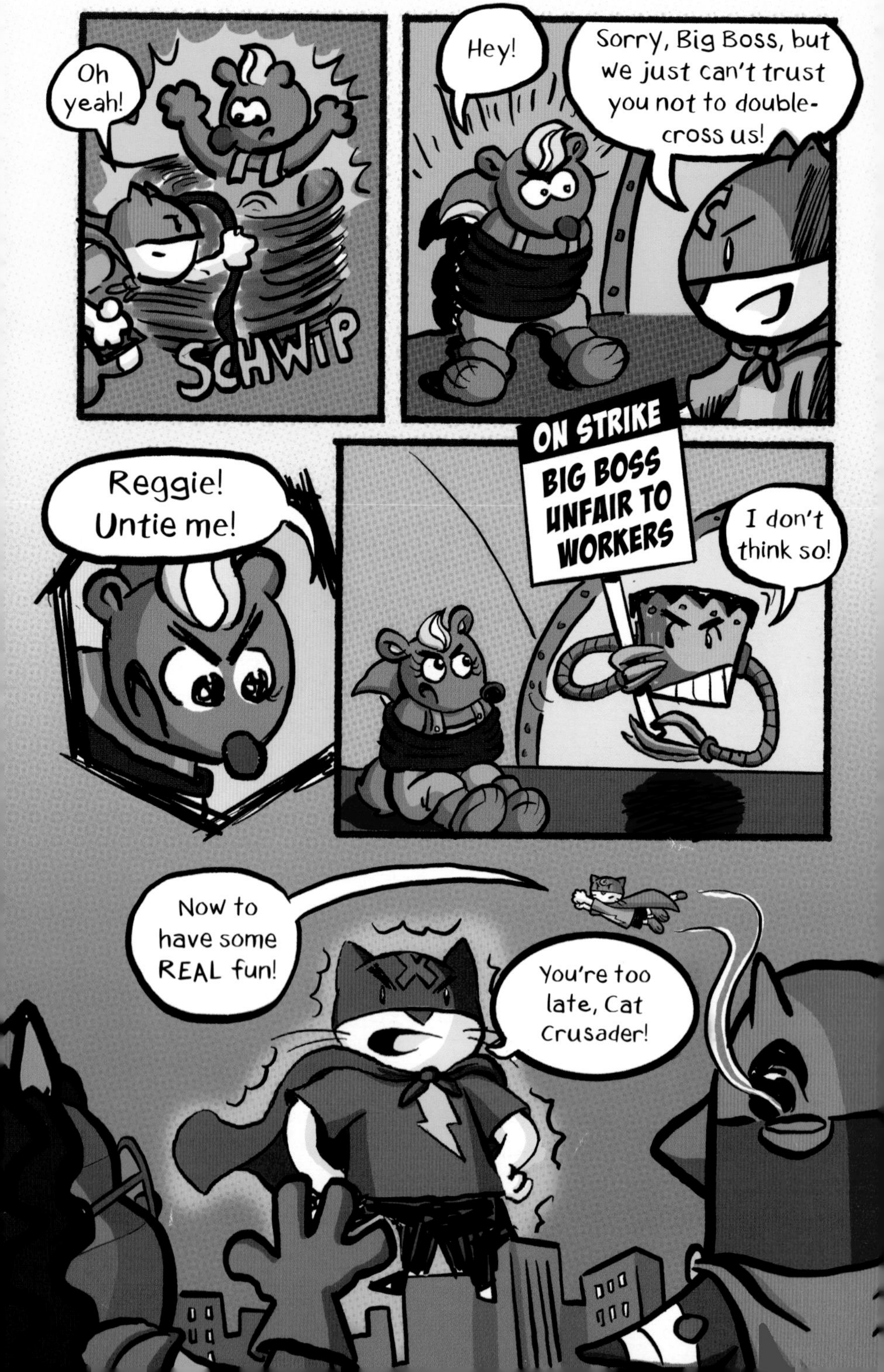
Oh yeah!
SCHWIP
Hey!
Sorry, Big Boss, but we just can't trust you not to double-cross us!
Reggie! Untie me!
ON STRIKE
BIG BOSS UNFAIR TO WORKERS
I don't think so!
Now to have some REAL fun!
You're too late, Cat Crusader!

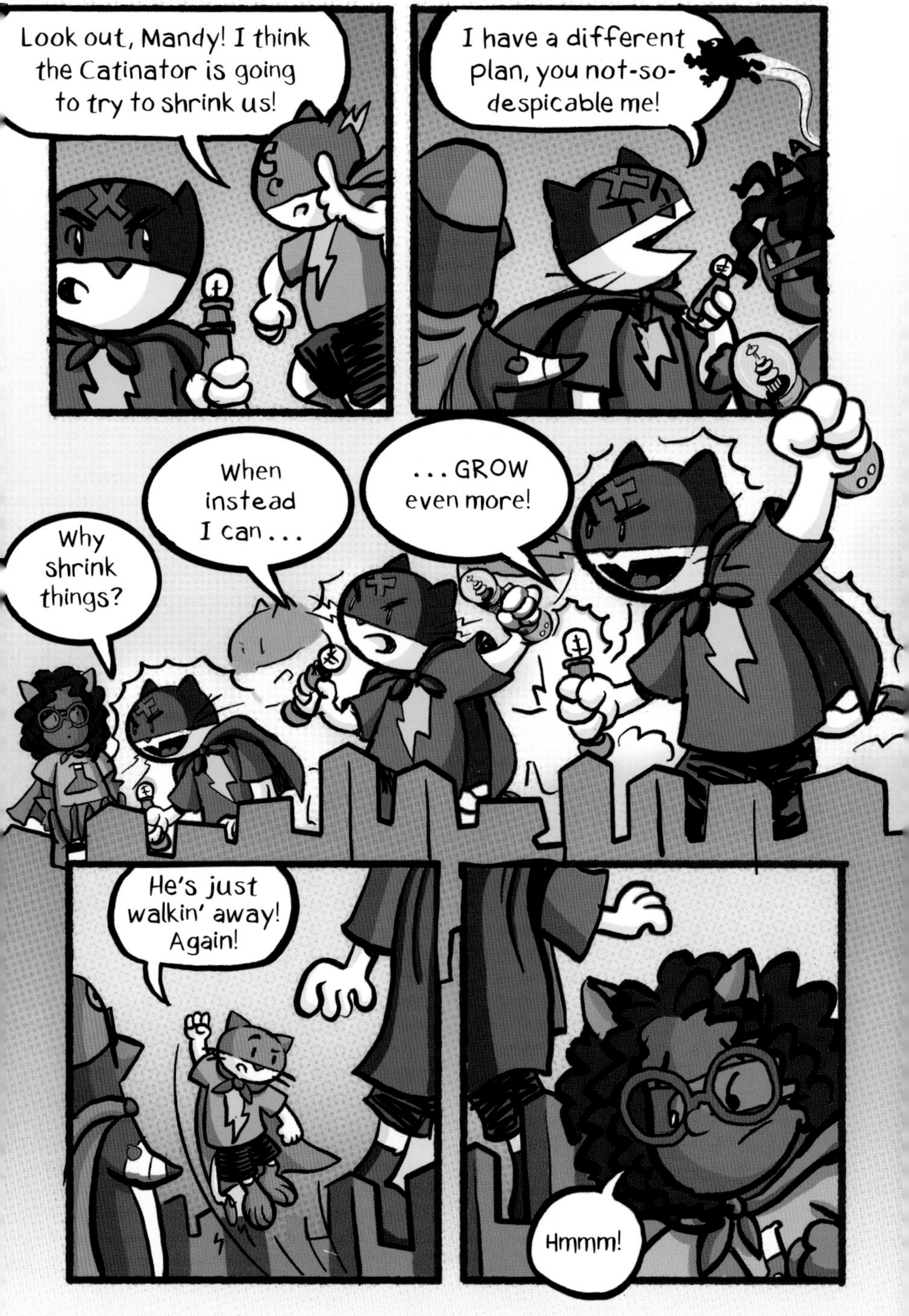
Look out, Mandy! I think the Catinator is going to try to shrink us!
I have a different plan, you not-so-despicable me!
Why shrink things?
When instead I can . . .
. . . GROW even more!
He's just walkin' away! Again!
Hmmm!

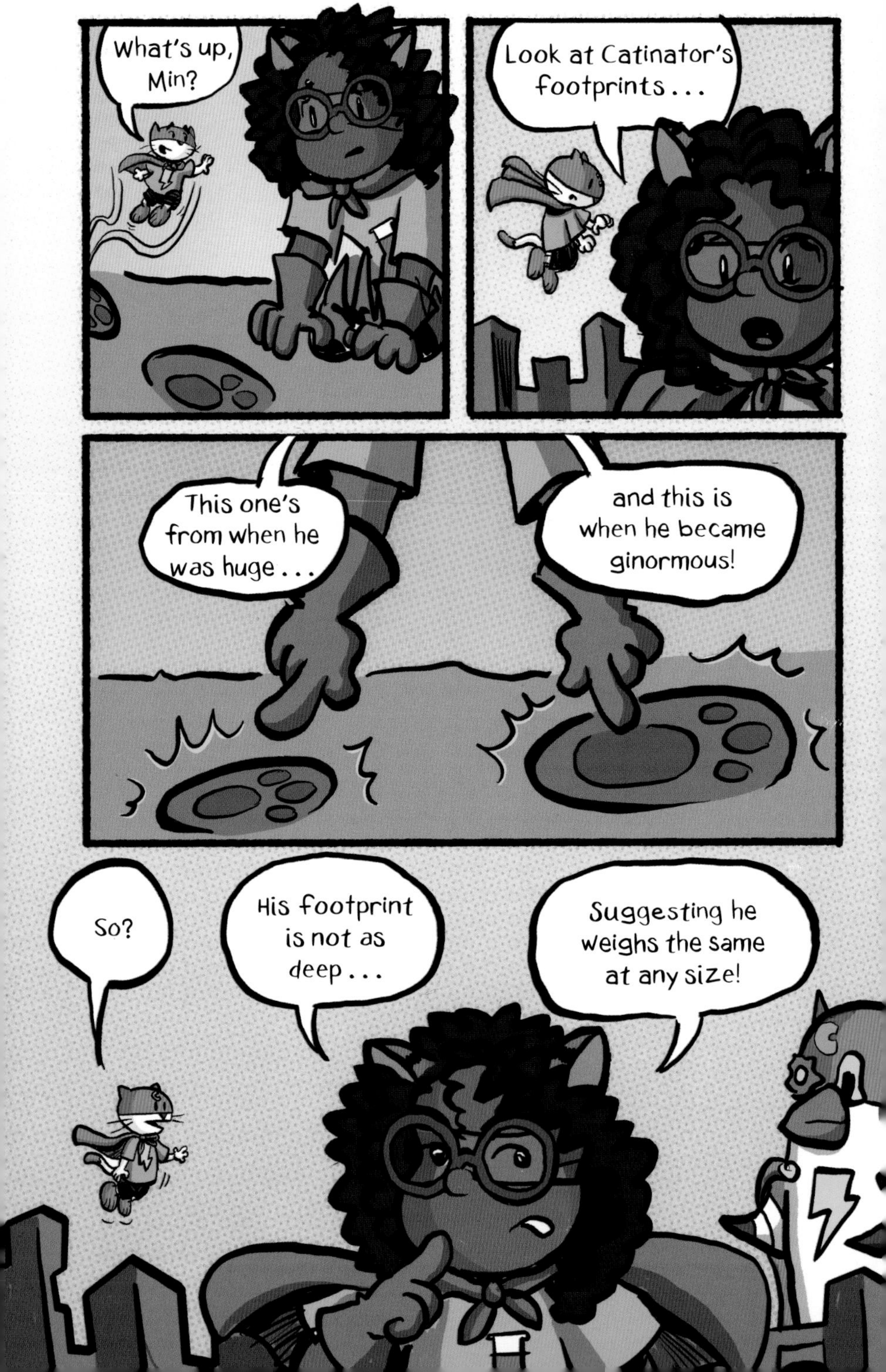
What's up, Min?
Look at Catinator's footprints . . .
This one's from when he was huge . . .
and this is when he became ginormous!
So?
His footprint is not as deep . . .
Suggesting he weighs the same at any size!

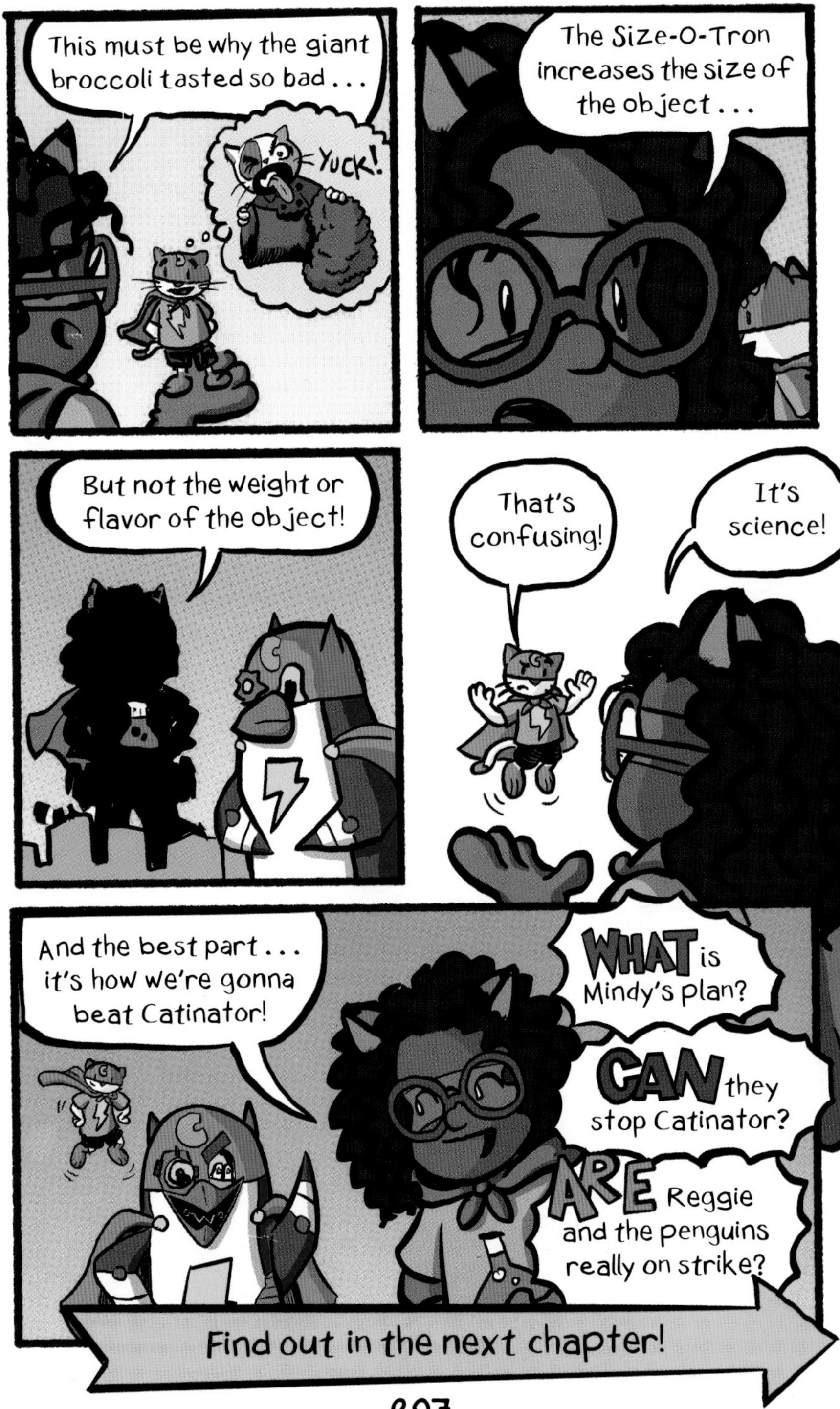
This must be why the giant broccoli tasted so bad . . .
YUCK!
The Size-O-Tron increases the size of the object . . .
But not the weight or flavor of the object!
That's confusing!
It's science!
And the best part . . . it's how we're gonna beat Catinator!
WHAT is Mindy's plan?
CAN they stop Catinator?
ARE Reggie and the penguins really on strike?
Find out in the next chapter!

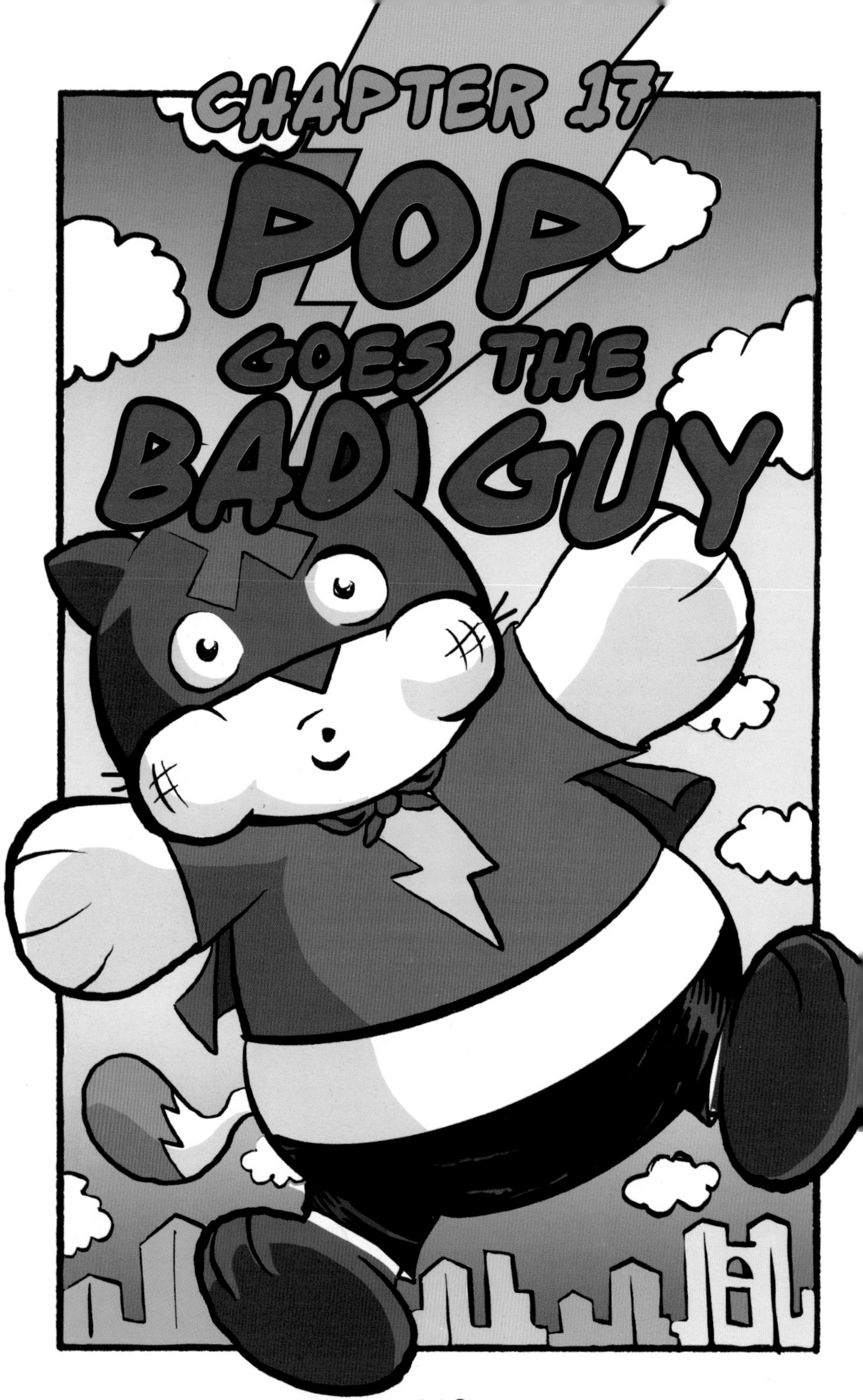
CHAPTER 17
POP GOES THE BAD GUY

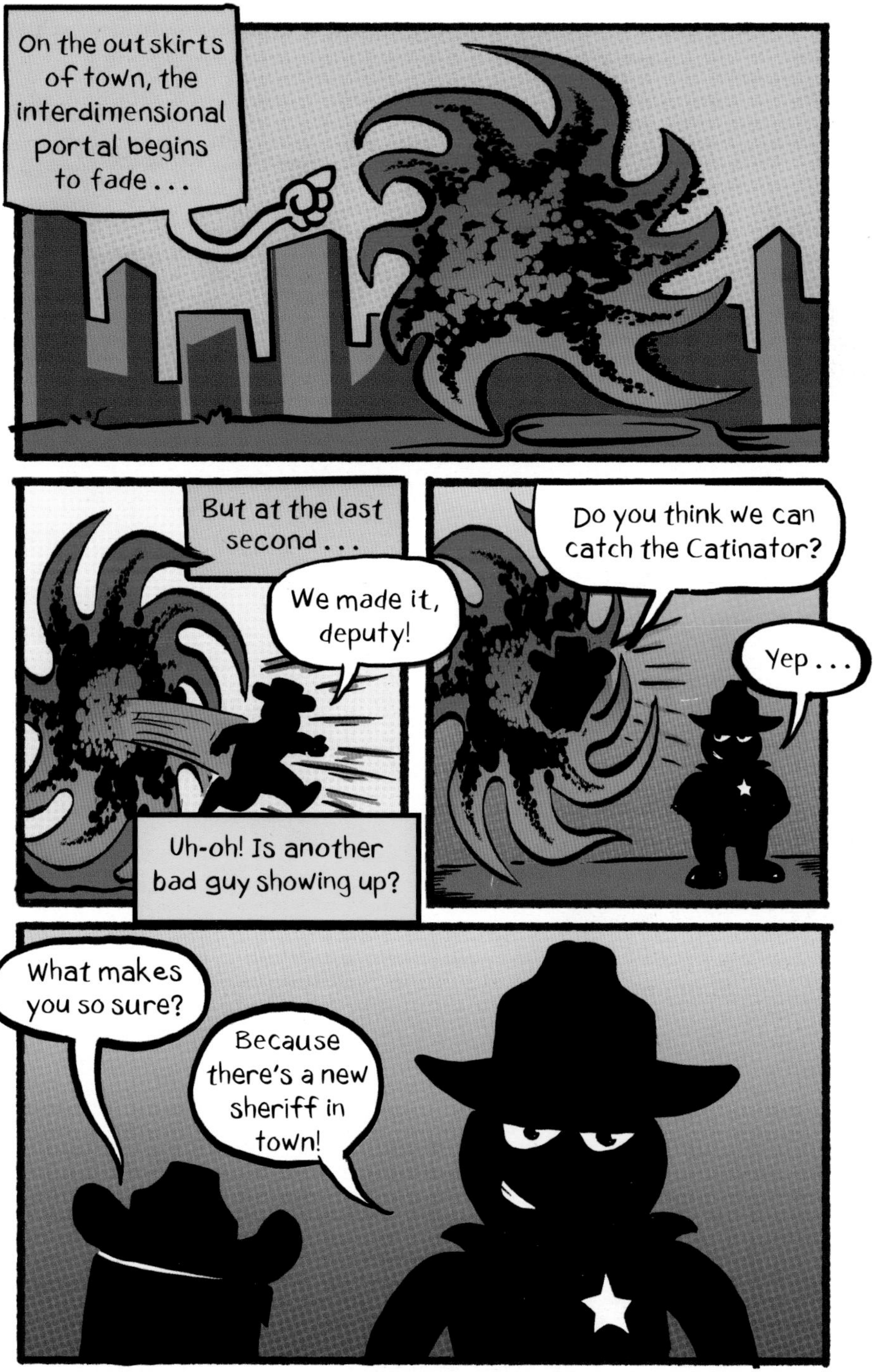
On the outskirts of town, the interdimensional portal begins to fade . . .
But at the last second . . .
We made it, deputy!
Uh-oh! Is another bad guy showing up?
Do you think we can catch the Catinator?
Yep . . .
What makes you so sure?
Because there's a new sheriff in town!

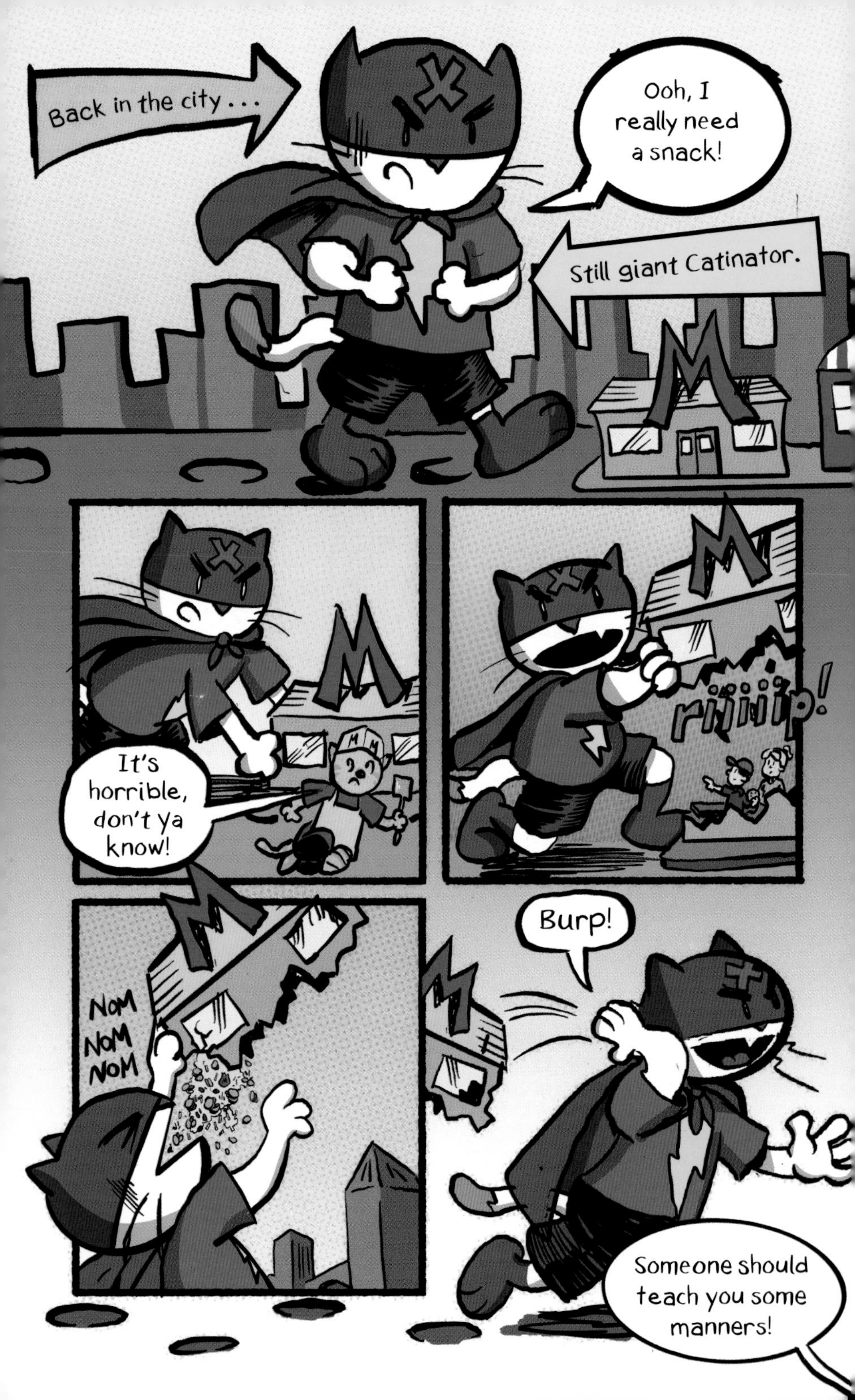
Back in the city . . .
Ooh, I really need a snack!
Still giant Catinator.
It's horrible, don't ya know!
riiiiip!
NOM NOM NOM
Burp!
Someone should teach you some manners!

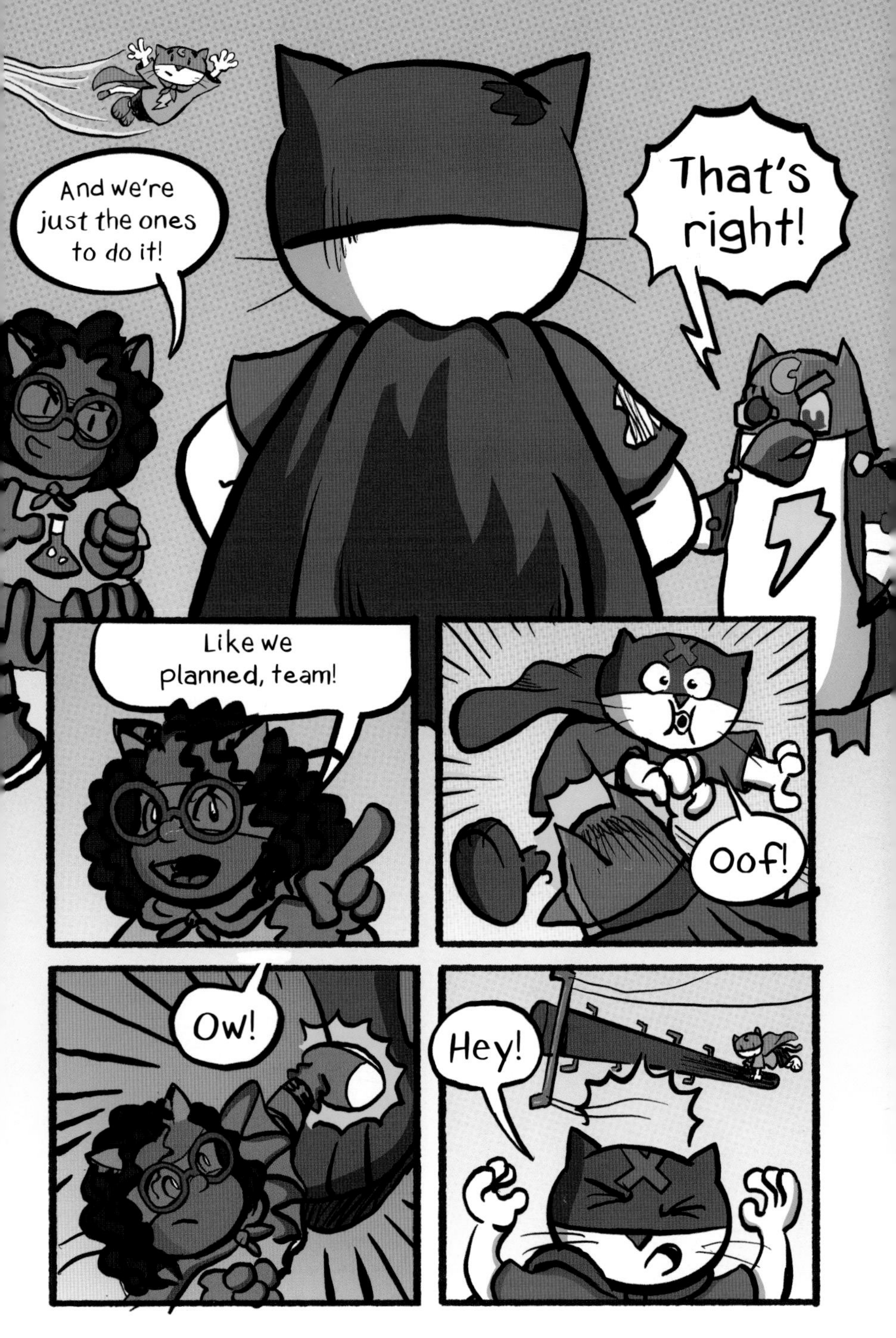
And we're just the ones to do it!
That's right!
Like we planned, team!
Oof!
Ow!
Hey!

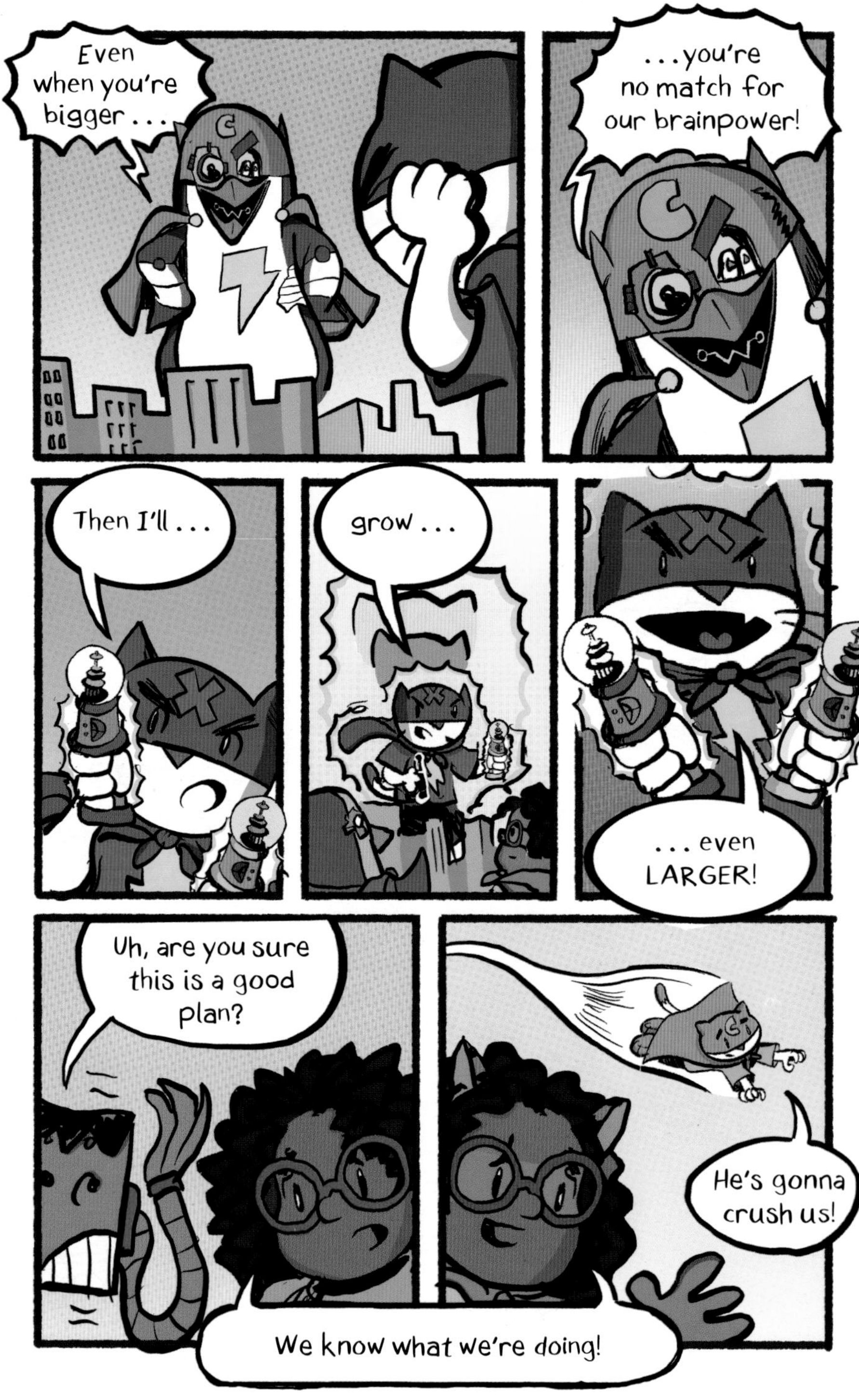
Even when you're bigger . . .
. . . you're no match for our brainpower!
Then I'll . . .
grow . . .
. . . even LARGER!
Uh, are you sure this is a good plan?
He's gonna crush us!
We know what we're doing!

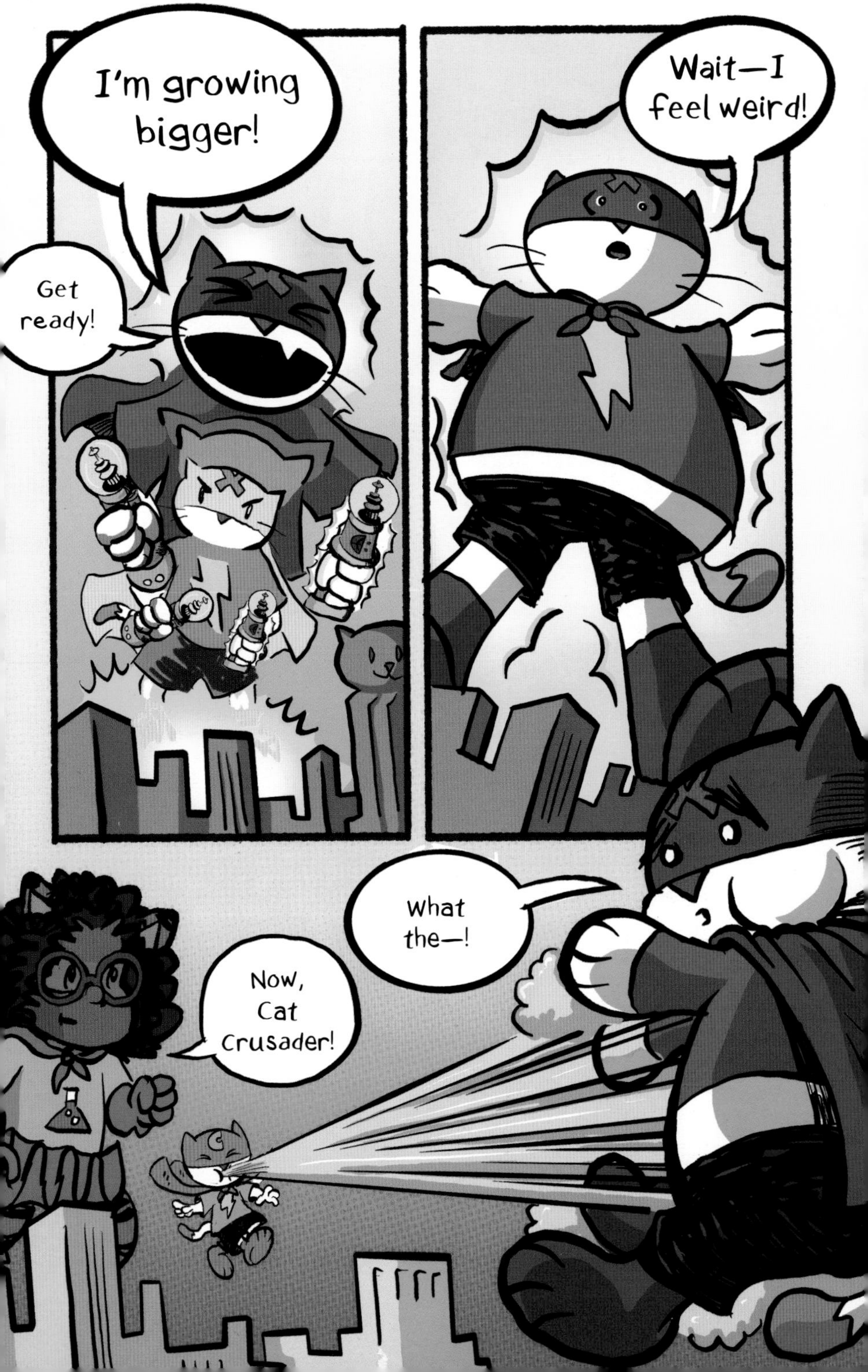
I'm growing bigger!
Get ready!
Wait—I feel weird!
What the—!
Now, Cat Crusader!

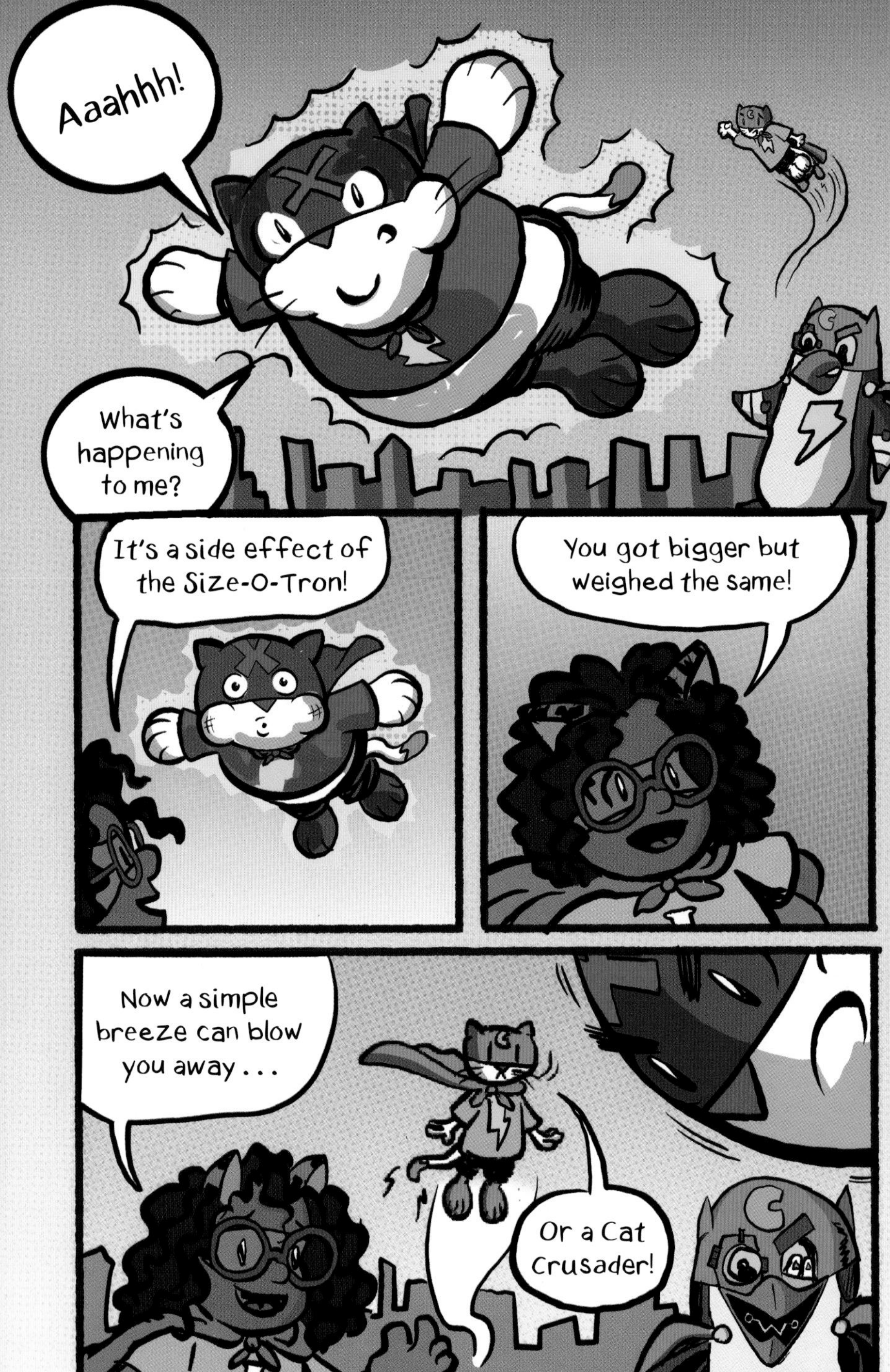
Aaahhh!
What's happening to me?
It's a side effect of the Size-O-Tron!
You got bigger but weighed the same!
Now a simple breeze can blow you away . . .
Or a Cat Crusader!

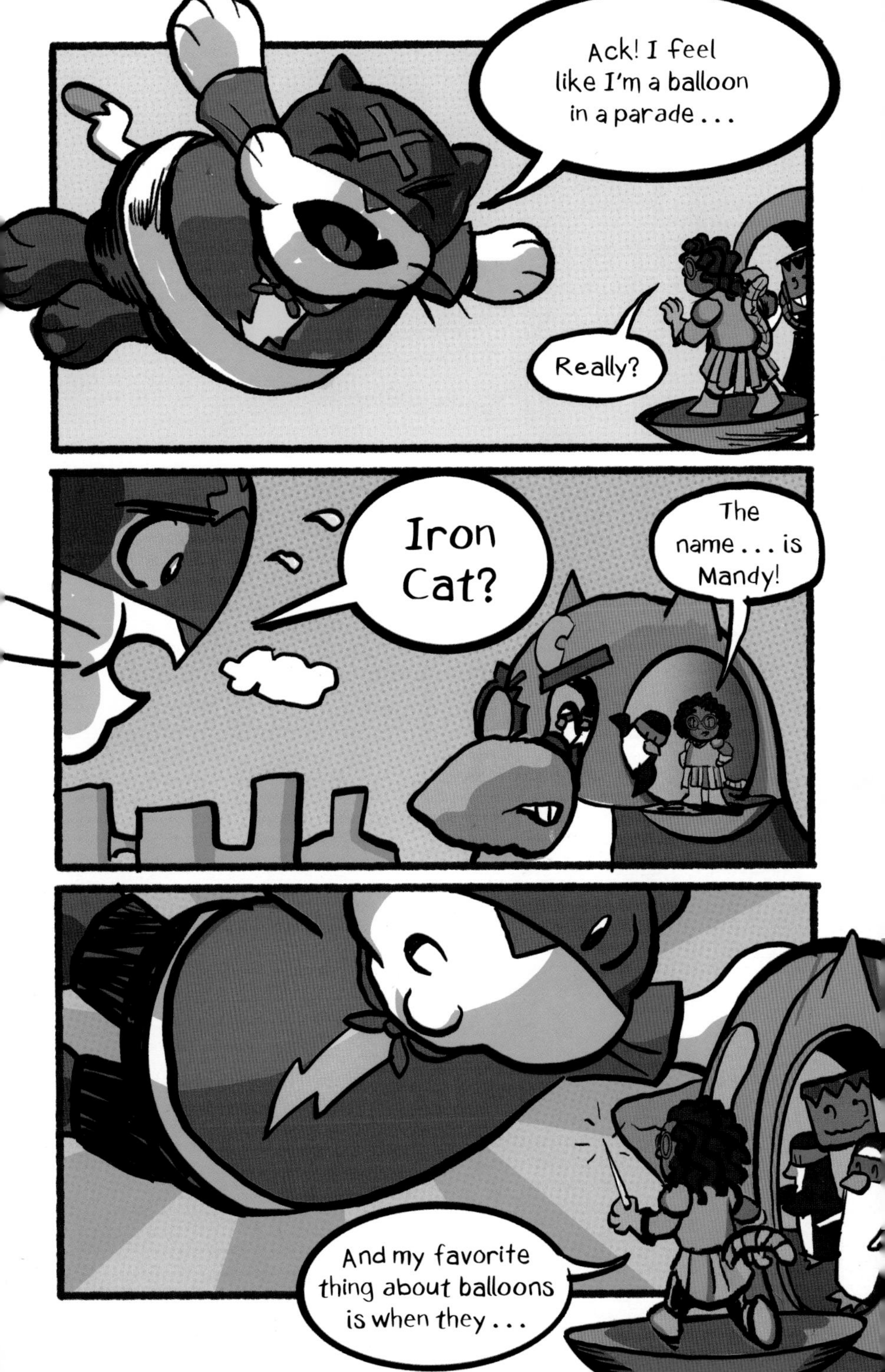
Ack! I feel like I'm a balloon in a parade . . .
Really?
Iron Cat?
The name . . . is Mandy!
And my favorite thing about balloons is when they . . .

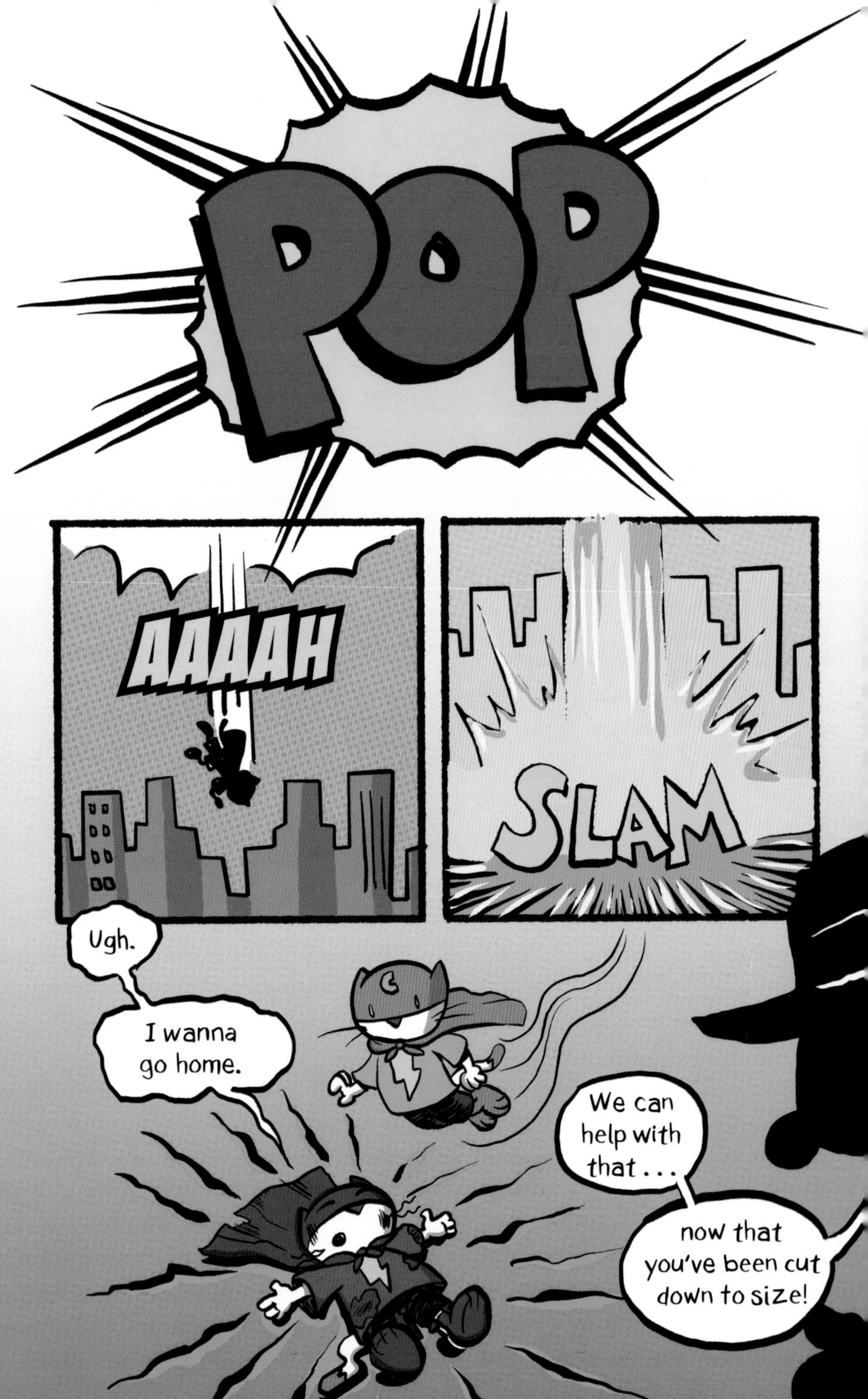
POP
AAAAH
SLAM
Ugh.
I wanna go home.
We can help with that . . .
now that you've been cut down to size!

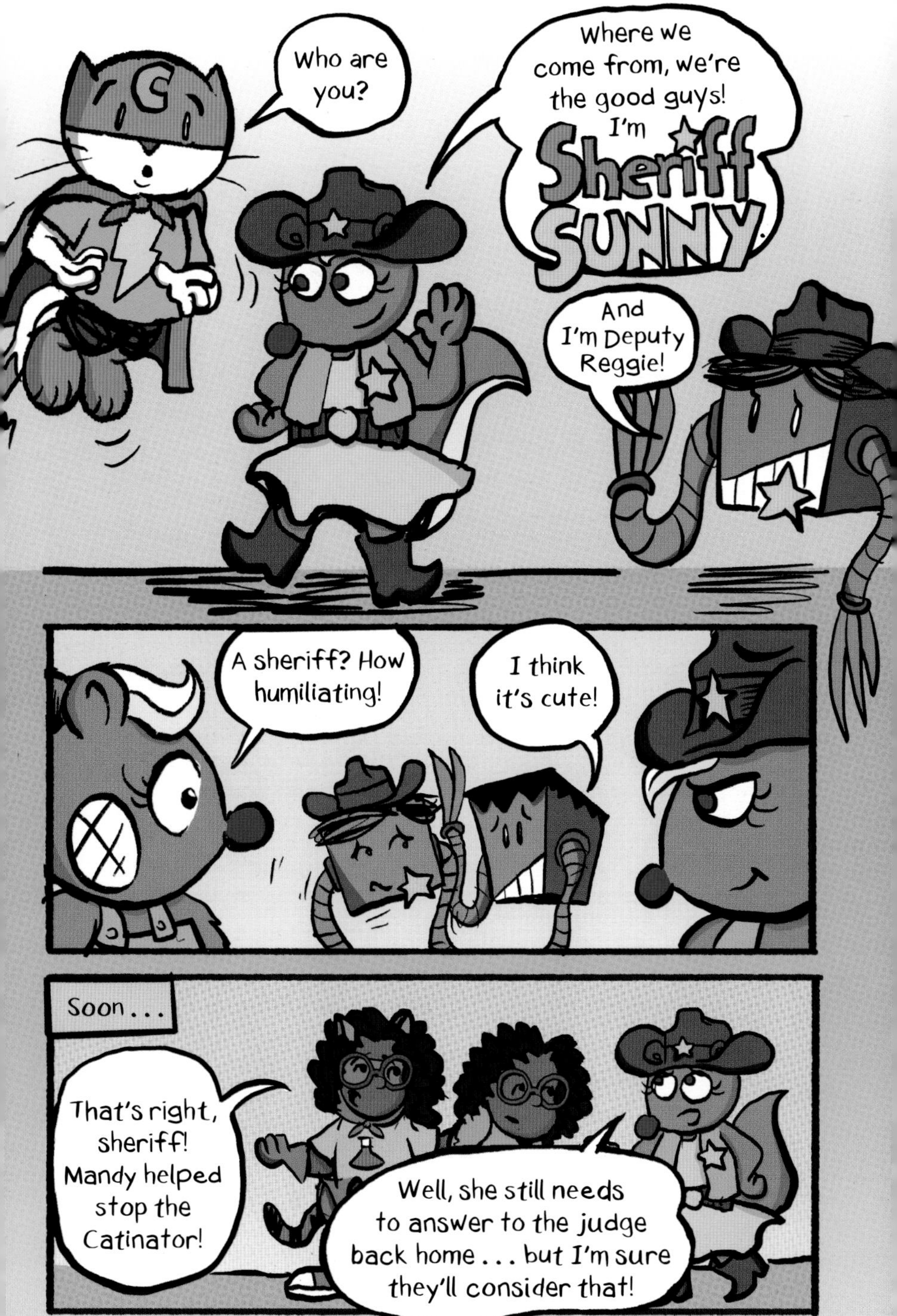
Who are you?
Where we come from, we're the good guys! I'm Sheriff SUNNY.
And I'm Deputy Reggie!
A sheriff? How humiliating!
I think it's cute!
Soon . . .
That's right, sheriff! Mandy helped stop the Catinator!
Well, she still needs to answer to the judge back home . . . but I'm sure they'll consider that!

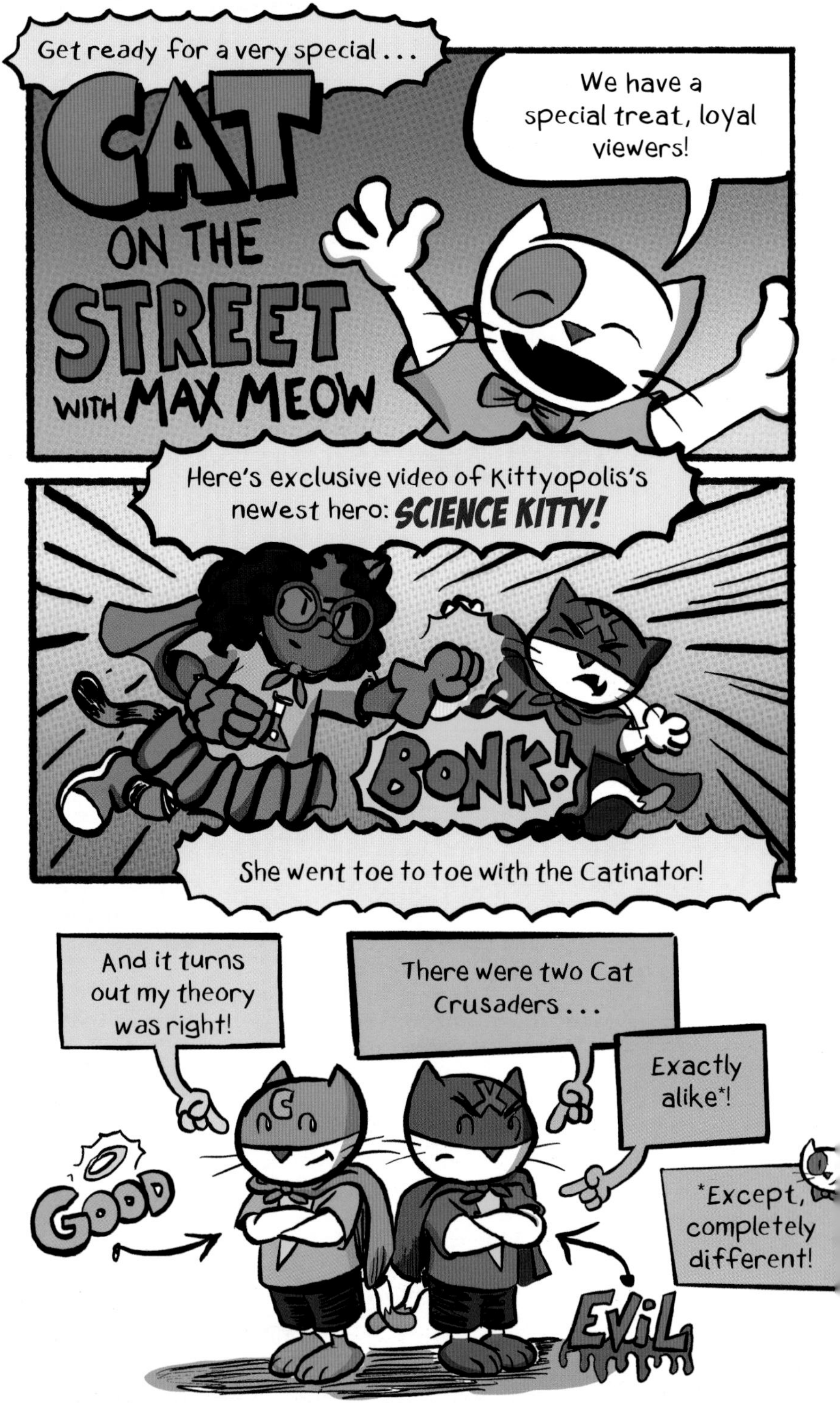
Get ready for a very special . . .
CAT ON THE STREET WITH MAX MEOW
We have a special treat, loyal viewers!
Here's exclusive video of Kittyopolis's newest hero: SCIENCE KITTY!
BONK!
She went toe to toe with the Catinator!
And it turns out my theory was right!
There were two Cat Crusaders . . .
Exactly alike*!
GOOD
EViL
*Except, completely different!

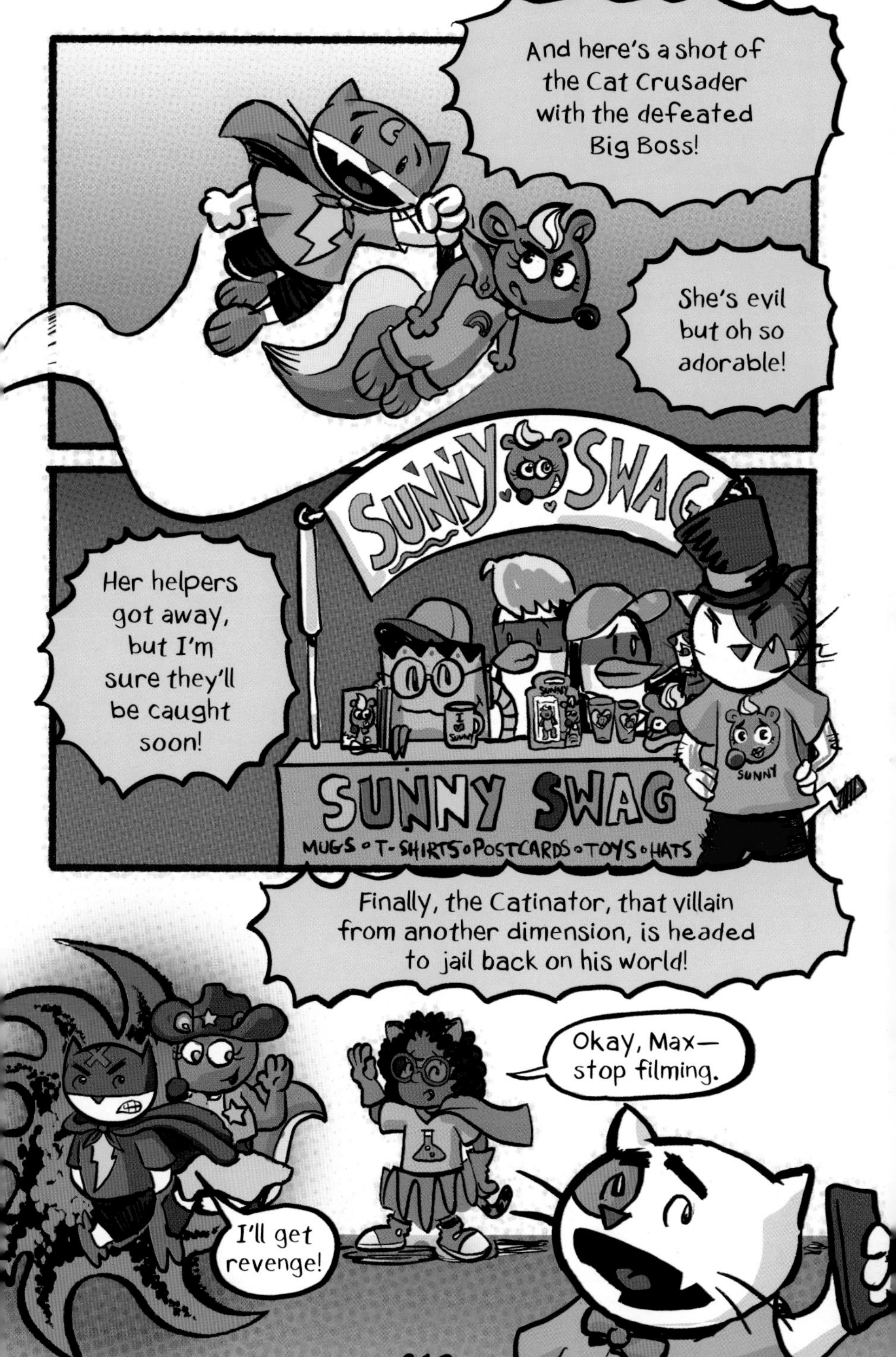
And here's a shot of the Cat Crusader with the defeated Big Boss!
She's evil but oh so adorable!
SUNNY SWAG
Her helpers got away, but I'm sure they'll be caught soon!
SUNNY SWAG
MUGS • T-SHIRTS • POSTCARDS • TOYS • HATS
Finally, the Catinator, that villain from another dimension, is headed to jail back on his world!
Okay, Max— stop filming.
I'll get revenge!

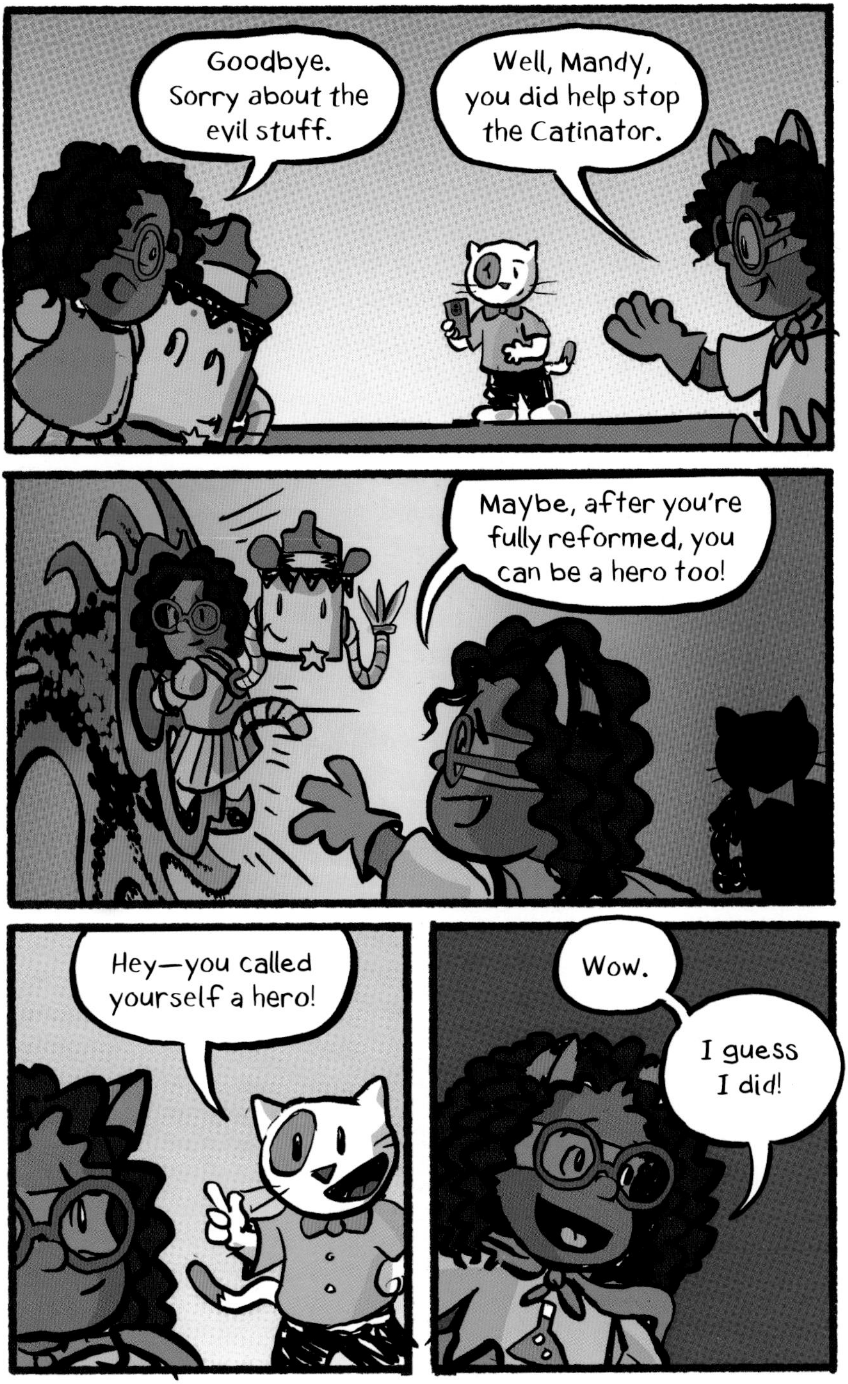
Goodbye. Sorry about the evil stuff.
Well, Mandy, you did help stop the Catinator.
Maybe, after you're fully reformed, you can be a hero too!
Hey—you called yourself a hero!
Wow.
I guess I did!

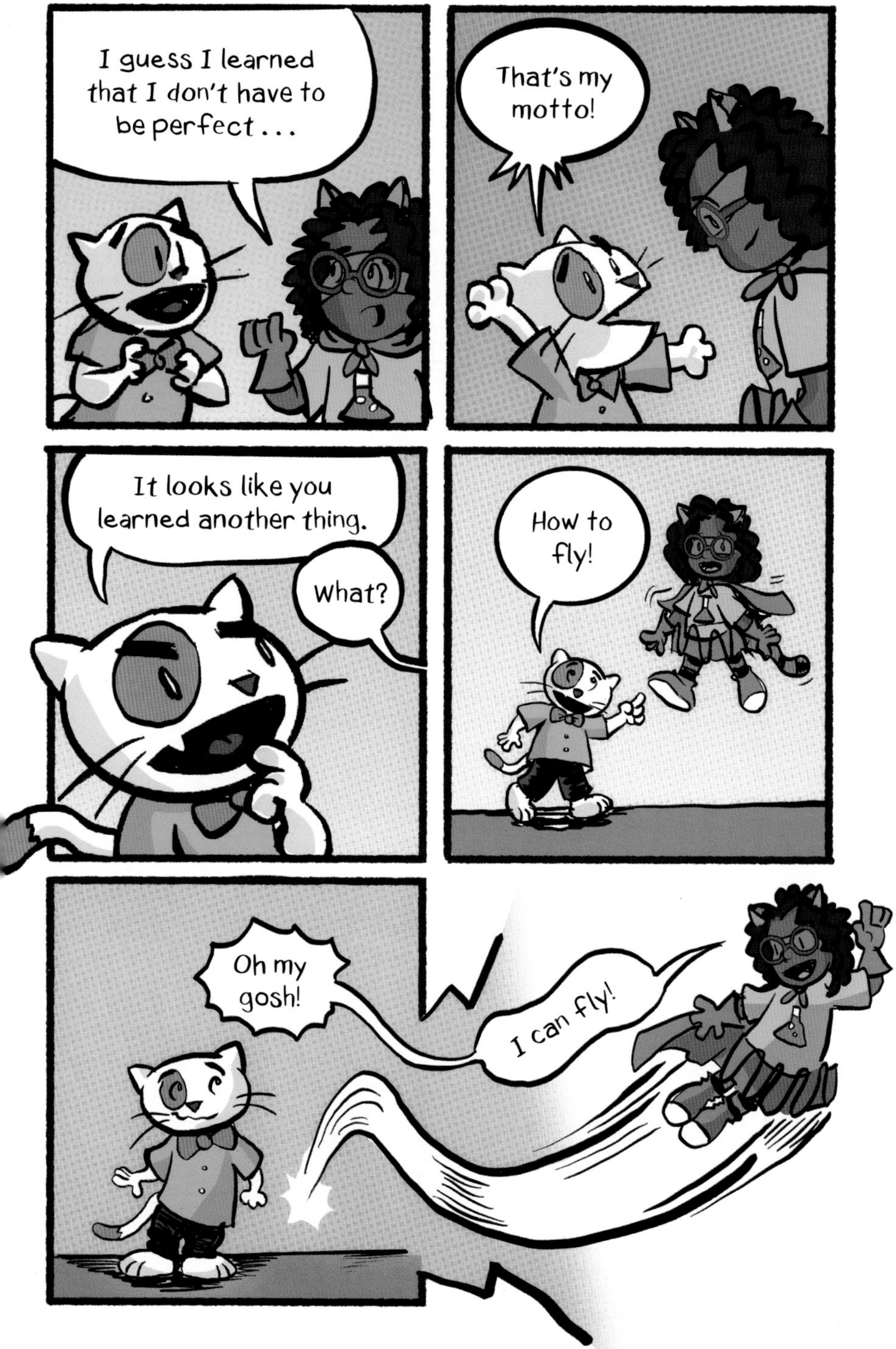
I guess I learned that I don't have to be perfect . . .
That's my motto!
It looks like you learned another thing.
What?
How to fly!
Oh my gosh!
I can fly!

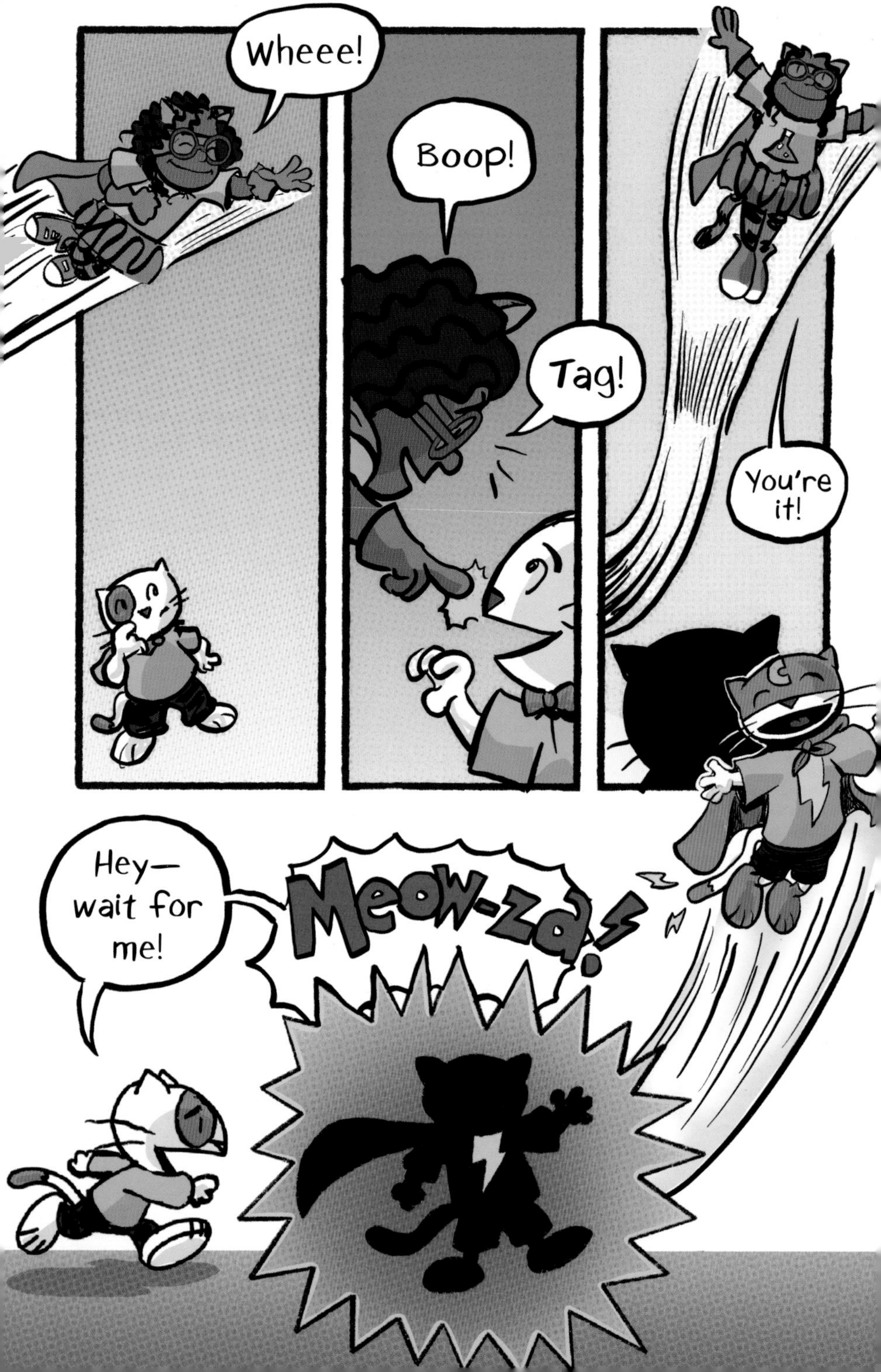
Wheeee!
Boop!
Tag!
You're it!
Hey—wait for me!
Meow-za!

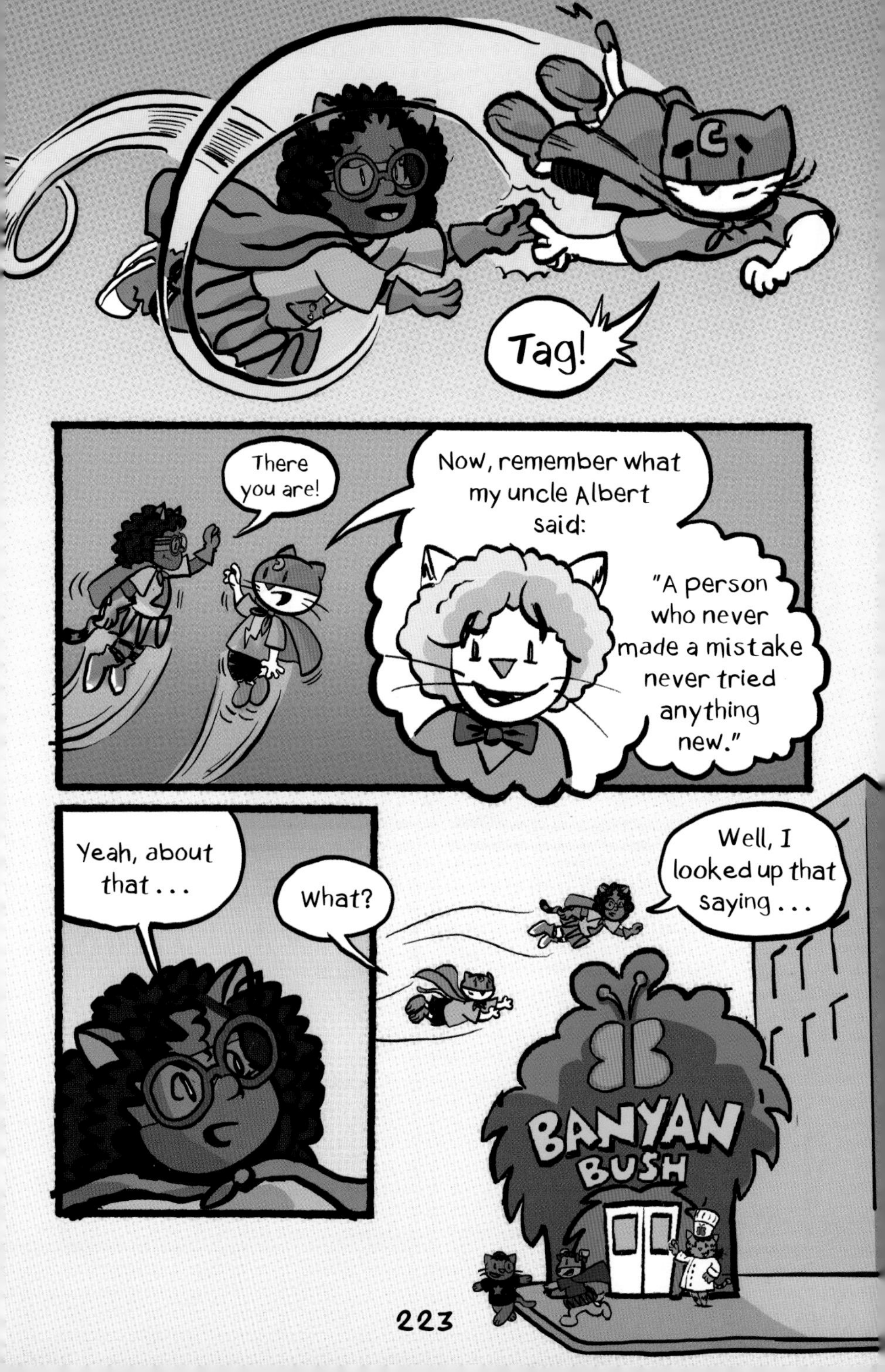
Tag!
There you are!
Now, remember what my uncle Albert said:
"A person who never made a mistake never tried anything new."
Yeah, about that . . .
What?
Well, I looked up that saying . . .
BANYAN BUSH

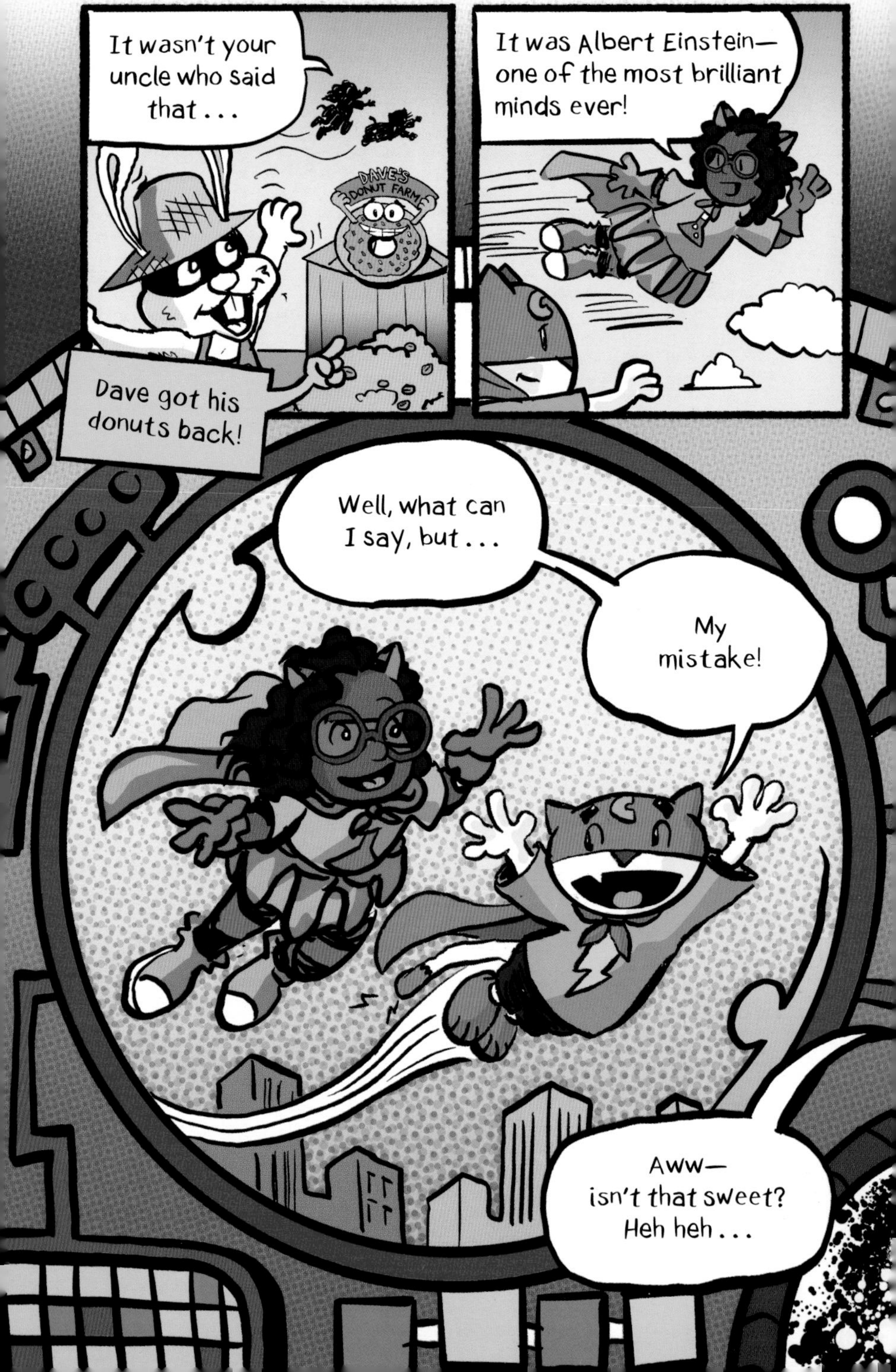
It wasn't your uncle who said that . . .
DAVE'S DONUT FARM
Dave got his donuts back!
It was Albert Einstein— one of the most brilliant minds ever!
Well, what can I say, but . . .
My mistake!
Aww— isn't that sweet? Heh heh . . .

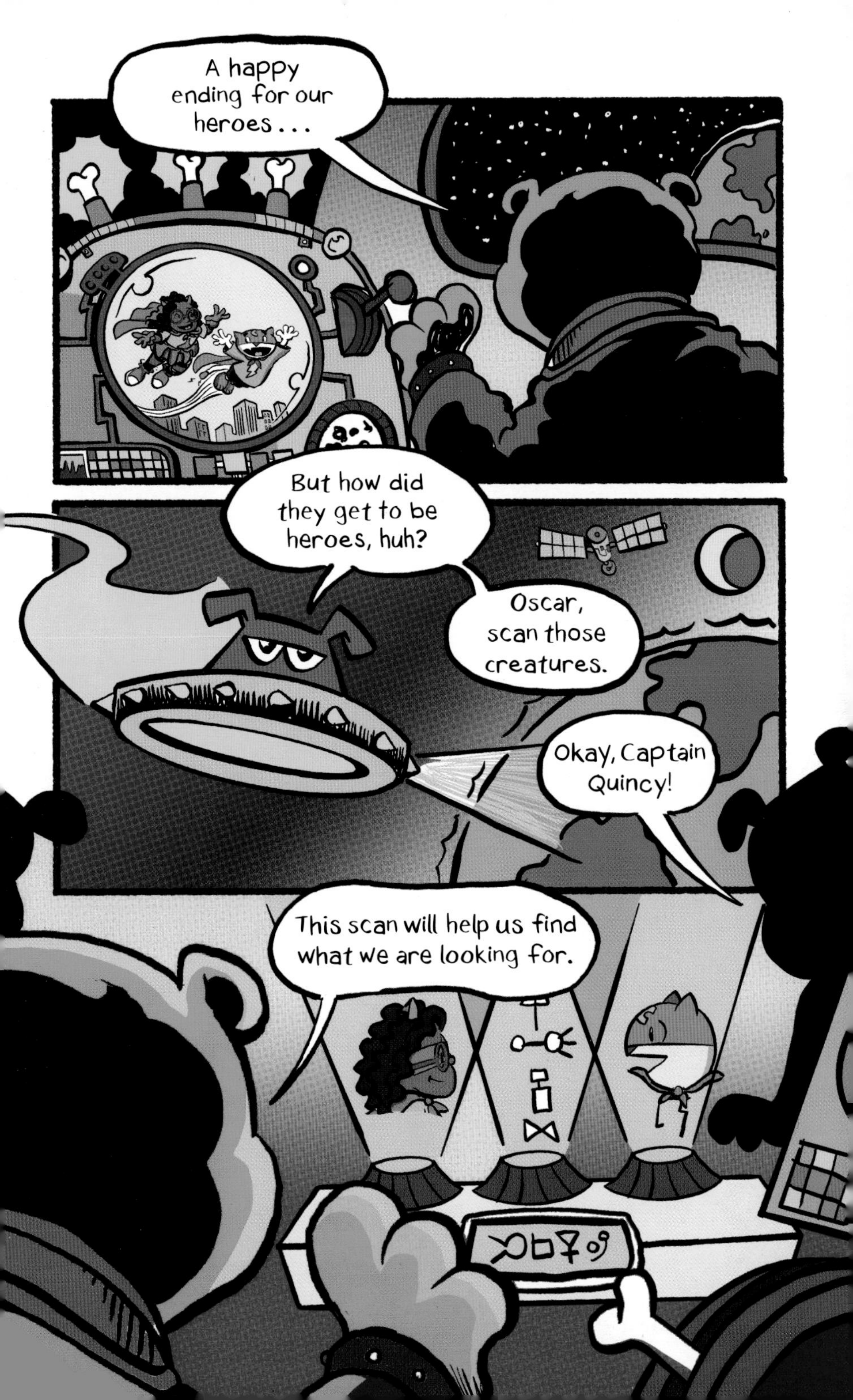
A happy ending for our heroes . . .
But how did they get to be heroes, huh?
Oscar, scan those creatures.
Okay, Captain Quincy!
This scan will help us find what we are looking for.

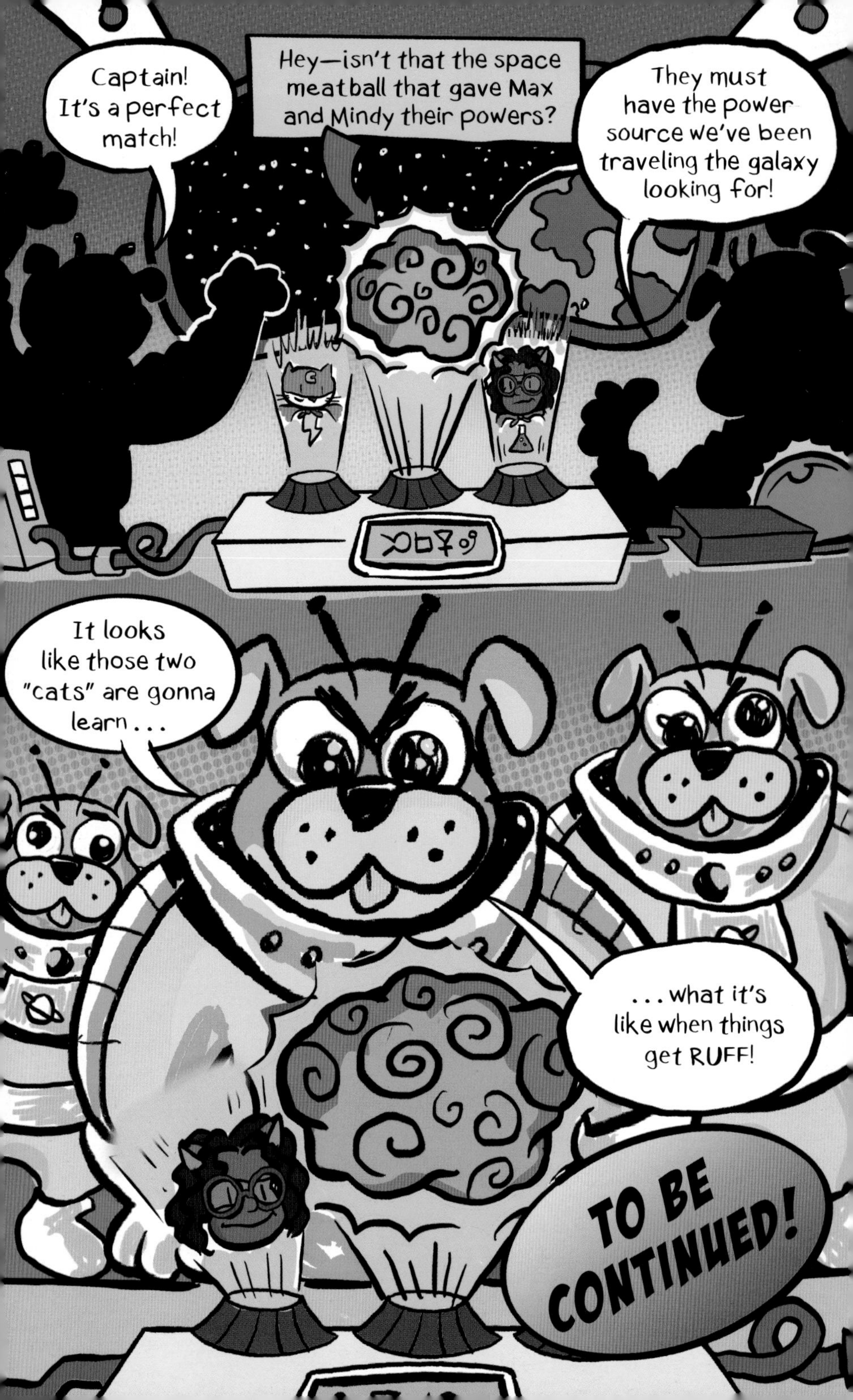
Captain! It's a perfect match!
Hey—isn't that the space meatball that gave Max and Mindy their powers?
They must have the power source we've been traveling the galaxy looking for!
It looks like those two "cats" are gonna learn . . .
. . . what it's like when things get RUFF!
TO BE CONTINUED!

FIND OUT WHAT HAPPENS NEXT IN

MAX MEOW!
PUGS FROM PLANET X

COMING IN
FALL 2021
TO A PLANET NEAR YOU!

Four paws up!

Oh my pug-ness!

Can you find the six checkered donuts that were hidden in this book?*

Paws-itively pawesome!

PSST!
DONUT SCAVENGER HUNT ALERT!

*Go to maxmeow.com to see if you're right!

MAX MEOW CAT CRUSADER

Learn to draw Mindy Microbe!

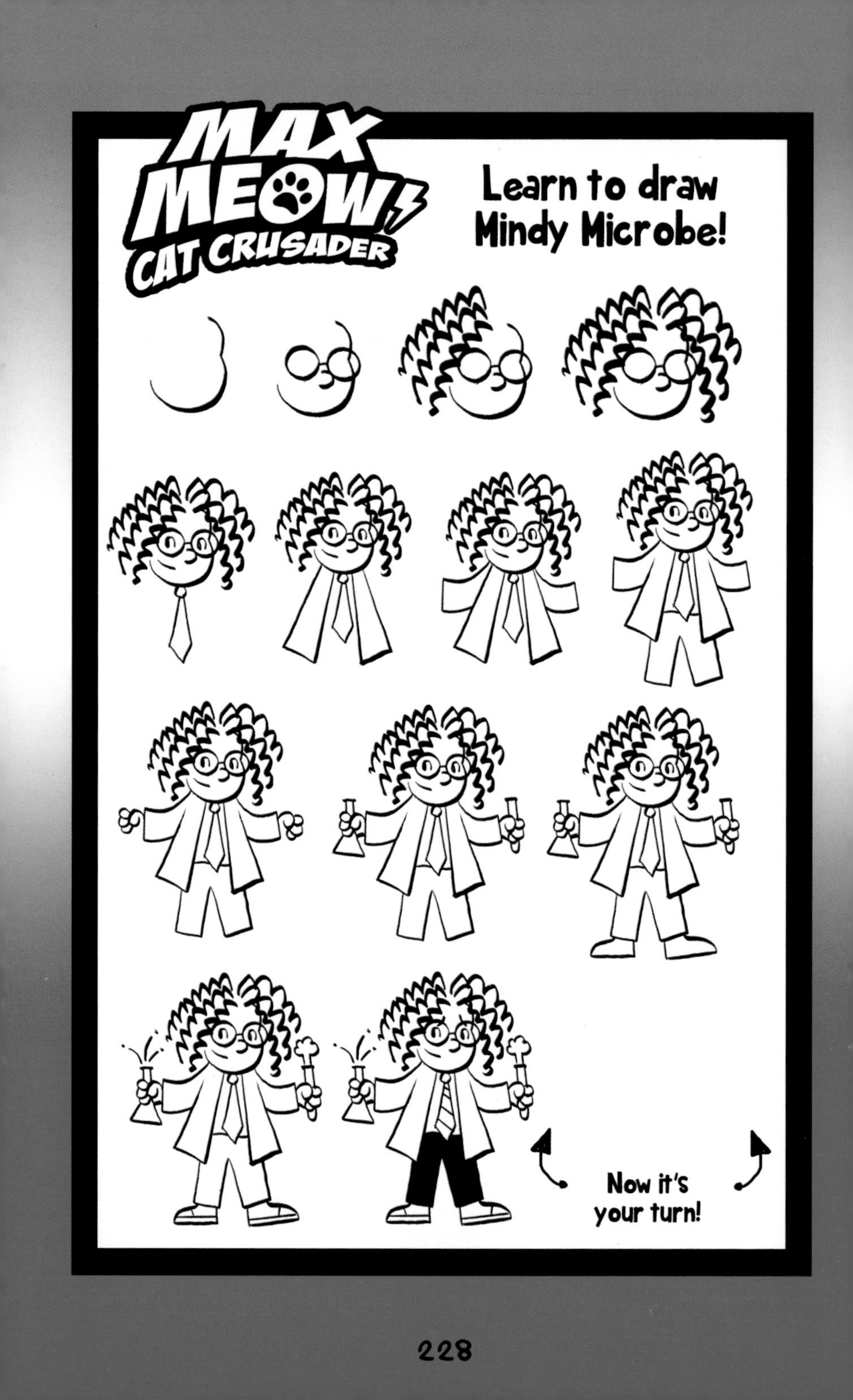
Now it's
your turn!

JOHN GALLAGHER has loved comics since he was five. He learned to read through comics and went on to read every book in his elementary school library. When he told his mom there was nothing left to read, she said, "Just because a book's over doesn't mean the *stories* end. Why don't *you* tell me what happens next?" And so John began creating comics to continue his favorite stories. John never stopped drawing comics. He's now the art director of the National Wildlife Federation's *Ranger Rick* magazine and the cofounder of Kids Love Comics, an organization that uses comics and graphic novels to promote literacy. He also leads workshops teaching kids how to create their own comics. John lives in Virginia with his wife and their three kids. Visit him at MaxMeow.com and on social media.

@JohnBGallagher @MaxMeowCatCrusader

@johngallagher_cartoonist

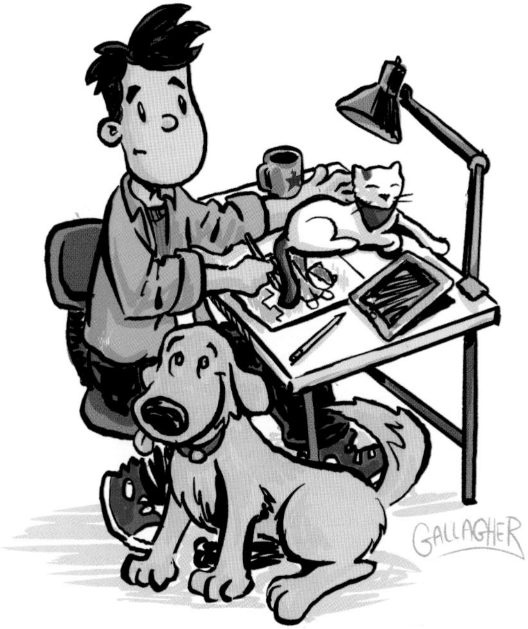
GALLAGHER

ACKNOWLEDGMENTS

STORY ASSISTANT
William Reese Gallagher

COLOR AND FLATTING ASSISTANTS
Sydney Cluff
J. Robert Deans
Ryn Gallagher
Allyson LaMont
Raen Ngu

SPECIAL THANKS

My wife and partner-in-fun, Beth, and my three purr-fect
kids, Katie Ryn, Jack, and Will; my agent, Judith Hansen;
my editor, Shana Corey; my art director, April Ward; Max's
sensitivity reader, Shasta Clinch; as well as Jenni and Matthew
Holm, the Kids Love Comics crew, Deb Werrlein, the Carmody
and Beldon families, Pinecrest School, Oak View Elementary
Comic Class students, and the *Ranger Rick* magazine team.

And thanks to all the teachers who inspired me to look at
the world in different ways (and embrace those differences),
including Kathy Irwin-Lentz, Rodney Ries, Dorothy Masom,
George Cravitz, Fred Hooper, and Alex Gruenberg. And
finally, to the King of Rock-and-Roll, Elvis Presley.